The Mar Saba Codex

A Novel

T0302985

The Mar Saba Codex

A Novel

Douglas Lockhart

BOOKS

Winchester, UK
Washington, USA

First published by O-Books, 2011
O-Books is an imprint of John Hunt Publishing Ltd., Laurel House, Station Approach,
Alresford, Hants, SO24 9JH, UK
office1@o-books.net
www.o-books.com

For distributor details and how to order please visit the 'Ordering' section on our website.

Text copyright: Douglas Lockhart 2010

ISBN: 978 1 84694 618 9

A CIP catalogue record for this book is available from the British Library.

Design: Stuart Davies

Printed in the UK by CPI Antony Rowe
Printed in the USA by Offset Paperback Mfrs, Inc

We operate a distinctive and ethical publishing philosophy in all
areas of our business, from our global network of authors to
production and worldwide distribution.

CONTENTS

ACKNOWLEDGMENTS

I owe a special debt of thanks to my partner Robin Mosley for her endless patience, support and encouragement as I wrestled this book into existence, Robert Cox for his skilful editing when all was complete, and Jeff Malpas for finding the time to read a bulky manuscript in the midst of an ultra busy life.

Also thanks to scholars of the Westar Institute in the US for their refreshing and technically exacting approach to Biblical problems, and the many, many others I've consulted in my attempt to makes this novel as thorough a study of religious attitudes, hopes, beliefs and aspiration as is permissible in a fictional context. And that, really, is the point. I've tried to break new ground in writing this book, and can only hope that readers will find something useful as well as entertaining within its pages.

Synopsis for The Mar Saba Codex

While attending a Catholic conference in the US to boost the faith in difficult times, Australian political journalist and ex-seminarian Jack Duggan is made aware of a controversial codex written by a 4th century Syrian bishop. Only photographs of the codex are available, the original having gone missing soon after its discovery at the Palestinian monastery of Mar Saba.

Within a few pages we are engaged in Duggan's struggle with his religious past, a past that furnished him with the expertise to translate the codex, but left him antagonistic to all things religious. From there we are carried into the thick of a story that reveals, step by step, what this ancient codex contains, and it contains not a few historical surprises.

Considered heretical and dangerous by Vatican specialists, the codex from Mar Saba is declared a forgery, those involved in bringing it to public attention accused of rabid anti-religious propaganda. The gloves are off. The Church feels itself under threat and reacts strongly in its own defense.

But all is not well in the Vatican's labyrinthine corridors. A new conservative Italian pope (Benedict X1V) has been installed, and he believes himself called by God in a dream to visit Jerusalem on behalf of the region's suffering children - a desire that turns into a bizarre and sometimes humorous reality. And alongside this are the antics of the "Children of the New Catholic Dawn", a powerful neo-conservative group whose beliefs and practices threaten to tear the established church apart from within. Sectarian forces are at work within the Catholic hierarchy itself, and these forces herald a return to a form of thinking that even conservative churchmen cannot in all conscience condone.

At once a kind of thriller, a romance and a slice of life, *The Mar Saba Codex* is a big story with many an unexpected twist that traverses the globe from Sydney to San Francisco, and from New York to Rome, reaching its grand climax in the old walled city of

Jerusalem where equally belligerent forces strive for dominance. Exploring the historical twists and turns of that belligerence in depth, and by the novel's end in situ, the author assists us to understand why both side are so intransigent.

This is a story that involves us in the historical, and even the theological, debates, arguments and discussions that take place between religious and secular specialists, and between individuals trying to make sense of the world around them. In doing so, it adds a rich and revealing seam of information to the novel's general mix. Delving into Christianity's obscure origins, and into the church's development as an institution, and into the religious factions that war for control of its gigantic resources, we are afforded an insiders glimpse of a church in crisis. In this sense the *Mar Saba Codex* is no ordinary novel - it challenges us to engage with our own religious views, or our lack of them, and determine their efficacy by engaging with minds schooled in the niceties of religious thought.

But again, *The Mar Saba Codex* is more than that, for at the heart of this tearingly realistic novel lies an oblique challenge to all of us - the challenge to wake up into ourselves as living beings.

RESEARCH ACKNOWLEDGMENTS

I should like to acknowledge my indebtedness to Lew Bretz for giving me access to his masters thesis on "Catholicism in America", and the following authors whose books, papers, essays and articles I have consulted during the writing of this novel. *The Mar Saba Codex* will herewith be referred to as MSC. If, by any chance I have overlooked anyone, I apologize in advance. The books and authors in question are: *The Human Situation* by Aldous Huxley, Chatto & Windus, 1977 p 71; *Evil and the God of Love* by John Hick, MacMillan, 1985, pp 201, 204, 209, 315, 216; *Evil and the Evidence for God/The Challenge of John Hick's Theodicy* by R D Geivett, Temple University Press, Philadelphia 1995; *Encountering Evil/Live options in Theodicy* edited by S T Davis, John Knox Press 1981; *The Family of Jesus/Family Feud or "Dynasty Two?"* by Arthur J Dewey, Forum, New Series 2, 1, Spring 1999, Polbridge Press, Santa Rosa, CA, p. 79-97; *Secret Mark* by Charles W Hedrick with Nikolaos Olympiou: The Fourth 'R', Polbridge Press, Santa Rosa, CA, vol 13, No. 5, Sept/Oct 2000; *Traditions & Faith in the New Era* by Roy W Hoover: The Fourth 'R', vol 17, No. 1, 2004; guest editorial by Thomas Sheehan on Vatican declaration *Dominus Iesus* by Cardinal Joseph Ratzinger: The Fourth 'R'. vol 13 No. 5, 2000;*Who Owns the Holy Land?* by Lloyd Geering, parts 2, 3 and 4, The Fourth 'R', vol 15. No: 2, 3 & 4; Who Hates the Jews Now?/*The New Anti-Semitism* by Mark Strauss, The Spectator, 29 November, 2003; *The Springs of Creativity* by H Westman (Chap 14 of *MSC* expresses Westman's view on Abraham's attempt to sacrifice his son); *The Pope's Armada* by G Urquhart, Corgi Books,1995, pp, 37, 80, 90-92, 93-95, 97, 98-99, 109, 111-113, 150-152, 191-192, 198, 209, 206, 221-222, 227, 229, 243-246, 293, 301, 339, 340 341,342-351, 290. 393-392, 397,540; *The Dark Side of the Papacy* by Peter de Rosa, Corgi Books, 1989, pp, 82-83, 202-205, 207-209, 333-334, 368, 370; *Reformation* by F Fernandez-Armesto and D Wilson, Scribner, 1996, p 9-13; *Canons in Conflict* by J E Brenneman, Oxford University Press, 1997, Intro, p 6-7, and pp 13-15, 19, 25; *Whicker's New World* by Allen

I

Whicker, Weidenfeld & Nicolson, 1985, p 96-98; *Lost Christianity* by J Needleman, Element Books, 1990, pp 42, 87, 175, 208; *The Ideas of the Fall and of Original Sin* by N P Willliams, Bampton Lectures, 1924, Longman Green & Co Ltd, London 1927; article on *Faith* by H Zwartz, *The Australian*, 12/7/01, and a paraphrasing in MSC of a statement in *Genesis in Exodus* by J Manyon, The Australian, 20/11/99; biography of Cardinal George Pell by Tess Livingston, Duffy & Snellgrove, 2002, p 70-71; *The Pell Papers/The Revolution in Catholic Classrooms/Return to the Dark Ages* by Martin Daly, The Sunday Age, 23 May 1999; *Divine Rights* by Richard Yallop, The Weekend Australian, Feb 14-15, 1998; *Vatican Uncovered* by Christopher Bantick (article on Paul Collins), The Mercury, March 18 2001; *Hellbent* by Andrew Dodd (article on Paul Collins), The Weekend Australian, 24 March 2001; *Alexander Solzhenitsyn and the West* by M Brander, Quadrant, March 2005; *Eminence* by Morris West, HarperCollins, 1999, pp, 120, 195-196, and *Lazarus*, Mandarin, 1990, p, 167;*The Inquisition* by A L Maycock, Constable & Company, 1928, p 61; *Theological Investigations* by K Rahner, vol 17, Darton, Longman & Todd, p 38; *The Passover Plot* by H Schonfield, Element Books, 1993, p 209; *His Holiness* by C Bernstein and M Politi, Bantam Books, 1997, pp 483-485; *The Truth about Eternal Change* by Peter Grant, *The Mercury*, Tasmania, 4/2/96; *Three Popes and a Cardinal* by Malachi Martin, Hart-Davis, McGibbon, 1973, *preface*, p ix; *Opus Dei* by John Allen, Allen Lane/Penguin Books, 2005, p 11; *The Vicars of Orthodoxy* by A. Sullivan, *Time*, May 2005; *Hick's 'Evolutionary' Eschatology* by John C McDowell, internet article; *An Irenaean Theodicy* by John Hick, internet article; *Catholic Church braced for another intervention*/AM Archive/ABC Local Radio/Friday, 29 Oct, 1999; *Catholic School Problems can be Solved* by Tom Kendell, internet article 1997; *New Spiritual Communities and Movements: An Inquiry into the Calling and Mission of the Church today* by Dr. Mariannee Tigges, 1998, internet article; *The psychological mechanisms of mental conditioning inside the neocatechumenate community* by Fundacja Antyk, Wszelkie prawa zastrzezone, internet article; *Neocatechumenate Community* -

2

Archdiocese of Melbourne/Report of activity in one parish by Paul Cooney, sm, 1990; *Report into the presence and activities of the Neocatechumenal Way in the Diocese of Clifton*/Summary Press Statement from Bishop's Office, St Ambrose, North Road, Leigh Woods, Bristol, also statement issued by the Right Reverend Mervyn Alexander, Bishop of Clifton concerning Neocatechumanate activities in Diocese of Clifton; *Is the Neocatechumenate Way Compatible with Religious Life* by Gerald A. Arbuckle, SM/Published in Religious Life Review, Jan/Feb 1994, vol 33, No. 164, internet article; Notes transcribed from a videotape of a debate on the Neocatechumanate held in Rome on April 20,1997, presented by Mario Frugiuele: internet article; *the Neoctechumanate*, a personal appraisal by Mgr. Joseph C. Buckley - Vicar General & Judical, Diocese of Clifton, England/Written in 1988 and sent to the bishops of England and Wales, and several in France: internet article; *The Pope's Contradictions* by Hans Kung/Spiegel Online/English Site, 2005; *Theologians at Risk/Ex Corde and Catholic Colleges* by R P McBrien: internet article; the Vatican, the Bishops, the Academy by P C Saunders: internet article; *Vatican Proposes More Control over Colleges:* A Today: Magazine Archives: Jan/Feb 1999; *Christian Colleges: A Dying Light or a New Refraction?* by M U Edwards, Jr., internet text by J C Purdy; *Dissent in Catholic Academia is 'out' says Vatican Instruction* by B Santamaria: internet article; *Who is Catholic?* by B Bollag: The Chronicle of Higher Education/Money & Management, April 9, 2004: internet article; *From the Holy Mountain* by W Dalrymple, Flamingo/HarperCollins, 1988, pp, 280-282, 288, and *In Judea*, a description of Dalrymple's visit to the monastery of Mar Saba used to build description of Mar Saba monastery in MSC: internet article; *The Strange Case of the Secret Gospel according to Mark*, or *How Morton Smith's Discovery of a Lost Letter by Clement of Alexandria Scandalized Biblical Scholarship* by Shawn Eyer: internet article; *A reply to Morton Smith* by Quentin Quesnell/ The Catholic Biblical Quarterly, April 1976, vol 38:2; *Highlights on the debate over 'Theodore of Mopsuestia's Christology'* by J S Romanides: internet article; *The Life and*

3

Writings of Theodore of Mopsuestia/Monastic and Liturgical Studies/Monachos.net; *Forgers & Critics/Creativity & Duplicity in Western Scholarship* by A Grafton: internet article; the *Quesnell-Smith* exchange on Morton Smith by R Cox, paraphrased in MSC: internet article; *Reconsidering Vatican II* by M Novak: internet article; *Massive Secret Mark Conspiracy?* by Yuri Kuchinsky: internet article; *the Jerusalem Syndrome,* the American Atheist's News, No. 26, Nov 1998: internet article; *Misunderstood Muslims* by Sheikh Palazzi, New York Review, 17 Nov '05, and observations by Sheikh Palazzi in the Jewish Virtual Library: internet article.

The greatest derangement of the mind is to
believe in something because one wishes it to be so.

- Louis Pasteur -

Part One

Give the Dog a Bone

I

Shades of Columbo

"Jack?"

Fr Timothy White was not immediately recognizable to Jack Duggan - twenty years had passed and the priest was now a portly ninety-five kilos.

"Have I changed that much?"

"Timothy?"

"Good for you!"

"I'll be damned!"

"I sincerely hope not."

They were standing in the foyer of 'The Bennington', a five-star hotel with five-star prices about an hour's drive from San Francisco. Duggan had just checked in. The Santa Rosa bus had got him within a short taxi ride.

"You look the same, Jack. How do you do it?"

"The mirror says otherwise."

"Except for the hair."

"I lost a bet. A colleague cropped it for me."

"Timothy too-many-potatoes," said Timothy, spreading the fingers of both hands across his stomach. Then, inquisitorially he said, "What are you doing here?"

"I got landed with it. I'm a journo these days. You?"

"Education. It's become an issue." Duggan was apt to incline his head when he concentrated; it was a trait Fr Timothy remembered all too well. "You're here because of Peters?"

"I've got the good bishop lined up for an interview."

Fr Timothy twitched a smile. "You'll like him."

The hotel chosen for the 2001 international conference on the future of Catholicism reflected its Santa Rosa setting. It was mildly Spanish in architecture, sprawling, and in the process of being painted rust red and cream. A two-storey wall of neatly stacked slate pieces dominated the foyer, and there was an elevated bar area with soft furnishings where, if it had been a church, an altar would have been. As Duggan and Fr White chatted, a flock of laughing priests swept into reception to complete the correspondences.

Priests are often likened to crows, and some three hundred crows were about to descend on Santa Rosa. Hailed as a landmark conference on Catholicism's conservative renewal in America, three keynote speakers and a handful of New Testament scholars had been primed with the theme *Returning to the Future* - a neat juxtaposition hatched by Archbishop Donaghue of Nevada on behalf of those struggling with modernity. Bishop Samuel Peters of Illinois, on the other hand, had stopped struggling with modernity. An advocate of Vatican II with a troublesome pen, he had forewarned the Archbishop that he intended to speak out on behalf of educational commonsense and the dignity of children.

"You were sorely missed, Jack."

"I was a misfit."

"You were brighter by half than any of us. You said what was on your mind." Timothy paused to scrutinize Duggan. "I thought you'd lecture."

"I did, for a while."

"And now you're a wordsmith."

"Political correspondent for *Quarterly Review* in Sydney. Forty-eight pages of pertinent comment on everything that matters." Duggan's smile was pained. "Someone fell ill and I got landed with this one."

"There'll be more than enough politicking around here. There's the promise of a bunfight if Peters does what he says he's going to do."

"It's a divided camp?"

"It's always a divided camp."

"Politicking imbued with moral certainty muddies already muddied waters. You can't shunt religious certainty onto the political plane, it bedevils debate. Peters is aware of that."

"He applies secular reasoning to religious education."

"We should apply religious reasoning to secular issues?"

"You know what I'm trying to say, Jack."

They were back exactly where they had left off all those years ago. Duggan did not hesitate to take the initiative.

"Peters is asking for open debate," he said. "Religious opinion elevated to the level of pronouncements from Mount Sinai help no one, Tim."

"He's perhaps bitten off more than he can chew."

"Donaghue hasn't?"

"Donaghue is Donaghue."

"You mean he's backed by Cardinal Menenger."

Fr Timothy's face crinkled into another short-lived smile. "The conservative push is on, Jack; Peters' doesn't stand a chance in this climate."

Duggan glanced at a group of laughing priests as they passed; they were jostling one another like schoolboys. His gaze swiveled back to Timothy. "May I ask whose side you're on?"

"I'm for sensible debate, Jack."

"Archbishop Pullman isn't. He's trying his damnedest to change the curriculum in Sydney's Catholic schools back to the old model. It's a bloody disgrace, Tim."

"The tendency has been to throw the baby out with the bath water. A correction was necessary." Fr Timothy blinked his concern at Duggan. "The faith's the faith, Jack."

"Yeh, I know," he replied.

There was an awkward moment; Fr Timothy came to the rescue. "You approve of the new Holy Father?"

"Can any good thing come out of Umbria?"

"The Holy Spirit has a mind of its own."

"He's an innocent among wolves. They chose him because neither side had the numbers."

"I hear what you're saying. . ."

"Come on! It would be laughable if it weren't so pathetic. Ratzinger's sudden illness threw them all into a tizz. The hard core had Ratzinger earmarked for the top job."

"I wasn't joking, Jack. The wisdom of the Spirit should not be discounted."

"That still leaves you with a decrepit old man and a school of scheming cardinals. Do you think the Holy Spirit's up to it? Well, do you?"

"You haven't lost your sting, Jack."

"I gave up believing in belief a long time ago." Duggan was faintly dismissive. "It's about power and very little else, Tim. You know that as well as I do."

"Benedict has already proved himself an astute negotiator."

"I agree. He's gone along with Cardinal Menenger's every wish."

"Not quite. And Menenger's not a complete ogre, Jack."

"Menenger wasn't made Prefect of the Congregation because of his boyish looks, Tim. He's as hardline as Ratzinger ever was."

A wooden crucifix had hung above Duggan's childhood bed, and halfway down the hallway, above a little half-moon table, a dangling Jesus full of torment had graced the floral wallpaper. And on a lumbering sideboard with brass drop handles, and on the dressing-room table with its corner-cracked mirror, and on a little wooden platform suspended above the kitchen table blue and white Madonna figures had stared sightlessly at the ceiling.

He had announced his desire to be a priest when he was sixteen. His mother had been ecstatic, his father concerned, the local priest patient in his examination. It was a great responsibility being a priest, the priest had said. Much prayer would be required, and he would have to do well at school. And so he did well at school, and at university, not because he intended to be a priest, but because he could not help himself. Prayer proved to be the greater challenge. Prayer was about submitting one's will to the will of God, and that, Duggan learned, was no easy thing to determine.

"Belief is the cement that holds the whole thing together, Jack.

What would you have us do?"

"That's no longer my concern."

"I remember you as an inspiration."

"I was a pain in everyone's arse!"

"You were a pain to Fr Michael and we loved it!" Timothy's delight was genuine. "You gave him a right run for his money."

"He hated me."

"Damn it, Jack, you had a doctorate and he didn't! What did you expect?"

"I expected honesty."

"He died three months after you left - may the Lord have mercy on his soul."

"He was a frightful man."

"There's no doubting he was tough." Fr Timothy paused; then with intent he said, "His replacement was a different kind of man altogether. If you had still been around, things might have turned out differently"

"I fell on my own sword, not theirs."

"You would have got on with Fr Martin."

"I doubt it. I was in self-destruct mode. I'd had all I could take of intellectual flannelling."

"Are you as bitter as you sound?"

"Bitter, but not twisted." Duggan's gaze was steady. "Best thing Fr Michael ever did was have me thrown out."

"I told him I didn't believe in a literal hell, Jack. He said I would by the time I had completed my studies. He wasn't wrong. From that moment he *made* my life hell."

"And here you are a priest and proud of it."

"I'm not a very good priest, Jack."

"If you thought you were you'd be in trouble."

"I sometimes wish they'd kicked *me* out."

"You don't mean that."

"I get disheartened at times."

"To have almost been a priest is not something I'd recommend."

A guffaw of laughter from reception caused Fr Timothy to look round. He looked back at Duggan and said, "You have no regrets?"

"Everyone has regrets." Duggan offered a qualification. "I don't mean by that that I regret what happened. My wanting to be a priest was an adolescent fantasy that got out of control."

Fr Timothy doubled back. "It's not *all* about power, Jack. You can't possibly believe that."

"Authority is power." Duggan snorted a laugh. "You either toe the line, or you don't."

"My reading of things isn't quite that bleak."

"I'd be surprised if it were."

"You're speaking as if the Church is just an organization. It's more than that."

Duggan conveyed disinterest.

"We can't just dump everything and start all over again."

"It could be argued that that's how Christianity got started."

"Yes, but – "

"But it's not an argument I would make."

Fr Timothy waited, but Duggan fell silent. It was as if a switch had been thrown.

"I'd like to chat further, Jack. Would that be possible? "

"You won't like what I have to say. I'm even more of a ratbag now that I was then."

The priest extended a hand. "I'll take that risk," he said.

* * *

Archbishop Donaghue's body twisted at the waist as he looked round at Bishop Peters' angular face on television - he would have known *that* voice anywhere, and *that* voice was dinning across the room at him. The conference was about to start and here was Sam sounding off on television. And such nonsense, too. The man could not see good Catholic wood for tree-trunks of Protestant apologetics.

"Why is he doing this?"

A rhetorical question to which canon lawyer Bob Carter, Donaghue's right-hand man, nevertheless replied.

"He thinks we're interfering busybodies."

"The Church does not interfere; it *instructs!*" A blunt appraisal of the truth. And then, "Is this really what we can expect?"

"*It's faith versus human experience,*" Bishop Peter was saying. "*What we're doing is overlooking a child's developmental stages and attempting to cram a particular religious view into their heads by the end of primary school. What is a year-one child supposed to think when told that the first parents of the human race - Adam and Eve no less - chose to sin? How are they going to take in literary forms later? How are they going to handle biblical myth when it crops up? These are just some of the questions that are not being thought through.*"

When the broadcast was over, Carter offered his thoughts on the Bishop's injudicious notions. Yes, the man was a menace, there was no doubt about that. He had not properly grasped the Church's intention in making such demands. It was not a matter of setting the clock back; it was a matter of rebuilding the almost shattered Wall of Faith so that people could rest easily again. Anyone with half a brain could see that. The new guidelines were not doctrinaire, they were a moral bulwark against relativism.

Switching off the television set, Archbishop Donaghue stood, hands in pockets, in the middle of the room and stared out at the golf course that flanked the hotel. Fresh wheel tracks were plainly visible on the wet grass, but he saw neither the tracks nor the course's emptiness.

"Should I talk to him, Bob?"

"Not advisable."

Donaghue collapsed back into a leather armchair. "He thinks I'm a crank. He thinks I don't understand the issues, but I do. What people believed in pre-Enlightenment times may seem naive by today's standards, but are we any better off? Are we less irrational than they were? I don't think so. I don't think this age's faith in materialism and freedom is getting it anywhere. Being rights-driven may sound good, but where's it carrying us? Straight down into the gutter, that's where. Did you pick up on that bit about religious education. . . what was it?

"Inculcating young people into the framework of the Church's defunct religious assumptions,'" said Carter, the bishop's words readily available because of their inbuilt cadence. "He's good at one-liners."

"How dare he!"

"Rhetoric," said Carter, who had compiled a thick dossier on Bishop Peters. "It's always easier to criticize than it is to do something constructive." He added quickly: "The other side are of course having the same problem. They've been forced to develop an accelerated Christian education program to combat what's going on out there."

The Archbishop could remember the swish of black habits in school corridors and the gentle clunk of wooden rosary beads as priests and nuns went about their business. Everyone had known their place then, their limits - particularly the laity. The laity was now flexing its muscles, and Bishop Peters was an advocate for that as well. With this in mind Donaghue said: "Laity involvement is a two-edged sword, Bob; they're beginning to think they can run the whole show just about." Borrowing a folksy idea from science, he added, "It's a virus, and it's spreading."

"Intellectual freedom has its own inbuilt brand of myopia," said Carter, delivering a favorite one-liner of his own. "That's what hasn't dawned on them yet."

"And we can't afford to wait for their enlightenment," said Donaghue, his face a study in seriousness. "The whirlwind is upon us."

* * *

Room 326 was spacious and in darkness when Duggan entered.

Drawing the drapes, he found glass doors and a small balcony overlooking a golf course. A practitioner of the art was moving down the fairway in an electric cart. He watched the man's progress for a moment or two, then, opening his duty-free, he poured himself a single malt and returned to the window to stare up at a cloud-riven Californian sky. He and Timothy had agreed to meet later that evening, after the theologian Peter Atkins's opening address, and as he contemplated that arrangement he wondered if he had done the right thing. If Timothy hoped to return him to the faith he would be bitterly disappointed. Closing his eyes, Duggan savored the whisky's soft rawness and the fact that if Fr Michael had died sooner rather than later, things might have been different. Would he have had the cheek to go through with ordination if given the chance? A wry smile formed. He could have carried the fight right into the heart of the enemy camp. The enemy? His smile faded. The enemy had once been the love of his life and the life of his love.

After a shower and a change of shirt he went downstairs again. The barman, a foxy-looking character, was talking animatedly to a man in a slightly disheveled raincoat - shades of Columbo - hunched over a glass of red wine. Glancing in Duggan's direction, this individual nodded, then looked away. Minutes later two clerics stopped to chat with this man. During the banter it was revealed that he was a journalist from San Francisco. When the crows departed, Duggan introduced himself.

"David Mayle," said David Mayle. Then, "Sydney? You're a long way from home."

"I'm filling in. I should be in Darwin sipping a cold one." He added quickly, "I'm a political correspondent." Mayle was about to reply, but Duggan interjected a second time. "Yeh, I know, plenty of politics around here."

An accommodating nod from Mayle, followed by an observation, "Your kind generally end up in New York or Washington."

"I got talked into this. Who are you with?"

"*San Francisco Tribune*," said Mayle "Fifteen years' hard labor."

His smile suggested contentment. "I'm here to keep an eye on the bastards."

Duggan laughed at the American's bluntness.

"My father was a Baptist minister," said Mayle "Okay, so that isn't the same as being Catholic, but it's a head start."

The barman was hovering. Duggan ordered a whisky and said that Mayle could help keep him on track

"I get the feeling that won't be necessary. I saw the welcome mat go out."

"That was Fr Timothy," said Duggan. "He's an Aussie. I haven't seen him in years."

Mayle pursed his lips. An Australian angle might be worth considering, he said. American interest in Australian was growing.

"You've been Down Under?"

"Never had the pleasure." Mayle changed direction. "So what made them send you?"

"Catholic education's become an issue in Australia," he said, parodying Timothy. "Bishop Peters's recent outbursts caught the attention of our editor."

"Rumor has it he won't survive the weekend. CDF already have him in their sights. You're familiar?"

Duggan gave a nod. The Congregation for Doctrine and the Faith was known to all Catholics. "You're sure about that?" he asked.

"Their claws are out."

"His book isn't all that threatening."

"He's come a long way since he wrote that."

"You've read it?"

"I helped edit it." Mayle changed direction a second time. "Are you Catholic?"

"You helped edit it?"

"He asked me to. I got to know him years ago." Mayle repeated his question.

"I was brought up Catholic."

"Does the name Robert Carter mean anything?" It being obvious from Duggan's response that it did not, Mayle continued. "He and the Archbishop are close, *very* close. He's a big-time lawyer and canon law expert. Set up the Catholic Watch Society in California about six months ago and hasn't been out of trouble since. It's rumored he has a network of spies at his disposal. Snoopers. There have been reports of strangers taking notes during the sermons of certain priests in the California area. Carter has been blamed for the intrusions and hasn't issued a denial." A smile from Mayle. "He made two trips to Rome during February lugging a heavy briefcase."

"You're keeping tabs on him?"

"Someone has to. Carter's Donaghue's adjutant. Donaghue's mission is to put Catholic America back on its knees. He's tipped to have a cardinal's hat before the end of the year." Mayle's smile became devious. "I have it on good authority that he and Carter report directly to Cardinal Menenger."

"Peters hasn't been barred from speaking at the conference."

"That was arranged months ago, before he laid into them." Mayle laughed. "His outburst on television this afternoon must have been the final straw."

"I didn't catch that"

"He gave it to them with both barrels."

"A Bishop taking up the cudgels is unusual."

"That's what's worrying them." Mayle swirled his wine round and round in his glass. "It's different for ordinary priests. Most of them favor an open Church, a sympathetic Church. It's the trend these days. A high proportion of religious are of the same mind. Human rights are to the fore. The laity have found their voice and won't any longer put up with the kind of nonsense that used to be dished out. Enter Donaghue, Carter, and a sprinkling of hardliners whose strategy is a return to the old certainties. Question the Church's authority and you're immediately in their sights. They're trouble-shooters. I saw Carter shred a local bishop on TV a few nights back for not holding to traditional teaching. Donaghue's been publicly haranguing Catholic intellectuals for over a year."

"Same thing is beginning to happen in Australia," said Duggan. He took a sip of whisky. "The new papa's probably too busy trying to be the new papa to take much notice."

"Seventy-two years of age and hasn't a thought of his own to play with, so I'm told," said Mayle. "It's rumored he's not a well man."

"It's rumored he had a bit of a turn when the final ballot came through. Can you imagine the shock of being told you've just been elected pope to someone like that?

Mayle chuckled into his wine.

"This Carter fella had a go at a bishop?"

"Have a go? He demolished the poor bastard with an avalanche of doctrinal legalese. Billy Graham couldn't have done a better job quoting Scripture."

"I've never had the privilege."

"You've never heard Billy preach?"

"I've seen him on television. In snippets."

"Billy was fabulous!" Mayle beamed at Duggan. "I got converted when I was sixteen."

"And?"

"Lasted about a year."

Duggan struck what he thought was a sensible note. "Believing that a man walked on water never struck me as a sound basis for a spiritual life."

Mayle came back in quickly, dexterously. "According to Carter's gospel you can't be that choosy."

"Choice is the essence of democracy."

"Choice is by definition heresy," said Mayle, reminding Duggan of an ancient truth. "You can't have choice if truth is a fixed entity. You either believe, or you do not believe."

"Then I am by definition a heretic," said Duggan. "I choose not to believe."

"You won't get away with that either. Everything's tied up with a doctrinal bow. In their book unbelief isn't a state of mind, it's a condition of the soul. You can't chop up Carter's kind of truth and get away with it."

"And the doors of the Bastille shut."

"Something like that," said Mayle. Then, surprising Duggan he said, "What is the basis of a spiritual life in your opinion?"

"I don't think I'm the right person to ask," said Duggan. "I'm not even sure I believe in God any longer."

"When Christians lose Jesus they generally lose God as well. I find that interesting."

"It's a package," said Duggan, impressed by Mayle's insight. "It's two for the price of one."

* * *

The conference got under way that evening, in the Grand Ballroom, with a blistering introductory address from Philip Atkins, theologian and sometime novelist. Atkins, it was soon evident, believed evil to be an intelligent force, a force that could invade a human life and destroy it. The fatal thread, he said, staring down at his audience of clergy and general religious, was secular society's unquestioning acceptance of evolutionary theory, its belief that we had evolved from lesser forms over many millions of years. Using this as its yardstick, society's interpretation of how the world worked had systematically undermined faith and eaten away at Christianity's core beliefs. Inch by inch we had lost out to a disabling spirit, a spirit of the times expert in its ability to make as nothing everything once held sacred. We were, according to this theory, brothers to the Earth and sisters to the stars, co-beings with plants and animals. We had emerged from the material world, and at death would merge again with our planetary mother. Redefining God's plan of salvation in terms of the evolutionary process, the historical Jesus had been turned into a metaphor, a point of reference in future time through which a self-perfected humanity would arrogantly stride.

There was no doubting Atkin's had his audience's attention; they seemed to be holding their breath.

The language of the lecture became philosophical at that point, the propositions offered sculpted in terms of this or that thinker, the arguments presented couched more and more in abstract formulae. Duggan's head reeled as Thomas Aquinas and Augustine were bashed off modern apologists and the question of evil was tapped into with ever increasing complexity.

Slightly dizzy from the bottle of red wine he had shared with Mayle over dinner in the hotel's restaurant, and from the heat generated by so many bodies in an already overheated banqueting hall, he fought off the desire to close his eyes and drift towards sleep. Mayle, legs askew, hands dangling, his body hunched forward slightly as if in search of a bar to lean on, was, conversely, all attention. Rallying, Duggan heard the lecturer say that Teilhardian concepts were no more than delicious mental play things used to reduce Christ to the status of a hero as pitifully mortal as Prometheus in the Greek myths. That's what we were left with, and it was high time we put things to right.

"Have you read Blackwell on possession?" Mayle asked quietly.

Duggan shook his head; he had little interest in such matters. He stared dully at the platform. What was the point of reading nonsense when you knew it was nonsense. If he had gained anything from philosophy, it was that questions were more important than answers. From theology he had gained nothing at all. Glancing at Mayle, he wondered why the lanky Californian bothered with such stuff.

What we were left with was a vacuum, the speaker was saying, a spiritual vacuum clearly detectable by the 1960s as the changes introduced by Vatican II took effect. Doing away with much of the Church's ancient symbolism, Catholics had been left all but shorn of mystery, their reliance on practices and associations that went back hundreds of years reduced to the twanging of electric guitars. Flushed with excitement as the Church modernized itself, congregations had been robbed of the external rites, words, actions and objects that had been so much a part of Catholic life.

Duggan had heard it all before; it was, as far as he was concerned, the chant of those to whom the quirky externals of the Catholic faith had become the faith itself, those to whom the movement of a hand or the swish of a vestment had taken on an almost magical significance. He himself was still infected with such nonsense, and that in spite of having not been inside a church for many years. Without looking at Mayle he said:

"I should never have taken on this assignment."

"Evil as an experience is a reality. All one has to do is read Camus, Dostoeyevsky or Hardy to realize this. Evil plays a distinct role in the lives of their characters."

Duggan closed his eyes and began to drift.

"We have to reject modernism's belief that it has solved the problem of evil."

A round of applause brought Duggan back to his senses.

"We have to remain sensitive to the philosophical questions that surround this subject, but we must not allow philosophy to blind us to the routine forcibleness of evil in human experience."

"If there be a God, from whence proceed so many evils?" said Duggan under his breath.

"What?" said Mayle.

Duggan got to his feet. "You know where to find me," he said, ignoring the stares of those in the rows behind.

His departure from the seminary had been equally abrupt. Betrayed by those he had trusted, by those from whom he had expected so much, he had stepped back into the world vowing never to have anything to do with the Church again. He was, he had been told, a mischief-maker. Head bowed, Fr Michael had sorrowfully delivered the Board's verdict, his podgy hands clamped palm down either side of the lengthy report he had helped compile. They had given him every chance. *Every* chance. But he had refused to listen.

Duggan headed down the wide, marquetry-floored corridor of the main lobby to the bar. The foxy-looking barman nodded, but did not smile - he was not the smiling type. Armed with a double scotch, Duggan chose a quiet corner, settled himself and took a few sips of the raw spirit. After a few minutes his eyes wandered in the direction of a dark-haired woman on his far right. She was reading a book, had taken off her shoes and stretched herself out on one of the heavily cushioned bamboo sofas.

That was when David Mayle turned up.

"I concluded you were having a better time than I was," Mayle said, easing himself into a low chair. "They're really getting down to it now. I think the devil's going to appear in person any second."

"It was too much for me," said Duggan. "Even the little I heard was too much."

"You don't believe in the devil?"

Duggan smiled and pushed himself up. "Shug pinot?"

A nod from Mayle.

When he returned, Mayle was smoking a cigarette. "I allow myself three per day," he said. "What are Jack Duggan's vices?"

"I have only one," said Duggan, reaching for his whisky.

They sat in silence for a moment, then Mayle said, "What was it you said before you upped and left?"

"'If there be a God, from whence proceed so many evils?' I don't remember who said it."

"You're full of surprises."

"You aren't?" said Duggan, remembering how the American had so deftly outmaneuvered him when speaking about Carter's hardline Catholicism.

"And if there isn't a God?" asked Mayle.

"Then it's how things are and that's the end of it."

"What caused you to break with them?"

"It was a gradual awakening; I began to notice things."

Mayle toyed with his glass. "My folks had been together for years before my father decided to train for the ministry." He glanced away, then back. "Wasn't her kind of thing at all."

"He saw the light."

"Saw something."

"You aren't tempted to hedge your bets?"

"That's nice," said Mayle. "I like the idea of being *tempted* to believe." Then with a smile he said: "Bottom's all but fallen out of my bucket I'm afraid."

The girl who had been reading got up and left. They watched her go.

"And here we are, the pair of us," added Mayle.

In the ballroom, the speaker was savoring a theological delicacy as if it were a hand-made sweet.

"I should be in Darwin," Duggan said for a second time.

2

Mother's Milk

Being early April, it rained heavily during the night. The noise woke Duggan and kept him awake. Switching on the bedside lamp, he lay thinking about his conversation with Mayle. It was just after three when he fell sleep again. He dreamt that the little electric cart he had seen on the golf course blew up, pieces of it shattering the thick glass of his balcony's sliding door.

There was no sign of Mayle in the crowded breakfast room. Duggan chose a side table and managed to order straight off - his coffee came immediately. When Mayle appeared, he looked as rough as Duggan felt.

"Get a decent newspaper," said Mayle, laying a blue folder on the table.

Duggan put the hotel's tourist newspaper aside.

"Carter's on this afternoon."

A nod from Duggan.

"Sleep well?"

"Like a dog. You?"

"Woke around two with the old heart doing the express train bit."

"Scotch is kinder."

"Yeh, I can see that." He picked up the menu. "What did you think of our rain?"

"Impressive." Mayle's hand shot up; a waitress acknowledged his signal but kept going. He looked back at Duggan. "Have you been following the Brindle case? Fr Brindle. The Australian priest who's taken on the CDF." Mayle opened his folder and pulled out a handful of newspaper cuttings. "This guy," he said, pointing at a bespectacled, middle-aged man with a face as rakish as his own. "He's been fighting off the Congregation for about three years."

Lifting the cutting, Duggan read about Fr Brindle, the priest who had incurred the wrath of Rome for speaking out against his Church's centralization of power.

"Makes for good reading," said Mayle.

"You think Carter's in with the CDF?"

"He keeps files on people."

"You know that for sure?"

"He's got a file on me and I'm not even Catholic."

Duggan stared at Mayle. "How could you possibly know that?"

"He told me." Mayle sighed. "I wrote a damning article on him a few months back. He tackled me on it. Put in a stiff complaint to my editor. When that didn't work, he phoned me at home."

"To say what?"

"To say that he had compiled a file on me because my bias was showing. In future, he said, I should be more careful when writing about the Catholic Church. I told him to mind his own business. He said it was his business, that there was a vendetta among print-media journalists to persecute the Church. I argued that it was our job to report on the Church's activities whether flattering or unflattering. He said we were consciously targeting the Church because we were, on the whole, a God-forsaken bunch of atheistic bullies who didn't give a damn about anything."

"Pugnacious."

"He called it the new anti-Semitism, said that he was setting up a Catholic anti-Defamation League." Mayle laughed to himself. "To be frank, I didn't know what to say to that."

"He's threatening legal action?"

"That's his pitch."

There was a picture of the Vatican's chief inquisitor - Frederick Cardinal Menenger - beneath that of Fr Brindle; it was the face of man confident in his own brand of truth. Duggan stared at that face for some seconds, then shifted his attention to Fr Brindle. The eyes looked pained, the mouth drawn. Then, realizing that all of the articles in the folder were from current Australian newspapers, he asked Mayle how he had come by such a collection.

"Cuttings service," said Mayle.

"And you just happened to have them with you?"

"I've got a campervan in the carpark stuffed with this kind of thing." Mayle laughed to himself. "Twenty volumes of cuttings covering eight subjects complete with cross-referenced index. I've got an obsessively tidy mind."

The waitress appeared with Duggan's scrambled eggs; it was an enormous helping with hash brown and what looked like a fruit salad on the side. Mayle ordered and Duggan asked about Bishop Peters. What kind of man was he. What had brought about the change in him.

"He describes himself as a left-brained mystic." Mayle paused, chose his words carefully. "He's deeply spiritual."

Duggan's brief had been slight - a book and two articles written by Peters. He looked up from his plate. "He's been fairly careful up until now."

"He broke the reticence barrier yesterday afternoon. Gave them a right old hiding."

"I'll need a transcript of that."

"I'll get you one."

"What's your angle?"

"The whole bag of tricks - as viewed from the bar."

"You'll send me a copy?"

"Of course. Likewise, please."

Mayle's coffee arrived.

"I'll never finish this," said Duggan.

"You're in America."

For want of something to say, Duggan said, "Married?"

"I was. My darling wife of twelve years ran off with the features editor of a rival newspaper about six months ago. You?"

"Never got round to it."

"I ought to have seen it coming. I tell a lie. I did see it coming but kidded myself on that it wasn't happening." Mayle took a sip of coffee. "I knew the guy. Got a lovely place top end of Chestnut in Frisco." A smile. "Nice area."

"I've got a hankering to see Haight Ashbury."

"Not much to see - apart from a few decrepit hippies and a second-hand clothes shop the size of an aircraft hangar."

Mayle's breakfast arrived; the waitress was stressed and hurried off. He poured maple syrup onto his pancakes: the pale yoke of a solitary fried egg bled out into the syrup to form a cloudy paste. The crispy bacon was the crispiest Duggan had ever seen. He asked for more information on Carter.

"Not much more to tell," said Mayle. "As I said, a big-time lawyer with a nose for trouble. He's been speaking to conservative Catholic enclaves all over the country for the last couple of years. A kind of roving ambassador without portfolio."

"But you think he's Vatican-backed."

"A personal mission that the hierarchy approves of." A piece of crispy bacon splintered and Mayle resorted to his fingers. "Question is, will the Donaghues and the Carters of this world succeed in slamming the stable door shut?" He corrected himself. "The door of the Bastille."

"They're running scared."

"Peeved, not scared. Those who know themselves to be in possession of the truth are seldom scared. Why should they be? They have a direct line to the Almighty."

There had been no shadow of doubt in Fr Michael Flynn's eyes as he pronounced the Board's verdict on Duggan. Out. Rejected. Ejected. How dare he question the Church's foundation doctrines and think he could get away with it. He had been warned on countless occasions to pull his head in, that a seminary was not the place in which to air those kinds of views. Not the right place at all. He had entered the seminary in the hope of becoming a priest, not a philosopher, to learn humility and submit himself to the will of his Maker, not argue the toss over issues amply dealt with elsewhere. So there was nothing else for it but to suspend him until he came to his senses. If he came to his senses and showed himself to be properly contrite then they might reconsider.

"I spent two years in a seminary."

Mayle did not reply.

"They threw me out for theological insubordination."

"They didn't pick up on your train of thought prior to entry?"

"I was an attractive candidate; I had a doctorate."

"Philosophy?"

"Ancient Greek and history. I ended up specializing in documents of the sixth century."

Mayle seemed more amazed by Duggan's subject choices than by his admission that he had been in a seminary.

"Most of us had good degrees," said Duggan. "I went in thinking a seminary was the place where questions of ultimate concern would be tackled. I was wrong. I found myself facing a system designed to smooth difficult questions out of existence. But you're right to have assumed that philosophy was the culprit, the battle's always been between religion and philosophy."

There was a queue standing at the open-plan entrance to the restaurant waiting for tables to be vacated. A roar of laughter went up from a large table crammed with clergymen.

"Some of their jokes don't bear repeating," said Mayle. He pushed his plate aside and reached for his folder. "Let's get out of here. I'll square mine up at the desk." As they rose, he said, "Carter's here. He's the big guy in the blue suit near the entrance. He's with two priests. Black hair. Built like a quarter-back. He saw me come in." A wry smile formed. "That's your cover blown."

As they passed, Carter glanced at Duggan.

Back in the foyer, Mayle checked his watch. They had half an hour before the first session started, time enough for an inspection of his mobile office. His office, it turned out, was a cream-and-brown Dodge with a coach-built rear.

"1990 and as good as new," said Mayle.

Everything had been so carefully arranged the interior appeared larger than it really was. There was even a fold-down single bed at the far end. The bed was down, and unmade.

"You're sleeping here?"

"It saves the chore of travelling in each day."

Computer gear on a narrow desk backed by a fax machine, a printer and backward-tilted shelves stacked with Mayle's boasted-of newspaper cuttings completed the scene. The cuttings books contained fifty folded A3 sheets, which in turn afforded one hundred sides per volume. A cross-referenced index gave Mayle full control over his little kingdom of facts and figures.

"You've put a lot of work into this."

"By the time I'm eighty I'll need a trailer. The electrical stuff runs off batteries; there are four big ones under the floor. I can change over to mains if I want."

"Have you always been this well organized?"

"It's a pathology." Mayle grimaced. "My marriage fell apart as a result of my fetish with order."

"Your bed's unmade."

"I'm learning to loosen up," said Mayle.

* * *

Bishop Peters arrived by taxi at 10-45, one hour and forty-five minutes after the first session of the conference got under way. As reception was momentarily unattended, he stood waiting, his mind preoccupied with a stabbing pain in his left knee. He would, he resolved yet again, have the damned thing seen to the moment he returned home.

The banqueting hall was packed. The platform was set out with a crescent of tables draped in wine-colored cloth. A grey-suited Archbishop Donaghue sat at the crescent's center, his grey-green eyes scanning the audience of clergy and religious as questions, answers and observations came from left and right. Robert Carter was on his right, sandwiched between a Fordham University man and one from St Francis College whose combined paper on the desert Fathers was at that moment under discussion. The paper had delicately set the tone Donaghue wanted for the conference.

Mayle and Duggan were at the very back of the hall, near an exit, the Australian having given in to Mayle when he realized that the paper being dealt with had to do with the early Anchorite communities. As a red-jacketed receptionist attended to Bishop Peters, an unexpected observation from one of the older scholars on the platform regarding this community caused Donaghue to snap his head round in the man's direction.

"Professor Donald Mercier, Pembroke, NC," he said, by way of introduction. And then: "It's certainly true that the early Anchorites behaved, prior to the introduction of the Pachomian rule, more like fakirs than Christians, but do you really think that what followed was entirely satisfactory? Was complete deference to superiors really the answer? Did not this, too, degenerate into an unhealthy practice?"

The scholar on Carter's left signaled to Donaghue that he would take up the question. Launching into a justification of the Pachomian rule, he said that it had brought stability to a large colony of monks at Mount Nitria in the Egyptian desert - some five thousand to be exact. Commendable as their solitary practice had been, it had, in essence, been about an exercising of the individual will. The obedience prescribed by the Pachomian rule had required a renouncing of the individual will and a strict observance of everything laid down by authority. It was true that this had later provoked a certain rivalry - some monasteries had gloried in their strictness - but on the whole it had been a move for the better: obedience had provoked humility. But at no time had the rule deteriorated to the extent of the fantastic competitions in spiritual perfection engaged in by the early Anchorites.

It was obvious from the questioner's reaction that this answer did not entirely satisfy, but he did not return serve, and the proceedings moved on. The next question had to do with St Basil's breaking up of the Pachomian community into smaller, more manageable units.

Duggan's expression was impassive, but his mind was racing. He did not agree with the view that all had been well in the Pachomian camp. It was true that some monks had been no better than Manichee heretics - Jerome had been taken aback by the ferocity with which many Anchorites had rejected the world at large - but it was a sweeping generalization to say that they had all been of the same ilk. The more probable reason for the Church's clampdown was that teachings banned by the Church were still being used by these communities. Free to do as they wished, these undisciplined searchers for truth had sought salvation by way of unregulated ascetic and contemplative practices, and the efforts of St Pachomius and St Basil, and later St Benedict, had been to stamp the Church's authority on the situation.

It was ironic to think that a collection of subversive manuscripts found in Upper Egypt had probably been hidden by monks belonging to the monastery of St Pachomius. Bishop Athanasius of Alexandria had been forced to purge the monasteries of heretical books, and that meant alternative views on Christianity's shape and purpose had been available. It hadn't just been a matter of monks trying to outdo each other in the spiritual stakes, it had also been a matter of documents antagonistic to Catholic doctrine being in wide circulation. With the four Gospels hailed as canonical, texts previously considered spiritually wholesome had, from that moment, been rejected and outlawed. Books that had previously been viewed as sacred had been placed on the Church's index of forbidden texts, many a monk being forced to live a double life.

When the session ended, Duggan and Mayle made straight for the bar.

"Heavy stuff," said Mayle.

"Mother's milk," said Duggan.

When served, they retreated to a table.

"They wouldn't have known what hit them." Duggan articulated his thoughts. "There's a lot more to what happened in the monasteries than you heard in there. It wasn't just a matter of a few regulations being added to the monastic mix to control enthusiasm; it was a full-scale blitz on an open-ended system of belief and practice backed by the threat of excommunication. What had been okay for you to believe on Monday was, by Wednesday, anathema. Any texts that contradicted what the ecclesiastics in Rome had decided was canonical were declared subversive, any person, or group of persons, continuing to use such texts were earmarked as disobedient to the faith - the 'faith' as it had been defined in Rome."

"Why didn't you say something? You had ample opportunity at the end."

"It's no longer my concern. I'm out of it. I'm here under protest."

"Is it possible to just walk away?"

"Arguing with them is pointless - they're inside a paradigm that has no exit." Duggan got to his feet. "Enough. I'd better check and see if Peters has turned up."

"Brindle's having a go."

"He'll go the same way as all the others."

"At least he'll go down fighting."

A shrug from Duggan. "I've got better things to do with my time."

"Sam doesn't believe Jesus walked on water."

"Sam? You're on first name terms?"

Mayle took a sip of wine and continued. "He believes in God, but not in a God who interferes in history."

"That's almost a contradiction in terms."

"Only if you think of God as a great big person out there somewhere. He doesn't talk about God that way. He says he gave up believing in that kind of God years ago, but only recently admitted to himself that it had happened." Mayle gave a little laugh. "He talks about that moment as a moment of discovery, a revelation almost."

"It's not how most people would describe it."

"Maybe they've missed the point."

"The point being?"

"That God has to die for Christianity to live."

Duggan blinked at Mayle.

"Nice twist, don't you think? He said it was the beginning of his spiritual life." Duggan made to turn away, but Mayle wasn't finished. "How can you ignore what's going on with these guys."

"With ease."

"Whisky's an alternative?"

Looking at Mayle with astonishment, Duggan said edgily, "Red wine's better?"

"I don't read ancient Greek."

"What the hell's that got to do with anything?"

"More than you could *ever* guess," said Mayle.

3

The Windle Woman

Bishop Peters agreed to see Duggan immediately after Bob Carter's afternoon lecture; he would be able to spare about an hour, he said drawlingly into the telephone. When Duggan hung up, the little bishop from Illinois turned to face the man in question.

"We have to have some idea of parameters," said Carter. "The press will be there in force."

"I understand your concern,"

"But not the need for circumspection, it seems." Carter's manner was that of a diplomat on a difficult mission. "Do you appreciate the position you will put Archbishop Donaghue in if you publicly reject Vatican policy? Can you imagine the repercussions of that?"

"It'll put this conference on the map."

"It will put *you* on the map," said Carter unflinchingly. "That's not quite the same thing."

"I can't in all conscience stand by and see decades of work discarded. I can't do that."

"I would remind you that decisions based on conscience alone can be in error."

"I'm well aware of the distinction between true and false propositions. Please do not lecture me!"

"I am not lecturing you. I am reminding you of your responsibilities as a bishop."

"I'm fulfilling those responsibilities by speaking out."

"Not in the Archbishop's opinion."

"I can't believe Michael sent you to do his dirty work."

"I'm not here at the Archbishop's instigation. I felt it my duty to speak to you on his behalf because —- "

"He doesn't know you're here?"

"*Because* I happen to know how deeply pained he is over this

35

matter."

"We *all* carry our share of pain, Mr Carter."

"Wouldn't prayer be more appropriate than a press conference?"

Staring at Carter, Bishop Peters terminated their discussion with a single word. "Out!" he said, and to drive the point home he thumbed the direction in which the door lay.

* * *

Bob Carter's lecture was, to say the least, unconventional and to the point. Lashing out with gusto at the liberal Catholic stance on education, he at the same time supplied some surprising facts and figures in relation to the Protestant educational system in America where, he said, the modernist approach had resulted in a backlash from parents against deteriorating standards. From mid-town Manhattan to Orlando, Florida, Protestant Christians were founding alternative community-based educational groups at an extraordinary rate, and Catholic parents were now asking the same fundamental questions about the education and instruction of their children. Middle-income parents on both sides of the religious fence had come out against the breakdown in standards of public schools and opted for institutions that demanded uniforms, dress codes, discipline and old-fashioned learning. And as old-fashioned learning included old-fashioned religion, there was now a move across the width and breadth of America to re-establish educational order and instill religious values. With that said he launched into a second volley of invective against liberal Catholic education policy, pointing out that the same concerns had arisen in Canada, Australia and Great Britain, and with a lawyer's dexterity catalogued just about every move made by educational modernists in America over the previous ten years. It was quite a performance, and when it ended, the audience showed its appreciation with a solid bout of applause and a barrage of questions.

Duggan scanned the audience, but there was no sign of Mayle.

Had he stayed away intentionally? That bothered the Australian. The American had refused to elaborate on his cryptic remark and had added insult to injury by reminding Duggan that it was only a quirk of circumstances that had changed a would-be priest into a journalist. If the seminary had been more flexible, he would have followed the vocation of priest and had to deal with his questions and his doubts at some other time. That. too, had not gone down well with Duggan - it had reminded him of a lost idealism. When the question period finished, he made his way out into the aisle and towards the exit.

"Stirring stuff."

"Where were you?"

"Over there on the right. I was buried behind that big guy."

"Look, I'm sorry . . ."

"Not your fault," said Mayle quickly. "I stuck my nose in where it didn't belong. I apologize."

"I was ungracious."

"You had every right."

They emerged from the hall and headed for Reception; neither spoke until they were there.

"I'm seeing Peters in a few minutes," said Duggan. "He's given me an hour."

"Give him my regards. And keep this evening free - there's someone I want you to meet." Mayle consulted his watch. "What say we meet back here at six?" Before Duggan could reply he said, "You like chicken?"

"Yup."

"Good. See you then."

Duggan watched the swing doors settle, then headed upstairs to collect his recorder. Glad to have cleared the air with Mayle, he strode down the long corridors with a sense of relief, his thoughts concentrated on the kinds of questions he would raise with Peters. Was he aware, for instance, that Carter had already stolen the march on him, that the audience for Carter's lecture had more than warmed to the lawyer's careful orchestration of conservative Catholic fears on education? There had been no mention of Peters' insistence that intellectual acuity was being undermined through myth being treated as incontrovertible fact. Just a barrage of statistics drawn from Catholic and Protestant sources supporting the notion of modernism's dire effect on Christian values. Secular education had its place, Carter had assured everyone, but when it systematically undermined the ability of our children to live a Christian life then it was time to call a halt. Duggan smiled to himself, collected his bits and pieces from his room and pulled the door shut behind him. Timothy had been right, there was more than enough politicking going on to keep the likes of him happy. Timothy? Duggan stopped in his tracks. He had forgotten all about Timothy.

* * *

Bishop Peters greeted the Australian warmly and commented on how far he had travelled. He was a small, lean man with greying hair and arresting grey eyes to match. When they were seated, Peters said that he had fond memories of Mel-bourne, which he had visited twice. He had been there to publicize his book, but had taken the opportunity to meet up with friends and see something of the countryside.

"You got to Sydney?"

"I had a day and an evening in Sydney, the same in Bris-bane. Four days and I was back home."

Duggan placed his recorder on the coffee table and switched it on. "Will you be heading back our way some time?"

"Yes, I think so. My book sold well in Australia."

"Contact me if you do." He handed over his card. "I read your book during the flight over."

"I should have been a little more forthright."

"You didn't know what was coming."

"I should have guessed."

Duggan doubled back. "When exactly were you in Australia?"

"May '99. Your draft proposals on religious education had just been released. That was when they moved up a gear."

"Perfect timing."

Bishop Peters smiled, but did not reply.

"You've been described by one American journalist as an intellectual mystic. Would you care to comment on that?"

A laugh. "I get high on ideas. I'm very much a left-brained animal."

"What decided you to take a hard line on education?"

"I don't see it as hardline. I see it as fundamental to the education of children that they be given the opportunity to develop a mental landscape in tune with reality. You can't function properly if you believe God suspends the laws of physics whenever it suits Him. The Christian God is not a resident of Mount Olympus."

"You're also sometimes referred to as a 'modernist'; recently as an 'obdurate modernist'."

"I'm unwilling to waste time on arguments that are patently absurd. The moves presently being made to reintroduce theological terms belonging to a time when it was believed Earth was flat is not, to my way of thinking, a move towards authenticity, it is a throwback curriculum specifically designed to undermine decades of hard-fought for advances in Catholic education. The educational materials now appearing are a prime example of the sharp divide that exists in the Church between faith and experience. Faith is more than knowing doctrine and Church teaching; it is discovering God *in* experience and allowing experience to inform conscience."

"You devote a chapter of your book to the developmental stages of young children, and suggest that the present movement in Catholic education all but ignores those stages. Why do you think they're taking this route?"

"Because they want the job of religious instruction completed before the end of primary school, which is ridiculous. Young children and abstract reasoning do not go together. Teach Genesis as a literal event to a child and see the trouble you have later trying to teach him the difference between literary forms and biblical myths. Now that ought to be obvious - obvious to any educated, thinking person - but it seems to have completely evaded those presently re-sculpting educational policy for the third millennium."

"As directed by the Vatican."

"Yes, as directed by the Vatican."

"Which I believe you spoke out against strongly on television yesterday."

"And which I will continue to do until the subject is properly debated."

"In his role as canon lawyer, Robert Carter has just given a stirring lecture on the need to return to doctrinal basics. " Duggan, consulted his notes. "He believes that moves must be made to redress the imbalance in Catholic education policy caused by, and I quote, 'the existentialism of the 60s and 70s'. Using your approach, isn't there a danger that the multiple theories of the modern secular world will simply swamp Catholic religious sensibility altogether?"

"If we refuse to change, then perhaps we *should* have our religious pins knocked from under us."

"That's a pretty daring thing to say."

Bishop Peters' smile was sardonic. "Death comes before resur-rection. If the Catholic faith is to survive, it will have to die to its old self. Resuscitation of the medieval corpse is not an alternative. The only reason J.F.K. got the presidency was because liberal intellectual non-Catholics were aware that his educational background was untainted by Catholic authoritarianism. In fact he had no Catholic education in his background at all. He attended an exclusive and expensive non-denominational preparatory school and then went straight to Harvard. If he'd had an old-time Catholic education he'd have been run out of town. I'll be talking at length about Catholic education in America tomorrow afternoon."

Intrigued, Duggan proceeded to ask questions on a range of issues, and Peters, firing from the hip, commented robustly on non-inclusive language, the exaggerated importance given to rules, the Church's obsessive interest in theological technicalities and a Church locked into an outmoded world view. What they were trying to do was stick Christianity back in the museum, he said, and that was not helpful. The three-tier universe and doctrines of the medievalist were no longer of practical use, and that being the case, we had to face facts and make every effort to transpose Christianity into a new key.

"And if we fail?"

"Then we will disappear without trace." Peters smiled. "Not in the sense of vanishing from the scene, that's unlikely. More in the sense of progressively ceasing to be relevant. If we don't get our act together, *that* will be our fate."

The interview ran overtime. When it was over, Duggan passed on David Mayle's greeting. Peters asked about Mayle's whereabouts, and on learning that he was at the conference said that he would like to speak to him. Impressed with the man's candor, Duggan thanked him and prepared to leave. But Peters wasn't finished. As they moved towards the door he asked Duggan how long he had being doing what he was doing.

"On and off for about twenty years."

"You have a good grasp of your subject."

Duggan smiled, but did not reply.

"Are you Catholic?"

"I was brought up Catholic."

"You've left the faith?"

"I'm in exile."

"Most thinking people are."

"That's not the impression I've got here."

"There's always an old guard."

"They're moving on a wide front."

"It will take time and a much prodding."

"You're optimistic about the future?"

"It's a failing."

As the door opened, Duggan framed a final question. "It's said that you don't believe Jesus walked on water."

Bishop Peters' smile had a weary edge. "Apples fell to earth in the first century just as they do now. What more can I say?"

"A lot of people here seem to have overlooked that fact."

"I'm not one of them," said the Bishop.

* * *

Duggan was a few minutes early for his appointment with David Mayle, so he walked down the corridor towards the restaurant and stood, hands in pockets, staring out through the picture window that afforded a view of a paved area complete with pergola. Workmen had been there during the day doing repairs, and that very afternoon the painters had dismantled most of their scaffolding, the cream and rust refurbishment of the hotel's facade being now all but complete. As he retraced his steps he glimpsed Bob Carter in the restaurant. As usual, the man was deep in conversation, his companion, a priest in full clerical garb in obvious agreement with some point being made. That was when Duggan decided to interview Robert Carter. When Mayle turned up, he let him in on his decision.

"He's been known to terminate an interview halfway through

"It would help balance things out."

"How did you get on with Sam?"

"Fine. He wants to speak to you."

A nod from Mayle. "You got what you wanted?"

"And more."

The American said something about eating at a nearby franchise house, but did not enlarge on who they were going to meet up with. They walked through the carpark in silence, crossed the road and headed for a shopping center at the hotel's rear. An octagonal building bursting with patrons was their destination. As he pushed open the door Mayle said that the grilled chicken was the best he had ever tasted. Making their way between packed tables, Duggan was led to where a woman in her late thirties sat by herself. She looked up and smiled when she saw Mayle.

"Jane Windle," said Mayle.

"Jack Duggan," said Duggan.

They shook hands and he sat down opposite. Mayle took up residence on Jane Windle's left.

"You were in the bar area of the hotel the other night," said Duggan. His gaze moved to Mayle. "What's going on?"

"A little necessary subterfuge," he replied.

"David says you're Australian. My father's been in Australia a number of times."

"Your father is?"

"Professor James Windle. He's an historian."

Duggan glanced at Mayle, but he was busy signaling to a waitress who was too busy to notice.

"He's just returned from the Middle East. He was doing research with Fr Paul Merle. Merle . . . "

"Merle is Professor of Semitic languages at the Sorbonne," said Duggan. "He's known to everyone in the field."

A waitress complete with baseball cap and stubby pigtails came and took their order. When she moved away, Jane said that her father and Merle had been doing Vatican-sponsored research on the letters of Ignatius of Antioch, and had stumbled on an additional handwritten letter in Greek pasted into the backboard of the 1646 Isaac Voss Collection. The letter had proved to be of such importance that Rome had put an embargo on news of the find getting out.

"And then the whole collection went missing." said Mayle. "The authorities haven't accused them of theft, but as they were the only ones in God knows how long to show any interest in that particular collection, and they photographed it extensively, questions are being asked."

"What does your father think happened?"

"He's at a complete loss; as is Fr Merle. There's a Vatican lawyer in Jerusalem right this minute trying to sort things out with the

Department of Antiquities."

"Point is," said Mayle, "if that collection doesn't turn up, then the photographs are worthless."

"Tell me about the photographs."

"There are three sets," said Jane. "One went to Rome with a translation, one to the Sorbonne with Merle, the other to the university of Essen in Germany with my father. He's visiting professor of ancient history there."

"Did Merle do the translation?"

"They worked on it together - my father's a Greek specialist in his own right."

"A translation went to Rome *before* they returned to their respective universities?"

"It wasn't a polished translation, but it was, as you can imagine, pretty thorough. Vatican specialists have taken over the task."

"Have you any idea what's in the text?"

"The barest idea," said Jane. "Anyway, I can't talk about it - it's *verboten.*"

"So what's this got to do with me?"

"There's a fourth set of photographs," said Mayle.

The little pig-tailed waitress returned with their drinks and swooped off again.

"So?" said Duggan.

"Merle doesn't know about the extra set. If the Voss Collection doesn't turn up we may have to leak the letter's contents to the media."

"Why the concern? The Department of Antiquities will publish the letter in their own good time."

"Exactly," said Mayle. "That could be some time never."

"Okay," said Duggan. Then, "Whoever publishes will have to explain how they came to be in possession of the photographs. Merle and your father will be implicated whether they like it or not."

"The fourth set is different from the other three." Jane's smile verged on the apologetic. "They were taken with a different camera."

Duggan digested the implications of that. "You want me to arrange for publication in Australia?"

"No. We want you to do a separate translation."

"Why? You've already got one."

"That would be to break the Vatican's embargo," said Jane, her tone careful; it was as if she were explaining something to the tax man. "If exactly the same translation turned up its origin would be immediately obvious."

Duggan accepted Jane's reasoning. They needed the idiosyncrasies of a fresh translation to draw attention away from Windle and Merle.

"A separate translation won't annul the fact that the original documents have disappeared."

"No, but we'll have the sworn testimony of my father and Merle that the photographs in their possession say fundamentally the same thing as the published photographs."

"You think Merle would own up to that?"

"He can't lie - wouldn't lie."

"He could stay silent."

"That would be tantamount to approval."

"It'll still be good night career if the photographs are traced back to your father. And need I remind you that we're sitting here in full view of everyone."

"These are locals," said Mayle. "They don't know who we are."

Duggan reached for his whisky. "There's more to translating this kind of thing than I think either of you realize. It isn't something you knock off in a couple of hours." He looked away, looked back. "The Jerusalem authorities will be on to this in a flash."

"Of course they will," said Mayle. "And they'll conclude that the theft of the Voss document is linked to these photographs. That'll take the pressure off."

"It would mean my taking the photographs back to Australia."

"We realize that."

"You're willing to take that risk?"

"You're the safest risk we've come up with."

Duggan huffed a laugh. "Friend of bishops *and* scholars? You're a man of parts, David."

"My father wouldn't be doing this if he didn't think it important."

"Obviously."

Jane completed her overture. The Voss document had obviously been stolen to undermine confidence in the photographs, she said. That could be turned to their advantage. On publication they would use that very fact to emphasize the importance of what had been found.

"You don't even know if I'm up to doing this."

"I'm sure you'd tell us if you weren't." Jane's look was quizzical. "Are you up to it?"

"I've kept my hand in."

"That'll do me," said Mayle.

* * *

Duggan slept well, woke early, breakfasted without seeing anything of David Mayle, and arrived late for the morning forum. Archbishop Donaghue was defending a paper he had written on the post-modern approach of scholars to Jesus and his intentions. But as Duggan listened, it was dark-eyed Jane Windle who occupied his mind. Donaghue's voice droned on. Liberationist, feminist, process, and post-modern theologians had changed the character of meaning-making in relation to Jesus in his time, and in our time, and this had all but destroyed the Church's two-thousand-year-old faith tradition in a matter of decades. Duggan smiled. The old guard were fighting back in the hope of a return to the simple faith, but the mishmash of history and mythology that underpinned that faith was no longer tenable. It would not be argument that would win the day, it would be empty pews that would bring the walls tumbling down.

When the forum's wrangle completed itself, he went out to the carpark in search of Mayle, but the campervan was locked and there was no sign of the man. The bar, too, afforded no success. Back in his room he lay down and again considered what had been asked of him. Perhaps he should get involved. A smile as he detected the real reason for his interest. Then a frown. Did he really need such a complication in his life? Everything had been moving along nicely until Dave Perry's pneumonia, then without warning he had been asked to acknowledge an old self, a self whose hopes and ambitions he had thought laid to rest. Duggan the would-be priest. Duggan the scholar. And now there was Jane Windle to complicate an already complicated situation, a woman with a wicked smile who knew he was attracted to her, a woman who had known it the moment their hands touched. And somewhere in the building Fr Timothy White waiting for his call, waiting to corner him for God and the Catholic Church.

* * *

The anteroom chosen for Bishop Peters's lecture was about one-third the size of the banqueting hall and not anywhere as well attended as hoped by those who sympathized with his viewpoint. But a good sprinkling of press people and photographers were present, and a television crew was in evidence. Tackling fear of change in his opening remarks, Peters said that such a fear had dogged the Church's footsteps for centuries, and not just in the sense of fearing that it might misinterpret the will of God, but in the sense of being unable to fulfill the urgings of the Holy Spirit. Why unable? Because fear of change was actually fear of fear itself, the fear of glimpsing our own vulnerability, our helplessness, our isolation, our weakness and fragility in a limitless and often incomprehensible universe. And so we barricaded ourselves in with mental constructs, and found it difficult to change our minds for fear of falling through the cracks in our own reasoning. That, more than anything else, was what we were afraid of, the cracks in our own reasoning. Fear of fire, fear of flood or terrorist bomb was bad enough, but fear of the danger lurking inside of us was worst of all, the danger of losing even the little bit of security we had.

From there he launched into an analysis of religious development in America, an analysis that suggested that the crisis undergone by American Catholicism in the 1890s had never been satisfactorily resolved. That crisis had been the so-called 'Americanist heresy', he said, his gaze ranging across that section of audience where Duggan sat, and the patterns of contention surrounding that heresy were still with us. Any major change in Church authority, or attitudes to that authority, were likely to be fought along similar lines to those of the heresy debate of that time, and it was our responsibility to familiarize ourselves with the issues involved.

In response to his own directive, he then ranged through a mass of historical detail to do with the development of the Catholic Church in America, and tackled what he described as the central issue, the issue of education and the change over for ordinary Catholics from being second-class citizens to that of equal partners in the shaping and building of American democracy. The Church's fear of democracy had lain at the heart of the accusation that American Catholics had abandoned their faith, and it was only when this unfair and treacherous accusation from the past was dealt with head-on that the present problem with Church directives on education could be properly understood. History was repeating itself, and it was our job to take a stand against the ultra-conservative faction that had, for the moment, usurped papal authority for its own unscrupulous ends.

A number of people walked out at that point; it was as if a prearranged signal had been given. One of them, a woman, shouted "Mirari Vos!" as she made for the door. On looking round, Duggan saw David Mayle standing at the back of the room. Mayle saw him in the same moment and raised a hand in salute.

"For those of you not familiar with 1832 Encyclical Mirari Vos," said Bishop Peters, "it teaches that throughout history states have perished as a result of excessive liberty, freedom of speech and constant reform. The Encyclical also condemns the liberty of the press, believes that the Apostles burnt books, and congratulates the Council of Trent on instituting an Index on which books believed to contain impure doctrine could be placed. If that is the direction in which you wish to travel, if that is the kind of Church you wish to see reinstituted, then feel free to join our brothers and sisters in the lobby."

The silence was electric; no one moved.

Showing little reaction to what had happened, he went on to talk of an illuminating experience he had had while doing research in the Paulist Archives in Washington DC, archives previously preserved in the 52nd Street Paulist Library in New York City. What had interested him were clippings dealing with the unofficial feelings of ordinary Catholics when accused by fellow Catholics in Europe of being dangerously close to a particular heresy, or insufficiently respectful of traditional values. The frank and sometimes gossipy tone of the information provided, and the strong feelings motivating their publication, had revealed a different stratum of thinking from that reflected in ecclesiastical correspondence. Put bluntly, these ordinary Catholics hadn't given a fig for the blinkered theological arguments being offered against the democratic freedoms they enjoyed. In response to the claim that they were in error, they had shown an unshakeable confidence in Republican values and directly equated those values with God's purposes.

A few people clapped, but the bulk of the audience remained silent. Smiling down at them, Bishop Peters said that good Catholics loved not only what was good and beautiful, but also what was true. The remedy for the confusions caused by a little learning was more learning, not less learning. Those who dreaded knowledge were as far away from the life of this century as the dead whose bones had crumbled into dust a thousand years before. Each century called for its own type of Christian perfection, and the call today was for a high standard of learning, not midnight flagellations or Compostellan pilgrimages. God had never at any time worked miracles to make up for human deficiency. We had to work as if everything depended on us, and pray as if everything depended on God. There was too much waiting on the actions of others. Laymen deferred continually to priests, priest to bishops, bishops to the pope, and while this was going on the promptings of the Holy Spirit were all but ignored. In this vein, it was time to establish a contemporary identity for the Church, and the only way in which this could be done was through the rejection of attempts to reintroduce some version of Pius IX's *Syllabus Errorum.* The idea that only absolutist policies could save Catholicism and, ultimately, Christianity, was a myth created by insecure, autocratic minds.

He ended his lecture by pointing out that two views of the Catholic Church were prevalent in American society: the communal and the hierarchical. It was believed by some that the Church's hierarchy exercised leadership through the communal, and that this worked well, but the truth was noticeably otherwise. As a self-enclosed hierarchical institution, the Church's behavior was often corrosive, its contribution to community an ongoing tension that many were now unwilling to ignore. Community, not hierarchy, was the key to a vibrant Church in the future, and attempts to hijack community by ultra-conservatives, or, to be more exact, *neoconservatives,* should be blocked at every turn. As the swamp of speculative theology had, in the past, been rejected as unhelpful in the building of American democracy, so the harsh, unbending and altogether unfruitful harangues of ecclesiastics bound to the autocratic model should be rejected in the present. In the autocratic model, community had no place in ministry; it was there simply to service and sustain the clergy's view of itself. In the community model, however, each and every person was a productive and essential element in the body of Christ, a point of contact with the Church as a living entity. On that challenging note, the lecture reached its conclusion. Having gone well over time, questions were few.

As his audience filed out, Bishop Peters gathered together his notes and placed them in a rather worn leather briefcase. When the buckles were done up, he thanked the young clergyman who had introduced him and turned to deal with the journalists who had gathered. Duggan watched as his colleagues went about their business, the photographers moving to and fro in search of an interesting shot. The hall was completely empty of its audience by the time they were through with him. Duggan and Mayle waited as a final question was dealt with, then walked down the aisle towards the little bishop and his helper. Seeing them approach, and recognizing Mayle's slouching form, Peters came towards them.

"David!"

"Hello Sam," said Mayle, astonishing the young priest who was deferentially hovering. "They haven't locked you away then?"

"I'm on a good behavior bond."

"Huh," said Mayle.

Turning to the priest who was now standing awkwardly to one side, Peters again thanked him, and by tone of voice intimated that he was no longer required.

"You've already met our resident Aussie."

"Mr Duggan," said Peters.

"Jack said you wanted to have a chat."

"Is the bar still open?"

"Yes, I think so."

"Then let's do it there. No, you too," said Peters, seeing Duggan's reaction. "There's more that has to be said."

4

Eating Glass

"A bishop's a damned sight more difficult to get rid of than an ordinary priest," said Peters, having chosen a spot in full view of Reception, "and I have no intention of making it easy for them."

"Is this off or on the record?" asked Duggan.

"On," said Peters. "If they're going to do me in, or try to do me in, then I want their every move put before the public. It's the only way I can hope to hold them in check."

"We're talking CDF?" said Mayle.

"We are," said Peters. He was leaning forward over the low table now, glass of whisky in hand, elbows on his knees. "They opened a file on me about six months ago - must be pretty thick by now." A laugh. "Palazzo del Santo Uffizio - the Holy Inquisition. Who'd believe it still exists?"

"*Inquisitio,*" said Duggan.

"The man has a little Latin," said Peters, glancing at Mayle, who was already scribbling. And then to Duggan he said, "Did you know that they imposed a new anti-modernist oath on priests and teachers in '89?"

"I'd heard," said Duggan.

"We all thought we'd seen the back of that one. The previous oath - the one introduced by Pius X - was dropped in '68. I, unfortunately, was ordained in '64." Another laugh from the little bishop. "As I said during my lecture, history is repeating itself. Catholic scholars at the turn of the twentieth century pointed to the need of coming to terms with modern, critical scholarship - particularly in biblical studies and church history - and here we are at the end of the twentieth making the same mistakes. They're even targeting popular writers and accusing them of doctrinal deviancy. Did you ever hear of anything so absurd!"

"And Menenger's head of the pack," said Mayle

"Cardinal Menenger is cozily ensconced in the little building next to the Basilica, just behind the left side of Bernini's colonnade," said Peters, having taken a close look at the Congregation for the Doctrine of the Faith's headquarters when last in Rome. "The CDF's previous prefect got things rolling and Menenger has taken up the task with enthusiasm."

Duggan came back in. "Weren't the CDF's archives opened to scrutiny last year?"

"Yes, but only up until 1903, a significant cut-off date if you think about it. It means that everything to do with the modernist crisis of 1907 is excluded. Not much of a treasure trove for scholars there. And as the French Revolutionary occupiers of Rome burned most of the Inquisition's records in 1798, a pretty thin haul for anyone trying to build a coherent picture of CDF behavior in the modern period."

"Are you sure you want to go public on this?"

"I have to; they do not engage in open dialogue. I might get a couple of words in about four years down the track, but it'll be too late by then."

"What are the charges?" asked Mayle.

"Questions, not charges; the charges will come later." He looked at Duggan. "They tried to get me on not appreciating the true harm of modernism, but that backfired. Even the CDF can't argue a case like that. They have the right to tackle me on theological interpretation, but observations dealing with historical reality are completely beyond their brief." A smile. "Then they got heavy. I'd been involved in a television debate - along with a fellow priest and a panel of literary experts - on the merits and demerits of a controversial novel on the life of Christ, and within minutes found myself involved in a silly discussion with the priest over whether Jesus had ordained his apostles to the priesthood at the Last Supper. The book denied that he had. The priest said that the book was in error. I said that such a belief was no more than that, a 'belief', and that belief for its own sake should never be taken too seriously. He said that not to believe that Jesus had ordained his apostles to the priesthood at the Last Supper was to deny the Holy Father apostolic authority. I said that such a notion

was deeply unhelpful to anyone trying to understand the Christian message. You can imagine what the press did with *that* the following day."

"I've got the cuttings," said Mayle.

"Bishop denies Pope's infallibility," intoned Peters.

A question from Duggan carried them back a step.

"How did you find out you were in the CDF's bad books?"

"Through my Archbishop. Clarification on my views was requested by the Congregation."

"You were delated?"

"I presume so; it's generally a complaint that starts the ball rolling."

"The priest you disagreed with?" said Mayle.

"Any arch-conservative who heard the broadcast could have been responsible."

"What do you think of the process itself?" asked Duggan.

"I think it's a travesty of Christian values. There's no place for inquisitorial procedures in the Church. Never was and never will be."

Mayle wanted to know about the ins and outs of the CDF's approach. Peters obliged. The Congregation was run, he said, by a *congregatio*, a committee of around twenty-three cardinals and bishops who, on the evidence put before them by a 'consulter', decided whether or not to take action. If action were required, then the delated individual was informed through a superior and asked to submit a clarification of his views. If the clarification were deemed adequate, the matter was dropped. If deemed inadequate, the process of doctrinal examination went ahead. A sigh from Bishop Peters. He had won the argument hands down in relation to 'modernism' as a stage of history, but in trying to unravel the intricacies of history in relation to theology and mythology, he had come unstuck. There was little room in CDF thinking for such niceties, no room at all for the suggestion that the Church's theologically driven traditions could, or should, be questioned.

"Can you really expect any other kind of reaction?" said Duggan. "The Church is the Church is the Church."

"I expect exactly what I get, but that does not stop me from being disappointed each time my expectations are realized. It is the cusp of the new century after all. We no longer believe that the sun revolves around the Earth, or that the Earth is the center of the universe. We no longer believe that women are merely receptacles for male sperm. We no longer believe that heaven is above our heads or that hell is beneath our feet. We've moved on. We've got rid of the idea that epileptics are possessed by demons or that sickness is a punishment from God because of sin. All of that is behind us, way, way behind us. Yet we persist in hanging on to religious ideas that by their very nature make a nonsense of everything we know. I can't ignore that. It is my duty as a human being to uphold intelligent inquiry, my duty as a bishop to encourage honesty over lies, love over hate, and, above all, courage over cowardice. If I fail in that duty, then I fail as a Christian."

The fluency and sincerity of the bishop's remarks impressed Duggan, as did the wave of energy that seemed to emanate from him. Mayle, too, picked up on the sudden change that had come over the man.

"If you go public you'll be censured automatically," said Duggan. "Is that what you want?"

"It's not what I want; it's what I can't avoid."

"They'll throw you out."

"They're going to have to throw an awful lot of us out over the next few years. It's the end of the line in that regard."

Mayle took up the question. "How does that translate? What would you say was the fundamental problem facing the Church?"

"Wornout formulas," said Peters without hesitation. "The Nicene Creed is a formula for Christ, it is not Christ. It is an attempt to define and express Christ through language at a specific time in human history. As such it is subjective and imperfect. End of story."

"We need a new formula?"

"Yes, I think so. And not just in the sense of juggling words. More in the sense of rediscovering the inclusive nature of Christianity, the Christianity of the Gospels, the Christianity that did not exist when the Gospel story was being acted out in real life. In a word, Jesus was not a Christian; he was a Jew who attempted to extend religious comprehension, not truncate it."

"The old formula's been around for a very long time," said Duggan. "Resistance will be considerable."

"This is not 1907; we're not going to fall back and toe the line."

"You could end up with two Catholicisms."

"It is my hope that we will not. Vatican II opted for a community model. That's the model I believe we have to nurture."

"You're pitting yourself against people of deep conviction, people of immense power and influence in the Church. Some of these people have been entrusted with the process of change itself. How can you hope to win?"

"Because the community model for Catholicism is already up and running. The hierarchy can threaten as much as it likes, but it can't halt what has taken place, and what is taking place. The Catholic cat is out of the ecclesiastical bag and it will not go back in again."

Duggan had scribbled a few notes at the back of his diary; he consulted them. "How would you define 'cowardice' in the sense you used it earlier? Your exact words were 'Courage over cowardice'."

"Courage in the sense of not falsifying reality. It's one thing to be afraid, to shy back from the vastness of reality, to feel inadequate and overpowered in the face of mystery; it is quite another to feign an irrefutable understanding of that mystery and foist that understanding on others for the sake of power. That's the bottom line here, not some great universal truth that has to remain unaltered for ever and ever, just power and the preservation of the status quo. The

Church is afraid of its own shadow, Mr Duggan, and so it ought to be; it has avoided the blatantly obvious for the last hundred years or more. What thinking men and women have to do is switch on the light of reason so that faith can complete its journey. Faith without reason is a travesty of every God-given talent that we possess. Blind faith is fear masquerading as courage. The truly courageous are not those who believe in spite of every reason to the contrary, they are those who trust in life and love and experience even when shaking to bits inside."

"You want people to stop believing in the Christian message?"

"No, I want them to realize that that message has been turned into a cheap replica of itself, and that the promises of a Christmas-cracker type faith won't see them through to the end. That's all."

There was a silence; it lasted some time. Mayle broke it. "So what's your next move?"

"More of the same until the dyke breaks." Bishop Peters glanced at his watch. "I have to be in San Francisco by six."

"Has Donaghue spoken to you?" asked Duggan.

"Not a word."

"I'm surprised he let you speak at all."

"Rope to hang myself with; it's to their advantage." He made to get up, but changed his mind. "Mr Duggan, it's been a pleasure." They shook hands across the table. "I look forward to reading your piece."

"I'm almost looking forward to writing it," said Duggan.

* * *

When he opened the door and found Jane Windle in the corridor he was, to say the least, surprised. David did not know she had come, she said. When the door closed behind her she came straight to the point - would he, or wouldn't he help them out? He said that there were responsibilities and questions of ethics attached to what they had asked him to do, and he was not at all sure that he wanted to shoulder such responsibility. Did she want a drink? She said No. He agreed that her father would not have done what he had done if the find had not been important, but there had to be someone out there better suited to the task.

"David wants you to do it."

"David be blowed!"

"My father will check whatever you come up with."

"Sorry, that's not a route I can take. Getting the nod from your father would be tantamount to collusion. I'd end up having to skew my translation to fit in with his opinions."

"Fr Merle had the last word, not my father."

"It was a rushed piece of work, Jane."

"My father agrees with Merle's findings."

"Your father might *want* Merle to be right. His liberal sensibilities have obviously been titillated."

She turned away, turned back and said, "Okay, so you don't want to do it."

"It's better that I just disappear back to where I came from."

"Aren't you even curious?"

"It's taken me twenty years to slip the noose."

"What's that supposed to mean?"

"It means I've developed an aversion to things religious."

"You wanted to be a priest!"

"We were kids. We didn't know our arse from our elbow."

"You must have had some idea of what you were getting yourself into. You're not exactly an idiot."

"That's your idea of flattery?"

"You were willing to contemplate being celibate for the rest of your life for God's sake!"

Duggan smiled in response. "It was a bit like an arranged marriage; devotion to the job was expected to come later."

"If you won't do it for yourself, then do it for me."

Duggan's expression was almost comic. "Why the hell should I do that?"

"Because it'll give you a way out of your dilemma."

"My dilemma being?"

"That you still want to be a priest and can't admit it to yourself."

"That's absolute rubbish!"

"Are you sure?"

"As sure as I'll ever be about anything. It was a young man's folly. I've hardly given it a second thought in twenty years."

Not quite the truth, but not far from it.

"Fine." Jane's smile was pragmatic. "You know as well as I do that you fit the bill perfectly." She gave a little laugh, stared at him. "I couldn't believe our luck when David described your background."

"I should have kept my big mouth shut."

"You know why this has to be done. If anyone knows, you know."

"You've turned into a pushy American."

"Pushy? You haven't seen *pushy*," she said back. Then, as if to prove her point, she said, "We'll pay you for your efforts. I should have said. Should I have said?"

"Don't be ridiculous."

"We wouldn't expect you to do something like this for nothing."

"The question of money never crossed my mind."

"Why not? You're a professional. We want to hire your services and services have to be paid for."

"You know what I mean."

She paused in her onslaught, pushed her slim hands into the pockets of her jeans and looked down for a moment. Her head came up. She had just assumed that he'd be interested, she said. It seemed like a foregone conclusion that he'd want to help.

"It's an aversion thing."

"Think of this as therapy."

"I'm not disabled; just pissed off."

"You mean angry."

He hesitated, then he said, "It wasn't all their fault, Jane. I should have known better. They put up with a lot before kicking me out."

"You stood your ground."

"I expected them to roll over in awe. They didn't."

She looked to the side as if searching for something, looked back. "I know you're the right person for this. You know it, too."

Duggan's smile was accepting of that possibility.

"I think you should take a look at the photographs before deciding."

"You don't give up easily, do you?"

"It's too important, Jack," she said.

* * *

Bishop Peters got into the waiting taxi with Archbishop Donaghue's perturbations following him. He had to think things through, the Archbishop was saying. He was good man and the Church needed good men, but there was a limit to the Holy Father's patience. Bishop Peters said that he would keep that in mind. The door closed. They stared at one another through glass, two men with the same steely resolve. They had never seen eye to eye - not even before the brouhaha over education - but Peters had always had a sneaky admiration for Donaghue's dogged stance on matters of faith: the man was like a rock when it came to questions of belief and tradition.

Yet the same man had shown himself capable of selling his faith short. A glaring example of this had been his unwillingness to warn against a report from Florida that an image of the Virgin Mary had appeared on the side of a building. Many thousands of people had visited Clearwater in the hope of catching a glimpse of this phenomenon, and all Donaghue had managed to come up with was something inane about it being the Blessed Virgin's right to appear wherever she wanted. That had shocked Peters. It had shown the Archbishop to be someone to whom keeping the faithful in tow was more important than facing reality. But his heart was in the right place; there was no doubting that. As a champion of the underdog and a strong advocate for women having a greater role in the Church he was courageous to a fault. As the taxi swept down the drive Peters closed his eyes and acknowledged that fact, took it into himself and allowed it to do its work. It was what he termed 'eating glass', and as he sped away it seemed to him that he was having to eat glass more often than he would have liked.

* * *

David Mayle and Bob Carter eyed one another with the kind of distrust reserved for dogs in an alleyway. Carter had just returned from Santa Rosa, and as luck would have it had bumped into Mayle in the carpark. He was the first to speak.

"It was my hope your paper would send someone a little more sympathetic," he said straight out, setting the tone for what was to follow.

"You're a bit of a mouth, aren't you," said Mayle.

"I speak my mind; I have that right."

"We all have that right ," said Mayle.

"Within limits."

"I know where the boundaries are."

"Not that I've noticed."

"I tell it like it is."

It was as if they had folded their arms and were pushing one another across a schoolyard.

"Your bias is an affront to journalism," said Carter. "You're selective in your choice of evidence."

"Everybody has a take on something. You have yours, I have mine."

"I try to be fair."

"You try to look as if you're being fair. That's not quite the same thing."

"At least I make the attempt."

"Yeh, before you ride roughshod over whatever poor bastard you happen to have set your sights on!"

"If you're saying that I defend the faith, then I accept that."

"You're out of step with what's happening out there. Hardly anyone agrees with you."

"That's not my impression."

"Try selling your brand of Catholicism on the street. You'd be laughed out of court."

"I've never once been laughed out of a court," said Carter, literalizing Mayle's metaphor. "You should perhaps keep that in mind."

"Is that a threat?"

Carter's smirk was unforgettable. "Read it any way you like," he said, turning away.

When Duggan heard the details of their conversation, it hardened his resolve to interview Carter.

"Nasty piece of work," said Mayle, tucking into his salad. A glance. "So what've you been up to?"

"I had a visit from Jane."

"Little hussy!"

"I've seen the photographs."

Mayle looked up. "And?"

"I've agreed to help"

Smiling into his salad, Mayle said, "I thought you might."

"What's that supposed to mean?"

"She obviously fancies you."

"She did everything but kick me in the chins."

"Exactly. She wouldn't have bothered if she didn't fancy you."

Duggan didn't know how to respond.

Mayle was smiling an odd smile; Duggan couldn't work out what that smile signified.

"You couldn't keep your eyes off her," said Mayle, glancing at Duggan. "I'm not blind."

"She's attractive. So what?"

"If you play your cards right you're in with a real chance there."

Duggan's perplexity over Mayle's tack was in his frown. He, too, changed tack. "How long have you known Jane?"

"As long as I've known her father. Nine, ten years? She's a good kid, but she's impulsive." A laugh from Mayle, and another glance. "But you've already found that out I think."

"I agreed for all the wrong reasons."

Mayle pushed the empty salad bowel aside. "She doesn't pull her punches."

Duggan huffed a laugh, but remained silent.

"So what did you make of the photographs?"

"If he was trying to make the special batch of photographs look unprofessional, he succeeded. They were obviously taken in a hurry."

"They were. Clear enough for your purposes?"

A nod from Duggan.

"Difficult?

"Everything will depends on how I construe the overall meaning of the text. If it was just a matter of translating words anyone with a dictionary could do it."

"What did you make of the script?"

"Fascinating."

"How long will it take?"

"Two, three weeks if I have difficulty dating the thing. There are three full pages of script. Windle's photographed them from different angles to show how the letter was attached to the main document. That's important."

"Any chance that it's a fake?"

"That's always a possibility."

"Will you be able to detect if it is a fake?"

"I'd need the original to be sure. All I'll have to go on is the text - photographs of the text - and the fact that Merle and Windle eventually treated that text *as if* it were authentic."

"And then it goes missing."

"Two possibilities. Someone knew it was there, or they put two and two together while Windle and Merle were doing their stuff."

"Could it have been a plant?"

"Unlikely. It's not the kind of thing you do at short notice. It's more likely to have been done years ago, even centuries ago. Concocted stories bearing important names were all the rage in the early centuries. The Gnostic heretics were into that kind of thing in a big way. It could be authentic as far as age is concerned, but still be a fake. There again, it could have been stolen to remove the possibility of it being identified as a fake. That leaves us with three possibilities. It's a bad fake, a good fake, or it's authentic. What I've got to do is read the damned thing through Merle's eyes. What would he look for? What would he be suspicious of? What caused him to freak out and send a hurried translation to Rome?"

"The fact that it's signed must make things easier."

"There were a lot of Theodores in the early centuries."

"It's a head start."

"It's a distraction, actually. The temptation is to filter everything through the signature. It's the text that's important." Duggan changed course. "How did they get the photographs out of the country?"

"They were lumped in with the general photographs of the Ignatius text. It would have taken a special set of eyes to pick up on that."

"How long afterwards before the original went missing?"

"Three days. Some monk noticed it wasn't in its usual place and informed a superior."

"What's Windle like?"

"First generation American. Jewish mother, German father. His wife was Jewish. She died of cancer a few years back."

"You knew her?"

A nod from Mayle.

"How long were you married?"

"Seven years."

"I've never met what I thought was the right person."

"I thought Emily was it. I was wrong."

Their main courses arrived. They ate in silence; then Duggan said, "She's not interested in me, David. I'm too old for her."

"Old be bold."

"She's said something?"

A shake of the head.

"Well, then . . . "

"Body language."

"I appreciate the vote of confidence."

"She's interested, Jack. I can tell."

"I think you're mistaken."

"Maybe I am, but I'm not mistaken about you. Am I?"

* * *

The scholars had their own private drinking hole in room 518; it had been set aside by management for that specific purpose. By ten that evening it was all but packed out. An assortment of wine bottles decorated the bar, some open, some yet to be opened, and an assortment of people talked and laughed and gesticulated as Archbishop Donaghue, deep in conversation with one of the keynote speakers, completed a point on Johannine Christianity's importance to the Church. Bob Carter entered the room in that moment. Donaghue acknowledged the lawyer's approach and showed little reaction to the confided titbit of information he delivered. Minutes later he excused himself and followed Carter out into the corridor.

"You're sure about this?" he asked.

"I checked. He's in the casualty section of the Santa Rosa Memorial Hospital."

"When did it happen?"

"Not long after he left here. The taxi collided with a private car. I heard it on the radio about twenty minutes ago. He was mentioned by name. They said he'd just come out of surgery."

Donaghue moved into gear. "Arrange for a car to pick me up in about fifteen minutes.

"It's a terrible night, and it's Saturday. It could take longer."

"Explain the situation. Use your charm."

"Shall I come with you?"

Donaghue said Yes, turned away, then turned back. "Convey my apologies in there first - particularly to Phil. But don't say anything about Peters. Keep that to yourself." With that said he walked off to get his coat and the odds and ends he might need if Bishop Peters' condition was as serious as it sounded.

With Donaghue gone, the topics in room 518 hotted up a little, a heated discussion breaking out between Phil Atkins - the theologian who had delivered the opening address on the reality of evil - and a visiting French cleric who believed that the question of evil had been handled badly by St Augustine. Suggesting that Augustine had introduced Manichaeism by another name, the Frenchman found himself on a losing wicket in spite of a spirited defense.

Housed in splendid isolation, a mass of tubes and wires sprouting from his body, Bishop Peters looked terrible, and felt worse. But the spirit that had driven him to speak his mind at the conference still burned bright, and the arrival of Donaghue and Carter further fuelled that spirit. A floating rib had punctured Peters' right lung, they were told, and he had a broken leg and an ugly gash down the right side of his face. Only just visible beneath a swathe of bandages, a metal cage making the bedclothes bulge, Peters signaled with a wan smile and the tiny movement of a hand that he was still in the land of the living. They had ten minutes, the nurse said.

"How are you, Sam?" asked Donaghue.

"Sore. I thought I was a goner."

"I think we're fated to have you with us for a little while longer."

"A warning shot across my bow, do you think?"

"Not for me to say," said Donaghue.

"My mouth's dry as an old bone. Is there any water there?"

"None that I can see," said Donaghue.

"I'll ask the nurse for some," said Carter.

"Proves I'm not in hell," said Peters, when Carter was gone. And then, "He makes an unlikely guardian angel."

"He's a good man, Sam. Give him a chance."

"That's what you said I was." Peters took a breath and let it out slowly. "What time is it?"

"It's after eleven. We were lucky to get in." Taking one of Peters' hands, Donaghue held it between his own. "You look done in, Sam. What you need is sleep."

"I doubt I'll be doing much of that tonight."

"You're alive; that's what matters."

"Is it?"

"You're not ready for heaven yet." Donaghue pressed the pale hand between his own. "What are we going to do with you?"

"You mean what are *they* going to do with me?"

Carter returned in that moment; he had a nurse with him. She checked her patient and went off to get some water.

"Could you leave us for a moment," said Donaghue. "Sam and I need a moment or two alone."

Carter removed himself and Donaghue turned back to Peters. He said that he was deeply concerned over what he had heard about the CDF's investigations, but that he, Sam, only had himself to blame. He could not expect to say the kind of things he was saying and hope to get away with it. Criticism was one thing, castigation of the hierarchy was altogether another.

"When I was a child, I thought as a child."

"They're tearing the heart out of the faith, Sam. We can't let them get away with that."

"An unexamined faith is worse than no faith at all."

"You're not up to this, Sam."

"There's more to faith than a string of beliefs."

Donaghue released Peters' hand; it flopped back onto the green counterpane. "They've, *you've* gone too far, Sam. We're called to a specific service, and only a Church convinced of its own truth can deliver that service."

Peters sucked in breath and changed position; it was an agony to watch him. "I won't go quietly," he said.

"Six, seven months from now it'll be as if you'd never opened your mouth." Donaghue's smile was that of man well aware of how things worked. "Faith is more important than facts, Sam. I would have thought you'd have learned that by now."

"I'm talking change."

"You're talking about a free rein and that's not possible. You know it isn't. A diluted faith is no faith at all."

"You're still confusing faith with belief."

"Faith without belief is a ship without an anchor."

"A permanently anchored ship belies its purpose," said Peters. He closed his eyes and tried to wet his lips. "Where's that nurse got to?"

Donaghue got up and went to the door, which was open, but there was no sign of anyone in the corridor. "I'll be right back," he said.

The nurse, when he found her, was in a little office just off the corridor. She apologized for the delay. They were short-staffed and another patient had needed urgent attention. There was a jug of water on the desk. Donaghue suggested that he deliver it. When he got back he found Carter hanging around in the corridor.

"I thought you were still with him," said Carter, eyeing the jug Donaghue was carrying.

"Won't be a minute," said Donaghue.

Bishop Peters studied Donaghue's face as he ministered to him. It was a kindly face, but he knew it could set hard as concrete.

"That better?" asked Donaghue.

"Much," said Peters.

"More?"

"A little."

Donaghue repeated the procedure.

"No sleep for the wicked, I suspect," said Peters.

"Then I suggest a little pray," said Donaghue.

5

War in Heaven

Although weak, Bishop Peters was precise in his choice of words, and at first surprisingly energetic in his delivery. "Atkins is now their theological front-man," he said, looking at Mayle, who was seated nearer to him than Duggan. "He's an Aquinas-besotted medievalist." He shifted position carefully, the discomfort of the move showing on his face. "Got two quite awful books to his name."

"Jack walked out of his lecture," said Mayle, squinting a look at Duggan.

They had heard about Bishop Peters's accident by accident the next morning and headed straight for the hospital.

A grunt from Peters, then an observation. "It's necessary to know what they think, and why they think it."

"I find that kind of thinking offensive," said Duggan. "I feel suffocated when I hear it."

"Loss of breath in the face of God's truth is a sure sign that the Devil has you in his grasp," said Peters, his own breathing less than certain.

"My mother would have agreed with that."

"It's a difficult mindset to give up."

"And when you do?" asked Duggan.

"Then the chances are you'll end up like me." The bishop's smile broadened. "Struck down for impudence!"

"So what drives someone like that?" Duggan's question was more rhetorical than actual. "He's obviously a clever man."

"The need for certainty bedevils us all," said Peters; "it becomes a disease with some. Thinkers like Atkins desperately want life to be meaningful, so they stuff it with their own brand of meaning - a mixture of imagination and contortionist reasoning - and spend the rest of their lives ironing out the endless incongruities that arise. At its most obtuse, that's what theology has become - an elaborate system of justification. And so you have a Church that claims to have been at the back of God's mind prior to the creation of the world, a plan of salvation envisioned before Eve reached for the apple, a moment in history nominated as the precise moment in which that plan was set in motion. It's simplistic nonsense, but it's easier than having to face ambiguity and uncertainty on a vast scale."

"Science likes certainty," said Duggan, amazed by what he was hearing.

"Science likes clarity," said Peters; "there's a difference. You can be clear about something without being certain. To know that you don't know something is to know something, it is to know that you do not know. The Church's problem is that it won't admit to not knowing; it feels compelled to answer all questions on the basis of a mythology which contradicts just about everything known about the universe and its workings. Faith in God has been swapped for the ability to accept the incredible, the improbable, the distorted *and* the deliberately forged. Open-ended trust in God has been replaced with a closed system of belief; the belief that 'belief' is all that matters. No wonder we're in the state we're in." He took a gulp of air, then another. "Did you know that Aquinas based his *Summa* on the *Decretals*, and that the *Decretals* are forgeries? A French scholar let the cat out of the bag in the mid seventeen hundreds, but the *Summa* sailed on, and continues to sail on. Pius VI eventually admitted that they were forgeries, but his confession was nine centuries too late, and it hasn't made a whit of difference to people like Atkins."

"Hence your stand on education."

"Precisely." Peters broke off, the effort of speaking proving difficult. "Censorship has plagued Catholic scholarship for centuries. The Frenchman who identified the *Decretals* as forgeries ended up on the Index. The old *Imprimatur* on the flyleaf of books didn't signify care or caution, it signified narrow-mindedness." A cough, and a bit of a laugh. "Of course it depended on who you knew. The *Decameron* was taken off the Index and given a double

Imprimatur because Cosimo de' Medici had the ear of the pope."

"There's no great truth underpinning reality?" Duggan was staring hard at Bishop Peters. "There's no ontology?"

"If you mean by that a God who takes sides and interferes in history like a meddlesome child, then no. I find such a God singularly unattractive."

"So what do you actually believe?"

"I believe in love."

"Isn't the Christian God 'love' by definition?"

"Indeed He is; but where is this love to be found? Is it hanging in interstellar space like a bunch of grapes? Is it to be found in theological wranglings or sermons that exclude more than they include? I do not think so. So where is it? Does it have an identifiable source? Is that source the Holy Father? The Church? The Curia? Cardinal Menenger? The theological ravings of a Philip Atkins? I see little evidence for that view. The source of God's love would seem to be people, Mr Duggan, and that explains the idea of incarnation to me more accurately than any bit of theology I've ever studied. Jesus didn't refer to himself as 'Son of God' - he called himself *Son of Man.*"

"Where two or three are gathered together."

"Yes, but not in the institutional sense; in the sense of community. Neither Church nor pope can be equated with God speaking directly to the world. God cannot be limited to an institution or a person; He is a presence in the midst of the people when they attend to questions of ultimate concern. Religion is questions of ultimate concern shared by men and women of good faith. And not just in the sense of discussion, or debate, or argument, but in the sense of a life lived fully. Experience is the greatest teacher of all."

"The Church denies that it is an institution."

"It has to if it wants to hang on to the idea of a special revelation sent down from above. But that is to gild the lily. The Church looks like an institution, it acts like an institution and it speaks like an institution, so why shouldn't it be called an institution and treated like one?"

"Because it's spiritual authority rests on it being more than that."

Bishop Peters turned his attention back on Mayle. "There's nothing like a well-schooled Catholic, David," he said, glancing at Duggan, "they know their basics." His gaze swiveled back to Duggan. "The problem with that kind of authority is that it ends up believing it can do and say anything it wants. God is in my pocket, so everything is permissible. I possess God, so God must do my bidding. I can *conjure* God into existence on my own behalf at any time." A pause. "That isn't divine authority, Mr Duggan, it's megalomania."

"Instilled with a rod of iron over the last two thousand years."

"And about to self-destruct on the very premise that could save it, community - community run amuck. There are now three factions in the Church: the conservatives, the neoconservatives and the liberals. This is what you have to understand if you want to make sense of what's going on. Donaghue is a conservative of the old school. He lauds tradition and holds to the faith as it has been handed down since the fourth century. Carter is a different breed of man altogether. As a neoconservative he embraces - along with the Creed - a Protestant-type fundamentalism laced with practices and tactics that would make your hair stand on end. He may look and sound like Donaghue, but they are in fact miles apart, a fact that Donaghue hasn't quite appreciated yet." A smile. "For myself, I am now a liberal who wants the Church to face historical reality. I want my Church to grow up. I want it to find the courage to redefine the whole spiritual canvas of Catholicism as we move into the twenty-first century."

"Community run amuck?" Mayle's perplexity was evident. "A moment ago you were talking of community as harboring the presence of God."

"I was advocating the experience of God *in* community, David, not *as* community. That sounds like semantics, but it's much more than that. What Carter's involved in is purely ideological; it's the equivalent of National Socialism's attempt to make community the bedrock of Nazism. It is the deification of the collective all over again. It is individuals reduced to the level of ciphers and community set up in the place of God. Transferring its waning institutional authority to artificially created communities, the Church gives the impression of being open and modern, but it is in fact a closed shop. At first glance these communities appear to be guided by a spirit of genuine renewal, by a desire to shrug off the past and embrace the future; but the motivation behind them is not renewal, it is subjugation of the human spirit on a massive scale." A bitter laugh from Peters. "But for the best possible reasons, of course. It's being done in the name of the family, social cohesion and a return to religious basics."

"Answerable to whom?" asked Duggan.

"The neoconservative leadership, all of whom are in Menenger's pocket."

"How long has this been going on?"

"Years. John Paul II's first encyclical proclaimed a program of renewal, a program based on a vision which saw Church and world as deeply opposed to one another. The world was conceived of as *death;* a definition based on the fact that Western democracy is in favor of divorce, birth control, homosexual reform, abortion, equality for women and freedom of speech. The pope's aim was a new Christendom, a new Europe united from the Atlantic to the Urals. The fundamentalist movements filled the bill. They were already up and running; all that was required was focus and official recognition."

"Donaghue doesn't know what Carter stands for?"

"Donaghue is an old-school conservative; Carter's using him as a front. The community movements are top-heavy with men like Carter. It's said that they have more lawyers than theologians. Why? Because lawyer-speak is the new theology. Canon law allows baptized Christians to form movements without a mandate from the hierarchy, and that loophole has been used to form a new power bloc within the Church. The movements are interpreted as *spontaneous expressions of community guided by the Holy Spirit*, and on that basis are left to their own devices. And all done with the pope's official blessing before he died."

"Where does our new pope stands on all this?"

"No one knows; the little Umbrian is an unknown quantity. And it won't make much difference even if he is against the movements: the movements are now too powerful to stop. They're thought to have in the region of fifty million adherents between them, plus an estimated fourteen thousand priests who have been released by their bishops to work in their ranks. Add CDF backing to that and you're talking in terms of a serious power bloc. There's even talk of the movements having their own seminaries, a fact that belies their supposed community-based status. It's clever stuff."

"Yet I've never heard of them," said Duggan. "Apart from Opus Dei, which I thought had been brought under control."

"They keep a low profile. But you can be pretty certain that any large gathering of Catholics anywhere in the world has more than its fair share of neoconservatives pulling the strings."

"Menenger's in favor?"

"Cardinal Menenger has allowed the movements to avoid becoming orders so that they can stay outside of Church supervision - they're each the equivalent of a floating diocese, a diocese with no geographical center. Having no fixed center allows them to function without interference or criticism."

"I find it hard to believe that the CDF has never questioned what these groups are up to."

"They were tested by the CDF in the mid eighties; they passed with flying colors. Menenger continues with his predecessor's quest for rigor. "

Duggan was incredulous. "How is that possible?"

"It's possible because Menenger, too, has recognized their potential. The good cardinal has reinvented pluralism in the name of the movements. Pluralism is *diversity of ideas*. He has changed it to mean *diversity of movements and their ideas.* This allows him to sound modern when he is in fact a convinced medievalist. What his predecessor and John Paul did was creatively link the movements with the mendicant monks who moved freely between one diocese and another in the thirteenth century, monks who ignored the authority of the bishops and made the pope their sole authority. This is what the whole thing is about - the undermining of the bishops and the centralization of power in the papacy. Gregory VII is the model being used. Gregory claimed jurisdiction for the papacy over *all* spiritual and temporal matters in the thirteenth century. He was a madman. He considered himself beyond judgment, believed that the Church had never erred, and that for all eternity it would never err. He even changed his title from 'Vicar of Christ' to 'Vicar of God'. By having the neoconservative movements answerable only to himself, our dear-departed pope wrested control from the bishops and centralized control of the Church in himself."

"Where it continues to reside," said Mayle.

"Exactly. It's war in heaven, David. Reject what the neoconservatives stand for and you're an outsider, a Catholic with no rights. It doesn't matter who you are. You can be a cardinal or an archbishop, a bishop or a priest, a religious or an ordinary Catholic going about his or her business. If you reject the movements and their aims, then by definition you reject the papacy's officially documented aims and ambitions. Some of the Church's most distinguished thinkers have failed to clear that hurdle." Peters closed his eyes, opened them again. "We're being pushed into involuntary exile, Mr Duggan, and it's time to fight back. We *must* fight back."

"Can I quote you on that?" asked Duggan.

"Why not." A bit of a smile from Peters. "I'm hardly likely to do more damage to myself than I already have, am I?"

* * *

Duggan spent part of the afternoon trying to recapture what Bishop

Peters had so carefully articulated, a paraphrasing that, as it grew in coherence alongside previous notes, made him wonder how the man had managed to remain a bishop for so long. Being liberal was one thing, holding the views that Peters held was quite another. Then came the telephone call to Sydney and his editor's resistance to the idea of his staying on for another few days. Did he really think the situation warranted extra time? Duggan said that it did. Giving nothing away, he said that he had been made privy to information that required further investigation. In the banqueting hall Philip Atkins was saying that the idea of 'soul-making' in relation to man and world was unacceptable. Such an hypothesis was logically possible, but was it probable? He did not think so.

Jane's stare was without focus: there was a subject, Atkins, but he had no bearing on her thoughts - he was a voice without meaning. It was Duggan that concerned her. What was it about him that interested her? An image arose: Duggan sitting by himself in the bar, his jaw set, his fingers bunched round a whisky glass, his pugilistic head slightly raised. She had watched him get a drink and choose a quiet corner, watched him on and off as he raised the glass to his lips. A man alone with his thoughts. A man whose every movement and expression had radiated a subtle irritation. It had showed in the way he held his glass, in the way he looked around, and in the way he sat. If she had had her pad she would have sketched him. And then his eyes on hers, watching without watching. Then David turning up and the shock of realizing that the stranger might not remain a stranger.

"Life is simply too short for soul-making to make sense; there is simply not enough time for the process to reach completion."

She came back to herself and heard Atkins articulate his belief that the idea of evil as a necessary ingredient in the maturing of a soul was deeply problematical. Given the shortness of life, it necessitated more than one life for completion, and that overlooked the fact that such a life, or, to be fair, lives, would not be qualitatively different, merely quantitatively different. Why hadn't God simply made us live longer in that case? A short life-span such as we had militated against such a theory. It was a possible, but it was not probable. It was more probable that both approaches were sheer nonsense. There was not, as far as Jane could see, a skerrick of evidence for the world being a training ground for anything.

"Children who die young haven't been given much of a chance on God's racetrack, have they?"

Duggan again usurped Atkins. Haight Ashbury? Why Haight Ashbury in particular? She had never ever been in Haight Ashbury. They would complete their negotiations there, she would hand over the photographs and they would go their separate ways.

Atkins's voice went up a pitch; he was getting into stride.

"Given the nature of the world, is God to be thought clumsy in his choices?"

The theologian was closing in on his premise: a world as evil as this one was difficult to justify on the basis of a process for perfecting souls, particularly as destruction seemed to be it's main strength. Was God the gradualist really being fair?

Her Catholic upbringing had been strong enough to instill Christian values, but not at all strong on the doctrinal front. James Windle had treated the Gospel Jesus with respect, but had avoided literalisms. God was in His heaven, probably, and that was enough as far as he was concerned. What mattered was how the whole edifice of belief had come about, how it had formed, and from what it had formed. Duggan seemed to be cut from the same cloth. With a true believer for a mother, and an uncertain father, he had emerged with the characteristic limp of someone who had wrestled with an angel.

"If evil is necessary for growth, then a certain balance of evil would be necessary."

Balance was, however, according to Atkins, nowhere evident. The demands of evil were excessive, the intensity of evil overpowering. And so we had to wonder about the purpose of such a God, and, more to the point, wonder about the validity of such a theory in the face of evil run rampant.

Jane registered these words, but as she had opted for evil being solely a human affair, they had little meaning to her. Men like Atkins belonged to a Catholicism with which she had had little truck; she suspected they were still trying to count how many angels could dance on a pinhead.

* * *

Mayle's excuse for not attending the banquet was that he would have to pay for it out of his own pocket - his expenses were of the very ordinary kind. Anyway, he had work to do; the conference was not the only thing on his plate. And he wanted to see Bishop Peters again before returning to San Francisco; the old bugger deserved more than one visit. They agreed to meet for a drink afterwards. Having arranged earlier to interview Carter, Duggan headed for the elevator wondering what kind of reception he would get. But he needn't have worried. Carter, as it turned out, was the epitome of good manners. Handsome in his dark suit, and studiously careful in his responses, he batted Duggan's questions back and posed a few of his own; it was like playing verbal chess. What was obvious to Duggan from the start was that Carter was a self-conscious man; he wanted to be perceived as sincere and fair-minded, and he worked hard to create that effect. He was a performer who could not stop performing. The first question was hardly out of Duggan's mouth when that performance started.

"There are two models of Church and Gospel at large," said Carter, leaning forward, his large, immaculate hands intermeshing, "and that is what is causing concern in many quarters. There are those who want radical reform in relation to the Church's hierarchical structure, and there are those who feel that the present structure is exactly what is required to combat deteriorating values. There are those who want to update the Gospels and the Gospel Jesus, and there are those who feel that past interpretations of

Gospel events and of Jesus' status are just fine the way they are. The gulf between these parties is considerable."

"There's no possibility of accommodation?"

"Yes, of course there is; but not on the basics. Give up on the basics and you are in deep trouble. A case in point is the Catholic Church in Holland. Prior to Vatican II it was stronger than the Irish Church; post Vatican II it has all but collapsed. It's estimated that only about five per cent of Dutch Catholics are practicing Catholics. At the last count it had three seminarians for one million Catholics. Not a happy state of affairs, and directly the result of rampant modernism."

"It could be argued that it's Christendom that's falling apart, that the vigorous imposition of papal government in the old imperial style is no longer tenable in Western democracy. "

"Western democracy is drowning in counterfeit compassion, Mr Duggan; it needs the steadying authority of Peter's successor to survive. The boundaries of reform have to be carefully analyzed - utopian optimism will not deliver the goods. What's the point of satisfying an itch for reform that continually runs beyond the boundaries of possibility? It's one thing to consider modifying some aspect of liturgy, some aspect of historical interpretation, some aspect of laity involvement; it's quite another to unthinkingly undermine the faith's foundational doctrines and end up with no Church at all. The post-modern desire for relevance equals doctrinal irrelevance for the Catholic Church on just about every level. We can't sit back and let that happen."

"You've been referred to as an authoritarian bully; how does that sit with you?"

"Personal feelings play no part in this; it's a matter of standing up for what one believes. Revelation is not opinion; it is truth granted to us from the Divine through the Church."

"Shouldn't belief be tempered by the facts of existence?"

"There are spiritual facts, and there are temporal facts; they do not belong in same box. It's a mistake to think that doctrine can be handled in the same way as scientific theory. Salvation is not a theory; it is an experience."

"At the international level, Pope Paul VI encouraged collegiality. Over the last few years collegiality has been discouraged in favor of a uni-directional vision. Discussion has been discouraged, papal authority imposed. The Synod has become nothing more than a rubber stamp. Do you really think that is the best way to go?"

"Subjectivism and relativism are sweeping our culture; we have to stand firm on the basics. Sartre may have believed that the life of a drunkard equaled that of a great statesman; we, I, do not. "

"Isn't individual conscience a basic?"

"Conscience is being used as an excuse for doing one's own thing; in that sense it has no primacy."

"None at all?"

"Excuse me sounding like the canon lawyer I am, but conscience is by definition a proximate norm in relation to truth; it is not in and of itself the truth. We stand under the word of God, the teachings of the Gospels and Christ's teaching. We are not at liberty to paint our own moral canvas whatever our individual feelings might be."

"Isn't what you're advocating a return to an earlier stage of moral reasoning and development? Like it or not, the Church has had to update much of its thinking as the centuries rolled in. Why should it stop now?"

"It hasn't stopped; it's doing what it has always done. It's holding the barque of Christ steady during a period of transition. Today's opinions are seldom tomorrow's opinions. Tomorrow's opinions will displace today's opinions and millions will go rushing off after the Lord knows what. That's how the world is."

"There are progressive theologians within the Church who see things differently."

"Mimicking secular society's desires is hardly progressive."

Duggan glanced at his notes. "Bishop Peters has called Catholic education policy into question. Would you like to comment?"

"You were at my lecture?"

"Yes."

"Then you know what I think of Bishop Peters' approach."

"Anything you would like to add?"

"Catechism and Scripture used to be the basis of the educational curriculum; we have got to get back to that. Ultimately, it is not what we want, it is what Jesus wants that matters."

"What does Jesus want?"

"Recognition. He is the Son of God."

"No other route can be taken?"

"We can't rewrite the Gospel message."

"How about reinterpreting it?"

"To suit ourselves? I don't think so."

"People are leaving the Church in droves."

"They'll come back when we put our house in order."

"Back to hell, sin and fear?"

"Fear of God is the beginning of wisdom."

Duggan changed tack. "Now that the white smoke has cleared, what do you imagine the future of the Church will be like?"

"I imagine nothing. The Holy Father is the Holy Father. Benedict XVI will decide the direction in which we go."

"With or without the College of Cardinals? The bishops?"

"With anyone and everyone who loves God and respects His truth."

"Is it true that the CDF has spies checking up on what is being said from pulpits right across California?"

"There have been complaints, that's quite true. As complaints against priests have to be taken seriously, the Church has had to follow through on those it has received. There are priests out there who think they can say more or less whatever comes into their head."

"Isn't it just that some priests are thinking things through?"

"We have trained theologians for that. A priest trained in theology has the right to submit his thoughts to a superior for consideration."

Another change of tack from Duggan, and an unexpected one. "It's rumored that a document has been found in the Middle East which seriously threatens Catholicism's interpretation of the Christian faith. Have you heard anything along those lines?"

"I have not." Carter's tone was harder, crisper. "Where did you hear this?"

"Here in this hotel; it's part of the gossip that's flying round. There's a lot of gossip flying around."

"I've heard nothing to that effect."

"If such a document has been found, what will the Church's reaction be?"

"We seem to have moved from the substantial to the hypothetical."

"There would be no attempt to suppress it?"

"That's the kind of accusation we have come to expect." A sigh from Carter. "What exactly is your point, Mr Duggan?"

"My point is that reality has a bad habit of catching up with us when we least expect it. When it does, there's generally all hell to pay."

"You perhaps speak a truth greater than you know."

"Perhaps we all do."

Carter paused. "I sense something personal in what you're saying. Are you Catholic?"

"Born and bred."

"Will your article be an attack on the Catholic Church?"

"Both sides of the question will be fairly represented. That's why I'm here talking to you."

Carter glanced at his watch. "I have a meeting in exactly twenty-five minutes."

"We're almost there," said Duggan, going in for the kill. He took a breath. "Can the Church continue to make thirteenth-century moves in the twenty-first century and hope to survive? A lot of people don't think it can; not in the face of what we now know about ourselves and the world. Very few people are going to put up with a return to the old ways."

"The truth, Mr Duggan, is that people haven't changed all that much since the thirteenth century; they're basically much the same. The sound of thunder still frightens them. A shadow can still spook them. Take away a loved one and they spin on the spot. Hit them with a disaster and they flee back to the Christian God for comfort. They're not certain about anything. The modern world hasn't convinced them that God does not exist, or that heaven and hell are imaginary; it's just distracted them with its toys and its noise. Scratch the surface and you find the same fears, the same superstitions. The old stuff has been repackaged, that's all. Gnosticism, astrology, tarot, witchcraft and pagan cults are still with us. The distant past is firmly embedded in the present and we'll never ever get rid of it."

"It could be argued that the Church itself is responsible for that kind of thinking, that it panders to superstition."

"All kinds of things can be argued; that does not make them right, or true. The universe and we humans are much more complicated than we're made out to be. The best brains on the planet are unable to explain what consciousness is, or how it arose."

"There was a time when we didn't know how the heart worked."

"And now we do. But do we know *why* it works? What is this thing called 'life' that makes the heart beat? We don't know. So the prime question is not what happens to us when our heart stops beating, but how did we ever get to be alive in the first place? What is *life*, Mr Duggan?"

"What is anything?"

"Well may you ask."

"It's a non question."

"Not to the Church it isn't. The Church safeguards life at every turn. It views life as a sacred mystery."

"Yet it has engaged in the murder of millions down the centuries."

"The secular world has done better?"

"The secular world does not lay claim to a two thousand-year-old revelation straight from God."

"We are all subject to the tenor of the times."

"You're supposed to know better when you've got God whispering in your ear."

"The will of God has to be interpreted."

"By the Church alone?"

"The Church is God's instrument in the world."

"In the Church's own opinion it is."

"Sanctioned by Jesus Christ."

"An interpretation of New Testament events at odds with modern scholarship."

"With the modernist interpretation of New Testament scholarship."

"Which is trying to face up to the fact that the Church's interpretation of first-century events has more to do with faith than history."

"The Church is founded on faith, Mr. Duggan."

"St Paul suggested that we should reason together."

"He also said that the truth about Jesus Christ is as foolishness to the world."

Duggan smiled at Carter. There wasn't going to be a winner, and they both knew it. Reaching forward he pressed the stop button on his recorder. "I think that takes us about as far as we need to go," he said. "I'm obliged to you for your time."

"You'll send me a copy of the article?"

"Of course."

They got to their feet.

"You'll be reporting on the conference as a whole?"

"By way of an introduction to my piece on Bishop Peters."

A smile. "So it's back to Australia?"

"I've got some business in San Francisco first."

"Then enjoy your stay." Carter's smile remained fixed; it was of the wholly manufactured variety. For a big man his handshake was surprisingly limp. "And may God go with you."

"And with you," said Duggan.

* * *

The banquet that evening was a massive affair. Duggan and seven others found themselves seated at a round table in the middle of the hall, the many priests in attendance shunted off to the right-hand side of the room. Donaghue, Carter and the three keynote speakers had been given a table all to themselves.

It was a jolly gathering with speeches, votes of thanks and many a joke from the podium. The hum of almost five hundred voices gave the impression of a room filled with bees. "Sydney, Australia!" The woman on Duggan's left was impressed. She was from Florida, although originally from Oregon, which was much closer to California, she pointed out. Marriage had carried her away to St Petersburg, which sounded so grand, but was in fact quite a small place on the Florida coast. Sydney was quite a big place, Duggan said. They laughed and chatted on about Sydney and St Petersburg, and then about the Oregon trail, and Duggan learned, apropos of nothing in particular, that Sally Hicks was a charismatic, and that she had experienced speaking in tongues.

Jane Windle was on the far left of the hall. She looked around on the offchance of spotting Duggan, but he was obscured by those at his table. It was not until much later that she saw him, and again he looked alone, those to his left and right talking to others, he, glass in hand, apparently disconnected from what was going on.

The truth was quite the opposite. Duggan had spent ages probing Sally Hicks on the question of charismatic renewal, and the man on his right, a dentist from some outlying Frisco diocese, had joined in, his experience of those who wanted to promote a similar kind of fervor something he viewed with dismay. There had been ructions over the splitting of the congregation into 'insiders' and 'outsiders', the outsiders being anyone who dared disagree with the hardliners on just about any level. Sally Hicks had been indignant.

Did he not want to be part of God's salvific initiative today? Not if it came down to a few lording it over the many through a policy of exclusivity, was the reply. It was one thing to promote prayer and confession, it was quite another to make prayer into a chore and confession into a debasement of the self. That was where he had drawn the line: a return to pre-Vatican II guilt dressed up in the guise of experiences shared was not high on his list of priorities. Sally Hicks had clammed up for a moment, leaving Duggan and the dentist to parlay on. And then the woman on the dentist's left had asked him a question, and Duggan had found himself with no one to talk to. But not for long. Sally the charismatic turned back and pressed him with information on the 'New Catholicism', and the dentist - Daniel Phelps by name – on hearing the term being used, said that missionaries advocating such renewal had all but wrecked his diocese.

"So what would you rather have," asked Sally Hicks, staring past Duggan with belligerent fixity, "a dead church, or an alive church?"

"We weren't in the least dead - there was excellent community feeling before the other stuff got going." He feigned a laugh, glanced at the woman he had been talking to, but she was now otherwise engaged. "It began with a prayer meeting that got out of control, and I *mean* out of control. Some new members suggested that we meet for an extra hour of prayer per week. I was all for it, as were others. The first three or four sessions were fine; then, slowly, things began to go wrong. Within a couple of months we were experimenting with open confession, something I wasn't against in principle, but something I quickly came to loathe. It was demeaning. People began to admit to all kinds of things; and they were encouraged to go even further. I dropped out and complained to our priest. He amazed me by saying that it would all sort itself out in good time. When I asked him what he meant, he was evasive. The second time I approached him he was rude. When I put in an complaint in writing, he got angry with me."

"Maybe you should look into your own heart," said Sally.

"Maybe *you* should learn to mind your own business."

"Jesus is at hand."

"Jesus would not have wanted to hear some of the stuff I heard."

"You don't believe in honesty?"

"Honesty without discrimination is dangerous."

"You mean things should remain hidden."

"It's better that some things remain hidden."

"You can't hide from God."

"Who said I wanted to?" Daniel Phelps looked nonplussed. "You're barking up the wrong tree, lady. I don't want to hide from God. I just think that personal stuff like that should remain personal. You don't have to wash your dirty linen in public to qualify as a Christian."

Undaunted, Sally Hicks said that confession before others led to self-control, self-control to revelation, revelation to the experience of Jesus being at hand. Confession before others was part of the purification process. If you were serious about your faith, it was something that could not be avoided.

"Are you saying that I'm not serious about my faith?"

"We're each being asked to renew ourselves; we have to decide whose side we're on."

"Side? Since when has there been *sides* within Catholicism?"

"Having a faith is not the same thing as *having faith.*"

"This is exactly the kind of nonsense I've been alluding to," said Daniel, glancing at Duggan. "It's tearing our congregation apart." Another bemused laugh. "That's what brought me here - I wanted to find out what was going on."

"Have you?" asked Duggan.

"I've heard stuff I haven't heard in twenty, thirty years, if that's anything to go by."

"Jesus is at hand."

"The Jesus you know isn't the Jesus I know," said Daniel. His face was a study in seriousness. "My Jesus doesn't hate the world, he loves it."

"That's liberal nonsense," said Sally Hicks. She was keeping her voice low, but others were listening in. "You'll be telling me next he approves of homosexuals."

Daniel was momentarily at a loss; he blinked rapidly, then he said, "We're all sinners."

"Amen to that," she said back. And then, as if canvassing for a political party, she added: "We have to become as one if we want to change the world. Unity of vision is what's required." She looked at Duggan. "Isn't that right?"

Duggan nodded sagely, but did not reply.

"You can't bludgeon people into unity." Daniel sounded tired; he even looked tired. "Pushing people around has never worked - it always backfires. We've got two separate congregations now, each with their own mass - that can hardly be described as unity."

"I bring a sword," said Sally, truncating a biblical text.

That was when Duggan came in; he asked Sally to explain what she meant by a changed world.

She was referring to the millennium, she said. We had to prepare ourselves for the thousand years of peace, a time when a new world order would be inaugurated by the Church. Acting as guides to presidents and kings, the Church triumphant would usher in a worldwide spiritual utopia.

"Not through the kind of nonsense I've witnessed," said Daniel.

"You'll be left behind," said Sally, speaking in code. "We have to learn to bend the knee, to submit. Obedience to the Holy Father is the key."

"Obedience to God is the key, surely."

"The Holy Father is God's representative on Earth."

"In conjunction with the magisterium."

"Which is also in obedience to the Holy Father."

Daniel Phelps shot a glance at Duggan. "I thought we had moved away from this kind of thinking."

Sally Hicks had the last word. As Archbishop Donaghue mounted the podium to give his closing address, she said, "You won't win. Jesus is at hand and we are headed for heaven."

He was, the Archbishop said, delighted and gratified by the turnout; particularly by the number of clergy and religious who had managed to attend; and by the high standard of debate that had been sustained throughout. The Church was in a state of transition, and it was good to see and hear men and women from all walks of life answer God's call for renewal. Getting back to basics was what it was all about, and in that respect the conference had been a resounding success. We were living in dark times, and it would take everything we had to overcome the spirit of deceit that was abroad in the world. Sally Hicks nodded in agreement, and Duggan wondered what it must be like to speak in tongues, and how this little Catholic women from St Petersburg, Florida, had come to do so.

6

This is America

They were on a highway flanked by green fields and stretches of forest; Mayle's Dodge was humming along. Up ahead, a bus drew into the curb to pick up a passenger. What Duggan saw was America going about its daily business. Swinging the Dodge out and around a small Japanese car, Mayle asked how he had got on with Carter.

"I caught him out on the old problem of the Church claiming to have a divine revelation, but at the same time being subject to the perceptions of a particular age. The second statement makes a nonsense of the first."

"You'll be on his hit-list for that."

"He handled the general stuff well."

"Ask to see your article?"

"Yup."

"Before or after publication?"

"Didn't say." A set of lights turned against them. "Carter said we hadn't the right to paint our own moral canvas. I got the impression he'd said that hundreds of times before, that just about everything he said had been endlessly repeated."

"You sensed right."

"What do you sense about me?"

Duggan was not at all sure why he had asked such a question, and now that it was out he was not at all sure that he wanted Mayle to answer.

"You're unhappy; and you're stuck." The lights changed and they moved off. "Jane's in the same boat. None of her relationships have worked out."

"You expect me to succeed where others have failed?"

"She's intrigued by you."

"I've never been skilled in that direction."

"She'll find that refreshing." A glance. "You handled things fine first time round. You were straight in there, hand out, big smile."

"It's a different situation."

"Just be your usual quarrelsome self."

"Quarrelsome?"

"You frown a lot."

"I do?"

They crossed the Golden Gate Bridge soon after, struck off onto Chestnut from the top of Lombard and headed down the upmarket shopping strip towards Chinatown. Mayle glanced at his watch. They had three-quarters of an hour in hand, time and plenty to get out to Haight Ashbury where Mayle had to interview someone mid-afternoon.

"She could have got the photographs to me at the hotel."

"She has business in Frisco."

They passed through the Chinese quarter on Stockton. The buses were crammed tight, the streets packed and full of color. Trucks added to the bedlam, crates of chickens and ducks being unloaded and carted into market-type warehouses where housewives jostled as they picked apart the sidewalk displays of Chinese vegetables. Mayle edged the Dodge carefully through the dense traffic, the automatic drive delivering new sounds; the smell and sight of food reminded Duggan that he had not had breakfast.

"It's the largest Chinese community outside of Asia," said Mayle.

"Reminds me of Marrickville in Sydney."

"We'll be turning off just before we reach the Stocton Tunnel. That's the center of things."

"I wish I had longer."

"Next time," said Mayle.

Some time later Mayle swung the Dodge off to the right. A shortcut, he said. Within minutes everything changed; it was as if someone had waved an architectural wand. Walk one block and you were in a completely different world, Mayle said.

They climbed a steep hill and began the descent; it was like coming in on a flight path.

"I told her she was pushy."

"She's a *very* successful artist, Jack. Mixes it with the best. She's had an exhibition running in one of the prestigious New York galleries for the last couple of weeks. Most of the stuff sold before it hit the wall."

Another corner; another set of lights.

"I feel like a schoolboy."

They found a parking spot on Haight, walked back to where Ashbury connected and found Jane already there. She had been in the area for about an hour, she said, and had done some shopping. She opened a plastic carrier and produced a sleeveless waistcoat made from some furry material. It was very sixties, brown with whorls of lighter brown and beautifully made. It had a crimson lining.

"Snazzy," said Duggan.

She dug back into the carrier and produced a second-hand copy of the life of Bernard of Clairvaux. Something to read on the plane, she said, handing it to Duggan.

"Thank you *very* much."

"He's one of my father's favorites."

"He was as influential as Athanasius."

They ended up in a newly opened wine and cocktail bar on Haight with a more than decent menu. Seated on an elevated platform of polished aluminum overlooking the bar area, Jane said without preamble that they wanted Duggan to handle publication.

Duggan absorbed the announcement.

"Australia will be the perfect surprise."

"It would keep everything tidy," said Mayle

"How would I explain having the photographs?"

"They were pushed under your hotel room door by an unknown benefactor." Mayle's grin was boyish. "This is America."

"We're small beer in your terms."

"You've cornered fifteen per cent of the Australian market in two years. That's pretty good."

"You've been checking."

"What do you think?"

"I think it's going to very much depend on what I find when I do the translation."

"He suspects it may be a fake," said Mayle.

"I didn't say that. I said it *could* be a fake."

"In the end it's your decision," said Jane.

A waitress arrived to take their order. When she left, Mayle said, "It would sure as hell simplify things if you handled publication."

"Have you spent any time in the Middle East?" Jane's question came with an uncertain look. "Not that it matters. . ."

"Twice while I was doing my doctorate."

"You know Mar Saba?"

"Hagios Sabas," he replied, giving the monastery its alternative name. "I'm familiar with its history."

Her brown eyes swiveled to Mayle, then back to Duggan. "My father mustn't get hurt as a result of this."

"He's put his career on the line," said Mayle.

"He can be very stubborn . . . " She broke off. "He doesn't suffer fools gladly."

"It's my bet he and Jack will get on just fine." Mayle was smiling, but there was an element of judgment in his tone. "Great guy when you get to know him."

Jane's concern surfaced. "Your editor can be relied on?"

"He'll put this through the wringer - he'll put *me* through the wringer." Duggan added a rider. "*If* I let it go that far."

"Merle's gone into retreat," said Mayle. "That'll draw attention to Rome's involvement."

"You mean it was to their advantage that the Voss Collection went missing." A quick shake of the head signaled Duggan's position on that. "I really don't think they would be so foolish. It's more their style to rubbish a text like this. They'll dismiss it with airy disdain."

"When do you leave for Australia?" Jane cut back in as if by way of an apology. "I leave at six this evening for New York."

"Her agent's screaming," said Mayle.

"I head out Wednesday morning." He watched her face. "You trained as an artist?"

"I did three years fine arts in Berlin. After arts school in New York. I was brought up in New York."

"You speak German?"

"My parents spoke German at home."

"Hebrew?"

"A smattering."

Their drinks arrived, but not their lunch.

"If it hadn't been for artists I don't think Catholicism would have got off the ground." The memory of Duggan's great Roman adventure returned. "Mind you, I thought the Sistine was awful. It reminded me of a Victorian scrapbook."

He had travelled up to Rome from Ancona, having come in by ferry from Patras in Greece - the contrast had hit him immediately. Instead of glittering, icon-infested churches where blues and whites dazzled the eye, he had been faced with a dark medievalism and dour, candle-illuminated spaces. A heavy gloom struck through with candlelight had been the norm, the occasional flash of light from a tourist's camera the only relief. It had felt as if a huge hand were pressing down in an attempt to flatten the genuflecting, praying, staring faithful.

He had expecting to sense the presence of God, but had instead been confronted with vertiginous spaces that left him empty and abandoned inside. The scale and intensity of the place had stunned him. The endless corridors, artworks and brilliant fakery saddened and completed the change in him. For no matter how beautifully executed each picture or piece of sculpture had seemed, or how breathtakingly set, the result had been the realization that it was all propaganda turned maniacal. Overcome by the spectacle of hand-illuminated books, sarcophagi, frescoes, monstrances, gravestones, mosaics, globes, reliquaries, plaques, chalices, lecterns, tiaras, hassocks, tapestries, maps, documents and seals, he had fled the place in search of fresh air and an open sky.

"You're no longer religious?"

"I even have an antipathy to red wine."

She imagined him in a priest's dark vestments . "David says you taught for a while."

"I taught, wrote, and travelled." He paused as another wave of memory rolled in. "My mother and I were reconciled at the last minute." He touched his solar plexus. "Way down here she still felt betrayed. Guilty." A smile. "I was bone of her bone and I had failed, so she had failed." He added lightly. "If the pope himself had sent her a letter saying that she could stop believing, she would have kept right on believing."

"It's all some people have," said Mayle.

"Thanks to the Church's myopia it is." He reached for his glass. "What they need is a good dose of history."

"A history lesson instead of the Eucharist?"

"Get the history right and the theology takes care of itself."

"That's a big ask," said Mayle.

"Dishonesty has a habit of catching up with you. If you pander to the lowest common denominator, you shouldn't be surprised when that attachment ends up carrying you in a direction you have no wish to go in."

"You still think there's something serviceable in it all? An authentic core."

Choosing his words carefully, Duggan said that the Council of Nicaea's fourth-century formula for Jesus' inherent divinity had been badly worded, that the discrepancies in that formula had developed into theological absurdity and historical distortion. As Bishop Peters had said, the Nicene formula was a formula for Christ, it was not Christ. We were still suffering from the repercussions of that formula, repercussions that had rocked both the Western and Eastern world on a number of occasions. Yes, the heart of

Christianity was about the human and the divine meeting in a man called Jesus, but not in the sense of the transcendent God being shoe-horned into a human form. The Catholic Church knew full well that it could not argue such a case - its own theology dismissed such a notion as heresy - but it had allowed the folksy idea of Jesus being literally God to blossom unchallenged throughout Christendom, and everyone was paying the price for that. We would discover the core of Christianity when we stripped the Jesus story back to basics. It was there, it just had to be excavated."

"You sound like Peters," Mayle said.

"If I'd stayed on I'd have ended up like Peters." Duggan added a qualification. "If I'd had the courage."

"Don't you sometimes wish you had stayed on?" Jane dug gently down into the flesh of his past. "You could have done a lot of good."

"Skepticism is acceptable; cynicism is not. I didn't think then the way I think now." His smile tailed off. "Let's get something straight. I do not enjoy being viewed as the priest who could have been. The only reason I told David about my past was because we were being honest with one another; it's the first time I've been that honest in years. Truth is, Jane, I would have made a bloody awful priest. I was a self-centered smartarse who thought he knew it all. I came out of university thinking I was God's gift to the world, and that's how I acted. I walked away from my vocation on the 20th of May 1979, and I've hardly given it a thought since. Some vocation."

Jane continued to probe. "Did it take long to get back into the flow of things?"

"About a year." He remembered a face, a body, a tangle of yellow hair. "I had a bit of a fling with someone I'd known when I was nineteen. Lasted about six months."

"I wasn't prying."

"That's generally what people want to know about."

"Now that you mention it," said Mayle.

"It turned into a big fat nothing."

Jane knew all about big fat nothings.

It was as if they were assembling a complex jigsaw and there was not yet sufficient picture to instruct them in the pieces to select. Mayle chose a piece at random.

"Being a journalist is enough?"

"I have other interests."

"A secret life," said Jane.

"My passion is literature." A different waitress appeared with their meals and shot off again. Duggan surveyed his plate, looked up. "Your mother didn't mind the Catholic thing? The 'Christ' thing?"

"She celebrated his Jewishness. I was brought up to respect both traditions."

"We were sold the blue-eyed paragon with russet brown hair. I was in my teens before I realized Jesus was a Jew."

"Hollywood," said Mayle. His smile was sardonic. "Did you know that ten per cent of Americans believe that Joan of Arc was Noah's wife? I kid you not."

"Some of the major studios act as propagandists for the Christian Right," said Duggan. "Their films are orchestrations of conservative religious ideas disguised as entertainment."

Mayle narrowed his response to an evangelical film he had seen as a youngster. Well acted, and in color, it had shown Americans going about their business in a world rotten to its core. Scenes of gambling, violence and sexual attack had been superimposed on the banality of family life, the powers that be portrayed as working consciously, or unconsciously, on behalf of principles that were often demonic. And then, suddenly, Christ had returned from heaven, and the evildoers had been left to their own devices. Caught up to meet Christ in the air, Christians from all over the world had vanished from home and workplace, those left behind mystified as to where they had gone. Mothers had been left without children, wives without husbands, brothers without sisters. One such disappearing act had involved an on-duty airline pilot. There one minute, he had been gone the next.

"Some of America's top politicians are evangelicals," said Mayle. "Some are fundamentalists. They believe in a literal return of Christ, a literal Armageddon and a literal Day of Judgment. Which means that they believe Christians will go 'pop' some day."

"Pop-theory," said Duggan.

Mayle's laugh was sour. The whole world had to be informed of the Christian message before Christ could return. Hence their evangelizing fervor. When that was accomplished, *voila*.

"My father only ever talked the history of religion," said Jane. "He said it was up to us to work out what we believed, or did not believe."

"If you believe God interferes in history, then it all makes perfect sense. If you don't . . . " Duggan's despondency surfaced. "When I hear an Atkins laboring to raise the specter of dark forces over which we have no control I have my doubts about the Church ever being able to change."

Addressing Mayle, Jane said that her father was returning to the States mid May. It would be good if he and Jack could get together.

Mayle was in agreement.

"If things work out." Duggan marshaled his thoughts. "I think your father should take the initiative and break the story before it has the chance of becoming a problem. He's got nothing to lose. The original photographs are locked away and I've never met him. Break the story before publication and you create the conditions for publications *and* for a meeting - if that proves necessary. We'd be seen as two hapless souls discussing how we got dragged into an academic bun fight against our will. Taking the initiative would give him the edge and force Rome into admitting that an important document had surfaced."

"Sounds right," said Mayle.

"It would give him a chance to participate. I get the feeling he'd welcome that."

The girls behind the downstairs bar were working flat out now; the whole area was packed with lunchtime drinkers and snackers.

"My father's a pragmatist," said Jane. "He rationalized the difference between Christianity and Judaism for my brother and I when we were young. It was great fun having two lots of festivals to look forward to."

"You have a brother?"

"Paul. I'm the older. It was a Jewish-Catholic household. My father was brought up Catholic because of his father. His parents got out of Germany just before the horror started. My mother's family weren't so lucky." A pause. "My mother died of cancer last year."

"I'm sorry to hear that." Duggan chose his words carefully. "You were close?"

Jane glanced at Mayle.

"Peas in a pod," said Mayle.

"He's in Israel right this minute discovering his roots."

"Has he been there long?"

"Three months. I get the impression he feels quite at home."

"He was there when his father was there?"

"Yes."

"That doesn't strike you as interesting?"

"It was a fluke. He had the trip planned ages before my father agreed to accompany Merle to Mar Saba."

"It might be viewed as suspicions."

"No one knows he's there. Was there."

"Let's hope it stays that way."

If they wanted another drink they would have to get it themselves, Mayle said, looking down at the hubbub. Yes, he was volunteering.

They decided on what to have and followed Mayle's progress in silence. When he reached the bar, Duggan said:

"There's no chance at all of you staying on until tomorrow?"

"More than my life's worth."

"Your first exhibition in New York?"

"My first successful exhibition in New York."

Her smile and the tilt of her head were quizzical.

"I might not get back to the States."

"There'll be a good story in it whichever way it goes."

"If it's a dud I won't be back."

Her quizzicalness became a frown. She looked down and away, then back at him.

"I'd like to know you better," he said.

He didn't know how she would react to that.

"I can't stay on," she said. The frown was still there, but it had relaxed a little. "Not much I can do about that."

"I suppose not," he said.

7

Like a dog after a bone

Duggan's return journey was shortened due to flying out of San Francisco instead of Los Angeles. High winds and a heavy fall of snow had brought everything in the entertainment belt to a standstill, thousands of passengers being re-routed to avoid the icy chaos. Following Mayle through the crowded passages to the international terminal, he had been thankful to have only one small suitcase to handle. Hello America, goodbye America. No more than an hour's wait before the call to board came. A few last words and out through the departure gate to sleep and read for a cramped thirteen hours, the photographs examined over and over again as the packed 747 droned its way across vast expanses of ocean. Another whisky and the realization that Theodore's letter was, as Windle and Merle had indicated, very important indeed. When he got home his cat came in from next door to check who had entered her domain.

In the morning, after a long, hot shower, he shaved and stared at his image in the mirror. An hour later he was explaining what had gone down in Santa Rosa to Elliot

"Hitler diaries?" said Elliot.

"If it's a hoax someone's gone to a lot of trouble to set it up."

"We'd have to get Windle and Merle involved."

"I've already suggested Windle take the initiative - but he can't be seen to be breaking Vatican trust."

Hands in pockets, Elliot stared at the photographs. "You can really read this stuff?"

"It'll mean another trip to the States if it works out. Windle's due back in New York mid-May."

Elliot's look of uncertainty returned. "Dave has the right to expect consultation on this."

"It would have to remain my story."

"I'm talking protocol."

"As long as he understands the situation."

"Bit of a turnaround given what you were saying before you left."

"It's a delicate situation."

"Dave isn't a threat, Jack. He's a reasonable man." Elliot switched tracks. "How did you get on with Bishop Peters?"

Duggan gave an edited account of his interaction with the lung-punctured bishop.

"Sounds formidable."

"I also interviewed a canon lawyer by the name of Robert Carter - he helped Donaghue set up the conference. I would like to amalgamate the two points of views."

"How long will the translation take?"

"You'll have a draft by the end of the week, a detailed translation in two." He felt the desire to explain, but desisted. "I'll need a few hours off to help deal with this."

"And if it turns out they've been hoaxed?"

Duggan's smile belied what he felt about the situation. "It'll make a good yarn whichever way it goes," he said.

Elliot moved back behind his desk. He would get someone to research Windle's and Merle's backgrounds. He scribbled a note to that effect. In a situation like this nothing should be taken for granted. He changed tack. He would want the piece on Peters and Carter by the end of the month. Was that possible? And Dave would want to see it. A smile. He had volunteered on Duggan's behalf. It had seemed like the right thing to do. A glance, and another change of tack. Windle and Merle were buddies?

"Not particularly. Having Windle around probably helps the priest look even-handed. Windle's a Catholic liberal from a part-Jewish background."

"What's he doing in Germany?"

"Research. University of Essen."

"Will your journalist friend want something in return?" Elliot was covering all contingencies. "He has just handed over what could be a very good story."

"It's convenient for them to do it this way. He's a friend of the family."

"Helluva fluke someone like you turning up."

"Downright mind boggling."."

"Could they be setting you up?"

"I think that highly unlikely."

Elliot stared at the litter of papers on his desk, then he said, "Tongues will wag here if you shoot off back to the States."

"We've got a couple of weeks before that becomes an issue."

"Dave will have to be told." A smile. "He was absolutely amazed when I told him it was you who would take over." Elliot jumped back in with a promised assurance. "I told him not to say anything to anyone."

"I appreciate that."

A crinkly kind of look from Elliot. "You didn't commit a crime, Jack. Must have happened to lots of young men."

"They made me feel as if I'd committed first degree murder. It's how things were, then."

"What made you tell David Mayle?"

"We got friendly, drank a bit. He's a really nice guy. He opened up and I followed."

"So he dashes straight round and tells the daughter."

"As you said, a fluke."

"What does she do for a crust?"

"She's an artist. Just hit the big time in New York." He could see Jane's face as he spoke. "She badgered me into doing it."

"I imagine Merle's in a bit of a quandary over what to say when the story breaks."

"He's in retreat."

"I'll bet."

"He's just being careful. He's a scholar with an international reputation being forced to juggle realities."

"Who would win if push came to shove?"

"I've got no way of telling."

Elliot put the photographs back in their envelope. What would the Vatican do to Peters, he wanted to know.

"They'll rubbish him in much the same way as they'll rubbish the contents of these photographs. They're very good at that. Mind you, Peters is media-savvy. He'll give them a run for their money."

Handing over the envelope, Elliot said, "He might turn out to be the better story."

"You could be right," said Duggan.

* * *

He woke after a restless two hours and shuffled his way through to the bathroom. It was six in the evening, but it felt like six in the morning. Out in the big bad world the sun was shining brightly. He relieved himself, turned towards the sink and was again confronted by his image in the mirror. Turning on the tap he bathed his face with cold water, dried it on a minimally fresh towel and headed for the lounge. Looking around for a lost sock, he realized that the elation he had felt as he flew across the Pacific had evaporated. He was back in his old routine, his old pattern, the light and warmth of an early evening sun an irritation because it contradicted his darkening mood. Bent over to tie a shoelace, his fingers busily engaged, he was, for a brief moment, a boy of fifteen heading off to school again, a boy for whom the Catholic scheme of things had been intact and inviolable. Intact. *Intacta.* A mysterious word applied to Our Lady that no one had ever thought to explain. He straightened, turned, and the boy turned with him.

Dave Perry's approach to religion was of a completely different character. He was a traditionalist who gloried in Church music and architecture, and was said to have a large collection of books dealing with liturgy, altar cloths and Church vestments. But it was really history that marked him out as a specialist; he had an honors degree in medieval history. A lanky fifty-year-old in John Lennon spectacles, he brooked no nonsense when reviewing authors dealing in the vagaries of New Age spirituality. A traditionalist on the one hand, he was, on the other, a man ever tweaking the Church's authorial intrusion. But only playfully. For what would happen if everyone turned their back on Christ's crazy injunction to love one's neighbor? What would happen if the heart-withering cruelty of reality was allowed to seep into society's bones? Knowing the answer to that, he kept the more serious of his questions to himself and allowed the beauty and harmony of the Church's imagination to soothe away his fears.

Duggan's mind flipped back to Jane Windle, and for a moment he was back in Santa Rosa, back in the hotel bar where he had first seen her. A shake of the head as he made his way through to the kitchen. An American? Another shake of the head as he poured boiling water onto a teabag and stared at it. A Catholic-Jew? Two generations of Catholic-Jews? Too much to contemplate on an empty stomach. A laugh as he made his way back into the lounge to order a takeaway. He would play the situation by ear and try to avoid an unseemly tangle.

* * *

As he entered the hospital, Duggan wondered how Dave would have handled Philip Atkins's vision of the world, a vision in which the Earth, infused with hints of heaven, served as a kind of preparatory hell. How would the man they had secretly labeled 'Trotsky' have reacted? Would he have walked out and headed for the bar? Or would he have accommodated Atkins's dour Augustinian preoccupations? When he found Dave he was lying back, eyes closed, his El Greco hands holding a book by the edges. Venturing the man's name, Duggan waited, but there was no response. Then, as if sensing a human presence, Dave opened his eyes.

"Jack?"

"How's it goin' fella?"

"I was asleep, I think."

They shook hands.

"You look okay?"

"I feel wretched."

"So what's the verdict?"

"They want to do more tests. Something isn't right. In here." Dave prodded at his chest. "Damned nuisance."

"What are you reading?"

"Johannes Weiss." He turned the book right way up. "Weiss is my favorite."

"Schonfield was mine. He said the only reason the Church had got away with its lies was because they were thumping big ones. His *Passover Plot* reads like a crime thriller."

Dave's little round spectacles glistened with reflected light. His look said: If you know something I don't, then tell me, but I doubt that you do.

That set the tenor of their interaction. Duggan said that he had enjoyed reading Weiss's two-volume history of the early Church, but that he'd got much more out of Schonfield. It was a matter of perspective. Weiss was all clever twists and turns; Schonfield's intention had been to reinstate Jewish history at the core of Christianity. Weiss had in the end sidestepped that issue.

"You think that ultimately important?"

"Don't you?"

"I think it muddies the waters a bit." Dave's smile was cautionary. "I mean, Christianity is something that's grown out of itself. Hasn't it? It is its own invention. The great strength of Christianity is that it is a self-perpetuating myth. I'm using 'myth' in the sense of something interpreted into reality as a great and lasting truth. Christianity's truth is not historical, Jack; it is epistemological. It's knowledge is grounded in vision and method."

"You can't just discard history."

"Schonfield disliked anything Catholic. He used history for his own ends."

"He didn't dislike Christianity, Dave. He took the time to do his own translation of the New Testament. He was a New Testament scholar of distinction."

"He ceased to be objective, Jack. He turned into a . . . a novelist?"

"He was nominated for the Nobel peace prize."

"He resorted to facts. Christianity isn't about facts, it's about vision. Christ is the vision of man perfected." He looked down, up again. "Anyway," a half smile became a half laugh, "you didn't come here to argue. Tell me about the conference. What was Donaghue like? What did it feel like to be back amongst it all?"

Duggan paused to accommodate the change in direction. "Regular-issue Archbishop that Peters thinks is being taken for a ride by the neoconservatives." A sheepish smile. "I ended up enjoying the conference in spite of myself."

"Bishop Peters?"

"Heading for the chop. He's in hospital right this minute with a punctured lung. A car accident."

"He's okay?"

"He's still talking. He's a big talker."

"Elliot said you didn't want to go."

"To put it mildly."

"What did you make of Atkins?"

"Frightful man. You're familiar?"

"A robust doctrine of evil makes everything comprehensible, don't you think?" Dave's smile was playful. "There's got to be a dark side to the vision, Jack."

"I found his theodicy scary."

"Elliot tells me you have a doctorate."

A nod from Duggan.

"You're no longer a believer?"

A shake of the head.

"You're an atheist?"

"I'm at one with the ancient Fathers; I prefer to contemplate what

God is not, rather than what some intellectually constipated theologian thinks he might be. Teilhard de Chardin said that at this present moment in history no religion proffers us the God we need. I'm with de Chardin."

"The God of our fathers is so easily dismissed?"

"The God of our fathers was an interfering busybody. That's Atkins's God."

"It's most people's God, Jack. It's the Jewish God as well as the Christian. It's the Islamic God. What's the point of being God if you can't break the rules?"

"A God capable of putting round pegs in square holes doesn't interest me. Anyway, why should he expect human beings to obey divine law if he's going to circumvent natural law whenever it suits him?" A fierce look. "None of it makes any sense, Dave."

"Making sense might not be the point. De Chardin admitted that a humble believer in the catechism was more likely to lead a life of real charity than he was." The playfulness had gone out of Dave's tone. "He was aware of an ethical dilemma."

"Aware of it, but not fooled by it. He also said that his sophisticated faith was the only type of faith he could tolerate."

"*He* could tolerate."

"That doesn't mean he was willing to put up with crowd control at any price, Dave. He saw the need to drag simple believers up out of their ignorance, not further embed them in it. He knew from experience that the catechism's simple-minded summary of Christianity wasn't enough, that mouthing the Creed does not constitute a spiritual life however good it might make one feel."

"A stirrup-cup of heady wine is how one writer described him."

"He was a threat to everything the Catholic Church stood for."

"His theories are laughed at by both sides now."

"He was a transition thinker. Transition thinkers don't have to be right to be important."

"That's a very generous view."

"They won't silence Peters the way they silenced de Chardin.

He'll fight them all the way."

"To be thrown out is to be silenced. No one listens to you with any seriousness when the collar comes off."

A small truth, but a truth nonetheless.

"The dilemma is theirs, not ours," said Duggan. He felt as dejected as he sounded. "Reality's caught up with them and they damn well know it."

There was an awkward moment as they emerged from the conversation they ought to have had months before. Giving Dave a weary-edged smile, Duggan said that he was sorry he had missed out on America. A wave of the hand absolved him.

"I may have to go back to the States in May."

Dave had removed his spectacles and was rubbing at his eyes.

"Something happened over there you should know about."

The spectacles settled back into place.

"Have you heard of Professor James Windle?"

* * *

Duggan's cat liked fried lamb's liver best; it was an experiment that had turned into an ongoing thing. Pig's liver would not do. She, Phoebe, turned up her nose at pig's liver. Fish was okay. Certain types of tinned meat were okay. Dry biscuits were acceptable in emergencies. Tonight it was lamb's liver and her purring was loud and strong, her tail erect, her circling of his feet constant. "In a minute," he kept saying, trying to pacify her. Later, when they were both fed and watered, and he was sitting at his desk poring over the photographs, she leapt up beside him and took to rubbing her head off his cheek, her sleek, striped body planted firmly on top of Theodore's exposition. He moved her, but she kept coming back, so he was forced to take her out of the room. Closing the door of his study, he set up his Greek-fonted typewriter (an old battered manual he'd paid next to nothing for at auction) and settled to the task of transcribing Theodore's letter.

He had stripped his library of inessentials. Devotional texts were out. Historical texts bolstering religious ideas were out. Speculative theology was out. Texts dealing with religious hopes and aspirations, whatever their origin, were out. The only books allowed were comparative studies, Greek and Latin lexicons, dictionaries, concordances and grammars. He had hung on to old worthies like Nestle's *Novum Testamentum Graece,* and Westcot and Hort's *The New Testament in Original Greek.* And although his Latin had not reached the same level of perfection as his Greek, he treasured Bover's *Novi Testamentum Graece et Latina.* The rest of his shelf space was taken up with political commentaries, a sprinkling of philosophy and a host of novels.

It had been a long and difficult road from classical Greek to New Testament Greek to Byzantine Greek, but he had loved every minute of it. His mother had been pleased, for a while. She had informed anyone who would listen that her son was learning the language of the Scriptures. But when informed that the Gospels had not been recorded by Jesus' disciples as they travelled around Galilee and Judea, but at a much later date, and by strangers who had assumed the names of the disciples, she had flatly refused to believe a word of it. What a lot of nonsense, she had said, pounding at him with her eyes. The Gospels were clearly marked Matthew, Mark, Luke and John, and as the Scriptures couldn't lie that had to be the way of it. He had tried to explain the ins and outs of historical exegesis, but she had refused to listen - not even to the parish priest when he tried to help out.

A moment's reverie as Theodore's observations sprang from the page and Duggan again caught the dramatic unfolding of the man's thinking. Whoever Theodore had been, he was attempting to correct what he believed to be historical and theological anomalies in relation to the Jerusalem Church and the growth of St Paul's charismatic assemblies. This might explain why a large body of Christians in fifth-century Syria had repudiated the patriarchs of Antioch as heretics and set up their own alternative patriarchs. Arguing that the

relationship between the human and the divine should be interpreted as the conjunction of two persons - the Messiah as ordinary
man *indwelt* by God the Son - these Syrian Christians had rejected
the notion of the Jewish Messiah being divine in his own right.

What intrigued Duggan was Theodore's insistence that the early
Church in Jerusalem had, at all times, remained true to its Jewish
roots and not fallen back into Judaism by way of a descent into error.
Yes, orthodox Jewry had viewed the Apostolic Nazoraean's choice of
Messiah as mistaken, but that had not resulted in rejection or
exclusion from the Temple. Up until the war with Rome in AD70
they had attended the Temple regularly, and after the invasion
regrouped as best they could. By the fourth century they had
founded synagogues that extended from the Syrian coast through
northern Transjordan down to Peraea. Duggan was reminded of
Hugh Schonfield's disgust over the question of Nazoraean identity,
the so- frequently-used term 'Jewish Christians' being ridiculed by
this scholar as inaccurate and misleading. Jewish sectarians, yes, but
not 'Christians', he had pleaded. That was a misnomer that should
be struck from the record.

He worked until late, then with the aid of a sleeping tablet and a
cup of hot chocolate, attempted to sleep. Phoebe lay with her back
against his calf, moving when he moved. No dreams that he could
remember next morning, just a slight numbness in the head and a
parched throat. After breakfast he went back into his study and
stared at his evening's work. An educated man, Theodore. Sculpted
prose. Someone to whom wielding a pen was second nature.
Duggan's guess was late fourth century given the allusions and
language. A reference to the hierarchy in Rome as 'debauched' was
a useful marker, and mention of a friend of the recipient's being
indicted for heresy on six charges helped narrow the possibilities.
When the 'phone rang, he reached for it absentmindedly.

"Thought I'd give you a few hours to settle in." Jane's tone was
bright; she had fortified herself with a gin and tonic. "You got off
okay?"

"I flew out of San Francisco instead of Los Angeles." He was now alert. "That cut the journey somewhat."

"I'm still in New York. Half the country's snowbound."

He searched for something to say. "Successful visit?"

"Beyond anything I expected." She hiccupped a laugh. "*Everything* sold. I can't get over it."

"Congratulations."

She was standing at the window of a large second-storey apartment looking down on pedestrians gingerly making their way along frozen pavements. It was snowing heavily, the illuminated flakes dancing in all directions. She turned back into a stylish room.

"How did your editor react?"

"He's waiting to see what I come up with."

"My father says it's a very important letter."

"If it's genuine, it's certainly that."

"You still have doubts?"

"All I have are a few photographs," he said, reminding her. She didn't reply, so he continued. "Don't expect the scholarly community to welcome this with open arms, Jane. They won't. They'll go after it like a dog after a bone. Theodore's letter will be automatically written off by Christian scholars as heretical rubbish - if it ever surfaces. Secular scholars will tiptoe around it for fear of upsetting the status quo."

"I think you're being overly pessimistic."

"I'm being realistic."

"You think my father isn't? He wouldn't be doing what he's doing if he didn't think it was worthwhile."

The mental picture he had of her was dominated by a mass of crinkly hair, and by expressive brown eyes. So different from the women he had known, the women who had punctuated, and on occasions punctured, his life.

"I admire him for what he's doing."

"He doesn't expect to change the world overnight - he isn't naive." She cut back in with what sounded like a personal criticism.

"Aren't you even a little bit excited by this, Jack?"

"Try *intrigued.*" He was sitting on the edge of his desk; Phoebe joined him with a squeak. "A gospel thought to be first or second-century was discovered in the Egyptian Museum in Berlin in the early nineties, Jane. It contained conversations between Jesus and his disciples. It was written off as heretical, as Gnostic in origin, and hasn't been heard of since. That's what could happen here. They don't listen to what they don't want to hear. When she did not immediately reply, he added in a softer tone, "It's not how I want things to be, it's just how things are."

"My father wants to meet up with you in New York. I told him he was in good hands."

"Do I detect irony?"

"From an American?"

He smiled into the receiver.

"Was that a cat I heard?"

"That's Phoebe," he said, lifting her. "Say hello, Phoebe." Phoebe obliged. "She's a stripey female. Lives next door when I'm not here."

"I've got two Burmese. Chips and Rafferty. One's grey, the other's brown."

"Too aloof for my taste," he said back. "Phoebe's a little smooch."

"Aloof?"

"Intelligent."

"They're very loving."

"In between planning bank jobs they are."

She laughed, and he came back in with an apology for having sounding so negative. He had felt pretty flat since returning, he said, aware of that flatness as he spoke.

"You'll be back in May."

"All going well, I will."

"It'll work out; you'll see." The muffled sound of a door closing made her look round. "I'll have to go, Jack. The people I'm staying with have just got back from the theatre."

"I know which Theodore wrote the letter, and to whom it was

sent."

"Now you tell me!"

"If I'm wrong, it's me who'll be classified as naive."

"You sound very certain."

It'll be one helluva fluke if it isn't right."

"Can you give me a name to pass on?"

"Coelestius," he said, testing the water.

8

Le Milieu Divin

"You should have come with us; it was a *marvelous* performance. I don't think I've heard Domingo in better voice." The speaker, a tall woman with black hair piled high tossed a white fur cape onto the sofa and headed for the drinks cabinet. "I *adore Carmen.*"

"I called Sydney."

Elspeth Bentley turned; her expression was one of expectation. "And?"

"We spoke for some time."

"And?"

"We talked mostly about the work he's doing for my father."

Did he say anything. . . *nice?*"

"He said he was glad that I'd rung."

"That's not very romantic."

"It wasn't that kind of call."

Elspeth looked round as George Bentley entered the room. "He isn't romantic, George," she said, reaching for the scotch.

A look from George. "Who isn't?"

"Jane's young man."

George smiled his smile; it was dismissive of Elspeth's attempt to embroil.

"A priest could be *fun,"* she ventured.

"He isn't a priest. Wasn't. He got thrown out."

"Once a priest. . ." said George, whose hearing was not the best.

"I think she's smitten," said Elspeth. And then, "You're obviously smitten, you're blushing like a teenager."

Jane's smile was laced with mild frustration.

"Enough," said George.

"It's the accent; she's fallen for the accent." Scotch in hand, Elspeth settled into a corner of the large white sofa that dominated the room. "Your description of him was not exactly enticing."

"He's not not good-looking."

"Cropped hair?"

"He did it for a bet."

"Irish?"

"Irish stock. He's *all* Australian."

"Is that good?"

A smile from Jane.

"It really is snowing now." George was standing at one of the big casement windows. "Even heavier than when we came in."

"You may not be able to fly out for days," Elspeth beamed, "so why don't you just stay on? We *love* having you."

"I've got work to do."

"You deserve a rest."

"I enjoy what I do." Jane corrected herself with a laugh. "In between going crazy over things that haven't turned out right."

"You can pull out all the old stuff now," said George. "Isn't that what one does? Novelists republish all of their old novels after a best seller."

Elspeth joined her husband at the window.

"Isn't it *superb!*"

"Very grand," said George, looking up into the blackness.

A financier, George was also a collector of artworks; it was he who had happened upon one of Jane Windle's paintings and realized her potential. Elspeth had trained as a ballet dancer, but failed to make the grade because of knee problems.

"He has a cat called Phoebe."

They looked at her, then at each other.

"Smitten," said Elspeth.

"I look forward to meeting him," said George.

"He's got a cleft chin, but no hair," said Elspeth, who had wormed the information out of Jane.

All three were now standing at the window.

"When is he coming to New York?" asked George.

"May. It depends," said Jane.

"On what?" asked Elspeth.

"Whether what he's doing for my father works out or not."

"What is he doing for your father?" asked Elspeth.

"Something to do with a translation."

"He must be very good," said George, who knew a lot about Jane's father. And then, "He's a religious correspondent?"

Jane explained the circumstances behind Duggan turning up in Santa Rosa.

"But he's never met the man," said Elspeth. "Your father, I mean."

"It's . . . complicated," said Jane. She smiled and deflected two more questions from Elspeth.

"*Dinner!*" said Elspeth, raising a slim finger.

"Only if you promise to behave," said Jane quickly.

"We'll invite a few friends."

"Just the four of us," said Jane, who had no desire to see Duggan drown in the Bostonian pool. "

* * *

There were a number of calls on Duggan's answering machine, but only one was of interest: it was from Elliot. Dave Perry's condition had been diagnosed as bone cancer. He rang the office immediately.

"It isn't necessarily a death sentence." Elliot scribbled something on a pad as he spoke. "It's chemotherapy followed by radiation, then stem cells. If that works out, he might survive."

When he rang off, Duggan poured himself a whisky and stood staring at nothing in particular. Might survive? He went into the kitchen and stared some more, Dave's lean face conjured vaguely to mind - it was as if the man were already dead and was glowering at him from beyond the grave. Then, donning his jacket, he set out reluctantly for the hospital. The moment Dave saw Duggan's expression, he knew Elliot had passed on the news.

"Come to give me absolution, Jack?"

Duggan smiled, but did not respond to the remark.

"I suspected all was not as it should be. "

"Elliot says the prognosis is good."

"All things being equal it is." A bit of a laugh. "It's an extraordinary feeling. I keep forgetting. I wake up, then after a minute or two I remember. Then I forget again. It's been like that all day."

"They're absolutely sure?"

"Oh yeh, they're sure."

"When do you start chemo?"

"This is it. The little bag?"

"I thought . . . "

"You're thinking radiation. That comes later."

The remains of Dave's evening meal lay on a plate. Duggan could smell it. As they talked, a woman collected it and moved off.

"Are you in pain?"

"A bit."

"How long has that been going on?"

"Some months."

"You've been in pain for some months?"

"Discomfort." A throwaway smile. "When I broke my leg, then my arm, that was why. Brittle bones?" He looked away, then back. "They'll be bringing round tea and biscuits in a minute. Would you like a cup? The tea lady and I are buddies."

When the trolley arrived, Dave negotiated an extra cup. Extra biscuits were palmed in their direction as if eyes other than their own were present.

He had not intended to tell Dave anything about the American trip during his first visit, but in the end had opened up because he felt he owed the man something. Dave had plagued him with questions. He sat in silence now wondering what to say next.

"How are things at mill?"

"Steve's in Elliot's bad books."

"Again?"

"I think he's for the chop."

Dave's expression indicated that that did not surprise him.

"I've worked out which Theodore it is."

"You have?"

"I got lucky." Duggan put his mug of tea aside and lifted a biscuit. "I got a fix because of something said in the letter about a disciple of the receiver's being a lawyer and a loudmouth. Theodore asks if the receiver has managed to bring his outspoken pupil under control. I'm betting on the pupil being Coelestius, a lawyer turned priest indicted for heresy on six counts at the end of the fourth century. That would make the receiver Pelagius, Augustine's adversary, and the writer of the letter Theodore of Mopsuestia, a Syrian bishop with a finger in just about every major debate of his time. It all fits. Up until now there's been no known link between Pelagius and Theodore."

"What does Windle think?"

"I don't know yet. I've only just told his daughter."

"I'm not familiar with your Syrian Bishop."

"Born Antioch 350. An eminent Christian theologian and bishop of the Church in Cilicia from around 392. Studied rhetoric alongside John Chrysostom under the celebrated pagan sophist Libanius. Contemplated entering the law, but changed his mind and ended up as a monk in a monastery in Antioch." Duggan took a sip of tea. "He became an important figure among the patristic authorities, was a bishop for 36 years, and was active in all of the Greek-oriental debates. The Nestorian scholar Abdisho mentions no less than forty-one books written by him, and that doesn't include the fifteen he wrote on the incarnation."

He had counted off each point on the palm of his left hand as he spoke.

"He was considered a heretic in the West?"

"He insisted on a separation between Jesus' divine nature and his human nature. He argued for a voluntary, moral union between the two, and likened it to the physical union between husband and wife.

He did not believe in a complete union of the two natures. What makes him unique is his interest in biblical evidence. He was probably the first Christian scholar to build a psychological profile of Jesus. His methodology was scientific, critical, philological and historical. He anticipated modern scholarship on just about every level."

"An arch heretic by the sound of it."

"That's how he was perceived in the West. But he did manage to influence the Council of Chalcedon into accepting, in principle, Christ's fundamental humanity. He foreshadowed Bishop Gore on that."

"So what's in the letter?"

"A mixture of history, theology and philosophy. The historical perspective is particularly strong."

"What were the charges against Coelestius?"

"That Adam would have died whether he had sinned or not, that the sin of Adam was personal, and therefore not communicable to others, that newborn children were as Adam was before the Fall, and that the human race did not die because of Adam's sin." Duggan searched the air for a moment. "That before Christ there had been human beings who had attained a sinless state, and that the law gave access to heaven as well as the Gospel."

Dave stared at Duggan, then in an almost awestruck voice he said, "What were the odds against them bumping into someone like you?"

"Fairly high, I would say."

"You have a very good memory."

"I refreshed it recently."

"The master believed what the pupil believed?"

"It would seem so. Pelagius argued that the human will was free and God-given, and that human beings could consciously avoid sin. Which is to say that he believed in individual responsibility. Augustine believed that God punished infants with eternal damnation if they died before baptism."

"Physician heal thyself."

"Exactly."

"Jesus was an ordinary man?"

"An ordinary man *indwelt* by God at his baptism. Theodore says that Christ must have known the agony of wrestling with bodily appetites. The Epistle to the Hebrews concurs."

"In all points tempted like as we were."

A smile from Duggan.

"So what's the bottom line?"

"The Nazoraean sect's view of Jesus. Theodore claims to be quoting from a fragment of an alternative gospel written by the second-century bishop Irenaeus."

"Is that likely?"

"It's possible, but it's problematical. Irenaeus is known to have held views at variance with standard teaching, but he's also famous for his five-volume treatise against the heretics, and that complicates things. He's even thought to have been the final arbiter on what went into the gospels. So what's he doing writing a gospel that flatly contradicts the accepted canon?"

An alternative story regarding the early Jerusalem Church had emerged as Duggan delved into Theodore's letter. Gone had been the notion of the Nazoraean Apostles being 'Christian', or of their having acquiesced in the Apostle Paul's interpretation of Jesus' life and purpose. They had, according to an irate Theodore, been sectarian Jews who believed Jesus to be the promised Messiah of Israel, but not in any literal sense Israel's God paying them a personal visit. Any such idea had been anathema to these guardians of the faith of Israel. And it was precisely this idea that had caused the rupture between the Jerusalem Apostles and the Apostle Paul - a fact detectable in the book of Acts. Jesus had been perceived as a man like any other man, but a man indwelt by the spirit of Messiah at his baptism. He had undoubtedly been a man of profound spiritual perception and tenacity of will, but to the extent that he had hungered and thirsted, grown weary and exhibited anger he had been a man like any other man. Yet simultaneously the promised Messiah of Israel, a man chosen by God to lead Israel out of bondage. But alas, only the Nazoraean sectaries had perceived Jesus in this way. Orthodox Jewry had dismissed him as a false Messiah, and under the influence of Paul's hyperbole the fourth-century Council of Nicaea had made him consubstantial with the supreme deity.

"Is it really possible to be sure what went on way back then?"

"Merle's running scared and Windle's put his career on the line - that speaks for itself. This isn't just theology, it's an alternative history and there's sufficient proof available from other sources to make his letter a key research document. Theodore is trying to set the historical record straight, and by claiming Irenaeus as his source he's drawn attention to someone the Church would prefer to ignore."

"They won't take the bait."

Duggan smiled as his own reading of the situation returned to mock him. "I agree," he said, lifting another biscuit, "but Theodore's letter confirms the suspicions of liberal scholars, and that could be damaging to the status quo."

"Is that what you want to see happen?"

"I'd like to see things straighten themselves out."

"What would you replace the old, old story with?"

"That's not my problem."

"Someone on the point of death might not be interested in your idea of intellectual integrity."

Duggan stared at Dave for a moment, then he said, "You want to believe whatever the truth of the situation?"

"I'm not talking about myself. I'm talking about some poor bugger who's never heard of the Nazoraeans. What does he or she care about the niceties of historical accuracy, Jack? Believing that their soul is saved because of Jesus' death on the cross might be all they've got to hang on to."

"If they don't understand the question, it's unlikely they'll be affected one way or the other."

"And if they do understand the question?"

"Then hopefully they'll make the appropriate adjustments." Duggan hesitated. "I known what you're saying, Dave, but we can't ignore the difficult questions just because some people have difficulty assimilating the answers. Life is about assimilation and adjustment on multiple levels of experience. We've got to keep on ditching Santa Clause."

"Jesus Christ isn't Santa Claus."

"If you accept without question some of the stuff Christianity dishes up, he might as well be."

"You're advocating facts over faith."

"If you retain any sense of mystery it's more a case of trust over belief."

"That sounds rather vague to me."

"You think Christianity's claim to possess revealed truth is true?"

"I've decided to believe that that is the case."

"Decided?"

"I've decided to ignore the epistemological prejudices of modernity."

It was a startling reply; Duggan stared at Dave Perry.

"I'm a Barthian, Jack. Barth believed the whole of reality lay within Christianity's sacred enclosure. He followed the Vincentian Rule."

"Which was?"

"That in the worldwide community of believers *every care should be taken to hold fast to what has been believed everywhere, always, and by all.*"

"Sixth century?"

"Fifth."

Duggan was silent for a moment; then, tentatively, he said, "I think you've just changed the clergy into antiquities dealers."

"The model works; why change it?"

"It works for you because you've decided to consciously ignore the obvious: we no longer live in a three-tier universe."

"You're still talking facts, Jack."

"Sorry. It's the best I can do."

"What keeps you going?"

"Bloody-mindedness?"

"The pugnacious Celt rides to our rescue."

"My superiors in the seminary called me a mischief-maker."

"Were you?"

"I was twenty-five and had a doctorate in classical studies. I thought I was God Almighty."

"You've never regretted leaving?"

A shake of the head.

"Not once?"

"It was an unrealizable dream."

"It was a dream you believed in once."

"I woke up."

"Into what?"

"What is."

"And what is that?"

"*Le Milieu Divin?*" said Duggan, half in jest.

He stepped into the evening sunshine feeling uneasy about his interaction with Dave Perry. Should he have talked more with the man about his predicament? Empathized more? Reaching his car, he got in and sat for a while trying to appreciate what it must feel like to be Dave right that minute, then with a disconsolate sigh reached for his seat belt. There was nothing more he could have done, or said, that would have alleviated the unacknowledged terror of the situation. What Comrade Trotsky needed more than anything else was distraction, and that he had managed to supply.

9

The Naive Child

"So what have we got?"

Duggan handed over the draft of Theodore's letter and the completed article on Bishop Peters. Putting the article to one side, Elliot leafed through the translation with interest.

"It contradicts the Church's opinion of its own origins. It's an indictment couched by a good mind in terms that will be difficult for historians to ignore. He accuses the Western Church of historical and theological misrepresentation. He argues that the Roman Church lost touch with what the original Jerusalem Church of the Apostles stood for, and as a result falsified its message to the world."

"Now you're talking."

"He also associates the Church of the Apostles with a Jewish sect - the Nazoraeans. Jesus is associated with this group in the Gospels." Duggan smiled. "The most telling part is where he shows how the Western Church got its theological sums wrong. He is explicit. He details the moves made and castigates the Roman hierarchy for holding to the belief that their authority came directly from the Apostles. I've never read anything quite like it."

"It'll be taken seriously?"

"It'll raise hackles."

"You think it's authentic."

"As far as I can tell from a few photographs."

Elliot nursed his coffee. "A Jewish sect?"

"The group St Paul was accused of belonging to by orthodox Jews prior to his arrest by the Romans. After the war with Rome in AD70, orthodox Jewry accused the Nazoraeans - alongside the Christians - of having caused the debacle. They also accused them of being heretics. A special prayer/curse called the *birkat ha-minim* was

composed and offered in the synagogues. The prayer was designed
to expose secret Nazoraeans and Christian followers of Jesus who
were mixing with fellow Jews. Note how the Nazoraeans and
Christians are lumped together, yet at the same time kept apart. So
what was going on? Who exactly are we dealing with here. *That* is
the prime question."

"And?"

"It seems there were three Nazoraean groups, or camps, two of
them pacifist, one militant - I'm working from inferences in
Theodore's letter and from other sources in saying that. The
Jerusalem group led by Jesus' brother James was, as is believed by
historians today, pacifist. The Damascus group with which St Paul is
associated also seems to have been pacifist, but at odds doctrinally
with the Jerusalem group over the status of Jesus. The third group
appears to have been in league with the ultra-militant Zealots, and it
is *this* group that eventually tarnishes the reputation of the other
two. Hence the *birkat ha-minim* curse. After the war with Rome,
during which the whole infrastructure of Jewish life and culture was
destroyed, they were lumped together and held to be equally
responsible for the debacle." Elliot's expression suggested that he
was finding the ins and outs of the business difficult to follow. "Bear
with me," said Duggan. "One more point. The title 'Christian' was a
term of abuse given to followers of St Paul by opponents at Antioch
in the early sixties of the first century. It had no meaning in relation
to the Jerusalem Apostles, and it is this basic mistake in group identification that has caused endless misunderstanding throughout the
history of the Church."

"What are your other sources on this"

"Two Jewish historians. Hugh Schonfield and Hyam Maccoby."

"You mentioned the status of Jesus?"

"Paul had a very different notion of Jesus' status from that of the
Jerusalem Apostles. To them he was the Messiah of Israel, a man
adopted by God to fulfill a role. To Paul, and one has to suppose
those who schooled him, Jesus was a species of divine being. And so

Theodore, being of the Jerusalem school, fought for the recognition of Christ's basic humanity at the Council of Chalcedon. Without his intervention Jesus' raw physical existence would have disappeared altogether. Everything in his letter points to the necessity of Rome's Christians accepting and appreciating the fact that Jesus was a flesh-and-blood human being called to a mighty task, not God himself hiding inside a human body."

"It's standard Christian teaching that he was God."

"It's actually heresy to suggest a complete identification between God and the man that Jesus was."

"It's heresy to believe that Jesus was God?"

"It's heresy to believe that Jesus the flesh-and-blood man was *literally* God in every sense."

"You've lost me."

"Nestorius - bishop of Constantinople, and a heretic like Theodore - put it best. He said he could not think of God as a two or three-week- old infant. The Council of Chalcedon affirmed the full deity *and* the full humanity of Christ in 450, but it did so with a plethora of qualifications. Truth was, no one knew what the words meant. It was a statement; it was not an explanation. It was a formula created in desperation, not, as some believe, a revelation. Prior to the Council of Nicaea in 325, God was prayed to *through* Jesus; he was perceived as an intermediary. After Nicaea, with the elevation of Jesus to the position of Second Person in a divine trinity, the new orthodoxy took to praying to Jesus *as if* he were God."

"The heterodox view was thrown out."

"By the *new* orthodoxy it was. There were lots of Christian groups in 325 who did not agree with the Nicaean formula. A religious faction gained the upper hand and imposed its view at the point of a sword. It systematically stamped out all opposition and set up a system of thought which looped back into itself for verification. God and Jesus and the Holy Spirit had conceived of the faction's triumph since before the foundation of the world. Rejection of the faction's point of view was to question the divine will. The circle closed - escape was impossible. Even if you were outside the circle you were part of the circle. The whole universe hinged on the faction's conception of itself. Truth was what the faction nominated to be the truth, and this truth, by its very nature, confirmed the faction's right to make such a claim. The faction's grocery list of beliefs was immutable."

Elliot stared at Duggan for a moment. "You sound bitter."

"I get annoyed when I think about it."

"You think about it much?"

"Not really. It just pops up from time to time."

Elliot drained his mug. "So what's your take on Jesus?"

"From what I can make out the Nicaean formula wasn't based on Jesus at all; it was based on a speculative figure created out of promises found in the Old Testament. Jesus was eventually perceived as *embodying* those promises; which is not the same as saying that he *was* this speculative figure. He may have identified with this figure, but as a Jew it's highly unlikely that he thought he was this figure. And as orthodoxy did not equate this figure with God, the Nicaean formula for Jesus' inherent divinity falls flat on its face."

"Neat."

"Obvious, I would have thought." Duggan's smile conveyed an element of pleasure. "What Christians don't realize is that prior to the Council of Nicaea the Eastern Church held to views of Jesus quite different from those of the Western Church. The tendency at Antioch was Adoptionist: Jesus had been possessed by the Spirit of God at his baptism. In Asia Minor it was Sabellian: Jesus was to be directly identified with the Father. At Alexandria it was Platonic: Jesus was the divine logos or link between God and creation. In the Alexandrian version the Son was subordinate to the Father, in Asia Minor consubstantial with the Father; whereas at Antioch these diametrically opposed ideas were sandwiched together to create the notion of Jesus as a specially created human being taken over by the Divine Logos, but unable to redeem humanity in his own right."

"Complicated."

"You don't know the half of it; it's been a mess from the very beginning. A hazy theological glow surrounds the happenings of the first century. In diminished form that glow is responsible for stories about Jesus worthy of Hans Andersen. Behind it all lies a welter of theology purporting to explain how a living, breathing, defecating man was also God." Duggan grimaced. "Everyone's concerned about sexual abuse in the Church, and so they ought to be, but what about the abuse of people's minds? Does that count for nothing? Wandering hands are one thing, minds dedicated to the task of telling attractive lies in the name of some imagined truth is, in my opinion, measurably worse."

"I treat the whole thing as poetic license."

"Fine. What if you can't?"

Elliot's tone became quizzical. "So how come they don't see it the way you do? They must be aware of what people like you think."

"They're inside a belief bubble - everything is filtered. They're psychologically incapable of separating history from theology, of distancing themselves from doctrine. Some make the attempt, but not wholeheartedly. They end up tying themselves in epistemological knots."

"I don't think my parents believed in anything." Elliot laughed to himself. "It just sort of petered out for me."

"Apart from a few weddings and funerals I haven't been inside a church in two decades."

"They can't turn the clock back, Jack. Not now."

"Every generation is a new generation. It's a merry-go-round packed with children who aren't allowed to get off."

"I wouldn't have thought many people gave a rat's arse about what the Church teaches these days."

"They don't. On the street it can be ignored; but it isn't ignored in newspaper articles or on television. Another level of reality kicks in. The Church as an institution looms large. Tell one of its representatives that you're an unbeliever, that you do not accept his interpretation of first-century events and you'll be accused of attacking God's revealed truth - the truth nominated by the Church *as* the truth. You'll find yourself at an immediate disadvantage no matter what you say, or how you say it."

"Theodore's view of Jesus sounds blasphemous."

"In the sense that it denies him divinity, it is. He insists on separating Jesus' divine and human nature. He argues for a voluntary, moral union or *synapheia* between the two natures. He likens this union to the physical union of husband and wife and rejects the idea of a complete union between the two. But he's more concerned with the identity of the Nazoraeans and the problem of Rome's claim to absolute spiritual authority. That's what bugs him."

"Are we heading for stormy water over this?"

"We are merely conveyors of bad news."

"You're the translator."

"That need never be known."

"How did we come by the document?"

"That'll be part of the story, part of the mystery."

"Windle will confirm the find?"

"He'll protest, then reluctantly accept that the cat is out of the bag."

"How will you explain knowing that he was involved?"

"A tip-off; which is true." A smile. "Conferences are hotbeds of rumor and scandal."

"What do you expect the Church's reaction to be?"

"They'll use the old argument that the document is worthless because written by someone outside of the consensus fold. The fact that Theodore was, in their terms, a heretic, will be used to undermine the document's historical worth. They'll use every trick in the book including attacking the competency of the translator to discredit the find. If Windle is too forthright, they'll drag Fr Merle in to muddy the waters."

"You'll admit to being the translator?"

"Only if I have to."

"What happens next?"

"I put Theodore's text through the wringer."

Elliot reached for a paper on his desk. Windle had been involved in some kind of controversy a few years back, he said, handing the sheet over. The Jewish lobby in the States had got huffy over something said about the Palestinians.

"Merle?" said Duggan.

"We're still digging." Elliot frowned. "I didn't even know Jesus had a brother."

"He had four brothers and at least two sisters. James, known as the 'Just', is a well-known sectarian figure in Jewish history. Catholic scholars interpret Jesus' siblings as cousins. The Catholic view is that Joseph was a widower with children, and that Jesus was the only child born to Mary, his second wife. Whatever the truth, the family Jesus was part of was no ordinary family; it was sectarian in belief and served as a model for church organization in the first century because of its dynastic nature. Some scholars refer to it as a *Caliphate*. Theodore refers to heirs of Jesus in his letter. He speaks of them as being in charge of the Jewish-Nazoraean Church throughout Palestine, Syria and Mesopotamia after the Roman invasion in AD70. That's quite a claim. It means that the Jerusalem church after James's death was governed by a succession of bishops or presbyters, and that the Nazoraeans were a rival group to that of Paul's charismatic assemblies. These Nazoraeans believed Jesus to have been possessed by the spirit of Messiah *after* his baptism. That's not what Paul was teaching. And it should be remembered that it was to James and the Jerusalem Council that Paul had to present himself when called to explain his theology. Rumor had it that his teachings were at variance with Nazoraean doctrine. What most scholars forget is that Paul only visited Jerusalem *twice* in, I think, fifteen years after his conversion. He was a rank outsider."

"There's been an upsurge in fundamentalist belief. Sydney's an evangelical stronghold. Not a few are dragging their beliefs out into the community."

"Faith belongs to another category of reality; an overworked category which most people see through. Either that or they ditch one set of supernaturalisms and take up another. But on the whole I think people are more discriminating, more insightful than they were a couple of decades ago. They're a lot more cautious than they used to be. It's when they start talking about having direct access to Jesus that the trouble starts. What to other Christians is a relationship with God through the life and teachings of Jesus turns into a literalist nightmare where God *as* Jesus becomes a private possession. That brings us back to the difference between what James and Paul believed about Jesus, and that's why Theodore's letter is so damned important."

"I haven't looked inside a Bible for years."

"You and the bulk of the population."

"You still read your Bible?"

A shake of the head from Duggan.

"So why should Theodore's letter matter?"

"Because it helps straighten out a forged reality. We've been living with a forged religious reality for centuries and it's all but bankrupted us. Hardly anyone takes the Church seriously now because it's plainly evident that that Church - whether Catholic or Protestant - has forfeited its right to be taken seriously." Duggan's sigh was edged with frustration. "They talk mostly drivel and expect us to come back for more. That's insulting."

"I'm surprised you got as far as entering a seminary."

"I'd read about the great Catholic intellectual tradition and wanted to experience it for myself. It turned out to be a hall of mirrors. Intellect was used to create a verbal smokescreen. I was up to my neck in trouble in the first week. They did not warm to my questioning the Irish school of romantic conservatism."

"Which is?"

"The idea that a correct interpretation of doctrine is naturally conservative. They were selling a pre-Vatican II Catholicism that restored the old Catholic sub-culture. It was *us* against the world."

"Your fellow students went along with that?"

"Some did, some didn't. Most kept their mouths shut."

"You were the only one to get turfed out?"

"The difference between them and me was that I refused to shut up."

"You still wanted to be a priest?"

"Good question." Duggan paused. "I don't quite know what I'd have done if they hadn't thrown me out. I may have gone through with it."

"You've never asked yourself that question?"

"Someone else did recently." A smile. "They'd have forced me out eventually." The emptiness he felt in that moment was profound. He looked away, looked back and found Elliot staring at him. "The answer to your question is that I don't give a damn for any of it now, not even the good bits."

"You don't accept any of it?"

"I no longer believe in belief."

Liturgy had helped Duggan understanding Christianity's evolution. Liturgy reflected degrees of emphasis in relation to the salvation story, and that in turn had revealed the transitional stages in theological thinking. The Great Church had emerged, not from some magically precise doctrinal state, but from three centuries of doctrinal chaos during which factions had struggled for superiority. Heterodoxy, not orthodoxy, had been Christianity's primary state, orthodoxy defined in relation to choices made by the most powerful of those factions. Christians had believed all kinds of things about Jesus in the early days. The so-called canonical view had been introduced in the fourth century at the point of a sword.

The question was, to what did one turn if the great truths of Christianity were based, not on revelation, but on no more than argument and debate? In what alternative could one put one's trust? Judaism? Islam? Some smiling guru sitting in a gold-plated Cadillac? Duggan had considered these alternatives, but decided that they were not for him. Dave Perry had travelled a similar route, but emerged with a different answer. Conservative to his carefully manicured fingertips, he had gone along with Christianity in spite of its obvious failings, for in the end, he believed, it mattered only that one was true to oneself. It was the opening up to something beyond the self that mattered, the transcendent interaction, not the pros and the cons of the religious path chosen. Standing before Christianity's God was, for Dave, better than standing before no God at all. Accepting the Christian story *as if* it were literally true was better than abandoning oneself to the idea that there was nothing worth believing in. It was, in the end, a matter of angles, not of angels, a matter of human energy positively directed, not a matter of truth or falsity. There was no one great unalterable truth, there were only little truths, and every human being had his or her share of them.

Duggan had his share of little truths, and he treasured them. He above all treasured his father, the man who had silently instructed him on the question of religion. Not once had his father told him what he should, or should not, believe - these were questions he would have to work out for himself, when he was older, the man had said. According to his mother his soul's salvation depended on what he believed right that very minute. For what if he died in an accident? Or in his sleep? What then? Throughout all the years of his youth the man in the big armchair had remained non-committal, but what he thought about God and the Church had sometimes filtered through. "You don't believe in *anything,*" his wife had railed on one occasion. "Why should I listen to you? Why should I listen to an atheist?" On that occasion his father's soft voice had been raised, and something of what he believed had percolated through from their bedroom.

His mother had delighted, for a while, in the contradiction of an atheist husband and a son training for the priesthood. Then had come the bombshell of Duggan's suspension, and the realization that he had joined his father in his rejection of Christ and his Church. A nervous breakdown and the accusation that his father was responsible for the debacle had followed, the storm of her emotions reaching its climax in a barrage of abuse where his father's atheism was blamed for allowing the Devil to take up residence in their little household. Duggan had already come to the conclusion that there was no such person as the Devil - the mystery of evil was no mystery at all. Duggan's father had been of that opinion, too, and Dave Perry was in agreement. All three had concluded, in their own way, that evil was not an intelligent force out to subvert God's good creation, merely human beings who had lost the plot on their own existence. Evil was human, not cosmic. Its center was not some force external to human beings, it was, in every respect, humans failing to appreciate the value of other humans.

Duggan had argued in seminary against the idea of evil being an intelligent force, and had been howled down. How dare he contradict two-thousand years of Church teaching! So what were they going to do with Irenaeus, he had asked. Had not this early Church Father repudiated the idea of Adam and Eve being tempted in the garden of Eden? Had he not, at one stroke, shown that the idea of human beings falling into sin as a result of a talking snake was superstitious nonsense? His tutor in theology had suggested that Irenaeus, like so many other primitive Christians of the second century, had been 'feeling his way' towards the truth. Duggan had rejected that contention on the grounds that Irenaeus's approach had been grounded on the down-to-earth realization that snakes simply do not talk, and that the perfect state that Adam and Eve were later supposed to be in was nothing more than the natural ignorance shared by the sub-humans of the prehistoric period. There was nothing 'primitive' about such an approach, it was about as modern as it was possible to get. If Irenaeus's common sense had won out over the idea of Adam and Eve existing in a state of supernatural perfection - an idea borrowed from Rabbinical Judaism - Christianity may even have been spared the later conflict with Darwinism. As this perceptive Father of the Church had observed, if the Devil had had the ability to make snakes talk, he would have enlisted the help of the whole animal kingdom to subvert the human race.

His parents' relationship had been instrumental in settling many an issue for Duggan. His mother's inflated claims and his father's careful silences had formed his opinions as readily as any textbook. He had at first believed what she believed. He had believed in hell, demons and the Devil, and had had no problem with the idea of Jesus floating off majestically into the heavens after the resurrection. So also with Jesus changing water into wine, walking on water and raising the dead. All perfectly sensible if you believed that God had personally entered the human domain in the form of Jesus of Nazareth. And that was the catch, for his mother's conception of Jesus had been of God thinly veiled in flesh and ready to burst into sight at any moment, her grasp of the theological difficulties inherent in such a view non-existent. And there were, he had discovered, priests who thought just like his mother, men of the cloth to whom the Gospel story could be gulped down whole, its every nuance an obvious confirmation of the Creed. No need to bother with the fact that snakes do not talk, or that apples fell to earth in the first century just as they did now. No need to bother with the fact that Christianity did not arrive on the planet full-blown and ready for consumption, but developed, piecemeal, until such times as Athanasius, Eusebius and the Emperor Constantine decided that the man Jesus was not only more than he seemed, but much, much more than anyone had ever guessed.

What annoyed Duggan was the idea that a more practical inter-pretation of Jesus' life and intentions somehow disallowed one from having a spiritual life. Repudiate Catholicism's reading of the New Testament and the Church automatically threw you on the scrap heap. Take a stand for a more historically based approach to the Scriptures and you were perceived as being in league with unsavory spiritual forces. There were many Catholic scholars who did not think like this, but the Catholic hierarchy was not in step with its scholars; it had hitched itself to the masses and was in trepidation about losing their support. Common-denominator beliefs had to remain intact, the academic tendency to question well-established principles something that had to be quashed. Ignore the fact that much of what passed for doctrinal innovation in the Church had come from the masses in the first place, that it was they who had dictated the direction of Church thinking and forced the hierarchy, century by century, to accommodate strange and anomalous ideas.

In Duggan's opinion it all depended on what you thought a spiritual life was in itself. Was it believing a grocery list of unbelievable things about a Jewish teacher who lived two thousand years ago? Or was it having the courage not to buckle in the face of a universe that gave little indication of caring whether human beings lived or died? Some argued for an anthropic principle, a principle of intentional design behind the fact that planet Earth was so favorable to human survival, others that it was all a pure fluke. Duggan fell between stools on this question: he sensed something untoward in the way things had come together, but suspected that the connection he felt had to do with the fact that human beings were composed of physical matter. Our sometimes mystical sense of connection with the world was probably due to that fact, the idea of being united with God as 'father' an expression of our intrinsic relationship to the Earth as 'mother'. A tenuous spirituality to be sure, a spirituality that few Churchmen would find meaningful, but hard fought for in his case, and curiously rewarding in spite of the great blackness that sometimes engulfed him.

He had, at first, attributed his bouts of depression to unhappiness, but realized, after a bit of thinking, and a bit of drinking, that it was his unwillingness to give in to easy solutions that was the trouble - religion was a sphere in which half-baked ideas could arise. But it wasn't the only one. The conversations he had with other people were often peppered with folksy, homespun nonsense - talking was an inexact science. Not that he expected everyone to be rigidly logical, that was not the case, but he did expect intelligent people to be sensitive to the danger of mangled categories. It amazed him that people for whom he had the greatest respect could sometimes wander into subject areas for which there was not a skerrick of evidence, link those areas to well-defined subjects and not expect to get pulled up. Sometimes it was ignorance of historical or scientific evidence that led them astray - a rectifiable problem for most, himself included - but sometimes it was a hidden naivety, an underlying immaturity of mind upon which experience and education had had little effect. It was as if the child in them were still operative, as if some bit of their brain were still blank. He was convinced that religious beliefs were often the underlying reason for this ongoing naivety.

To Duggan's way of thinking, Catholicism's support of the naive child was a crime of some proportions. Jesus may have said that we had to become as little children, but he had not meant by that that we should forfeit our capacity for adult thought. It was clear thinking that had made Jesus challenge the stultifying religious opinions of his day, and if given half a chance it was clear thinking that would rescue Christianity from its moribund state. The conservative dream of a return to pre-Vatican II values was the dream of minds afraid to face the facts of existence. Faking reality to make it fit some predetermined plan was the business of totalitarian states. Attempt to reinstate the old dogmatic Catholicism and you would cause the death of the very thing you were trying to save. Amputate yourself from the struggle to understand what it meant to sense the beating heart of creation, and you turned your back on the possibility of transcending pettiness. It was pettiness that was the problem, and the Church, in spite of its grandiose claims, had more than its fair share of this all too human commodity.

Part Two

A Time of Testing

10

Axis Mundi

Bob Carter's expression remained impassive; he had Duggan's fax cupped in his large pink hands. Better than expected, he admitted, turning a page, but biased nonetheless. A smile and a shake of the head. Accurate in terms of reportage, and certainly clever in the way it juxtaposed Peters with himself, but highly critical of the conference's attempt to deal with the vexed question of evil. The Australian had come up with the old chestnut of evil being no more than individual or collective human failing loosed on the world, but it was much more than that - it was a palpable force, a diabolical presence that could look out at you from a man's eyes. Experience that presence once and any doubt you had about the Church's role in the world immediately vanished - there was a war going on behind the scenes, and we were all involved. To understand this was to experience liberation; it was to know beyond a shadow of doubt that we were more than a cosmic joke born out of helium, hydrogen gases and amino acids. A mystery we certainly were; an evolutionary accident we were not.

And again it was Bishop Peters who was threatening from the sidelines - Duggan's article was riddled with the bishop's special pleading. Young children should not be subjected to doctrines that made nonsense of what they would learn later as adolescents and teenagers. It was incumbent upon us to prepare children to live in a multicultural society, and that required a more open-minded approach to religious education. On and on it went, the liberal agenda popping up in every other line, what appeared to be a concession to religious education (many Australian parents were quoted as wanting a values-based curriculum) no more than a journalistic ploy to discredit the values-based approach of religious schools. That, to Mr Duggan's way of thinking, was an excuse to teach 'creationism', and that was tantamount to building an ethical tower on a foundation of epistemological sand. Values as an outworking of beliefs found in the Bible were too narrow; they did not help the individual to cultivate the broad-based values of respect, tolerance and equality that underpinned Western society.

Laying the article aside, Carter pondered what he had just read. If only they knew what it was they were facing. If only they knew. Evil was not some amorphous influence arising from the vicissitudes of human behavior, it was an independent, intelligent and altogether beguiling influence that had backgrounded human nature from the very beginning. It was a contagion that leapt from mind to mind, and from continent to continent in the minds of those whose pagan instincts had in some sense remained intact. Over thirty-eight million people had immigrated to the United States between 1820 and 1930, almost one-sixth making the Lower East Side of New York their home, and that contagion had come with them in the form of folk mores, and in social and familial traditions. Mainly Christian, Jewish or Muslim in belief, they had also carried with them powers and spirits belonging to the Old World, ancient entities belonging to the European and Middle Eastern pre-Christian period. Much that was assumed by Americans to be the work of alien abductors was in fact those entities working their mischief in the depths of human consciousness, ancient forces attempting to break out into the world again.

Carter had read a great deal about exorcism; his library bulged with documented cases. People's heads revolving on their shoulders, such as in the film *The Exorcist* was, in his opinion, to go too far. But other bizarre happenings had been carefully recorded by priests and specialist observers. These included acts of prodigious strength, the ability to speak in dead languages such as Latin, contortionist movements of the body, the production of unimaginable volumes of urine and vomit, and, last but not least, words and signs written into the very skin of the human body. And as if this were not enough, some individuals had interacted with the Devil in person, or with an angel. In the case of the little boy on which *The Exorcist* had been modeled, that angel had been none other than the Archangel Michael. According to the boy's own report, Michael had pointed down into the pit where the Devil, surrounded by demons, had stood amidst flames.

The fatal flaw in liberal, secularist reasoning was that all such happenings were seen as the result of psychological disorder and naught else. Priests were biased, observers gullible because of their catholicity. The case was closed before it was even opened, the evidence sneered at because it did not fit in with consensus scientific opinion. There were no such things as demons, no such person as the Devil, no such being as God - we were no more than chemical compounds set in motion by complexity, animals carrying the pretension of selfhood. Carter could not accept such a dismal view; he saw the diminuition of human beings as diabolical in origin, the attempt to undermine established doctrine as the Devil's oldest trick. Herein lay the axis of the world, the *axis mundi,* the pivot of falsity and truth where life was either conceived of as a game of chance or intuited to be a majestic enterprise. What did the Duggans of this world know about that? When would they wake up to the fact that their vacuous interpretation of reality was itself a symptom of the very thing they denied?

The e-mail from Bob Carter was congratulatory, sort of; it commended Duggan on his accuracy, but condemned him for his all-too-obvious liberalism. A proper balance had been struck with regard to quotes, and a general attempt at fairness was evident, but the basic mistake of equating progressive ideas with the language of secular humanism, and the marginalizing of anyone who used the language of religion to express similar or even identical ideas was something that could not be tolerated. Exclusion of the religious viewpoint was a sectarianian act, it devalued the Christian ethic and disallowed the religious beliefs on which Western society had been founded. Religion was intrinsic to culture, and as such it was a vital element in any debate that arose within a culture.

"Take that," said Elliot.

"I don't disagree," said Duggan. "What I object to is the religious lobby's claim to have access to the mind of God. It's one thing to have an informed opinion, it's quite another to claim that that opinion is an extrapolation of the will of God. For goodness sake, it gives you the right to say just about anything and expect to get away with it. Both opinions can be analyzed for content, that's true, but that is not the point. The point is that when religion enters the debate there's generally a price to pay later - an irrational demand of some kind is just around the corner." He laughed and continued. "Expecting others to ignore the fact that your argument is attached to a grocery list of religious beliefs is, in my opinion, downright naive. It took enormous courage and a lot of pain to separate Church from state, and it was done for very good reasons."

"But you agree that religion has a role to play."

"Yes, but not as the final arbiter of ideas. The tendency of the religious lobby is to veto things, not create them. It acts as a blocking mechanism. Now there's nothing wrong with that, it's a slowing-down process that is often valuable, but it should never be allowed to become the final arbiter."

"What do you make of his point that secular liberalism is often libertinism in disguise, that liberalism is often complacent in the face of moral outrage?"

"If he's saying that a secular society runs the risk of making horrible mistakes, then he's right. But I'll tell you something for nothing, a religious society wouldn't do the job any better. Too much liberty can be a real headache, but you try lack of liberty some time. Hand over the reins to those who believe themselves to be in possession of absolute truth and see where you end up." Another laugh. "I'll take my chances with a secular, liberal-minded society any day of the week."

"Dave's approach is very different from yours."

"Dave's high church Anglican; he's a gentleman thinker with a liking for ritual. I'm an opinionated ratbag."

"It's unlikely he'll return, Jack."

Elliot's expression carried an offer.

"I'm perfectly happy doing what I'm doing."

"You could do both standing on your head."

"I'm not sure I want to stand on my head."

When he got home, Duggan poured himself a whisky and collapsed into the old armchair he had found in a local secondhand shop. Just about everything in the room was secondhand. The lampstand with its bulbous stem and yellowed parchment shade perfectly matched the armchair and the rather chunky sideboard he used as a bar top. The round dining table with its equally bulbous and chunky central pillar merged harmoniously with the brass coal scuttle, and the treble-chained light-fitting with its apricot glass basin mellowed the glare of a one hundred watt bulb. Underfoot, a large axminster drew the whole conglomerate together, a scattering of rugs adding depth and comfort. Only two things were missing: curtains and a china display cabinet. Only one thing jarred: a large, black-bodied television set.

Having finished his whisky, he closed his eyes and drifted. When he opened them again, Phoebe was sitting on the arm of the chair staring at him. Almost an hour had elapsed. Followed by Phoebe, he went into the kitchen and set about making himself an omelet. He prided himself on his omelets, and on this occasion added a sprinkling of herbs and grated cheese. Carrying his plate through to the lounge, he switched on the TV and returned to his chair pleased that he had forced himself to cook, the accompanying salad drenched in olive oil appeasing his conscience over endless takeaways. Phoebe took up position on the chair arm and began to clean herself. The news rambled on, further questions being asked about the government's speculation on the currency market, then, after a barrage of news items, he heard James Windle's name being mentioned.

Professor Windle, it seemed, had caused a minor sensation in Germany by revealing that he and a French colleague had made an important discovery while conducting a Vatican-sponsored research program in the Middle East. This discovery, in the form of a letter that threw new light on the formation and beliefs of the early Church, had been stolen not long afterwards, and it was because of this unfortunate incident that he was now speaking out. When approached to confirm Windle's statement, a Vatican spokesman admitted to a document being found, but declined to confirm Windle's outline. As preliminary investigations had shown it to be fourth- century, and the writer held views similar to that of the Nestorian heretics, it was unlikely that any dramatic change would take place in church thinking. The interview had ended on that note.

The telephone rang almost immediately; it was Elliot.

"Yeh, I caught it. I suggested to his daughter that he should take the initiative. He has."

"They didn't get much out of Rome."

"It's the line I expected."

The second call came through at two in the morning; it was Jane Windle. Phoebe opened her eyes as Duggan reached for the telephone. She had news she had to share, she said. Her father had been contacted by someone who claimed to know something important about the stolen document. They had arranged to meet and her father wanted Duggan to be present.

"When? Where?"

"This Sunday in New York."

"That's two days away!"

"He wants you there, Jack."

"How does he know it's for real?"

"Certain things were said that convinced him."

"He could be compromising himself."

"He doesn't think so."

Duggan blinked his uncertainty. "Elliot may not come at this."

"Accommodation is laid on."

"That'll help, but. . ."

"You were right about Coelestius."

It took a split second for him to digest that piece of news. He would talk to his editor first thing, he said. He might be able to persuade Elliot now that his choice of candidates had been confirmation.

"Get back to me the moment you know."

"I'll do that." And then, realizing, he said, "Will you be there?"

"What do you think?" she said back.

* * *

He was in the air and well out over the Pacific by two o'clock the following afternoon, Elliot having reluctantly given the trip his blessing. Not the best way to complete his scrutiny of Theodore's letter, but beggars could not be choosers. Having already made copious notes on points to be checked, he now double-checked each item and made a list of things to ask Windle about. Later, after a meal, and a nap, his thoughts returned to Theodore's take on Jesus and the sectarian milieu from which he had sprung. Smiling to himself, he caught the attention of a passing attendant and ordered a soft drink. Two authorities, two presentations of Messiah, two inspirations and two gospels - no wonder there had been a tussle. Paul had written off his theological rivals as 'Judaizers', Torah-bound Jews who had not appreciated his expansive, world-enveloping theology. But according to Theodore, these so-called 'Judaizers' had been none other than the Messiah's remaining disciples led by James, Jesus' younger brother, and that supported the suspicion of some scholars that all was not as the book of Acts seemed to suggest. Through the truncation of texts and a misrepresentation of the Jerusalem Church's relationship to St Paul, we had been led into accepting a portrait of Jesus that contradicted Jewish tradition and made a mockery of monotheism's basic premise - the God of Israel is one God, and there is none other like unto him.

But was knowing any of this going to change anything? Theodore's interpretation would be written off as garbage, his attempt to reinterpret a well-established view of Jesus' messiahship regarded as revisionist nonsense. And all because the Hebrew word for 'Messiah' had been swapped for a Greek word, and that word had been allowed to transmute into a conception of messiahship that eclipsed anything envisaged by orthodox Jews then or now. In Paul's hands, the term 'Christos' had been used to create a God-man, a theologically inflated figure that, even in Theodore's day, had generated bitter conflict for Christians and pagans alike. Exactly the same problem had arisen with the word 'Nazoraean', the association with the town of Nazareth having been shown to be spurious. No such town had existed in Galilee at the time of Jesus.

The plane droned on, the blue-grey light from Duggan's laptop illuminating his face in the darkened cabin, the scanned-in photographs appearing at intervals as he doubled back again and again to check an individual letter or group of letters. Was this or that a legitimate fourth-century usage? Was this curve or slant in Theodore's script stylistically of the late fourth century? He had painstakingly transcribed Theodore's letter, but feared a transcription error. Contending with scholars of international reputation - Merle in particular was revered - he searched his translation wondering if he had missed something, if he had overemphasized something, if he had perhaps failed to grasp something glaringly obvious. In as far as any translation could be 'perfect', it was possible to produce a perfect translation and discover later that the text itself was a hoax, a deception constructed by an expert, or experts, to fool fellow experts. That was his greatest fear, his only consolation being that Merle and Windle had grappled with the same possibility and concluded that all was well. He slept, eventually, if moving position every few minutes could be called sleep, Theodore's words going around and around in his head as they ploughed further and further into the night, and then into the light. A fitful sleep, a constantly disturbed sleep, but a welcomed few hours given what lay ahead.

It was nine in the morning and snowing when he arrived in Los

Angeles; a gentle flurry masked the thick glass of the 747's windows as they taxied towards disembarkation. Then came the chaos of overhead lockers being opened, and the interminable wait as over three hundred passengers shuffled their way to freedom. After customs, he made his way through to the domestic terminal and caught his connection for New York. When he arrived it was late afternoon and Jane Windle was waiting for him. She was altogether different-looking. Dressed in a fitted black woolen coat with the collar turned up, a Russian-styled fur hat and laced-up leather boots, she looked like something out of Vogue magazine. What to do? How should he greet her? A peck on the cheek and a little hug? A peck on the cheek and a big hug? When the moment came it was she, not he, who took the initiative, and in a way he did not expect. There was no kiss, just a long embrace, and Jane saying: "Hello, Jack Duggan. Good to have you back." When they separated, all that had to be said seemed to have been said.

Elspeth Bentley's reaction to a bedraggled Jack Duggan was one of amused interest - she had never been to Australia but had heard *lots* about it. Would he like a drink? Yes, of course he would. A whisky? She opened a rosewood cabinet and waved vaguely at a cluster of single malts. That one? How clever - that was George's favorite. Seated on the big white sofa with Jane next to him, the spirit warming his innards, Duggan allowed Elspeth's polite chatter to envelope him. Only a few days? All that distance for a few days? A glance at Jane. Something would have to be done about *that*. He could not *possibly* return so quickly.

"It's purely a working visit," said Duggan.

"You'll need a week at least," said Elspeth firmly. And then, "Surely you could arrange it?"

He slept for two hours and awoke at eight in the evening feeling numb. When he came into the lounge, Jane, who was reading, and alone, looked up. She asked how he felt.

"How do I look?"

"Awful."

"That's how I feel."

"Coffee?"

"I'd love a coffee."

Had he imagined the invitation to intimacy? Her attitude and chat during the taxi ride had been maddeningly mundane, but not those first few words - in articulating his name the way she had, she had communicated something deeply personal. At least that is how it had seemed at the time.

"How do you take it?"

"Black with one." He registered the expensive cut of her skirt and blouse. "You look different."

"I'm in New York," she replied, as if that sufficed as an explanation.

"Elspeth's out?"

"Resting."

"I feel like a country hick around her."

"She likes you."."

"Money and class."

"The other way round, actually."

He paused. "You're obviously very much at home here."

"Is that a criticism?"

"No."

She made to turn, but changed her mind. "When you get to know them, Jack, you'll feel the same way I do."

He moved on. "How much do they know?"

"You're helping my father with research."

"About me, I meant."

"Everything."

He sat blinking at her.

"Having trained for the priesthood isn't the end of the world."

"I prefer to keep that to myself."

"You told David."

"It was unlikely I'd ever see him again."

"Well, there you are," she said. And then. "Dinner will be served at eight-thirty."

"You seem very distant," he said straight out.

There were pockets either side of her skirt; she pushed her hands down into them and looked at him for a long moment. When she spoke, it was with an altogether different note in her voice.

"I'm nervous."

"Why?"

"You know why."

With that said she bent down and quickly kissed him on the cheek. When she straightened, he tried to get up, but she stopped him. From there on it was as if nothing had happened between them. When Elspeth appeared, they had more drinks. George would be with them in time for dinner, Elspeth said, lighting a cigarette.

She was a tall, good-looking woman in her late fifties, dark-eyed and dark-haired like Jane, and as elegant as a swan. It became obvious after only a few minutes that there was also a restless intellect at work, a searching through wordplay that could engulf if you weren't careful.

"I wanted to invite some people to meet you, but Jane wouldn't let me do that." An accusing glance thrown at Jane. "She's *extremely* protective of you."

"I'm not exactly at my best."

"But before you leave, perhaps," she persisted.

"Jack's time is at a premium," said Jane.

"It's all *very* mysterious," said Elspeth. "I can't get *anything* out of little miss here."

Duggan smiled, but kept his mouth shut.

"Flying in like this to meet up with Jane's father?" She blew a perfect smoke ring as if it were a commonplace, and turned back to Jane. "You know I wouldn't tell anyone."

"Jack's helping my father with some research."

"Huh," said Elspeth. "Since when has your father required help with anything" And then, "Are we going to see him while he's here?"

"He's on a tight schedule."

Elspeth turned back to Duggan. "You're here because of that business in Palestine, aren't you?"

Voices in the corridor heralded George Bentley's arrival; he was talking to Martina the cook, who was Puerto Rican, about fifty years of age, and garrulous. Shorter than his wife by a few inches, stockily built and of a quiet disposition, George came into the room smiling at what had passed between himself and Martina.

"They won't say what's going on," said Elspeth.

"It's a delicate situation," said Jane.

On being introduced, George said, "First time in New York, Jack?"

A nod from Duggan.

"Sydney?"

"Sydney town," said Duggan.

Elspeth moved in. "You must be very good at what you do," she said, pulling the conversation back to where she wanted it.

"It was more coincidence than confidence," said Duggan. "He needed someone and I just happened along."

"Really," said Elspeth.

George poured himself a small scotch and stood sipping at it.

"It's good of you to put me up at such short notice," said Duggan.

"Any friend of Jane's," said Elspeth.

Dinner was about to be served, Martina announced. They trooped into the dining room, Elspeth insisting that Duggan sit next to her. There were a number of paintings on the walls.

"Do you cook?" asked Elspeth.

"A little."

"*All* of the men I meet these days seem to cook."

The banter continued and Elspeth returned to the length of Duggan's stay. He said that he was out on a limb as it was, that it was unlikely his editor would give him an extension.

"The two great oppressed tribes," said George, apropos of nothing. Duggan smiled a frown. "The Irish and the Jews, Jack. Both noted for their natural intelligence, their passion, their sense of family and their sociability."

"Ah," said Duggan.

"And the Italians, of course. Irish, Jew and Italian versus the prosaic German." He mulled over the question of origins. "Yet we've ended up nearer to Central Europe, I think. The American habit of smoking between courses at meals originated in Vienna, and our hats are definitely Central European."

"The melting pot," said Duggan.

"*Bagdad-on-the-Subway* is how O. Henry described Lower Manhattan," said Elspeth.

"That's no longer the case," said George. "The Syrians and Armenians have all but vanished."

"The standardized New Yorker," said Jane.

"Not altogether standardized. New Yorkers are less brutally standardized than in other cities. We're proud of our mixed cultural origins. Privacy on that level is all but impossible; in fact privacy is suspect."

"That seems to apply to money as well," said Duggan.

"Correct. We talk about money the way a Frenchman talks about women - that's where we diverge from our Central European roots." He gave a little laugh. "In New York, money parades its excess."

They talked on about money, then quite suddenly Elspeth returned to the subject of Duggan's skills. Could he *think* in ancient Greek, she wanted to know, having got that much out of Jane. Over rare roast beef he tried to describe what it was like to read Sophocles in the original and have no sense of the English language as one did so.

She moved on, getting closer and closer to the question she really wanted to ask. When conversational protocol was exhausted, she came to the point.

"So what drove you out of the church?"

"Disappointment. They proved to be afraid of their own shadow."

"You didn't have to think about that, did you?" she said. And then, "I lost faith when a priest put his hand up my skirt. I was fifteen and as innocent as a lamb."

Duggan could not imagine Elspeth ever having been as innocent as a lamb. He said that it was only a small number of priests who went off the rails in that way.

"Being deprived of a sex life isn't natural."

"It's not difficult for some."

"You would defend celibacy?"

"For some, not all." A sigh from Duggan. "They'll eventually be forced to separate celibacy from ministry. It wasn't always a requirement."

"What do you make of our new pope?" asked George.

"He's a compromise candidate - it'll give the factions time to fight it out."

"It amazes me they don't see the absurdity of the whole thing," said Jane. "All those *men* in pointed hats."

"Their principal purpose is the preservation of the Church," said Duggan, "and never more so than during a Conclave. When a pope dies these *men* are left without a superior; there's nothing between them and God Almighty. We Catholics are born into a fixed hierarchy: Parents. Priest. Superior. Cardinal. Pope. To be without a superior is almost to be without a brain. When Cardinal Pacelli, as organizer of the 1939 Conclave, turned to face the cardinals, it's said that there were beads of perspiration on his forehead. An arrogantly self-confident diplomat he may have been, but in that moment, without a superior to bow to, he was at his wits' end."

"Hence papal infallibility," said George, who was used to hierarchies. "That helped cover contingencies."

"They're not infallible *all* of the time," said Elspeth, who was a stickler for detail.

Duggan looked across at Jane, who had not contributed much to the conversation. "Do you ever paint religious subjects?" he asked.

"Occasionally." She gave a little laugh. "I'm apt to mix up the symbolisms though. Stars of David in the background?"

"Some of her stuff's quite pagan," said Elspeth.

George attended to a bottle of wine while they chatted about Jane's paintings. When he sat down again, he looked across at Duggan. "Jane is deeply archetypal as an artist," he said. "One can sense something bubbling up out of the depths in just about everything she does." He turned, and pointed to a painting on his right. "That's one of Jane's. It's the first one I bought of hers."

The painting was hauntingly beautiful

"I used the head of a child's doll as model," said Jane. "Dolls sometimes carry an extraordinary charge."

"The face looks human."

"It's the eyes I'm referring to."

It was quite a large painting, and heavily framed. The subject was a child of around three, a girl in a whitish-blue dress with dark hair and large staring eyes who seemed to float as she ran. The background was indistinct.

"She sold every painting in her recent exhibition," said Elspeth.

"So I believe," said Duggan. They were looking at one another across the table. He huffed a laugh. "I was useless at art."

"Did you want to help people?"

It was the question Elspeth had wanted to ask right from the start.

" . . . I was just a kid when I decided," he said, sensing her intent. "It never occurred to me that I might one day doubt what I was being taught." A pause. "I'd like to say that I wanted to help suffering humanity, but I don't think that had anything to do with it. Maybe I sensed the power they had." A laugh. "The only time my mother ever showed deference to a man was when the local priest showed up."

Turning to Jane, Elspeth said, "Bleeding hearts are to be avoided, they're an *absolute* bore." She looked back at Duggan and smiled. "I'm of the opinion that people should be helped because it is the *right* thing to do, not because of pity."

Duggan knew Elspeth had decided to flush him out. As if in response to his thoughts, she said that in their eyes wealth carried responsibilities divorced from liberalism. Duggan's response was to say that such an approach was potentially paternalistic. Which was the worst? A liberalism that ran out of control because it lacked a pragmatic perspective, or a conservatism that seldom went far enough because its perspective was affectively deficient?

"Very clever," she said back.

"My family was Irish working class," he said, scratching for a truth. "My father didn't develop a taste for wine until he was in his seventies. My mother believed there was something like a telephone line between Christ and the Pope, and that non-Catholics went automatically to hell." He scratched on. "When you come from that kind of background you have to fight your way to the surface. I was lucky enough to have a good education, others were not so lucky."

"What was it J.F.K said about McNamara and Sorenson?" George consulted his memory. "'You can't beat brains'" To Duggan's surprise, he added, "My father was a banker, Jack, but he was also a racist. My mother did not hold with his view of Afro-American worth, but she was just as odd. We all have to fight our way to the surface. Inherited wealth can wound a man as surely as poverty can."

"McNamara's Vietnam policy was a disaster," said Jane. "He didn't know what he was doing."

"He was holding on to a job at which he was very good on every other level," said George. "He had a machine-like intellect."

"You think that's good?" asked Jane.

"We New Yorkers love machines," said George, smiling.

The fuse lighted by Elspeth's reference to 'bleeding hearts' continued to smolder. Duggan said that he had no problem with wealth, or privilege, but that he did have a problem with snobbery. Of all the human failings he had been unfortunate enough to run into, snobbery had been one of the worst. To assume superiority because of wealth, education or social standing was to reveal one's self a bankrupt in the midst of plenty. And he was not speaking as a socialist, but as a humanist. We were all naked under our clothes, and we ought not to forget that."

"The little girl in my painting has the eyes of a doll because they're unseeing eyes," said Jane.

"Eyes that see not, ears that hear not," said Duggan.

"She's obviously dreaming," said Elspeth.

"She's dead," said Jane.

When Elspeth recovered her composure, she said, "You ought not to have told us that, Jane."

There was a silence.

"What an extraordinary thing to have happened," said George. "The letter going missing like that."

"Someone with a grudge?" said Elspeth.

George turned attention back to Duggan's past. "It must have been difficult to go that far then change your mind."

"I didn't leave of my own volition. I was suspended, then unceremoniously chucked out."

"Excellent," said Elspeth.

Martina appeared. She dealt expertly with the dishes and vanished again. A bowl of raspberry mousse arrived soon after.

"It's an old recipe of my mother's," said Elspeth, who liked occasionally to dabble in the kitchen. "*Lots* of cream I'm afraid."

Duggan wondered where Martina had managed to find raspberries.

They talked about dieting for a moment or two - Elspeth the eternally thin could get away with eating anything, apparently. Then the conversation swung round to the city itself. The engineers had defeated the architects, George said. Someone had described New York as a *jaw load of rotting teeth,* and they had not been all wrong. Who was it that had said that? he asked. Elspeth could not remember either, so they moved on.

Duggan looked across at Jane. She smiled back.

"Did you return to being an *ordinary Catholic?*" Elspeth asked, tilting her head at Duggan.

"Not quite."

"I often talk to God, but he never replies," she added.

"Elspeth does not like to be interrupted," said George.

"A New York trait," said Jane. "If you interrupt a New Yorker, Jack, they'll wait politely until you've finished, then pick up on precisely the word at which the break was forced."

"It's an American trait, actually," said George, "just as interrupting is an English one."

"Australians are apt to jump in as well," said Duggan. "Conversation is a bit of a tussle Down Under."

"My father's fond of monologues," said Jane. "An anecdote can sometimes take ten minutes."

"If you have something worth saying . . . " Duggan stifled a yawn, and apologized.

"Your father's a *fascinating* talker," said Elspeth. "I could listen to him for hours, *have* listened to him for hours."

"Gorki!" said George suddenly. "It was Maxim Gorki who said that New York resembled a jaw load of rotting teeth."

"Not an image I care for," said Elspeth.

A wave of tiredness hit Duggan; he took a breath and closed his eyes for a moment, opened them again.

"You okay?" asked Jane.

"I'm a bit tired."

"A bit? You look all in," said George.

"I think I've had it." Duggan smiled apologetically. "I've had it. Sorry." He got to his feet. "I really do appreciate your putting me up"

"Our pleasure," said Elspeth. Her expression said that she meant it. "Isn't that right, George?"

11

Metamorphosis

It took them three-quarters of an hour to get from Upper West Side to Downtown Manhattan. Dressed in the same outfit she had worn to the airport, Jane reminded Duggan of Pasternak's Lara.

The meeting with Windle and his informer took place in the Astoria Hotel, a nineteen-forties building restored to former glory. Her father always stayed there, Jane said, as they traversed the foyer. When the door to room 345 opened, there was no doubting that it was James Windle who filled the opening - the man's enthusiastic greeting for Jane confirmed his identity. A full six foot three in his soles, bearded, dark-eyed and with a shock of greying curly black hair even more unruly than his daughter's, this bear of a man greeted her in German, then turned to Duggan.

"Welcome to New York, Dr Duggan!"

They shook hands and Windle stood aside. At the far end of the room stood a small, elderly man in a dark suit. There was no sign of David Mayle.

"This is Dr Weisel," said Windle. Weisel came towards them. "I'm afraid Dr Weisel has only a few hours to spare."

Weisel had piercing blue eyes and a firm handshake. His accent was minimal.

Armchairs and a sofa had been strategically placed for the meeting. Removing her hat and coat, Jane handed them to her father. Placing the folder he was carrying on the low table which separated them, Duggan chose the armchair next to Jane's. When Weisel was seated, Windle took up the opposite end of the sofa and got down to business.

"Dr Weisel has broken silence because he felt he had to. I'm deeply grateful to him for that." Windle's glance of respect elicited a curt nod from Weisel. "Not that he knows exactly what is going on.

He does not. But he has an interesting story to tell, and I want you to hear it from his own lips. Doctor?"

Weisel got straight to the point. He had been tipped off about the Ignatius document's textual passenger and told to pass on the information to Windle, but only when given the green light. He had not been told the nature of the discovery to be made, just that something of great importance was there to be found. A smile and a shake of the head. Why had they chosen him? Because of an article he had written in the early nineties critical of the attitude of Vatican historians. He had become a target of the conservative lobby because of that. Anticipating Duggan's question, he said that he was presently senior lecturer in ancient history at the University of Geneva.

Windle interjected at that point. The research proposal he and Fr Merle had lodged with the Vatican's Department of Antiquities had not, at that point, been given the go-ahead. Only when it had been accepted had Dr Weisel been instructed to make contact. Duggan wanted to know the exact nature of the project they had had in mind.

"Our project was to search *all* printed books - as opposed to handwritten manuscripts - for manuscripts hand-copied into them."

"You thought you might find something of interest?"

"There's almost always something of interest to be found. If not what you're after, then something else. The libraries in these places are veritable gold mines."

"Did you tell Fr Merle about the tip-off?"

"Of course. He was as intrigued as I was. I of course did not know that my informer had himself been informed by a separate party, or that that party had waited until our sponsored research trip was signed and sealed before giving the go-ahead to contact me."

"Could it have been a set-up?"

"I don't think so." Windle's frown showed uncertainty. "We were out of the country before the Ignatius letters were found to be missing."

"Dr Weisel?"

"I became uneasy because of the *don't move until I tell you* aspect of the situation. When news broke of the Ignatius document going missing I began to have second thoughts."

"Why?"

"It struck me that I had been a little naive."

"A little?"

"I'm indebted to Dr Weisel." Windle's tone had an edge of warning about it. "He didn't have to do what he's done."

Ignoring Windle concern, Duggan continued to probe. "We have a situation that doesn't make any sense and we have to get to the bottom of it."

There was a uneasy silence.

"It's almost certainly a Vatican faction we're dealing with," said Weisel. His expression was stony. "How else could they have known when to make their move?"

"Did you go straight for the Ingnatius document?" Duggan asked of Windle.

"It was one of a number of documents we looked at."

He turned back to Weisel. "What made you go along with such a strange request?"

" . . . I had the strong impression that someone wanted to help. *I* wanted to help." A pained look. "I could not see what could go wrong. Either there was something worth finding, or their wasn't."

"You didn't wonder at being tipped off like that?"

"I didn't know what to make of it at the start."

Duggan looked at Windle.

"I took it with a pinch of salt right up until the moment we found Theodore's letter. That was when I began to wonder."

"It was visible?"

"The opening section of the letter was visible. And before you ask, it was integral to the document. It was part of the backboard and it hadn't been tampered with."

Duggan stared at Windle for a moment. "You removed it?"

"With difficulty."

"And replaced it?"

"Of course!"

"Fr Merle will vouch for it being integral to the Codex?"

"If it comes to that, yes."

"And you mentioned what you had found to no one?"

Windle's smile suggested Duggan's question was superfluous.

"What did you think might happen if you did?"

"We thought someone might be tempted to remove it permanently."

"Could the librarian have suspected something?"

"We photographed numerous documents and returned them. The Ignatius document was returned intact and without comment. The librarian had no reason to think anything unusual was going on, and there was not the slightest indication that anything was wrong when we left."

"Someone knew why you were there."

"Obviously." Windle raised a hand. "If entrapment had been the intention they could have planted something on us."

"The letter's not sufficiently important to warrant that level of subterfuge." Duggan's look was searching. "It'll be dismissed by Christian specialists as heretical nonsense the moment it appears."

"I think not. There were six pages to Theodore's letter, not just the two you have. Theodore's claim is that he's working from a document written in the second century by Bishop Irenaeus, a document in the bishop's own hand, no less, That makes his letter eminently more important than it otherwise would be. As Theodore also directly addresses the concerns of Pelagius Britto, who seems to have been a friend, or pupil, its contents take on further significance." An apologetic smile. "I didn't drag you all the way to New York to . . . interrogate Dr Weisel?"

"You want me to complete the translation?"

"It has to be consistent."

"Shouldn't you have a look at what I've done first?"

"I've already read two papers published by you in the mid-nineties. Their thoroughness is impressive."

"You didn't know that earlier."

"Your having only a piece of the cake was our safeguard."

"I could still have caused trouble."

"Jane was pretty sure you wouldn't. David was of the same opinion."

"You had someone else in mind?"

Jane's smile was of the Mona Lisa variety.

"Dr Weisel and I have discussed the situation at length." Windle sounded tired suddenly. "He did what he did for the very best of reasons." A pause. "Isn't as if we were arrested or anything. We weren't. We sailed out of Palestine without a hitch."

"They could have miscalculated."

"Precise one minute, slipshod the next? No, I don't think so. Whoever set this in motion was probably as surprised as we were when the theft took place"

"Someone watching the watcher."

"That's my guess."

"Why you and Fr. Merle?"

"We just happened along. I don't think there was anything more to it than that."

"First you, then me."

"Your turning up was less likely."

"Less likely is hard to imagine." Duggan moved his attention back to Weisel. "I'm sorry if I sounded a little brusque. I'm forced to wear two hats in this situation."

A curt movement of the head from Weisel acknowledged Duggan's apology, but whether it excused him or not was unclear.

"Why Ignatius?"

Jane's question elicited a detailed explanation from her father. The leg bone was connected to the hip bone, he said by way of an intro. Ignatius of Antioch had warned against 'Judaizers', and that mirrored Theodore's and Irenaeus' concerns. Ignatius may have been referring to Gentiles who had converted to a loose form of Judaism, or to a form of Samaritan Gnosticism, but that hardly mattered. It was the use of the term 'Judaizers' that was important. That was the link, and that was where it got tricky. It was the opinion of scholars uninfluenced by Christian apologetics that St Paul's mention of 'Judaizers' was a reference to the Jerusalem Apostles led by Jesus' brother James. Christian scholars did not agree. They interpreted 'Judaizers' to mean meddlesome Jews of the orthodox school. To get around this problem they argued that the early Apostolic Church under James had fallen back into Jewish ways after James's death. That allowed them to discount the Nazoraean succession of bishops and transfer their allegiance via St Paul to Rome's succession founded on the Apostle Peter. But the truth of the matter was that the Apostolic Church had not fallen back into Judaism, it had simply never ceased in its affiliation to everything Jewish. The Jerusalem community had been composed of sectarian Jews of Nazoraean persuasion who viewed Jesus as a man called to fulfill the role of Messiah on behalf of the Jewish nation. He had not in any sense been viewed as Israel's God hiding inside a human body. It was this that lay at the heart of Theodore's theological and historical investigations, and Irenaeus' style of thinking had helped clarify the situation for him.

"The Irenaeus claim is probable?"

"They had the same concerns. Irenaeus had a very down-to-earth view of the Christian faith. He rejected the idea of a fall into sin by our first parents. Adam and Eve had not been, in his view, perfect beings who had sinned against God and passed on some terrible contagion to the human race. In his scheme our first parents were simple souls who disobeyed God in much the same manner as a child disobeys a parent. He thought the story of Eve's temptation utterly ridiculous. He said that if the devil had had the power to make snakes talk, he would have used the whole animal kingdom to subvert the human race. He was a progressivist. He believed human beings had grown towards perfection through a system of covenants initiated by God. Each covenant had marked a further degree of enlightenment in human experience. Christ had completed that process through his death."

"Yet he's viewed as a founder of Christian orthodoxy," said Duggan, recognizing Windle's argument as his own.

"Exactly. So the question is, how can such beliefs be reconciled with the idea of Atonement and Redemption. Answer? Only with difficulty. Augustinian dourness is not evident in Irenaeus. There's no doubting that he believed Christ had initiated God's final covenant with human beings, but given his view of Adam and Eve as naughty children it's difficult to reconcile that with the Church's idea of sin's indelibility. If he believed each covenant with God was a stage in our growing up into the truth, then the final stage of that growing up was an awakening of the self to the revelation of God's intent, not an abandoning of the self to a formula based on the idea that sin was endemic to the human race. What he believed about our first parents did not resonate with Catholic teaching then or now. And that drives me to conclude that either he was a very bad theologian, which I do not think he was, or that his non-standard view of things was perhaps nearer to what the early Church believed than anyone has so far suspected."

"I'm reminded of Helvetius."

Duggan's statement made Windle smile. Launching into another monologue he said that they had just jumped to the eighteenth century. Helvetius was thought by some to have reaffirmed the Pelagian idea that man was born without hereditary characteristics, that he had become what he was in virtue of what he learned, and of how he had reacted to the world. The only problem with that was that it led to undiluted behaviorism. A curt laugh from Windle at that point. The truth was of course somewhere between those extremes. It was downright unfair to associate Pelagius with what Helvetius advocated. Or, for that matter, with the beliefs of Lamarck or Lysenko. All Pelagius had been saying was that Augustine's idea of an original sin damning the whole human race was overblown, and that seemed to be Irenaeus's view as well. To say that Pelagius should have been held responsible for the idea that human beings were born without hereditary characteristics was the equivalent of saying that Augustine should be held responsible for the views of modern genetics. That was ridiculous. The most important point was that the theology surrounding Israel's Messiah had not yet settled into a final shape when Irenaeus was alive. Yet it was Irenaeus, as Duggan had said, who had initiated that theology's final shape. So what had this man really believed about Jesus and the early Church? That was the question that had to be answered. His general writings appeared conventional, but his sounding off like Bertrand Russell when speaking of Eve's temptation by the serpent gave pause for thought.

"His tutor was Polycarp of Smyra," said Duggan, availing himself of some water from a carafe on the table. "Polycarp was a disciple of the Apostle John. That lends a certain credence to his statements about Jesus."

"Fact is," said Windle, "all four Gospels were only just in circulation. So what I think we have here is a version of Jesus' life still in vogue, but about to be overcome by Gospels more in tune with theological developments elsewhere. Apart from a few fragments, only two complete volumes of Irenaeus's writings have survived, and they're not in their original Greek. Hence the importance of Theodore's claim to have writings by Irenaeus in his own hand."

"Maybe that's why he insisted on a fixed canon," said Weisel. "He may have been attempting to derail the very opinions about Jesus that Christendom now takes for granted."

"Exactly," said Windle. "His appeal to the Churches of the Apostolic foundation suggests access to writings belonging to the Nazoraeans - hence his staunch support for the Jewish scriptures." Windle's gaze shifted to his daughter. "The later Nazoraeans had documents backing their claim that the Roman Church had usurped the authority of the Mother Church in Jerusalem by borrowing the Apostle Peter and making him a convert to Paul's way of thinking. In the fourth century documents reflecting third-century problems appeared. The compilers of those documents spell out Nazoraean grievances by creating a pseudo-Peter who railed against what the Church had said and done in the Apostle Peter's name. Neither Paul nor the Church in Rome is mentioned by name, but it does not take much imagination to work out who is being referred to." Windle paused to gather his thoughts. "Pseudo-Peter condemns those who have set up an authority other than the Nazoraean Council. Teachers lacking Nazoraean credentials are not to be believed; only teachers from the Jerusalem Church carrying the testimony of James, the Lord's brother. Or, interestingly, *whosoever may come after him.* All teachers are to be approved by the Jerusalem Council, and there are no Apostles other than the original twelve."

"So much for the Apostle Paul," said Jane.

"Indeed. These writings allege that Paul killed Jesus' brother James by throwing him down the steps of the Nicanor gate in the Temple. Now whether true, or untrue, the vehemence of the writing suggests an unbridgeable gulf between what Paul and the Nazoraeans believed about Jesus, and it is this same gulf we detect in the writings of Pelagius, Theodore, and even in Irenaeus when the Roman Church's reinvention of the Jesus story begins to surface. Yes, both Paul and the Nazoraeans revered Jesus, but not at all in the same way. And yes, they were at first in partial relationship, but it was a relationship doomed to failure due to what Paul was preaching about Jesus and atonement.

"But let's get back to Irenaeus. Irenaeus believed Jesus was divine, but who knows in what sense? He believed that God had brought humanity forward in a long process of development culminating in the incarnation of Jesus, and that clearly suggests stages of moral development. It suggests, that for Irenaeus, the experiences of daily life were necessary for the development of conscience. The Church's view was that Adam and Eve had fallen from a state of perfection and that forgiveness of sin could only be found in Christ through the auspices of the Church. Irenaeus believed, or seems to have believed, that God had allowed our first parents to fall for the express purpose of discipline and experience. That is not orthodox teaching. To explain the discrepancies in belief held by Christians in the second and third century, the Church came to view those early decades of its existence as - and there's a terrible irony in this - *a growing up process*. By the third decade of the fourth century what they had determined to be the truth as a result of this process had been legislated into existence *as* unchangeable truth. Theological scrying had produced, they believed, what had not at first been fully appreciated about Jesus - he had been God visiting humanity in the form of a human being. Hence the Council of Nicaea's need in AD325 to legislate that Jesus was co-equal with God."

"And that's been the story ever since," said Jane.

"Not quite. It was up for grabs again within a few years. Ten years after Nicaea a second council reversed the decisions of the first and Arianism - the belief that Jesus had been created by the Father - became the flavor of the day. But only until 337. On Constantine's death each of his three sons took up the theological position of their area, and this resulted in a Nicene West and an Arian East. Geographically, Constantine II ruled in the area west of Italy, Constans in Italy and Greece, and Constantius in the East. As the West was divided between two emperors, the Nicene approach weakened, but with the elimination of Constantine II it triumphed, only to fail again with the assassination of Constans and the rise of Constantius as ruler of the East. And so another shuffling of bishops took place, and Athanasius, champion of the Nicene formula, found himself banished for the sixth time. In 381, however, as a result of dissension between opposing Arian splinter groups, the Emperor Theodosius summoned the second ecumenical Council at Constantinople, and this resulted in a ratification of the original Nicene formula with only slight alteration."

"Which is why it is so important to get the Nazoraeans into perspective." Duggan's words, too, were directed at Jane. "To not understand who these Nazoraeans were, or not know what they believed, is to be robbed of vital intelligence when trying to make sense of Paul's and the Jerusalem Church's claims about Jesus, and the Roman Church's reinterpretation of those claims. What people don't realize is that the Nazoraean Council at Jerusalem functioned as the de facto government of Israel. In form, it was the equivalent of the Jewish Sanhedrin which it regarded as pro-Roman and apostate. Jesus was executed as a rebel against Rome and designated a pretender to the Jewish throne. We shouldn't forget that. Close association with the Nazoraeans convinced the Romans that Jesus had been keeping bad company. The story of Jesus' temptation by the devil in the wilderness is either a meeting with a Zealot commander, or it's a record of Jesus being tempted to join the militant branch of the Nazoraeans. He's offered the known world if he'll join the other side, but he refuses. The whole story reeks of nationalism."

"Jesus as closet politician?" Jane's tone was ironic. "He did not die on the cross to save us from our sins?"

Duggan glanced at Windle, who waved him on.

"Not in the sense Paul's interpreters would have us believe. He died to redeem Israel - at least that's what the Nazoraean sectaries believed. Gentile God-fearers who accepted that Jesus had been Israel's Messiah were made part of an extended Israel; it was the equivalent of gaining Jewish citizenship, but not quite. The Nazoraean Council was willing to compromise on circumcision and the dietary laws with Paul, but they would not give in to the idea that believing non-Jews should be given full recognition as Jews if they did not comply with these observances. If non-Jewish believers in the Messiah did not fully surrender their Gentile state, then they could not be awarded full membership of Israel. To have done so would have been to nullify the whole idea of the Jews being the chosen people of God. It was this that caused the rift between Paul and the Nazoraean Council, and it was this that eventually caused Paul to preach a whole new conception of atonement - an atonement estranged from its Jewish sectarian roots. This is why Christians harp on and on about *believing in Jesus*. What they're unwittingly referring to is the Nazoraean demand that non-Jews *believe* in the

Messiah of Israel so that they can benefit, with certain provisos, in the same manner as regular Jews. Everything's been turned on its head. Christians expect Jews to recognize Paul's Christ figure as their long-awaited Messiah and convert to Christianity, but that is in fact to reverse the historical premise. It's Christianity that has to recognize that Gentile believers in Jesus came under the extended cloak of Jewish spirituality, not the other way round. Jesus' sacrifice of himself as the Messiah of Israel was supposed to inaugurate the Kingdom of God on Earth, but it did no such thing. The Roman backlash to Jewish expectations of victory was devastating - the whole infrastructure of Jewish life was destroyed. Instead of the Kingdom of God, they got Roman occupation. And so we have the final breakdown between Paul's ideas and those of the Nazoraeans, ideas later taken up by the Roman Christians and progressively misunderstood because of the disconnection with Nazoraean tradition. By the end of the first century the Roman Christians had either forgotten, or conveniently shelved, what they knew of Nazoraean beliefs. By the middle of the second century they had rationalized those beliefs into an overview which made them, and them alone, the custodians and dispensers of Jesus' propitiatory act. What had once been Israel's gift to the pagan world had turned into a rod that would be used by Christians to break Jewish backs for the next eighteen hundred years."

If Jane Windle had wished to set up a situation in which to determine what kind of man Duggan really was, then this would have been her situation of choice. His annoyance with theologically oriented scholarship had bubbled to the surface as he spoke, his pugilistic pose, when he fell silent, identical to that that had first attracted her to him.

"David *bumped* into you in Santa Rosa?" said Windle.

"He was having a drink at the bar when I wandered in." Duggan glanced at Jane and smiled. "And here we all are - except for David."

"Thanks to Dr Weisel," said Windle.

Weisel smiled, but said nothing.

"So what's your next move?" asked Duggan.

"We set you up with the requisite tools so you can complete the translation of Theodore's letter. I've already made arrangements to that effect."

"I'm supposed to leave first thing Monday morning."

"You'll have to get an extension."

"I don't think my editor will agree."

"Do you want me to talk to him?"

"I don't know if that would help."

"We need you, Jack." Windle's sudden informality underlined his seriousness. "It's a matter of priorities."

"I could lose my job."

"Snap," said Windle.

* * *

They ate at the Astoria that evening, in the big gold dining room with its chandeliers and stiff white tablecloths. There was still no word of David Mayle's whereabouts. With Dr Weisel on his way to Kennedy, they went down to the ground floor bar for a drink, then into the restaurant where the conversation turned to the problem of how to interpret the Christian message for the modern world. Windle was forthright in his condemnation of literalist thinkers. In a voice a fraction too loud for comfort, he said that the literalist smorgasbord of fallacious arguments led the unsuspecting searcher for religious truth into a blind alley. Finishing off his second glass of red as if it were lemonade, he said that literalists were a menace to themselves and everyone around them. Duggan chose the position of Devil's Advocate. Belief in a God-man did not seem like a blind alley if you were a believer, he said. To the believer, Jesus was God and that was the end of the matter. It was also the beginning of the mess, said Windle. Didn't any of them ever stop to think what such a claim meant in real terms?

"Faith papers over the cracks."

"Faith is as much an ass as the law."

"The law works, on the whole."

"Justice, like salvation, sometimes comes at too great a cost." Windle knew his metaphor had reached its limit and abandoned it. "I know what you're saying, Jack, but you know as well as I do that faith divorced from history bedevils the faithful at every turn. Believing against the odds that something is true when it is patently untrue may afford the believer buckets of satisfaction, but in the end it scrambles his or her wits to the point of lunacy."

"I think we have to appreciate the mental dilemma they're in. *Not believing* is not an option to the believer. To *not believe* that Jesus was divine, or that he died on the cross for our sins is, in their terms, to reject God's offer of eternal life. Wiggle your way out of that one if you've gone through the conversion process, or had the faith hammered into you since the day you were born."

"Believing against the odds becomes a point of honor," said Jane. "Blessed assurance, Jesus is mine. I had a girlfriend at university who took that route."

"If you sidestep the questions that have to be asked, then you're forever in danger of caving in." Duggan's tone was of someone who had given this question some thought. "It doesn't matter what age you are, or what your educational background is, if you've ignored the questions that really matter, you're a sitting duck."

"A lot of Christians backslide," said Jane. "They know deep down that the faith is not all it's made out to be."

"That way lie dragons," said Duggan. "Life either knocks the stuffing out of you, and you lose your faith, or your faith melts away without your noticing, or you consciously examine its claims and set aside the sillier bits. If you think your way out, then its unlikely you'll return to anything like what you once believed. If you're knocked out of your faith by the uncertainties of life, or are simply too lazy to question its claims, then you may well return to the literalist fold when the going gets tough."

"Unfinished business," said Windle.

"And you pay the price on other levels." Duggan's smile was terse. "Scratch a lapsed believer and you'll find all kinds of confusions."

"Few of us are rational all of the time," said Jane.

"That's not what I'm getting at. I'm saying that superstition still has a place in the lapsed believers mind because they've never properly dealt with the supernaturalisms in Christianity. Christians vilify everyone else's superstitions and endlessly justify their own as God-given. A mythology gulped down in a literal way is just superstition by another name. Hence the quite extraordinary contortions of theology. It's wall-to-wall miracles and magic. It's priest versus magician just like in the story of Moses at Pharaoh's court except that Moses was just as much a magician as any of the others. What does he do? He turns his staff into a snake and it gobbles up all the other snakes."

"When did you know you were safe?"

Windle's question made Duggan blink.

"The past is obviously no longer a threat."

" . . . I was talking to my father. We were sitting in the dark and he was smoking his pipe - it was summer and the kitchen window was all the way up. I could see the glow of the burning tobacco when he drew on it. He asked me what my plans were and I said that I didn't know, that right that minute I didn't much care what I ended up doing. There was a long silence, then out of the blue he asked me if I still believed in God. My mother had accused him of being an atheist so often I had come to think of him as one, but as we talked it dawned on me that he was the believer and that I was the unbeliever. In losing Jesus I had lost God as well. They had bound Jesus and God so close together it was hard to separate them." Duggan shook his head as memory of that conversation flooded back. "That's when I got my first proper lesson in theology, the theology of what God is not. My mother thought my father an atheist, but he wasn't. He had simply stripped his God of projections."

"His nothing was different from your nothing," said Windle.

"Radically different."

"And if you succeed?" asked Jane.

"Then it's back to square one."

"Which is?"

"Jesus," said Duggan. "We have to rediscover him. We have to wake up to the fact that Christianity killed God off when it divinized a human being. The moment Jesus became God in the human imagination, God was dead."

"The trinity includes God," said Jane.

"The Godhead is not quite the same thing as God," said her father. "God becomes a *quality* shared with two others. Theism is the belief in one divine creator, Christianity split the one into three and made the human better represent God than the invisible God did himself. Only problem was, the human ended up inhuman - Jesus the human being became more God than human being in spite of what was said about his human side being equal to his divine side."

"Christians still pray to God." Jane was frowning. "God is still at the back of their minds."

"Christians stumble backwards and forwards between Jesus and God not knowing to whom they pray most of the time. One minute they're using the term God in the Jewish sense, in the theistic sense, then they're back to Jesus, then God, then Jesus again. It's a form of spiritual schizophrenia and it took the Church centuries to make it stick. It was the Church's final solution in the face of Gnosticism's challenge, and it resulted in those who didn't agree being excommunicated, or worse. It was no more than a formula devised to combat the many views of Jesus circulating at that time."

"So it's back to Jesus as Jack said."

Father and daughter were staring at one another.

"There's no other route. Jesus underwent a metamorphosis at human hands - his raw humanity evaporated. He was promoted from man to God and had a contortionist theology thrust on him. He's had so many theological facelifts he's only barely recognizable as a human being - he's turned into a language event. At Pentecost -

which as you know is a Jewish festival, *not* a Christian one - Peter speaks of Jesus as *a man sent from God,* and that, in spite of theological hyperbole, is how Paul saw Jesus as well. In Pauline terms Jesus was the New Adam; he was the human state perfected in the sense of having become complete. That's how Arab thinkers see Jesus. In Paul's scheme he was a replacement figure for the old Adam who had been *incomplete.* It is the problem of *incompleteness* that is passed on generation after generation, not some indelible stain requiring a blood sacrifice. I don't think Paul was offering the world a God-man when he said 'put on the Christ', I think he was offering Gentile God-fearers and Diaspora Jews the possibility of a new awareness. It is a renewing of the 'mind' that lies at the heart of his thinking, not possession by a phantom. The human and the divine had been intuited by Jewish scholars to be very close in Messiah, but the inner significance of that union was lost to the Christian mind at Nicaea. A great metaphorical truth was changed into a sad literalism. In that moment of debate and physical coercion a thoroughly Hellenized Jesus triumphed over the Jewish Jesus. Jesus the Jew was dead; Jesus as paragon of the Christian imagination was on the loose."

Duggan's reaction to Windle's summary was much the same as Jane's reaction to his own impassioned outburst. The man's eyes had burned as he spoke, his hands cutting the air as he attempted to explain the underlying problem. Our collective dilemma was not disinterest in Christianity, it was Christianity's disinterest in dealing with its own scrambled perceptions of the past.

12

The deep end

There was a media scrum around Windle the following morning - his statement to the German press had been syndicated, his presence in New York detected as he supped at the Astoria. A female journalist wearing pink earmuffs asked if the lost manuscript had turned up again. He replied wondering if she could hear what he was saying. She came back at him quickly, jostling to hold her place. Who did he think was responsible for the document's disappearance? He said that her guess was as good as his. A barrage of questions followed. Windle batted back his answers with ease, smiling all the while. Then came a question from Miss Earmuffs that stopped him in his tracks. Was it true his son had been arrested by the Jerusalem police?

"My son was holidaying in Jerusalem. I informed the police of that fact and he was questioned as a matter of course."

"*You* informed the police?"

"Of course."

"Quite a coincidence his being there as well."

"No coincidence at all. We planned to meet up there." Windle's smile returned. "Parents and children do that kind of thing."

A young man with flaming red hair was next.

"Fr Paul Merle can't be contacted. Do you know why that is?"

"I believe he's on retreat."

A snicker ran through the pack.

"Professor Merle is not the kind of man to retreat from anything," said Windle, reading their reaction.

"Are you Jewish, Professor Windle?"

It was Miss Earmuffs again.

"My mother was Jewish."

"Do you think of yourself as Jewish?"

"I was brought up Catholic."

"But do you think of yourself as Jewish?"

"I have no particular religious affiliation."

"You're an atheist?"

"I'm a professor of history."

"Do you believe in God?"

"I don't quite see what that's got to do with anything."

"Do you think the Catholic Church is behind the document's disappearance?"

"I think that highly unlikely."

A booming voice from the back of the crowd wanted to know to what extent the letter they had discovered threw new light on the origins of the Christian Church. Windle replied carefully. It supported the contentions of *some* historians, but not all, he said. That was about as far as he could go under the circumstances. The same voice said that the Vatican had already written off the letter as heretical nonsense. So was it a case of faith versus fact? Windle sidestepped the question by saying that the Church had it's own highly qualified specialists. He was sure many of them would be chagrined by such a remark.

Little Miss Earmuffs returned to the fray soon after. Was it true that his son's passport had been confiscated by the Jerusalem police?

"Where on earth did you hear that?"

"That's the rumor."

"And *that* is all it is," said Windle.

"You had plenty to say about John Paul II's apology to the Jews. Do you still think it was an inadequate response?"

"What's that got to do with anything?"

"You were also extremely vocal about the plight of the Palestinians a few years back."

"*Mea culpa.*" Windle's confusion over the line of questioning was apparent. "What exactly is the point you're trying to make?"

"You're known for speaking your mind."

"So?"

"So would you take the law into your own hands if you thought it necessary?"

Windle's smile returned, then faded. "I suggest you tread carefully from here on in," he said.

"I'm not accusing you of anything, Professor. I'm simply asking a question. The piece you wrote for the *New York Times* on Israel's treatment of the Palestinians was, to say the least, pointed. You're obviously a man of strong convictions."

"I was speaking as a historian, as a man, *not* as a Jew."

"So you do think of yourself as Jewish?"

"You know exactly what I meant by that. The Church's apology to the Jews was inadequate and anyone with a grain of historical sense knows that to be the case. You can't conjure away fifteen hundred years of . . . *harassment?* with a few slick sentences. Yes, I have Jewish blood in my veins, and Gentile blood. Most of you here have mixed backgrounds unless I'm very much mistaken. So what? I argue on behalf of what I believe to be true and I back my observations with properly handled evidence. If the Catholic Church fails to do its duty, I say so. If Israel fail in hers, I say so. If the Palestinians or their backers act like idiots, I say so."

A flurry of questions unrelated to why they were all there followed, then settled again on the issue of the discovered document.

"Can we expect the Vatican to release the photographs fairly soon?"

"I can't speak for the Vatican."

"There are copies being held at the University of Essen?"

"Correct. And at the Sorbonne."

"If the Vatican decides against publication, would either you or Professor Merle break the embargo?"

"The Vatican's Department of Antiquities will, I'm sure, publish in their own good time. We'll just have to be patient."

"You're not known for your patience, Professor."

Little Miss Earmuffs smile was angelic.

"Time is precious. I try not to waste it," said Windle, turning away.

* * *

Elliott said he hoped Duggan knew what he was doing. The purpose of his visit was not to be at the beck and call of James Windle, it was to get the rest of the story and get his tail, or tale, back to Sydney as quickly as possible. Duggan said he could not go into detail, but that it was imperative he remain. He would willingly take leave without pay to get the extra time he needed. That would very much depend on how long he stayed away, and what he arrived back with, Elliott said, his tone dry as toast. If he pushed management's patience too far they might throw the book at him.

The very next day saw Duggan hard at work, the photographs of Theodore's extended text laid out alongside the tools of his trade in Windle's hotel room. The big man had insisted that he do the translation there for security reasons, and had laid on snacks and lunches at his own expense. And what a text it turned out to be. There was no doubting Irenaeus' influence on the Syrian bishop's thinking; his so-modern contentions about our first parents had been amalgamated with materials from other sources, some known, some unknown. In Theodore's reading of things, alarming distortions of historical reality had taken root in Church thinking since the end of the first century, and he was determined to straighten things out. This was evident from the urgency of his writing, and from the thrust of his logic. History made subservient to a theology embedded in superstition and supernaturalisms was not for him. That such an approach was comforting to many was evident in the Church's success, but it was robbing whole congregations of that excellent vision which had sustained the Apostles. Where was the deep connection with God that people craved? Where was the depth of communion with God and 'other' that ordinary people sensed could exist, but could not find in the ramblings of ecclesiastics?

Duggan's smile was tinged with irony. Today's Protestant hardliners were well aware of how Rome had distorted first-century events; what they were not aware of was the extent of those distortions. The view of Jesus trumpeted by evangelicals and fundamentalists was itself a distortion built on a distortion, the heavily conservative approach of Catholic hardliners similarly flawed. What each of these groups claimed as the original beliefs of the Church were actually second, third and fourth-century interpretations of Nazoraean doctrine filtered through St Paul's extended theology - a theology reflecting a fundamentally Jewish approach to God ripped out of its historical context. In the Nazoraean view, which was the Apostolic view, Jesus had not been the Second Person in a divine trinity, he had been the awaited Messiah of the Jews, a Messiah rejected by his own people and taken up by God-fearing Gentiles wishing to enjoy the heavenly rewards and earthly benefits of Jewish citizenship. Only later, as Windle had explained, had this *act of believing* in Jesus been transformed by St Paul into the magical rite of salvation through faith alone. The Epistle of James flatly contradicted that view.

The heart of the problem was that Gentile believers in Jesus had chosen a Messiah orthodox Jews had rejected, and although this did not debar them from becoming honorary Jews - Orthodoxy held to the opinion that a Messiah figure would arise - it had been expected that these Gentiles would, however mistaken in their choice of Messiah, adhere to Jewish law on all points. Orthodox Jewry had rejected Jesus, but it had not rejected the Nazoraeans because of their choice of Messiah - at least not until after the war with Rome. The Nazoraeans were considered part of Israel and allowed to worship in the Temple. What orthodoxy would not accept was the idea that since orthodox Jews had rejected Jesus, Gentile believers could step in and reap the rewards promised to the Jews without fulfilling the requirements of the law. On this point orthodox Jewry *and* the Apostolic Nazoraeans had been in agreement - hence the two meetings St Paul had had with the Jerusalem Council to thrash out the pros and cons of the situation. At no point had there been a cozy relationship between Paul and the Jerusalem Council. Compromise had been reached, that was clearly recorded, but it had concerned how far God-fearing Gentiles could penetrate into the Temple, not whether they were saved for all eternity through believing in the Nazoraean Messiah. From the very beginning there had been suspicion and distrust. From being a persecutor of the Nazoraeans, Saul of Tarsus had turned into Paul the Nazoraeans' heretical helpmate, the man who eventually inflamed them into an outright rejection of his extended theology.

As he worked with Theodore's complex text, Duggan's respect for the man grew. Here was a thinker who had appreciated the slow and painful process of life, a man of experience who recognized human experience as a vital and necessary part of human growth. For Theodore, as for Irenaeus, attaining the 'likeness of God' had been an altogether different proposition from having been made in the 'image of God'. Image and likeness were at the extreme poles of experience. They were the Alpha and Omega of existence, one freely given, the other attained. Life was inherently free and self-directing; it was a creative process and could not be perfected by divine fiat. There was no such thing as an off-the-peg reprieve for sin through faith alone. Salvation was the accumulation of responsible choices, not a form of spiritual camouflage supplied by Jesus.

* * *

Archbishop Donaghue's temper frayed as he read an article on the Resurrection published by Bishop Peters. As usual, the bishop's thinking was a travesty of Church teaching and a slap in the face to all sincere believers. Reducing that greatest of all historical happenings to the level of a misunderstood event, Peters showed himself to be at odds with the heart of the Christian faith. How could the man bear to put his name to such rubbish? Either Christ was resurrected, as the New Testament stated, or everything about God's son come down from heaven to save humanity from sin and death was a monstrous lie. The question was: How could a lie of such damnable proportions have changed the lives of so many people? If Jesus Christ had not been who the Church said he was, then how in the name of all that was sensible had the Church managed to deceive so many people for so long?

Dealing with wayward colleagues had become a way of life for Donaghue, but few bishops had strayed from the path in quite the way Peters had - he had raised 'straying' to the level of an art form. Donaghue could remember Peters laying down the conservative viewpoint at conferences, so how had he got to where he was now? The change in him was astonishing. In what seemed no time at all he had transformed himself into an apologist for every crackpot radical idea threatening the people's faith. And he wasn't doing himself any favors publishing this kind of thing while under suspension - Cardinal Menenger would throw a fit when he read this his latest excursion into speculative truth.

In Donaghue's mind, Bishop Peters had quite simply lost his faith and was attempting to dress up his loss as a necessary and worthwhile condition. The dilemma for people like Peters, Donaghue reasoned, was that their reductionism made no sense to ordinary believers; it fell flat in the face of human suffering. Try comforting a grieving widow with the news that Christ's resurrection should not be taken literally, or that his promised return was wishful thinking. How help the sick with a Gospel shorn of miracles, or calm a devastated town with biblical criticism? It was all too silly for words. The New Testament brimmed with evidence for Jesus having been who he claimed to be, and in every century thousands of lives attested to that extraordinary historical fact.

The odd thing about Peters was that he wanted to continue within the Church. He believed the Church could be useful, but not in its present form. A rejigging of its theological notions would have to take place, he believed. An updating of its image and its ideas would allow it to accommodate the modern age. According to

Donaghue that was exactly what should not take place. Selling out to modernism would undermine and eventually destroy everything the Church stood for. It was not a matter of returning to a defunct medievalism, as some misguided souls believed, it was matter of remaining true to the heart of the Gospel as revealed in the life, teachings and death of Jesus of Nazareth.

The big mistake was that thinkers like Peters postulated a Christ of Faith *and* a Christ of History. By creating two figures they hoped to show that history and faith were separate entities, incompatibles that no amount of manipulation could bring together. But this was in itself a form of manipulation; it was an academic ploy designed to create problems where problems did not exist. History and faith were not separate entities. God had entered history through his son, and history had taken on a sacred dimension. Modernists could not understand this. Starting from the premise that Jesus had been an ordinary flesh and blood man, they rejected his obvious divinity and made its existence dependent on the eye of faith. To them, the eye of faith was not spiritual discernment, it was subjectivity enthralled by make-believe.

Sitting back into the leather swivel chair that made hours of desk work bearable, Donaghue pushed Bishop Peters's article aside and reached for the letter he had received from Bob Carter that morning. It was in a handcrafted envelope with a discreet gold-embossed logo on the back flap - the logo was of a phoenix rising from its own ashes. This image was repeated in a slightly larger version on the letterhead, and there was a reference in the letter itself to this mythical bird's capacity to renew itself by fire. Reading the letter through for a third time, the Archbishop weighed Carter's tone and decided that the man had overstepped himself. It was one thing to uphold the old values, it was quite another to use those values to impose a new-fangled conception of mission on others. There was also a sense of threat in Carter's words, a delicately constructed reminder that the previous Holy Father had sanctioned the movement he, Carter, represented, and that members of this movement should be given every assistance when visiting a parish.

The problem had arisen when a local priest had written to his bishop, and the bishop, in turn, had written to Donaghue complaining of interference in parish affairs by visitors sanctioned as missionary by Rome. Carrying the title Children of the New Catholic Dawn (CNCD), they had quickly shown themselves to be divisive in their dealings with parish members - within two months they had split the parish in question into opposing camps. As a result, Donaghue had written to Carter asking that the matter be looked into. In a long and considered response, Carter ignored the pros and cons of the situation and suggested, after a minor sermon, that a little pain was sometimes necessary when dealing with an infected community. Infected? Donaghue was chagrined. Fr Brentano ran one of the more successful Nevada parishes - it had been a model community up until the movement's missionaries arrived. The rest of the letter was a lecture couched in the language of a friend. He, Carter, understood how difficult it could be when a favored community began to reveal its flaws, but that's what the new drive towards repentance was all about. It was a chance for everyone, from the lowest to the highest, to face the reality of how they had been infected by modernism's poison.

Donaghue's problem was that he was in full agreement with Carter about the challenge of Modernism, but not with some of the movement's rather odd theological propositions - particularly its insistence that feelings of love and affection for others should be sublimated. According to CNCD representatives operating in Nevada and elsewhere, attachment to family or friends was to be discouraged, as were the more troublesome feelings of love and desire between partners. Why? Because emotional attachments displaced God. Had not Christ himself disowned his family on behalf of his Father in heaven? As this was Christ's own injunction, how could it be argued with? Directly commissioned by the previous pope to deal with the Modernist threat in America, Donaghue was at a loss to understand how CNCD had sneaked into such a position of authority without his noticing. There were rumors coming out of Rome that anyone who publicly criticized the movement rapidly found himself in trouble, and that this applied to bishops as well as priests and theologians. As he lifted the phone, Donaghue wondered if it also applied to archbishops.

Fr Brentano listened attentively as Donaghue fluffed his way round the issue; the matter was being looked into and he would just have to be patient.

"The whole community is in an uproar, Your Grace."

"Yes, I understand that, but —-"

"Something has to be done."

"That's why I'm ringing you. I —-"

"These people have to go."

"I can't authorize that. They're part of a missionary program blessed by the late Holy Father."

"Then it's high time the present Holy Father was informed as to what's going on in his predecessor's name."

Donaghue tried to terminate the call with the promise that he would give the matter his full attention, but Fr Brentano wasn't finished. If nothing happened within a week, the whole messy business would be put into the hands of the local press.

"Are you threatening me, Father?"

"I'm merely a mouthpiece, Your Grace."

"You mustn't allow this to happen."

"It's beyond my power to stop it."

"Then disassociate yourself."

"That will be difficult, Your Grace."

"You have no option."

"Truth is always an option."

"Don't be impertinent!"

There was a silence.

"Fr Brentano?"

"Yes."

"You mustn't be seen to take sides. Distance yourself."

"Yes, Your Grace."

"I can rely on you to do that?"

"Yes, Your Grace."

Donaghue replaced the receiver and sat back. There was no denying that Fr Brentano was in a very awkward position, but if he joined the breakaways awkwardness would be swapped for official censorship. The Children of the New Catholic Dawn might be a pain in the neck, but they were an official pain in the neck, and that could not easily be got around.

* * *

"Tell me about Mar Saba. I know a little of its history, but I've never been there."

Duggan and Windle were sitting side by side in the hotel bar; they had been there for some time.

"It's a helluva place. Beautiful. Austere. Crazy. Its history as a Christian monastery dates from the end of the fifth century." Windle took a sip of bourbon. "It was founded by St Sabas, a Cappadocian ascetic. It's situated about fifteen miles southeast of Jerusalem in the Kedron valley. Dry as a bone most of the time. Sabas was a disciple of the famous Palestinian monk Euthymios the Great."

"Wasn't there some kind of connection with Origen?"

"A breakaway group of Origanist monks took over in 507. Their ideas were later condemned by the Council of Constantinople. The Mar Saba scriptorium churned out manuscripts right up until the twelfth century. St John of Damascus was holed up in a cell there for thirty years. Have you read his critique of Islam?"

A shake of the head.

"It was the first ever penned by a Christian. He regarded Islam as Judaeo-Christian in form, but heterodox because it believed, as the Arian heretics believed, that God could not have become human without compromising his divinity. He grew up in the Ummayed Arab court in Damascus, the hub of early Islamic thinking. His father was chancellor of the new Islamic capital."

"I believe it's quite spectacular."

"All the way down to the Valley of Dreadful Judgment where a river of blood will flow on Judgment Day." Windle's tone had become musical, his smile wistful for the chapels, cells and oratories that hung in layers from the rock face. "The monks believe the Kedron will become a river of blood on Judgment Day - a river of heretics, whores and Freemasons headed for everlasting damnation." A pause, and a glance.. "The mouth of hell is believed to be near the Dead Sea."

"How on earth did you manage to photograph these documents without anyone realizing what you were up to?"

"I did it at the same time as I did the official ones. It got hairy at times. Fr Merle would duck out and I'd snip-snap away. The lighting, everything I needed, was already in place."

"You were the official photographer?"

"I'm semi-professional."

"That could raise difficulties later."

"I'm aware of that."

Duggan's next question was in the form of a statement. The fifth century was well known for its textual creativity, he said, returning to the possibility of forgery, so the skulduggery of an imaginative fourth or fifth-century monk could not be ruled out. The flawless scribal handwriting, subtle abbreviations and complexities of the letters could mean that both were early, rather then late, forgeries.

Windle's reply was that that was perfectly possible, but not probable. These guys, he said, referring to Theodore and Irenaeus, had confirmed what a growing number of scholars thought to be the case - one unholy row had been going on between the Nazoraean sect and the Roman Church for centuries. And the inclusion of Pelagius in the argument was exactly what one would expect. The very fact that the Pelagian and Nestorian heretics had later appealed to Theodore's writings strengthened the possibility of a connection between the two men.

"It'll still be argued that you're between a stone and a hard place."

"They can argue all they like, Jack, but you know as well as I do that we're on track. There are sufficient examples of Theodore's writings in existence for a comparison to be made."

"You had time to make such a comparison?"

Windle laughed his laugh. "Merle was already an expert on Theodore. His *Essai sur Theodore de Mopsueste* appeared way back in '48. It's an exhaustive study of the theological factors that led to Theodore's condemnation by the Fifth Ecumenical Council in 553. His conclusion was that Theodore was the father of Nestorianism."

"We're talking handwriting, not theology. And you can't say the same about Irenaeus's writings."

"True. But Merle was familiar enough with Theodore's original work to consider it authentic. Computer analysis did the rest within 24 hours."

"How did he react when he realized the letter was probably authentic?"

"I think he was deeply shocked. I think it began to dawn on him that his Church's attempt to write the Nazoraeans off as incompetent Christians, and therefore rightly superseded by the Roman Church, was at best a mistake, and at worst a deliberate policy of deception."

"Irenaeus doesn't mention the Nazoraeans in his writings."

"No, but he does talk at length about an older theological tradition, a tradition which asserted that humanity and divinity did not exclude one another. He says that God became man in order that man might become God. The trinitarian relationship is extended to all humanity. Christ is still unique, but human beings have the opportunity to take on a divine aspect - they can share in Christ's divinity for the simple reason that Christ had also been a human being. And he clearly anticipates and undermines Augustine's notion of original sin; he allows for the working of conscience in our earliest ancestors. Yes, Christ is seen as the incarnate Word of God, but not in the sense of Jesus the man being literally God. He's an apologist for the Eastern, rather than the Western, conception of Jesus' divinity. I think he saw Jesus as someone who *carried* the Word of God within himself, but was not himself that word in any literal sense."

"You'd have a devil of a time proving that."

"It's there by inference in his theology. You can't hold a progressivist theology like he did and be mainstream Roman in your views. The whole business of those he describes as attempting to establish their false opinion *regarding that which is written* about Jesus and his ministry speaks for itself. He knew damn well that something had gone wrong."

"He was never indicted for heresy."

"Better to overlook his second-century peccadillos and enforce his five-volume refutation *of* the heretics. Almost everything written about the heretics after that point relies in some way on Irenaeus's writings, writings not in Irenaeus's hand or in the language he wrote them in. The earlier works of Agrippa Castor and Justin Martyr against the heretics are lost to us, so Irenaeus is the only substantial informant on heresy the Church has, and he was working far from the real scene of action, and with limited information. Not that that's ever concerned the hierarchy - at least not until the Nag Hamadi Scrolls turned up." Windle's laugh was deep. "That must have caused a few of them to turn in their beds!"

"Yes, but —-"

"You didn't have any problem with this when we were talking to Weisel." Windle's stare was direct. "Why object now?"

"I'm not objecting, I'm trying to anticipate objections." Duggan placed his glass carefully in front of him; his action mirrored his attitude. "You suggested that afternoon that Irenaeus had access to Nazoraean writings."

"He couldn't have appealed to the Churches of the Apostolic Foundation without some awareness of what the Nazoraeans believed. He certainly knew of a Nazoraean gospel written in

Hebrew."

"Then why attack the Ebionites? The Ebionites were a direct off-shoot of the Nazoraeans headed by the Apostle James."

"The early Ebionites were. The later Ebionites were Nazoraeans of extreme view who believed Jesus to have betrayed their secrets. Irenaeus rejected them because they seemed to reject Jesus. It was as simple as that."

"Paul's Jesus."

"The Jesus the Church borrowed from Paul *after* the destruction of the Nazoraean community in Rome by Nero, the Jesus the Church eventually legislated into existence *as* God at the Council of Nicaea in the fourth century. The later Ebionites didn't reject the Azorean Jesus, they rejected, as did the later Nazoraeans, the theological distortions forced on Jesus by the Roman Church. Irenaeus' disgust with the Ebionite sect does not cancel out his acceptance of views belonging to the original Nazoraean community in Jerusalem, it highlights the fact that the Church had lost all sense of Nazoraean importance by the end of the first century."

"But not Irenaeus."

"I think he knew what was going on. He rejected any view that did not concur with what the original Apostles and Elders had taught about Jesus, and he had some odd ideas in that direction. Hence his angry reaction against those who tried to push a reinvented Jesus into circulation. That's the crunch point. He would not put up with Jesus' teachings being hijacked.

"You discussed this with Merle?"

"He's not a big talker, Jack. When it became obvious we were in possession of a document that seriously questioned the Church's origins, he clammed up all together."

"And reported straight to Rome."

"The *facts*, not his fears."

"You've communicated since?"

"He's incommunicado."

"Even to you?"

A nod from Windle, then a silence.

Looking down the length of the bar to where a group of men were drinking and chatting, Duggan wondered what it must be like to wake in the morning devoid of questions. Some people lived as if the questions he and Windle were discussing had no meaning at all, others as if institutionalized Christianity's version of the Jesus story was beyond criticism. Jesus walking on water was acceptable to many, to others it was plainly a nonsense, or at best a metaphor. If taken at face value, however, such stories ruptured the fabric of reality and reduced all of us to pawns in some unimaginably silly cosmic game - the game an Atkins or a Carter reveled in. The question of where the line should be drawn was a question all thinking men and women had a responsibility to address. The brandishing of literalisms had caused much pain and suffering down the centuries, and the present attempt to reinstate belief in the devil, in miracles, in weeping statues, in visions of Jesus or Mary as shadow play on a building or in a bush spoke of an institution interested only in sustaining a doctrinal smokescreen. It was time to wake up. It was time to grow up. It was time to start asking questions again.

"You find America congenial?

The tone of Windle's question surprised Duggan.

" . . . I like what I see."

"You could return to the fold. You could get a post here in the States."

"I've no particular desire to return to the fold."

"You'll be fighting them off when they find out how talented you are."

"I won't be advertising my talents."

"It'll get out sooner or later."

"I'll deal with that if and when it happens."

Windle's next remark made Duggan look at him.

"You're working way below capacity, Jack."

"I'm where I want to be."

"But not where you should be."

"I started out wanting to be a priest."

"That doesn't mean everything you were doing was a mistake."

"It's all related."

"Related, but not fixed. You don't have to think like a priest to work in our area. You know that as well as I do."

"I know what you're saying."

"I'm saying you've got a first-class mind and you ought to be using it on first-class problems."

"It's as a result of my being a journalist we're sitting here discussing this."

"*Touché.*" A smile followed by a non-sequitur. "She's the most contented I've ever seen her."

"Jane?"

"Who else?" Windle signaled to the barman. "It's nice to see her at peace in herself." He continued with his observations. "She's been a bit wild at times. Headstrong. Particularly after her mother died."

"She seems very capable."

"She needed a break and she's got one. With her art. That helped settle her a bit." A glance. "And then you turned up."

Duggan looked at Windle with interest.

"She hasn't mentioned you."

"That's meaningful?"

"Not a single word."

Duggan waited.

"Is it meaningful?"

"I'm not sure I can answer that."

"Can't, or won't?"

"Can't. She hasn't said anything to me either." He corrected himself. "She's admitted to being nervous, that's all."

"That'll be first," said Windle. And then to Duggan's surprise he changed tracks. "I liked the way you tackled Weisel."

"I rather got the impression you were annoyed with me."

"Good policeman, bad policeman."

"You don't trust him either?"

"Love many, trust few, always paddle your own canoe." A smile. "I learned that from my father."

13

The Winds of Necessary Change

Elbows on the fake wood surface of the cafeteria table, little Miss Earmuffs sipped at her cappuccino and listened as David Mayle marveled yet again at their running into one another. Intrigued to see her old colleague in the foyer of the Astoria, Holly Parks had followed him to reception and heard him ask for the very man she was hoping to ambush.

"You came up from Washington because of Windle?"

A shake of the head. She had been covering something quite unrelated when the story broke.

"Windle and I go back a long way. He's completely in the dark as to what happened out there."

"Could you arrange for me to talk to him?"

"And let you waltz off with my bloody story!" Said half in jest, but only half. "I don't think so."

There was a pause; she seemed to have run out of strategy.

"So what were you working on before this came up?" he asked.

"Something . . . *tasty*." A smile distorted her face slightly. "What's good for the goose?"

Mayle laughed and said that they had all known she would make it; she had had that extra something.

"Why have you hung around so long?"

"I left it too late."

"It's *never* too late."

"I'd never find anywhere to park my van."

"You've still got that van!"

A laugh of resignation from Mayle.

"A crumb or two from the master's table?" Holly's blue-green eyes were full of humor. "Do I have to beg?"

They were looking at one another; Mayle liked what he saw.

"Windle's not got a lot of patience with journalists," she said, remembering how he had rounded on her. She followed up with an observation. "He's very handsome."

"He's brighter by half than he is good-looking."

"How did you meet?"

"It's a long story. What matters is that he's a regular guy and he's in a fix." Mayle ploughed on conscious of her stare, conscious of the dangers. "His daughter's just hit the big time as an artist."

"So what's it all about?" Her expression was a mixture of innocence and guile. "The letter. His son being out there at the same time."

"They weren't even in the country when the theft took place.""

"He and Merle were the last people to handle the Ignatius document."

"Wrong. The librarian was ."

She moved on undaunted. "The son hasn't been arrested?"

"Not that I'm aware of."

He could almost hear her brain working.

"You know what's in the letter they found?"

"No more than you do."

"He must have talked to you about it."

"In general terms only."

"Surely . . ."

"I'd be guessing if I said more than that. *That* would not be helpful."

"An English tabloid thinks it's a letter written in Jesus' own hand."

Mayle's laugh was derisory.

"It's obviously an important find."

"Obviously."

Holly's lips formed a smile without parting; she was getting nowhere and that annoyed her. "So how's Frisco?" she asked by way of distraction.

"Broke," he said.

"You're with someone?"

A shake of the head.

"Me neither."

"It isn't compulsory."

Her crinkly smile returned; it was full of innuendo. "Speak for yourself!"

"I'm not exactly the catch of the year."

"Some women like the disheveled type." Her tone was playful, her stare disconcerting. "You've always underestimated your attractiveness, David. The Christmas party?"

"Don't remind me."

"It was only a kiss."

"You'd been drinking."

"So had you!"

"I'm not saying I didn't enjoy it."

A pause. "You changed into my father."

"I'm as old as your father."

"How old are you? Forty-seven? Forty-eight?"

"What are you? Twenty something?"

"I'm twenty-eight."

"Twenty years is a lifetime."

"It's a lifetime later on, but who's talking later on?" Holly's eyes sparkled with mischief. "I saw the way you were looking at me."

Mayle forced a smile and Holly jumped tracks again.

"We could work together on this."

"You'd steal it from under me! I haven't forgotten the things you got up to."

She shook her head, pursed her mouth. She would be good. She would play the game. She had learned her lesson.

"Is that what this is about?"

"Of course not!" Her expression was scornful. "I like you, David. I've always liked you."

"You're trying to muscle in."

"Don't write off the idea until you think about it. It would be fun.

I have resources you don't have."

"If I could, I would, but I can't." A sigh from Mayle. "It's way too complicated, Holly."

"In what way?"

"He's a friend."

"So you keep saying."

"The water's muddy enough."

She considered that; then she said, "Can I stand you lunch some time? For old time's sake. You looked after me when I first arrived."

"We saw your potential."

"*You* saw my potential." The crinkly smile returned. "How did you ever put up with me?"

"You were a breath of fresh air."

"I was a kid."

"You're still a kid."

"Is that how you see me? Still?"

He chose his words carefully. "Relatively speaking."

"Relative to what?"

"Me."

She looked away, then back. "If you think you're old, then you *are* old."

"I'll keep that in mind."

The pup reporter came back on line. "I need a little something to set me off, David."

"I'll help if I can."

"I need something yesterday."

"That's the price you pay for working out of Washington."

She paused in her machinations, then almost desperately suggested that they meet up later over a bottle of something really nice.

"I'm with Windle this evening."

"Monday?"

"I doubt if I'll be free."

"Tuesday?"

He smiled at her persistence.

"Ring me." She produced a card and scribbled the name of her hotel and room number on the back. "I mean it, David. It could be a lot of fun."

* * *

Bishop Peters chose a book from his library, opened it at random and began to read. What he read was unexpectedly appropriate.

In the religious tradition, inherited variability has been expressed in the doctrine that individual human souls are of infinite value, although this has not prevented the organized churches from trying to dragoon the faithful into a single pattern. We always have this tension between the fact of genetic variability and the fact that society does on the whole like to create a single manageable pattern for human life. The problem, as usual, is to make the best of both worlds, to find how we can have a stable and viable society which yet gives scope to the enormous variations which, as a matter of empirical fact, do exist between human beings.

This was what Cardinal Menenger's demand for doctrinal conformity did not properly address: 'soul' and 'creativity' were closely related. A Church following through on Menenger's vision of the future would not result in Christ's return and the birth of a society governed by Catholic values, it would result in a second Reformation and a tearing down of much that was held dear. In Bishop Peters's scheme of things. the winds of necessary change would bring that about. In spite of our collective fear of change, there was, he believed, simultaneously a drive towards change, and 'thought' was its trigger. Think one thing and you were liable (tempted?) to think its opposite. Human beings were condemned to sin because they were capable of creative thought. Become holier than thou and the result was an incursion of images and ideas antithetical to pet religious notions - witness St Augustine *Confessions.* A Philip Atkins was inclined to interpret such compulsions as the devil trying to undo God's work. A psychiatrist saw it as no more than attitudinal imbalance. A theology grounded in the idea of cosmic conflict saw everything as potentially in the clutches of the devil. Dump such an idea and life took on an almost innocent charm.

The trick was to let God off the hook. But before that could happen a number of thorny issues had to be dealt with. As human beings trying to understand our place in a large and complex universe, we had by necessity conjured into existence a series of explanations culminating in the great faiths of antiquity. These faiths had sufficed until the present moment - they were the crowning achievement of centuries of thought and exploration - but they were now being challenged at every turn. What had once been sacrosanct was now being trashed nightly on television. What had once been viewed as incontrovertible truth was now the subject of cruel jokes. Everything was up for grabs. So what to do? Give in and allow centuries of delicate searching to be washed away? Or stand one's ground in the face of spiritual decadence and fight for the Church's survival? Thinkers like Donaghue, Carter and Atkins had lumped for the latter - they saw themselves as guardians of the true faith. For them, cheap New Age sentiments and devil-inspired religious forms incubated in the East did not in the end satisfy. Or for that matter the utilitarian rhetoric of scientists and philosophers. No matter how clever, such messages could not contend with Christianity's transcendent vision. In the face of social breakdown and the challenges facing individuals at every turn God's eternal truths had to be restated in the terms he himself had supplied.

Attaching a yellow sticker to the top of the page where Huxley had so eloquently stated his case, Bishop Peters put the book aside and returned to the task of teasing basic truths out of an elaborate religious fiction. The hierarchy would be furious with him for continuing to write in such a manner, but he had little choice - his mission now was to see the process of emptying through to the bitter end. Bitter? Casting off so much had at times left him dispirited and unsure, a mere shell of a man in comparison with what he had once been. What he had once been now seemed distant and unreal, his certainty of faith a memory too faint to be resurrected. He was undergoing change, and it was going to take all the courage he had to let happen what had to happen. Empty was anything but empty, he was discovering.

His ribs hurt. He rubbed at them with the index finger and forefinger of his right hand - it was as if he were delivering an off-angle benediction to himself. Getting to his feet, he stretched, eyes closed, arms hanging out from his sides like spindly wings. That seemed to help. Straightening, he took a breath and let it out slowly, then another, then another. Eyes closed still, he stood listening, the background hiss of his hearing joining with the occasional sound from beyond the window. A car. The sound of a horn. In the distance a siren wailing. Back to the hiss and its immediacy, then out onto the street again. Then back to the hiss of his personal space and the sense of euphoria stacking up in his middle. Yes, they would strip him like a disgraced soldier and disparage everything he said, but none of it mattered a jot. It was to be expected. A defrocked bishop would receive special attention, more so than any recalcitrant priest, or theologian. He was in the Congregation's sights and could expect no mercy.

* * *

Duggan stretched in much the same manner as Bishop Peters, then leaned forward again to worry at Theodore's script. The Gospels gave only a glimmer of what had been going on in Jesus' life, so it came as no surprise to read that the Church's version of that life was at odds with the reality of that life. Claiming to have a letter in Irenaeus's own hand, Theodore had examined the early Church's sectarian origins and concluded that Christianity had gone off the rails. Irenaeus's was acknowledged in this context, but it was not clear to what extent. Theodore had, like many modern scholars, extrapolated from Irenaeus's basic theology and concluded that the Nicaean formula was a gross exaggeration. One thing was clear, however, Irenaeus's had all but ignored St Paul's preoccupation with justification and atonement, and that spoke volumes about his perception of Jesus and his intentions. Referring only to one side of Paul's thinking, Irenaeus had promoted the Gospel of John and acknowledged no break between the early Church and Jewish religious practice. This was now accepted by most scholars, but its full significance had dawned on only a few. As Irenaeus also contended that Jesus had lived beyond the age of forty - whether before or after the crucifixion was unclear - a new set of possibilities loomed large.

Duggan warmed to the idea of an old Jesus. A Jesus with greying hair and a few wrinkles was a Jesus people could relate to. Perhaps 'resurrection' had signified something altogether different to Jesus' disciples. God in the form of a man overpowering death, and then gravity, was not an easy thing to digest; whereas a human being rising out of limitation into limitlessness because of a profound closeness to God made perfect sense. To the conservative mind this was to rob Jesus of his inherent divinity, but what it actually did was reinstate his forgotten humanity. Convinced that Jesus was God paying humanity a visit, believers ran the risk of being possessed by a phantom of the imagination, a phantom who whispered only what they wanted to hear.

Duggan's mother had been delusional in this respect, the priest who attended her equally so. She and he had talked about Jesus as if he were in the room, particularly the bedroom, and the result had been decades of quiet misery for his father. And if it wasn't God *as* Jesus who was listening in, or playing peeping Tom, then it was the Virgin Mary, or an angel, or some saint plucked out of the pantheon of God's helpers. We were surrounded by a cloud of witnesses, she had believed, and as a child Duggan had accepted her reasoning without question. Later, when he had awakened to the absurdity of that idea, she had dumbfounded him with the news that her love for him was the same as that of a mother whose son had committed murder. Yes, she loved him, but she could not forgive him for murdering Christ all over again.

There was no doubting there had been saintly individuals in the Church who had done much good, but while they had exercised their beautiful natures their Church had harassed and slaughtered whole communities on behalf of ideas turned manic. Duggan had drunk deeply at the well of history and could not ignore such goings on. At it's best the hierarchy had been incorrigibly naive, at its worst bestial. The problem with believers today was that they thought their Church's past had nothing whatever to do with them. The Church was no longer like that, they said. These had been brutal times, they said. You had to make allowances, they said. The problem with that kind of reasoning was that you couldn't make allowances for a brutal past and argue for a sensible present in the same breath. It was, after all, the same God either end of the puzzle, the same system of ideas, the same basic interpretation that in other centuries had led to unbelievable violence. Weaken the laws separating Church and State and the old propensity for excess would reappear.

So what had happened? Had God forgotten to mention that he did not like butchery? Had he forgotten to mention Christ's injunction to love one's neighbor as one's self? Had he decided to overlook the fact that his Church had taken to torturing and burning human beings in the name of truth? Whatever the reasons given, all of it warranted close investigation, and that, as Theodore's insightful letter made plain, was no new idea.

14

A Blow from Within

In alignment with the Vatican's hardline approach, Robert Carter damned a journalist in San Francisco for perpetrating the new anti-Semitism, namely, Catholic-bashing. According to Carter, religious correspondents wrote mostly post-modernist, relativist drivel; they were secularist preachers to whom God was a stranger and the religious viewpoint no more than an opinion. The idea that all religions were equal, that they were merely differing routes to the same source was a monstrous lie. Christ had died to take away the sins of the world, but the world had to respond. Belief systems like Buddhism, Hinduism, Islam or any of the other religious forms could not deliver the human soul from sin. There was only one great truth, and the Roman Catholic Church was the custodian of that truth. Christ had not founded a plethora of churches, he had founded only one Church. It followed, therefore, that Protestant Christians were living in error. Being tolerant of another's religious point of view was one thing, but when tolerance was turned into a euphemism for equality between religions, or between Catholic and Protestant interpretations of the faith, then committed Catholics should speak out.

"*He* ought to be committed," said Mayle, who had pocketed the cutting for Duggan.

"Actually, he has a point," said Duggan. "Tolerance in this sense isn't asked of other religious leaders."

Duggan's reply prompted Windle to say that Carter's gripe was not with the media, but with Western democracy. When democracy worked to the Church's disadvantage, it set her teeth on edge.

The three men were relaxing over a late afternoon beer and sandwiches in Windle's hotel room.

"It's pluralism that's the problem," said Duggan. "The Church's definition of cultural pluralism hangs on the old idea of cultures geographically separated from the West. That's not how things are any longer. We're now a mix of cultures and religious systems. And on top of it all there's the challenge of secularism. On the one hand you have irreconcilable truth claims being made by the major religions, on the other you have a secularist definition of freedom which these same religions find almost impossible to live with. Western Christianity is buckling under the pressure of it all. So also are our politicians. Some mainstream Australian politicians are daring to ask - in conjunction with the far-Right - how much pluralism a society can bear. What Carter's trying to do is defend his Church's right to speak out against a pluralism of truths."

"No one's stopping him from speaking out."

"Pluralistic tolerance can be *very* intolerant - it's now a theoretical system with it's own rules of practice. Contravene those rules and you're immediately in hot water."

"The Church is any different?"

"The Church is the Church."

Windle laughed. "Whose side are you on?"

"Not Carter's, that's for sure." Duggan paused; then he said, "The Second Vatican Council never envisaged the kind of pluralism we're faced with today. I don't think any of us did. Hence the unease in our society and the Church's retreat into dull obduracy. It detects nihilism and bland relativism on all fronts. It's one thing to expect a religion to refine or redefine its ideas from time to time, it's quite another to expect it to sit back and ignore the fact that it's being relativized out of existence."

There was a silence.

"Carter's a menace," said Mayle. Then, as if wishing to push Carter out of his mind he said, "What was Herr Weisel like?"

"Small," said Duggan.

"Jack gave him a hard time."

"I asked questions that had to be asked."

"Remind me not to get in your bad books, Jack!"

Windle's frequent use of 'Jack' was not lost on Mayle; the two men had obviously hit it off.

"Jane?" inquired Mayle.

"She's with Elspeth this evening," said Windle. "They've been together all day."

Mayle looked at Duggan.

"I saw her last night for a couple of hours. She asked about you."

"We were almost in the air when it was decided we should turn back. Some light was flashing that shouldn't have."

"Better late than not at all," said Duggan.

The contrast with the previous afternoon's formality was stark. Windle was shoeless and in shirt sleeves, his big frame sprawled out on the sofa. Duggan, beer in hand, was slumped in one of the armchairs. On the table by the window a litter of papers and books added to the atmosphere of relaxed industry.

"Worth waiting for?" asked Mayle.

"Oh, yes," said Duggan.

"East versus West," said Windle. "Theodore and Irenaeus were bishops in the Eastern Church. That's the key, David. The Eastern Church didn't develop a systematic theology; it was more interested in icons." Windle laughed. "I mean by that that it had a contemplative rather than an intellectualist approach. As a result, Eastern Christians had a tangentially different view of sin and salvation from the West. They saw the world as the place where human beings developed towards perfection, not as a place of punishment. In the Eastern scheme our first parents weren't corrupt, they were just weak and immature. The West believed in universal human guilt, the East in an inherited sinfulness, or *tendency* towards sin. These are very different concepts. Clement of Alexandria agreed with Irenaeus, as did quite a few others. To Clement, Adam was a child made in the image of God not yet capable of exhibiting the likeness of God - he believed that would come later. Sin did not necessitate universal guilt. Adam and Eve had not fallen into sin from a state of perfect righteousness - an idea borrowed from Rabbinical Judaism they had fallen into sin because they were primitive souls lacking experience. That's all there was to it. The world of toil and experience was not God's punishment for some unimaginable fault, it was God's remedy for underdeveloped minds."

"That's a helluva jump from the idea of an original sin carried by all humanity."

"It's implicit in Irenaeus' thinking that the world is a divinely appointed environment, not a place of retribution. I think it's fair to say that Irenaeus saw salvation as a gradual process, not a sudden crediting of righteousness to someone who believed Jesus Christ to be God. That's the Catholic position, and it's also the evangelical or fundamentalist Protestant position. The only difference between the two is that Catholics accept the Church as an indispensable intermediary."

"Irenaeus only hints at gradualism," said Duggan, mindful of the cross-currents in Irenaeus' thinking. "But I agree, he was no Augustinian."

Windle was accepting of the point, but dismissive of scholarly attempts to disallow the Irenaean approach because of theological stasis. Irenaeus represented the ecumenical phase of Christian thought, he said gruffly, and *that* should be expounded whenever possible. Augustinian theology had thrown up acres of unresolved problems and it was high time the Church faced that fact.

"The whole business leaves me stone cold," said Mayle. He reached for a sandwich. "Sin is a religious term; it doesn't reflect how we view wrongdoing nowadays. The idea of the world as God's remedy for underdeveloped minds is as much inside the believers camp as the idea of the world as a place of punishment. Atkins attacked the gradulist approach in his opening lecture at the conference. Most people don't give a fig either way."

"It's a matter of perspective," said Windle. "The presumption that God is behind everything wasn't under question then the way it is now. The Romans called Christians atheists because they only had one God. They arrested St Polycarp - Irenaeus' mentor - for that very reason. What's important is the underlying sense of the Ireneaen formula; it merges with, rather than contradicts, our present interpretation of reality."

"It's still an apologetic mindset."

"True, but it's a step in the right direction."

"Ecumenical or just underdeveloped?" asked Duggan, musing on an earlier point.

"The early Church let sleeping dogs lie for over a century. In my book that's ecumenicalism."

"It isn't how ecumenicalism is envisaged today."

"They weren't conscious of being ecumenical," said Windle. "It's just how things were. The closer you get to the first century the more fluid Christianity becomes." Knowing that he had covered Duggan's point, Windle directed the rest of his comments at Mayle. "They hadn't got to the point of dogmatizing the faith. That came later. This is what fundamentalism and evangelicalism are all about. These guys are trying to get back to the simple faith, problem is, the nearer you get to the early Church the more complex it becomes." He laughed again. "The freedom of interpretation that existed between Christians in the first two centuries would scare the living daylights out of today's literalists! And we're not talking pluralism of styles, we're talking real difference. What today's literalists don't understand is that for around twenty-five years after the crucifixion what we now think of as the New Testament didn't exist. No one had determined what was or was not holy Scripture. There were dozens, if not hundreds, of gospels available. In about the middle of the second century Polycarp suggested a general standardization, an idea taken up and made good by Irenaeus in the face of Gnosticism's challenge. Even the Apostle Paul's writings didn't have much influence during the first hundred years. His letters to the Churches weren't thought to be anything other than letters. During this period sin was blamed on the sinner, not on our mythical first parents."

"So how come Atkins doesn't see it that way?"

Mayle's question had an aggressive edge to it; it was as if he were saying: If you're all so damned clever why can't you agree on anything?

"Again it's a matter of perspective," said Windle. "You referred to sin as 'wrongdoing', but ultimately it doesn't matter what one calls it. What matters is our interpretation of evil."

"That was exactly Atkins's point."

"He's right. That's where the whole thing hinges. Is evil an independent force, or is it just a word? That's the question that has to be addressed. During the first two centuries the emphasis was on temptation by evil spirits. Evil spirits were believed to infest the world. Guided by the desire to subvert the human race, these spirits were believed to be a source of temptation *beyond* that of individual weakness. Led by the fallen archangel Satan, these spirits were thought to have been the enemy of the human race since the beginning of time."

Duggan raised his hands in abdication; he was, he said, no expert on how the concept of evil had developed in Judaism. In seminary he had been more interested in how the world of spirits and demons had been confused with what we now understood to be psychological complexes and libidinous pressures. That had not gone down well.

In response to that, Windle quickly identified the three developmental stages of evil. Stage one was the reason given by God in Genesis for destroying humankind with the flood, namely, sexual intercourse with angels and the wickedness of men's hearts. Stage two was where the angel story had been transformed into the 'Watcher' legend by Jewish thinkers in the last two centuries before Christ, and stage three was where the Jewish reassessment of the naughty angel story had been dropped in favor of Adam's fall from grace. The giveaway was Eve's seduction by Satan in the form of a snake. The snake, for obvious reasons, mirrored the more direct angelic seduction of women in the earlier myth, and that had been the state of play when St Paul was writing his Epistles. Using current perceptions, Paul had used the Adam and Eve story to good effect.

What he, and later Augustine, had imagined the Genesis story to mean, however, had in the end had little to do with what the ancient writers were actually saying.

"Why were human beings blamed when it was angels that were to blame?" Mayle's expression was one of annoyance. "Angels should have had more sense."

"Given that two thirds of them are said to have rebelled against God, the answer is plain: they, like human beings, were free agents."

Mayle considered that. "Two-thirds is an *awful* lot of angels!"

"And not exactly ethereal if you consider that they physically seduced humans," said Windle. He came back in quickly. "Actually, physical seduction by angels is questioned by Christian apologists. They think it more likely that the reference to 'sons of God' in Genesis refers to men of the godly line of Seth mating with women from the Godless line of Cain. The only problem with this explanation is that it doesn't gel with references in the Book of Job to 'sons of God' presenting themselves in heaven before God, or with the fact that 'Satan' - believed to be Eve's temper in the Garden - just happens to be among them. Genesis goes as far as to suggests that these illicit unions produced a race of beings in which divine and human essences were mixed."

"Two natures in one," said Duggan.

Windle's throaty laugh recognized Duggan's aside.

"Does any of it matter?" asked Mayle

"To the extent that it's what people believed, and to some extent still believe, it matters quite a lot," said Windle. "It's the only way we can grasp how things have turned out the way they have."

"And the Watchers?" said Duggan.

"It's a term used in 1 Enoch during the last two centuries BC In II Enoch, which was written around the time of Jesus, the fall story has replaced the Watchers legend. Some think the Watchers are the 'sons of God' of Genesis vi and Job i where, specifically, we're told that the 'sons of God' *and* 'Satan' presented themselves before God. Satan, who comes across more as a tester than a tempter, describes himself as someone who spends a lot of his time going to and fro on the Earth - he seems to be in God's pay. The basic idea is that humanity is being watched by God, by angelic beings, and by Satan on behalf of God. But we're getting away from the point. If sin isn't caused by an objective evil, an evil out there somewhere, then what causes it? The rabbinical school's interpretation was that it results from an evil imagination - *yecer ha-ra* in Hebrew. What's fascinating about that is that the energy of the *yecer ha-ra* is said to be morally neutral, it can be used for good as well as evil."

"The Jungian libido?" ventured Duggan.

"Something like that."

"There's a helluva difference between a tester and a tempter," said Mayle. His tone had softened, but he was still edgy. "Job was tested to destruction."

"Not quite to destruction," said Windle.

"Damn near it."

"There wouldn't have been much point in bumping him off."

"It's a *horrible* story."

Raising a finger patrician style, Windle intoned some ancient lines for Duggan's benefit. *"In the mansions of Hades, upon the left . . . a spring wilt thou find, and near it a white cypress tree."* He corrected himself. *"A white cypress standing. Before it are watchers: To them shalt thou say . . ."* He stopped in triumph. "They had watchers too. The Greeks, that is. It's thought there may have been a Pythagorean Book of the dead."

"They wrote those words on tablets and placed them in the graves of Orphic and Pythorean initiates," said Duggan.

"With thirst I parch, I perish; quick, give me to drink of the water fresh flowing from memory's lake!" Windle smiled to himself. "God that takes me back, Jack."

"If we'd known how much we'd remember we'd have learned heaps more than we did."

"Youth has all the luck."

"Stuff-n-nonsense then and now," said Mayle. And then, "Sorry. I left in a bad mood and arrived in a bad mood."

"Your coming at all is appreciated, David. You know that."

"Yeh, I know."

Duggan broke an awkward moment by saying that to believe sin had any other source than the human imagination was to live inside a horror story of unimaginable proportions.

"A horror story with compensations," said Mayle.

"I've always been the first to admit that."

"No hangover from your seminary days?"

"Put me in a dark, lonely place and I'm as subject to fear as anyone else."

"We're hardwired for fright and flight," said Windle.

"But why angels and demons?" asked Mayle. "Why a belief in good and bad spirits?"

"We react in a similar way because we're wired up in a similar way," said Duggan. "We're constitutionally similar."

"And so we end up with a God who resembles human beings in temperament," said Windle. "He hates, he loves, he kills, he saves."

"The anthropomorphic drift," said Duggan. "Our dreams carry the same pattern."

"Goup delusion?" said Mayle,

"What we have to ask ourselves," said Windle, "is why God would give us free will and intelligence, then force us by dint of a fore-ordained and inflexible plan to accept doctrines that make a nonsense of both our intelligence and our free will? What would be the point of that? - apart from proving that God can't be bucked? That's what all of this comes down to. God is either a big bad bully, or there is no God at all, or he - excuse the ongoing anthropomorphism - is *very* different from how we've imagined God to be. If God is the big bad bully he's made out to be in the Old Testament, then two-thirds of the angels in heaven had no option but to bail out. In terms of how human beings thought in the past, these stories were simply an attempt to solve moral and ethical problems. We used story to maneuver our way through the blind spots in our comprehension."

"Cardinal Newman defined human beings as rebels who had to lay down their arms," said Duggan. "Not much room for maneuver there."

"That's why I love the story of Abraham and Isaac." Windle had swiveled round and was sitting, rather than lying, on the couch now. "Is the story true? I don't know. What I do know is that it captures something important: Abraham's decision to *not do* what his murderous God appears to have told him to do. It's thought that Abraham would have killed Isaac if God hadn't let him off the hook, but that's to read the surface of the story only. On this occasion the story carries a charge in the same way that a dream can carry a charge. I mean by that that dream sometimes contains glimmers of comprehensions not known to the conscious mind. The story of Abraham trying not to question his God's command is of that quality - it reveals a being in torment, a being in the process of moral and ethical transition. What we have to do is identify the archetypal meaning of such stories - we're being spoken to on more than one level. In English, the Greek word archetype - *archetypos* - is used in a pretty ordinary fashion; in Greek it carries another level of meaning altogether. On that other level it means *a mark left by a blow, an impress, or mold*. Now that wouldn't count for much if it referred only to a physical act, but it doesn't, it refers to a psychological state. It is *a blow from within* that leaves a deep impression on the mind. *That* is what Abraham experienced on Mount Moriah."

"*Libidinous pressure* doesn't sound quite the same, does it?" said Duggan.

"No, it doesn't. The story of God's command to Abraham to kill his son was a transition point in human understanding. In primitive psychology the sacrifice of a child symbolized the stopping of time - the child's ritualized death was thought to delay the future. A child offered to the Gods warded off old age and death. And so Chronos kills. his children because they reminded him of his age, and

Oedipus is exposed on a mountain because it is believed he will kill his father. From there it becomes more complicated. Agamemnon, for instance, sacrifices his daughter Iphigenia for political reasons. In Abraham's case the impulse is religious - it comes from God himself. But it comes in a rather peculiar fashion. The text says that God *tempted* Abraham to commit infanticide. That allows us to look into the depths of Abraham's mind and feel the presence of an old pagan brutality. The pressure is on from word one, and it doesn't diminish until he makes his leap of faith, a leap *away* from literalisms towards the symbolic. The wood is stacked, Isaac is tied down and the knife is in the air, but the blow is never struck. Why? Because at the last moment Abraham wakes up to what is going on in his life and makes a choice, a choice that revolutionizes his whole conception of God. But only after a three-day journey during which he has had time to think, time to ponder the meaning of what he is about to do." Windle sat back, his big hands spread out either side on the sofa. "We know from contemporary achieves that Abraham came from a legal background. To people like Abraham it was mandatory to seal a contract or covenant with an animal sacrifice. That's the clue we need to understand this story. Abraham isn't let of the hook by God, it's God that's let of the hook by Abraham. He asserts a more humane prerogative to human sacrifice, and in doing so allows a whole new conception of God to evolve."

Duggan's response was immediate; he thought Windle's explanation of the story excellent.

"It tells us we have a duty to create other ways of defining God, his purposes and the reality at large," said Windle. "It's crude, but it's effective."

"Do you think it may have been written with that in mind?"

"I think it's a travesty to see it as some kind of justification for Jesus getting himself crucified by the Romans in the Ist century, that's what I think. "

* * *

"George's father was an absolute horror" said Elspeth. "I hated being in his company. He said something heartily disagreeable every time we met." It was early evening and the two woman were having pre-dinner drinks in the lounge. "He couldn't resist challenging you with what he believed to be the truth, and he made a point of invaded your physical space to do it. You could see the conversation being bent to accommodate his prejudices." A shake of the head, and a sigh. "How George avoided turning out like his father is a mystery to everyone."

"George is special."

"As is Jack."

"You think so?"

"He's sensitive to other people's feelings and not afraid to speak out when he has to. That's a rare combination."

"He hasn't had many relationships."

"He's none the worse for that."

"I really am smitten."

"As is he."

"You think so?"

"You know so."

"An Australian?"

"We hunt out the best foil we can find."

"In my case that's generally the best folly."

"You have the enviable habit of looking into the darkness and making it work for you." Elspeth's smile tugged at the corners of her mouth. "You transpose folly into art."

"At a price."

"The wages of sin, my dear. Without sin we would be insufferable!" Elspeth took a breath and huffed it out into the room. "There are only two sins that have to be avoided. Betrayal and lying. There's no way back from betrayal - it's an acid that works its way through to the bone. Lying is its handmaiden."

"We're sometimes obliged to lie."

"Yes, but it should not become a habit."

"When you met George you knew that was it?"

"Meeting George was the equivalent of walking out of a dark tunnel for me. Everything made sense after that. When I was told I could no longer dance I retreated into an alcoholic haze. That's when you find out what people are really like."

"I saw that when my mother was ill. My father devoted himself to her."

"What age were you?"

"Seventeen. Paul was eleven." Jane paused. "Paul went through a very difficult two years after her death. I went quiet; I'd lost a friend."

"She'd be proud of you."

"I miss her terribly. She knew better than I did what was going on in my head most of the time."

"My mother was altogether different. I don't think she had a serious thought in the whole of her life."

"You were close to your father?"

"As close as he would allow. He was not an affectionate man. Neither of them were. I'm not all that affectionate myself."

"I think you're marvelous."

"I can be a terrible bitch."

"You say what's on your mind."

"Too frequently, it's been suggested."

"I've been accused of the same thing myself."

"Giving short shrift to the ramblings of idiots is not a sin."

The two women sat in silence for a moment.

"I sometimes think I'm one of those idiots," Jane said.

"You've avoided stasis, that's all. With most people *nothing* is on the move.'"

"Jack's on the move?"

"Oh yes."

"How can you be so sure?"

"You can't. You have to keep checking." Elspeth's laugh matched her glance of warning. "People fall asleep you know."

They had been talking all day, in shops, on the street, in cabs, even as they walked up the staircase and into the flat. Jane had enjoyed every minute of it. There was nothing that could not be said, they discovered, as they made their way through the glittering department stores. Over coffee, and then lunch, their chat had taken a more personal turn, Elspeth admitting that even George could be insufferably masculine at times.

"Jack's very much a man's man," Jane said, picking up on that observation. "He won't be easy to live with if it ever comes to that."

"Ease isn't at all what we're after," said Elspeth. "That's what I meant by *stasis*. Easy men annoy the hell out of women whatever they might say to the contrary."

Jane smiled at Elspeth's slant on things.

"It's true!"

"That certainly isn't Jack."

"No, it isn't."

"You really are in favor, aren't you?"

"I too admit to being smitten. He's quite delicious in spite of having no hair."

"He's hard to read at times."

"I would have thought that half of the attraction."

"I mean . . . I don't know what he's thinking."

"Do we ever know that? "

They were back to the possibility of betrayal, back to the lying, back to the uncertainty that sat at the heart of human relationships. There was no escaping the fact that most people seldom said what they meant, or meant what they said. Relating was a constant subterfuge, a careful shuffling of the cards to avoid detection.

"Jack said he'd be late in, to not wait up."

"Men *busy* at being men," said Elspeth. Then in the tone of someone irked at being kept in the dark, she added, "You know I won't say anything, Jane. Not even to George."

"It's a very complicated situation."

"I gathered *that*."

Jane eyed her companion.

"If you can't, then don't."

"It's not that I can't; it's that I shouldn't."

"Then that's it. Fine." A wave of the hand dismissed Jane's reluctance. "I'll just have to put up with being kept in the dark for once."

"It's also a delicate situation."

"So it would seem."

"There are forces at work." Jane drew breath. "Jack was a totally unexpected bonus, Elspeth. We got lucky. He's invaluable. And on top of everything he's a journalist."

"Why is that important?"

"He'll handle the story when it's time to break it."

"Which will be when?"

"When he finishes the translation."

"That's the bit I don't understand. Why does your father need Jack for that?"

"To take the pressure off. As I said, it's . . . complicated."

Elspeth smiled and reached for Jane's empty martini glass. She would probe no further, she said, getting up.

"I wish I could tell you everything. I really do."

"When you're ready," said Elspeth.

15

Distant drums

"Our new pontiff's behaving much as expected." Duggan turned his folded copy of the *New York Times* over to catch the final paragraph of the article he was reading. "Seems he greatly admires his predecessor."

The peach-colored silk dressing gown Jane was wearing opened provocatively as she reached for the coffee pot. "They would say that whether it was true or not," she said back, clutching vaguely at a lapel.

Angelo Cardinal Rinaldi's elevation had been greeted with little enthusiasm. The indeterminate smoke rising from the Sistine reflected, some said, the disappointment and uncertainty everyone felt. As at the election of Albino Cardinal Luciani, Vatican radio had been forced to issue a special 'bianco' announcement. Aged 72, and in uncertain health, a fretful Rinaldi had accepted his fate, his reservations about tiaras and coronations being dealt with gently, but firmly. With the required two-thirds majority assured, the little-known cardinal from Umbria had donned the wool cloak presented to popes and metropolitan archbishops on the feast of St Agnes and stepped, gingerly, onto the stage of world affairs.

Except for a reminder at Easter warning Catholics from sharing communion with Protestants, not much had been heard from the new pope. Everything issuing from the Vatican had the touch of John Paul II about it, and if not John Paul, then recognizably that of Cardinal Menenger. John Paul had labeled divorced Catholics *dark clouds of unacceptable doctrine and practice,* and oddly similar pronouncements had been issued by Benedict. The announcement that surprised everyone, however, was that the new Pontiff had a burning desire to visit the Holy Land. When news of that got out, a Vatican spokesman immediately poured cold water on the idea: the escalating violence in the Middle East made such a visit highly unlikely.

"Why Benedict XVI?" Duggan's question hung unanswered in the air. "The previous Benedict didn't amount to much."

"When was he around?"

"Beginning of World War I. He was hardline conservative straight out of the diplomatic corps. He was characterized by his detractors as an intellectual and spiritual featherweight. But it's thought Woodrow Wilson's 14-point peace plan was based on a plan he cooked up."

"Then he wasn't altogether useless."

"Thirty-five million Catholics died during that debacle, Jane. " A shake of the head. "Peace declarations written in the safety of the Vatican fell somewhat short of what was required."

There was a silence.

"Elspeth isn't up yet?" queried Duggan.

"We had a tiring day yesterday."

"David's in a hotel on 21st Street. I've got a number for you."

"I'll meet him for lunch."

He smiled brokenly at the suggestion, admitted to irritation over the idea of Mayle having her all to himself.

"We're together now."

"How about this evening?"

"Wouldn't be polite , Jack."

"No, I suppose not," he said.

"More coffee?"

He held out his cup, but kept his eyes on her face. She glanced at him, but looked away again quickly.

"How was your day with Elspeth?"

"We talked non-stop. She's marvelous company. David arrived okay?"

"Yeah." A pause. "Pretty tetchy at having missed out on meeting with Weisel. Stayed that way for most of the afternoon.

"He can be quite dark at times."

"That why his wife bailed out?"

"A contributing factor." She hesitated, decided to go on. "He became enamored with someone. Jack. It was all very silly."

"Really? Did you ever meet his wife?"

"No."

"He told me she ran off with the editor of a rival newspaper."

"She did. Eventually. But it was his own stupid fault. He told her about the other woman."

"About the affair?"

"There was no affair. Didn't happen."

"You've lost me."

"Guilt, Jack. His conscience got the better of him."

Duggan chewed on that for a moment; then he said, "He thinks the world of you."

"He's a dear, but over-protective."

"Someone at work?"

"A shake of the head, and a glance that spoke volumes.

"You?"

She took a breath, held it for a moment. She hadn't known anything about his infatuation until months after the split-up. It had come as a complete surprise.

"What did you say to him?"

"What could I say?" An uncertain laugh. "It strained things for a while. It's the kind of thing that generally happens to young girls. It happened to me at least twice during my teens."

"Is he over it?"

"I think so."

"He may have been punishing you for causing the break-up of his marriage."

" . . . That never occurred to me." She looked troubled. "I suppose it's possible, in a twisted kind of way."

"Or he may have been testing the water on the off chance you would respond."

"I've never given him any reason to think I might."

"It may also have something to do with the way he's pushed us together. He's been *very* encouraging this end."

"He's talked about me?"

"He told me you were stuck in the same way that I was stuck. There was no suggestion of what he felt, or had felt for you in anything he said. He was quite objective."

She took another audible breath. "I went through a relationship rough spot a couple of years back. David would ring and we'd talk for ages. He may have misconstrued something I said."

"You're an attractive woman, Jane."

"I didn't lead him on, Jack."

"Your confiding in him was a form of intimacy."

"So what's he up to now?"

"If *he* can't have you . . . "

"That's . . . disquieting." She flopped back in her chair. "So how did our mutual *stuckness* happen to come up?"

"We were en route to San Francisco and got to talking. One thing led to another." Their eyes met and held. "I *was* stuck, Jane."

"That's changed?"

"What do you think?"

She stared at him for a moment, then, rising, she leaned across the breakfast things so that they could kiss. After a moment or two she drew back slightly. "Elspeth says you're okay."

"Elspeth is a woman of discrimination."

"Has my father said anything to you?"

"Not much. He said you were more contented than he'd seen you for some time. He seemed relieved."

A non-committal smile. "He approves of you ."

"I'm more interested in what you think."

"Elspeth says I'm smitten."

"Are you?"

A searching look. "You know I am."

They kissed again and the crockery rattled. She surfaced laughing. "This is ridiculous!"

"Cue Elspeth," he said back.

"She's staying out of our hair."

"By arrangement?"

"Good sense."

Pulling away, he came round the table to her. When they came together again he could feel the warm contours of her body through the silk dressing gown.

"I think I'd better get dressed," she said, smiling into his face.

"I like you just the way you are."

"That's why I think I'd better get dressed."

"I could take the rest of the day off."

"That would be too blatant."

"Would that matter?"

"It's delicious the way it is."

"There's no arguing with that," he said, intoxicated with the taste and smell of her.

"Then take it as it comes," she said back.

* * *

"Professor Windle?" As James Windle turned, Holly Parks generated her most winsome of smiles. "Could I possibly have a minute of your time?"

"You are?"

"Holly Parks. *Washington Post.*"

"I've nothing more to say than I've already said."

"It's your daughter I want to talk to actually."

Windle blinked down at the smiling face.

"I'd like to interview her if that's possible. About her exhibition."

"Oh, I see," said Windle. "Sorry. I thought . . . "

"If she could spare me . . . half an hour?"

"I'll ask her." A frown, then a question. "Haven't we met before?"

"I was part of the media pack that interviewed you on the street a couple of days ago."

"Ah yes," said Windle. And then, "You were the one wearing pink earmuffs."

"That's right!" Holly's smile was all-encompassing. "I thought you handled things really well."

"Where on earth did you get the idea that my son's passport had been confiscated?"

"I came on to the story with hardly any brief." Holly laughed. "Think of it as a working hypothesis."

Windle smiled in spite of himself, "Is wanting to interview my daughter a working hypothesis?"

"I've moved on. I think everyone has."

Windle stared at Holly for a moment. "When did you decide you wanted to talk to her?"

"Yesterday afternoon around two," was the prompt reply. "Someone you know told me about her newly found fame."

"That someone was?"

"David Mayle?"

"You know David?"

"We worked on the same newspaper a few years back." Holly's smile turned to mild astonishment. "Can you believe we bumped into one another here! In New York! I couldn't believe my eyes."

"Then you found out he knew me."

"You came up after three coffees and a lot of chat."

"That must have been a surprise."

"To say the least." She came back in quickly. "He wouldn't tell me anything. I couldn't get a thing out of him."

"There's nothing to get."

Holly's smile was non committal.

"Where can you be contacted?"

She scribbled the name of her hotel and room number on the back of one of her cards and handed it over. She would be there for another three days, she said, looking up at Windle with blue-green innocence.

"I'll be seeing my daughter this evening," he said, glancing at what she had written.

"Many thanks." Holly extended a slim hand. "I've got to rush off, I'm afraid. An appointment. Thank you for your time."

"You're welcome," he said, watching her turn and walk smartly away.

* * *

A Vatican press-release denying Windle's involvement in the removal of the Ignatius document appeared in US newspapers that very morning. The idea that someone of his standing would stoop so low was unthinkable, the Vatican communiqué said. Professor Windle's reputation was of the highest caliber, the attempt to question his professionalism and impugn his character utterly unwarranted. Although rigorously defended by the Vatican, Windle knew the claim of self-promotion being refuted in the article would stick when all else was forgotten.

"There's no mention of who's responsible for the claim," said Duggan.

"Of course there isn't." Windle tone was gruff. "If they can't get me one way, they'll get me another."

"And there's no mention of Fr Merle."

"They look after their own."

"You really think it's a ploy?"

"I think it likely they've decided to discredit me by any means prior to publishing their take on Theodore's letter."

"Praising you to the heavens is a pretty oblique approach."

"I'm being set up for public disgrace. "

"They categorically deny your involvement."

"But fail to mention that I wasn't in the country when the manuscript went missing. That's the key omission, Jack. Without that small fact up front their belief in me is purely academic."

The more Duggan thought about it, the more he found himself in agreement with Windle. The press release seemed wholesome enough, straightforward enough, but it subtly undermined Windle at the same time as it vindicated him. Concentrating on the denial, the writer of the piece had cleverly masked the facts and emphasized the very negative the press release was supposed to counteract.

"Your response will be?"

"If I respond I'm dead in the water."

"The press will badger you to respond."

"I don't mean that I won't respond, just that I won't respond the way they want me to." The big man smiled. "They'll expect me to come out guns blazing. I won't. I'll simply point out that Fr Merle and I were not in the country when the document went missing. It'll be Fr Merle this and Fr Merle that until they're fed up hearing the name of the saintly Fr Merle."

"Innocence by association."

"It's the only defense I have." Windle drew breath and changed direction. "Has David mentioned anything to you about a Holly Parks?"

"No."

"She's a journalist. She approached me in the foyer this morning. Seems she had coffee and a long chat with David yesterday afternoon. She wants to interview Jane. She was one of the pack that interviewed me outside the hotel."

"You think she's snooping?"

"It's likely; she's with the *Washington Post*. Worked with David in Frisco years ago."

"What's she like?"

"Blonde. Good on her feet."

"She's using Jane as an excuse."

"I'd put a small bet on it."

Duggan paused. "What do you suggest we do?"

"Wait until David mentions her."

"And if he doesn't?"

"I'm sure he will." Said quickly, and with confidence. "She admitted to not getting anything out of him. I challenged her interest in Jane. She looked me straight in the eye and said she had moved on from me to her."

"Plausible."

"You think so?"

They talked on about Holly Parks, then about the work in hand; then almost irritably Windle said, "I don't know why David's here, Jack. There's nothing he can do but sit around."

"It makes him feel part of what's going on."

" . . . I appreciate that, but he isn't needed and he must realize that."

"I think he realizes it only too well. I think that's why he was in such a bad mood."

"Then why come?"

"Fear of redundancy?"

"He knows how grateful I am to him. Finding you was a stroke of genius."

"You've told him that?"

"In as many words."

"Tell him again."

Windle studied Duggan for a moment. "He's jealous of you?"

"He was the center of things before I turned up."

"He found you."

"Journalist and Greek specialist doesn't generally come in the same package. It's a wonder he mentioned me at all."

"Ah," said Windle.

They sat pondering that for a moment.

"Any idea where he is?"

"Jane said she'd ring him and arrange lunch."

A nod from Windle. He would book a table in the hotel restaurant for that evening. It would give them a chance to tie off a few loose ends. Returning to the question of Mayle's injured sensibilities, he said, "It may be because you and I have so much in common, Jack."

"That's how I read it."

"Should I ask him about the *Washington Post* woman?"

"If you don't he'll wonder why you haven't."

Windle smiled his trepidation. "She's a sexy little thing. Big blue-green eyes. I smell opportunism."

It was possible David had suggested an interview with Jane, Duggan said, weighing up the possibilities. Or he may just have mentioned her in passing.

"And she decides to use it as an intro to get to me."

"Or she intends to augment the original story with a little family seasoning." Duggan laughed. " She could be after a Pulitzer."

"Lovely little butt," said Windle, remembering the backview of Holly as she walked away. "She uses everything she's got, and then some."

"You'd think David would be in a better mood."

"Maybe he smells trouble." said Windle.

16

Holly go-lightly

"Wasn't I supposed to phone you?"

"I'm back in Washington Thursday." A smile from Holly Parks. "I didn't come up with the goods. Did I?"

They were sitting in a high-backed cubicle eating Thai food. Holly had ordered an expensive bottle of wine. She was partial to a good red herself, she said, when he commented on her choice

"I'm sorry I couldn't help out with Windle," he said after a moment. "There wasn't really anything I could do."

"I talked to him this morning," she said, glancing at him as if over spectacles. "He's very nice."

Mayle stopped eating and stared at her.

"He said he would talk to his daughter on my behalf, but I don't think he will."

"You mentioned me?"

"I said we'd bumped into one another. That we'd had coffee together. That you'd mentioned his daughter and that I'd got interested." Holly was frowning. "You have a problem with that?"

" . . . No."

"Why the long face?"

"What was his reaction?"

"Surprise." Holly laughed to herself. "He was suddenly quite attentive."

"You aren't interested in his daughter."

"Yes I am. She's a celebrity in her own right, *and* she's Windle's daughter. I can do something with that."

"It won't get you what you want."

"I'll play it absolutely straight, David."

"I should have guessed."

"I haven't done anything except my job." Holly's look was

earnest. "I wasn't kidding about having to return to Washington."

"It would be better all round if you did."

"That's unfair!"

"Not from where I'm sitting."

"Have you seen this morning's papers? Windle's accused of being a publicity hound."

"The piece I read vindicated him."

"I think the term is 'damned by faint praise'."

"Hardly faint."

"Try feigned."

Mayle stopped eating and sat back. "You've met him. Is that how he comes across?"

"No."

"Well, then. . ."

"Well then what?"

"Well then leave him alone for Chrissakes!"

It was Holly's turn to stare. "It isn't a vendetta, David. I'm not after his blood."

"What are you after?"

"The truth?"

"Huh," said Mayle.

"Don't be unfair. I could be of help in this."

"Why would you want to help Windle?"

"I didn't say I wanted to, I said I could. It's up to you what happens next."

"That sounds like blackmail."

"Silence signifies guilt in a courtroom."

"So what's he guilty of?" asked Mayle. "He wasn't even in the country when the damned thing went missing!"

"He could have arranged to have it removed."

"That's preposterous. There's no precedent for thinking Windle would do something like that!"

"He's known to be a bit of a hothead."

"He speaks his mind; there's a difference."

"He's thought of as arrogant in some quarters."

"He's bright. He's made enemies."

"He's being targeted. Why?"

"I'd have thought that obvious."

"Not to me."

"He's in a sensitive area of research, Holly. He tells it as it is, as it was. There are those who'd prefer sleeping dogs to remain asleep."

"The document he found is said to contradict Church teaching."

"Augments would be a better description."

"It's been written off by Vatican specialists as something cobbled together in the fourth century."

"That surprises you?"

She sat back, elbow on wrist, her mouth shielded by the fingers of her right hand. When she spoke, it was to say that she had been brought up Catholic, but that she hadn't been inside a church in years.

"You're no longer a believer?"

"I'm no longer interested in trying to believe."

He frowned his incomprehension.

"It doesn't work for me." An innocence that was not manufactured surfaced. "It's probably just me."

"It's probably just a lot of people."

She smiled at his offer of absolution. "I think I'm what used to be referred to as a reprobate."

An unnerving thought occurred to Mayle in that moment - Holly Parks might actually be of use. He smothered the thought and said: "There's probably a belief gene."

"That would explain predestination."

He smiled his appreciation.

"Were you ever religious?"

"I flirted with the evangelicals when I was young. Didn't last. I'm not the happy-clappy type."

"No, you aren't," she agreed.

After a sip of wine he surprised both her and himself by saying that an honestly written article in the *Post* might not do Windle any harm.

"You've changed your mind?"

"Options are always of interest."

"You were saying only a moment ago that everyone would be better off if I left town!"

"Collaring Windle like that was a provocative act. He would have seen through you at a glance."

"He was supposed to." Holly's look was one of quizzical incomprehension. "What did you expect me to do, David? Sit on my fanny?"

Mayle forked a piece of chicken into his mouth and chewed on it. Then, in a more conciliatory tone he said, "I'll talk to Windle this evening. But I can't promise anything."

"I'm obliged, David," she said back. Then, "What's the daughter like?"

He stopped chewing to think about that. "Very much the individual. Talented."

"And the other guy with them in the Astoria a couple of nights back?" Holly's smile was restrained. "The one with cropped hair?"

"You were hanging around the Astoria?"

"I was a having a meal in their esteemed restaurant."

Mayle smiled. "I'm surprised you didn't collar Windle there and then.".

"I was working. An interview."

"A colleague."

"Miss Frizz is the daughter?"

A nod from Mayle.

"Couldn't keep his eyes off her. The colleague. Windle was quite animated."

"That's the kind of man he is."

"He was very restrained this morning."

"You accosted him."

She looked away laughing, looked back, "You really will speak to him on my behalf?"

"I said I would."

"What made you change your mind?"

"The look in your eye," he said back.

* * *

Robert Carter's next attack came in the form of a late-evening television broadcast during which he savaged a Protestant theologian for advocating free will theism. Free will theism was the result of libertarian thinking, he said, identifying what to him was the principal weakness in his antagonist's argument. Libertarian thinking imagined a God who could not know everything because the human will was intrinsically free - to know in advance what a human being was about to do was thought to annul that freedom. Carter objected and counteracted with the argument that humans were undoubtedly free, but in terms of how they lived their lives it was a freedom contingent on the vicissitudes of fashion and whim, therefore not free in the sense that libertarians believed. With that as his premise, he then scornfully set about the business of dismantling his opponent's claim that God was limited in his predictive powers. So virulent was the attack that bits of the program become prime-time news items the following day.

Of more interest to Duggan, however, was Mayle's announcement that he had just had lunch with Holly Parks. He appeared mid-afternoon with a red-wine look about him.

"I thought you were having lunch with Jane?"

"Was I supposed to?"

"She was going to ring you this morning."

"Holly rang first thing. I went out not long after."

Duggan nodded, waited.

"I think she could be useful." He corrected himself. "I didn't think so to begin with, but I do now."

"How much have you told her?" Asked with all the innocence

Duggan could muster.

"Next to nothing," said Mayle. Then as his wits came on line, "Nothing at all, Jack. I'm not an idiot!"

"What do you have in mind."

"Back-up. She could be useful if things get rough."

"She'd play along?"

"If she thought there was something in it for her. She's ambitious."

"Having the *Washington Post* on side would certainly be useful. She can be trusted?"

"Within reason."

Mayle's reply elicited a smile from Duggan. "I believe she used to work with you?"

"Jumped ship after three years. Straight to the *Washington Post* like a bee to nectar. We were sorry to see her go." A second correction. "Well, not all of us. Some found her a little threatening."

"How's she shaped up?"

"Professional, and very canny."

"And cute, from what I've heard."

"Oh yes, *and* cute." Mayle's smile took on a lascivious edge. "She has the look of the eternally young." His expression became a grimace. "I felt guilty talking to her even though I had nothing to feel guilty about. "

"You're beginning to sound like a good Catholic."

"Holly's Catholic."

"That might not be to our advantage."

"She's dumped it."

"You discussed religion?"

"A bit. That's what gave me the idea she might be of use - that and the fact that we need someone out there looking after our interests. She'll need a tit-bit or two to keep her on side of course."

"Like what?"

"Rome? We can't dig in that area without being noticed. She can. She'd be the perfect cover. She will of course want to interview

Windle at some point."

"He may refuse."

"I told her that." Mayle rambled on. "Don't get me wrong, Jack, Holly's a nice kid. She's ambitious, but she's not dishonest. She's just . . . tenacious?" His laugh had the past in it. "When she gets her teeth into something . . . "

"We'll feed her with an eye-dropper." Duggan decided to be frank. "My editor will crucify me if a slip of a girl edges me out of this."

"There's story enough for two."

"She'll want to profile Windle."

"We can't stop her doing that."

"The monastery bit is *mine*, David."

It was the first time Mayle had sensed the steel in Duggan. "Of course," he said. He moved on. "I'd better ring Jane."

"We're eating here at seven. Okay with you?"

A "Yup" from Mayle. Then a question that took Duggan by surprise. "How's it going with you two?"

"I've seen hardly anything of her since I arrived." Duggan waved a hand vaguely at the table. "*That* has taken up most of my time."

"Things are okay?"

"They're fine. Coffee?"

A nod. "How far have you got with the translation?"

"I'm pretty well through the first draft."

"James behaving himself?"

A quizzical glance from Duggan.

"He lives very much in a world of his own."

"Don't we all."

"I think you'll find Jane takes after her father."

Duggan wondered what Mayle was getting at.

"Her perceptions are sometimes idiosyncratic."

"I haven't noticed that trait in Windle."

"You haven't been around him long enough."

"If you mean he moves fast mentally, I'll give you that."

"He can be quite hurtful at times."

"He thinks the world of you, David."

"I'm useful."

The Russian doll quality of Mayle's words was not lost on Duggan; he waited to see where Mayle would go next.

"He couldn't have been very pleased with what was in this morning's papers."

"He saw it as an attempt to sully his name."

"That was Holly's impression."

"You discussed the article?"

"Peripherally."

Duggan hesitated. "She could be trouble, David."

"Out there on her own she would be trouble." Mayle smiled his second smile of the afternoon. "I'm beginning to think I should have stayed in Frisco."

"I think it's just as well you didn't."

Later, when he was alone, Duggan stood by the windows and watched a flock of pigeons weave an erratic dance in the space between the buildings. As he watched, a bird of prey dropped into the center of the wheeling flock. Wings closed one second, it wheeled round the next and clamped its talons onto the body of its victim, its wings thrashing the air for lift, its prey flapping helplessly in its grasp.

* * *

Archbishop Donaghue's letter to Bob Carter came straight to the point. Preserving the religious status quo would always be one of his priorities, he said, acknowledging the need to hold the barque of Christ steady in a mad, bad world. But you could not equate the denial of love relations in a family with serving the best interests of Christ's Church. CNCD's argument that love given to another was love denied Christ, or God, was just about as ludicrous a piece of reasoning as he had ever come across. The movement may have the

Holy Father's general approval, but given the nonsensical nature of that pronouncement, it was unlikely His Holiness would have gone along with what was being perpetrated in his name. On the basis of this fact he had decided to intervene in favor of Fr Brentano, the priest who had complained about the movement's missionaries, and would be writing to Rome for further guidance on the matter. Pleased with himself for taking what he saw as a principled stand, Donaghue signed his letter with a flourish, sealed it, and placed it in his out tray.

* * *

"Is taking her on board advisable?" Windle's question was directed at Mayle. "I must admit to not being happy with the idea, David."

"Better that her instincts are used on our behalf."

They were sitting in the lounge area of the Astoria's grand bar. Jane had ordered an exotic cocktail.

"What do you think, Jack?" asked Windle.

"She's got resources and she's smart. If she starts nosing around it'll look natural. She could be useful."

"I should let her interview me?"

"Yes, I think so. But I'd want to discuss parameters with you."

"When do I get to meet this little hustler?" Jane's tone was playful, but there was an edge to what followed "She's got you all on the hop."

"Hardly," said Mayle.

"She can have an hour tomorrow afternoon," said Windle, deciding. And then, "Will she still want to interview Jane?"

"I'll ask," said Mayle.

"I'd want her to interview Jane as well. She could perhaps do that first. In the morning."

A nod from Mayle.

Their drinks arrived. Jane lifted her bedecked cocktail and smiled at Duggan through fruit and plastic accoutrements.

"I'll ring Holly later and set things up," said Mayle.

"Fr Merle still hasn't been in touch?" asked Duggan.

Windle shook his head.

"Did he voice any misgivings before you parted?"

"His silence was eloquent testimony to how he felt."

"They may have shut him up."

"That's unlikely. He's not the kind of man you can easily bully."

"If he accepts the Church's line that heretics have no legitimate voice then the whole thing's a foregone conclusion."

"He's a complex individual," said Windle.

"He's a priest," said Duggan.

"He's also a scholar with a reputation to safeguard. He'll find a way round the problem."

"You mean he'll obfuscate."

Tread carefully is how I'd put it. Catholic scholars like Merle have to safeguard tradition at the same time as they force the Church to abandon some of its more idiotic ideas."

"You badly need his support."

"His having been at Mar Saba is support enough."

"Not if they silence him."

"I try to give human beings the benefit of the doubt, Jack."

Duggan felt reprimanded.

"Merle could be Holly's starter," said Mayle.

"Not suitable," said Windle. "Better that she use her wits on the question of what Rome is up to."

* * *

Fr Brentano ordered the New Catholic Dawn's missionaries to leave his parish that same evening - the furore had been such that he had been forced to exercise his priestly authority. Donaghue was informed within the hour.

"If only you had waited!"

"I had no way of knowing Your Grace's thoughts on the matter."

"How ironic." Donaghue drew breath. "I will need a full explanation in writing."

"You will have it, Your Grace."

"And a complete breakdown of everything said and done by these nincompoops."

"Yes, Your Grace."

A sigh from Donaghue. "They'll try to make something out of the fact that you jumped the gun."

"They?" said Brentano.

"Those in favor of the movement. Direct any communication you have with them back to me. Do you understand?"

"Yes, Your Grace."

"And keep away from the press!"

"Yes, Your Grace."

"That's all, Fr Brentano. May the Lord go with you."

"And with you, Your Grace."

On returning the telephone to its cradle, Donaghue sat rock still and considered his position. His rebuff of Carter would produce a reaction, of that he was certain, and his letter to Fr Brentano, although carefully worded, would further complicate matters. But what had he to fear? The notion that all natural affection had to be severed so that one might wholly love God was, to say the least, idiosyncratic. And the attendant notion that emotional involvement between married couples was of little importance was equally odd. Affection between human beings was fundamental to the smooth working of society, as was love between husband and wife. So on the basis of what kind of theology did these people justify their thinking? And why hadn't he heard more about them prior to their appearance on Brentano's patch? Carter had spoken highly of the movement while helping to set up the Santa Rosa conference, but as he was now exhibiting the same elitist attitudes, and had, since the conference, admitted to being a long-standing member of CNCD, the only conclusion possible was that the Children of the New Catholic Dawn were acting outside of their pontifical brief. Good

Catholics they may be, superb Catholics they may be, but there was a marked difference between upholding the great truths of the Church and using those truths to bemuse and abuse others. Truth was not a weapon, it was revelation, and the sooner they were reminded of that fact the better.

* * *

"I've got an in." Holly Parks reached for her drink. She was standing at the window 39 floors up in the Marriot-Marquis Hotel in Times Square; it was a corner room and larger than most. "I got lucky."

"Yeh, of course you did." Her editor's laugh was all-knowing. "What's Windle like?"

"Dishy." She took another sip of whisky. "There's also a daughter who paints. I've to interview her first."

"How the hell did you swing that?"

"There's a journalist from Frisco in tow. I worked with him years ago. He helped talk Windle round."

"What's he doing there?"

"He's a friend of Windle's."

"He doesn't mind you stepping in?"

"He's using me."

"To what end?"

"To help take the pressure off Windle."

"You've agreed to play along?"

"What do you think?"

Max Spearman knew exactly what to think.

Holly rang off soon afterwards and stood gazing out over Manhattan, the illuminated skyscrapers glittering like sculpted spikes against the black backdrop of the not-so-faraway river. It *was* Mayle's intention to use her, she knew that. But things hardly ever worked out the way people intended - life, as she had discovered again and again, was full of surprises.

17

Life's a Bitch

Dr Hubert Weisel's body was found in an alleyway off Fifth Avenue at 6am on the Thursday; there was sufficient bruising about the man's face and neck for the police to conclude that he had been attacked. The question, however, was what had killed him. As Windle's hotel and room number were found neatly inscribed on a piece of paper in the man's pocket, Homicide was at the Astoria within the hour.

The two detectives who turned up were Lieutenant Marcelo and Detective Mendelsohn. The lieutenant was a small, thickset man, his offsider lean and almost six feet in height. Marcelo did most of the talking to start with, but it quickly became apparent to Windle that they were practiced interviewers.

"You met with Dr Weisel here on Sunday?"

"That's correct. "

"Why was he here?"

A sigh from Windle. "He admired my work and wanted to meet me, poor man. I'm a historian. He —- "

"Had you met before?"

"No. Never."

"Where was he from?"

"He was a senior lecturer at the University of Geneva. You don't have his passport?"

"Wasn't on him," said Marcelo.

"He was Swiss?" asked Mendelsohn.

"I think so," said Windle. "It's difficult to say for sure, we spoke English from the moment he arrived."

"How long were you together?"

"Most of the day. He left by taxi for JFK around six. "

"Was anyone else present?"

"My daughter and a colleague. Dr Duggan will be here any minute. He and my daughter are in New York temporarily. As I am. I flew in from Germany only a few days ago. I'm a Research Fellow at the University of Essen."

"When are you scheduled to return?"

"I was hoping to leave on Monday."

Lieutenant Marcelo's smile suggested a change of plan. "The others live here in New York?"

"No. My daughter's come in from Ohio. Dr Duggan is an Australian. Sydney. He's here at my invitation."

The questioning went back to Windle's left. "Dr Weisel seemed okay while he was with you?"

"Very much so. We had a very pleasant afternoon together."

"When did he first contact you?"

"About . . . ten days ago. He rang from London."

"He rang you in Germany?"

"Yes."

"How did he know to ring you there?"

"It's not difficult if you're in the academic loop."

Marcelo came back in. "He travelled to New York specifically to meet up with you?"

"If you're asking what else he did while he was here, I have absolutely no idea."

"If he was carrying his passport, then it's a goner," said Mendelsohn. "He was stripped of cash and credit cards."

Windle shook his head in disbelief. "I know nothing at all about the man other than that he had read some of my papers and wanted to meet with me. That's the only information I have."

"The others were present?" asked Marcelo.

Windle said that Dr. Duggan was working daily with him on a project - hence his imminent arrival - and that his daughter, whom he had not seen for months, had, on that particular day, decided to tag along. She and Dr Duggan were staying with a friend. As his meeting with Dr Weisel had been informal, their being there had not been a problem.

"Did he have any luggage with him?"

"A briefcase. That's all."

"And you think he headed straight for JFK?"

"That was my understanding. But I suppose he must have had luggage to pick up some where."

"You saw him off?"

"We said goodbye here in this room."

"And that was the last time you saw him?"

"Yes," said Windle.

Slipping his keycard into the slot, Duggan waited for the green light to flash. As he entered the room Windle got to his feet. "It's okay, Jack," he said, raising a palm. "These gentlemen are detectives. Something *awful* has happened."

The news of Weisel's death left Duggan feeling sick, and not a little on guard. He knew Windle would have avoided mentioning the photographs, but what else had he avoided?

The questioning started immediately. He batted his replies back hoping each time that he hadn't committed a faux pas.

"You thought he was heading for the airport?" said Marcelo. "That's what Professor Windle led us to understand when we arrived."

"He obviously didn't come all the way from London just to see Professor Windle for a few hours," said Mendelsohn. "He must have had other business to attend to in New York."

"One would think so," said Duggan.

"Did you know he'd be here?" asked Mendelsohn.

"Yes. Professor Windle mentioned that he'd be here," said Duggan.

"In what context?" said Mendelsohn.

"A fellow academic passing through?" said Duggan, hoping that that would suffice.

"How did he seem? Was he in good spirits?"

"Cool as a cucumber is how I would describe him. He was a very precise individual. Small, neat, and precise. He talked about Professor Windle's work with great admiration."

"So he didn't seem worried about anything?"

Duggan frowned at Mendelsohn's question.

"It looks like he was mugged, but you never know," said the Lieutenant.

"What we want to find out is who he met and spoke to besides yourselves," said Mendelsohn.

"And where he was holed up," said Marcelo.

"You've checked the major hotels?" asked Duggan.

"That's being done as we speak."

"The most likely explanation for his death is a heart attack," said Mendelsohn. "He'd been roughed up, but that's unlikely to have killed him."

"Will there be an autopsy?" asked Windle.

"I expect so," said Marcelo.

Duggan winced at the thought of Weisel undergoing the indignity of a postmortem.

"You're an Australian?" asked Mendelsohn.

"Yup.".

"Dr Duggan's a specialist in early sixth-century Greek texts," said Windle. "He's helping me with a project."

Both detectives stared at Duggan with renewed interest. Then Marcelo said to Windle that they'd need to speak to his daughter. Windle went immediately to where his jacket was hanging, retrieved his address book and handed it to Marcelo open at the requisite page. The lieutenant produced a mobile, but Jane was busy being interviewed by Holly Parks and there was no response.

"We'll go to her," said Mendelsohn. "Got an address?"

"I'll write it out for you," said Windle. He retrieved his diary and headed for the table to get pen and paper. "What shall I say if she rings here?"

"Tell her to stay put. Or ring us," said Marcelo. He produced a card and handed it to Duggan. "Only use the precinct number if you can't get through on the other."

"We'll get back to you on this," said Mendelsohn. A glance at his partner and half-smile. "Sorry to have been the bearer of such bad news."

"It's too bizarre to take in," said Windle.

"Life's a bitch and then you die," said the lieutenant.

Jane, too, was stunned by the news. She listened as her father rattled off what could and what could not be said, then asked what he intended to do about his interview with Holly.

"It goes ahead as planned."

"And when she finds out about Weisel?"

"I'll handle that."

"You'll tell her?"

"Better that it comes from us direct. It's unlikely she'll jump to any outlandish conclusions then."

"How's Jack taken it?"

"How do you think? He's devastated."

"What happens now?"

"You wait for the arrival of the police."

"Should I say you 'phoned?"

"Yes, but don't mention my using the Bentleys' line. They'll wonder why I didn't suggest that."

Windle rang off and turned to Duggan. "We've got two hours before Holly turns up."

"You'll tell her about Weisel?"

"I'll have to. She'd find out and wonder why I didn't. Safer to tell her than not tell her."

"She does sound like a right little hustler."

"Then let's hope we can make her *our* little hustler," he said back.

* * *

It was as if time had been suspended; everything slowed. Duggan went to his place at the table and attempted to take up where he had left off, but nothing seemed real - Dr Weisel was dead and their little world had all but stopped spinning. When Holly Parks arrived he was absent and there was nothing on the table to suggest industry. She glanced around with approval and concluded that Windle wasn't short of a dollar. A separate bedroom and a well-appointed lounge with a large corner window said it all.

"Nice," she said.

Windle smiled, but said nothing.

"It's good of you to see me."

Holly's two-piece suit was expensively tailored and traditional in cut, her coat dark brown and fur-collared - it was a far cry from slacks, anorak and pink ear-muffs, and it was not lost on Windle.

When they were seated, Windle said straight out that events had overtaken them. He explained about Dr Weisel and she stared at him in stunned silence. They were, he said, in a state of shock.

"If this got out . . . "

"I've been assured that won't happen. It's got nothing to do with us. Poor man just happened to be in the wrong place at the wrong time."

"Where do I fit in?"

"That's up to you," said Windle. "We'll handle the basic story when it breaks - the text and its significance. You might be interested in tracking down those attempting to discredit me. We have reason to believe there's a Vatican faction out to discredit both the text and myself."

"You think they were involved in its disappearance?"

"I think that's an unlikely scenario, but who knows," said Windle,"

"It's such an important text?"

"It confirms suspicions about the nature of early Christianity." A smile from Windle. "Things weren't as theologically tidy in the early centuries as some would have us believe. The early Church is suspected of having been Jewish sectarian, not 'Christian' in any sense that Christians today would understand."

"That's what this is all about?"

"It's *part* of what it's about."

"That alone would cause an upset?"

"It doesn't take much to ruffle feathers in this area. The merest tweak to the tail of consensus thinking and they come out flailing."

"Yes, but —-"

"Until Rome lifts its embargo, that's about all I can say. I'm bound by protocol. We all have our masters."

"What's to stop me pursuing this on my own? I could, you know. I've got the resources."

"You wouldn't have access to myself *or* Fr Merle."

"I don't like the idea of being tied to someone's coattails."

"No more than we like having a *Washington Post* journalist breathing down our necks. Truth is, we need you as much as you need us. If the tabloid press found out about Weisel's visit to me they'd come out with a storm of nonsense. I would need someone like yourself to take up cudgels on my behalf. It's a trade-off pure and simple."

"You're being very frank."

"Would you have it any other way?"

She observed him as she would have done something behind glass. "You expect this faction to take the gloves off at some point?"

"They'll have no option."

"You seem very sure about that."

"I know how they go about things when pressed."

"You don't know me at all."

"That I can rectify," said Windle.

* * *

They got together that evening in Windle's hotel room and had their meals sent up. Elspeth had been full of questions, Jane said, picking at some curried chicken. One interrogation had followed another and she wasn't sure what her host had made of her explanation.

"I rang the Bentleys the moment the police left, and got George," Windle said for Mayle's benefit. "It was lucky Jane had her mobile switched off." He glanced at Duggan. "Jack managed to flannel his way through without arousing suspicion."

"It's not an experience I'd wish to repeat," said Duggan.

"How was it with Holly?"

Mayle's question was directed at Jane..

"I liked her. She seemed genuinely interested in my work. I didn't expect that."

"Did she mention your father?"

"Only that she was interviewing him later in the day." A smile from Jane. "She's going to use my publicity photographs from the exhibition for her article."

For a brief moment it was as if things were normal again. That moment passed.

"Being upfront about Weisel gave me the edge," said Windle. "I think it was the right thing to do."

Mayle was sitting forward, elbows on knees, his hands dangling. "She's clever enough to suspect a connection between Weisel and the codex. Was there any indication of that?"

"None," said Windle.

"She's got nothing to go on," said Duggan.

"Did she ask any questions about Weisel?"

"Not one."

"Are the police aware of your involvement with the codex?"

"I don't know. They might be. They didn't say."

Mayle's questions continued. "So what did he do in New York besides meeting with you?"

A shrug from Windle.

"Strikes me as naive of him to have contacted you the way he did. At first, that is. He didn't know for certain there would be something for you to find at Mar Saba."

"He accepted that he'd been a touch naive," said Duggan.

"But why give the impression he was about to fly out that

evening when he had no intentions of doing anything of the kind?"

"He obviously changed his mind," said Windle. There was a weariness about his reply, a tiredness. "People do that kind of thing."

"He must have had some other reason for being here," said Mayle, continuing to worry at the problem.

"Couldn't you have met more easily in London?" said Duggan. "Why trail all the way to New York?"

"I said when I'd be in New York and he said straight off that he'd meet me there. Here." A pause. "It was convenient for me."

"He could just as easily have flown to Germany," said Mayle.

"Okay," said Windle. "So we don't know what he was up to. If anything. I think we should leave this to the police."

Duggan pushed his plate aside. "I agree," he said. "It's Fr Merle we should be concentrating on. Where did you two meet?"

"At a conference in Paris about ten years ago. I found him intriguing. He has a very unusual mind."

"He was presented to us as an authority on Platonic and neo-Platonic mysticism," said Duggan. "I studied him while doing my Ph.D"

"He has a very fine grasp of how the early Christians thought and behaved," said Windle. "That's become his specialty, his pet endeavor. He's been criticized for being too lenient on the Gnostics."

"So where's he's hiding out?" asked Mayle.

"In a monastery somewhere, I suspect," said Windle.

"Was it his intention to go into Retreat the moment he got back?" asked Duggan.

"I don't think so."

"Could he be being held incommunicado?"

"It's my guess he's biding his time, waiting for the right moment to surface."

"They can hold someone incommunicado?" said Jane.

"They have the right to demand silence of a priest or theologian if they think they're jeopardizing the faith," said Duggan. "They locked Hans Kung up for God knows how long."

"How can anyone in their right mind put up with such nonsense?"

"It's a contract," said Duggan. "If you change your mind, it's just your bad luck."

"Bishop Peters isn't putting up with it," said Mayle.

"Bishop Peters is about to run out of steam," said Duggan. "It's only a matter of time."

18

Water off a Duck's Back

Fr Brentano clasped his hands and waited for the archbishop to continue; Donaghue was clearly agitated. When he spoke again, it was in a low, grinding tone. Who in their right mind would say that marriage was an inferior state to that of the priesthood? Marriage was a sacrament! It was a blessed state. A whole society practicing celibacy would be disobeying God's command to go forth and multiply.

Brentano was specific in his reply. The New Catholic Dawn were in danger of negating their Catholic heritage, he said. Some of their ideas verged on the heretical.

"Your report is deeply disturbing, Father."

"Some of it is straight from the horse's mouth."

"And the rest?"

"Partly from those in my congregation who have reported the movement as a disruptive influence, and from making some enquiries of my own. Everything seems to hinge on their notion of what is, and what is not, authentically Catholic. In the light of their new-fangled vision, they've accused other Catholic organizations of not being authentically Catholic - particularly in the realm of education. Of more immediate concern, Your Grace, are their methods of recruitment. Basically, the difference between them and other Catholic organizations is that CNCD rites are performed behind closed doors - transparency of rite is considered *modernist*. Individuals are psychologically assaulted in private, coerced into the movement with an avalanche of disciplinary demands that undermine confidence and disallow the individual's right to choose freely. They subject would-be members to brutal scrutinies and group confessions."

"There must be a high attrition rate."

"There is; at least there was. They're more careful now, but their aim remains control of the individual. Their policy, ultimately, is that individuals sell their goods, detach themselves from husband, wife and children, and devote themselves to the movement's needs and aspirations. That may sound like the early Church in action, but it isn't really. In the form CNCD have developed, it's enslavement, and it's more often than not brought about by stealth and cunning. 'Cunning' is described as a virtue to be practiced because of Jesus' injunction to be *as cunning as foxes.*"

"You can't be serious!"

"It was explained to me without a blush that everyone has to be rescued from the Devil. On the basis of that insight members are encouraged to achieve their end by deception if deception is deemed necessary."

The archbishop remained silent; his expression spoke for him.

"Total commitment to the movement is demanded. To offset the possibility of failure - there's a trial period of one year followed by two years in a CNCD school. That in turn is followed by two years in a community where temporary vows of poverty, chastity and obedience are taken. These vows are renewed yearly for five or more years until final vows are taken." Brentano's delivery was flat and emotionless. "The most interesting aspect of it all, Your Grace, is that they deny being a movement. They refer to themselves as a *service.* I presume because a 'service' does not require approval or examination."

"That in itself is a form of deception."

"Exactly, Your Grace. The movement has achieved complete autonomy in spite of its dubious character. So the question is, how? Rome must be aware of what's going on."

"What was Bishop Harrier's reaction when you first voiced your concerns?"

"Puzzlement. He said that CNCD had the approval of the appropriate ecclesiastical authorities and that I was perhaps 'overreacting to their very disciplined approach to the faith'. I'm quoting. When I suggested there was more to the faith than discipline, he got angry with me."

"It must have sounded as if you were questioning his judgment."

"I gave him every respect, Your Grace."

"What were his instructions?"

"To give the movement's missionaries a second chance. It was after all yourself who had initially opened the door to them. Everything would sort itself out in the end, I was assured."

"You followed Bishop Harrier's instructions?"

"To the letter, Your Grace. I called an extraordinary meeting of those disenchanted with the missionaries sent to us and asked them to be patient. After about an hour's discussion they agreed to give CNCD a second chance."

"But it didn't work out."

"I'm afraid not, Your Grace. If anything, the two missionaries we were dealing with became even more belligerent."

Aware that he was dealing with a situation that could easily backfire on him, Donaghue said that CNCD had been described to him as part of the new evangelization policy put together to counteract the dechristianisation of modern society. An earlier incarnation had had John Paul II's blessing, and as far as he could make out, Benedict XVI was also in favor.

Brentano's response was again specific. CNCD was not just one movement, he said, it was hydra headed. It had its own network of priests and even a sprinkling of bishops. At the last bishops' conference in Rome some disgruntled bishops had voiced concern over priests whose vocation had developed in the context of a particular movement. The charge had been that some movements were building their own parallel hierarchies. CNCD had been mentioned in that context.

"You're very well informed, Father."

Fr Brentano did not immediately reply, then with a note of challenge he said, "I don't think Rome cares where it gets its priests from as long as it gets them. From what I can make out, Your Grace,

Rome is turning a blind eye to CNCD and its offshoots."

"Your source for that extraordinary suggestion?"

"My brother, Your Grace. He's presently studying at the Gregorian University in Rome. He moves in exalted company."

"I wasn't aware you had a brother."

"He's the bright one, Your Grace. He'll make a very fine priest some day."

Donaghue was impressed; two priests in the one family was a sacrifice of some proportion. Smiling, he remarked on this, then proceeded to enlarge on what he had said before about the movement's conceived role. According to his sources, CNCD's aggressive missionary activities were proving effective in combating the secularization of Europe, not to mention the Protestant advance, and as its adherents professed complete obedience to Peter's throne, it stood in direct contrast to other groups within the Church. As it was also a rapidly growing source of vocations, and a staunch supporter of traditional teaching, it was, to put not to fine a point on it, the answer to any pope's prayers.

"Not to mine it isn't," said Brentano.

Donaghue smiled at the priest's unconscious effrontery. "Rome has to deal with the larger picture, Father."

"They almost destroyed my parish, Your Grace."

"It may only be a case of over-zealousness."

"Being over-zealous is their hallmark, Your Grace.

"You can't know that for certain."

"I know it firsthand, Your Grace. First impression is that they are there to assist and support. That changes almost immediately. Anyone who gets in their way is brutally pushed aside. Their principal method of communication is confrontation, their aim, dominance. This seems to be their style wherever they are."

"Yes, but – "

"They've been carefully schooled, Your Grace. You can tell that from their parrot-like responses. And they've been taught to distrust and ignore *all* emotion - that distorts just about everything they say and think. Hence their rather odd theological notions, notions you yourself are uncomfortable with." Brentano paused, then he said what he believed had to be said. "They think of themselves as the embodiment of a perfect society, a society that *all* Catholics should be part of. That, Your Grace, is the height of arrogance."

Donaghue chewed on that for a moment, then with characteristic caution he said, "A truly Christian society *would* be a perfect society, Father. Wouldn't it?"

"Of course, Your Grace. I'm not questioning that. What I'm questioning is CNCD's right to be classed as the only legitimate route to that perfect society."

The archbishop blinked at Brentano's forthrightness; that was perhaps to push CNCD claims too far, he said, frowning. Yes, he had qualms about the movement's behavior and attitudes, and not a few questions to ask of the ecclesiastical authorities concerning their sometimes oddball theology, but their unquestioning allegiance to the Holy Father, and their unrelenting energy in a world gone mad, could not be overlooked. Whatever their faults, and they certainly had a few, they were ardent workers for Christ and that had to mean something.

"There's resistance to them within the Vatican itself, Your Grace."

"There's also strong support."

"I have it on good authority that resistance is growing daily."

"That is your brother's verdict?"

"That of those my brother talks to."

"And they are?"

"I'm not permitted to say, Your Grace, but we're apparently in very good company."

Donaghue kept his eyes on Brentano's face. "Watch your step, Father," he said, alarmed by what he was hearing, "and keep me out of your machinations. There are powerful forces at work here, and they should not be underestimated."

"I'm aware of that, Your Grace."

"Complain by all means, but do *not* antagonize. That is I think the best advice I can give you."

Fr Brentano was silent for a moment; then to Donaghue's horror he said, "The Church appears to have spawned it's first officially sanctioned sect, Your Grace."

"I beg your pardon?"

Brentano's expression remained blank, his tone even. "According to my sources CNCD has Cardinal Menenger's blessing."

"I would have thought that unlikely given some of their more bizarre notions. Cardinal Menenger is the Grand Inquisitor, Father, not some New Age lunatic."

"The Catholic community has developed a mind of its own, Your Grace; it is no longer willing to believe for the sake of believing."

"All the more reason to hold to established truth, Father - *that* is the brief I was given by the Holy Father before his death."

"Remove love from the equation, Your Grace, and you remove the heart of the Christian message."

"In spite of appearances, I'm sure that is not the movement's intention, Father. But I assure you, I will look into it."

"If you look deeply enough, Your Grace, I think you may be in for a shock."

Donaghue had been about to rise; he hesitated. "What exactly are you suggesting, Father?"

"The possibility of schism, Your Grace. That's the rumor."

* * *

Lieutenant Marcelo's squat form filled the doorway; he was smiling, but it was a smile lacking in humor. He was alone on this occasion; his partner had a touch of food poisoning, he said. When they were seated, Marcelo came straight to the point. As suspected, Dr Weisel had died as a result of a heart attack brought on by the bashing he had received. All of his valuables - money, credit cards, etc - had been taken. They had even taken his shoes,.

"His shoes?"

"Were they distinctive in any way?"

"Black and shiny that I remember."

"There's still the problem of his luggage. And of course the black leather briefcase he had with him when he visited you."

"I'm afraid I can't help you there."

The lieutenant's eyes strayed across the room. "Your colleague isn't working today?"

"He and my daughter are in town somewhere. It's Jack's first time in New York and he's hardly had a minute to himself."

"He's sightseeing?"

"Not quite how I'd put it, lieutenant. He needed time off. Dr Weisel's death has deeply affected all of us."

Marcelo nodded slowly; he seemed genuinely sympathetic. "Has anything at all occurred to you that you think might help us with our investigations?" he asked. "It's often something small and seemingly unimportant that opens things up."

"It's the same in my field," said Windle. "An interpretation can sometimes hinge on a single word."

"Exactly." Lieutenant Marcello's smile was collusive. "Maybe we should share notes sometime."

Windle laughed not knowing whether the detective was serious or not.

"So nothing comes to mind?"

"Nothing strikes me as useful in the sense you mean," said Windle. "We covered a lot of territory that day."

"I was thinking more in the lines of general conversation. Comments he may have made about his journey. His previous time in New York prior to meeting with you. If he was heading for the airport, how did he end up dead in an alleyway off Fifth Avenue a few days later?"

"That's something I can't help you with."

A pause, then a surprise question. "Did you discuss the document that went missing during your last dig in the Middle East?"

Windle absorbed the detective's skillfully placed question, then offered a correction. "I'm not an archaeologist, Lieutenant. I'm a historian. And I should point out that the Voss edition of the Ignatius Letters went missing *after* Fr Merle and I left the country. Yes, the subject of the missing document did came up, as you would expect, but it was merely one subject among many."

"The guy working with you out there was a priest?"

"Fr Merle is Professor of Ancient History and Semitic Languages. He lectures at the Sorbonne in Paris. We've been on a number of . . . *digs* together."

Lieutenant Marcello's smile was one of feigned confusion laced with humor. "You didn't think we'd be interested in the Palestine thing?"

"I saw no reason to complicate matters. Neither Fr Merle nor I have been accused of anything, Lieutenant. It was a matter of association. We just happened to be the last people to handle the document that went missing. But as we weren't in the country when the damned thing went missing. . . "

"There was a context."

"It would have been an unnecessary complication to mention it."

"I like complications," said the detective. "The more complications there are in a case the greater the chance there is of someone slipping up."

"Or of arriving at an erroneous conclusion," said Windle.

Lieutenant Marcelo smiled his appreciation. "His flight back to London was for 8-30 pm on Thursday the thirtieth of April. He cancelled at 6-20 pm on that day. That was directly after he left here."

"He may have decided to stay on and see something of New York."

"You don't think he would have mentioned that to you?"

Windle remained silent.

"We've talked to the taxi handlers downstairs. They don't remember a little guy in a blue suit freezing his butt off in the taxi queue." A smile. "That's how he arrived. Right? In a suit. No scarf or gloves?"

A nod from Windle.

"He was wearing a green, blanket-lined overcoat when he was found."

"Really?"

"So why wasn't he wearing it the day he met you? It was eight degrees outside. So either he had a car, or someone picked him up."

"I suppose," said Windle."

The lieutenant looked down, then up again. "There's an Interpol alert on the document that went missing *after* you left Palestine, Professor. When we checked you and Dr Duggan out - we had to under the circumstances - it came into play." A frown." Dr Duggan is a journalist?"

Windle absorbed the shock of NYPD thoroughness. "He is also, as I've already said, a specialist in early century Greek texts. It's in that capacity he's engaged here."

"His entry card says he's on holiday."

"He's doing what he's doing for love of the job and to help me out. There's no money involved, Lieutenant. He hasn't broken any laws."

Lieutenant Marcelo's smile reflected inner conflict "All I'm trying to do is iron out what I thought was a straightforward situation a few hours ago. But it isn't, is it? Guy gets mugged and dies of a heart attack as a result. Right? That was how I saw it. But what do I find when I start digging? I find there's a problem in your recent past related to antiquities, and that our Australian friend isn't what he seems. What am I supposed to make of that?"

"We're beset by circumstances over which we have little control," said Windle. "If it wasn't all so pathetic, it would be funny."

"Make me laugh," said the lieutenant.

"I doubt if I'll manage that," said Windle, aware that he would have to tread very carefully indeed. "But if you'll give me a minute, Lieutenant, I think I can put your mind at rest."

"Be my guest," said a smiling Marcelo.

* * *

A heaving mass of people, an avalanche of talking, laughing, munching humanity coming towards them. Above their heads a forest of neon-lit signs, some of them as big as the screen in a picture theatre, blinking out their assorted messages in a glitz of color and movement. And lording it over all of them a single word in scarlet scrawled with the upward sweep of an audacious hand: *VIRGIN*. A paean to the innocence of youth? An indecent reference to the Holy Mother? Duggan found it difficult to look away. It was such an unlikely word to find floating in a sink of desire.

"Fifth Avenue intersects with Forty-Second Street," Jane said, slipping a gloved hand out of Duggan's for a moment. The temperature had risen a little, but not a lot. When their hands joined again, they glanced at one another as if surprised by the renewed intimacy.

"If it wasn't for Weisel I'd be the happiest man on Earth," Duggan said, his bit of a smile carrying the same message.

Jane did not reply; it seemed superfluous.

They had taken the subway to Times Square and walked for what seemed like miles, Duggan struggling to digest the vast number of new sights and sounds. What amazed and amused him most was the fact that steam really did issue from gratings in the streets.

And at every other corner an NYPD presence, either a couple of officers laden with the accoutrements of their trade chatting to each other, or to a member of the public. Or a squad car or van prominently marked and parked. Duggan remarked on the high profile the police had and received a two-word reply: zero tolerance. Last she'd heard New York had the lowest crime rate in the world for a large city.

In an Asian cafe crowded to the door where every imaginable combination of food could be had, they scoffed what to Duggan was a mountain of rice and chicken curry and chatted about nothing in particular. He would have to see Central Park, that was a must, she said. You couldn't say you had visited New York without a walk in the park. Or they could take the bus through Harlem to the Cloisters. He'd love the Cloisters. Rockefeller Junior had had it built to house a fabulous collection of fourteenth-century artifacts. Or they could head in the opposite direction, stop off in Greenwich Village for an hour then take the ferry out to Ellis Island. It wasn't a bad day for that.

As it turned out, they did the park and nothing else. It was as if they had engaged neutral gear, Duggan said later, when they returned to the Bentleys'.

"They're at a fund raiser," Jane said, in answer to his question. Her look of innocence was anything but innocent. "Elspeth thought they'd be back around eight. It's Martina's night off."

"We're alone?"

A smile. What would he like to drink? He said whisky, and she got him one.

"You like whisky too?"

"Thought I'd try some of your poison."

"You're on the slippery slope to ruin, Jane."

"You think so?"

"Eight o'clock?"

"Eight o'clock," she said back, smiling.

* * *

The Bentleys were as good as their word. When they arrived home, Jane and Duggan were sitting side by side on the couch watching television.

"Not *another* program on Kennedy," said Elspeth, after a moment's watching.

"It's about the fears some Americans had about a Catholic being president," said Jane.

"Some thought Kennedy wanted to do away with the divide between church and state," George said, staring at the screen. "He was accused of being as much a prisoner of a religious system as

259

Khrushchev was of a political system."

"In American, the Church is forced to accept the status quo. This accep-tance is based on the French distinction of 'thesis 'and 'hypothesis' put forward by Cardinal Gibbons of Baltimore. Rome frowned on republican sentiments, hence Cardinal Gibbons' attempt to clear himself of the charge of heresy by invoking the thesis/hypothesis argument. According to this argument, in a perfect world (thesis), a strict medieval theocracy could function, but in an imperfect world (hypothesis) that theocracy had to give way to the status quo. In his day, Kennedy was faced with much the same dilemma: to be a good Catholic, or a good American. He chose to be a good American and uphold the American ideal."

"Wouldn't have got far if he hadn't," said George,"

Jane made to turn the television off, but George wanted to hear more. Kennedy's unequivocal statement upholding the American ideal followed:

"I believe in an America where the separation of Church and State is absolute - where no Catholic prelate would tell the president (should he be a Catholic) how to act and no Protestant minister would tell his parish-ioners for whom to vote . . . an America that is officially neither Catholic, Protestant nor Jewish - where no public official either requests or accepts instruction in public policy from . . . any ecclesiastical source."

His declaration ended with the words:

"I do not speak for my Church on public matters and my Church does not speak for me."

"We seem to have lost sight of that somewhat." Elspeth turned away, her tone scathing. "Patriotism and religion cannot but be in conflict. John Paul killed off any hope Catholics had after Vatican II, and this idiot, Benedict whatever, is of the same ilk." Her eyes settled on Duggan. "The Church is all for openness and freedom of worship when it comes to how the state should handle its affairs, but when it comes to its own affairs it's a different story. In relation to the state, freedom and truth are bedfellows; in relation to the Church never the twain shall meet. Catholics have to put up with secrecy and unaccountability at every turn. There are no checks and balances.

Explanations are taboo. Honesty in discussion is viewed as a watering down of the truth. And we can't have that, can we! The Church pleads for freedom everywhere except where it's most needed - *in* the Church itself!"

She was addressing Duggan, but he knew she was actually speaking through him to the Church that had wronged her. For a moment, a brief, frightening moment, he was a conduit for her loathing. "They're prisoners of their own imaginations, Elspeth," he said, looking up at her steadily.

"Damn them all!" was her response.

"American's mission, Emerson said, was to 'liberate, to abolish Kingcraft, priestcraft, caste, monopoly; to pull down the gallows, to burn up the bloody statute book.'"

Elspeth turned to look at the screen again.

"In 1832 Gregory the XVI described liberty of conscience as a form of madness. He condemned freedom of worship, the press, assembly and education as a filthy sewer of heretical vomit." Fear of Rome's influence sank the presidential ambitions of Al Smith, Demoncratic Governor of New York State . . . "

Duggan was reminded of the woman who had stormed out of Bishop Peters's lecture with the words *'Mirari vos'* on her lips. The same onslaught had been kept up by Pius IX, he said. It was Pius they had to thank for the *Syllabus of Errors* where any form of religion other than the Catholic was condemned as unfit to represent the state.

"They haven't changed their tune by much," said George.

"They confidently restate their claim to be the only true religion on the planet." Duggan laughed a bitter laugh. "The sixteenth century is where you see them at their best. Leo X condemned Luther for saying that it was against the will of God to condemn heretics to the fire. Gregory XIII rejoiced over the memory of the Massacre of St Bartholomew when thousands of Huguenot Protestants were killed. Clement VIII attacked the Edict of Nantes because it gave equality of citizenship to all, regardless of religion.

And Innocent X condemned the Peace of Westphalia for granting toleration to all citizens whatever their religion. The Edict of Nantes was later revoked and fifty thousand Protestant families had to leave France and flee for their lives."

"We Americans democratized religion," said George, his tone matter of fact. "Jefferson brought in the statute of religious freedom in the eighteenth century, the first ever passed by a popular assembly. But believing in something religious was only half the point being made. The more important point - at least to my way of thinking - was that an individual had the right to *not believe* in *any* form of religion. It was no longer a matter of toleration. It was a matter of individual liberty and equality. Part of Jefferson's statute was that no one should be compelled to attend a place of worship, or support any form of religion if he or she did not wish to. *That* was the big break."

Duggan was nodding vigorously; it was a point too seldom made, he said. Tolerance was a form of hypocrisy; it was an insult to those being tolerated. It implied inequality. What was tolerated today might not be tolerated tomorrow. And having the right to not believe was just as important as the right to choose between belief systems.

"Kennedy was fortunate to be campaigning for the presidency during the pontificate of John XXIII, the least bigoted and most truly catholic pope in history."

"It's all so arbitrary, isn't it?" said Elspeth. "Almost seems as though God prefers the bigots."

"If he's at all like what they say he's like, then it stands to reason that he does," said George.

"Europe altered; Catholic teaching did not. Liberty was un-Christian; only law and order mattered. Church and state were indissolubly consummated in marriage."

"Bad enough when I was a girl," said Elspeth.

"Told by his advisors that the Christian state was a fourth-century creation of the Emperor Constantine, Kennedy was probably not fully aware that he was contradicting centuries of Catholic teaching."

The program ended soon after. The credits scrolled across John XXIII's beaming face. In the background, Kennedy's personal declaration of independence from religious interference was repeated. It was a moving finale.

"Water off a duck's back," said Elspeth. She turned away. "They'll never admit to inadequacy."

"The facts are getting out," said Duggan.

"The scared will always be with us," she replied.

19

A Kind of Madness

"Quite a view," said Mayle.

"Doesn't mean much when you're by yourself." Holly's smile was wry. "I *hate* being alone."

"You should see my place."

"I remember."

"Not my flat. My hotel room."

Her smile broadened. "No one who ever visited your flat in Frisco forgets it," she said.

"My wife was an ultra untidy person."

"You're a hoarder, David."

"An organized hoarder."

She had visited his flat only once, out of curiosity, and more at her own invitation that his. He had apologized for what he termed 'the muddle'.

"Top up?"

He held out his glass and she filled it with St Francis pinot noir. Most of the wines downstairs seemed to have the names of saints.

"Okay," he said, watching her. "What's so important you had to talk to me right away?"

"I want to know what's going on? You're holding out on me."

"No one's holding out on you."

"Pull the other one."

Mayle grinned and sipped at his wine. "You're becoming paranoid."

"I smell subterfuge."

"You're new on the block. Take your time."

"Meaning?"

"Don't rush things."

"There's more, isn't there?"

"There's always *more*, " said Mayle.

"You'll bring me up to speed when you can?"

"Of course."

He felt important, suddenly. "Your being with the *Washington Post* has its advantages, Holly," he said, smiling wearily. "Being *you* has its advantages."

She looked away smiling, then back. "They even took the poor bastard's shoes. Did you know that?"

"I didn't know that," he said, watching her face.

"Could be there's quite a few things you don't know about."

"Meaning?"

"Windle might not be squaring with you either."

Mayle's smile withered.

"Tell me what's going on, David."

"Nothing's going on."

"I don't believe you."

"Believe what you like." He decided to sit down, and did so carefully, his glass of wine held out for fear of spilling it. "Is that what this is all about, Holly?"

"I don't like wasting time."

"Weisel's death was a horrible coincidence. Nothing more. Wrong place wrong time. End of story."

"You really believe that?"

"He was a fan. The unthinkable happened." He raised a finger of warning. "Don't you go putting two and two together and getting six!"

"You weren't there. Right?"

"My plane developed mechanical problems."

Holly didn't say anything for a moment; she just stared at Mayle. Then she said, "That must have been a disappointment."

"It was unfortunate. I missed out."

She had chosen to sit some distance away, on the end of a slim table used for tourist brochures. One foot was on the floor, almost, the other dangled. Due to the angle of her body, her camel-hair skirt had ridden up a little. In spite of himself, Mayle could not keep his eyes off the little bit of extra flesh that that revealed.

"The others met with Weisel?"

"They spent most of a day together."

"Why?"

"Why not?"

"Wasn't he there to talk to Windle?"

"Politeness? I don't know!" Mayle sensed that Holly was closing in. "Jack's there just about every day. I don't know why Jane was there. Ask her father."

"From what you said a moment ago you obviously think you should have been there as well."

Mayle remained silent.

"Why else be disappointed?" Holly's expression was one of veiled triumph. "You were supposed to be there, weren't you?" He was about to answer, but she cut back in. "It's my guess that's what you flew in for." She reached behind her for the bottle of wine and her skirt rode up outrageously. "If we're going to work together, David," she said, bringing the bottle to her glass, "you're going to have to be honest with me."

"You're jumping to conclusions."

"Am I? I don't think so. I'm being used."

"There's no doubting we gain from having you on board, Holly. I haven't denied that. But you gain, too. It's a two-way street."

"Is it?" She was looking at him with the same intensity as before. "I don't see any evidence of that yet."

"We told you about Weisel straight off."

"What did he have to share that was so important?"

She was back on track and he tried to draw her away. "Your imagination is getting the better of you."

"If you don't level with me David, I'll go for it."

"Go for what?"

"Windle's dilemma and Weisel's death in the one article. That would put the cat among the pigeons."

"There's no connection and you know it."

"There will be if I make a connection."

In a tired voice, Mayle said, "I should have known better."

"It's you who's playing games, not me!" she said energetically. "I knew you were holding out on me the moment you changed your mind about letting me in. It was too damned quick."

"I was trying to avoid nonsense like this."

"Keep her busy and she won't cause trouble?" Holly drained her glass and slid off the end of the table with something resembling a laugh. "That's an old trick of yours and it doesn't work any more."

Mayle's smile was sheepish. "You were a handful, Holly. The stuff you got up to helped age me ten years."

"I got results."

"I won't deny that."

"You told me once you were proud of me."

"I remember."

"You do?"

"You came back with the goodies when no one else could."

"You taught me how to do that."

"You were a natural."

"You disciplined me.,"

Mayle sighed into his wine. "It's still about discipline, Holly," he said, looking up at her. "A good journalist does not jump to rash conclusions."

"You know I haven't done that."

"Threats aren't the best route."

"Threats sometimes help focus the mind." She turned away and reached under the table. When she straightened, she had another bottle of St Francis in her hand. "You know I wouldn't do anything to hurt you, David." Mayle remained silent, so she continued. "You're the last of the gentlemen reporters, if you'll forgive the term." He watched her insert the corkscrew and lever out the cork. "Great word 'reporter'." she said, picking at the lead foil around the neck, "it conjures up the past." Coming over to where he sat, she filled his glass. "That's what you taught me. How to report. I haven't forgotten that, David."

He felt vulnerable suddenly, with her standing there so close. "You're a one-off, Holly," he said.

"You'll have to tell me what's going on eventually, so it might as well be now."

"I'm not in a position to do that."

"A hint?"

"God, you're tenacious!"

"I'm a little bit drunk."

"You don't sound drunk."

"Drunk enough to want you to kiss me."

He stared up at her not knowing how to respond.

"There's no little wife at home this time, David."

"Behaving like this won't get you anywhere."

"Depends where you think I want to go."

He didn't dare consider what she was implying; it was too ridiculous. "I think it's time I left," he said.

"You're turning me down?"

" . . . I find it hard to believe you're serious."

"And if I am?"

He studied her face for a moment. "Are you?" he asked.

"Try this," she said, bending to kiss him.

* * *

On being suspended from duty for entertaining ideas 'not commensurate with his role as a senior churchman', Bishop Peters launched the first of three broadsides that immediately hit the national press. Leafing through the New York Times over breakfast on the Saturday, Duggan was confronted with a full-page article by the little bishop that blasted the Catholic hierarchy for what he termed 'intellectual subterfuge'. By definition, 'subterfuge' meant any attempt to escape censure or defeat in argument by evading the issue, wrote Peters, and Rome had been guilty of subterfuge ever since Copernicus and Galileo initiated their epochal shift in perception. That, in essence, was what the Copernican revolution had been, an epochal shift the repercussions of which we were still trying to absorb. A new era in human understanding had resulted, and it was our collective responsibility to further that understanding by all means possible.

Duggan turned the paper so that Jane could see the heading. It read: *The Erosion of Religious Credibility and Meaning.* "Listen to this: 'Reading Scripture canonically, that is, in accordance with the Vincentian rule where the community of believers everywhere is expected to believe exactly the same thing, may be deeply reassuring, indeed comforting, but it is a practice that denies and belies reality at every turn. The Vincentian rule offers refuge to those who prefer a stifling orthodoxy to the challenges of the modern world. This is the faith-model being touted by the Holy Office, and it is a model all thinking Catholics should reject if they are to remain true to themselves as people of intelligence and integrity.'"

Jane had not heard of the Vincentian rule; it shocked her to think that some Catholics deliberately chose to think that way.

"Vincent of Lerins was a fifth-century monk who hid himself away on an island off the coast of southern France," said Duggan. "The nearest thing we have to him is Stanley Hauerwas and Karl Barth. Hauerwas's claim is that we are no longer confident in our use of Christian speech about God. Barth's drive was toward . . .'" He searched his memory and found the line he wanted. "' . . . enclosing the whole of reality within the sacred precinct of revealed truth'." Duggan reached for the coffee pot. "Barth set out to prove that the message proclaimed by the Church *as* true *is* true no matter what we discover about the world and ourselves. He said we should be proclaiming now what they proclaimed centuries ago *in spite of* Copernicus and Galileo."

"That would make the Christian faith purely self-referential."

"Exactly. What the Vincentians do is withdraw into a grotto of belief hoping against hope that belief by itself will be sufficient. It's an illusion, but it's a powerful illusion. Instead of language being subservient to meaning, meaning is made subservient to fixed modes of language. Faith becomes no more than a system of creedal affirmation." Duggan sipped at his coffee. "Systematic theology is out; dogmatic theology is in. We're back to a fixed revelation, a circle of ideas from which there is no escape."

"It's hard to believe anyone would want to return to that kind of thinking."

"It's been described as turning the ordained clergy into antiquities dealers. That's an apt description of what these people are up to."

She had crept into his bed in the early hours, and they had made love. He had fallen asleep holding her, and wakened to find her gone.

"Here's a point not often made." Duggan shook his head in admiration. "'At its worst, the Church makes the same pseudo-scholarly pronouncements as those who tout fantastic theories about Jesus. They claim as irrefutably accurate a New Testament that is riddled with mistakes, exaggerations and interpolations, and in doing so blithely advocate impossibilities that lead Christians away from, rather than towards, the fundamental message of the gospels. In doing this they undermine Jesus' teachings and make him into a puppet of their own imaginings.'" He beamed across the table at her. "*That* is right on the button."

"What will they do to him, Jack?"

"Drop him like the hot potato he is."

"You should write to him."

"I will. He'll need all the support he can get."

He had lain awake for some time wondering where their love affair would take them, what with her being American, and him Australian. What had they set in motion, he wondered. Were her expectations as a woman, as an American woman, different from his? If they decided this was it, would she expect him to live and work in America? In Ohio for God's sake? Or would she follow him

back to Sydney and add Aussie charm to her list of accomplishments? A small knot of alarm had formed as he weighed the possibilities. With her career blossoming she might reject Australia out of
hand. What would he do if it came to that? He loved her, of that he
was certain, but did he love her enough to turn his life inside out
and upside down?

He had fallen asleep again and dreamt that he was soaring over
some desert or other. He hadn't had a flying dream in years, and the
exhilaration and freedom of the experience had stayed with him
afterwards. A desert? Had his dream been trying to tell him
something? A laugh and a shake of the head as he took on the day
realizing that everything, but everything, in his life had changed.
Whatever the future held, it had to be better than the past.

"Most of them carry on as if nothing's ever happened in the
world," said Duggan. He had returned to the subject of
Christianity's dilemma. "They enter a kind of holy narcolepsy and
hardly ever awaken."

"And if they do?"

"Then they face the possibility of losing everything in one hit.
Jesus. God. The whole works. You can't put all of your hopes in one
theological basket and expect them to survive if that basket gets
flattened. Knock the pins out from under Jesus and that's what
happens to most Christians, they lose the lot. That's the price they
pay for belonging to a personality cult. I've spent the last twenty
years of my life in a spiritual wilderness as a result of their *overloaded*
Jesus."

"Is that a glimpse of the inner man?"

Duggan paused to consider that. Was he still in the wilderness?
Perhaps not. He had felt less estranged from himself since attending
the conference in Santa Rosa, but did not know why. He had arrived
fretful for having been sent, and had left sensing that a phase of his
life had completed itself. The result of having met Jane? Perhaps.
But more than that, he suspected. Something had shifted in him, and
that shift had left him feeling less abandoned, less empty. Reminded

of this, he said that the Jewish scholar Hugh Schonfield had noted back in the sixties that Christians who lost their belief in Jesus generally lost God at the same time. Not surprising, really. They had invested Jesus with divine attributes and when he crashed, God crashed too. That's what had happened to him. As Jesus had taken on truly human proportions, the God he was supposed to have been had receded into greater and greater obscurity.

"And now?" asked Jane.

"He blinked out years ago for me"

"Altogether? You're an atheist?"

"I'm an a-theist."

"There's a difference?"

"I think so," said Duggan. "My definition of an a-theist is a person who rejects the idea of a God with human characteristics. That's the God of history, and he's a right old bastard. If you believe in that God, then you believe in a God who gets angry, a God capable of jealousy, a God who interferes in history, a God who heals some people and leaves others to rot, a God who favors one particular group of people over all others. I refuse to have anything to do with that God. He's a pain in the neck and he should be dumped."

"You prefer the wilderness?"

"You get used to being in the wilderness." He offered a qualification. "The wilderness is involuntary exile, Jane. It isn't the nicest place to be, but it's preferable to living in bullshit land."

"Am I in the wilderness?"

"I don't know. Are you?"

She looked away, looked back and said, "I guess I must be. I certainly feel as if I am at times."

"We each have our own route."

"To what, the Promised Land?"

"An excuse isn't a promise."

"Theism came out of the desert, Jack."

"Theism came out of the need of human beings to better regulate their lives. Problem is, it's well by it's use-by date. What was once a benefit is now a stumbling block."

"What would you replace it with?"

"I don't think that's something we can work out in advance."

"We can solve our problems without Christianity? Without God?"

"I don't think we have any option. We've come to see the world in ways incompatible with Christianity. Humanism no longer means the study of the humane arts, it means people can solve their problems without reference to religion. Secular thought has revolutionized our approach to just about everything."

"Some would say for the worse."

"In some instances, yes; but not in all instances. Crass materialism and consumerism is offset by good science, good philosophy and good law. Rational thinking has encouraged people to see transcendence in ways incompatible with Christianity. That's important. Our liberal democracies promise satisfaction in this world, not some nebulous salvation in the next. The Reformation is in full swing in spite of the Robert Carters of this world. People are questioning and reassessing religious belief as never before; they're no longer willing to accept the old pat answers."

"What about morality?"

"It's been replaced by secular ethics. Morality is inherently tribal. Ethics - secular ethics - is inherently democratic. It straddles all cultural and social norms. The question on most people's lips today is not 'how can I be good?'; it's how can I find the courage to face the vicissitudes of reality without flinching?"

"Maybe that's why religion is making such a comeback. It's just all too difficult for most people."

"All we can hope for, Jane, is that in stripping away the lies and the exaggerations we'll hit on something authentic within ourselves. The buck stops with ourselves. If we can't face ourselves there's not a lot of hope for us."

"Existential angst versus blessed assurance?"

"I prefer to think of it in terms of honesty and dishonesty."

"Transcendence might not always be so tidy."

"I agree. But there a point in untidiness where you simply can't find what you're looking for. That isn't much good either. A muddle is a muddle is a muddle."

Jane said nothing for a moment; then she said, "You're very cerebral, aren't you?"

"That's a problem?"

"It's an observation."

"Analysis is my bag, Jane. It's what I do. It's what I did. It's my life, more or less."

"I'm not complaining, Jack. I like the way you think."

"You probably know as much about art history as I do about Church history. You must have covered a lot of theoretical ground while doing fine arts here in New York and in Berlin."

She acknowledged that that was true, but suggested there might be more to life than facts.

"I agree entirely," he said, watching her face.

"You said in San Francisco you thought Christianity had an authentic core. Do you really believe that?"

"You may have misunderstood what I was saying. Christianity's authentic core may not be worth buttons, Jane. Its core may be no more than convoluted Jewish sectarianism distorted beyond recognition by Christian thinkers."

"You think that's the case?"

"I think Theodore's letter harbors the answer to that question."

"In a positive way?"

"In a quite unexpected way."

* * *

Archbishop Donaghue sat transfixed as Bishop Antonio Pia - an about- to-retire friend of many years - explained the New Catholic Dawn's financial shenanigans on the telephone. On receiving Donaghue's letter, Pia had made discreet enquires into CNCD operations in Italy, and had come up with some startling accusations. The pressure on followers to give money to the movement was apparently incessant, he said, quoting a priest who had reported the movement's greed to his superiors. Over and above donating a tenth of their income to the movement, new members were encouraged to give generously during 'fixed collections'; that is, when specified amounts of cash were asked for from groups. If the amount asked for did not immediately materialize, the bag, box or whatever kept going round until it did. If still it did not materialize, the sum required was surreptitiously added to the collection and a miracle of generosity was announced. Later, in the guise of teaching full members 'love of community', the movement stripped individuals of just about everything they owned. Cars, jewelry, savings and even property were handed over, this 'act of devotion to Christ' leaving individuals utterly dependent on CNCD mercies.

"How can they possibly hope to get away with such behavior?" asked Donaghue.

"*That* is the question on many people's lips."

"It's been suggested to me that the Holy Office is involved."

"*Involved* is an understatement!" exclaimed Pia. "Cardinal Menenger is up to his neck in it. Huge amounts of money are said to be pouring into the Vatican. There's even talk of parish priests and bishops receiving generous donations from CNCD."

"Hush money?"

"Depends on how you look at it. Look at it one way and it's utterly innocent. Look at it another and that's exactly what it is. And it goes all the way to the top. The European Bishops' conference in Vienna was paid for by the movement, as was the meeting in Rome for African bishops. CNCD paid for everything."

"And on the positive side?"

"Is there a positive side?"

"Their devotion to Christ is beyond question."

"Fanaticism isn't devotion, Michael, it's a form of madness. CNCD isn't about giving, it's about taking. They screw every last dollar out of their membership. The whole organization is based on cunning and deceit. Members are 'unhooked' - *sganciati* - from their money and belongings through a process that's identical to brain-washing."

"Would you go as far as to call it a sect?"

"It has all the hallmarkings of one. It exploits members and pays no attention to trade unions, regulations or codes of practice. It's a law unto itself. I'd go as far as to call it a deadly infection."

Donaghue was silent for a moment, then he said, "There are those who would combat this infection?"

"Yes."

"Are they powerful enough to deal with it?"

"I would say so."

"Then why isn't something being done to curb these excesses!"

"Rome wasn't built in a day, Michael."

"Huh!" said Donaghue. Then, "The Holy Father is unaware of what's going on?"

"The Holy Father is preoccupied with the demands of office."

"He hasn't been told?"

"He sees and hears only of the movement's success."

"I think it's time I came to Rome with some observations of my own."

"That would be most welcome, Michael. I will arrange for you to meet some interesting people while you're here."

"Thank you, Antonio. I'll will look forward to that."

"As will we, Michael."

20

An Honest Man

The telephone call from Lieutenant Marcelo was taken by Windle around seven in the evening. There was a hint of triumph in the lieutenant's voice. They had located Dr Weisel's briefcase and they would like him to go through its contents with them. Could he spare half an hour?

"Will you come to me?" asked Windle

"Be with you in twenty," said the lieutenant.

Replacing the receiver, Windle stood contemplating what this might mean, then he dialed the Bentleys' number and got Elspeth. Yes, it had been hectic since he arrived. Yes, he would try to get over their way before returning to Germany. No, he wouldn't forget. Another few seconds passed before he was able to ask if Jack was there. Yes, it was important.

"They've gone to the theatre, James. Left at least an hour ago."

"Could you get Jack to ring me when they come in."

"They'll be late back, I'm afraid. Said so."

"Well, tomorrow morning first thing," said Windle.

"You could ring Jane on her mobile."

"The performance will have started by now."

"You could check when the show finishes."

"No. It's okay. It's important, but it's not that important. It'll keep till morning."

"What shall I tell them?"

"That there's been a development. No, really, Elspeth, it's okay. I'll be seeing Jack in the morning anyway. Yes. Of course." He smiled into the receiver. "I'll ring you back with a time."

He rang off and tried to contact David Mayle, but had no luck there either. When Lieutenant Marcelo and his partner turned up, he opened a bottle of red wine and offered them some. They both accepted. They were off duty, Detective Mendelsohn said.

"I'm surprised you've included me in this," said Windle.

"Truth is we can't make head nor tail of what's in his case," said the sergeant. "There's not a single thing in English."

The lieutenant placed Weisel's case on the table Duggan used as a desk and opened it. His first question was rhetorical:

"Is it personal? Should it be returned to his university?"

"It wasn't locked?"

"No one expects to get mugged."

"Where did it turn up?"

"Weisel's shoes turned up first. They were on the feet of a sixteen year old questioned in connection with something entirely different." Marcelo laughed to himself. "He was one of those kids who likes to wear fancy suits. Weisel's shiny black shoes proved irresistible."

"Someone noticed?"

"It's the kind of detail people remember. We put out a description of the shoes based on what you told us and got lucky."

"The case turned up soon after, in the home of a fellow traveller," said Mendelsohn. "They didn't know the guy had died. The other kid's just turned fifteen."

Windle shook his head at the thought of what lay ahead of these youngsters. Fascinated, he watched as the lieutenant extracted the contents of the case. Along with a couple of paperback books - a thriller in English and a history text in German - there was a sheaf of notes in a minute German script stapled at one corner, two unposted letters - presumably opened by the police - and a faded notebook in copperplate handwriting in a clear plastic sleeve.

"All yours," said Marcelo.

Windle lifted the sheaf of notes, scanned a couple of pages and moved on to the addressed envelopes. One was for a Dr Herbert Moyer in Berlin, the other for a Fr Grosjean in Rome. Moyer's letter was in German, Grosjean's in French. Extracting the notebook from its sleeve, Windle scanned a few pages and replaced it.

"So what have we got?" asked Marcelo.

"At first glance it's all personal." Windle looked back at the table. "The notes are mundane. The unposted letters look as if they're to friends. The notebook's something he probably picked up in a market somewhere."

"It's dated 1889," said Marcelo. "There's a date in ink on the flyleaf."

You read French as well as German?" asked Mendelsohn.

"I get by," said Windle.

"I can handle Spanish," said Marcelo, "but not this stuff."

"In my case, Yiddish," said Mendelsohn. "And Hebrew." A smile. "My father was a teacher."

"You don't have German?" asked Windle.

"He wouldn't teach us German."

Windle did not have to ask why.

"If we sign this lot over, could you have a look at it and decide where it should be sent?" Marcelo's expression was one of someone in need. "We haven't managed to track any of his family yet."

"His university will probably have next-of-kin details," said Windle.

"We'll check that," said Marcelo.

"This is a good drop," said Mendelsohn. "My father said is was better to drink one good bottle of wine than ten mediocre ones."

"Your father was a wise man," said Windle.

"Were you born in the States?" asked Mendelsohn.

"I was born here in New York. My father was German Catholic, my mother German Jewish. They escaped from Germany late '34. They were lucky. My mother's parents were not so lucky." Windle glanced at Mendelsohn. "I get the impression you two have worked together for some time."

"Almost four years," said Marcelo. "I can't get rid of the bum!"

"What'll happen to these kids?"

"They're for the high jump." said Marcelo. "Just their bad luck to mug someone with a dicky heart."

Apropos of nothing, Detective Mendelsohn said, "We've had a *Washington Post* journalist sniffing around. Wanted to know about Weisel, but wouldn't say how she knew about his death."

"Talk to you?" asked Marcello.

"It's complicated," said Windle

"I thought it might be," he replied.

Windle explained how Holly Parks had bumped into his friend David Mayle, who was also a journalist. They had thought it better to take her into their confidence. The greater risk was that she found out later about Weisel and made his death a component of the story she was working on.

"You were the reason she was in New York?" asked Marcello.

"I was added to her original assignment. She was here to interview some senator or other when it was discovered I was in town."

Mendelsohn cut in. "We had no reason to tell anyone about Weisel's visit to you. The guy was mugged and that was it as far as we were concerned."

"You've met Holly, Sergeant. You must surely get my point."

"She came snooping in spite of your declared trust?"

"Professionals double-check everything."

"What we need to know is where Weisel was holed up," said Mendelsohn. "His luggage'll be there."

"No address book or diary?" said Windle.

"Nothing," said Marcello

* * *

"It's to our advantage that they keep digging," said Windle. He was standing, hands in pockets, in the middle of his lounge, his shock of black hair particularly unruly.

Duggan and Jane were at the table, the contents of Weisel's case spread out for inspection. "

"The investigation is closed?" said Duggan.

"As to how he died, yes. But to quote the lieutenant, there are *loose ends.*"

"What's in the letters?"

"Nothing much. The one to Moyer is to say thanks for some bit of research he sent to Weisel. There's no way to determine what that might have been. Similarly, the other letter mentions research at Harvard, but again does not specify." Windle's laugh was of the bemused variety. "It's almost as if he knew his letters were going to be read by outsiders."

"At least we have a couple of names," said Duggan. "That's more than we had this time yesterday."

Jane lifted the letter to Fr Grosjean and scanned it. "His French is excellent," she said immediately. Then after a moment, "His avoiding the subject does almost seem deliberate, doesn't it?"

"Moyer's reputation took a bit of a tumble some years back," said Windle. "He came out with a theory that some considered ill-advised."

Duggan turned from the table, Weisel's diminutive notes in his hand. "You've met Moyer?"

"We've never spoken. He turned up at a symposium I attended in the eighties. Caused a bit of a stir by suggesting that Christ may not have died on the cross. It was the old resuscitation argument refashioned and it earned him catcalls. He retired soon after. Just as well, perhaps."

"And the ill-advised theory? Or was that it?"

"Along the same lines. Jesus was married to the Magdalene and there was a blood lineage."

"He came up with that old chestnut?"

"That was a couple of years back. He was considered a respectable historian up until the mid-seventies."

"Shades of Allegro," said Duggan. And then, "Hugh Schonfield speculated that Jesus survived the cross and died in the tomb as a result of the spear thrust."

"Moyer wasn't a Schonfield," said Windle. "Schonfield was the last of the gentleman Jewish scholars. I talked with him in the eighties. In London. He was an original thinker, but he was no scatterbrain. He dismissed the lineage idea as unworkable."

"And now we have Weisel thanking Moyer for services rendered. Wonder what was going on there?"

"Interesting address for Fr Grosjean?" said Jane, holding up the envelope. "Isn't just anyone who can handle teaching philosophy at Gregorian University.

"What intrigues me," said Windle, "is the contrast between Grosjean and Moyer."

"That forces one to ask what kind of man Weisel was?" said Duggan. "His doing the bidding of an unseen master suggests he was a bit of an innocent."

"I would imagine that's why they chose him; his notes suggest an interest in esoterica." Windle changed direction. "But nothing stands out. The letters are interesting, but they give nothing away. The diary is an oddity belonging to some nineteenth-century priest. Weisel's notes, although suggestive of *avant garde* interests, are in every other respect respectable."

"My bet's on the philosopher priest," said Jane.

"What kind of esoterica?" asked Duggan.

"He had an interest in contemplative methodology," said Windle. "Not that that means he was a nutcase. He gets quite technical in places. That's probably why he bought that old diary. Bits of it deal with mystical experiences had by the writer."

"He didn't strike me as a budding contemplative," said Duggan.

"He was compiling case notes on states of consciousness. Some of his observations are quite insightful." Windle's laugh contained an element of respect. "I think he was a man driven by the desire to prove there's more to life than most of us think there is. But yes, I agree. It's unlikely he was a practitioner. He was fundamentally a theoretician."

"A dead theoretician," said Jane.

Windle opened his eyes wide in an attempt to accommodate that thought; it was something he still found difficult to accept.

"Cute of them to hold back on Holly Parks until the last gasp," said Duggan.

"A policeman's mind is a suspicious mind," said Windle. "They consider every angle."

"Must have thought they were onto something when Holly turned up."

"I rang the number she gave me last night," said Windle. "No response." A smile, then, "I also rang David. Three times. No response from him either. His mobile was switched off."

"You think he was with Holly?" said Duggan.

"That's my guess," said Windle. "And why not? He knows her too well to fall into any kind of silly trap." He turned to Jane. "I'm off back to Germany tomorrow afternoon," he said, grimacing. "I don't want to, but I have obligations."

"The splitting of the ways," said Duggan.

* * *

The temperature in New York rose over the next few days. On the Sunday it jumped a good five or six degrees. Jane assured Duggan it would hit twenty-something in June and around thirty in July. He would not be there to experience that, he said. Whether he liked it or not, he would have to return to Sydney. He had no option. He could feel his editor's growing discomfort radiating across the Pacific.

That evening, as if in response to his forebodings, Elliot's voice sounded in his ear. "Jack? Hi. Sorry, but it's bad news, fella." A pause during which Duggan imagined all kinds of things. And then the completely unexpected. "Dave didn't make it, Jack. He died late last night. Doc said he was riddled with it."

"Christ!" said Duggan.

"The funeral's Tuesday. Any chance?"

"Not a hope," he said back.

Another pause. "Questions are being asked, Jack. What do I

say?"

"I should be back in a week. I'll explain everything then. It's bigger even than I thought." Duggan paused. "Was it quick for Dave?"

"'I'm afraid not, Jack. It was horrible."

"You were there?"

"Sort of. They moved him to a room by himself in the final hours. Wasn't really meant for what was going on." A pause. "I could see him through the half glass door, Jack, but I couldn't hear anything. He was sitting up. Talking. He knew I was there; glanced out at me a couple of times." A bit of a laugh. "It was like he was in a business meeting and couldn't get away."

"Who was with him?"

"A brother and a couple of relatives. His folks died years ago. The whole thing was utterly surreal."

"He was sitting up?"

"Bobbed up would be a better description. I don't know what was going on. Nurses kept coming and going."

"Sounds *awful.*"

"It was." Another pause. Duggan waited. "He asked about you a couple of times. Earlier in the week. I saw him every other day."

Duggan said nothing.

"You still there?"

"Yeh, I'm here."

"He left you his books, Jack."

"He did what?"

"There was a letter saying that his library had to go to you."

"What about his family? His brother?"

"There's a lot of religious stuff. The brother said they didn't mind."

"They could sell them."

"They won't go against his wishes. They asked about you. I said you and he were close."

"That isn't true."

"True enough, Jack. He liked you. Told me."

Duggan drew a shaky breath. "I visited him twice in hospital. I got the impression he didn't approve of me."

"You got that wrong."

"Could you organize some flowers? A card?"

They agreed on the wording and Elliot rang off. On his way back to the lounge from George's study, Duggan pondered Dave Perry's gift. An act of friendship? An aberration? A nudge in the ribs from a dying man? Opening the door to the lounge, Duggan stepped back into his life. Jane smiled up at him and he smiled back.

"Everything okay?" she asked.

"Yeh, fine," he replied. Then to Elspeth he said, "Do you mind if I help myself to a whisky?"

* * *

James Windle was engrossed in Duggan's almost completed translation when Mayle turned up. The Californian came in looking sheepish and immediately apologized for his disappearing act. He and Holly had spent the whole day together doing research, he said. A smile that wasn't a smile. She was a real goer. If anyone could get to the bottom of the Rome thing she would. Could. Anyway, it was probably better that he use his time that way than hang around under their feet. Windle smiled at Mayle's convolutions. No one expected him to be around twenty-four hours a day, he said back. Even Duggan had time off.

"How's Jack doing?"

"A few more days and he'll be finished."

"What you hoped for?"

"Exactly what I hoped for. It's got a hand other than mine stamped all over it. I'm always amazed by how stylistically different two translations of the same thing can be."

"I slept with Holly."

Windle blinked the sentence down.

"I won't give anything away. Haven't."

"I trust you implicitly, David."

"I just wanted you to know."

"I know you too well to think you'd do anything foolish."

"It won't last, but what the hell." Mayle's smile broadened into a grin. "Haven't felt this good in years!"

"Drink?"

"Wouldn't mind."

Windle opened a bottle of red and they seated themselves. "I seem to be the only one left. Who'd have thought Jane would go for an Australian!"

"A *bloody* Australian," said Mayle, attempting the accent.

"Its a relief to see her happy. At last."

"You think he's it?"

"I think so. Don't you? It's in her face, David." A generous sip of wine. "I've never seen that look before."

"What are their plans?"

"Didn't ask. I don't think they know themselves."

"Australia?"

"It's possible." Another laugh. "Can you see Jack laboring in Ohio? I can't. It'll be either New York or Sydney."

"He's a lucky guy."

Windle mused on that. "There's a lot of her mother in her; more than she knows," he said, remembering the vivacious dark-eyed woman he'd fallen in love with.

"I knew they'd hit it off the moment I set eyes on him," said Mayle. "Well, within twenty-four hours I did."

"What made you think so?"

"I saw the look of interest on her face even before they were formally introduced." He explained about Duggan swapping the lecture hall for the bar during the conference in Santa Rosa. "When I turned up she was watching his every move."

"Holly obviously thinks you're a bit of all right."

"I don't know what Holly thinks. I don't think Holly knows what she thinks half the time. She's pure instinct."

"Then she's probably more true to herself than the rest of us."

"Yeh, I suppose," said Mayle. A laugh. "The moment she's back in Washington it'll be as if I never existed."

"You can't be certain about that."

"Trust me," said Mayle.

There was a silence.

"So what have you decided about Rome?"

"She's wants to make it a *Washington Post* exercise. Blessings of her editor and all that. She's talking about going over there to get a handle on the situation."

"The police found Weisel's case. There's a letter in it addressed to a Fr Grosjean in Rome. It's in French. It might prove useful."

"She could deliver it," said Mayle. "That would give her a head start. Anything else of interest?"

"Nothing that tells us much." Windle doubled back. "You really think she might get to Rome?"

"If it's in Holly's head, it's happened already."

Windle refilled their glasses. "Holly's going to ask questions when Jack breaks the story in Australia. How should we handle that?"

"He was here in New York to authenticate the illicit photographs he picked up in Santa Rosa. Right? You and he became friends because of his academic background."

"That would make me a collaborator."

"An *unwilling* collaborator. A bad translation of the text would have led to all kinds of confusion. You had a duty to the text to see that it was handled with the correct sensitivity."

Windle was silent for a moment, then in a tired voice he said, "I'm beginning to regret ever having clapped eyes on the damned thing. I'll end up having to lie my head off."

"For all the right reasons."

"'Do not tell lies, and do not do what you do not wish to do.'" Windle smiled. "It's one of Jesus' sayings in the Gospel of Thomas."

"Some lies are permissible."

"I wake up some mornings feeling distinctly uneasy about it all."

"You're a man of honor."

"Am I? I sometimes wonder."

"It took courage to do what you did."

"It seemed right at the time."

"They're the real liars, not you, James. You're an amateur, that's why it bothers you."

Windle put back his head and laughed.

"It's true! You feel guilty because you're an honest man."

"That's a nice way to put it, David."

Mayle turned on a passable Jewish accent. *"Would I tell you a lie?"*

They finished the bottle of red and opened another.

"Comfort yourself with the idea that what you've done is for the greater good," said Mayle. "Politicians void ordinary morality on that basis day in and day out."

"There a point where that argument ceases to work," said Windle. "It can only be taken so far."

"Tell them that!"

"That's why democracy works as well as it does. It safeguards us against the tyranny of those who think only in terms of the greater good. It's sometimes necessary to think that way, but it's full of dangers. Make it the moral constant in your politics and the whole of society ends up suffering."

"I don't think you're in any danger."

"It's a slippery slope," said Windle.

21

Roma

"The Holy Father has a brain tumor, but it isn't immediately life-threatening." Cardinal Antonio Pia's smile was non-committal, his grey eyes were not. "They say he's in unusually good spirits."

"When was this discovered?" asked Donaghue. He had not long arrived from the airport, and was still flustered.

"A few days ago. He has been complaining of headaches for some time. A brain scan revealed the cause."

"It's benign?"

"It's small."

"I won't be able to speak with him?"

"It's unlikely he'll have returned from the Gemelli Clinic by the time you leave."

Archbishop Donaghue twisted slightly in his chair. "They must have known an audience wouldn't be possible. It's only a couple of days since I arranged this visit."

"Telephones are dangerous things, Michael. Only a handful of people are aware of the Holy Father's predicament."

"I've come all this way for nothing?"

"Hardly for nothing. There are people to meet. Things to discuss. We look forward to your company over dinner this evening."

"I feel like a damned conspirator!"

"You *are* a conspirator, Michael! As for being damned, well . . ." Antonio Pia's laugh echoed around his vaulted study. It was his way of reprimanding Donaghue for supposing that he could single-handedly change the Holy Father's mind on anything.

"I have no wish to sup with the Devil, Antonio."

"There will be only two liberals at the table: Cardinal Bettino Craxi and Cardinal Graziella Gammarelli."

"The others will be?"

"Bishop Lamberto Furno and Cardinal Flavio Benedetti."

"Benedetti's involved?"

"He and Gammarelli are the principal players. They have been forced into a truce. There are others, of course. Quite a few. It was Benedetti who suggested a circle to deal with this matter."

"Where are we to meet?"

"In the Old Quarter. At the home of a friend. A car will collect us at seven." Antonio Pia's gaze did not budge from Donaghue's face. "There's nothing to fear, Michael. No one will as much as breathe your name in these halls."

"How many supporters do we have?"

"Enough —- "

"Others will find their courage in time."

Having been diagnosed with a virulent form of lymphatic cancer, Cardinal Flavio Beneditti of Milan's chance of becoming pope had melted away. A handsome man with a winsome smile, the sixty-two-year-old had won support from both the liberal and conservative wings because of his clarity and humility. But all the talking and whispering had been for nothing: the report on Beneditti's health had led to the infinitely more manageable Cardinal Angelo Rinaldi feeling the weight of the golden miter bite into his brow. Similarly concerned with the Church's survival, but a conservative in his approach, Rinaldi had become a sacrificial pawn acceptable to the two most powerful Vatican factions.

"I could never have imagined myself in this position," said Donaghue. "To think that it has come to this!"

"You were unaware of what was going on?"

"I didn't believe the rumors. They sounded like extraordinary exaggerations." Archbishop Donaghue's natural pomposity deserted him for a moment. "It was only when Fr Brentano alerted me to what was happening in his own parish that the reality of the situation hit home."

"We're dealing with maniacs, Michael. Clever maniacs. They've been building their empire for over fifty years and hardly anyone has noticed. CNCD looks like a movement, sounds like a movement and acts like a movement, but it defines itself as a *spirituality.* That's how they've avoided censorship for so long. You don't *join* CNCD, you *become* a child of the New Catholic Dawn through the auspices of the Holy Spirit. That, as I'm sure you realize, is to claim a species of infallibility." Cardinal Pia halted for a moment to let what he was saying sink in. "The Holy Office has shown no interest in CNCD's excesses, just in its successes. Cardinal Menenger seems willing to put up with just about anything in the hope of turning the tide of atheism and secularism."

"It is our combined hope that that tide will some day turn," said Donaghue, whose brief from above had been to put Catholic America back on its knees inside one decade, "but we cannot in all conscience ignore how that is accomplished." A sigh from Donaghue. "It is Fr Brentano's assertion - he has a brother at Gregorian University who knows something of the matter - that CNCD is building its own parallel hierarchies. It's already noted for its pool of clergy."

"There's even a sprinkling of bishops - two are Vatican advisers." The Cardinal laughed, but it was a sour laugh. "Some argue that it's better to take this route than contemplate relaxing the celibacy laws or allowing the ordination of women, but I for one think it is equally dangerous. Allow this to go on unchecked and we'll be faced with the possibility of CNCD cardinals and even popes in the next century!"

"The CDF refuses to act?"

"The CDF is up to his neck in it."

"Surely not," said Donaghue, who suspected Cardinal Menenger was being misrepresented. "The Holy Office is presently investigating an American bishop for not holding to the proper line on Catholic education."

"I'm sure it is," said Pia, "but I think you'll find the policy being advocated violates the necessary freedoms a college or university requires to function in the modern world."

"Christ's freedom is perfect bondage."

"Christ said knock and it will be opened unto you. Education is about knocking on the door, not slamming it shut!"

"It's only in the area of theology that an embargo has been placed."

"You accept the idea of having to have a license to teach theology in a Catholic Institution?"

"I don't see why not. We've been debating *Ex Corde Ecclesiae* in the U.S. for almost a decade," said Donaghue. "The bishops have agreed only recently that licenses are required."

"Michael, you know as well as I do that the American bishops are anything but happy with *Ex Corde Ecclesiae*. They felt they had no choice in the matter. If they had voted against the guidelines it would have signified disloyalty to the pope."

"You can't say the Holy Father wasn't patient."

"The Holy Father knew no single document could prescribe norms for Catholic colleges and universities worldwide. There were too many variables."

"Agreement has nevertheless been reached," said Donaghue, surprised by his friend's skeptical tone. "Anyway, Catholic colleges and universities have been subject to regular scrutiny by external accrediting agencies for years."

"The American bishops reached agreement back in '96," said Pia. "Problem is, the Holy See rejected their conclusions and forced them into their present dilemma."

"It's only a dilemma for the modernists!" exclaimed Donaghue.

"That's *far* too easy," said Pia. He gave an irritated sigh and continued. "You're confusing properly regulated accreditation with a policy of educational suppression. The difference between what is being demanded now and what was acceptable to colleges and universities over the last decade is that those rendering judgment for the accreditors were academically qualified to do so. In the present climate it is the bishops themselves who will issue the licenses. Who ever heard such nonsense! The bishops aren't qualified for such a task."

"There's been a steady erosion of Catholic character in our colleges and universities. We had to do something to stop the rot."

"That's a claim I no longer find tenable."

Donaghue did not immediately reply; he stared hard at the neatly laden surface of Antonio Pia's massive desk, then in a troubled voice he said, "You seem to have developed a more . . . *lenient* approach."

"Correction, Michael: I have awakened to the fact that we conservatives have been manipulated towards a form of thinking that could and will bring the Catholic Church into disrepute unless we move against it. It's not just a matter of CNCD excesses, it's a matter of the whole conservative value system having been hijacked by a bunch of unscrupulous rogues."

"I'm not sure I follow you."

"We've been infected by a doctrinal virus, Michael."

"You can't possibly believe that!"

"A form of thinking has developed that does the conservative cause *no* favors." Pia's grey eyes glittered with intent. "It's time to weigh the consequences of our actions, Michael. We're in danger of setting something in motion that we later won't be able to control."

"The Holy Father was mistaken in his directives?"

"The Holy Father was desperately ill and in need of better advisers."

Thunderstruck by what he was hearing, Archbishop Donaghue drew back into his heavily ornamented chair. "If I didn't know you as well as I do I would doubt I was hearing you say such things."

"Do not fear, Michael. I'm the same man I always was. I'm not trying to infect you with a parallel contagion."

"Beneditti agrees with you on this?"

"Beneditti was the source of my enlightenment."

After a moment, Donaghue said guardedly, "Your Eminence has given me much to ponder."

"Then I have done my duty," said Pia. He got to his feet smiling and extended the hand of friendship. "I can promise you an Upper Room experience this evening, Michael. Cardinal Beneditti is one of the most remarkable men I have ever met." His smile broadened. "And of course some *excellent* Tuscan wines!"

"Seven o'clock," said Donaghue.

"Seven o'clock *sharp*," said Pia.

* * *

Lieutenant Marcelo's expression warned Windle of an impending revelation. Ushering the lieutenant and his partner into the room, Windle glanced at Duggan and closed the door behind them.

"We've got Weisel's luggage," said Marcelo. "He was reported missing the day after we found him by someone claiming to be a sister." Giving Duggan a nod, he continued. "You can imagine her reaction when told that her missing brother was dead."

"He has a sister here in Manhattan?" Windle's eyes strayed to Duggan, then back to lieutenant. "That explains everything."

"There was only one small suitcase at the sister's place," said Mendelsohn. "Weisel's address book and passport were in the pocket of a suit hanging in the wardrobe."

"Two suits and some underwear," said Marcelo. "If you discount the books, he sure travelled light. The winter jacket he was wearing on top of his suit belonged to the sister's husband."

Windle pushed away the thought of how shocked the woman must be and suggested coffee. Duggan set about the task.

"So that's it," said Marcelo, planting himself in a corner of the sofa. "No more loose ends."

"The only interesting thing in Weisel's briefcase was that old diary," said Windle. "It's was written by a Catholic priest critical of his Church *and* of orthodox Christianity. He gets quite heated in places. I can quite see why Weisel bought it."

"Weisel was interested in Christianity?" said Mendelsohn.

"We all are. You can't lecture in ancient history and ignore

Christianity. That's why I was ferreting about in the Middle East. The history of Christianity is integral to our understanding of Western culture. Western civilization."

"Was Weisel Jewish?" asked Mendelsohn.

"I have no idea," said Windle.

"I knew a Jewish kid in the Bronx called Weisel. When I was a kid," said Mendelsohn.

'The sister's an American citizen," said Marcelo. "She's married to an Austrian-American by the name of Neumann. Nice guy. High school teacher. She hadn't seen or heard from her brother in years. Family tiff, it seems. He used his meeting with you to mend a few fences."

"And this happens to him," said Mendelsohn.

Lieutenant Marcelo was about to say something, but Windle cut in. "Life's a bitch," he said dryly.

Marcelo's smiled his response. Then he said, "The sister wants to speak to you. There's something of Weisel's she thinks you ought to have."

"Did she say what?"

A shake of the head.

"When does she want to meet?"

"Said she'd prefer to meet here at your hotel."

"Of course," said Windle.

Marcelo took out his diary and scribbled a number on one of his cards.

"So you're free to leave whenever you want," said Mendelsohn. He looked across at Duggan, who was pouring coffee. "Is it back to Australia?"

"Sydney town," said Duggan.

"Back to being your other self?"

"For my sins," said Duggan.

"Which are?" asked the lieutenant.

"Many," said Duggan.

* * *

When the black limousine carrying Archbishop Donaghue and Cardinal Pia reached the Ponto Sisto bridge, it turned right into the Piazza Trilussa and edged its way into the narrow backstreets of the ancient city. Within a few minutes it had entered the Piazza di Santa Maria where the softly illuminated colonnades of an early Christian church seemed to welcome them.

"Santa Maria in Trastevere," said Antonio Pia. "It was the first church to be dedicated to the Madonna."

"How old is it?" asked Donaghue.

"Third century. It was founded by Pope Callixtus I. Some think it the oldest in Rome."

"There are so many," said Donaghue.

"It has some remarkable mosaics," said Pia.

Santa Maria Trastevere slid from view.

"We're almost there," said Pia.

Minutes later they entered the Piazza Cosimato and came to a halt. To Donaghue's horror the place was littered with parked scooters and mopeds belonging to the patrons of busy restaurants. Not a few souls had braved the evening chill and were sitting outside.

"They have a marvelous market here," said Pia.

"We'll be recognized," said Donaghue.

"In Rome we are invisible," said the Cardinal. He laughed and waited for their driver to open the car door.

Shielded by the car, they entered the adjacent building and were greeted by a small, immaculately dressed man who ushered them into an elevator. After what seemed an age they alighted two floors up and were shown into an apartment that belied the building's deteriorating exterior. Someone had lavished care, attention and money on every aspect of the apartment's decor and furnishings.

"Magnificent!" said Donaghue.

"It belongs to Gammarelli's brother," said Pia. "He has opened his home to us."

Donaghue recognized Cardinal Flavio Beneditti immediately; his athletic form was difficult to miss. To his surprise, Beneditti also recognized him. Rising from his chair at the fire, the dying cardinal greeted the American archbishop warmly, and in English.

"*Eminencia*," said Donaghue.

"We're grateful to Antonio for bringing you here this evening," said Beneditti. "We need American support in this."

"I'm honored," said Donaghue.

"You had a good journey?"

"I had work to distract me," said Donaghue. And then, solicitously, he asked after the cardinal's health.

"They say I'll be off the planet in a year."

"May the Lord sustain you, Eminence."

Beneditti's bow of the head was infinitesimal, the look in his eye that of a man more amused than fearful. "It comes to all of us, Archbishop," he said matter of factly. "No one escapes."

Cardinals Craxi and Gammarelli were examining a delicate bronze recently acquired by Gammarelli's brother when Pia and the archbishop approached. They both turned, smiled, tilted their heads in recognition, for the Archbishop of Nevada was known for his stern views,

"It's good of you to spare the time," said Craxi, his English almost accentless. He extended a hand. "We're going to need all the help we can get, Archbishop."

Donaghue copied Beneditti's bow of the head. "Difficult times are upon us," he replied.

"American honesty is what we need," said Gammarelli.

"Isn't she beautiful!" said Craxi, standing aside so that Donaghue could glimpse the bronze they had been admiring. It was of a young girl, a naked young girl. "It's by Fabio Zago," he added, his eyes alight with respect. "He died last year aged eighty."

"It's . . . very fine," said Donaghue.

Lifting the bronze, Craxi stroked it as if trying to extract its beauty through his fingertips. "You're interested in art, Archbishop?"

"I . . . *dabble* in porcelain," said Donaghue, hoping that that would suffice. On seeing the look of interest in Gammarelli's eyes, he added, "I'm very much the amateur, Eminence."

"As are we all," said Gammarelli. He turned to Pia. "I have a treat for you, Antonio. A '97 Banfi Brunello di Montalcinos."

"Ah!" said Cardinal Pia. He turned to Donaghue. "Italy's finest vintage," he said. "Sangiovese at its best." The look on Donaghue's face made him add: "Sangiovese is the primary red wine in Tuscany, Michael. It has the most variations of any single grape."

"Six hundred and fifty, to be exact," said Gammarelli.

"It sounds wonderful," said Donaghue.

"Tastes even better," said Gammarelli.

"It's a Tuscan menu with Tuscan wines in honor of Bishop Furno this evening," said Craxi. "He's Tuscan, and it's his birthday." He turned laughing to Cardinal Pia. "Little sense in wasting the occasion on worrisome things alone. Eh, Antonio?"

The cardinal smiled, but did not reply.

As if on cue, Bishop Furno arrived. He made straight for Cardinal Beneditti, grasped his hands in his and bent to kiss them. Beneditti attempted to rise, but Furno wouldn't let him. It was as if he were paying his respects to the pope himself.

"He loves him like a brother," said Gammarelli.

Donaghue said little over the next half an hour. He listened, watched, smiled and nodded, and every so often ventured something in Italian. It was not that he felt out of place, or inadequate, it was that he felt uncomfortable. He was in the presence of powerful men, men whose reputations went before them, men whose intentions were undoubtedly honorable, yet at the same time oddly contradictory. For how was it possible, he wondered, for liberals like Gammarelli and Craxi to sup with the likes of Beneditti and Pia? They were poles apart. Beneditti was a man of faith, a man who held the Church's traditions and doctrines in high esteem.

Gammarelli and Craxi were known dissenters, Vatican II advocates harboring policies of radical change. Donaghue knew nothing of Bishop Furno's background, but Antonio had assured him that he was a man after their own heart, a man who would stand his ground for doctrinal purity. And so, when the call to table came, and Donaghue found himself sandwiched between Gammarelli and Craxi, he felt as if he were the butt of an insensitive joke.

"Bruno is a restaurateur, hence the menu," said Gammarelli. "My brother," he added, to remind Donaghue.

"He'll be joining us?" asked Donaghue.

"Not on this occasion." A smile. "He supports our needs invisibly."

The menu was impressive. Donaghue read it silently and the words rolled off his tongue like poetry: *Aperitivi e Antipasti della traditione toscana. Straccetti de pasta fresca ai funghi porcini e xucchini. Risollo ai fiori di xucca. Maialino di latte servito in bellavista con patate rosolate e sformatino alle erbette.*

"Suckling pig?" said Donaghue.

"Not the whole thing," said Gammarelli. "Bruno puts that on with great pomp for the tourists."

"Risotto rice with pumpkin blossom sounds delightful."

"His chefs are creative," said Gammarelli.

After a welcoming toast and birthday greetings by Gammarelli, the meal got under way. Waiters in immaculate white jackets materialized. As the evening progressed, Donaghue began to wonder if they would ever get down to the business of discussing CNCD behavior. "Waiters have ears," said Craxi, when he ventured a remark in that direction.

And so the wine flowed, and Antonio Pia waxed lyrical over the Brunello de Montalcinos, and a sorbet *di Caterina De Medici* and sweet pastries completed what had been a gastronomic experience.

"Caffe," said Donaghue. He watched the waiter pour and move on. Then, turning to Craxi, he said, "I would have imagined such a meeting of minds unlikely only a few months ago, Eminence."

Cardinal Craxi's laugh was low-key, his reply equally subdued. They were in an unprecedented situation, he said softly. The Pontifical Council of the Laity had affirmed the Vatican's unqualified acceptance of CNCD at the recent bishops' conference, and that had removed the possibility of debate. The bishops had assumed they would be discussing laity participation in Church government, but had instead faced a *fait accompli* - CNCD's centralized structure, ideology and multiple projects had the pope's blessing, they had been told, and that meant they were above discussion.

"It's gone that far?" said Donaghue.

"Further than any of us could ever have anticipated." The Cardinal's tone became scathing. "The Children of the New Catholic Dawn think they've got God in their pocket. Hence their extraordinary abuses. When questioned, they evoke God as if He is theirs and theirs alone." Craxi corrected himself. "*Conjure* God would be a better way to put it. They're magicians of the worst ilk who have come to believe that their movement not only reveals God, but that in some inexplicable sense it *is* God."

"Surely not!" said Donaghue.

"A whole new idea of community has been spawned; it's spreading like wildfire."

Donaghue was reminded of Antonio's reference to CNCD thinking as a virus. With Robert Carter's insolent letter in mind, he said he himself had experienced CNCD's overbearing tactics.

"They're turning human souls inside out," said Craxi. "The spiritual life has been defined as belonging to the community, not to the individual."

A burst of laughter came from across the table. Cardinal Pia was trying to tell a joke he had heard that morning, but it had come out back to front and it was causing more mirth than if he had told it right way round.

And then, suddenly, the doors of the dining room closed and they were alone. There was no immediate reaction to this, everyone went on talking as before, but there was a gradual lowering of tones, and within a few minutes, complete silence.

Cardinal Pia was the first to speak. He remained seated. Laying a hand on Beneditti's hand for a moment, he said a few words about the cardinal's health, then directed their attention to CNCD and its insidious effect. They were confronted by a problem so deeply rooted in so many quarters it would take radical surgery to get rid of it, he said gravely. No one had foreseen the hidden agenda enacted at the recent bishops' conference, and 700 million Catholics worldwide ought to be made aware of what had happened there. The Curia's responsibility for the laity was not in question, but there were rules, and these rules had been flouted. Lay representation had been stacked with CNCD members, and no one knew by what criteria they had been chosen. There had also been an attempt to force CNCD values onto the conference through vehement directives, and this had been backed by an attack on laity involvement in Church governance, a habit disparagingly described as *meddling.*

"Fear of the democratic process," said Gammarelli.

"CNCD has all but been given the right of binding and loosing," said Pia. "They're a law unto themselves."

"The South American Church argued that the movement's missionaries should work in obedience and communion with the pastors of the local churches," said Craxi. "Their argument was that coming with the pontiff's blessing wasn't enough. The ordinary and immediate power of local pastors had to be respected."

"That exactly describes the problem I've faced," said Donaghue. "One of my local priests has been pushed aside as irrelevant by CNCD missionaries. They've succeeded in splitting his congregation in two, and have claimed papal authority for their actions. I'm informed that similar tactics are being used elsewhere."

"That authority has just been renewed by the Holy Father," said Benneditti, whose expulsion of CNCD operatives throughout Milan was well known. "It all but places the movement and the bishops on the same level."

"New wine bursting old wine skins," said Craxi.

"Exactly," said Benneditti.

"Bishop Pasquale's attack on his fellow bishops for being skeptical of the movement's qualities was vicious," said Bishop Furno, who had championed what Pasquale had later described to Furno's face as 'hostile forces'. "He warned me off in no uncertain terms."

"How did you respond?" asked Donaghue.

"I suggested we should perhaps pay a little more attention to what we loosed on Earth."

"That must have gone down well," said Pia.

"It earned me a salvo of carefully constructed . . . " Bishop Furno searched for the correct English expression, *"twaddle,"* he said with relish. "I was told in all seriousness that the Children of the New Dawn constituted a 'channel of freedom for today's Church'."

"What on earth does that mean?" asked Donaghue.

"You tell me," said Furno.

"It is the Church's . . . *final solution* to the problem of Modernity," said Benneditti. "It is a license to use whatever means are available to save the world from the perceived ravages of Satan."

"Which are real enough," said Donaghue.

"Indeed," said Benneditti. "But we are mostly concerned with human folly, not with diabolical machinations. Satan is only as real as we allow him to be, only as effective as we are ineffective. Evil resides in exclusivity, in the logic of power, in the belief that God's creation is not as good as He himself declared it to be. Perceive it as bound to Satan and you have loosed Satan. Perceive it as incapable of good in its own right and you cripple its God-given capacity to do the right thing. The only reason CNCD has been so successful is because its generous and self-sacrificing members have been milked of their inherent capacity for service. Their deep humanity has been harnessed to the imaginings of a self-appointed elite, their capacity for spiritual discernment trashed in the belief that CNCD authority equals an unchallengeable truth." Beneditti paused; it was as if he were drawing sustenance from the air. "We're dealing with an attitude of total militancy that will overpower the magisterium if left to its own devices. *That* must not be allowed to happen."

"Their stated aim is to reawaken the Church and bring about a new dawn," said Bishop Furno. "Many find that an attractive idea - around thirty million according to CNCD figures."

"Their estimates are always on the generous side," said Pia.

Donaghue took a sip of wine and replaced his glass carefully. "CNCD has been referred to as the pope's shock troops," he said, his gaze settling on Benneditti's handsome face. "How do you respond to such a claim, Eminence?"

"It's a strategy of centralization that should be discouraged," said Benneditti. "John Paul was in favor of the movement, but only because he was unaware of its true nature. If he had known what these scoundrels were up to he would have halted their advance."

"He didn't know?"

"We must presume that he didn't know."

"And the present Holy Father?"

"He is under the influence of the same advisers."

"No one else has his ear?"

"He sees only the need of the Church."

"Michael and I were discussing the problem prior to coming here," said Cardinal Pia. "To my way of thinking, what we're witnessing is a seeping through of CNCD policies into the general forum. They've somehow managed to capture the imagination of the Holy Office."

"The Holy Office is singularly lacking in imagination," said Benneditti. "Cardinal Menenger's failure to deal with what is going on is a disgrace. I've remonstrated with him on a number of occasions and have received no satisfactory response. His arrogance is monumental."

"And here we are, closeted like a bunch of criminals," said Gammarelli, who had been listening intently. "Isn't it time we made our move? We've got the numbers."

"We have many promises," said Benneditti, "but the tongue is often more courageous than the heart."

"We should wait?"

"For the right moment. There is always a right moment. Move too soon and you will bring about disaster. Move too late . . . "

"Who shall decide the moment?"

"They will decide. We will watch, and wait."

"Our Lord asked that of his disciples in Gethsemane," said Donaghue. "They fell asleep and were awakened by the temple guard."

"We will watch for one another," said a smiling Benneditti. "I will watch for you, you will watch for me."

"I was speaking metaphorically, Eminence," said Donaghue.

"I was not," said Benneditti. He turned to Cardinal Pia and left Donaghue to ponder his meaning. "CNCD's intention is to capture the laity and coerce the Church into accepting their fundamentalist vision. But what they've overlooked is the already active spirituality of the laity, a spirituality based on criteria of lasting worth. There are millions of good Catholics out there who have decided that a centrally controlled faith - a faith controlled by the papacy alone - is no longer tenable. The Holy Father has every right to expect deference in matters of doctrine and faith - courteous regard for his opinions is a historical given - but that is not the same as claiming sole authority in such matters. CNCD's parallel claim through obedience to the Holy Father alone is equally untenable."

"We're made free through our bondage in Christ," said Donaghue, cutting a careful path into Beneditti's argument. "The Church is the custodian of that extraordinary revelation."

"Indeed it is," said Beneditti, "but it is an ever deepening revelation, It is not, and never has been, static. The New Catholic Dawn claims to be waging war on rationalism - rampant democratic rationalism, to use their exact words - but

they're doing much more than that. They've waged war on the intellect itself, and that makes a nonsense of our God-given faculties. There's evidence galore that rationalisms are the bane of Western society, but that does not cancel out as a diabolical conspiracy. We no longer believe the world to be flat. We know for certain that the Earth revolves around the sun. We no longer confuse disease with demon possession and we accept without question that democracy is better than dictatorship. Things have changed. The flower of human understanding has opened and we are obliged to accommodate the bewildering complexity that faces us. Deny that complexity and you deny Christ as surely as St Peter did."

"The Church's stance on Christ is immutable," said Donaghue.

"I'm not talking about Christ. I'm talking about denying the shape and form of reality. Reality, too, is immutable - it does not suffer phony constructions, and neither does our Lord's life or teachings. When our interpretation of Christ causes endless conflict in the world, when it is exclusive and not inclusive of the sinner, then we are on dangerous ground."

"We love the sinner, but not his sin."

"Was it a sin to believe that the Earth revolved around the sun, or that epileptics were in the clutch of evil spirits?"

"We were children."

"Children then, children still."

"The battle is between the spirit of Christ and the spirit of dissolution."

"The truth gulped down whole chokes as surely as a chicken bone does," said Benneditti. "To not understand *that* is to not understand anything."

Donaghue's eyelids fluttered. Was this the 'Upper Room' experience promised by his friend?

"Cardinal Menenger's apocalyptic vision of CNCD's struggle is unique," said Gammarelli. "In his construction of things the opposing forces include cardinals, bishops, priests and laity. He sees the fight the Church is engaged in as fundamentally internal."

"And so with CNCD," said Benneditti. "Forces of renewal in the Church are portrayed in their literature as subject to internal persecution. Past reformers such as Anthony of the desert, Athanasius,

Francis and Ignatius are held up as examples of those who had to fight against obstinate resistance at every turn. They see any form of opposition as devil-inspired."

"The threat of modernism is real enough, Eminence," said Donaghue, trying to hold the line.

"But equally often imaginary," said Benneditti. He waved a hand vaguely in the direction of Gammarelli and Craxi as if to confirm the present company's breadth of vision. "CNCD is afraid of its own shadow!"

"The arch inquisitor's regime is wholly repressive," spat Gammarelli.

"I think that is to go too far!" said Donaghue.

"You think so?" said Gammarelli. "Let me tell you something, Archbishop. We're back in the time when walls had eyes and ears, and that is no exaggeration. Menenger's spies are everywhere."

"Truth must be safeguarded at all cost," said Donaghue, confused and worried by what he was hearing.

"But not at the cost of truth itself," said Benneditti. A sigh indicated his impatience with Donaghue. "There are some basics that have to be grasped here. It's become a matter of you pat my back and I'll pat yours. The movement recognizes the Holy Father and the Holy Father recognizes the movement. The movement's growing importance gives new relevance to the papal office, and the papal office returns the favor by strengthening the movement's hand in the parishes. Its a symbiotic relationship, and it grows stronger by the day."

"It's rumored that the Holy Father is about to recommend membership of the movement to *all* lay people," said Craxi. "That would be an unmitigated disaster for the Church."

"And there's now an army of canon lawyers dedicated to the task of sustaining CNCD's privileges," said Antonio Pia, who had been listening and watching intently. "Past religious orders produced theologians, Michael, this lot have produced an armada of lawyers."

The mention of canon lawyers caused Donaghue to relent

slightly. He admitted to having had first-hand experience in that quarter.

"*Centratura,*" said Craxi, describing the quality of 'self-centeredness' required of CNCD members. "Their leaders are chosen for their fidelity to the party line. That is all that matters to them."

"It's basically a brain-washing technique," said Benneditti. "A professor of philosophy at Gregorian University described the language of the movement to me as a system of elaborate codes 'designed to confuse the uninitiated'. The jargon they've developed provokes guilt, obedience and a sense of belonging through the use of trigger words."

"This can be proved?" said Donaghue.

"Father Grosjean is preparing a detailed study for publication," said Benneditti. "It'll cause a scandal when it's released."

"Is that what you want?"

"It's what has to be. The movement's grip is tightening."

"A book can be refuted."

"The signatures of some thirty cardinals backing the book's contentions will be difficult to ignore."

"You yourself will sign?"

"Of course."

Donaghue looked at Pia, then back at Benneditti. "It doesn't worry you that the Church could be split in two by this?"

"It's already split in two," said Benneditti.

"But not yet known to be," said Donaghue.

"If you mean we should attempt to save face, then I have to disagree. This is not something that can be sidestepped or accommodated, Archbishop. It's a cancer, and as such it has to be dealt with before its grip becomes too strong."

"It will bring the Catholic faith into disrepute."

"Not if we clean out our own stable," said Benneditti. "If we do that, we'll survive."

22

Full Circle

Marcia Neumann was a small, neat woman in her mid-forties with dark hair, a sallow complexion and, like her brother, piercing blue eyes. Unlike her brother, her European accent was quite pronounced. "Thank you for seeing me," she said, extending a hand. When seated, she produced a black leather diary from her pocket and got straight to the point. "Under the circumstances I think you should have this. It tells the whole story of how Hubert came to know about the codex."

"I thought I already knew the whole story."

"Not quite." Marcia Neumann's smile was wan. "My brother kept a little bit back . . . " She looked down at her hands, which were clasped, and up again. "He was shielding someone, Professor."

Windle fingered the diary open and scanned a few lines. "What should I be looking at, Frau Neumann?"

"The entry for 2 February. He talked to me about it."

Windle leafed through the pages of neat German script until he hit the entry in question. After a moment's reading, he looked up and said, "Fr Grosjean was his source?"

A nod from Marcia Neumann.

Windle read on, Weisel's detailed description of his telephone conversations with the priest revealing not only a long-standing friendship, but a behind-the-scenes conspirator of some importance. "I'm in your debt, Frau Neumann," he said, looking up. "This answers questions that have been bothering me.

Marcia Neumann's dip of the head reminded Windle of her brother's sometimes silent acknowledgment of a point. "May I offer you tea, Frau Neumann?" he asked.

A shake of the head, and a smile. She would have to go soon.

"I haven't said how shocked I was to hear of your loss. I can't imagine how you must have felt when you were told."

"I hadn't seen Hubert in years," she replied. "And of course we quarreled almost immediately. It was our habit."

" . . . I can't help but feel partly responsible."

"As I do!" Her blue eyes opened wide. "He accepted your invitation because of *me*. He said so. If anyone should feel guilty, I should."

Windle said nothing for a moment, then he said, "I can't just let you go like this. Let me make you some tea." He was on his feet. "You've got no idea how helpful you've been."

She hesitated, then assented. As he prepared the tea, she said, "I saw you being interviewed on television."

"*Grilled* would be a better word."

"Your son is still in Israel?"

"He's having a wonderful time." Windle glanced at Weisel's sister. "I get worried when I hear what's going on out there. It looks like things are getting worse."

"You also have a daughter?"

"Yes. Jane's here in New York at the moment."

"We have a son at university."

"I'm sorry, would you prefer coffee, Frau Neumann?"

"No, no," she said quickly. "Tea. Black. No sugar."

"How long have you been in the States?"

"Twenty-two years. My husband's Austrian." She corrected herself. "He was born in Austria. He's much more American than I am. He teaches German. We met in Munich a lifetime ago."

"You're Swiss-born?"

"Yes. You?"

"New Yorker through and through. My parents were German." He came across with their tea. "I've got a research post in Essen. This was supposed to be a flying visit." A smile, then the question he really wanted to ask. "There's only one thing I do not understand, Frau Neumann . . . Your brother's reason for meeting with me here. He didn't have to do that. Did he?"

"He thought it his duty to look you in the eye," she replied. "He said so. It was his way of dealing with the injustice of the situation. It was also important for you to realize there was a cabal, that you were a pawn in a much larger game." The irony of what she was about to add twisted her mouth. "He had to lie to tell you the truth, to safeguard his informer and ease his conscience."

"Did he say how Fr Grosjean came to know about the location of the codex?"

"I don't think he knew."

"I'm a pawn in a much larger game?"

"It's a power struggle, Professor. The liberal and the conservative factions have joined forces against the neo-conservatives."

"Your brother told you this?"

A quick nod. "The neo-conservatives are considered dangerous to the faith even by the conservatives. Fr Grosjean is a key player."

"Did your brother ever mention a Professor Moyer?"

"Moyer? He studied under Moyer in Berlin. As a young man. They were still in contact?"

"There were letters in his briefcase to Grosjean and Moyer."

"You already knew about Grosjean?"

"We knew the name, that's all. The letters were non-specific thankyous for services rendered."

"Moyer filled his head with a lot of nonsense during his student days. My father was livid when he found out."

"Your brother found Moyer's ideas interesting?"

"He described himself as open-minded on certain questions. I had no idea they were still in contact."

"He's not mentioned in the diary?"

"I haven't read it all. I knew about Grosjean because Hubert talked to me about him.

"Grosjean is liberal?"

"Oh yes," she replied.

"You're in favor?"

"Very much so." She made a face. "Moyer was an idiot."

310

Windle moved on. "You're sure about this . . . alliance?"

"Yes, I'm sure."

"It sounds improbable."

"The neo-conservatives have alienated just about everyone with their puritanical nonsense. CNCD's claim is that it has returned to basics; it has done nothing of the kind. It has returned to the madness of the thirteenth century." She drew breath and continued. "If they aren't stopped there's no telling where the Church will end up."

"CNCD?"

"Children of the New Catholic Dawn."

"There's an actual movement?"

"A hydra-headed movement. CNCD is the brain."

"The acronym is new to me."

"That's why I brought you Hubert's diary. It explains the larger picture; it's a disturbing one. Hardly anyone realizes what's going on outside of the hierarchy itself."

"I would have thought the conservative and liberal viewpoints almost impossible to reconcile."

"Not all conservatives are literalists, Professor. Quite a few take a more symbolic approach to doctrine. By that means they are able to straddle the fence between tradition and good sense. It's a tightrope, but it safeguards the faith from wanton destruction. There are vandals on both sides of the fence."

"Some would say I'm one of those vandals," said Windle, eyeing Marcia Neumann's angular face. "There is certainly a temptation in that direction at times."

"You don't strike me as an arrogant man, Professor."

"We all have our moments of weakness, Frau Neumann."

"To know that is to be tempered from within," she replied.

* * *

"Bishop Peters articulated much of what you've just told me about

CNCD when David and I visited him in hospital," said Duggan, watching Windle scoff a late breakfast. They were seated in the hotel's almost empty breakfast room. "We seem to have come full circle."

"Grosjean's written a book detailing CNCD excesses," said Windle, who had only just completed reading Weisel's diary. "He's even got a publisher lined up."

"But nothing on how he knew about the codex?"

A shake of the head from Windle.

"You'll contact him?"

"Of course."

"What will you say?"

"That I have the full story in Weisel's own hand. That I know what's going down in Rome. That I'd like to know what he hopes to achieve with Theodore's letter given that the Vatican will do everything in its power to rubbish it the moment it's released. *And,* " said Windle, jumping back in, "I'll want to know if he has the original Voss document, or if he knows where it is."

"You'll frighten the life out of him. "

"He doesn't sound like the kind of man who frightens easily."

"Beware of telephones."

"I'll be careful in what I say."

Duggan watched Windle eat for a moment or two, then he said, "What was the sister like?"

"Good-looking, in a thinnish kind of way. She had her brother's eyes. I think her hair was dyed. It was too dark for her complexion."

"They didn't get on?"

"Mending fences was part of his reason for coming to New York." A mouthful of scrambled egg before Windle continued. "She didn't approve of the way I was being used, Jack."

Accepting Windle's evaluation, Duggan said, "Peters talked of a serious power bloc."

"So does Weisel. He describes it as hydra-headed." Windle's expression became one of bemusement. "It's scary stuff, Jack. They're rampant lunatics from the sound of it, and they've got the backing of some of the most powerful figures in Rome."

"But not Benneditti?"

"Apparently not. Benneditti may be dying of cancer, but according to Weisel he intends to go out with a bang."

"No other names are mentioned?"

"There are hints, but nothing specific."

"Benneditti is backing Grosjean?"

"That's the story." Pushing his empty plate aside, Windle reached for his coffee. "There are also some scathing remarks about Cardinal Menenger in the text. He seems willing to sustain the status quo at almost any price. "

"'Pluralism of ideas . . . changed into pluralism of movements and their ideas,'" said Duggan. "That was how Bishop Peters described the Prefect. It allows him to sound modern when he is in fact antediluvian in his thinking"

"You think it's that conscious?"

"It has to be. He can't not know what's going on."

"Power at any price."

"Plenitudo potestatis," said Duggan, referring to the fullness of power enjoyed by the pope as head of a sovereign state. He smiled and added: "It would be more accurate to talk about order at any price. The whole thing's about the sustaining of order through the giving of orders. "

"There's been an attempt at reform since Vatican II."

"Vatican II recognized the Church as a community in constant need of reform. It's my guess that's what Menenger is playing games with."

Windle was silent for a moment, then he said, "There's no doubt in Grosjean's mind the codex is authentic. Weisel gives an account of the priest's pleasure in being able to set up a situation where Theodore's letter is made known to the world. He obviously knew enough about its contents to know the kind of impact it could have."

"Which suggests there's another mind at work here. Grosjean's a philosopher; it's unlikely he's also a paleographer. Could be he has a friend in the Department of Antiquities."

"That's a nice thought," said Windle. Then, realizing, he said, "What do you suggest we do about Holly Parks?"

"Leave things as they are? Whatever she finds out about the factions is to our benefit."

"David will have mentioned the Grosjean and Moyer letters found in Weisel's briefcase."

"Yes, but only in that context. He doesn't know about Grosjean's connection with the codex."

"He's slept with her," said Windle. "Came straight out with it. Plus assurances."

"You know David better than I do."

"Yes, I do, and there isn't a problem," said Windle. Taking Weisel's diary out of his jacket pocket, he flicked at its pages. "Some of the stuff in here is explosive, Jack. Seems John Paul II's long-term plan had as much to do with Western culture as it had to do with the spiritual. His plan was to change the whole mentality of Western culture. That's what lay behind *Christifideles laici,* his 1987 official report on the Laity. A section of that report is devoted to the movements as agents of cultural change, and it's Benedict's intention to follow through on John Paul's aims."

"Nothing new there," said Duggan. "The hierarchy perceive themselves as the embodiment of a perfect society *in potenti,*"

"It's an attempt to engineer the whole of Western culture away from hard-won democratic values."

"The hardliners don't see it that way," said Duggan. "All they see is a culture of death, a civilization of death. That was the actual description of modern society used by John Paul II. In their mind Western democracy equals rampant secularism and the death of the soul. They believe themselves to be the antidote to a society gone over to the devil. They're theological literalists. All they see is decay and breakdown. What normal people think of as Western society's strengths - pluralism, feminism and minority rights - they categorized as its greatest weaknesses. And so you end up with moral hobbyhorses in every direction. If they had their way we wouldn't be able to blink without permission."

"Weisel writes of fanaticism, blind obedience, sloganeering and manipulation of the media as CNCD's bread and butter. He also mentions denunciations as common practice, and of a rigid ideology based on a personality cult centered on the pope. It's wild stuff, Jack, but he gives chapter and verse for what he says."

"I didn't fully appreciate what Bishop Peters was saying when David and I visited him in hospital. I do now. He said there were three factions in the Church: the conservatives, the neo-conservatives and the liberals. He described the neo-conservatives as being the Catholic equivalent of a Protestant fundamentalist sect. He said the idea of community had been usurped and turned into a tool of oppression by the movements. He likened what was going on to National Socialism's use of community as the bedrock for Nazism." Duggan smiled. "I thought that was a bit strong, but from what you've just told me, it seems he was right."

"Jane passed his recent article on to me," said Windle. "He didn't pull his punches."

"We may have to invest a little more trust in Holly at some point," said Duggan, sensing complications ahead. "We don't have to let on that it was Grosjean who had you tipped off about the codex, just that he was known to Weisel. Translate some of the stuff in Weisel's diary for her. If she gets her teeth into CNCD that'll keep her busy. And I'd let David pass that on; it would strengthen his hand."

"And if she digs a little too deeply?"

"That's something we'll just have to live with if it happens. Weisel protected his source at every stage. We should do the same, I think."

"Grosjean's playing two difficult bridge hands at once, Jack; he shouldn't be surprised if things go awry."

"Leave Grosjean to Holly. Better that you keep your distance."

"I want to know how this whole charade got going."

"Telephoning Grosjean isn't the way to go. He may already be under scrutiny. He's certainly under pressure."

"So what do you suggest?"

"What I said a moment ago. Prime Holly and let her loose."

"That wouldn't answer the questions I want answered."

"No, but it would force Grosjean to the surface. Talk to him direct and he may clam up. Let David in on what you've discovered. He'll appreciate the trust and he'll be one big step ahead of Holly. He'll like that. It'll put him back in the frame. It's a game of wits. It's chess. The other side's well practiced at it and shouldn't be given the slightest advantage."

Windle was silent for a moment, then with a shrug he said he would go along with Duggan's suggestions. David would know how to get the best out of the situation.

Later that same afternoon Duggan handed Windle the completed translation of Theodore's letter. It had turned into a fifteen-page document. Flinging himself down onto the couch, he sighed a sigh of relief.

"It's a brilliant piece of work, Jack. Congratulations." Windle had read each page as Duggan produced it, but had kept his opinions to himself. He leafed through the pages of neat transcription now with obvious admiration. "Excellent work."

"Glad you think so."

"Drink?"

A nod from Duggan.

Windle returned with two large whiskies; he took up the other end of the couch. "To Theodore," he said.

"Theodore," said Duggan.

They sipped in silence.

"Elliot will have my scalp when I get back," said Duggan. "Difficult questions will have been asked."

"You've got a big story out of it."

"Which is something we have to discuss now that Holly's in the picture. When the story breaks in Australia with my name on it she'll what to know what the hell has been going on."

"Leave Holly to David; he'll smooth the waters. You came to New York to authenticate the photographs. We became friends because of your academic background. There's no great mystery in that."

"Too many journalists spoil the broth," said Duggan.

Part Three

The storm Breaks

23

Lull Before the Storm

Jane's tone was playful, but Duggan knew she meant business. She was coming to Australia and that was that. To see Sydney. To see how he lived. To get a few pointers from his cat Phoebe. She had shown him New York; it was his turn.

They were seated in Central Park not far from the rink, the swish of skates audible in spite of the line of onlookers at the rail.

"Just when it's warming up," he said, conscious of the change in temperature May had brought. "It's winter in Sydney."

"I can help you subdue Elliot."

"That'll be the day. Elliot's a force to be reckoned with."

"He's been very patient"

"I haven't given him much option."

She paused. "What's David working on now?"

"The American Church's relationship to the Vatican. History of. He's already got a lot of what they need in these files of his."

"They?"

"He and Holly. They've teamed up." Duggan smiled. "Sort of."

"Why that particular angle?"

"To show why a fundamentalist Catholicism will never work in America, or in any tried-and-true democracy. It was tried in America a century ago, and failed. Bishop Peters's lecture tapped into that fiasco."

"I gave that one a miss."

"Pity. It was a thumper. In the 1890s Rome accused American Catholics of having abandoned their faith - they were accused of heresy no less. American democracy was blamed. We seem to be headed back in that direction. But there's a twist. It seems that papal authority has been usurped by an equally petulant ultra-conserv-ative lobby from within the Vatican. American Catholics rejected the 'swamp of speculative theology' at the end of nineteenth century - to quote Bishop Peters - and we now have to do the same at the end of the twentieth."

"I'm surprised my father isn't on a plane to Rome given what you've just learned about Grosjean."

"It's something we'll use only if we have to."

There was a silence. Duggan watched the queue at the hot-dog stand move forward another notch.

"Do you really think she cares for David?" Jane's frown was searching. "They make a strange pair. I'd hate to see him get hurt."

"She's broken the drought."

"Is that how you read it?"

"You get out of practice."

Jane was looking at him with interest.

"I wasn't stuck in the way he was stuck, but there's no doubting I was out of practice. I kept hoping the next face would have in it what I was looking for."

She tilted her head and watched his eyes, smiled as he began to smile. "I feel as if I've always known you, Jack."

"We met twenty-six days ago," he said, having calculated their time together that very morning. "We met on the evening of the eleventh of April. You were wearing a brown skirt and a red polar-necked sweater. I couldn't take my eyes off you."

"We met the evening before, actually," she said back. "In the hotel bar? You were nursing a whisky and you were in a foul mood."

"You were sprawled out on one of the bamboo sofas reading a book. You had taken your shoes off."

"I was aware of you looking at me."

"I didn't think you had noticed."

"We *always* notice," she said, breaking another smile.

He absorbed her playfulness and asked what they would have done if he had refused to join them.

"I really don't know." She blinked her uncertainty at him. "We took an awful chance telling you about the photographs the way we did. I realized that later."

"Why did you?"

"David felt certain you'd be willing to help."

"I distinctly remember you bitching at me because you thought I was going to walk away."

"Did you seriously think of doing that?"

"I'd probably have robbed a bank if you'd asked."

"That's not the impression I got from you."

"It's what David sensed. He wasn't wrong."

Her reply was to lean right across the table and quickly kiss him. He liked that. It told him a lot about her as a person. When she drew away, he suggested they go back to the apartment.

"You're forgetting something. My father's coming to dinner this evening." She made a face. "It'll be a madhouse, Jack. Elspeth and Martina will be in the thick of preparations."

"A last supper."

"I hope not."

"I meant in the sense of partings."

"A lull before the storm is what I sense."

"He's not exactly a wilting violet, Jane. He'll take whatever comes in his stride."

She looked down at the table as if what she had to say next was written there. "He's a funny mixture." Her gaze lifted to his face. "He's got a soft centre, Jack. I've seen him shed a tear over a news item."

"He's as determined about this as I've ever seen anyone about anything."

"Yet hates having had to do what he's done. It bothers him that he's had to use such tactics."

Duggan's reply was oblique. "I love Durer's woodcut of the little man with his head stuck through a hole in the Earth's crystal sphere," he said, smiling at Jane. "He's broken out of his circumscribed reality and he damn well knows it. Theodore's letter carries the same sense of astonishment. To not know about that letter would be to be robbed of vital intelligence."

"But will it make any difference? Will it hit the mark?"

"Scholars with a theological axe to grind will debunk it. Anyone with a modicum of historical sense will see it as seminal to our understanding of the make-up and intentions of the early Church. It throws a lot of light on the sect backgrounding the Apostles and St Paul. It explains in explicit terms how the juggernaut of Christianity got under way. Yes, it's only one man's opinion, but he just happens to have been one of the outstanding intellects of the fourth century."

"There must be a sense of anticlimax. You've been living inside someone else's head for almost a month."

"He's a wonderful stylist."

"You make him sound as if he's still alive."

"He is. He's not just on the page, he's *in* the page. I can feel his presence as I read what he's written." A smile from Duggan. "He was once as real as I am, Jane. As real as you are. It's not just meanings that come across when you translate something like this. It's also tone. You can tell a lot about someone from their tone."

"Christians will buck at the idea of Christianity having sprung from a sect."

"When that's properly understood everything will fall into place."

"They won't buy it, Jack."

"They're not all tarred with the same brush."

"The evangelical lobby here in the States is as strong as it's ever been."

"They're still a minority."

"A vocal minority with growing political clout."

"They thought a Baptist like Carter would initiate their policies. He didn't. They made the same mistake with Reagan. Any democracy worth its salt rejects foisting minority opinions on the majority. It will always be thus. It has to be. Kennedy understood that better than anyone. Hence his categorical promise to ignore any religious directive from Rome that jeopardized the democratic freedoms of non-Catholics. Carter and Reagan tried to have it both ways, but in the end they realized that simply wasn't possible. Future administrations will be faced with the same dilemma."

"The evangelicals admit to having a ten-year plan. They're set on developing political consciousness among their followers."

"Faster the better as far as I'm concerned. Why? Because to be politically conscious is to see and understand things you didn't see or understand beforehand. To be politically conscious is to wake up to reality whether you like it or not. It's to appreciate the needs of others alongside your own needs. You can't just use the democratic system for your own ends. You can't legislate others into accepting your idea of God. You can try, but it won't work."

"You're putting a lot of faith in the system."

"It's what makes the West the West. For all its faults, it's the best system around."

She smiled and reached for his hands. "How do you get on with my father? Really?"

"I like him. He's gruff at times, but he's fair."

"Your translation?"

"Gave it a big tick."

"He says you're very disciplined."

"I had a job to do."

"I wasn't much help."

"You kept giving out mixed signals. I didn't know where I was with you for ages. Or what seemed like ages."

"I was afraid of making a mistake." She was looking at him intently. "*Another* mistake," she added, letting his hands go. "I've made a few in my time."

"You think I haven't?"

"I kept thinking I'd got it right when I hadn't." She gave out a hopeless little laugh. "My father despaired of me!"

"He hasn't thought of marrying again?"

"Of course. He's an attractive man."

Duggan paused; then jumping ahead, he said, "I think you'll like

Sydney. It isn't New York, but I don't think you'll be disappointed. It's a friendly place. A bit mad, but friendly."

"You're reputed to be not unlike Americans."

"There's some truth in that," he admitted. "We're pretty laidback, and we're garrulous. But I warn you, we aren't respectful of authority."

She was leaning on the table now, arms folded, her head up and slightly tilted. "Your haircut accentuates the point," she said.

"I've came to like it. You?"

"It's how you were when I first saw you. It's the only *you* I know." She looked away, then back. "You like New York?"

"It's different from what I expected."

"What did you expect?"

"Sirens and chalked bodies on the pavement." He corrected himself. "The sidewalk."

"You've seen too many American movies."

He laughed and passed on a story he had heard from a friend. A mate of his had came to New York in the mid-seventies, he said, his face already creased with humor. When he came out of his hotel on the first morning there had been police everywhere and the chalked outline of a body a few feet from the entrance. That had scared him. What happened next had scared him even more. He had gone walking in Central Park, and within minutes had been accosted by three black guys who stripped him of his valuables. Watch. Money. Credit cards. The lot. Then the most extraordinary thing had happened. Realizing that he was an Australian, they'd given him everything back. Everything. Why? Because they hadn't wanted their city to get a bad name. And then they had escorted him to the nearest exit and told him to be more careful in future.

They sat in easy silence for a moment or two considering the likelihood of that ever happening again, then Jane suggested that they walk for a bit. It was just after three.

"When are we expected back?" asked Duggan.

"By eight." Jane grimaced at the thought of what lay ahead.

"Elspeth will be in her element. She's already guessed you're here because of the codex, but hasn't been able to fathom why my father needs you." They were on their feet now and heading back the way they had come. "She asked me point blank about you on one occasion. Wanted to know what we were all up to."

"What did you tell her?"

"That I didn't know the ins and outs of what you were doing, but that you were proving very helpful. She more or less gave up after that."

They watched a hired horse and buggy go by, its Japanese occupants sitting as still and stiff as manikins in a shop window. That was when something struck Duggan. "Passport," he said, staring at her.

"I brought it with me; I thought I might need it." Her smile broadened. "I've got my father's pragmatic genes, Jack."

* * *

Cardinal Menenger's tone was even and precise. The Children of the New Catholic Dawn were like undesired children, he said, eyeing Robert Carter across his desk. They were not wanted, but they could not be aborted. Something resembling a smile infused the Prefect's face. It was a matter of educating the bishops to understand that the movements, in conjunction with the Holy Father's wishes, constituted the only viable solution to the Church's present crisis. The bishops' jibe that new wine was bursting old wineskins had to be countered with the observation that the movements were indispensable and co-essential with the hierarchy. The primacy of the pope distilled *through* the movements - particularly CNCD - would eventually still the clamor of dissent. The movements were the Church's shock-troops - as the Jesuits had once been - and if the Church ever needed shock-troops it needed them now.

Carter nodded in agreement, but did not reply. The Prefect of the Congregation for the Defense of the Faith was on a roll.

"The situation we face can only be resolved through the primacy of the pope, Robert. Theologians who continue to differ with the Holy Father on fundamental issues have to be dealt with."

A thick sheaf of reports on local clergy in California who had refused to toe the consensus line lay on the Prefect's desk. It contained lines from sermons, bits of conversation with parishioners, letters, tapes of broadcasts and, in particular, detailed accounts of those who had refused to co-operate with CNCD's missionary efforts. As the bearer of those reports, and others, Carter knew from experience that dire consequences would result for those who continued to buck Vatican directives.

The Prefect's voice continued rhetorically:

"Deep reforms are necessary. We have to take back the initiative. We've become detached from history because our brave Vatican II reformers lacked a historical perspective. Catholicism isn't a culture, Robert, it's a creed, and as such it makes objective demands on *all* of us. *That* is what has been forgotten. Dissent against the Church's official teachings on faith and morals cannot be tolerated."

To anyone listening at the door, Cardinal Menenger's remarks could have been taken as a reproof of something Carter had said, but it was in fact his normal method of talking to subordinates. Empowered to correct, the Grand Inquisitor took every opportunity to fulfill his office.

"Catholicism *is* true humanism," he then ventured. "That's what we have to sell to the world. Without the truths of faith humanism is a denigration of what it means to be a human being."

"The crown jewels," said Carter, referring to the life-giving data of the Christian revelation. Emboldened by the sound of his own voice, he added, "We are beset by secular disciples unsuited to the task of deciphering our Lord's intentions."

"Exactly," said Menenger. "There are givens that cannot be tampered with. They carry the force of principles. Eliminate them and you cease to do theology in any real sense."

The two men were looking at one another; it was as if they were resonating on the same frequency.

"We can't have a parallel magisterium made up of theologians who dismiss the Gospel story as a fairytale." Menenger's face was set hard with intent. "They have a duty to teach what the Church has always taught, and the Church has a duty to see that they do it. They have no legitimate claim to existence outside of the framework of the Church."

Carter, whose whole existence was dedicated to the task of sustaining the Church's two-thousand-year-old claim to possess divine truth, nodded vigorously in support. It was shocking to think, he said, that so many Catholic institutions had ceased to be places where the fullness of Catholic truth was joyfully taught, defended and proclaimed.

Menenger's eyes brightened as if through a surge of electricity. "It is our stated mission to help as many people as possible to get to heaven," he said, quoting something he had downloaded from the net that very morning, "and I frankly don't see that being accomplished by those who advocate either a watering down or a rejection of Catholicism's great truths. The existence of God's objective truth is being denied at every turn, and we have to put a stop to that."

The eyes that had brightened dulled; it seemed to Menenger that everything sacred was under threat. God's truth had been through the fire of human experience and had proved itself hardier than any half-baked theory spawned by disillusioned minds.

Having allowed Cardinal Menenger time to unburden himself, Carter then made his move. It was his unpleasant duty, he said, producing Archbishop Donaghue's letter refuting CNCD priorities, to call in question the suitability of the man appointed by the late pontiff as guardian of the American soul. The Archbishop of Nevada was a good man, and a doctrinally sound man, but he did not seem to have the stomach for implementing the late Holy Father's vision of the American Church revived and ready to meet the challenge's of the twenty-first century. His categorical unwillingness to support CNCD's missionary efforts was proof of that, as was his concern with the vicissitudes of public opinion rather than with God's so clearly intended purpose for his people.

"Fr Brentano joined the recalcitrants?"

"The priest has been vocal in his condemnation of the movement in the local press." Carter's expression was one of deep concern. "Those he supports have turned a simple situation into a scandal with serious repercussions for the Church, Eminence."

"The archbishop did nothing to stop this?"

"I'm not privy to the archbishop's response in relation to Brentano, but if what he wrote to me is anything to go by, I would say they are of the same mind."

"I'm informed he's in Rome this very minute seeking an audience with the Holy Father."

"Is it your Eminence's intention to speak with him?"

Cardinal Menenger's gaze returned to Donaghue's letter for a moment, then lifted again. "On seeing this I think perhaps I should." The smile returned. "I'm grateful to you for you bringing this to my attention, Robert."

"I thought it an important matter, Eminence."

"I'll need a copy of this letter for my files."

"Of course," said Carter. He looked suddenly uncomfortable, guilty almost. " . . . Could what has passed between us be kept in confidence, Eminence?"

"Of course. The Brentano affair will suffice as an excuse." Menenger glanced at his watch. "I'll ask the archbishop for copies of all relevant communications. Was there anything else you wished to draw my attention to?"

"Nothing, Eminence. I think the reports speak for themselves."

"Then I'll bid you good day, Robert. May God go with you."

"And with you, Eminence," said Carter.

* * *

"It's thought that the basic conventions of Islam grew out of Eastern

Christian practice." Windle cut into his steak. "The Muslim method of prayer is thought to have developed from the earlier Syrian Orthodox tradition." The steak headed for his mouth, but did not enter. "Even the architecture of the earliest minarets - they were square rather than round - probably sprang from the design of church towers in Byzantine Syria."

"*Fascinating,*" said Elspeth.

"What's Mar Saba like inside?"

George's question caused Windle to smile. "Dark and dingy. Many of the corridors are cut out of the solid rock. The whole place hangs from a rock face."

"The monastery's still in use?"

"Oh yes. You can still hear Vespers being sung." Windle turned to Duggan. "Did I mention that St John of Damascus believed Islam was a form of Christianity related to the heterodox Christian doctrine of Arianism?" Duggan shook his head and Windle turned his attention back to the others. "The Arian heretics rejected the idea of God becoming fully human."

"They had a point," said Duggan.

"It's Sufism that interests me," said Windle. He looked from George to Elspeth. "The more I study it, the more it comes across as a strand of Eastern Christianity. Sufi forms of dress were used in pre-Islamic Christianity, as was the use of heavy chains for purposes of mortification. It's been suggested that a monk from sixth century Byzantium would be more at home with a Muslim Sufi than with a contemporary American evangelical."

"Theodore's slant is that the so-called Christian heresies developed out of Nazoraean doctrine," said Duggan. "Maybe the Sufis fit in there as well."

"The smoking gun," said Windle.

"Is that how you read it?"

Windle reached for his glass of wine. "Might be that the Sufi's are what's left of the Ebionites." After a sip of wine he offered a further insight. "I read a paper some years back in which it was suggested that Islam's primary reason for coming into existence was to counteract Rome's false ideas about early Christianity. There might be something in that. Kamil Salibi - he was Professor of History at the American University in Lebanon a few years back - argued that the Koran contains an independent tradition concerning the origins of Christianity. He did original research on Nazoraean origins and traced them to the Hijaz mountains of western Arabia."

"The Hijaz?" said Duggan.

"He distinguishes between two groups of Nazoraean, and says that the Koran condemns one for maintaining that God is a trinity, but praises the other for teaching that God is one, not three."

"Does he offer a date for these groups?"

"Circa 500BCE?" Windle laughed to himself. "It gets better, Jack. The first group worshipped their founder - a prophet called Issa - as a divine being. When transliterated from Arabic through Aramaic into Greek, the name Issa emerges as *Iesous*. *Iesous* is the Greek name for Jesus in the New Testament," said Windle, glancing at his hosts.

"Transliterated?" said George.

"The way in which the name has traditionally moved from language to language," said Windle. "It wouldn't be accurate to say *translated*."

"If he's right, they'll have to drop the notion of Christianity being unique." Duggan was staring at Windle. "His findings are trustworthy?"

"He's dismissed by some as a crank, but I think that's a bit harsh. He's done his homework, and there are too many coincidences. He's also got the requisite languages under his belt - he's fluent in Arabic and Hebrew." Windle paused for another sip of wine. "The Arabian home of the Nazoraean sect was Nasira. Nasira translates as *Nazareth*. The location of the Arabian Nazareth was *Wadi Jalil*. That translates as *'valley of Galilee*. There's more. Salabi's conclusion is that there was an early migrational wave into Palestine from the Hijaz area. The basic story is that after the community of Israel was given the Torah by Moses, two prophets appeared: Ezra and Issa." Windle pushed his plate away and placed his elbows on the table. "The followers of Ezra became the Jews, the followers of Issa became the Nasara, or Nazoraeans. Both groups are said to have called their leader a son of God, but the Nazoraeans took to worshipping their founder as divine in his own right. Salibi's research suggests that the Nazoraeans were not an extension of Judaism, but a kind of sister religion, a parallel set of religious ideas that eventually surfaced as Pauline Christianity."

"That would explain a few imponderables," said Duggan.

"Indeed." Windle explained further for the sake of George and Elspeth. "Palestine is a geographical extension of western Arabia. The Jerusalem of Judea is a possibly reflection of an older Arabian Jerusalem known as *Uri Shalim*. The political history of the Israelites came to an end in western Arabia with the destruction of Judah by the Babylonians in 586BCE. The Persians allowed Israelite exiles to return to their Arabian homeland. There was a whole community of Arabian Israelites in the Hijaz region, and they were divided into three distinct groups: Those who remained true to Israelite monotheism; those who became Jews as defined by the prophet Ezra; and those who became followers of the divine Issa. Jesus is referred to as *Issa* in Arabic to this day."

"How do you *remember* it all!" said Elspeth.

"Might explain why St Paul's claim to be an Apostle 'born out of season' was so readily accepted by the other Apostles in Jerusalem," said Duggan. "His Galatian Epistle suggests he spent some time in Arabia."

"Arabia was also a code name for Damascus."

"Really?"

"Which seems to have housed a more radical set of Nazoraeans to those resident in Jerusalem."

"Believers in a divine Jesus," said Duggan.

"It helps solve the puzzle of what St Paul believed about Jesus. They quite simply converted him to an ancient variation of Nazoraean belief."

Duggan's cogs were whirling, Paul's road to Damascus experience had taken on new significance.

"What it does do," said Windle, addressing the table as a whole, "is give us a handle on why there are different Jesus figures in the New Testament. What I would suggest is that the Gospel Jesus is a composite figure, a figure composed of three elements: The historical Issa of the ancient Nasara, or Nazoraeans. The historical Jesus of the Christian Gospels. And of course the phantom Jesus who walked on water and worked miracles. This particular Jesus wasn't real - hence the tendency of some scholars to say that Jesus never existed at all - he was the result of the other two being sandwiched together. Seen that way the problems surrounding Jesus' historical existence, and his existence as a divine being, evaporate. Yes, he existed. Yes, some of his followers believed him to be divine. But that was the result of beliefs stemming from an ancient heretical branch of the Nazoraean sect grafted onto the flesh-and-blood Jesus who existed in the first century CE."

"*Brilliant!*" said Elspeth.

"Yes, but is it true?" Windle sat back into his chair. "I myself think it's a plausible theory."

"It still leaves open the question of why the original Nazoraeans thought Issa was divine," said Duggan.

"My guess is that Issa and Jesus underwent some kind of trans-formative experience," said Windle. "It's the only thing that makes sense."

There was a lull in the conversation; everyone retreated into their shell for a moment or two. Then George said: "Do you think Theodore knew anything about this?"

"He probably didn't known about the Hijaz Nazoraeans, but he knew a lot about the Jerusalem branch. Hence his take on sin. Unlike Origen, who believed man's sinfulness was the result of misconduct in a previous existence, Theodore believed sin was an incidental part of human education. He was written off as a Nestorian heretic by the Council of Constantinople in 533CE. During his lifetime his orthodoxy was regarded as unimpeachable."

"How is that possible?" asked George.

"It's possible because the view of Jesus held by Christians today took the Church the best part of four centuries to cobble together. Christian doctrine wasn't at all neat and tidy in the early centuries. Some thought Jesus was divine, some that he was a prophet, others that he was a man who had transcended his human limitations."

"I really don't know how you keep track of it all," said Elspeth. "I'm finding the few bits you've talked about difficult to follow. There are so many twists and turns."

"Tracking the ideas becomes a passion," said Windle.

"Scholars are still arguing over Theodore's orthodoxy," said Duggan, who had run numerous computer checks to clarify what this fourth-century bishop had believed about the nature of Christ. "It's still an undecided issue for many."

"An issue to which we are about to add a generous historical footnote," said Windle.

"We?" said Elspeth.

" . . . Fr Merle and I," he replied, correcting the drift of Elspeth's suspicions. Windle's smile became disingenuous. "Although a combined paper with Jack isn't out of the question."

"So what *exactly* are you working on?" Elspeth's question came at Duggan with a manufactured innocence equal to Windle's. "You've never really said."

"Research," said Duggan. "Everything Theodore says in his letter has to be weighed against his other known statements and opinions. If there's no echo, there could be a problem in getting anyone to accept what he says in this letter."

"Are there echoes?"

"Quite a few."

"Theodore held that evil was permitted by the Creator because it was to man's advantage to experience it," said Windle. "It's at exactly that point that he connects with Bishop Irenaeus, and with the early Apostolic Church's idea of Israel's Messiah being *visited upon by God.*

What we've found in Theodore's letter is a fundamentally Jewish conception of messiahship integrated with an historical perspective that confirms that perspective. That's in alignment with what's known of his theology. The Messiah of Israel isn't perceived as a dying Savior in Theodore's theological scheme, he's glimpsed as a living illustration of what we can all become."

"Perfect?" ventured Elspeth.

"Complete," said Windle. "Can you imagine a complete human being who hasn't experienced sin?"

"I'll drink to that," said George.

"It also throws light on how scholars like Theodore perceived Jesus. They didn't see a dying God, they saw proof of God's continuing covenant with man. The appearance of Jesus was interpreted as the final step in a series of covenants designed to raise human beings from the lower levels of awareness."

"Atkins rejected the idea of evil as necessary for human growth in his final lecture at the conference," said Jane. "I don't remember much of what he said, but I do remember him saying that the demands of evil were excessive, and that on that basis the destruction of souls rather than the perfecting of souls was the more likely outcome."

"It all comes down to how you view Jesus' nature," said Duggan.

"Some think the Eastern Church was forced into a position of diplomatic compromise over the question of Christ's true nature," said Windle. "It was a case of Eastern Christianity versus Western Christianity complicated by the belief of some that Christ had only one nature, not two. It's referred to in the West as the 'problem of appropriation. In the East, the tendency was to view Christ as having had a human nature *and* a divine nature. In the West, he was believed to have 'appropriated' a human nature." Windle smiled at George's expression. "I agree, that sounds like semantics, but it isn't. In Eastern thinking the human part of Christ's nature was an individual called Jesus the Nazoraean. In the West, Christ's human nature was perceived not as a person, or as a named individual, but as a *principle*. There's a heck of a difference between these two approaches. One is a literal possession of the human by the divine; the other is a subtle *appropriation* of human characteristics by the divine. That's a whole different ball game."

"Which takes us dangerously close to the idea that Jesus was more divine than human in spite of his having had a human body." Duggan's laugh was sour. "It was only a short hop from there to the belief that Jesus could do miracles, that he in fact could do anything. Indeed, that he was actually God paying planet Earth a visit in disguised form."

"For the purpose of making us perfect," said Elspeth dryly.

"Exactly," said Duggan. "The whole thing's an inflation. And an obvious one at that when one considers Jesus' words in the Garden. *'Father, if it be possible, take this cup from me.'* That's not God talking to himself; that's a human being buckling as he contemplates the horrors of crucifixion. Theodore plainly understood this. He's faithful to the principle that Mary could not have given birth to God, only to a human being. On that score he was in alignment with the Nestorian heretics."

"You think Jesus really said these things?" said Jane, frowning a crinkly kind of smile. "How can we know for sure?"

"We can't," said Duggan. "But it's more likely that that particular incident happened than that he walked on water. An incident like that gives us a glimpse of the flesh and blood man behind the image. When you read that Jesus was tired, or angry, or that he wept, that's the human being peeping through. Only by keeping that flesh and blood individual before our eyes can we ever hope to dismantle the public relations figure that's been foisted on us."

"Ultimately," said Windle, extending the theme, "the whole thing's about determinism and free will. Believe that Jesus was God come down to save us from sin and you're nothing but a poor hapless creature caught up in a gigantic cosmic game. It's human responsibility versus divine supremacy. Accept the latter and you descend into a demoralizing fatalism. It's a controversy that's been going on for centuries. Luther took on Erasmus and Whitefield took on Wesley over the same issues. Every age does battle with it."

"Hence Pelagius's friendship with Theodore," said Duggan. "Pelagius argued against Augustine's jaundiced view of man as a fallen creature. The doctrine of original sin was sheer nonsense, he said. The first sin had been single and insignificant; it was an excusable, not an inexcusable act. And it was not transmissible. It had not had the power to corrupt the human species and necessitate a divine sacrifice. Every sinner had his own individual fall, and the possibility of recovering from it. To believe otherwise was to exaggerate the potency and influence of sin."

"There's no fork-tailed Devil?" said Elspeth.

"Just our own stupidity," said Windle.

"Then what's the *point* of it all?" she asked.

"The point is that the point has been lost," said Windle.

"You still think there is a point?"

Windle paused, then he said, "According to Fr Merle there is."

24

Cat Among the Pigeons

A formal letter from the Vatican's Department of Antiquities arrived for Windle on the Thursday morning. It informed him that a general report on the Mar Saba Codex was about to be released to the media. Windle rang Duggan immediately. The result was worse than expected, he said, staring at the cold hard type surmounted by the Vatican's ubiquitous logo. The department's specialists had concluded that the codex was either a hoax or a forgery.

"They've gone straight for the jugular," said Duggan.

"Without offering a skerrick of evidence either way," said Windle. "They've merely stated that that's how the codex is being viewed. It's a clever move on their part, Jack."

"To the extent that you could say that about any old manuscript, it's meaningless."

"They cite Grafton: 'Argument based on form and content alone cannot eliminate the possibility of contemporary hoaxing. . . Any such argument can uncover the hoaxer only by detecting his mistakes.' They add that a contemporary might always possess as much information about plausible form and content as the would-be detector, possess the same tools, know as much about the uncovering of earlier hoaxes. As both Theodore's and Irenaeus's letters can be authenticated using the appropriate concordances, they argue that they could also have been forged using the same conconcordances." A laugh from Windle. "It's textbook stuff, Jack. Forgery as the criminal sibling of higher criticism. Higher criticism grew out of the detection of forgeries therefore just about anything is a potential forgery until proved otherwise by higher criticism."

"That's to misuse Grafton's point."

"You don't say!"

The twists and turns of the forger's mind had been outlined for

Duggan during his studies. It had been noted that the motives for forgery were varied: money, ambition, careerism, amusement, love for a heroic figure, malice, support for one's beliefs or sheer mystification. And it didn't matter how deft the forger was, there was generally a tendency to imprint the pattern and texture of their own period of life, thought or language on the past. It was this tendency that made the trickery stand out in bold relief. The details used by the forger to impress the victim more often than not revealed the forger's period superimposed on the forgery.

"The Vinland map case comes to mind," said Duggan, referring to the controversy surrounding the claim that North America had been discovered by Norse explorers in the fifteen century. "The paper and ink tests they resorted to weren't conclusive either way."

"Exactly." A laugh from the big American. "Proving authenticity is now more difficult than proving that something is a fake."

"How are you going to react?"

"Respectfully."

"Has Merle contacted you?"

"He rang me first thing this morning."

"Where from?"

"Rome."

"What's he doing there?"

"Being interrogated, I would imagine."

"And?"

"He knows what they're after."

"He's sticking by his guns?"

"As best he can."

"What does that mean?"

"It means he's standing by his earlier judgment on the codex, but that he's accommodating the department's approach." Windle's sigh was one of resignation. "He's informed them of the tip-off. He had to under the circumstances."

"And?"

Windle did not immediately reply. He drew a long breath, then he said, "I'm caught between the Devil and the deep blue sea, Jack."

"Merle standing by his previous evaluation strengthens your hand," said Duggan, "but there's a helluva difference between something being called heretical and it being called a hoax or a fake. It's a situation that could turn very nasty."

"Don't I know it."

Duggan's brain was racing. "They're releasing only a general report on the codex?"

"They've bought themselves time in which to perfect their strategy." Windle's tone was contemptuous. "They sense real danger in this one, Jack."

"They intend to mention the tip-off in their report?"

"Didn't say."

"Why not?"

Windle took a moment to answer. " . . . It's their cute way of silencing me on what the codex has to say, Jack. They hold back, I hold back."

"Except that you haven't."

"That's why I did what I did."

"You were one step ahead."

"I *thought* I was," said Windle, admitting to a measure of naivety. "I didn't expect them to take this particular route."

"It suggests panic on their part."

"Which makes them all the more dangerous."

"You're having second thoughts?"

"About publishing? Not at all. It's too late for that, Jack. It's too important a text to let them scare me off now."

"And when the connection is made between you and I, as it inevitably will be?"

"I'll be able to say with a clear conscience that I did not assist with the translation, and that what you ended up publishing was wholly the work of another mind."

"And if they find out that I am that other mind?"

"I knew there'd be risks, Jack."

"It's you who'll have to explain the coincidence and take the flak."

A sigh from Windle. "I'll write a thriller and make a lot of money. Isn't that what one does these days?"

"I think it's time we spoke to Holly," said Duggan.

"You think so?"

"Insurance for the future," said Duggan. "A voice strong enough to take on your ever-so-respectable foes if things get out of hand."

* * *

Archbishop Donaghue closed his eyes and listened to the drone of the Boeing's engines, his friend Cardinal Pia's parting words uppermost in his mind: *Ecclesia semper reformanda* - the Church is always in need of reform.

He had glanced back sensing Pia's eyes on him as he moved down the gilded corridor *en route* for the airport, and found the aged cardinal watching him like a father would a difficult son.

"The New Catholic Dawn's vision is riddled with a deep-seated loathing for the world," Pia had warned over a lunch of sandwiches and strong black coffee. "They view *all* human activity as empty and without purpose. That isn't Christianity, Michael, it's Manichaean fanaticism masquerading as Christianity. It is the faith turned manic and self-destructive."

"It is sometimes difficult to know where to draw the line," Donaghue had ventured. "The basics have to be enforced."

"Enforced?" Pia's frown had an element of scorn about it. "Anything that smacks of doctrinal coercion has to be ditched, Michael. It's one thing to teach the basics, it's quite another to teach those basics as if the slightest veering from a fixed interpretation warrants hell and damnation for all eternity. Truth is by necessity multifaceted; it is not a fixed quantity that has to be endlessly weighed in the manner CNCD weighs and distributes it - that is a return to old-fashioned absolutism and it has no place in the twenty-first century Church." The Cardinal drew breath and continued. "The recent pontiff's fear of moral relativism played havoc with Italian sensibilities, Michael. We Italians are the masters of what a writer I read only recently called 'finding a workable concordance between two notions'. That is an accurate description of the Italian soul. In spite of what some may think, it is that capacity which separates us from the Germans and the Anglo-Saxons."

For four days Donaghue had listened to Pia, and others of similar mind, talk such talk while damning CNCD for its grim, apocalyptic view of Western society. Overawed by such exchanges he had eventually submitted to the collective wisdom of his peers. CNCD would have to be dealt with, he had agreed, and that in spite of Menenger's unwillingness to see any fault in the organization's controversial theology and behavior. For how could any right-thinking person go along with the idea that Catholics outside of the movement's ranks were, as CNCD members believed, pagans because uncommitted in the way they were committed? Such a notion was ludicrous, the belief that what the movement taught had to be swallowed whole before the term 'Catholic' could apply nothing more than hubris run riot. Fanaticism of this sort had to be confronted, the more ridiculous theological claims made by CNCD challenged and brought to the attention of . . .

The Holy Office?

Opening his eyes, the archbishop summoned an attendant and asked for another glass of the airline's excellent Australian red. He had done his Christian duty, he told himself. He had done what conscience and common sense and the demands of his office asked of him, and that in spite of the fact that it would mean colliding with the Holy Office. He blinked at the thought of that, felt his heart begin to pound in his chest. What would Cardinal Menenger's reaction be, he wondered. What would the Church's Grand Inquisitor make of the fact that he of all people had joined the rebel camp?

* * *

"So what else aren't you telling me?" Holly's gaze was fixed on Windle. "Each time any of you decide to talk to me I find out I only know a bit of the story."

"It's only a matter of days since we ourselves got Weisel's diary from his sister," said Windle. "Marcia Neumann came to me on Monday evening; it's now only Thursday afternoon."

"Weisel's diary is written in a difficult hand, and it's in German," said Duggan, his tone less conciliatory. "It wasn't something that could be done in a couple of minutes."

Holly glanced at David Mayle as if to say *you ought to have told me this*. Then she said, "I get the feeling I'm being used."

"Accommodated," said Windle. "Because of your friendship with David. And because of your reputation." He manufactured a laugh. "Truth is, Holly, we weren't quite sure how to react when you turned up. You were a complication we could well have done without."

"What's changed your mind?"

"Circumstances. Dr Weisel's death left us no option but to level with you."

She blinked at his forthrightness.

"It's a tricky situation," said Windle, his tone fatherly. "It requires finesse."

She offered him a lopsided smile in return.

"Weisel's diary is illuminating," said Duggan. "We have the name of someone in Rome who knows what's going on with the factions, and we have a handle on the faction that's causing consternation among many of the Vatican's high-rankers."

"That sounds promising," said Holly.

"Your target would be Sebastian Grosjean," said Windle. "He teaches philosophy at Gregorian University. According to Weisel's diary he's written a rather damning book on the factions."

"Weisel is explicit in his condemnation of one particular group," said Duggan. "Grosjean has earmarked it as the most active and the most dangerous of the charismatic movements."

"Children of the New Catholic Dawn," said Windle, Duggan's

interjections reminding him of how Lieutenant Marcello and his off-sider had similarly cut in and out of their first conversation with him. "CNCD for short. If a tenth of the accusations made by Grosjean against this movement are accurate, then the papacy is in real trouble." He held up a hand. "There's more, Holly." He paused, then to everyone's surprise he said, "Grosjean tipped me off about the now lost codex's location at Mar Saba. Weisel was Grosjean's conduit."

An astonished Holly glanced at Mayle, then at Duggan.

"It was suggested that I examine the back cover of the 1946 Isaac Voss Collection of Ignatius of Antioch's letters. That's the only pointer I was given."

"What you would find wasn't specified?"

"No."

"How were you contacted?"

"By telephone."

"You took the call seriously?"

"I treated it as a practical joke to begin with, then began to wonder. You see we had only just received confirmation that the trip was on, that we had the funding. My caller was obviously aware of that fact."

"Why are you telling me this?"

Duggan, too, was interested in the answer to that question. "Because I don't want you turning up later as my enemy. Because I think I can trust you."

Holly dipped her head in acknowledgment.

"There are those who would have a field day with what I've just told you. That and the death of Dr Weisel could be whipped up into something quite bizarre."

"Anyone with half an eye can see Weisel's death was a fluke of circumstances," said Holly.

"He was murdered for next to nothing by a couple of unfortunate youths who will, I'm sure, spend the rest of their lives regretting it." Windle's incomprehension at how something so awful could have ended up being so useful registered on his face. "The gods are fickle, Holly." He smiled and returned to his confession. "My principal reason for telling you about the tip-off is because I think things are going to get difficult for me over the next few weeks." Reaching into the inside pocket of his jacket, he produced the Department of Antiquity's acidy letter. "Unless I'm very much mistaken, this is their initial salvo."

Holly glanced at the Vatican's logo, then back at Windle.

"It raises the specter of forgery, or hoax." Windle's laugh was half-hearted. "Hoax is the more kindly expression of the two, but when all is said and done, it too cancels out as forgery."

"They've accused you in some way?"

"If they've accused me of anything, it's of being a dupe. Professor Merle and I decided to hold back on telling the department about the tip-off until after their specialists had delivered their verdict, but it hasn't worked out that way. Merle had no choice but to tell them."

"Then you're safe."

"Not quite. Telling my partner could have been a ploy on my part. That's how some will see it."

Holly's frown was again laced with a smile. "That's how you reckon they'll end up reasoning?"

"The greater their sense of threat from the codex, the greater the possibility they'll jump in that direction. And they would be justified. The whole thing has the hallmark of a carefully planned set-up."

"With you as the fall guy."

"That's how it would look to some."

"So what's going on?"

"I don't think the codex was supposed to disappear. I think that came as a complete surprise to everyone."

"If the Department of Antiquities feels as threatened by the codex as you suggest, then doesn't it disappearing the way it did play right into their hands?"

"That's already crossed our minds."

"We thought at first it had been removed to highlight its importance," said Duggan. "Then perhaps by arrangement through the Vatican. But neither scenario seems likely now. Not unless the department's playing a really subtle game."

"Why pick on you and Merle?" asked Holly.

"I think it was a matter of first come first served," said Windle. "Could have been anyone doing our kind of research at Mar Saba."

Holly was silent for a moment, then she said, "How did Grosjean come to know about codex?"

"That's something we've yet to find out. You could perhaps ask him if you get to Rome."

"I'm surprised you aren't heading there yourself."

"I have to get back to Essen. I have obligations."

There's a fair chance I can swing Rome," she said. Then, tongue in cheek, "Anything else you would want me to do while I'm there?"

"You could deliver a note of thanks from Weisel to Grosjean that never got posted."

"That could prove handy."

"I'd expect you to use what you're told to help vindicate me." said Windle.

"Of course," said Holly. "But I'll need a translation of those parts of Weisel's diary dealing with the accusations against CNCD. That and what's happening to you should keep my editor happy."

"Consider it done," said Windle.

25

Shot Through With Arrows

"Voltaire!" Flavio Cardinal Beneditti's laugh was deep-throated and good-natured. "Galileo did the basic work a hundred years before Voltaire. He offered the Church the means to understand Genesis, but they wouldn't listen."

Sebastian Grosjean, priest and professor of philosophy, sipped at his cognac and continued with his theme. "Voltaire's assessment was that the Church was feeding its children acorns," he said, conscious of the fiery liquid washing its way down into his inners. "He also took us to task on the question of Noah's Ark. He suggested, satirically, that getting animals from other parts of the world must have been a miracle."

"Fifty years after Darwin published the *Origin of Species* we were still teaching the first three chapters of Genesis as historical truth!" Beneditti smile was laced with irony. "We've been forced to play Galileo's game of hide and seek for centuries."

As a biblical scholar, Beneditti was considered one of the best in Italy, his reference to Galileo another way of saying that the Church had a responsibility to straighten things out in accordance with reality. And not just in connection with CNCD's theological and behavioral excesses, that went without saying, but with the way in which Catholic scholarship had been strangled decade after decade in the name of a truth that could not be questioned. In the mid-nineteen hundreds Pius IX's *Syllabus of Errors* had applied pressure to the throat of Catholic scholarship, and in similar fashion Leo XIII had tightening the papacy's grip on anything that smacked of scholarly freedom. Freedom and truth were incompatible, these men had taught. At the Church's command, the State had enforced Catholic truth by every means available, the fact that relativity entered into all moral judgments refuted and denied t every turn.

"*Lamentabili* was Pius X's attempt to stamp out anything that even hinted at scholarly progress," said Grosjean. "He treated progress in scholarship as though it were a heretical sect in its own right."

"A garbled document in anyone's terms," said Beneditti. "Pius labeled everything he didn't like as modernism and claimed that by simply looking at a Bible text he could divine its exact meaning." A laugh from the man who had banned CNCD missionaries from his diocese. "Of them all I prefer Gregory's *Mirari vos*." Beneditti raised a finger in fake sobriety. "'Freedom of worship, of the press, of assembly or of education is a filthy sewer full of heretical vomit.'"

The two men laughed heartily at the stupidity of it all, at the craziness of it all, then fell silent. It was as if a heavy hand had been laid on their hearts.

"Why do we bother having these conversations?" Grosjean's question was rhetorical. He laughed, and added, "Are we so afraid we may be proved wrong some day?"

"Doubt renders arrogance impotent," said Beneditti. "To be free of doubt is to be possessed by a devil."

A nod from Grosjean, and a smile; he liked the way Beneditti sometimes mixed categories to get his point across.

"The American seems to have found his courage," added Beneditti. "He has agreed to support you if he finds your text acceptable."

"What's he like?"

"Pompous, but well-meaning."

"It's rumored he has the ear of the Holy Father."

"The late Holy Father."

"He's still in line for a red hat?"

"I believe so." Beneditti returned to the question of Donaghue's character. "He's deeply conservative. A man of old-fashioned sensibilities faced with the dilemma of having to deal with conservative fanatics who make him look and sound like a paid-up liberal." The cardinal's smile blossomed. "Must be shocking for him to glimpse something of himself in their block-headed certainty."

"You trust him?"

"I trust him to take a stand against CNCD's one-eyed emissaries. He was incensed by what happened in one of his own parishes."

"You spoke with him at length?"

"We spoke for about an hour after Gammarelli's dinner. He was, I think, a little shocked by some of the views expressed that evening, but diplomatic in his responses. He's a close friend of Antonio's."

"I'd never have believed some of you would come to relate in the way you have."

"Needs must when the Devil drives," said Beneditti, resorting to an English expression.

"Antonio vouched for him?"

"Recommended. There are those in our midst how would find the archbishop's views quite acceptable."

"And if he tells of his experience with you and your friends in the wrong quarter?"

"I think he has more sense than that. He can be a pompous fool at times, but that does not mean he is a fool."

Grosjean digested that and moved on. "And your lunch with the Secretary of State?"

Grosjean's second question was not unexpected; Beneditti and Cardinal Secretary of State Valerio Maglione had been discussing matters to do with CNCD's doctrinal audacity for some weeks.

"His job is to hold a billion believers together as one unit, not allow that unit to splinter into a thousand pieces. As such he must remain an impartial observer."

"But he's sympathetic."

"Yes, very. He isn't blind to what's going on. He knows only too well what a disruptive influence CNCD has become throughout Italy, and beyond. He describes the New Catholic Dawn as composed of deluded fanatics who have to be dealt with before they gobble up the whole Church."

Grosjean took another sip of cognac. "'Prepare war, stir up the warriors,'" he said, quoting the prophet Joel. Then, in a sad voice he said, "It is war, isn't it, Flavio."

"Scripture is the battle of the powerless against the powerful," said Beneditti, extending Grosjean's premise, "hence the need for prophets and miracles and literary force. Scripture is community taking on the bully through story, and winning - it is community talking to itself. It is Midrash. It is the art of Jewish storytelling as overlooked in the rush by we Catholics to offer the world an unquestionable story, an unquestionable truth." Beneditti lowered his head and took a deep breath. "But truth, as any thinking person knows, is more than mere content, it is also context. In the final analysis context is greater than content. It doesn't really matter what the content of the story is, it is the ethical dimension of story that matters most of all. Scripture became scripture because it had an ethical context to leaven its all to human inadequacies. It is a democracy of words, it is *not* a mathematical formula applicable under ever circumstance. If that were the case we wouldn't need the rule of law. If that were the case we'd be free to drive spikes through the heads of our enemies!"

"We've done worse during our history."

"And we'd still be doing it but for the efforts of intelligent men and women - theocratic government is an unwitting Bastille."

Grosjean meditated on that for a moment or two. "Christians fear to usurp biblical authority above all else," he said at last. "It is conceived of as the greatest of the heresies."

"Yet that is how every believer lives in relationship to his or her scriptural canon. As I said a moment ago, Pius X believed he could divine a biblical text just by looking at it. Believers believe in a particular brand of biblical authority authorized by a particular section of community. In that sense Catholicism is in the same boat as Anglicanism and any other Protestant-based confession of the Christian faith. And so the fall of a set way of thinking evokes crisis. CNCD is the result of a crisis in Catholic thinking that is fast coming to a head. It is a flailing attempt by the fearful and the slothful to reclaim scriptural authority in what is regarded as a demon-possessed world."

"Fear of a non-foundational world?"

"Exactly. That's what's causing the panic. What we're experiencing, as a Church, as individuals, is a guided descent into a necessary chaos, an attempt to remake our world and ourselves in accordance with reality - a reality that does not respond to the paradigm on which our specific truth claims rest."

"God."

"The whole works. We have to find a new way to talk about God and everything associated with God."

"In what sense 'guided'?" asked Fr Grosjean.

"In the sense that we must assist one another in this extraordinary adventure." Beneditti took another deep breath. "The nearer we get to the radical plurality of language and the radical ambiguity of history the more we need one another. The antidote to our fear, our scaredness, our dread of contradiction and uncertainty is not madcap individuality, it is community in action. It is where two or three are gathered together that fear abates and sanity reigns."

"You've just described the Church as it stands, as it has always stood."

"Not quite. I've described a meeting of minds; that's not the same thing as believer sitting down with believer. The Old Testament contains multiple voices, contradictory voices. There is disagreement between the priestly and the prophetic, between wisdom and tradition, between varying shades of orthodoxy. In the New Testament, as you and I have often discussed, there is the argument between St Paul and Jesus' brother James - an argument not yet properly resolved by scholars. In the Gospels we are faced with a series of claims about what God was doing in Christ. They are contradictory claims. Christian scholars have spent centuries trying to explain these contradictions. Catholic and Protestant scholars of a fundamentalist hue have done their utmost to smooth away these embarrassing irregularities. The problem with that kind of approach is that it undermines our ability to deal with any kind of reality at all. Only *in contra dictus* do we come to know what we know with any certainty. Contradiction and ambiguity are vital to our understanding of anything. Everything! The Scriptures are only adaptable to everyday life because they reflect the contradictions *of* every day life. Remove all Scriptural contradictions and you remove the ability of the Scriptures to communicate age by age."

In his last bible class, Beneditti had referred to the Bible as an interpretive battleground. Erasmus had insisted on the discernment of reason, Luther on Christ, the early Anabaptists on the role of the Holy Spirit, and Calvin on the belief that God spoke directly to the reader through Scripture. This idea - the idea of *sola scriptura* - had freed readers from Roman dogma, but it had also unleashed a plethora of views that obscured more than it revealed. To understand what had been going on century by century, we had to follow the interpretive journey from sacred story to sacred text and not lose sight of it for a moment. To do so was to remain forever in a historical and theological fairyland where everything about the Bible remained magical and untouchable.

"Everything depends on the competency of the reader," said Grosjean.

"Only if they're obeying the same linguistic rules," said Beneditti, to whom the question of intertextuality was also important.

"As believers do," said Grosjean, throwing a stone into Beneditti's pond.

"I'm talking thinkers, not believers," said Beneditti. "Different kinds of believers deal in subjectivisms, idiosyncratic readings of Scripture upon which they happen to agree; thinkers share a system of rules that allow them to appreciate the interplay between text and response."

Grosjean did not immediately reply, he merely smiled to himself. Then he said, "You should come and speak to my students some time, Flavio. They badly need to hear this from the horse's mouth."

"*In contra dictus,* " said Beneditti, repeating what had become a mantra. "We only know through difference."

There was a silence.

"The codex found at Mar Saba has set the cat among the pigeons," Grosjean said at last. The Department of Antiquities is about to publish a damning assessment of it in *Sala Stampa*. It's to be syndicated. Their verdict is that it's a probable forgery."

"They may be right."

"Their argument is pure sophistry. A verdict like that should not go out without solid evidence to back it up - it could ruin the careers of the scholars involved." Grosjean's countenance clouded over. "The Secretary of State can't do something about it? The Press Office is under his jurisdiction."

"Cardinal Maglione has charge of it, but when it comes to materials submitted by departments or congregations via the Holy Office or the Holy Father, he has little say in the matter."

An irritable sigh escaped Grosjean's lips; then a change of direction. "My contact at Mar Saba is as puzzled by the codex's disappearance as anyone else," he said, toying with his empty glass. "He's searched every inch of the library and come up with nothing." A half laugh. "It's either been shifted or lifted."

"You're still in contact."

"Of course."

"Beware of Greeks bearing gifts."

A smile from Grosjean, followed by an emphatic assurance that his contact in Palestine could be trusted. He had studied alongside him while at the Sorbonne and knew him to be of sound character.

"Yet willing to enter into intrigue over the codex," replied Beneditti, fingering the flaw in Grosjean's argument.

"It's an important document - *too* important to leave hidden, or to chance destruction. It carries important clues as to the nature of the Early Church, Eminence." Grosjean's use of title reinforced his claim. "It would be beyond price for that reason alone, but it also sheds light on other equally important issues."

"There may be a perfectly innocent reason for its disappearance."

"It was thought it may have been taken to the Patriarchate library in Jerusalem for repairs, but checks run there were fruitless."

"Someone else knew of the codex's existence?"

"That's uncertain."

"It disappeared."

"Some monk may have checked up on the Voss edition of Ignatius' letters when the scholars left, found the codex, realized its significance and concealed it for reasons of piety."

"The chief librarian didn't know about the codex?"

"Swears blind that he didn't."

Beneditti sucked in a breath and grimaced, then returned to the question of the codex's authenticity. "The scholarly community will be the final arbiters on whether it's genuine or not."

"Are you in pain, Flavio?"

"It comes, it goes."

"Would you prefer to be alone?"

"Stay, my friend. Stay. It passes."

The pains had been coming more frequently of late, tiny knives arbitrarily stabbing him from within. He had been warned that this would be the case, but was surprised by how quickly his condition had deteriorated.

"If they took the codex seriously, it could lead to a radical rethinking of Christian origins," said Grosjean.

"Others have hoped for a similar result, but to no avail," said Beneditti. He motioned that Grosjean should help himself to more cognac. "The route to real change perhaps lies in a different direction."

"History is important."

"But in the Church's scheme of things not the final arbiter of what is true, or untrue." Beneditti looked as though he were gathering his energies for some great onslaught. " . . . Objectivist attempts at history are often deeply flawed because of prejudice."

"I think I should take my leave of you," said Grosjean, alarmed by Beneditti's obvious distress..

"Yes, perhaps. Perhaps," said Beneditti.

"Shall I send for a doctor?"

"There's no need; it's what's expected." An ironic laugh from Beneditti. "Isn't it *you* who should be shot through with arrows?"

"My apologies, Eminence."

"I should think so!" said Beneditti, feigning annoyance. And then, "Pray for me, Sebastian."

"I have hardly ceased," replied Fr Grosjean.

26

Dissipation

It amazed Duggan that he had become so attached to New York in such a short time; he had quite simply fallen in love with the place and everything about it. But to say 'New York' was perhaps to range too widely; what he had really fallen in love with was the island of Manhattan, apex of the American myth and home of strangers. To walk its streets was to engage in something other than mere pedestrianship, it was to encounter *energy*, and lots of it. That, above all, was what Duggan was carrying away with him, a sense of indefatigable resolve, an almost manic concentration on being a success, *any* kind of success.

"It's *so* sad you're going," Elspeth intoned from the front passenger's seat of what she called 'George's car'. "You've no idea how I'm going to miss you both!"

They had taken to the back streets of Queen's to avoid a serious snarl-up on the highway, and were making good time for the airport.

"They're so little," Duggan said, peering out at the rows of neat, box-like houses, some of which resembled mansions shrunk to economy size.

"It's a nice little neighborhood," said Elspeth.

"But not as serene as it looks." George glanced at Duggan in the central mirror. "Some of the nice white middle-class kids from here are right tearaways."

"He's talking *years* ago," said Elspeth.

"True," said George. "There were incidents at the skating rink in Central Park in the mid-eighties. Posh kids would come in from Queens and get up to all kinds of mischief. One of them threw a lighted liter bottle of something straight into the middle of the rink one night. There were lots of reports of well-spoken Queen's kids causing trouble."

"In New York insanity is close to the surface for everyone," said Jane, more to Duggan than to anyone else. She was snuggled up close, and was holding his hand. "It's the environment. People are the weak link; they can appear sane one minute and explode the next. Scream. Do all sorts of mad things. Kids are vulnerable to that kind of atmosphere."

"Not to mention the drugs," said George.

They crossed suburban intersection after intersection, the highway becoming visible at points, and eventually rejoined the main highway. Crossing a toll bridge, they ploughed on, sometimes at a snail's pace, sometimes speedily. Duggan had no idea where he was, just that he was on his way back to Australia and that Jane Windle was going with him. He marveled at the thought and glanced at her.

"What?" she asked

"Nothing," he said, smiling at her.

"We're making good time." Elspeth half turned her head, elevated it slightly. "Promise me you'll *both* come back soon."

"Whenever possible," promised Duggan.

George's car was a mint-new black BMW 5 Series that the financier handled with relaxed aplomb. He seemed not to be driving at all, merely another passenger idly chatting as the car, self-propelled, headed for its destination.

Windle had left early that afternoon for Germany via London, Holly for Washington DC, and Mayle, reluctantly, for California. Duggan had felt sorry for Mayle as he and Holly left the Astoria to catch a taxi together. Was it the end of their relationship or the beginning, he wondered. Windle had bear-hugged his daughter and muttered something in German Duggan had not managed to catch, then with a smile that was half warning he had turned to the Australian. "Look after her, Jack. She's all I've got."

At Duggan's side rested a sleek, gun-metal computer case containing his translation of Theodore of Mopsuestia's letter to the arch heretic Pelagius Britto. A damning letter in anyone's terms. A letter that loosed the historical cat among the theological pigeons. Had the Early Church been so different from what was now thought, and taught? Had the second-century Church Father Irenaeus's idea of salvation really been so markedly different from that of bishops only a few decades later? These questions, and a host of others, were being debated by a growing band of Christian scholars worldwide, but for clergy on the whole, it was business as usual. For some, however, it was a matter of life and death. The Church's survival as an institution was at stake. It was a matter of believe, believe, believe in the old, old story whatever the cost. Panic was in the air, and it was spreading rapidly.

Some saw this as proof that God was heralding in a great spiritual revival, a return to tried-and-true Christian beliefs and values, but it was really just fear of the unknown run amuck. Human beings were in the throes of a second Reformation, and most were unprepared for its singular demands.

Windle and Duggan had discussed this observable fact many times, it being their conclusion that in its deep-rooted fear of change the Church had betrayed the trust put in it by so many. Instead of being fed meat and potatoes, Christendom had had to survive mainly on a diet of milky sops. Hence its dilapidated state, its pretense that all was well with the patient when the patient was in fact in a terminal state.

"How long is the flight to Australia?" asked George.

"Should be around the thirteen-hour mark from here," said Duggan. "It's fifteen from Los Angeles depending on tail winds."

"Sounds *dreadful!* " said Elspeth.

"I'll be busy all the way."

"Busy, busy busy," said Elspeth.

Jane's smile revealed her perfect teeth.

"I thought you were finished with work," said George.

"Loose ends," said Duggan. "There are always loose ends."

"And *still* we don't really know what you've been up to," said Elspeth.

"You will. Soon. I can promise you that."

"If the press contacts you for any reason, you know nothing," said Jane. "Particularly about Jack."

"And the missing document, I suppose," said George.

" It's a complicated business," said Duggan.

"Lawful?" asked George playfully.

"If you mean by that do we have the codex, the answer is no. The damn thing really has gone missing."

"You're hopeful of it being returned?"

"That depends very much on who took it in the first place," said Duggan, stating the obvious. "But yes, we are hopeful."

"Must have been a dreadful shock when that friend of your father's was murdered," said Elspeth. "What did that make you think when first you heard about it?"

"We thought the unthinkable," said Jane.

"And it turns out to be a mugging," said George. He shook his head at the thought of how uncertain life could be. "Couple of kids short of a dollar and you're dead."

"Poor man," said Elspeth.

"It's a lottery," said Duggan.

"What is? Life?" Elspeth's frown was quizzical. "You think the whole shemozzle is a matter of chance?"

"You can't have free will *and* a Grand Design" said Duggan. "They're mutually exclusive. That, you may remember, was what Jane's father was on about. Believe for one minute that we're all involved in some grand cosmic game and you give away your right to think anything other than what the game dictates."

"We are the arbiters of our own existence," said George.

"Not even a *little bit* of a Grand Design?" pleaded Elspeth.

"That's up to you. If you can find a way to juggle them, then fine. But I doubt that you can."

Elspeth was silent for a moment; then she said, "You don't believe in any kind of God?"

"I don't believe in a God who every so often pulls strings in the background. I find that a grotesque idea. It's just another way of saying that everything is part of a predetermined game of cosmic proportions"

"Or plan," said Elspeth.

"Game? Plan? Does it make any difference?"

"The universe is a meaningless blob?"

"I don't feel particularly meaningless. Do you?"

Duggan's reply surprised Elspeth so much she turned round to look at him.

"That's what we're still trying to understand, Elspeth. Our capacity for meaning directly contradicts the idea of the universe being meaningless in itself, or to itself. "

"Now I'm really confused."

"Welcome to the club!"

"We are the stuff that stars are made of," said George.

"Matter *matters*," said Duggan, articulating something he considered of great important. "For all we know eternity may well reside in a grain of sand."

"Hitler isn't roasting in hell for all eternity?"

"You have to weigh up the cost of believing that. Accept that that's the case and you have to accept the whole package. Are you willing to do that?"

"People have, and do."

"Perhaps we're about to come of age."

She looked round as if trying to penetrate his skull with her dark, expressive eyes. Then in a mocking tone that Duggan knew carried no ill-will, she said, "You're a *tricky* little Australian, aren't you?" Then to Jane she said, "I think you may *just* have met your match with this one."

* * *

Holly had spent an hour over coffee trying to convince David Mayle that together they could come up with a story strong enough to make the front page of the *Washington Post.* Dr Weisel's diary was a smoking gun, his having died by misadventure an added pathos. They had just about every piece of the jigsaw for an expose on Vatican factionalism. All they had to do was bring those pieces together, add some lively interviews and the whole thing would take off of its own accord. She rebaited her hook. With the paper's backing and his knowledge of American religious life they could produce a much-needed foil to neo-conservative aspirations. And not just on the religious front - the political hawks were also gearing up for a confrontation of their own, and there were connections between the two.

Was she suggesting he give up his job, an astonished Mayle wanted to know. Yes, exactly that, she said back. The moment had arrived for them to make their move.

It was an attractive offer, Mayle had admitted, but not a very secure one. If it didn't work out she'd still have a job and he'd be out on his ear. She countered with flattery. His talents were wasted where he was, she said, looking at him intently, almost savagely. It was now or perhaps never for him to make his mark.

He stared at her not knowing what to make of her offer, but aware of a terrible truth in her words. To further persuade him, she resorted to an old tactic. "It'll be fun, David! We'll have a ball!" To which he replied: "I don't doubt that for one minute, Holly."

* * *

Photographs of the Mar Saba Codex lay on Cardinal Menenger's desk face up. Scowling at them, the Prefect of the Congregation for the Doctrine of the Faith vented his displeasure at having to bother with them. The codex was a distraction, he said to those present. It was also a nuisance and an impertinence. Theodore of Mopsuestia had been condemned by Pope Vigilius and declared a heretic by the Fifth Ecumenical Council. That, surely, was enough to put an end to the matter.

Along with Valerio Cardinal Maglione, Secretary of State, two others were present for the hastily summoned curial committee meeting: Monsignor Francesco Rossi, chief paleographer from the Department of Antiquities, and Paolo Cardinal Pironio, editor of *Sala Stampa,* the official Press Office of the Holy See.

"It's the letter's unusual historical slant that will attract attention," said the monsignor. "Theodore's view of Christ's nature - a view we are already familiar with from his other writings - is now made to hinge on the belief that the early Jerusalem Church was Jewish sectarian, not Christian. Theodore - if indeed the letter is in his hand - arrives at the conclusion that Christ was a messiah figure in the Jewish mold, not a divine being in his own right."

"Yet with redemptive power in the sense of being the completion of the redemptive process initiated by Adam's fall into *necessary* experience," said Cardinal Pironio with exaggerated emphasis. "The text follows the notion of stages of redemption."

"I thought the letter had been discredited?" said Maglione,

"It's considered a probable forgery."

"Probable?"

"Theodore of Mopsuestia was a gifted thinker, Eminence. He was one of the few capable of using historical argument in this fashion at that time."

"And Fr Merle's confession as to how the document was discovered?"

"He thinks the letter genuine in spite of the circumstances surrounding its discovery. He's sticking by his earlier assessment."

"And so he should he if he thinks it authentic," said Maglione. "It's his scholarly duty to stand by what he believes to be true."

"It's also his priestly duty to avoid creating stumbling blocks for the faithful," said Menenger.

The Secretary of State blinked at Menenger's words. "Supporting the American in his belief that the letter is authentic does not authenticate the notions it contains."

"Merle is a recognized expert in this area," said Menenger, who had checked Fr Merle's credentials. "The scholarly community will take notice of what he has to say. On that basis I have prepared a statement revealing the facts for publication. I think the facts of the situation speak for themselves." A smile from Menenger. "The very fact that the original document has disappeared suggests a ploy to highlight the letter's existence. That suggests it's likely to turn up again, and that in turn suggests further manipulation. Manipulation with intent."

"The so-called facts may not be enough to dampen scholarly interest," said the Secretary of State.

"Fear of being associated with a forgery, whether old or new, will, I think, temper enthusiasm." Menenger kept his gaze on the Secretary of State's face. "The letter is a concerted attack on our Lord's nature, Valerio. Whoever wrote it had it in mind to undermine the way in which Christ's nature is perceived. Our Lord is made out to be no more than a role-playing Jewish Messiah whom we have mistakenly inflated to the level of God Almighty."

"There are Catholic scholars who would not in essence disagree with that description," said Maglione.

"And it is grist to their Satanic mill," said Menenger. Then, as if by way of rebuke, he added, "There is no question mark hanging over our Lord's nature as far as I'm concerned. Christ's nature hinges on one small realization, doesn't it, Valerio? The human appropriated by the Word. Not a particular human. Not a person or an identity. Just the human untainted by Adam's sin. The definite article is where it all rests." He turned to Cardinal Peronio. "Insist too strongly on a distinction between Christ and Jesus, Paolo, and you end up with too great a distinction of subjects. Correct?"

"Correct" said Peronio, who was known to be close to the Prefect.

As the Vatican's leading theologian - some said the Church's only theologian due to his having silenced all the others - Cardinal Menenger was a law unto himself. Questioning even the theological legitimacy of the bishops' conference, but ignoring the Curia, which, according to the same criteria, was equally questionable, he strongly advocated a centralized authority. The pope, and no other, he insisted, had primacy in matters of faith and doctrine, the Holy Office a duty to bring any recalcitrant Catholic thinker to heel.

The Secretary of State's smile had been of the fixed variety. It melted away, and he said, "There was a particular matter you wished to speak with us about?"

"The American professor," said Menenger.

"He has responded?"

A shake of the head from Menenger.

"He is known to be a stubborn man," said Pironio, answering for the Prefect.

"We expect a less than positive reaction from him," said Menenger.

"That is hardly surprising," said Maglione.

"He has only himself to blame," said Menenger. "The circumstances alone suggest a deception of some kind. And his holding back on how he knew where to look further condemns him."

"You suspect him of being involved in some way?"

"It's possible. If he's telling the truth, then a third party is certainly involved."

"And if he isn't telling the truth?"

"It would not be the first time a scholar of repute has decided to help his career along with a little bit of fakery."

"You think that likely?"

"Fr Merle is the specialist on Theodore, not the American. To produce Theodore's letter *and* the letter's Ireanaean content, the American would have needed an expert accomplice. Perhaps two, or more. It would have taken years for him to set it up the ruse by himself"

"You've ruled Fr Merle out?"

"If Merle is anything, he is Professor Windle's dupe, not an accomplice. He is an internationally respected scholar."

"So is Professor Windle."

"They're not comparable."

The Secretary of State paused, then he said, "Prior to arriving in Palestine, the American admitted to Fr Merle that he had been tipped off. Why do that? Why lessen the impact of the find in that way? Why complicate it with such an admission? That doesn't sound like someone involved in a deception that's taken years to perfect."

"Reversed psychology?" said Menenger. "A method of drawing attention away from himself?"

"Or the simple truth," said Maglione.

Menenger turned to Monsignor Rossi with a plea. "Tell us what your department has decided about the American professor, Fransesco."

"He would have to be an epigraphic genius to have produced a forged text of this quality," said the palaeographer, pleased to have the floor at last, "and we know for sure that he is not a genius. Hence his need of Fr Merle to authenticate the text. So, two things are possible. He has either masterminded the whole affair with the help of others, or he is naively caught up in someone else's crooked little scheme. Either way, he is responsible for trying to loose this garbage on the world."

"Not such a little scheme," said Menenger, whose whole task in life was to defend the Catholic faith from threat. "If taken seriously, this supposed fourth-century text could seriously affect the thinking of scholars with a secular axe to grind. It's exactly the kind of thing they relish."

"So what do you intend to do about it all?" asked an intrigued Secretary of State

"Find the American's accomplice, if he exists, or show him up for the gullible fool he is," said a smiling Menenger. "Whichever way it turns out, Valerio, he *is* guilty. The only remaining question is, to what extent is he guilty?"

27

Birds of a Feather

Elbows resting on the marble counter top, his cup held in both hands before his bearded and bespectacled face, Fr Paul Merle sat drinking black coffee alongside Fr Grosjean in a crowded coffee-bar. It was a white beard, and like his white hair, severely trimmed. The face turned towards Grosjean was, to any casual observer, a stern face, but to those who knew Merle, more a self-contained face, a face within which something indefinable had happened. In his standard clerical suit and Roman collar, Merle was just another priest in a city crammed with priests, but as Sebastian Grosjean was about to realize, that was about as far from the truth as it was possible to get. Priest, Merle certainly was, any old priest he was not.

"He was a fellow student," said Grosjean, remembering a black-bearded Greek by the name of Takis Kostakidas. "I don't think I would have passed my Greek language studies without him."

"I remember him," said Fr Merle.

They were speaking French, glad to be back in their own tongue for an hour or so.

"He contacted me by telephone about six months ago. Out of the blue. He'd already spent three years at Mar Saba cataloguing the library and shifting sections of it to the Greek Orthodox Patriarchal Palace in Jerusalem."

"Time enough in which to create Theodore's letter and affix it to the end of the Ignatius letters," said Merle.

Sebastian Grosjean did not reply; he stared at Merle and waited for him to continue.

"Given the content of Theodore's letter, and the circumstances, that's the conclusion many scholars will come to."

"*If* they knew about Kostakidas's involvement," said Grosjean.

"They'll jump to that conclusion on the basis of Professor

Windle's mysterious benefactor. That'll set tongues wagging." Merle placed his now empty cup on its saucer. That's where the problem rests, Father. That's the kind of reasoning about to be applied by Monsignor Rossi to my American colleague. The department hasn't actually accused him of anything, but it's only a matter of time."

"And I'm responsible," said Grosjean. A grimace from the philosopher-priest as the seriousness of his own words struck home. "I knew there would be difficulties, but I didn't think they'd take this form."

"At least you've been honest enough to admit what you've done to me - however belatedly. I thank you for that."

"I had no option," said Grosjean. "With the claim of forgery floating about it's turned into a potentially damaging issue for both of you. And now that Menenger's involved . . . "

"We've . . . spoken," said Merle.

"What made you tell Monsignor Rossi about the codex being located on the basis of information received?"

"It would have come out later and made us look as guilty as sin," said Merle, resorting to a cliche. "It was our intention to tell the monsignor about our benefactor *after* publication."

"Will the codex ever see the light of day?"

"Only after they've thoroughly poisoned the waters."

Another sip of coffee before Grosjean replied. "Seeing your name on the list of proposed visits to Mar Saba seemed like an omen."

"You didn't think I would respond if contacted directly?"

Fr Merle's question caused Grosjean to hesitate. " . . . I didn't want to involve you in that kind of way."

"It was okay to involve Professor Windle in *that* kind of way?"

Grosjean again reconsidered. "I was relying on your expertise keeping Professor Windle on track and out of the kind of trouble he's now in. You're a recognized expert on *Theodore of Mopsuestia*, he isn't. If anyone could judge the codex's authenticity, I knew you could."

Fr Merle looked away, then back at Fr Grosjean. "So you used

Professor Windle to get to me, then used me to get to Professor Windle."

An uncomfortable Grosjean nodded. He had reasoned that it was better for a secular scholar to make the initial find, he said.

"You were safe-guarding Mother Church in the offchance of the codex being a forgery?

"I was safeguarding scholarship in the offchance that Mother Church succeeded in shutting you up."

Fr Merle absorbed the blow without comment. Then, in a softer tone he said, "Your friend Kostakidas would have had access to the files and known who was scheduled to visit the monastery." He broke off and signaled for two more coffees. "But I'm certain he wasn't there when we visited. I think I'd have recognized him."

"He must have realized that and kept out of your way."

"Did he suggest you contact Professor Windle?"

"No. He left the choice of contact up to me."

"Knowing of course that you would check the department's lists and discover what he had discovered."

"Yes, I suppose so," said Grosjean. An embarrassed laugh. "It seems obvious now."

There was a silence Merle broke back in. "It hardly seems likely you'll be broadcasting what you've just told me, but you may in the end be forced to admit your involvement."

"It's my hope it doesn't come to that."

"Did your friend Kostakidas spirit the codex away?"

"I have no idea. We haven't spoken since I become involved."

"Why did you become involved?"

" . . . It seemed like the right thing to do."

"And now?"

"Now I'm not so sure."

They were bent over their coffee and speaking in low tones, the background noise of the bar all but blotted out by the intensity of their engagement. Fr Merle continued to probe.

"Have you tried to contact Kostakidas?"

"He said not to contact him. I doubt he called me from the monastery."

"What exactly did he tell you about the codex?"

"He described it in very dramatic terms. He said it was a bomb ready to explode. An unfortunate metaphor given the state of things in Israel."

"You trust him?"

"I've no reason not to."

"How well did you know him?"

"As students we were quite close."

"You remained in communication?"

"We'd drop each other the occasional postcard, but I lost contact with him after a couple of years. He stopped replying, I stopped writing. Then out of the blue there he was on the telephone."

"With an extraordinary suggestion to which you agreed?"

"Not immediately. It took two long telephone calls before I agreed to play intermediary." Grosjean's smile was of someone perplexed by his own actions. "His excitement over the codex seemed genuine."

"He told you what was in it?"

"In some detail."

"He had no doubt it was from Theodore's hand?"

"He seemed pretty sure."

"Did he mention Irenaeus?"

"He said the letter contained another major surprise, but didn't say what it was. There's an Irenaean connection?"

A nod from Merle. Then, "Why didn't he claim credit for finding the codex himself? Did you ask him that?"

"He said he didn't want to jeopardise his position at Mar Saba. He liked what he was doing and wanted to keep on doing it. He loves what he's doing. It gives him the chance to immerse himself in the ancient writings."

"I remember him as a dedicated student," said Merle, lifting the fresh cup of coffee that had arrived. "Talented. Unusually non judgemental when it came to Catholicism. The same could not be said for most of his companions at Mar Saba."

"That was his point, I think. He didn't want to ruffle feathers."

"Almost anyone at the monastery had good reason to remove the codex, destroy it, or at best hide it away for reasons of piety. They're an austere lot. The divide between East and West is very pronounced."

"They gave you and Professor Windle access to the library"

"I've been doing research at Mar Saba on and off for over two decades. They know me. Perhaps even trust me." Merle smiled. "I cease to be who I am when I'm there. I become a monk. I eat their terrible bread and join them in prayer - when I can muster the strength to rise at some ungodly hour. And I listen. I listen mostly. They're wonderful storytellers. They eyes burn with passion as they tell their stories of demons, devils and *djinns*." Merle laughed a kindly laugh. "They hate three things with a perfect hatred: the Devil, Catholicism and Freemasonry. They're of the opinion that Freemasons are the pope's stormtroopers, that the late Holy Father was president of the Freemasons, and that on Judgment Day a troop of popes will lead the damned - sinners and the non-Orthodox - down into hell. They have a very interesting slant on things."

"What on Earth do you say when they come out with stuff like that?"

"I smile and nod my head sagely, bite on another piece of hard bread and promise in my heart to examine yet again my own most cherished beliefs." Merle paused; then almost dreamily he said: "It's an extraordinary location. Austere. Dry. Forbidding. Two Byzantine watchtowers are the first thing you see. Then a jagged wall dropping almost vertically into a deep *wadi*. The wall encloses a crazy bundle of turquoise domes and cupolas, cells, balconies, staircases and platforms hanging on the cliff face. It looks so implausible it's almost visionary."

"Where do you sleep?"

"In a cell with white walls and a blue dado. There's no electricity.

The monks are up at two in the morning. They sing their office for five hours, rest until eleven, then eat their one meal of the day. Their asceticism is severe. After a couple of weeks in one of these cells you begin to appreciate their unshakeable belief in demons."

"The *intifada* wasn't a problem?"

"Our taxi driver hung a Palestinian *keffiyeh* on the windscreen. Without it we could easily have been mistaken for Israeli settlers and stoned." Merle's face twisted in a personal agony. "Something like a 150 Jewish settlements have been built in the West Bank since '67. In plain numbers that's around 280,000 settlers. The Israelis have syphoned off 80 per cent of the West Bank's drinking water." A huffed laugh. "All done in defiance of international law I might add."

"You see no solution to the problem?"

"There's only one solution - stop the tit for tat. One side or the other has to wake up to that glaringly obvious and uncomfortable fact. If they don't, the whole region could go up in smoke."

There was another silence. Grosjean returned to the question of the codex's authenticity.

"I don't think it's a forgery," said Merle, "but it'll take more than my assessment - and that of Professor Windle - to convince the scholarly community. Without the actual document there's little hope of convincing anyone of anything."

"You saw it, handled it, studied it."

"If I pushed that point too hard they might think I had a private agenda." A smile, and a laugh. "Reputations aren't worth buttons when pet beliefs or theories are being trampled on. It's eggshell territory for everyone."

"You've discussed the situation with Professor Windle?"

"I informed him of developments."

"And?"

"He's as ready for the onslaught as anyone can be." Merle came back in quickly. "I stand by my assessment of the codex. It's an extraordinary document. Theodore was an extraordinary man. He was truly *Magister Orientis*. His theological compositions at the age of twenty - at eighteen according to Leontius - are exegetical in the extreme. His commentary on the Psalms is almost exclusively grammatico-historical in exposition. The codex discovered at Mar Saba is a perfect example of his polemic."

"A man ahead of his time."

"Way, way ahead of his time. Apart from Bishop Irenaeus in the second century, I can't think of another thinker so down to earth in his explanations."

"He was influenced by Irenaeus?"

"He claims to be working from a fragment of an alternative gospel written by Irenaeus. There are quotes. Some are recognizable, some aren't. Hardly anything by Irenaeus exists in his own hand."

"Such a gospel is likely?"

"I think so. Irenaeus wasn't into fairy tales. More than anyone else I know he kept to the historical facts - those available to him. He enumerated all the Roman bishops up to the twelfth, and named the first bishop of Rome as Linus, not Peter or Paul. The Apostolic Constitution of 270 agreed with him. And neither did he believe that Jesus' mother was without sin. Irenaeus, Origen, Basil, Cyril of Alexandria and others accused Mary of many sins. A lot of nonsense stems from believing the opposite." A laugh from Merle. "It's interesting that it was in Lyons - Irenaeus's home turf - that a new feast celebrating the Virgin's conception so angered St Bernard of Clairvaux that he wrote a stinging letter to the Canons of Lyons warning them that a sinless conception for Mary meant that a whole line of sinless conceptions would have to be postulated."

"Absolute power fashioning absolute truth."

"Exactly. Papal infallibility was on the loose. It had been conveniently forgotten that not even a pope has the right to decide Catholic doctrine, only the entire episcopate in council." Merle's cropped skull shook with indignation. "Pius IX's claim that he encapsulated tradition not only made a nonsense of tradition, it has worked to the detriment of a sensible theology every since. We are now in the hands of fantacists!"

"Are you familiar with CNCD?"

"We've . . . collided. Some of them invaded a lecture I gave in Paris. There was a fracas."

"Grosjean explained about CNCD mischief in Italy and linked the *New Catholic Dawn* to what Merle had said about a pope-centered faith. They were probably the most dangerous group of literalists to have surfaced within Catholicism in the last hundred years, he said.

"I've heard rumors to that effect," said Merle.

"You'll be hearing a lot more about them in the near future. I'm about to publish a book on their exploits."

"You've named names?"

"Names were unavoidable."

A slow nod from Fr Merle.

I've got support from within the curia. "

"You'll need more than promises of support if your book is as forthright as it sounds."

"I also have signatures. Cardinal Beneditti's is one of them."

Merle's glance became a frown.

"It's potentially a major split," said Grosjean. "If they gain control the Church will no longer be recognisably Catholic, it will have turned into a Protestant-styled fundamentalist sect."

"And you would prefer to see what exactly?" asked Merle.

Grosjean did not immediately reply; he looked away for a moment, then back. "I sense where you're headed with that." he said, staring at Merle. "You suspect the liberal scheme of things isn't much better."

"Is it?"

"It attempts to be honest."

"And in being honest destroys the faith from a different direction."

"You prefer dishonesty?"

"I prefer gnosis. "

It was Grosjean's turn to frown.

"It isn't the first time we've lost our way."

"You're a closet heretic?"

"I'm talking *gnosis*, not Gnosticism. Gnosis is an understanding of the spiritual life passed on by the early Christians - the so-called *Jewish Christians*. Gnosticism is a heresy of gnosis. Gnosticism wasn't a distortion of Church doctrine, it was a distortion of a teaching all but unknown to the Church, a lost teaching. Hence Theodore's attempt to straighten out the Church's early history - it isn't possible to understand what happened to that teaching until you understand that early history. Theodore was aware of that, and Irenaeus's writings were instrumental in helping him towards a deep appreciation of what he already knew about that earliest form of Christianity."

"Which was what?"

"That they understood what was meant by 'the God beyond God' - the God of the developed soul." Merle's face lit up for a moment, then clouded again. "Most of the Gnostic sects misunderstood this to mean that there were two separate Gods, a creator God in charge of morality and religious sanctity, and a God alien to the Church who existed beyond the cosmos. In literalizing a great truth - the truth that a developed soul's perception of God is different from that of someone who merely gulps down a religious formula - they slammed the door shut on a body of teaching passed on orally since the earliest days of the faith."

"Many scholars today consider Gnosticism to be early Christianity's message to the world."

"And they are both right, and wrong. They are right to think that Gnosticism reflects a secret teaching, they are wrong to think that Gnosticism's many versions of that teaching properly reflects what became lost to Christianity. There are gems galore in Gnosticism, there's no doubting that, but they are mostly embedded in imaginative dross - hence the hotch-potch delivered by exponents of the New Age. What we have to do is extract those gems and carefully examine them."

"And if one does?"

"Then an extraordinary thing becomes apparent: we learn that the soul is not a given in human nature: we don't automatically have a soul at birth, we have to build a soul out of our interaction with the world."

"If you believe in a soul at all."

"And why do we doubt the soul's existence?"

A Gallic shrug was all Grosjean could offer.

"Because in most cases it is so paltry a thing it might as well not exist, or in fact does not exist!" Another beaming smile from Fr Merle. "Souls and babies have a lot in common; they have to be fed and nourished. Without food they do not form, without food, even if they have formed, they wither away and die."

"Are we really talking about soul?" Grosjean's tone had an edge to it. "You could just as easily say that about the human mind."

"They're not dissimilar. An uninformed mind is a sorry thing to behold, and a soul starved of nutrients is no different. The difference lies in what they feed on. The mind feeds on information; the soul on energy. We abort the soul a thousand times every day through squandering our energy. This is what the Scriptures mean when they say it's possible to gain the world and lose our soul - that's the price we pay for squandering our sacred energies. "

"How can you possibly know such a thing?"

"It's all a matter of gathering, or not gathering." Merle paused, then as if reciting a formula he said, "If, as we interact with the world, we lack the ability to properly attend to what we are engaged in, then we are asleep - *consciously* asleep. The oftener we realize we have been asleep, the more awake we become. Being awake feeds soul with the energy of attention; being asleep systematically empties soul of life. Soul is an accumulation of energy. Waking up gathers energy; sleeping scatters energy. There is a threshold of attention that has to be visited over and over again before the light of attention can light up the whole being."

"It's a contradiction in terms to talk of conscious sleep."

"*Submerged* in conscious activity," said Merle, refining his definition. "When we surface from the submerged state, from the state of being consciously engaged in the world, then and only then are we awake."

"We're consciously engaged at all times, surely?" said Grosjean. "Except when actually asleep."

"No, we come *back* to ourselves at intervals," said Merle. "We surface from conscious engagement every so often and *re-member* ourselves. If we didn't, our energies would fail and we would die. We do exactly the same when physically asleep - we come back to ourselves *as if* from another world and pick up where we left off. The two states are similar, except that actual sleep refreshes, whereas conscious sleep tires us out. Our daily lives are the equivalent of a far country from which we intermittently return. We are, as the Scriptures say, prodigal sons and daughters in need of a father's mercy."

Intrigued by what he was hearing, Grosjean returned to the question of soul. Merle's reply was in the form of a metaphor.

"The more often we surface, the more money we have in the bank. It's a matter of opening a savings account and making regular deposits. Opening an account is easy; finding the will to save regularly is not so easy."

"A teaching unknown to the Church?" said Grosjean.

"All but unknown to the Church. The rudiments are there, but they have become scrambled. Adjustments are necessary."

"Even to our idea of salvation?"

"Particularly to that idea."

"In what sense?"

"In the sense of jettisoning the idea that Jesus' death on the cross was a once-for-all-time sacrifice demanded by God to appease himself. Did you ever hear anything so ridiculous? I'm sorry, it won't do. Human sacrifice was a pagan practice. Abraham woke up to that fact on Mount Moriah and refused to murder his son. We have to do the same with Jesus."

"That's not how the Abraham story reads."

"It's been tampered with. Most of our stories have been tampered with."

"So what is of use in the stories we have?"

"Almost everything; we just have to detect what lies behind what they say."

"And if we can't?"

"Then we learn nothing and perish for want of a soul."

Grosjean laughed and looked away. When he looked back it was to say that that turned the whole idea of losing one's soul on its head.

"And that's a perfect example of what I'm getting at. You can't lose what you've never had. You don't perish because you lose your soul to the Devil, because you're bad or evil and deserve eternal punishment. You perish because you never properly existed in the first place." He paused to let his words sink in. "There's a huge misunderstanding here. Christian teachers are forever warning us to avoid paying the world too much attention. They think the world is the problem. It isn't. It's the way in which we pay attention to the world that's the problem. Lock yourself away from the world of experience and interaction and you lock yourself away from the chance to balance your inner traits with the energy available in the world. It should not be a one-way street; it should be a two-lane highway. The world is a huge energy source that can be tapped into if we're awake to it, if we can wake up *inside our interactions with it*. Pour your energies out into the world through submerged conscious engagement and you end up with a deficit in your bank account. Wake up to what's going on and the situation is reversed. That's what the whole business of fearing the world is about. Our deep-seated fear is not about involvement leading to moral breakdown, it's about identification resulting in a submerged state of consciousness. Identification is our mutual sleeping draught."

"The spiritual life is about nothing more than accruing energy?"

"Nothing more than?" Merle stare was almost comical. "Father, *everything* is about energy! Beliefs are secondary to the process of waking up to that fact *as* an experience. The prodigal son squandered his substance, we have to gather ours."

"Where did you learn all this?"

"From a man I met in the desert."

"A monk?"

"He may have been a monk; I didn't ask. He turned up one day and we got talking."

"He was Christian?"

"I didn't ask that either."

Grosjean stared at Fr Merle.

"Christians existed long before Christianity appeared on the globe, Father. I learned that a long time ago. Christianity isn't a grocery list of things to be believed, it is a process of transformation through which the forces of good and evil are reconciled over and over again. It is not a one-off experience; it is an ongoing experience, a discipline of mind. Wake up to what waking up means and the process swings into action. Remain submerged and unaware and the process of transformation never really gets going."

"It sounds daunting."

"It's more rewarding than trying to be good and failing all of the time. At least you get something immediate out of it."

"Like what?" asked Grosjean.

"Energy," said Merle. "How else could you awaken again one minute from now?"

* * *

Holly Parks stepped out of her camel-hair skirt and headed for the bathroom; she was back in her Washington apartment and pleased with her efforts. In her spacious lounge, contemplating a moment of recklessness, David Mayle was flopped on the sofa clutching a glass of red wine. One side of a minute he had been headed for Frisco and grey routine, the next, for Washington DC and he knew not what.

The sound of water cascading over Holly's body brought Mayle back from his reverie. Getting up, he wandered into the bathroom and stood, glass in hand, watching the movements of her body through the rippled glass.

"How in God's name did you ever get me to agree to this?" he asked rhetorically.

"It's compulsory to lose one's marble, at least *once* in a lifetime, David." Holly poked her head round the shower curtain and glowered at him "You're not going to back out on me, are you?"

"I'm throwing away a perfectly good job."

"A dead end and you know it," she shot back. Then, from within the shower again, "It'll work, David. You'll see. What we have on CNCD's machinations will make *beautiful* copy."

Her earlier suggestion had been that she head for Italy and that he concentrate on CNCD happenings at home - she had already earmarked a disturbance in Nevada. He had argued against the idea because of what he thought lay behind her offer, but as they argued it had become obvious that she was genuinely interested in breaking the CNCD story, and that her wanting him on board had to do with that and not with the codex. At least that's how it had seemed. He gulped down some wine wondering how she would react when she discovered that it was Duggan who had control of the basic story. Deciding to test her on that, he broke the bad news.

"Jack's a journalist?"

Holly's head appeared a second time.

"And a specialist in early-century Christian writings. He's political correspondent for a magazine in Sydney."

"So what are you saying?"

"I'm saying that Jack will be the one to break the story of the codex, not me. Windle can't be seen to be breaking the rules, and I'm a known friend."

"He's been seen endlessly in Jack's company."

"Jack was tipped off about the codex. He got hold of some

photographs and contacted Windle. Windle agreed to check his translation when it was complete."

"Why would he do that?"

"Because he didn't want some garbled version of the Codex getting out, and because it served his own purposes."

"Which were? Are?"

"To publish sooner rather than later. There are those who would prefer the codex to evaporate as an issue. They're working hard to bring that about."

Emerging from the shower, Holly wrapped herself in a bath towel and headed into the lounge. "Australia?" she said, glancing back at him. And then, "I knew something was going on."

"We have to tread carefully."

She turned to face him, scrutinised him for a moment. "Why tell me now?"

"I didn't want you thinking I had something to offer when I hadn't. Fair's fair." He added quickly: "If that changes things I'll understand."

"You think it might?"

"I don't know what to think."

She stared at him, then said quite unexpectedly, "I could ask you a very awkward question at this point, but I won't. I think I already know the answer." She turned away and poured herself a glass of wine, spoke with her back to him. "I'm not as cutthroat as I used to be, David. I've changed. Not a lot, but enough to make a difference." She turned back. "I don't expect you to believe me."

"You were never ever cutthroat."

"I was an opportunistic little miss; still am at times. You have to be to survive in this business."

"I'm no saint."

"You're more conscious of the rules than I'll ever be."

"The rules have changed . . . the world has changed." A bit of a laugh from Mayle. "Very little of what I was taught applies now."

"I couldn't believe you could do proper shorthand."

"It was compulsory when I started."

"You were *so* patient."

"You were the daughter I didn't have. That's how I saw you at first."

"This is incest?"

"Hardly," said Mayle.

"What is it then?"

"You tell me."

"You don't know?"

"I don't know what you want it to be."

"What about you?"

"I don't feel I've got much of a say in the matter."

"It's just sex?"

"Isn't it?"

"Is it?"

She tilted her head at him; it reminded him of Duggan. "I don't want to spoil it," he said apologetically. Then, by way of a confession, "You're the best thing to have happened to me in a *very* long time."

"But thought I was letting you fuck me to get at the story behind the codex?"

"I thought it unlikely you were attracted to me for my *disheveled* self, as I think you put it."

"You've changed your mind about that?"

"You seem genuinely interested in unmasking the *Catholic Dawn* thing. My instincts tell me that's more important to you than the codex."

"You couldn't be more right." Her smile was congratulatory, her look quizzical. "It's by far the more important of the two stories, and it's my bet your instincts told you that straight off."

"I admit to sensing its potential."

"And so reluctantly agreed to join me here when you realized I did, too." She turned with a laugh and reached for the wine bottle, filled her glass and turned to fill his. "Who's the whore now?" she asked

"My hesitation was genuine."

"You could have told me about Jack at Kennedy."

"True," he admitted.

Reaching out, she touched his cheek. "Birds of a feather," she said, smiling at him sweetly.

* * *

Bishop Peters' second article in the *New York Times* took a surprising tack. Cardinal Menenger's recently published declaration *Dominius Christos* was not, he claimed, theological in nature, it was unashamedly political. For reasons as yet obscure, the Prefect of the Congregation for the Doctrine of the Faith had laid down a set of political markers, and those markers suggested an attempt to influence opinion before the next conclave. *Dominius Christos* was, in effect, a sunset document, a *documento ditramonto,* as the Romans called it, and that suggested some kind of crisis in the papal household. So was the pope ill? Was the recently elevated son of Umbria preparing, perhaps, for even greater elevation? Rumor had it that he had visited the Gemelli clinic earlier in the week, and had not yet returned.

As Peters' general point of attack was theological sloppiness in high places, his opening gambit involving Menenger's curious offering constituted a rap over the fingers for Rome's inquisitional overlord - an act of considerable daring given the bishop's tenuous hold on office. Broadening his canvas, the little bishop from Illinois then accused Menenger and his supporters of working overtime to severely contain, if not shut down, the intellectual renaissance that Catholicism had experienced in the last century. With one exception the papacy's proud achievement had been to reduce great religious truths to the level of shoddy literalisms, its contribution to a needy world little more than a barrage of embarrassing second-rate pronouncements. If the Church wanted to be taken seriously, it would have to take back the reins from men whose vision for the future was a return to wilful ignorance.

At the end of his article he again questioned Menenger's theological competence, describing it as a faltering, flat-footed attempt to disguise in-house politics as *a return to basic religious truths*. Nothing was further from the truth, he said. The battle for succession had started. The land that had produced Machiavelli and the Mafia was preparing itself for the Holy Spirit's next pontifical surprise.

28

Half a Story

"So what do you think of Sydney?"

"Marvellous light," said Jane.

"So speaks the artist," said Duggan.

They were sitting in Elliot's office drinking coffee. Elliot was perched on the edge of his desk, palms down, his attention on Jane Windle. How long was her stay, he wanted to know.

"I've allowed a month."

A nod from Elliot. He had scheduled publication of the codex for the June issue, which meant working flat out over the last two weeks of May. A glance in Duggan's direction. Would the piece be ready on time for the printers? It would, Duggan said. He'd prepared the ground-plan for the whole thing on the flight back and had already put quite a bit on paper.

"Finished by the twentieth?"

A nod from Duggan.

"So what's the overall state of play?"

"The Vatican's Department of Antiquities is saying it's a fraud, or a hoax - a *probable* fraud or hoax." Duggan's laugh was artificial. "Take your pick between those two."

"You still think it's for real?"

"I only had photographs to work from, but yes. Fr Merle's the expert, and he's continuing to back Jane's father."

Elliot's attention swiveled to Jane. "This is one very naughty boy we have here," he said, feigning a smile. Then to Duggan he said, "We'll have to cover our back."

"Of course, but it's a win-win situation," said Duggan. "If the codex is kosher, it'll be a big story. If it isn't, it'll be just as big a story. Whichever way it goes, we'll come out on top."

"I wish it were that way for my father," said Jane, resenting

Duggan's pragmatism. "It's his head that's on the block. His involvement in this could ruin his career."

"It's just as difficult to argue fraud from photographs as it is to argue authenticity," said Duggan. "Someone would have to detect a glaring error to make any such suspicion stick."

"Mud sticks," said Jane. "The Department of Antiquities knows about the tip-off. That gives them the upper hand."

"They can't ignore Merle's reputation," said Duggan. "He's a recognized authority on Theodore's literary output. He's one of the giants in the business."

"They can, and they will," she said sullenly. "It looks like something that's been setup with the intention of hurting the Church."

"And if the codex doesn't turn up?" asked Elliot.

"Grosjean's the key to that," said Jane.

"Who the hell is Grosjean?" asked Elliot.

"Fr Sebastian Grosjean," said Duggan. "He teaches philosophy at Gregorian University in Rome." He explained as quickly as he could about Dr Weisel's diary, and about the man's unfortunate demise. Elliot's eyes widened as the turns and twists of the story fell out. "And then there's Holly Parks." Duggan glanced at Jane before divulging that a *Washington Post* journalist had stumbled into their patch. "We had no option but to compromise," he said, offering Elliot a disarming smile.

"To what extent did you compromise?"

"She knows Grosjean was Weisel's contact, but she doesn't know about the extra set of photographs. She's headed for Rome right this minute trying to find out from Grosjean who tipped him off about the codex, and about the factions. She's James Windle's insurance policy if things get rough. There's also the possibility of a major split in the Vatican hierarchy and that's what really interests her. A major split. Grosjean's an activist. He's about to publish a book on a possible schism."

"It's you who should be interviewing Grosjean."

"Confirmation from the *Washington Post* won't do us any harm. Anyway, I can't be in two places at once. I've got to get that bloody article written."

"You trust her?"

"She doesn't know enough to jeopardise what we're about to do. Grosgean just happens to be the intersecting point in two quite separate stories."

"Are you sure you can trust her?"

"She's an old workmate of David Mayle's."

"The *other* journalist," said Elliot, his sarcasm obvious. Then, in a tired voice, he said, "It sounds far too complicated. Who's keeping tabs on Mayle for God's sake?"

"You don't have to worry about David" said Duggan. "He's been a friend of Jane's family for years."

Elliot's gaze travelled from Duggan to Jane and back again. "I don't like what I'm hearing. Is there more?"

A shake of the head from Duggan.

"Let me get this straight," said Elliot. "The *Washington Post* woman is going after Grosjean, it's Grosjean who tipped off Weisel about the codex, and it's Weisel who tipped off your father. Right?"

"Correct," said Duggan.

"Then what's to stop her breaking our story wide open from the opposite end? She knows just enough to take a crack at it."

"She thinks Mayle's going to break the story in California. They're friends - more than friends. She doesn't even know I'm a journalist."

"She could work backwards and know everything she needs to know within twenty-four hours. She might make him an offer he can't refuse."

"She can't get at the codex. Without the codex and a translation she can't make the thing work. It would be half a story. Holly Parks would *never* be satisfied with half a story. She's got enough to keep her happy. More than enough

"Let's hope you're right," said Elliot.

* * *

They had gone straight to bed and slept for a couple of hours when they arrived, awakening to find a purring Phoebe kneading the bedclothes. Jane had gathered her up in delight, and Phoebe had turned on her special brand of charm for the occasion.

"She's *so* beautiful, Jack!"

"So are you," he said.

Jane Windle in his bed, in his flat, in Sydney town. He could hardly believe his luck.

"She seems none the worse for your not being here."

"She's a survivor. I found her wandering in the rain when she was only a few weeks old. She looked like a drowned rat."

"How long have you had her?"

"About three years. She's used to me disappearing for days at a time. The occasional week. This is the longest I've been away."

"Chips and Rafferty have one another, plus a mother who puts up with them when they visit."

"I look forward to meeting them."

"Do you think you will?"

"Will I ever come to Ohio? Can't see why not." She was looking at him over the top of Phoebe's head; Phoebe, too, was looking at him. "Why so uncertain?" he asked.

"Just that the cards seem to have fallen this way rather than that." She buried her face in Phoebe's neck for a moment. "I'd like you to see where I paint. Where I live. The woods I walk in. The lake." She placed Phoebe on the bedspread, continued to pet her. "Just so you know I had a life of my own."

"I've never doubted it."

"See it for yourself," she said without emphasis. "Touch it. Smell it."

"And then?"

"Make love to me in my own bed."

Duggan did not reply; he sensed the importance of what she was saying, waited for her to continue.

"So that when I mention something later you'll know what I'm talking about."

"I understand what you're saying," he said.

"Do you?"

"You weren't finished with it. It was an alchemy that was still working for you."

She nodded slowly, smiled a tight smile. He thought she might cry, but she didn't.

There was a silence.

"I'd better ring Elliot," he said. "Let him know we've arrived in one bit."

"He knows about us?"

"I think he's guessed."

Phoebe headed over to Duggan.

"She must have missed you."

"She hasn't said."

"Some cats give their owners a hard time for desertion. They aren't as self-contained as they seem."

"Yours probably spend up big on your credit card."

She laughed at the idea, admitted that her Burmese would probably watch him for hours before approaching. If indeed they ever did.

He got up and made coffee, brought it to her in bed. Elliot would expect him to knuckle down now that he was back, he said. It was a wonder he still had a job.

"He obviously believes in you."

"I've pushed him about as far as it's safe to go."

"I'll go exploring," she said jauntily, responding to his warning.

"Are you hungry?"

"Not in the least."

"Mind if we eat out tonight? I couldn't face trying to cook something. Greek okay?"

"Greek's fine." She took a sip of coffee. "Can you speak modern

Greek?"

"A bit. I'm not terribly good. I keep lapsing into ancient forms."

"So many skills."

"You speak German, French and Hebrew."

"My French is terrible and my Hebrew is rudimentary."

"Your father's linguistic skills are impressive."

"He had Hebrew drummed into him as a child. It was a multi-lingual household. I was brought up speaking German and English interchangeably. I did French at school. I found Hebrew very difficult."

"I had a crack at it years ago, but didn't continue. It's taken me all my time to keep my Greek up to scratch."

"Why did you bother?"

"I'd invested too much in it to let it slip away. It was my prize secret. The identity no one knew about."

"What made you choose journalism?"

"I needed an income."

"That was it?"

"I enjoyed writing." A self-deprecating laugh. "I thought I might try writing a novel at some point."

"Did you?"

"It's in a drawer somewhere."

"Show me!"

"It's not worth looking at."

"It was rejected?"

"I didn't send it anywhere."

She did not immediately reply. When she did, it was to say that artists were not always the best judge of their own work. Some thought it good when it wasn't, some thought it bad when it was actually very good. A friend had had to badger her before she'd exhibit.

"And now you're famous."

"Hardly."

"You've just sold out in one of the most prestigious galleries in

New York."

"It took ten years of hard slog to get there. Wouldn't have happened without George. He spotted one of my pictures in a tiny little gallery in the Village and contacted me. Wanted to see everything I'd done. I thought he was up to something to start with."

"They're an extraordinary pair."

"He bought six other paintings on the basis of nothing more than color slides. Paid good money for them." She shook her head as if still trying to take in what that had meant to her. "He put the one hanging in their dining room into one of the big gallaries through a friend and waited for a reaction. There were three enquiries in the first week."

"It wasn't for sale?"

"It was bait. The original sold sticker was still on it. "

"Clever."

"So let me read your novel."

"You'll give me handfuls of cash for it?"

"Will you settle for a kiss?"

"Can I have it now?"

"Later. I have to see if it's any good first."

She kissed him anyway, and he kissed her back. As they smooched, Phoebe took to pouncing on Duggan's bare feet. She would do some sketching, Jane said suddenly, as if in answer to a question. She had her work pad with her. Then, doubling back, she said that her brother Paul had been trying to write. He had published some short fiction with a small publishing house in Maine.

"Short is difficult," said Duggan.

"You've tried?"

"It's where most people start." A laugh. "Doesn't take long to realize it isn't as easy as it looks."

"Have you had anything published?"

"Only articles. Isn't much of a market here for short fiction. Unless you're a big name. And there's no money in it. They pay a pittance in Australia."

"You should try your luck in the States."

"It's crossed my mind."

"Paul's an English teacher."

"Why the sudden interest in his roots?"

She stopped to consider that. "I think it had to do with his wanting to write."

"I can relate to that," said Duggan. "My novel has an Irish background."

"You've been to Ireland?"

"Never."

"UK?"

"Twice."

"You didn't think to visit Ireland?"

"I was young. I was Australian. Ireland was some Godforsaken place my mother and father had escaped from. I think I saw it more in terms of a gulag than a country."

"Hardly Godforsaken."

"No, certainly not that. Riddled with God one could say. Like an old cupboard is infested with woodworm." A laugh. "Not a very good metaphor, but it'll do."

"They didn't try to sell you the old country?"

"My mother did; not my father. I think he was glad to see the back of the place. My mother regretted coming to Australia. He didn't. She brought her brutal God with her and kept him alive through hating everything around her. He kept his mouth shut right up until the day she died. At least in front of me he did."

"She sounds awful."

"It's a hard thing to say about one's own mother, but she *was* awful. Everything was okay as long as you went along with her way of seeing and doing things. Question her judgment and you got what-for. And don't forget the local priest was in there as well. He was there every other day backing her stupidity. If you include God, it was a *menage a trois.*"

"I'm surprised you got as far as going into a seminary."

"I was on a career path and couldn't get off. She saw to it that I didn't. Everything I studied from the age of fifteen was grist to the priestly mill."

"Your father never interfered?"

"In his own quiet way he did. He would talk to me about life, counteract her nonsense with stories about people he had known. I learned a lot about story from him."

"The Irish are good at stories."

"It's the accent. They can make a load of rubbish sound important because of the lilt. They're gossips with a flair for the dramatic."

"I would like to read your novel. You might be another Joyce."

"I doubt very much that that's the case."

"So who's your favorite writer?"

"Among the greats? It would have to be Thomas Mann."

"You read him in German?"

"My German isn't good enough. I tend to skim. You shouldn't do that with Mann. Every word counts with that kind of writer."

"Which novel?"

"*The Magic Mountain.* It's a masterpiece. I think I've read it six or seven times."

"And your favorite artist?"

" . . . El Greco."

"Why?"

"His use of light. His intensity. His portrayal of the human condition through the elongation of form. He knew what suffering was about."

"You think suffering is important?"

"Depends what you mean by it." Duggan drew breath, let it out in one. "Mature reflection? You begin to glimpse more and more of what's really going on inside yourself."

"You know this from experience?"

"Not enough by far." A self-contained laugh. "It happens to all of us all of the time but we don't let it register much. When we do, things look very different."

"And you equate that with suffering?"

"It's the most honorable form of suffering available to us. The most useful, if you like. You see and understand what you did not see or understand seconds before. It's simultaneously the most enlightening *and* the most challenging experience you can have. In seeing what you do not want to see you're forced to consider what it is you're up to moment by moment."

"It's said we experience something like that at death," said Jane. "A last and final glimpse of what we are before the lights go out. Or come on, depending on what you believe."

"Everything in one searing glance," said Duggan. "Past, present and immediate future in one frame."

"You think that's likely?"

"I think it's a possibility. Might be that the dam bursts and everything breaks through in the last few seconds."

Jane blinked her consternation at Duggan. *"That* is a scary idea," she said. "How would you explain it?"

"Judgment Swedenborg-style. Self-judgment? The way it has to be if God, whatever God might be, is even vaguely democratic. Or, more probably, the brain's last mad attempt to ward off the inevitable." She was studying his face as if hoping to detect something beyond what was being said. "Question is, what happens to this little mite?" Duggan reached for Phoebe, who was busy nuzzling her fur. "Does she just snuff out and that's it? I'd hate to think I went on and she didn't."

"You're using that as a yardstick?"

"Why not. We're both conscious. I'm no more conscious that she is most of the time. It's only occasionally I glimpse what I'm avoiding."

"Which is what?"

"Myself." Duggan's smile was mischievous. "It's the old Socratic problem come home to roost, Jane. I'm only just beginning to understand what he was on about."

"We know more about ourselves now than we ever did."

"In quantitative terms, yes. I think Socrates was talking about something quite different."

"Like what?"

"Knowing *as* the self, not just *about* the self."

"You've lost me."

"Exactly that, but from a different angle. We get lost to ourselves. We disappear. We fade out. We . . . turn into the equivalent of cats cleaning themselves."

She laughed and asked him what he meant.

"I'm not really sure." He laughed along with her and tried again. "It's a little something I glimpsed and don't quite know what to make of. An *anomalia,* as the Greeks say."

"Will it keep to after breakfast."

"I'll make you Greek eggs."

"Socrates *and* Greek eggs!"

"It's that kind of household," he said back.

* * *

Archbishop Donaghue's dilemma was that he agreed with most of CNCD's aspirations and objectives, but not with their methodology. It was one thing to advocate a return to prayer; it was quite another to turn prayer into a confessional battleground. It was permissible to advocate obedience to Christ as a first principle; it was not permissible to denigrate the love of one human being for another. The missionary-children of the New Catholic Dawn had every right to confront parishieners with their sloth, but they did not have the right to coerce, threaten or attempt to brainwash them into a homogenous entity. Enforcement of basic Catholic doctrine was a given in Donaghue's book, but only in the sense of challenging priests and their congregations to recognise that Christianity's core doctrines could not, and should not, be tampered with. There was an irreducible core to Christianity and it should be guarded at all cost.

Enforcement did not entail bullying people into submission, it entailed offering them something that helped shift their mind into a higher gear. In terms of the soul, there were questions that mattered, and there were questions that did not matter. Questions that did not matter came to an abrupt halt within themselves - once answered there was no more to them - whereas questions that mattered continued to expand and develop. Knowing the exact distance between the Earth and the sun ended in knowing just that, a mere measurement, whereas the questions generated by one reading of Tolstoy's *War and Peace* blossomed into a thousand other questions. So with Scripture. That was the key to Christianity's success: it always carried the eye to the horizon. The modern mind found it difficult to appreciate how believing that a man walked on water could be of benefit, but they had quite missed the point in thinking like that. Faith was not about stubbornness, or about facts and figures; it was about focusing the mind beyond utilitarian concepts and glimpsing eternity.

Donaghue's distrust of facts and figures was well known. Aware that every verse of the Bible could not be read literally - genres such as poetry, prophesy, aphorisms and exhortations existed alongside history, biography and autobiography - he nevertheless expected faithfulness to the New Testament story of Christ's saving death and resurrection. That was the core of St Paul's message, and it could not be got around. Wrapping a withered and withering humanism in counterfeit Christian terminology, liberal-minded Christians hoped to undermine that directive, but in doing so they offered nothing to the thirsting soul. Abandon a personal God and a divine Christ and you ended up as deprived as any inhabitant of the Third World.

So what of those mighty men in Rome he had been privileged to sup with? What of their beliefs, hopes and ambitions? Gammarelli and Craxi were declared modernists, so could be excused their liberal excesses, but Benneditti and Furno were supposed to be conservatives like himself. So, too, Cardinal Pia, his friend and confidant of many years. Pia professed not to have changed, but he had at times sounded all too modern in his thinking. Certainly

Benneditti's views on Satan had been an eye-opener, as had his thoughts on a laity-based spirituality beyond papal control, but his notion of an ever-deepening Christian revelation had left Donaghue feeling uncomfortable. Ever-deepening? What exactly had he meant by that? Spiritual discernment was always a factor in the spiritual life, that was a given, but Donaghue sensed something quite different at the back of Benneditti's mind: he detected the occursed doctrine of *relevance*.

It was all Fr. Edward Schillebeeckx's fault. Schillebeeckx, a Dutch Dominican teacher of history and theology at the University of the Netherlands, and a favorite son of the radical left, had taught relevance to the world as an improvement on divine revelation. Everything to do with Church doctrine had to be brought up to date and reworked, Schillebeeckx had believed. A Church that was not relevant to the needs and beliefs of the twentieth century was not a properly functioning Church. So had Cardinal Benneditti drunk at the Dutchman's infected well? Had he, too, succumbed to the idea that *relevance to the world* could extend what was already understood as Christ's mission on Earth? Were these so-called conservatives paying no more than lipservice to the old doctrines, playing the ultimate game of deception as they prepared to deal with CNCD extravagance? And was it perhaps for that very reason that CNCD had received papal recognition and Cardinal Menenger's backing in the first place?

A distraught Archbishop Donaghue got up from his desk and stood by the window contemplating that possibility. Hardly the elevated experience promised by his friend as they chatted over sandwiches and coffee. More an oblique assault, he now realized, an assault on his simple faith dressed up in the language of expediency. There was more going on than had been admitted, more afoot within that odd assemblage than he had been able to determine over a few slices of suckling pig.

29

The Imaginings of Men

"Which paper did you say you were with?"

"I didn't." David Mayle put his cards on the table. "I'm freelance - since yesterday. The paper I was with in Frisco reached its use-by date."

Fr Brentano's suspicions remained intact.

"The *Washington Post* is interested in CNCD machinations." Mayle smiled his hang-dog smile. "*Very* interested. I tracked you down through your local paper's report on what the movement got up to here."

"I got into a lot of trouble over that."

"You stood up to them. That took courage."

"There isn't much I can add."

"It's the details we're interested in."

Mayle's use of the plural was not lost on the priest; it seemed to lessen the vagueness of the situation somewhat. He responded with a request that what they discussed be off the record.

"Off the record it is," said Mayle. Another of his disarming smiles. "Just point me in the right direction - I already have a couple of addresses."

And still the priest hesitated. "Why the interest in something that happened weeks ago?" he asked.

"Seems they're having much the same trouble with CNCD in Rome. Big ructions looming there."

Brentano stared at Mayle for a moment, then stood aside so that he could enter. As the door closed behind them, he asked what Mayle's connection with the *Washington Post* was.

"I'm working on the story alongside one of their journalists." Mayle laughed his laugh. "It's also a matter of her not being able to biolocate."

"That's an interesting choice of word."

"I'm a fan of Padre Pio's."

A glance, and a half-smile from the priest. "Your partner's headed for Rome?"

"She's there now."

"She is?"

"Holly Parks. She worked with me years ago in Frisco. We've teamed up for this one."

They entered Brentano's lounge; it was littered with books and was none too tidy. The priest's breakfast dishes were still on the table.

"My housekeeper's ill. Flu. It's been over a week." Still apologising, Brentano cleared a chair so that Mayle could sit down. "Coffee?"

Mayle nodded and the priest went into his kitchen. Hidden from view, he spoke through the open doorway. CNCD's emissaries had caused him endless sleepless nights, he said. Their leaving had been an answer to prayer. But in many ways it was as if they were still around.

"Your local bishop didn't put up much of a fight."

"They had letters of approval from competent ecclesiastical authorities in Rome. Bishop Harrier couldn't say no to them, and Archbishop Donaghue had recommended them. We didn't known what we were taking on at that point."

"You went over your bishop's head?"

"I had to. He wouldn't listen." Brentano appeared in the doorway. "I was accused of exaggerating a problem of my own making. If I'd let things take their course everything would have been okay, I was told. Truth is, if I'd let things take their course years of work in this parish would have been destroyed overnight. Almost were, in fact." The priest's face reflected the torment he had been through. "It was a nightmare I have no wish to repeat."

"How did the showdown come about?"

"I was confronted one evening by a deputation of very angry

parishioners; they demanded that I act immediately." A sigh from Brentano. "I'd promised the archbishop to keep what was happening out of the press, to remain neutral, but that proved impossible."

"What was happening?"

"High-handed nonsense. The movement's stated aim was to make us into *real* Catholics. Or, as they put it in their strangled volcabulary, bring us to a full and integral catholicity. Most of my congregation found that quite insulting. As I did."

"How long before you realized what was going on?"

"A month? Six weeks? Didn't take them long to get into gear. They were sweetness and light for as long as it took to establish themselves, then all hell broke loose. First thing they did was inaugurate extra prayer meetings. These turned into rabid confessionals. Then came meetings for this, that and the next thing; endless meetings that went on endlessly. Turned out we had to believe what they believed to the letter to even be considered Christian never mind Catholic."

"How are things now? Everything's back to normal?"

"I don't think they'll ever return to normal. Not completely. They accomplished what they set out to accomplish - a split."

"There's still a split?"

"A few recovered their wits, but it'll never be the same around here. You could say we've been robbed of our innocence." A shake of the head. "About a third of my congregation is still under their influence."

"Their missionaries are still around?"

"Not in person. The breakaway group set up a parallel ministry in the Church hall. They follow proscribed CNCD services and even have a separate mass."

"Who takes the mass?"

"A priest sympathetic to the movement. They bus him in twice a week. There are a lot of strangers around now. I would imagine some of them are CNCD. It's how they set about building one of their damnable communities."

"They're doing this under your nose?"

"Gleefully under my nose. It's only a matter of time before we're back where we started." Brentano disappeared again. When he reappeared it was with two mugs of coffee.

"You've obviously been looking into how they do things," said Mayle. "I'd be interested in your sources."

"I have a brother studying at Gregorian University in Rome. He's been keeping tabs on the movement."

"And?"

"You probably know as much as I do."

"Another perspective is always useful."

"You musn't use my brother's name either."

"Understood," said Mayle, amazed by Brentano's trusting nature. Then, "When did this lot get going?"

"They fired their first serious shots in '87 with documents prepared by the Curia for the synod on laity. The key statement during that Synod was that the laity were to strive to overcome . . . *the pernicious separation between professed faith and daily life."* Brentano expression was ironic. "That's the basis of their thinking, and it's proved to be an insidious directive ever since."

"In what way?"

"By dint of its ambiguity. You can make it mean just about anything. My brother desribes CNCD's approach as over-spiritualised. He means by that that it's inward-looking to the point of idiocy."

"Your bishop's aware of the new developments here?"

"He granted the breakaway group the right of assembly the moment they asked for it. He's scared stiff of CNCD. It's pathetic. I confronted him and was reminded that they had the backing of the Roman authorities." The priest swapped irony for cynicism. "I sometimes think we're as reliant on bits of stamped paper as the Third Reich."

Mayle added a few more squiggles to his pad.

"You mustn't quote me on that. You musn't quote me on anything!"

"What I write won't be traceable back to you - at least not to anything said this afternoon." A smile of assurance from Mayle. "I'm old-school, Father. I keep my promises." Then, "Your archbishop's reaction to all this?"

"If you question archbishop Donaghue's authority you have to wear a tin hat. He also is old-school. He's a stickler for obedience and does not take kindly to being told by those he considers subordinates what he can or cannot do. Their arrogance has to be experienced to be believed."

"Your local bishop has gone against the archbishop's wishes?"

"Donaghue's been in Rome for over a week and has just returned. A full report on the latest madness is on his desk."

"That may make him amenable to talking to me."

"I doubt it. He's probably been reeled in."

"I have it on good authority that Cardinal Menenger fully endorses CNCD methodology. He's been quoted as saying that the movements are Vatican II's only positive result."

"It's a wooden horse," said Brentano. "It's *everything* the second Vatican Council attempted brought to nothing."

"You've made your views known to the archbishop?"

A nod from Brentano.

"His reaction?"

"A plea for caution at first. It was only when things spiralled out of control that he was forced to intervene."

"How did he handle the situation?"

"He argued for a modification to their pastoral methods on the basis of their being a foreign import. It was, he said, necessary to sit down with the local bishops and talk through how the missionary thing should be handled. It was a commonsense approach and it got him absolutely nowhere."

"They wouldn't listen?"

"One of them sat where you're sitting now and told him that how they went about their business was none of his business. They were sanctioned to teach and preach in America and that was the end of the matter."

"That must have gone down well."

"Donaghue blew his top. I don't think I've ever seen him so angry. He ordered them out of the diocese on the spot."

"Yet it's said they're highly succesful."

"They supply firm answers in a time of uncertainty. They're never stuck for an answer. They're fundamentalist with a theology as hardline as any Protestant sect." Brentano paused to take a sip of coffee. "There are always those who need that kind of assurance." Another sip of coffee. "What you may not realize is that CNCD has been building its presence within the Church for decades. They're not a recent phenomenon. It's just that they've decided to spread their wings in earnest over the last six months or so."

"They really think of themselves as missionaries?"

"That's their official title."

"Missionaries to the Church?"

"With the task of making us all into *real* Catholics." Brentano's tone was tinged with disgust. Then, for no apparent reason, he began to laugh. "I put it all under the rubric of Donaghue's dilemma."

"Why?"

"Because he's thought of as leading the charge for Catholic renewal in this wonderful country of ours."

"I was at the conference he chaired recently in Santa Rosa. He came across as a bit of a hardliner himself. Imagine my lack of surprise when I discovered he was your archbishop."

"He keeps faith with the faith."

"I rather got the impression he wanted to turn the clock back."

"Not in the manner CNCD wants to. The New Catholic Dawn is rabidly anti-intellectual. Donaghue's got a doctorate in philosophy."

"He sounded pretty hardline to me."

"Not when compared with CNCD."

"Enlighten me."

Brentano considered Mayle's request, then launched into a scathing description of CNCD ambitions. They saw themselves as the repository of all truth, he said. They were messianic in that respect. It was their intention to renew every aspect of society. Their stated mission was to infiltrate existing social structures and bring them to heel, create a self-contained culture covering the entire gamut of human experience. In that respect they were identical to hardline Protestant evangelicals and fundamentalist. They carried the same agenda as radicalised Moslems and enforced that agenda by whatever means they thought necessary. The gloves were off. Whatever it took to reinstate Catholicism's past glory would be considered valid on the basis that it was successful. This included the destruction of families who did not see eye-to-eye on CNCD practice. It was a matter of indoctrination at any cost.

"You're talking theocratic state."

"I'm talking social experiment and the machinations of men taken to the nth degree."

"Donaghue doesn't see it that way?"

"He realizes his mistake, I think. Hence his dilemma."

"Hoist by his own petard," said Mayle.

Fr Brentano finished his coffee and put his mug down. "The charismatic movements offer a fatalistic vision. Everything happens by the grace of God. A beautiful day, the birth of a child, a hurricane that destroys a city and kills thousands is ultimately God's will. So you have to accept that conflict and war and human suffering are all part of a divine plan." Brentano drew breath and added. "Such a view breeds passivity, then conformity to the sect's wishes. They consider unquestioning belief and obedience a virtue."

"Many a pope has thought the same way."

"It is a sin to relinquish our capacity to think and question."

"Even if you believe in a great cosmic plan?"

"We see through a glass but darkly."

"Not according to your archbishop. He believes in a cosmic plan. He believes evil and good are battling it out behind the scenes. The conference he chaired was about just that. They had everything tied up with a theological bow."

"He's a man of simple faith."

"You just told me he has a doctorate in philosophy."

"Doctorates in philosophy are part of the scenery among churchmen."

Mayle hiccupped a laugh. "You're very frank, Father!"

"There's a need for frankness in this matter."

"You're obviously liberal in your views."

"I'm perceived as such by some."

"By the Archbishop?"

Fr. Brentano considered Mayle's question. "The archbishop has been very patient with me. He's backed me when many another would have thrown me to the wolves. I'm in his debt. I put my misfortune down to an incident that took place here about six months ago." A shake of the head from Brentano as memory stirred. "We were visited by a particularly nasty character who took it upon himself to scold me in public for not being rigorous enough in my ministry."

"Visited by?"

"We invited him to speak at one of our evening gatherings and got more than we bargained for. The archbishop introduced him as a personal friend."

"A hardliner."

"And cheeky with it. He ticked me off for allowing elements of evolutionary theory to stand as true."

"You challenged something he said?"

"I suggested diplomatically during his question time that he was perhaps a little behind the times in his thinking. That did not go down well. He's a canon lawyer with an authority complex big enough to trip over?"

"Wouldn't be Robert Carter by any chance?"

"Why yes. Your paths have crossed?"

"He helped set up the Santa Rosa conference with your

archbishop. He's had a go at me personally. He's known to arrange visits to parishes thought to be theologically suspect. Didn't know he was connected to CNCD, though."

"You're saying I did this to myself?"

"It sounds like it. CNCD turned up soon afterwards?"

"About a month later."

Mayle digested that, said that Carter having links with CNCD added a whole new and interesting dimension to the puzzle.

The priest fell silent, then admitted that he'd heard rumors about odd goings-on in other parishes. But if something didn't affect you directly you were apt to push it aside, weren't you?. And he had been the only one targeted among a couple of dozen parishes in Donaghue's diocese. Then, apropos of nothing, he said that the archbishop's heart was in the right place.

"I don't doubt it," said Mayle.

"He's caught between a rock and a hard place."

"It'll be interesting to see which way he jumps."

Fr Brentano smiled and surprised Mayle by doubling back to something said earlier. Why the sudden decision to go freelance, he wanted to know.

"The only difference between a rut and a grave is that one is deeper," said Mayle, quoting Holly Parks. He added quickly, and with a twist, "Call it a crisis of faith, Father. Faith in myself."

"You obviously think there's a big story in this."

A nod from Mayle. CNCD's shenanigans were worth more than a casual glance, and Carter's likely involvement with the movement was, as far as he was concerned, an added bonus. The man's intentions were downright sinister.

"It's a Catch-22 situation, isn't it," said Brentano. "We're being pushed into an impossible position."

"Utopian beliefs have a habit of backfiring," said Mayle.

"Is that how you read Christianity's promises?" asked Fr Brentano.

"No, it's how I read the imaginings of men," said Mayle.

* * *

It was a strange feeling to be back behind his desk, back among known faces and know without turning that one face was missing. *Missing presumed dead.* Getting up, Duggan went over to the photocopier and placed Bishop Peters' second article on the glass plate. Some day Peters, too, would be dead. Dead as a doornail, whatever that meant. And Jack Duggan. And Jane. And Windle and Mayle and even Holly Parks. Dead and gone and most probably forgotten except for some snippet or other. He watched the blue light scan the page, watched it return to source and repeat the process. A laugh as the image translated itself into a metaphor. "What would be the point of that?" he said to himself. A glance round to see if anyone had heard, which they hadn't.

Three copies of Bishop Peters's article slid into the tray. He scooped them up and took them back to his desk. One for the file, one for himself and one for Elliot. A smile. Peters was still doing battle, as was Fr Brindle, the Australian priest who had accused the Catholic establishment of pettiness. Another smile and a half-laugh at Mayle having managed to conjure cuttings on Brindle out of thin air only hours after they'd met. A feat that had impressed him, as had Mayle's Dodge van with its computer gear and its unmade bed. Who'd have guessed, at that point, what lay ahead.

His thoughts returned to Jane; he decided to ring her. Hardly had he done so when her voice sounded in his ear.

"It's me," he said. "What ya doin? Have you been out and about yet?"

"I went for a wander. Glebe has the same feel as the Village in places. I found a good bookshop."

"What are you doing right this minute?"

"Phoebe and I are watching television. It's eighteen degrees and raining in Rome. I wonder how Holly's getting on?"

'If I know Holly she'll be busy."

"I like her. She's got guts."

"I've never doubted that."

Jane hesitated, then she said, "Did you ever return to Rome after that dreadful experience you described?"

"No. My interests have been wholly Greek. I think I'm a pagan at heart. Rome is just another city in my book."

"Will you show me the sights some time?"

"I'd love to."

"Before I return to the States?"

" . . . If that's what you want."

"It's what I want," she said back.

* * *

Sebastian Grosjean frowned a Gallic frown when Holly contacted him by telephone. Did he speak English, she wanted to know. Excellent. She was with the *Washington Post* and she had come all the way to Rome to interview him about his fourthcoming book.

"The *Washington Post* is aware of my book? How can that possibly be?"

"A tip-off," said Holly, offering a half-truth and a tap on the shoulder to Grosjean's conscience.

"I'm surprised you didn't think of contacting me first. I may not have been here."

"We checked on that."

"With whom?"

"Your department."

"But didn't think to speak to me?"

"You weren't available."

"Did you say who you were?"

"Under the circumstances we thought that unwise."

Grosjean fell silent for a moment; then in a low voice he said, "My book is not yet ready for publcation."

"When will it be ready?"

"A couple of weeks. Three? Look, I'm really not sure . . . There have been problems."

"What kind of problems?"

"It's not something I can discuss on the telephone." An audible sigh from the Frenchman. "Can we meet somewhere other than the university to talk about this?"

"Name it," said Holly.

He named the cafe where he had confessed his sins to Fr Merle, suggested that they meet immediately to avoid the lunchtime crush, and asked how he would recognise her.

"I'm blonde," she said, knowing that that would be enough when the moment came.

Grosjean turned out to be a small, slim man in his late forties. He raised a hand in recognition when Holly arrived, got to his feet and greeted her unsmilingly.

"You're a priest!" a surprised Holly said, eyeing the black soutane. "It never occurred to me that you might be a priest."

"It's possible to be both professor *and* priest," he replied, filling in the unspoken part of her response. "Would you like coffee?"

"I'd *love* a coffee," she said back.

He gestured vaguely at a chair, and summoned a waiter who was standing nearby. When she had his attention again, she asked his permission to record their conversation. It was granted. Having set things up, she came straight to the point. Was the papacy in as much trouble as he seemed to believe it was?

"There's the possibility of a schism if the movements aren't brought under control," he said, leaning towards the recorder. Then, irritably, he asked the question that had been bothering him. "By what means did you learn that I had written a book?"

"Through Dr Hubert Weisel," Holly said, knowing that that would rivet his attention.

"Hubert?"

"I'm afraid it's bad news," she said, knowing she'd just have to blurt it out. "Dr Weisel was mugged in New York less than two weeks ago. He died of a heart attack soon after. He left a diary. I gained access to that diary."

Grosjean's shock was patent; he sat back into his chair as if struck, but his brain was still working. "Under what circumstances did you gain access to Hubert's diary?"

"It came into the possession of Professor James Windle, who was in New York at the same time." Offering a half-truth, she added, "I was there to cover the story surrounding the disappearance of the Mar Saba Codex."

Grosjean sat blinking for a moment, then he said, "How did Professor Windle come to be in possession of Hubert's diary?"

"It was given to him by Dr Weisel's sister."

" . . . I'm sorry, I don't understand any of this." Grosjean's perplexity was patent. "Why would Hubert's sister do that?"

"Because she knew what had gone down between you and her brother and felt that Professor Windle should know the truth of the situation. She did not like the way her brother had gone about things."

Sebastian Grosjean's laugh was bitter. "Is it your intention to plaster my involvement in this matter across the front page of the *Washington Post?*"

"That is *not* our intention," Holly said back. "Professor Windle has forbidden it. In fact he sends his greetings, and his condolences on the loss of your friend." Reaching for her handbag, she extracted Weisel's thank you note and added, "He asked me to give you this."

After a moment's reading, Grosjean looked up, his eyes filled with tears. "This is all my fault, isn't it?" he said.

"He wasn't just in New York to see Professor Windle; he was also there to see his sister - a sister he hadn't see in years."

"Hubert met with Professor Windle?"

"Yes."

"Why?"

"To warn him about the factional infighting that was going on here in Rome. He had come to regret the deviousness involved."

"It's been said that the road to hell is paved with good intentions," said Grosjean. "You don't realize how true that is until you get involved in something like this." He raised both hands in an expression of hopelessness. "I should have been more forthright in my dealings with Professor Windle."

"Why weren't you?"

"It's one thing to criticize the Catholic Church, Miss Parks, it's quite another to threaten the fabric of its existence. Not that I believe the codex does that, I don't; but there are those who think otherwise." A sigh before he continued. "Imagine my surprise when it turned out to be Fr Merle who was headed for Mar Saba. I'd never heard of Professor Windle, but Merle had helped me a great deal during my Sorbonne years, so I was only too pleased to slide the codex in his direction."

"But you didn't; at least not directly. It was Professor Windle you landed that honor with."

"I was playing safe. I didn't want Fr Merle to carry responsibility for finding the codex if it proved to be deficient, and I knew he had the best chance of detecting any such deficiency. All in all it was a neat arrangement that I didn't think could go wrong."

"Why did you choose Weisel as intermediary?"

"I met Hubert in Berlin years ago. It was a chance meeting. We got on well in spite of his having some crazy ideas. Then suddenly there he was on the telephone talking research and asking for my help. One thing led to another and I enlisted his help."

"Why?"

Grosjean hesitated, then he said, "To steer the whole thing away from the Vatican's front door. Modernist I may be; Church-hater I am not."

"So who tipped you off about the codex?"

"I'm sorry, I can't tell you that. It's a matter of trust."

"You may have to break that trust if things get really nasty." Holly produced a copy of the Department of Antiquities' letter given to her by Windle. "As you can see, they're gearing up for something."

Grosjean read the letter through and handed it back. "They feel threatened. They're at their most dangerous when threatened."

"They're consciously targeting Professor Windle to shift attention away from the codex."

"It's the only option open to them," said Grosjean. "If taken seriously, the codex could stimulate intense scholarly discussion around the question of the Jerusalem Church and its origins. They want to avoid that at all costs."

"They're not interested in historical facts?"

"The Church believes itself to be in possession of a revelation straight from God, Miss Parks; what use has it for historical facts? In attacking the codex, and in particular Professor Windle, it believes itself to be protecting that revelation from the ravages of secularism and modernism."

"You obviously think otherwise."

"Let's just say that my profession has made me suspicious of packages that fall from heaven."

Holly waited for some noisy youths to pass their table, then she said, "You obviously gave the question of forgery some thought before contacting Dr Weisel."

"I trusted the scholarship and integrity of the person who informed me of the codex's existence."

"Someone at the monastery?"

"I can't say."

"Someone in the Department of Antiquities?"

"Goodness me no! The Department of Antiquities is a closed shop. Monsignor Francesco Rossi is well known as a pope's man."

"He's CNCD?"

"He's in favor of CNCD. Those in the top echelons of the hierarchy agree from a distance."

"It's faction against faction?"

"It's always been so. From the very beginning it's been a matter of who wins the day."

"What would it mean for Catholicism if CNCD won the day?"

"It would mean the end of the Church as we know it. She would continue to look and sound the same, but it would be an entirely different kind of papacy. It would devour all before it and use Christ's name as its excuse."

"Your book spells this out?"

"Clearly, and in considerable detail."

"Can I have a copy to read."

A nod from Grosjean; then a doubling back to what he had said on the phone about problems. There had been a break-in at the publishers, he said. A number of manuscripts undergoing editing had been trashed, but that was thought to be a blind. It was believed his manuscript had been the target of the break-in.

"It was generally known you were about to publish a book?"

"Only a select few knew of the manuscript's existence."

"Someone is not what they seem?"

"It's more likely to have been an employee of the publisher who got wind of it - someone with CNCD connections. It's being looked into."

"You think CNCD was responsible?"

"My researches show them to be capable of the most alarming things."

"Such as?"

"It's all in my book. Everything is documented."

"Could you arrange for me to talk with your publisher?"

"To what end?"

"Serial rights? Reviews? In-depth articles? It's in my power to make your book a best-seller overnight."

"You haven't as much as seen my book yet!"

"You're a professor; it can't be that bad."

It was a cheeky reply; it made Grosjean smile. Then, surprising Holly, he said that the Department of Antiquity's unexpectedly hardline approach on the codex meant that Fr Merle, too, was now in a difficult position..

"You know this for a fact?"

"He has refused to back down on his earlier evaluation of the codex."

"That was last week. What about this week?"

"There is no indication that he has changed his mind, or will change his mind. My sources assure me of that."

"What will happen if you're identified as the key figure in all this?"

"I'd be forced out of my job."

"And when your book's published?"

"The book is an academic exercise, Miss Parks. It's properly documented and its has the backing of some *very* powerful people. I have no fears in that direction."

"Do these same people have any inkling of what you've been up to with regard to the codex?"

"On the whole, no."

"What would happen if that got out?"

"The conservative element would immediately desert me."

"Does it worry you that that might happen?"

Grosjean's smile, when it came, was full-blown and devoid of calculation. Fixing Holly with a look, he said in a quiet voice, "The only thing I really have to worry about is you, Miss Parks. Isn't that so?"

30

More than a Hiccup

The Press Office of the Holy See (*Sala Stampa*) issued its bulletin on the Mar Saba Codex on May 12, a blustery Tuesday afternoon. The opinion it offered was that the codex was a modern forgery, an outrageous concoction designed to undermine decades of rigorous scholarship. Set up to hoodwink even the experts, the codex was a denigration of core Christian beliefs. The scholars who had found the codex had been notified of the department's conclusions, and further investigations were being conducted into the circumstances surrounding the discovery.

Alerted by her editor in Washington, Holly Parks arranged an interview with Monsignor Francesco Rossi, the Department of Antiquity's chief palaeographer, and on an equally blustery Wednesday morning found herself facing this imperious scrutiniser of sacred texts.

"I've just spoken with Professor Windle in New York," Holly said, eliciting a blink of surprise from the monsignor. "He didn't hide the fact that he had been tipped off about the codex's whereabouts. Would you care to comment on that?"

"It is a troubling element in the story," said Rossi, his English self-consciously precise. "It adds further substance to our suspicion that the codex is a forgery."

"Suspicion? Your bulletin gave the impression forgery was a foregone conclusion."

"A *strong* suspicion based on evidence."

"What kind of evidence?"

"The kind that is easily missed because it is so subtle." Rossi's smile became condescending. "The text is simply *too* perfect, Miss Parks. Someone has laboured to make it so."

"Wouldn't something genuine carry the same quality imprint?"

Rossi acknowledged Holly's jargonised point with a nod. "Yes, but not the same quantity of carefully arranged proofs. It is a problem of quantity, not of quality. The codex could be described as a masterpiece of scholarly objections anticipated. It's creator has laboured to be always one step ahead of the informed reader."

"Professor Windle doesn't agree with your department's findings."

Only when he had constructed another perfect sentence did Rossi speak. "Professor Windle's expertise is . . . perhaps not sufficient to judge," he said, his head tilted back slightly.

"Professor Merle is of the same opinion as Professor Windle."

"You've talked with Professor Merle?"

"Not directly."

"Professor Windle told you this?"

"In as many words." Holly flashed a smile and doubled back. "Your only evidence for forgery is that the codex is too perfect? You expect such a verdict to be taken seriously?"

"It is also counter-intuitive to what is already known on many levels of scholarship."

"You mean it offers a point of view not acceptable to your department's specialists." Holly's smile was accusatory. "It could be said you have little choice but to reject any point of view that does not coincide with your Church's faith claims."

Monsignor Rossi's head tilted back further still. "Let me put you in the picture. The codex offers a revisionist history of the Early Church that is totally fantastic. It is one thing to contradict the carefully sifted findings of scholars, it is quite another to rubbish those findings altogether and hope to get away with it."

"The codex does that?"

"It is an incorrigible piece of nonsense the like of which I have not seen in many years!" Monsignor Rossi sighed before continuing. "Our conclusion is that more than one pair of hands was responsible in its creation."

"People with expert knowledge?"

"*That* is our unfortunate conclusion."

"So what happens now?"

"Further investigations are being conducted into the circumstances surrounding the codex's discovery. It is imperative for all concerned that we find out who is behind this . . " Words failed the monsignor; his mouth clamped shut.

"The police are involved?"

"Of course."

"Pity you don't have the original manuscript."

"That would be of benefit."

"Your bulletin states that the codex is a modern forgery. How modern is modern?"

"That has not yet been determined."

"A twentieth century attempt to deceive? A nineteenth century attempt?"

"We'll have more to say about that quite soon. It is, as stated, under investigation. Further study of the codex may even reveals its creator's hand."

"How?"

"There are only so many people in the world with the ability to create such a document. Marry that fact to known attitudes of dissent in certain quarters and a profile may emerge"

"You would have to be very sure of your findings to pinpoint someone on that basis."

"The police also have experts in this area. Their investigations would complete the picture, I am sure. It is a matter of one small step at a time."

"How do you explain Professor Merle's conviction that the codex is not a forgery? And Professor Windle's for that matter?"

"It is a question on which many scholars will eventually adjudicate."

"It'll be open to scholars outside of your department?"

"Eventually, yes."

Holly paused, then calculatedly she said, "Isn't it precipitous of your department to make such a claim on the basis of a few photographs? Professor Windle and Professor Merle handled and examined the original document. Shouldn't their findings take precedence over yours?"

"They submitted their findings to the Department of Antiquities for confirmation, not automatic approval. Need I say more? The original document may never be found, but even if it were, the language, meanings and historical references it contains would be the same. Our findings are based on content, *not* on physical characteristics. There is sufficient evidence in the former to cast serious doubt on the latter."

"Doubt? Suspicion? Is that really sufficient for you to shout *forgery* from the rooftops?"

"In our world doubt is a powerful mechanism, it tempers enthusiasm and saves us from the ramblings of the incautious."

"How long before a translation of the codex is released?"

"That's hard to say. It depends on the results of our investigations, and on the police. It could be months."

Handing Monsignor Rossi her card, Holly said, "Professor Merle's stance on the codex doesn't bother you?"

"Fr Merle has taken the department's findings into consideration. He is aware of the implications."

"Is he still in Rome?"

"Not to my knowledge. I would imagine he has returned to France."

A big smile from Holly, and thanks for seeing her at such short notice. Was there any chance of a second interview if it proved necessary?

"The *Washington Post* is a very fine newspaper, Miss Parks. It would be my pleasure."

Holly made to turn, but appeared to change her mind. "One more thing," she said, as if just remembering. "What can you tell me about the New Catholic Dawn movement?"

* * *

Duggan completed his article on the Codex in three days; it was longer than Elliot had stipulated, but when he read it through any thought of cutting it vanished. It was a dexterous piece of writing, he admitted, controversial yet balanced, complex yet accessible. And underneath it all such a good yarn, a rollicking good story ending with a surprised James Windle being interviewed in New York. An unwilling admittance from Windle that the photographs Duggan had so mysteriously come by were authentic, that the translation he had somehow managed to secure was an accurate rendition of the text. A photograph of Windle looking stern and slightly perplexed would be added to the mix, his misgivings concerning this pirated version of the codex sounded loud and clear.

The artwork preceded the article, one of Windle's ellicit photographs (the final page of Theodore's letter) serving both as full-bleed centrefold and front cover. Pictures of the monastery and something of its history would be scattered throughout, special attention being paid to the Vatican's announcement that the codex was a modern forgery. They should expect a strong response from the Vatican, and from the churches, Elliot said during one of his staff briefings. The phones would ring hot and there would be the danger of being distracted from the other jobs in hand.

In Rome, Holly interviewed Grosjean's publisher and learned that an employee had been sacked on the suspicion that he had supplied an outside source with information deemed private to the company. Unabashed at being identified, this individual had faced-down his accusers and accused them in turn of publishing a book only fit for the flames. Nothing overt had been admitted by this employee, and a direct link between CNCD and those who had ransacked the publisher's offices could not be proved, but the man's attitude and behavior strongly suggested a connection. Having charmed her way into the affections of the publisher's spokesperson, Holly had emerged clutching the promised proof copy of Grosjean's book, the arrangement being that she wait until given the go-ahead.

Later that evening, in her hotel room, she opened *The End of Catholicism?* and stared at the august signatures it contained. Whatever the book's content, these signatures were, she knew, sufficient in themselves to blow the lid off CNCD's totalitarian ambitions. But more than that, much more. They also constituted a naked challenge to the pope's authority, and that signaled the unimaginable, a potential schism.

Mayle's Brentano interview was also rewarding; it led to a rather strained meeting between himself and Archbishop Donaghue, a meeting with a surprising conclusion. Huffing and puffing about how difficult it was to condemn the Children of the New Catholic Dawn over their ever-so-successful missionary activities - they were undoubtedly a movement dedicated to the task of reviving important aspects of the Catholic faith - Donaghue admitted that their excessive authoritarianism was sometimes something of a problem.

They batted that one backward and forward for some minutes, a slightly exasperated Mayle suggesting in the end that CNCD activity was tantamount to brainwashing. And still Donaghue tried to sidestep the issue, his premise being that things would eventually settle, the behavior of CNCD and parallel groups being nothing more than uncurbed enthusiasm. Such behavior would, he said, be brought under control in time.

That was when Mayle delivered his *coup de grace.* Why not immediately? he asked. Couldn't the Holy Father control the spiritual movements?

Donaghue's expression flickered like a distressed electric bulb. It was hard to say for certain how much the Holy Father knew about CNCD's activities, he said, unwittingly positing a breakdown in advice to the Pope. Then, realizing that he had committed a faux pas, he over-corrected with the extraordinary observation that it was not known to what extent the Holy Father actually approved of CNCD.

"You're seriously suggesting the pope might be in favor?"

"He may think such measures are necessary in these troubled times," Donaghue said, digging deeper still the hole he was in. "Particularly if he doesn't know the extent of the problem."

It was two for the price of one, and Mayle didn't turn down the offer. "Can I quote you on that?" he asked.

"Off the record, of course!" said Donaghue, diving for cover.

But it was too late; he had opened the stable door, and he knew it. Grimacing at his own stupidity, he said, "We've had enough trouble in this diocese, please don't add to it."

"It's a national issue as far as we're concerned, not a local one," Mayle replied. "My colleague is researching CNCD in Rome as we speak."

"I've just returned from Rome."

"You were there because of the movement?"

"They were one of the issues I had to deal with."

"And?"

"I reported what happened here and await a reaction."

"They must have had quite a few complaints by now."

"Others have come forward."

Mayle returned to the question of Pope Benedict's attitude towards CNCD, and to the fact that his predecessor had given the evangelizing movements an unqualified thumbs-up. It had even been suggested that John Paul II suffered from an excess of zeal in that direction, and that Benedict had picked up John Paul's baton.

"He realizes how serious the world situation is."

"In what sense serious?"

"Rampant relativism. The West's descent into an overarching relativity of ideas is evident on just about every level. It is now commonplace, indeed mandatory, to seek autonomy from God. The Church teaches that eternal separation from God is hell, Mr Mayle. Western culture all but teaches that separation from God is the beginning of wisdom! Come to terms with that kind of thinking and you make a nonsense of what for the last thousand years has been a civilization driven by Christian beliefs and values."

"The advances made on just about every level can't be ignored."

"And towards what exactly are we advancing?"

"A more equitable future for all human beings?"

"A designer society based on ideological fads is more equitable in your opinion?"

"Religious absolutism is better?"

"Ask Solzhenitsyn that question. The society he lived in was the result of absolutist political thinking shorn of Christian values. Soviet communism made human beings the measure of all things on Earth - human beings with a regrettable tendency towards pride, vanity and self-interest. The result was totalitarianism of the worst ilk." Donaghue drew breath and switched to a more accommodating tone. "Yes of course we want a more equitable future for all human beings. And yes of course we have enriched our thinking and our way of life since the Renaissance. But along the way we lost the concept of a Supreme Being capable of restraining our passions and our irresponsibility, and we're paying the price for that mistake."

"You can hardly equate what we have in the West with Soviet-style communism. There's no comparison."

"I can, and I do. The West's secularisation of human consciousness is producing a spiritual desert - *has* produced a spiritual desert. We are in the process of losing all sense of a spiritual life. The glories of Western culture are being swapped for a mess of New Age pottage. The result of that and the commercialisation of every aspect of life will be a society with its spiritual heart torn out, a society as grey and as forbidding as anything the Soviets ever cobbled together. What's being overlooked here is that the Soviet system was a direct consequence of modern thinking, not a development of Russian culture. Understand *that* and you immediately understand the danger we are all in."

Mayle was on the back foot; he had unleashed something unexpected in Donaghue and didn't quite know how to handle it. Attempting to put the interview back on its earlier rail, he said that

CNCD's evangelizing techniques were hardly the route back to spiritual sanity.

"In times of acute crisis one is apt to overreact."

"You'll put up with their behavior on that basis?"

"I've made my misgivings known to the appropriate authorities. I can do no more than that."

"What about Fr Brentano?"

"What about him?"

"He's at his wits' end. His parish is split down the middle. His authority as a priest has been usurped by strangers."

"I'm aware of his dilemma." Archbishop Donaghue sighed a sigh of resignation. "It's . . . an unfortunate situation."

"It's about to become ugly," said Mayle.

"With a little help from the media, I suppose," said Donaghue.

"They're back doing their dirty work in Brentano's parish. He knows they're there, but can't prove it. The bit of his congregation that went over to them is bussing in a priest at weekends."

"I'll look into it," said Donaghue.

"There's also a rather damning book on CNCD about to be published in Rome - a book carrying some very powerful signatures to back its claims."

Donaghue did not reply.

"You know about it?"

"There have been rumors."

"From what I've heard the lid's about to come off," said Mayle. "There's talk of a possible schism."

"I doubt it will come to that," said Donaghue, consciously ignoring Cardinal Benneditti's graphic warning. "The Catholic Church is not so easily rocked, Mr Mayle."

"What happened once could happen a second time."

"Are you proposing a second Reformation?"

"I'd say it was shaping up to be more than a mere hiccup, wouldn't you?" said Mayle.

* * *

The substance of a telephone call from Fr Merle to Windle in Germany was immediately passed on to Duggan. When told that Grosjean, too, had been the recipient of a tip-off, Duggan laughed and asked the obvious question.

"He wouldn't say."

"Grosjean wouldn't say?"

"Merle wouldn't say. He knows, but thinks it better that he keep it to himself - for the moment at least."

"Someone at the monastery?"

"That's the assumption one has to draw."

Another laugh from Duggan. "Holly will have asked him the same question by now."

"Probably. Grosjean didn't mention meeting her to Merle, so she probably hadn't got to him at that point."

"You didn't say anything?"

"We all have our secrets, Jack." A smiling Windle added, "Turns out Grosjean knows Merle; he was a student of his years back."

"Then it's probably someone known to Grosjean."

"Exactly."

"Merle's still on-side?"

"Hasn't budged."

"They've put him on the mat?"

"Monsignor Francesco Rossi put him through the hoop; he heads the Department of Antiquities."

"So where is Merle now?"

"He's in Rome awaiting Cardinal Menenger's call. Menenger's taken a personal interest in the codex." It was Windle's turn to laugh. "Having someone hang around for days waiting for an interview or audience is an old and tried tactic. They're trying to unnerve him."

Duggan's mind whirled. "As long as they don't publish the damn thing before we do."

"There's no chance of that, Jack. They'll take all the time in the world with this one."

"Nice of Grosjean to own up."

"He realized things could turn nasty for me when *Sala Stampa* issued their bulletin on the codex. He may be forced to step forward if things get really nasty. His book sales could plummet if that happens."

"Or skyrocket," said Duggan.

"He'll know about Weisel's death by now," said Windle. "It's my guess he's not a happy chappy. Have you heard from Holly?"

"Nothing. You?"

"Not a thing. What about David?"

"I tried to contact him last night but couldn't get through. His mobile was switched off."

"Same result here," said Windle. Then came a surprise. "I also rang his paper this morning. Guess what? No one's seen him since he left for New York. Not even a telephone call."

"What do you think he's up to?"

"Could be he's in Rome with Holly."

"I think that unlikely."

"They were *very* chummy when they left."

Duggan thought about that. "You'd think he'd have let his paper know where he was."

"He's in love, Jack. For good or ill, he's in love."

"He may have switched his mobile off so his paper can't make contact with him."

"Or had an accident."

"Holly may know what's going on. I'll ring her. There's probably a perfectly simply explanation."

"Let's hope you're right," said Windle.

* * *

As it turned out, Mayle rang Duggan that very evening. He was in

434

Nevada, he said. He had decided to join forces with Holly and go for the big one - namely, CNCD operations in America and elsewhere. She had made him an offer he couldn't refuse - a working partnership and the chance to move up the ladder. On that basis he had just interviewed a priest in Nevada who had been having real problems with CNCD. And guess who his archbishop had turned out to be - Michael Donaghue no less. Mayle's voice had faded at that point, returned, then faded again. Grimacing, Duggan had strained to catch what was being said. Then, suddenly, Mayle was loud and clear and saying something about cracking the story wide open.

"And if you don't crack it wide open?" asked Duggan.

"We will, Jack. It's begging to be cracked."

"Clever little Holly getting you on side," said Duggan. "Have you heard from her?"

"Every few hours. She's going great guns over there. She's even managed to winkle a proof copy of Grosjean's book out of his publisher. She says it's dynamite. She can't read it - it's in Italian of course - but Grosjean's filled her in. She's come to some kind of arrangement with Grosjean. She's also interviewed Monsignor Fransesco Rossi, head of the Department of Antiquities. Lots there that will be of use to you."

"Such as?"

"There's an email coming your way."

Duggan digested that. "I take it Grosjean wasn't forthcoming about his source."

"Did you expect him to be?"

A 'huh' from Duggan. Then, "Windle's been trying to contact you. So have I, for that matter. Your paper must be wondering where the hell you are."

"Let them wonder. I'll contact them when I'm ready. If it doesn't work out with Holly I'll concoct some cock-and-bull story. "

It was a whole new David Mayle speaking. Duggan frowned his concern into the receiver and asked how the interview with

Donaghue had gone.

"He's no fool. It's obvious he thinks CNCD is bonkers, but he knows he has to be careful. They're running riot in his diocese. At least they were. That's where the priest comes in. And guess what, our friend Carter's involved. I got the impression from Brentano he's no longer flavor of the month with Donaghue."

"Taste of his own medicine?"

"Something like that. He's still playing the arch-conservative though. Gave me a lecture on the secularization of Western consciousness. He's got a PhD in philosophy according to Brentano."

"Everything is made to fit," said Duggan.

"How's it going your end?"

"We're almost there. It'll be quite a splash."

"Jane?"

"She likes Sydney. She's off sketching as we speak." Duggan looked round as some colleagues took to playing AFL with a wastepaper basket. "The natives are restless," he said, knowing Mayle would understand. Then, "It's quite the leap of faith you've taken."

"It had to happen, Jack. I was stagnating. There's the chance of being picked up by the *Washington Post* if it works out. That would make a nice change."

"Holly's behaving herself?"

"As much as Holly can ever behave herself."

"She's a livewire that one." The wastepaper basket sailed overhead accompanied by a roar. "Look, I'd better go," said Duggan. "Keep me up to date with what's going on. And give James a ring; he phoned your paper and drew a blank."

"It's now or never, Jack," Mayle replied.

31

Oh, Jerusalem, Jerusalem

"It's the Holy Father's wish to visit Jerusalem," said the Secretary of State. "He won't budge. He's adamant that the trip should take place."

Cardinal Menenger turned tired eyes toward the window, then swiveled his gaze back to Valerio Maglione's unsmiling face. "We couldn't do it at short notice even if we wanted to, which we don't," he said. "There would have to be a clearly defined necessity for such a visit, and no such necessity exists. Personal whim is insufficient, Valerio. When he first mooted the idea he was immediately advised against it. It is a patently absurd notion."

"He speaks of it as being God's wish."

"Was it God's wish that he become pope?"

Maglione's lips twitched, but did not form words. Whatever one thought of the Conclave's choice of candidate, one had to believe the Holy Spirit had had some kind of hand in the affair. Think otherwise and you ran the risk of viewing the Church as no more than a corporation, a body politic within which men vied with one another for power and influence.

"John Paul's visit to the Holy Land completed the Church's mission in that part of the world," said Menenger. "A visit by Benedict so soon after would confuse everyone as to past intentions."

"The Holy Father's view is somewhat different."

"He has a view?"

"He fears the task of reconciling the Abrahamic faiths is not yet complete."

"The Jewish and Islamic lobbies responded well."

"There were not a few dissenters."

"There are *always* dissenters, Valerio."

The Secretary of State smiled; it was his patient smile, "There is perhaps room for improvement."

"You agree with this mad scheme of his?"

"I understand his concerns."

"What needed to be done has already been done," said Menenger emphatically. "John Paul resolved the major difficulties between the Abrahamic faiths by his presence in the Holy Land. If he had never uttered a word, that would have been enough. His visit was not a political stunt, Valerio, it was an exercise in peacemaking prefaced by the fact that he helped draft the Vatican II document recognizing that the Jews were not responsible for Jesus' death. And need I remind you that it was he, too, who pushed through the Vatican's diplomatic recognition of Israel in '93.

"So as to make a state visit possible."

"Each side gained, I would not deny that. But along with the overture he made to the Moslems by entering a mosque, it was an impressive tour in anyone's terms. He did not abandon the needs of the Palestinian people. When he spoke with Arafat in Bethlehem he recognized their right to a homeland."

"A homeland is somewhat less than a state."

"It was, as you know only too well, a delicate situation; he had to avoid being pushed into saying something he would regret later." Menenger sat back into his black leather chair with the air of a man hampered by idiots. "Benedict has to understand that a visit to Jerusalem in the near future is out of the question. A delicate truce has been set up between the three great monotheistic religions and it mustn't be jeopardized."

"He wants more than a delicate truce."

"He does not possess the skills to further the situation."

"His eyes are shining."

"His grasp of the situation is naive."

"He held my hand."

"So?" Menenger was momentarily lost for words. When he spoke again, it was in the tone of someone whose patience had run out.

"Inform the Holy Father that his request to visit Jerusalem has been rejected on the ground that it could serve no immediately conceivable purpose."

"I told him that would be your response."

"And?"

"He laughed."

"He laughed?"

"More of a chuckle, really. He was in very good spirits."

"He has a brain tumor and doesn't seem to realize how life-threatening it is."

"His fear has deserted him; perhaps because of that realization. He is a changed man."

"Good sense seems to have followed his fear."

"He's at ease in himself," said Maglione, remembering how they had sat together in silence for some minutes.

"The tumor is pressing on some vital area of the brain according to the Gemmeli's specialists," said Menenger, reinforcing his point. "It's inoperable." He clasped his long-fingered hands. "He's got a year at best, six months if he's really unlucky. He has to be made aware of his responsibilities."

"Which are?"

Menenger's expression was one of disbelief. "I hardly think you need that spelled out for you."

"Keeping out of people's way is a responsibility?"

"That's not what I said."

"It's what you meant."

"Benedict has had greatness thrust upon him," said Menenger, whose talent always was for the bigger picture. "I think the shortness of his time with us confirms the Spirit's directive and the rightness of the Conclave's choice. But as things stand he is a danger to the Church if he takes it upon himself to make decisions contrary to good advice."

The Holy Spirit was back in business, it seemed. But for how long, the Secretary of State wondered. And upon whom would the golden miter settle when the little Umbrian was neatly tucked away? On Menenger himself, perhaps? Maglione's smile underwent another subtle shift. "Some of the late Holy Father's decisions were not always to the Church's benefit," he said thoughtfully. "It's argued by some that his pontificate was marred by self-aggrandizement."

Menenger's surprise flared in his grey eyes. "John Paul was a man of *great* humility," he said. "His humility is an indisputable fact."

"Humble, yet incorrigibly self-centered," said Maglione, who, before becoming Secretary of State, had had the difficult task of being the pope's principal adviser.

Menenger's head came up at an inquisitorial angle. "In what way self-centered?"

"His belief that the Holy Virgin was overseeing his life. That verged on a mania at times."

"He was devoted to her."

"It became a mandate for him to do and say whatever he wanted without recourse to council. It suggested that everything he did and said had the seal of heaven on it."

Menenger absorbed the Secretary of State's barb. John Paul had had a purpose in life such as few men were privileged to have, he said. Who else but he could have resolved the dilemma of a divided Europe? Who else but he would have offered the Russians help with perestroika? As a champion of human rights he had had no peer, and his tireless commitment to world peace was unprecedented. If ever there had been a man touched by God, it had been the Polish pope.

"There's no doubting any of that," said an unrepentant Maglione. "He was the right man in the right place at the right time, but that was due to circumstances and the wisdom of the previous Conclave. His pontificate was not an appointment from on high ratified by the Blessed Virgin in 1917."

"The Holy Spirit was our guide, Valerio. It was an inspired choice. His ascendancy to the throne of St Peters surprised everyone."

The tables had been neatly turned; the Holy Spirit was back with a vengeance.

"A conclave battling it out behind closed doors is the Church in action, it is the Church as a whole concentrated into one stream of energy," said Maglione. "The belief that you and you alone have access to God's intentions is something quite other. For all of his gifts, John Paul was excessively certain on too many fronts. By the end of his pontificate he was a dictator worthy of the communist system he detested."

"That is an extraordinary statement!"

"You saw him humiliate those who didn't agree with him. There was a vindictive streak in the man. He changed into a smiling tyrant."

"He was not afraid to exercise his authority. He was a natural leader."

"You mean he was a bully. He created his own authority by ignoring everyone around him. The authority invested in others meant nothing to him."

"Do I detect a personal gripe in this?" said Menenger, attempting to deflect Maglione's criticism.

"You know the kind of incidents I'm referring to. You witnessed them. They were appalling."

Menenger stared at the Secretary of State for some seconds. Then he said, "And again you surprise me, Valerio. I had no idea you harbored such resentments."

"I doubt my views come as a complete surprise," said Maglione, alluding to the fact that Vatican walls again had eyes and ears.

Menenger leaned forward to adjust something on his desk. When he looked up his tired eyes seemed tireder, darker still. "Inform the Holy Father that Jerusalem is out of the question, for the time being at least," he said, his semblance of a smile followed by a request. "I would be obliged if you could keep me informed as to his Holiness's state of mind, Valerio. For his own good. We have to look after him in these troubled times."

"I suspect he is better balanced than any of us suspect," said

Maglione.

* * *

Fr Paul Merle leaned on the stone parapet and watched the wild cats of Rome skitter about in the ruin-strewn gully below. All around him the noise of city traffic contradicted what his eyes were registering - cats of all colors and ages playing, fighting or hiding among boulders and bits of broken masonry. Ancient grassed-over masonry where these feline rejects lived out their short, vicious lives.

No call as yet from Cardinal Menenger who, he had been informed, viewed Theodore's letter as nothing more than a bothersome blip on his theological radar.

Monsignor Rossi had signaled the department's attitude to the codex in one short, telling sentence: "Heresy and truth are not bedfellows, Father."

Turning from the scene, Merle viewed the busy street for a moment, then moved on, the words of someone a little wiser than Rossi coming back to him. "The language of the heart is veiled by the emotions."

It had taken Merle some time to understand what these words meant - they had sounded odd at first. Wasn't the heart the seat of the emotions? So what was the language of the heart if it wasn't emotion? And another strange statement from this other. "Do not speak of God, speak of presence; for you that is God."

The street was sharply defined for Merle as he trudged along, as was his breathing, as were the street's bustling inhabitants. It was as if everything had coalesced and now stood together as one.

* * *

Fr Brentano's blood pressure was on the rise; he had vowed to keep his cool, but was finding it difficult in the face of such an onslaught. It was two to one - a man to his right, a woman to his left: two declared CNCD catechists badgering him with practiced insensitivity.

"You can't stand in the way of God's blessing, Father. You have to get out of the way." The woman glowering at him, her face set hard, her eyes like flint. "You know what you have to do."

"Your idea of God's blessing is an affront to everything I've ever held dear," said the priest. "How you have the nerve to stand there and say the things you're saying is beyond me!"

"It is the End Time," said the man, as if that were argument enough.

"Maybe it is, maybe it isn't," said Brentano, "but that doesn't mean we can ride roughshod over people's sensibilities. The behavior of your people in this parish has been reprehensible in the extreme."

"We do the Lord's bidding," said the woman. "We are the final admonition."

"Final admonition my foot!" said Brentano. "Your movement is a blight on the face of everything ever thought to be spiritual."

"The Lord has heard my cry and lifted me out of the pit of death," said the man, intoning a psalm for reasons that were not clear.

"What you're witnessing here is an explosion of the Holy Spirit," said the woman. "Can't you feel it? It's in the very woodwork."

"What I'm witnessing is a community turned on its head," said Brentano. "We had a vibrant community before your people turned up. What we've got now is an unholy shambles lorded over by unscrupulous mischief-mongers. The havoc you've caused in this parish in the name of reviving Catholicism's deepest truths is beyond belief. I've never witnessed anything like it in all my years as a priest."

"And Pharaoh hardened his heart," said the man.

His patience having finally run out, Brentano told the man to shut up. Then he told the woman that things had gone far enough, that CNCD operatives weren't supposed to be in his parish, that they were trespassing, and that as parish priest he was ordering them to leave and not return.

"You haven't the authority," said the man.

"The archbishop himself sent you packing."

"That was yesterday," said the man. "Today is today."

"We were invited back," said the woman.

"By whom?"

"By men and women of your own community, men and women who have awakened to the Spirit."

"Men and women you've subjected to hours of mental coercion, you mean," said Brentano, who had spent almost as many hours counseling some of them.

"You know nothing and understand less," said the woman.

"When a mass turns into a frenzied pop concert I know something's gone wrong," said Brentano. Then, spittingly, he said, "We don't need your hyped-up Protestant nonsense here. Yours isn't a spiritual movement; it's a sect, and it's as dangerous as any I've ever heard of."

He didn't wait for a reply; turning on his heel he walked away from them, their eyes burning into his back. If looks could have killed, he said later to David Mayle on the telephone, he would have dropped dead on the spot.

Mayle had been surprised by the call at first, but when he heard what the priest had to say he understood the man's concern. "You sound as if you've reached the end of your tether, Father."

"I've got to put an end to this. It's gone far enough."

"What do you have in mind?"

"Something drastic."

"Like what?"

There was a silence.

"Father?"

"I'm powerless! They have clearance from a competent authority. Even Donaghue has piped down."

"He's waiting for a directive from Rome?"

"I can tell you now it'll be pro-CNCD. They have extraordinary influence in high places."

"Not quite," said Mayle. "The liberals aren't sitting on their hands." He decided to open up a little. "They've joined forces with the regular conservatives in Rome, and I can tell you, they mean business." A bit of a laugh from Mayle. "Believe me, Father, there's going to be one almighty explosion when this gets going."

It was the second time Brentano had heard the word explosion that day; he winced at it.

"You still there?" asked Mayle.

"I know something of what you speak," said Brentano.

"Your archbishop won't give in; I'm sure about that. He knows more than he's letting on. He tries to defend CNCD, but his heart isn't in it."

"He's a good man," said the priest.

"He's an old-fashioned conservative who doesn't know what's hit him," said Mayle. "The impression I got when talking to him was that he was unsure about things he had always been sure about. I'm not talking about his faith; I'm talking about that bombastic certainty of his. Something, or someone has got to him."

"Have you talked with the parishioners I suggested?"

"*Very* enlightening," said Mayle. "I thank you for that. *They* thank you for the opportunity to speak out."

"Others want to speak to you." A pause. "Will I be expected to confirm their stories?"

"Here I stand?" said Mayle, teasing Brentano.

"Yes, I suppose that's what it's come to, hasn't it," said the priest.

"You're not alone," said Mayle. "I can assure you of that."

32

The Land of Damascus

Integration of all the bits and pieces of information surrounding publication of the Mar Saba Codex was completed by May 20, Theodore's letter and its translation being given pride of place. Photographs of the monastery set the scene, and profiles on Windle, Merle, Cardinal Menenger and Monsignor Rossi added the human touch to what was, in essence, a fairly involved piece of journalism. When advance copies of the magazine arrived from the printers on the 27th, a delighted Elliot dished them out and broke open a bottle of champagne - they were in for an interesting ride, he said. Five days later the Mar Saba story hit the newsstands. There was very little reaction at first, but as they entered the second week of June the situation heated up.

"I got an irate call this morning from Monsignor Rossi demanding an explanation." said Windle, phone in one hand, coffee in the other. "He was under the impression this was all my doing."

Duggan said that that was to be expected, that by its very nature the rumor mill almost always got things the wrong way round.

"On this occasion the rumor mill's simultaneously right and wrong."

"What did Rossi have to say?"

"He asked me straight out why I had betrayed his department. When it became clear that it was you who had approached me, he quietened a bit, but not a lot. Why hadn't I contacted him immediately, he wanted to know. As someone funded by the Department of Antiquities it was my duty to inform him of any irregularity. No mention of Merle; it was me he was after. Not only had I held back on your approach, I had also said nothing about my mysterious informer until circumstances forced me to do so."

"How did you handle that?"

"I said it had all happened very quickly and that I had been more concerned to see an accurate, rather than a hopelessly garbled translation of the codex get out. A bad translation would have created the problem of their having to refute and correct endless textual misconceptions. It was also important that I try to gauge what kind of journalist you were. As for my mysterious informer, I had fully intended to tell him about that, and had only not done so for fear that it would adversely influence the department's view of the codex. As things stood, they could not be accused of using such information as an excuse to dismiss the codex out of hand."

"Clever little you."

"That's when I mentioned Merle. I said that he too had agreed to delay telling the department for fear that publication would be indefinitely postponed. We had believed then that the codex was genuine, and were still of that opinion."

"So what's their next move?"

"They want your magazine off the street. They're trying for a court injunction to have that particular issue removed from the shops."

"They're too late; the horse has bolted. The whole print run's gone. The shops are trying to re-order and our printer is bitching. It's the best response to a news story we've had in years. It's huge. My editor's in bliss."

"You made a good job of it, Jack. It's everything I hoped for, and more."

"It was important to me, too, as you well know. "

"The nonsense is just starting here," said Windle. "*Der Spiegel's* on to it. They want an interview." A laugh. "The theology department's just across the hall; I've been getting dirty looks."

"We treated ourselves to French champagne and salmon sandwiches. Jane and I went out to the theatre that evening."

"I had a long chat with her before ringing you. Sounds like she's enjoying Australia. I think she'll be sorry to leave."

"I've promised to visit her eyrie in Ohio the moment I can get away."

"She likes your flat. And your cat."

"She's being kind about the flat; it's not what she's used to. Phoebe adopted her straight off."

"You'll find she's quite adaptable."

"I've noticed," said Duggan, remembering the long black coat, boots and fur hat she had worn to greet him at Kennedy. He changed direction. "Have you heard from Merle yet?"

"He's back in Paris. Menenger read him the riot act when they finally got together."

"And?"

"Nothing's changed; he's standing by his guns. I'm thinking of paying him a visit. Pity you're so far away, Jack. I think you two would get on."

"What was Menenger's tack?"

"Undisguised intimidation. He brought in a couple of heavies to help soften Paul up, but it didn't work. I think they got more than they bargained for. Shades of Eckhart. He's a favorite of Paul's. He described him to me once as the bravest churchman of all times, and the most intelligent. He holds him in high regard."

"Merle's mystically inclined?"

"Not in the usual sense of that word. He's no contemplative. He's an intellectual, with a twist. That's the only way I can put it. He's . . . *available* in a way that most people aren't."

"Sounds like a nice guy."

"Not a word I'd use either. Paul isn't *nice;* he's just *there,* if you see what I mean. He's a force to be reckoned with. Doesn't put up with fools. I would imagine Menenger and his cohorts felt as if they'd walked into a brick wall. He's one of the cleverest men I've ever met."

"That must have worried them."

"Undoubtedly. They'll have him in their sights now. Not that he probably wasn't already; but they must have thought he'd be easier to handle."

"You've spoken to him since my article appeared?"

"Not yet. I'll ring him today. He can't have missed the furore."

"How will you handle that?"

"I've been puzzling over that one, Jack. Should I have said something was about to break? I don't know." A sigh from Windle. "Maybe I should have." A pause as he contemplated that. Then a note of disgust. "It's a *very* awkward situation and it isn't going to get any better."

"Is there any chance he knew what you were up to?"

"It's possible, but I don't think it's likely. There was no sign he suspected anything."

"What will his reaction be if he ever finds out?"

"I've got no idea. He's not predictable in that kind of way."

"You're close?"

"Again, not a word I'd use. I doubt he'd judge me. He'll understand my motive if it gets out."

"I'm surprised he hasn't been on the blower."

"He'll be waiting for me to contact him. Hence my proposed visit."

Intrigued, Duggan suggested that a meeting with Fr Merle might not be such a good idea. A telephone call might be better.

"It's more for my sake than his, Jack. I want him to see that I'm not afraid to look him in the eye. That whether he knows or not I'm not ashamed of what I've done. There are occasions when a certain level of dishonesty is the only available route. One lives with that as best one can. He's deeply intuitive."

"Isn't an intuitive intellectual a contradiction in terms?"

"Not in his case. He doesn't judge on the basis of virtue. He told me that once. He described virtue as the enemy we had to constantly crucify."

Duggan smiled into the receiver. "That's a unique perspective for a priest"

He meant it in the sense of something that obscures something much more important. He was fond of saying that not even God himself could help a man who had no proper level of attention. He puts a lot of stock by where a person's at in themselves."

"Cardinal Menenger must have found him interesting."

"I dare say. He'll have tried to browbeat Paul and failed. It isn't difficult to imagine how Paul reacted given the tenor of the meeting."

"Ditching virtue lets us all off the hook."

"You think so? I don't. Attention in the sense Paul means it isn't so easily come by." Windle's tone had changed. "But that's a conversation for some other time, Jack. I've got to get back to work - I'm still *way* behind the eight-ball here. It's been good talking to you. Any problems, let me know. And look after that girl of mine."

"I'll do that," said Duggan.

* * *

The publicity generated over publication of the codex caused Cardinal Menenger to enlist the help of Cardinal Pironio, head of the Vatican Press Office. As public relations spokesman, Pironio fended off criticism of the Department of Antiquities' decision to delay publication. Yes, the Mar Saba Codex was an interesting document, but the circumstances under which it had been found were, to say the least, unusual - being tipped off by a source that would not declare itself should have engendered caution. And anyway, the codex's basic thesis was preposterous - the Church in Jerusalem had been Christian in every sense of that word, not Jewish sectarian as claimed by the author. The apostles had been followers of Christ, and as such were Christian by definition. To say otherwise was to make a nonsense of the New Testament story. The ideas and supposed historical facts use to bolster this claim were therefore of no consequence.

The jump in Pironio's argument from unusual circumstances to that of preposterous thesis seemed to go unnoticed; consensus thinking was on the loose and the devil take him who questioned the accepted order of things.

It was also argued that the supposed writer of the codex - the fourth-century Syrian bishop Theodore of Mopsueastia - was unlikely to have come up with this particular arrangement of ideas. Yes, Theodore had been nominated a heretic by Pope Vigilius and declared a heretic by the Fifth Ecumenical Council, but there were good reasons to think this an unfortunate judgment, and the codex a forgery. In the opinion of Vatican specialists, the codex was more probably a clever modern-era concoction designed to sow dissent among scholars. Theodore's theological approach had been under review for some time, and it was likely he would be cleared of previous charges. Having spiked a ticklish problem, Pironio turned on his Latin charm and further demolished the codex's credibility with a grocery list of objections.

As a result of this attack, and others of similar ilk, scholarly acceptance of the codex fluctuated, then underwent a dramatic change - it was as if a switch had been thrown. Windle was inundated with calls and emails demanding further information on the circumstances of the find. Some were from colleagues in America. Had he seriously considered the implications of such a tip-of? As the rumor mill spun, the situation slowly turned nasty, the attacks more frequent, the bravado of Protestant hardliners more shrill. Whether authentic or not hardly mattered, thundered a Baptist pastor. The codex was a scurrilous document fashioned by whomever to cast doubt on Christ's divinity and undermine the credentials of the apostles.

The more moderate thought Windle naive, if not a little stupid, to have walked into such a situation without safeguards, the dubious that he might be implicated in a criminal conspiracy. When this idea took root in the tabloids, articles casting doubt on the codex's authenticity began to multiply.

In Sydney, Duggan reaped the rewards of success. In Washington, avalanched with testimony against CNCD from parish-ioners and clergy alike, Holly and Mayle launched their lethal exposé on Catholic fundamentalism. There was an immediate uproar. Going into damage control, the Vatican issued a series of statements denying that a fundamentalist sect was attempting to overthrow the Vatican hierarchy. It was all a terrible mistake, according to Cardinal Pironio. A few over-enthusiastic individuals were the cause of it all.

In reply to this, the *Washington Post* ran the first of three long extracts from Fr. Sebastian Grosjean's controversial book on the Children of the New Catholic Dawn - the translation had been done at breakneck speed. The furore intensified, it being noted by a journalist in Oregon that three of the most vicious attacks on Professor James Windle - discoverer of the controversial Mar Saba Codex - had come from high-ranking Roman clergymen earmarked by Grosjean as avid CNCD supporters. Could it be, he mused, that the professor was being hounded by a neo-conservatives lobby in the Vatican?

Picking up on this theme, *The New York Times* whittled away at Windle's adversaries, observing in turn that Professor Paul Merle, Windle's offsider at Mar Saba, and himself a priest, continued to vouch for the codex's provenance. As a recognized authority on the fourth-century bishop whose signature was on the codex, it was surely unwise to ignore this specialist's expert opinion. And how exactly had Windle gone about forging such a document? As highly specialised criteria were involved - special scribal ligatures, subscripts, complex abbreviations and coronis - how had he gone about it? Had he advertised on the shadowy antiquity market for an epigraphic genius? Not one scholar of repute (this was a backhander for Cardinal Peronio's attack on the codex) had so far griped about the letter's idiom, or about the myriad stylistic points that, if badly executed, would have glaringly revealed the codex to be a fraud. And quotes from Irenaeus further complicated the situation. To create the text, the good professor would have required the backing of high-level biblical as well as Clementine scholars, so a conspiracy involving three, four or more world experts in varies specialised fields of study would have been necessary. All in all, a lot to ask. And as Windle's accomplices would, by necessity, have included monks at the Mar Saba monastery (how else could he have planted Theodore's letter?), that carried the situation to the point of absurdity.

Attacks from the Protestant evangelical press proved to be the more venomous. Lacking, on the whole, the credentials to question the codex technically, ministers and pastors of differing congregations chose to attack Windle personally. Convinced that forgery was a foregone conclusion, they unleashed their paranoia and bile in a series of statements verging on the hysterical. How dare he attack revealed truth, they railed. Was it not obvious from the New Testament that Jesus was God's son? How else could the miracles have been accomplished? How else down the centuries could people's lives have been changed so dramatically if Jesus had not been divine? The Christian message was not a construct, it was a revelation, and as a revelation we did not have the right to reconstruct or alter it. The fact that Theodore's letter contradicted the New Testament was proof enough of forgery, or at best, deviance - the Bible was a self-authenticating, self-validating document from which everything else could be judged. And the claim that Theodore's letter containing rare Greek expressions was a furphy; the forger had obviously added these to hoodwink the experts.

In reply to this latter point, a letter to the *Washington Post* from a well-known biblical scholar said that such an argument was indefensible. It was the equivalent of saying that God had planted fossils in the ground to test our faith in the Genesis story. In reply to this, one writer said that that was exactly what God had done.

Then came the suggestion that it was Windle's partially Jewish background that was the culprit. Tainted by that background against believing that Jesus was the Messiah of Israel, he had succumbed to Judaism's rejection of Jesus and manufactured Theodore's letter in an attempt to discredit Christianity's faith claims. A letter from Windle's New York lawyer had produced a published apology of sorts from this individual. That was when Holly Parks ploughed into the debate. Not to be outdone by the *New York Times*, she trumpeted Windle's integrity, pointing out that in her dealings with him he had shown himself to be open and honest at all times. With characteristic flair she had then noted how Windle's informer had contacted him within hours of his Mar Saba trip being ratified by the Department of Antiquities. Was this a significant fact, she asked. Might it be that Windle's informer had insider information, or was himself an insider? Having cast her bread upon the waters, she sat back and waited for her fellow journalists to follow.

By the end of June things had settled sufficiently for Windle to visit Fr Merle in Paris - the rumor mill had something else to chew on. Primed with a good bottle of red, Windle sat facing Merle in his little kitchen and told of his involvement in the publication of the codex. The Australian journalist who broke the story had turned out to be an ex-seminarian and ancient Greek specialist, he said, elbows on the scrubbed deal table. Got himself thrown out of seminary after a couple of years for questioning the wisdom of his superiors. Photographs of the codex had come his way while covering a Catholic conference in Santa Rosa. Monsignor Rossi had accepted, albeit unwillingly, his excuse of safeguarding the department from endless wrangles over textual accuracy. That was of course true, as far as it went, but he had also, as was plain to everyone, been driven by the desire to see the codex in print. A smile as Windle teetered on truth's precipitous edge. Given the claims now being made about the codex he felt justified in having made that decision.

"Came his way?" said Fr Merle.

"Pushed under his hotel room door, to be exact," said Windle, sticking to the official story. "Took Jack only a few minute to realize their importance."

"Jack?"

"Jack Duggan. Nice guy, as it turned out. He decided to do the right thing and check his translation at source. Came all the way to New York to do it. "

"He's now a friend?"

"He's good company."

"Did you supply the extra set of photographs?"

nod from Windle, and a qualification. He had not passed on a copy of the originals.

Fr Merle chewed on that. "You've been following the *Washington Post* revelations?"

"I'm grateful to them. Long may it continue."

"My news," said Fr Merle, reaching for the bottle of red, "is that the writer of the book being serialised by the *Washington Post* was also behind their discovery at Mar Saba." He refilled Windle's glass. "It was Fr Sebastian Grosjean who set you, us, up to discovering the codex. But it doesn't stop there; he was merely the conduit." Windle's surprise at Merle knowing about Grosjean's involvement was genuine. "He was a student of mine years ago," added Fr Merle. "He arranged a meeting with me a few days ago and confessed all. He's willing to step forward if things get out of hand. He is, as they say, a man of conscience."

"What was *his* source?"

"A fellow student - a Greek now working to rationalise the Mar Saba Library. That's between you and I, of course. For the moment at least."

"He removed the codex?"

A shake of the head. Grosjean's friend was as mystified by its disappearance as everyone else.

It was Windle's turn to surprise Merle; he grimaced, then admitted that he had known about Fr Grosjean for almost two weeks. Grateful for the chance to level with Merle on that point, he then told the story of Dr Weisel's fateful visit to New York.

"Extraordinary," said Fr Merle.

"There was a diary and two letters in his briefcase. One was addressed to Grosjean. There were also numerous diary entries outlining Grosjean's researches into the movements. CNCD in particular. It was extraordinary stuff. I passed it on to a *Washington*

Post journalist in exchange for her silence on Weisel. It's a little detail the tabloids would have had a field day with."

You're responsible for the *Post* expose as well?" Another shake of the head. "You live a complicated life, James."

"It's just how the cards fell. The gods are unpredictable."

"It's said we attract whatever gods come to us."

"Grosjean was your pupil, not mine," said Windle, reversing what he sensed to be veiled criticism.

"I'm not judging you, James. Not for a moment. You were singled out to safeguard my reputation. Grosjean admitted as much."

"His job must be hanging by a thread."

"He's got powerful backing from within the Curia. The signatures to be released on publication day includes Beneditti's."

"I didn't know that." Windle was grateful for the intelligence. Then, "Isn't Beneditti a spent force?"

"Not quite. He is in fact the hub of a resistance movement. He, too, is a man of conscience."

"Acts of conscience which contradict the Church's teachings amount to nothing in Menenger's book," said Windle. "He considers conscience a vehicle for sin if it veers even tangentially from what is perceived as received truth. Benedict XV1 seems to be in agreement."

"The rumor is that Benedict is ill. Hardly anything's been seen of him over the last two weeks. Menenger is running the show."

Windle took a generous mouthful of wine and swallowed it. "Did he scold you?"

"He told me the Church's teachings were non-negotiable, that as a priest it was expected I would respect that fact."

"Keep your mouth shut, in other words."

"It's how I imagine chatting with the head of the KGB would have felt. Fr Merle's laugh was more internal than external. "I don't think the Holy Office has ever run so smoothly."

"He obviously isn't in favor of Aquinas's idea of sensible engagement with the world."

"He's an Augustinian. He believes human beings are too deeply flawed to figure out the meaning of life on their own. He believes in a world dominated by *ordo* - God's all-inclusive order. It's the Catholic Church's interpretation of things or nothing at all." A weary smile from Fr. Merle. "He offers nothing but the letter of the law, and believes himself to be in tune with the infinite."

Menenger's vision, as explained by Menenger during an interview, was simplicity itself. The Church, created solely by God, carried the authority of God. The Church was a heavenly reality superimposed on earthly reality. The only problem with this was that it required a total subjugation of the intellect to a scheme of things divorced from just about every sensible line of inquiry. To Menenger and his supporters, the Catholic Church's teachings were a spiritual *fait accompli,* a set of beliefs about Jesus, the Church and a host of other things that could not be changed, and should not be challenged. Questioning had no place in the Christian scheme of things.

It had been feared by many that Cardinal Menenger would be chosen as pope on the death of John Paul II, but that hadn't happened. Instead, the frail figure of Angelo Cardinal Rinaldi, now Benedict XVI, had mounted the balcony and blessed the crowd in St Peter's Square. Not that that had made much difference. Rinaldi had quickly shown himself to be Menenger's clone - *ordo* was still flavour of the day.

"I seem to have gained some ground over the last few days," said Windle. "Even the evangelicals have quietened." He placed his empty glass on the table. "Have you had any problems here?"

"None so far," said Fr. Merle.

"Which Retreat did they choose for you."

"I prefer the classroom to the cloister," said Merle. He poured what remained of the red wine into Windle's glass. "I had some leave due; I took it down south. I have an interest in the troubadour poets. I took the opportunity to do further research in Toulouse."

"Subversion through poetry," said Windle.

"Beautiful poetry. Their gifts were considerable. They single-handedly created European lyric poetry - their poetic style can be found fully developed in the verses of William IX, Duke of Aquitane. They were also responsible for introducing courtesy, politeness, refinement and manners into French society. The dour northerners hated their sophistication. They considered the princes of the Languedoc weak, superficial and spineless. The whole people was written off as decadent, the luxury and lightness of their society as subversive. One Catholic commentator describes them as 'effeminate and almost grotesque'. The question for many years was, whence came their considerable gifts?"

"You've answered that question?"

"The answer's been known for some time - Islam. Mystical Islam, that is. Sufism, to be exact. My researches have been a little more generic: Why has Sufism been considered subversive by the parent religion? Why the centuries-old antagonism between parent and child?" Merle looking down at the scrubbed surface of the table, then up again. "I think Sufism predates Islam. I think the sect is more closely connected with Christianity than with Islam. It's never gained Islam's full trust. Islam rejected the sect's spiritual indepen- dence and demanded doctrinal conformity - they're in much the same position today as they were centuries ago." He looked down again, up again; it was as if he were being invisibly prompted. "Catholic scholars conjecture that as the poetry of the troubadours was influenced by Sufism, so Sufism was influenced by the desert Fathers. They base their supposition on the fact that the oldest known representative of Sufi tradition - Ma'ruf of Bagdad - was the son of Christian parents. I think the idea has merit, but I would go further. I think Christianity and Sufism are more closely related than anyone has so far realized."

"I was talking about Sufism over dinner only recently," said Windle. "I had no idea they were an interest of yours."

"I tend to keep my more flamboyant theories to myself."

"John of Damascus believed Islam to be a form of Christianity related to the Arian heresy."

"He was on the right track. The connecting point between Islam and Sufism is their mutual rejection of the idea that Jesus was in some literal sense, God. A human instrument adopted by God, yes, literally God made manifest in flesh, no. That and their belief in successive appearances of the 'True Prophet' - Jesus being the penultimate prophet - more or less exhausts the relationship. What my fellow Catholic scholars ignore is that the term 'True Prophet' also links the Sufis to the Nazoraeans and their sub-groups in the second, third and fourth centuries. In the Clementine literature of the Ebionite Nazoraeans Jesus is described as the 'True Prophet'. Fleeing from the advancing Romans, the Nazoraeans entered northern Syria, northern and southern Iraq, Perea and southern Arabia. Fanning out into the Syrian and Iraqi deserts, they evolved into sects close in belief to the first century Nazoraeans, and from out of those who chose Arabia as their home emerged Islam. In whatever form Sufism originally existed, it came to support seventh century Islam's rebuff of Christianity's claim that Jesus was God, and that, as anyone familiar with the Nazoraean sect knows, was what separated the Jerusalem Church from St Paul's charismatic assemblies."

Windle remained silent for a moment, then he said, "It appears Theodore was trying to nut out the same problem in the fourth century."

"Yes, I think he was - hence my astonishment at his text. He was aware of the Church's attempt to erase the Nazoraeans from history, and why they thought such a move necessary. He knew that the Nazoraean Apostles of Jesus, and later groups such as the Ebionites, Ophites, Naassenes, Mandeans and Peratae had *all* rejected the idea of Jesus being Israel's God encased in flesh. It was heresy to their ears, just as it was heresy to orthodox Jews in Jesus' day, and later to Islam. The give-away was that these groups all held Jesus' brother James in high esteem, particularly the Ebionites. Their condemnation of the Roman Church's evaluation of Jesus was ferocious."

"All of which started with St Paul."

"All of which *appears* to have started with St Paul."

"The relationship between Paul and the early Church is something I've never fully understood." Windle made to reach for his wine, but his glass was empty. "Why try to accommodate his demands on matters of diet and circumcision when he was so obviously preaching a different Jesus from the one they were? He admits as much in reverse when he talks of those who preach a different Jesus from the one he's preaching."

"Things may not have been as clear cut as we've come to think they were. It's possible that what Paul was preaching about his 'Lord' didn't have anything to do with Jesus. Johannes Weiss's studies are worth looking at in this respect. He tells us that the term 'Kyrios', or Lord, as applied to Jesus at Antioch, denoted some kind of cult. What he finds difficult to explain is how the Churches came to apply a term belonging to the Hellenistic mystery schools to Jesus. Why, he asks, did those who had no personal experience of Jesus take to worshipping him? What was the trigger? Weiss's explanation is that it evolved out of the honor paid to Jesus by the disciples, an attitude of reverence that gradually spun out of control in a Hellenistic milieu. He argues that the term 'Kyrios' may only have been a Greek replacement for the reverential Hebrew term Maran."

"You obviously think something else was going on."

"Yes, I do. Antioch was a province in which diverse cultures existed. It housed churches with differing views of Jesus. The Jewish-Messianic in its Nazoraean form rubbed shoulders with the Gentile-Christian in its Pauline form. There were mixed churches where Jew and Gentile sat together. There may even have been pagans who worshipped Jesus for reasons of their own. It was the kind of mix within which just about anything could happen, and did. There's even evidence of a form of Jesus-worship unconnected with the historical Jesus being practiced there prior to Paul's arrival. That's intriguing; it suggests the 'Jesus' name stood for much more than an individual who happened to be called Jesus."

"A power name."

"Exactly. The disciples cast out demons in Jesus' name because his 'name' carried an archetypal charge." Fr Merle threw up his hands in mock despair. "There may never have been a person called 'Jesus', just a name called upon to trigger a release of creative energy in the caller. We don't even know the exact form of the name we're talking about. In Hebrew it's one thing, in Greek another. All we have is a translation from the Greek!"

"There may never have been a Jesus?"

"The idea of a power name is part of the puzzle; but I don't think it's all of the puzzle." Fr Merle paused, then in a pensive tone he said, "I think the Gospel Jesus existed. Why? Because I *sense* the presence of a real man in the Gospels. The real man peeps through in spite of endless attempts to theologise his nature and his deeds. Yes, he was on a mission, but it isn't the one the later Roman Church came to believe he was on. He's connected to the Nazoraean sect at some unspecified level of leadership, and that suggests his mission was messianic, but only in the strict Jewish sense of that word. Between AD70 and AD125 the compilers of the Gospels, backed by Paul's letters and Acts, superimposed Paul's 'Lord' and 'Christ' on the Jesus story, then adjusted Paul's letters so that the name 'Jesus' could be attached to either title. And so we end up with the 'Lord Jesus' and 'Jesus Christ', or an amalgamation of those two. 'Christ' became Jesus' surname, and its strict meaning in relation to the Hebrew term 'messiah' was engulfed in theology."

"So who is Paul's 'Lord'?"

"Given the form of Nazoraeanism Paul followed, his Lord may have been the long dead Teacher of Righteousness written about in Dead Sea scrolls, and in the Damascus Document. A growing minority of scholars is now of that opinion."

"You're talking a hundred years before Jesus appeared in the scene."

"Yes, I am. And that raises the question of where exactly Paul was when he says he was *in the land of Damascus*. Paul's vehement denial in his Galatian letter that he visited Jerusalem immediately after his conversion contradicts what we're told of the same incident in the book of Acts. Paul tells us in no uncertain terms that he did not immediately visit Jerusalem, but headed for Arabia, then returned to Damascus and spent three years there. Only then did he go up to Jerusalem and present himself to Peter. As 'three years' was the exact length of the induction period required of those wishing to join a desert community, and 'Damascus' is now known to have been a code name for such a community, it doesn't take much imagination to guess where he ended up. And that in spite of attempts by the editors of Paul's letters to lead us astray - Paul's second letter to the Corinthians has been altered to conform to what's written in Acts. In historical terms the Damascus mentioned in Acts could not have been the Roman-controlled city of the same name." Getting up, Fr Merle retrieved another bottle of wine from his little store on a nearby shelf and opened it. Reaching for Windle's glass, he filled it. "We know that a group of Essene-type sectaries quit the Temple cult a century before Jesus turned up. We're told that they followed their venerated Teacher - The Teacher of Righteousness - out into the desert where he was executed by a person, or persons unknown. The significance of that execution is only now beginning to dawn on us, and that in spite of knowing for decades that this community believed their Teacher would return from the dead."

"Kamal Salibi's researches tell us that the founding prophet of the Nazoraeans was executed and later came back to life," said Windle. "That's four hundred years earlier than the Teacher of Righteousness!"

"Salibi's researches are interesting, but I think it's the *Teacher of Righteousness* who will figure as more important in the scheme of things. He could well be the key to unlocking what was going on in the mind of Paul when he speaks so passionately about 'resurrection'. The sect led by the Teacher is probably the same sect Paul set out to persecute *in the land of Damascus*, but ended up joining. Question is, which desert sect are we talking about, and what changed Paul's mind?"

"They're thought to have been Essenes," said Windle.

"They were a desert community not unlike the Essenes, but they weren't Essenes in the sense we've come to understand that term. It's a term that's been misused in the same way 'gnostic' would later be misused to debunk groups opposed to the Roman Church. The group in question was called *Shomerim* - 'Keepers of the Law' - but their full title in Aramaic was *Natsarraya*, and that transliterates perfectly into Greek as *Nazoraioi*. Exactly - *Nazoraean*. Now I ask you, is it really too difficult for my peers to admit where Paul got his theology from?" Fr Merle lifted one of the dry biscuits he liked to nibble while drinking, and crunched on it. "It's a beautiful twist, isn't it. Christianity's story is that Jesus was executed and came back to life. The Natsarraya believed exactly the same thing about their Teacher. All in all, a remarkable coincidences given that the founder of the Nazoraean sect in or around 500BC was also said to have risen from the dead. And the fact that Paul relies on Old Testament material rather than on Jesus' own story when speaking about his 'Lord' supports the idea that this figure was not the Gospel Jesus. In Salibi's defense, Paul's use of the term 'Lord' may signify a growing perception among Damascus Nazoraeans that their Teacher was in some sense 'divine'. It was after all a term interchangeable with the word 'God' for both sectarians and orthodox Jews"

"The divine Issa strikes again," said Windle.

"The Jerusalem Nazoraeans weren't in conflict with the Temple authorities at the time Paul was persecuting Nazoraeans in so-called Damascus," said Fr Merle. "That tells us that the Nazoraeans *in the land of Damascus* were different in kind from those in Jerusalem. It stands to reason that if the Romans had just crucified Jesus for political subversion, then his disciples in Jerusalem would also have been categorized as dangerous. But if, say, they worshipped some vague spiritual being from some other age, then they wouldn't have constituted any kind of threat to the Empire. Paul's letters are silent on the circumstances of Jesus' crucifixion, so maybe it never took place. Or if it did, maybe not in quite the way the Gospels suggest.

Paul's knowledge of the historical Jesus is, as I've already said, all but non-existent, as is his knowledge of Peter's denial of Jesus or the fact that this apostle could apparently walk on water. Or of Jesus calling Peter 'Satan' on one occasions. Given the bitterness of his quarrel with Peter over the food laws, one would think tit-bits like that would have been used by Paul to put Peter in his place."

"Gratian said back in 1150 that Peter had compelled Gentiles to live as Jews and depart from Gospel truth."

"Which links directly into our situation. Or, to be more accurate, your situation. Gratian's Code of Canon Law was peppered with three centuries of forgeries plus the conclusions drawn from them. Not to mention his own fictional additions. Of the 324 passages he quotes from, only eleven are genuine. As a result of his handiwork, heretics came to be classed as 'forgers of the faith' and killed. Hence the treatment you're getting."

"*Tortured* and killed," said Windle. He shook his head and laughed. "It's an irony that Thomas Aquinas relied on Gratian's Code when writing his *Summa.* It's he who propounds the notion that forgers are equal to heretics. Little did he realize the documents he was working from were ninety per cent forgeries in their own right!"

"It's history conceived as a minor branch of theology from start to finish," said Fr Merle in a brittle tone. "Paul's letters and the book of Acts are a case in point. There's little doubt they were tampered with early in the second century. Paul's denial in Galatians that he presented himself to James in Jerusalem immediately after his conversion tells us that the writer of Acts was either unaware of the facts, or that the text was changed to eradicate Paul's three-year stay in *the land of Damascus.* I suspect the latter. The reference in Acts to Paul being blind for three days probably reflects that adjustment to the text. As for Paul talking with 'the Lord' while journeying to Damascus, that suggests something quite different to me. I think it refers to a meeting, probably later, between Paul and the venerated Teacher of the Damascus Nazoraeans - the 'Just One' they equated with the long-dead, but now resurrected Teacher of Righteousness.

The vision's content is too personal; it's more of a chat than a vision. The Teacher wants to know why Paul is so intent on persecuting him and his followers. One gets the impression the Teacher is at Paul's elbow, and maybe he was. It's the same with Paul's helper, Ananias. Ananias and the Lord converse about Paul as if speaking on the telephone. The editor of Acts betrays his presence when he says to Paul that he's been sent by 'the Lord, *even* Jesus' to remind him of his visionary experience on the road to Damascus. The name 'Jesus' has been added to the text."

"*Equated* with the long-dead *Teacher?*" said Windle.

"*Identified* as being the same," said Fr Merle. "It may all have had more to do with reincarnation than with resurrection."

"Whom say men that I am?"

The priest dipped his head in acknowledgment of Windle's lightning response. "That is exactly the context I had in mind. When asked that question by Jesus, Peter's suggestion, among others, is that some think he is Elijah returned to life. It may be a matter of that kind of thinking amalgamated with a figure who established himself as the Just One because of his holiness."

"It sounds like James the Just, Jesus' brother."

"But can't be. We know he belonged to the alternative Nazoraean group, the orthodox branch."

Windle remained silent for a moment, then in a puzzled voice he said, "May I ask how all of this affects you as a person, as a priest?"

Fr Merle hesitated for only a seconds. "I'm in agreement with the Church's radical theologian Karl Rahner when he says that every concept of the incarnation which views Jesus' humanity as the guise God takes upon himself is, and remains, a heresy. He tells us that the 'is' in 'Jesus *is* God', does not mean *identity*, it only means a unity or link. I find that a sensible description of Jesus' nature."

"Rahner said that?"

"Loud and clear. It's just a pity he doesn't pay a little more attention to his own words. He has Jesus as 'unsupersedable' in the next breath. I can't accept that. The Gospel Jesus says that after him others will be capable of doing greater things than he did. I trust the Gospels on that point. It reflects the man of limitation. *That* is the real Jesus."

"You really think there was a real Jesus?"

"I think he may have been living out the northern tradition of the 'Suffering Just One'. It had earlier been expected that the Elect of Israel, the Son of Man collective, would perform an atoning work for sin through faithfulness to the Law. In Jesus' day this expectation seems to have been applied by some sectarians to a messianic personality, the Son of Man singular. From what I can make out, this idea was based on the Old Testament story of Joseph. Abandoned in the desert to die by his brothers, Joseph turns up later alive and well. The sectarian Book of Jubilees confirms a connection between the idea of atonement and Joseph the individual. He emerges in later Judaism as 'Messiah ben Joseph'. Hence the use, perhaps, of 'Joseph' as Jesus' father's name in the Gospels, a father who does not 'father' in the usual sense, yet does 'father' in the sense of symbolising the dying/resurrecting role Jesus will eventually take on."

"And the second Joseph? Joseph of Arimathaea."

"He supplies Jesus with the tomb he resurrects from. I find that very interesting. If one wants to carry the Joseph story to its symbolic conclusion, then Jesus walking out of his tomb alive and well is Joseph being rescued from his pit in the desert. He's believed dead by the brothers who abandon him, but he isn't dead. And similarly, Jesus is believed dead by his disciples, who also abandon him, but he isn't dead either. Like Joseph, he turns up later and scares the wits out of them."

"You could almost build a convincing conspiracy theory on the basis of that idea."

"It's one the conspiracy-mongers have missed out on." Fr Merle gave a little laugh and continued. "What my Church doesn't realize, is that it borrowed a sectarian belief system, and in conjunction with Paul's letters and other sectarian literatures created the dying-resurrecting Jesus narrative. The New Testament is, in other words, a cut-

and-paste job, and it hasn't been so well done that the joins can't be detected. The Nazoraean idea of messiahship as a mantle taken on by some deserving individual was replaced by Paul's little understood *Christos*, the 'Christ' of his Gentile-oriented, cultic Christianity. The rest is history. They have no choice but to ignore Nazoraean importance. Emotionally embedded in a belief system from which they cannot escape, they turn a blind eye to the fact that no less than fourteen blood relatives of Jesus followed James as leaders of Jerusalem Church." Fr Merle took a sip of wine as if to wash away a bad taste. "The book of Acts was already written when the Roman Church got under way, but it was all but unknown for the best part of a century. The letters of Paul were written before Acts, but didn't come into circulation until after Acts appeared. The canonical Gospels had not yet surfaced in their final, church-approved form. So it's a matter of sequence, really. The Gospel Jesus wasn't yet up and running in canonical form, and a plethora of Gnostic texts were offering ideas about Jesus and his teachings which the Church viewed as heretical. That's when the skulduggery starts. By early in the second-century, confusing issues arose about Jesus' identity, his teachings, and his family relationships. Those in control of compiling the New Testament decided it was time to straighten things out. Changes made to key documents at that time influenced the development of Christianity for centuries to come."

"What a twisted tale it all is," said Windle

"And so we have to help untwist it," said Fr Merle. "I think we can do that with Theodore's help."

"If they'll let us," said Windle. "The roof falls in if you even suggest Christianity developed out of Nazoraeanism. Christian scholars are preoccupied with writing the Nazoraeans out of history, not into it, and secular scholars are frightened to question Christian origins with any kind of rigor. Tentatively suggest a connection with the Nazoraeans and you're immediately shouted down; and that in spite of the fact that Jesus himself is described as a Nazoraean in the Gospels, and Acts has Paul admit that he too is a Nazoraean. The idea that Nazoraioi as used in the Gospels refers to a village called Nazareth is patently absurd. No such place existed in Jesus' day. Nazoraioi is Greek for Nazoraean, not Nazareth. It's conscious suppression to state otherwise. The early Church of the apostles was Jewish sectarian and remained Jewish sectarian to the end, if indeed it had an end. When that's accepted as historical fact then maybe, just maybe, things will start sorting themselves out."

It's something I don't think they'll ever acknowledge."

"They'll have to at some point!"

"I don't think so. Along with the Protestant fundamentalists the Roman Church will never admit its origins to have been Jewish sectarian. Nazoraeanism was the source of Christian Gnosticism. As it was also the source of Roman Christianity they would have to admit orthodox Christianity developed out of a Gnostic milieu. They'll never do that."

"They'll cease to be relevant if they don't."

"I don't think Cardinal Menenger's terribly worried about relevance, James. He believes against all the odds that his Church is in possession of Revealed Truth. Who can argue with that?"

33

The Eye of the Storm

The host of Channel Nine's new, prime-time T.V. program rose to greet Duggan as he walked, accompanied by upbeat music, on to the set of *IN YOUR FACE*. Three others were already seated, two archbishops and a biblical historian known for his secular views. Behind them, on a giant screen, a back-projected image of the Mar Saba Codex dominated proceedings. Applauded on cue by a sizeable audience, a pugilistic-looking Duggan shook hands with Don Cooper, Australia's latest television phenomenon. As the music faded, a tanned and athletic- looking Cooper took up position between his guests and launched into an explanatory spiel about the Mar Saba Codex. It had taken the world of biblical scholarship by storm, he said, glancing at Duggan meaningfully. Not since John Allegro's claim that Christ was no more than a vision-inducing mushroom had the Church reacted with such fury. Well, maybe once or twice since then, he admitted. The claim by some British authors in the eighties that Jesus had married Mary Magdalene, sired children and founded a bloodline had been one such occasion. Another had been similarly bizarre claims made during the nineties by an Australian authority on the Dead Sea *scrolls*. So why all the fuss over a letter written by some bishop in the fourth century? When compared to those other events, the letter attributed to this bishop was pretty tame. Turning to Anglican Archbishop Robert Hutch of Sydney, Cooper posed the same question in a slightly different form. Why, for Anglicans, he asked, was the *Mar Saba Codex* considered such a threat?

"It's more of an affront than a threat," the dark-suited archbishop replied. "It's another of those tiresome attempts to denigrate the Christian faith, and it affects *all* Christians, not just Anglicans. We're mutually fedup with what's become sanctioned Christianity-bashing by the media and by academics."

Catholic Archbishop Pullman of Sydney's shock of white hair added slow assent to Hutch's pre-emptive strike. He and his Anglican counterpart did not see eye-to-eye on a number of issues, but they were as one when it came to defending Christianity from wanton attack. Both were steadfast in their belief that God was in his heaven and that the world should wake up to that fact before very long.

"But wasn't the writer of this letter a respected Christian bishop?" urged Cooper, looking from one archbishop to the other. "Why would a Christian bishop wish to denigrate his own faith?"

"The authorship of this letter is, to put it mildly, in dispute," said Hutch. "Specialists on ancient documents have already pronounced this hotchpotch of nonsense a modern forgery."

"Vatican specialists," said Cooper, stirring the pot a little.

"A specialist is a specialist," replied Hutch. "The Vatican's *Department of Antiquities* is a highly respected institution staffed by some of the finest scholars in the world. If they say the codex is a forgery, that's good enough for me."

"So it's a matter of . . . *faith?*" said Cooper, darting a smile at his audience.

"I'm not a specialist in ancient documents, if that's what you're saying. Few people are."

"True," said Cooper. He turned to Duggan, who was pleased to see Jane only a few rows from the front. "But there isn't actually a document at all, is there? Didn't it immediately go missing?"

"Yes, it did," said Duggan. "The Department of Antiquities had only photographs to work from. As had we."

"So why the fanfare? Why bother publishing something denounced by a whole team of specialists as a forgery? Is it, as Archbishop Hutch contends, just another case of the media giving Christianity a hard time?"

"I don't think it's that at all," said Duggan. "Those who found and studied the codex continue to believe that it's genuine. And I should remind you, they too are specialists. So the question of authenticity is still an open one." Leaning forward, Duggan looked directly at Archbishop Hutch. "Professor Merle is himself a recognized authority on the writings of Theodore of Mopsuestia. Some would say a world authority."

"What do you say to that, Archbishop Pullman?" said Cooper. "I think you would have to admit Mr Duggan has a point."

Taking an audible breath, Pullman huffed out his reply. He thought it unfortunate that the scholars involved were being so incautious, he said, ignoring Duggan and addressing the audience direct. Everyone should be reminded that the circumstances under which the codex had surfaced were, to say the least, extremely odd.

"You're referring to Professor Windle being informed of the codex's exact location by telephone?"

"And to the fact that the document in question mysteriously vanished soon after," said Pullman. "And to the oddity of copies of those photographs being passed anonymously to Mr Duggan whilst in America. I think all of it speaks for itself."

Cooper looked at Duggan expectantly.

"I just happened to be in the right place at the right time. I got lucky."

"You *and* the professor," said Pullman.

Don Cooper's gaze moved to the biblical historian. "Is it legitimate to claim something is a forgery from photographs alone, Dr. Fisk?"

Fisk, a small, neat man in a grey suit, said that it would be all but impossible to make any kind of definitive claim for forgery from photographs alone. Or for authenticity, for that matter. Scholars in this field often worked from photographs, but they did so knowing that an original document existed if clarification were required. No such document existed in this case.

"Criteria *other* than the obvious are operative in this instance," interjected Archbishop Pullman. "I talked on the telephone last night with Monsignor Rossi, the *Department of Antiquity's* chief palaeographer. He told me that given the voluminous amount of data available on Theodore of Mopsuestias's phraseology, style and vocabulary, forgery is only too possible. And I should point out that Cardinal Peronio, on behalf of the d*epartment,* has recently listed no less than ten carefully delineated objections to the codex's genuineness."

"One of which is that it's *too* perfect," said Duggan.

"That is a legitimate observation given the circumstances of the find," said Pullman. "The extraordinary perfection of the text suggests that every possible lexical circumstance has been anticipated by the writer."

"I take your point," said Duggan. "But it could also mean it's the real thing. Couldn't it?"

"Doesn't that suggests a certain rashness on the *Department of Antiquity's* part?" said Cooper, picking up on Duggan's lead.

"If the photographs are accurate representations of the original, and it's thought they probably are, then the same reasoning would apply to the original." Archbishop Pullman paused to let his reasoning sink in. "I'm instructed by the *Department of Antiquities* that few documents of this nature are ever this perfect."

"Which is of course to admit that some are," said Duggan quickly.

"Hardly *any,* from what I can make out," replied Pullman.

"We're not just talking a lack of scribal errors here," said Duggan. "This is a letter written in an identifiable hand, in a script from a known period. It's signed. We're pretty sure who the recipient was, and the theological drift of the piece fits with what is known about both individuals. But most important of all, Professor Merle *and* Professor Windle worked from the original document - *that* is an advantage the *Department of Antiquities* did not have."

"The lexical abnormalities of the document still stand," said Pullman. "Anyway, the question of Theodore's theology is a complex one."

"Lexical abnormalities?" said Duggan, staring at the archbishop "Isn't that to stretch a point somewhat?"

"It's a legitimate definition, Mr Duggan. If two letters baring the same signature prove to be carrying identical signatures, then it can be assumed that one of those signatures is a forgery. It simply isn't possible to produce two signatures that are perfect in every way."

"You can't use that kind of analogy in relation to the codex," said an annoyed Duggan. "It's not a parallel circumstance."

"I admit it's not a perfect analogy," said Pullman, "but I think it may help the audience to understand a technical point."

"Or help bamboozle them," said Duggan.

Laughter from the audience caused them to pause.

"Dr Fisk?" said Cooper.

"I tend to agree with Jack Duggan," said Fisk, introducing a note of informality. "There's a bit of game-playing going on here."

"*That* is insulting," said Archbishop Hutch.

"No one blames you for looking after your own corner," said a forthright Fisk, "but I don't think clouding the issues involved is at all helpful."

Cooper turned again to Archbishop Pullman. "Wasn't Theodore of Mopsuestia eventually classified as a heretic?"

"That's under review as we speak," said Pullman, whose brief from Monsignor Rossi had been thorough. "There are lots of complicated factors in this case."

"Theodore's ideas about Jesus were hardly conventional," said Duggan. "I imagine that's why he was so taken with Bishop Irenaeous's preference for early first-century views of Jesus."

"The Irenaean connection is highly improbable; particularly a letter that contradicts the canonical Gospels."

"The diversity of the text also arouses suspicion," said Archbishop Hutch, who had edgily waited to get back into the conversation. "The text diverges significantly from the acknowledged traditions of the Church. It is, in other words, a maverick document and should be treated with utmost caution."

Archbishop Pullman was in agreement. The codex was a revisionist history worthy of Britain's David Irving, he said, his words directed at Duggan. It contradicted everything known and accepted about the history of the early Church, and that had to mean something in itself.

"The historical origins of Christianity are no longer as sure as they once were," said Duggan. "Questions are being asked these days that didn't cross anyone's mind a decade ago." Then to Don Cooper, he said, "Not enough attention has been paid to Jewish scholars in this respect."

Cooper turned the question over to Dr Fisk.

"Quite right," said Fisk. "The work of contemporary Jewish scholars in relation to New Testament studies have all but been ignored by Christian scholars. Christianity's connection with Judaism's more adventurous groups is steered clear of by most Christian scholars."

"Geza Vermes is one of my *favorite* writers," said Archbishop Pullman by way of reprimand. "Vermes's work on the New Testament is used at every turn by Christian scholars."

"What about Hyam Maccoby or Robert Eisenman?" said Fisk. "Or the venerable Hugh Schonfield for that matter? I could name a dozen."

"Every field has its . . . oddities," said Pullman.

"You reject the scholarship of these gentlemen out of hand?"

"They've overlooked the fact of *revelation,*" said Pullman, reaching for that which no unbeliever could constructively contradict. "Christianity isn't a theory to be accepted or rejected, Mr Fisk. It is God's revealed truth to the world. Unless memory has failed me, Schonfield believed Jesus to have contrived his own crucifixion, survived the cross and died later in the tomb because of the spear wound! I ask you, what kind of nonsense is that?"

"It's the nonsense of a rational mind trying to work out what was actually going on," said Duggan. "Or, as a Catholic bishop said to me only recently, 'Apples fell to Earth in the first century just as they do now.' I think that pretty well sums up what we're talking about here."

A bursts of applause showed that the audience was paying attention.

"*Revealed* truth does not, and cannot, answer to the limitations of human reasoning," said Pullman. "St Paul teaches us that it is folly to think that it should. Hence the necessity for faith."

"Faith in *Jesus*," said Archbishop Hutch, who was renowned for his hardline evangelical views.

"Theodore woke up to the fact that the Church's whole conception of salvation was based on a topsy-turvy interpretation of Jewish history," said Duggan in a rush. "That's what he was trying to straighten out for Pelagius in his letter."

"Suddenly you're an expert in Jewish history?" said Archbishop Hutch.

"I've read my Maccoby *and* my Eisenman," said Duggan. "But I have to admit, Schonfield's still my favorite. He's one of the few scholars who really understood Christianity's dilemma."

Archbishop Hutch snorted in disgust. "I rest my case," he said.

"That's just not good enough!" said Dr Fisk. "Hugh Schonfield can't be so easily dismissed. Theodore's letter - let us assume for the moment that he is the writer - raises important issues, not the least of which is: was Jesus a sectarian Jew? When he refers to himself in the Gospels as the 'Son of Man' coming in clouds of glory he's quoting the *Similitudes of Enoch*. That, whether we like it or not, links him to the desert communities. It may be that before the time of Jesus, 'Son of Man' was already a term for the Messiah, a term used by Jesus to identify himself with the community of the saints who separated themselves from the Temple during the Hasmonean period."

Both archbishops were uncomfortable with such a notion; it showed in the way they moved in their seats.

"Hence the orthodox Jewish rejection of Jesus as the Messiah of Israel," said Duggan. "He was the wrong man for the job as far as they were concerned."

"Exactly right," said Fisk. "Problem is, no one's exactly sure when the *Similitudes* were written. They may not have been pre-Christian in the sense Christians suppose. They may in fact have been Jewish-Christian, and that points to them being a product of a Nazoraean-Essene-type community."

"Oh, not that tired old furphy again," said Archbishop Hutch. "There's no connection *whatsoever* between Christianity and the Essenes. Just about everyone admits that now."

"Essene-*type* community," said Duggan. "Dr Fisk isn't referring to the Qumran Essenes, Archbishop. There were a number of groups out there in the Judean desert, and the group calling themselves Nazoraeans may have been their hub."

"The Nazoraean are important to our understanding of how Christianity formed," said Fisk. "The codex is obsessed with this group. Its writer believes the Church of the Jerusalem Apostles to have been Nazoraean in orientation. That fits with the growing suspicion of many scholars today that the rift between Jerusalem and Antioch, the rift between Jesus' brother James and St Paul was sectarian in nature. That in turn fits with the fact that Jesus is referred to in the Gospels as a Nazoraean. As is St Paul on no less than six occasions in *Acts of the Apostles.*"

"*Nazoraioi* refers to the village of Nazareth, Jesus' home town," said a dismissive Archbishop Pullman.

"I'm sorry, but that's simply not correct," said Fisk. "It refers directly to the Nazoraeans sect - most scholars are now agreed on that point. There was no such place as Nazareth in Jesus' day. It appears on maps for a first time in about the third century."

"Not all scholars are of that opinion," said Pullman huffily.

Dr Fisk's laugh was derisory.

"*All* very fascinating," said Don Cooper, taking the reins, "but it carries us away from how an Australian journalist came to possess such important photographs in the first place. Why do you think that happened, Mr Duggan? Was it just a matter of being in the right place at the right time as you've suggested? Or is there more to this situation than meets the eye?" All eyes moved to Duggan. "I think what I'm asking you is this. Why choose to dump these photographs on someone from a moderately successful Australian magazine rather than one of the big American glossies? It doesn't make any sense, does it?"

"I've asked myself the same question a dozen times," said Duggan. "I think it really must have been a matter of pot luck. They may have liked my face. They may have overheard something I said in an unguarded moment. Who knows?"

"When you say an 'unguarded moment', what do you mean? Did you have such a moment during the conference?"

Duggan felt his chest tighten; he had just had an unguarded moment and was painfully aware of it.

"Nothing springs to mind?" said a smiling Don Cooper.

Duggan pursed his lips and shook his head.

"So what alerted you to the codex's importance? You obviously couldn't read ancient Greek."

"A hunch," said Duggan. "I reasoned that the photographs had been passed on to a journalist because they were controversial in some way."

"You weren't wrong about that. Were you?"

A murmur of laughter from the audience.

"Are you a religious man?"

"No."

"Not even a little bit?"

"We're all scared of something and need comfort," said Duggan.

"And when you found out the nature of the thing passed on to you?" Don Cooper expanded on his point. "The codex must have read like gobblydegook."

"The person who translated it understood its importance."

"Ah," said Don Cooper. "The mysterious translator. There's no way you're going to tell us who that is. Right?"

"Sorry, I can't," said Duggan.

"How did you go about getting the translation done? Did you find someone here in Australia?"

"I can't say. I have to protect my source."

"You're safeguarding the identity of someone who ought to have reported being offered such photographs?"

"Something like that." Duggan huffed an uneasy laugh. "That's not quite it, but it'll have to do."

"Professional ethics had been breached?"

"Yes, and no. Sorry, that's it."

"Then you travel all the way to New York to meet up with Professor Windle. Why did you do that?"

"To check that the translation I had was accurate in its drift."

"You doubted the person's ability who did it?"

"We had put two and two together by that time and realized who was involved. It was a matter of courtesy, really. I was about to break the Vatican embargo on publication, so I had to make sure I had the best translation possible - for my magazine's sake, never mind my own reputation as a journalist. What would have been the point of releasing a translation that was inaccurate?"

"Professor Windle didn't threaten to dob you in?"

"I told him we were fully aware of the codex's importance and that we were going to publish whatever he decided to do. Wasn't as if we were asking him to do a separate translation, just make sure that what we'd come up wasn't way off the mark."

"He agreed readily?"

"Reluctantly. But he knew it was to everyone's benefit that the translation be a good one."

A beaming Don Cooper turned to his audience. "We're going to take a short break and listen to the lovely voice of . . . " He mentioned a singer Duggan was unfamiliar with, then surprised everyone with the news that on their return they would be talking by satellite link to the Vatican's chief paleographer, Monsignor Rossi. It went without saying that the monsignor was not a happy man, said Cooper. Why? Because he considered the unauthorized release of the Mar Saba codex a provocative act, an act designed to do the Church harm. Combine this with the recent revelation that Catholicism harbored a sect of neoconservatives whose views and practices reflected communist tactics at their worst, and one could understand the growing nervousness of senior Churchmen. Add to that the deep unease over multiple claims of sexual abuse by priests worldwide, and you had a mixture volatile enough to shake the Church to its very foundations. With that hanging in the air, the lights dimmed and the band struck up again. Taking a deep breath, Duggan glanced at Jane and let it out slowly.

When engagement was resumed, it was with Monsignor Rosso's stern face looming above them, the booklined shelves of his sumptuous office plainly visible in the background. With their chairs arranged either side of the screen - the two archbishops were now on their own - Don Cooper greeted their guest, informed him of who was present, and got down to business.

"I would imagine you have a few things you would like to say to the journalist who published the Mar Saba Codex here in Australia, Monsignor."

Something resembling a smile crept onto Rossi's face, then in heavily accented English he said, "Good evening, Mr Duggan."

Duggan responded in kind.

"I'm afraid Mr. Duggan is quite unrepentant," said Don Cooper. "He justifies what he's done by pointing out that those who discovered the codex at Mar Saba continue to believe in its genuineness. Is that so?"

"Haste affords nothing in this matter," was Rossi's oblique reply. "Time and patient inquiry is required to do the Mar Saba Codex justice."

"Then why precipitously announce that it's a forgery?" said Don Cooper, turning the monsignor's statement about haste back on himself.

"My department's official statement was taken out of context, Mr Cooper. "The announcement made by Cardinal Peronio on our behalf was that preliminary studies of the codex strongly suggested forgery. That is not the same as saying that the codex is a forgery."

The hair-splitting had started; Duggan smiled to himself.

"Isn't it just as well to be out in the open," said Don Cooper.

Not in this instance, I'm afraid," said Rossi. "It is, in construction and intention, a particularly pernicious document which, in the wrong hands, could, and may well already have harmed the Church."

"In what way?"

"There are many simple souls who would find the codex's contents disturbing."

"If they understand it at all." said Don Cooper.

"The thrust of the letter's argument has been more than carefully outlined by Mr Duggan. There again, he had the good sense to check his translation with Professor Windle. We thank him for that. It was however . . . *precipitous* of him to publish the codex knowing, as he surely did, that such a document requires the input of many specialists."

Monsignor Rossi was playing a careful game; Duggan knew he would have to be equally careful. Smiling up at Rossi's gigantic image, he said he was reminded of the debacle over publication of the Dead Sea Scrolls. Catholic specialists had been accused of holding back on publication for decades, and what had undoubtedly been an embargo had been broken only when scholars of courage had taken matters into their own hands. It could be argued that some of the material published prior to this had had a detectable bias in relation to how Christianity was perceived to have formed and developed by believers.

"There is absolutely no foundation to such a claim," said Rossi mildly. "Those who published the Scrolls were lucky not to be prosecuted. It was only through the good grace of those so unfairly accused that that was avoided."

"The massive delay in publication was never properly explained," said Duggan.

"It was a hugely difficult and delicate task putting the many bits and pieces of text together. Conspiracy theorists like yourself ignore that fact."

"I don't consider myself to be a conspiracy theorist," said Duggan. "And I deeply resent being referred to as such, Monsignor."

"Your article suggests you are firmly in that camp," replied Rossi. "Your willingness to publish and be damned marks you out as at best naive and at worst an opportunist. I would imagine both Archbishop Pullman and Archbishop Hutch agree with that assessment."""

Archbishop Hutch responded immediately. Duggan's article was a farrago of nonsense, he said. How in the name of everything sensible could he have ignored the broad agreement among scholars about Christian origins? Why take a letter such as Theodore's seriously when so much scholarship flatly contradicted it's absurd claims?

"Because the Gospels and *Acts of the Apostles* can no longer be treated as wholly authentic, that's why," said Duggan. "As records go, they report not what happened at the time, but what the Church, at a much later date, wanted to convey had happened. You have to read between the lines. The past was overwritten to suit the needs of a later present. The idea that there's a strict line of continuity between the Apostolic, the sub-Apostolic and the Patristic age is pure invention. It's an illusion, Archbishop. It's a conjuring trick that allowed the Church to claim apostolic authority for its actions. It's highly unlikely that any such authority was ever passed on."

"What extraordinary nonsense is this!" said an irate Pullman. "You're referring to a handful of secular scholars out of thousands who have decided to clutch at straws, Mr Duggan. Your 'reading between the lines' is a blatant and unacceptable insertion of the academically imagined into the New Testament."

"Wrong," said Duggan. "It's painstaking research versus the vagaries of theological construction. I know which side I'm on."

Archbishop Hutch flapped his hands like a bird finding difficulty during take-off. This is what happened when journalists became involved in matters of biblical scholarship, he said to Don

Cooper. They ended up supporting some crackpot theory because they had no real sense of the subtleties involved.

"Are you a crackpot theorist?" asked Don Cooper.

"I didn't go hunting for this," said Duggan. "Whoever pushed these photographs under my hotel room door obviously feared the Mar Saba Codex might never be allowed to surface. Or if it did, only after the situation had been sufficiently undermined as to make its appearance of little or no consequence. Cardinal Peronio's out-of-court dismissal of the codex as a modern forgery is confirmation of the latter. As a journalist it was my responsibility to identify the nature of the document that had come into my possession. I did that, and in doing so I took every precaution to ensure that the job was properly done. My editor wouldn't have had it otherwise. As for the hypotheticals raised in my article, they arose from the nature of the material itself, *not* from my imagination."

"It didn't occur to you that the document you had in your possession might be a forgery?" Monsignor Rossi's question was laced with disbelief. "You just accepted it?"

"Professor Windle's comments in the German press had already alerted me to the codex's probable significance. And Fr. Merle, or Professor Merle as he is better known, did not at any point contradict his colleague."

"Fr Merle had the good sense to remain silent, Mr. Duggan."

"Silence is admissible in a court of law," replied Duggan. "Anyway, he has since given the codex the thumbs up."

That was when Monsignor Rossi decided to strike. After a pause and a theatrical sigh, he said, "You aren't being entirely honest with us, are you, Mr Duggan? Isn't there a little something you're neglecting to tell us? A little something you should have owned up to in your article?"

"Such as?" asked Duggan.

"The fact that you spent two years in a Catholic seminary training for the priesthood, but were eventually thrown out." Duggan made to reply but was cut short. "*AND* that you just happen to have a doctorate in ancient Greek."

There was a stunned silence as everyone present digested the implications of the monsignor's revelation.

"Thrown out is a little colorful, don't you think?" said Duggan. "I was suspended for asking questions no one could answer, or would answer."

"You were suspended for insubordination, Mr Duggan. You delighted in insubordination. You were, according to the *many* reports written at the time, a disruptive influence on your fellow students."

"I expected honesty, not theological shenanigans."

"Coming from someone like yourself, that's almost funny," said Monsignor Rossi. "You did the translation yourself, didn't you? You are yourself the scholar who decided to breach professional etiquette."

Don Cooper silently invited Duggan's reply with a sweep of his right hand.

Duggan's reply, when it came, was measured and steady. "I've spent the last twenty or so years of my life as a journalist, and prior to that was a university lecturer," he said to Rossi's inflated image. "I saw no need to tell anyone that I had spent a couple of years in a seminary as a young man. I'm a journalist first and last."

"You could have added to your credibility by revealing your hidden academic talents."

"I knew the priest thing would be used against me if it got out. I think you're proving my point, Monsignor."

"Come, come, Mr Duggan. Do you really expect anyone to believe such a tale? Is it not true that you carry a deep resentment towards the Catholic Church? Isn't that the truth of it? Has honesty deserted you altogether?"

"I think you've got a helluva cheek saying what you've just said."

"You've accused us of bias, and worse, Mr Duggan. But I think your own capacity for bias is much the more obvious."

"Then I'll be clearer in my condemnation," said Duggan. "The Church's main problem isn't bias, Monsignor Rossi, it's overt *lying*. No, hear me out! You've lied your way up through the centuries and there's no sign that you intend to stop. A question mark may occasionally appear in some study or other, in the occasional seminar, but when it comes to the pulpit everything's just *rosy*. There's no proper self-questioning by the bulk of clergy, no biting the bullet on crucial questions, no sensitivity to the fact that your congregations are dwindling to nothing because you're massively out of step with reality. Since the twelfth century forged documents have been used by the Church to justify its existence at every turn, so it's particularly galling when churchmen demote as forgeries, or as apocryphal, anything that even remotely questions their Church's theological constructions. Gratian's much lauded *Code of Canon Law* is, as I'm sure you are well aware, peppered with three centuries of forgeries, not to mention the utterly daft conclusions drawn from them by Aquinas and others. Of the hundreds of passages endlessly quoted, only *eleven* are genuine. Now I ask you , what –"

"I hardly think we are in need of a lecture," said Monsignor Rossi testily. "The problem here is not the attempts of scribes to strengthen rather than weaken the Church when history and much else was, to say the least, a fluid exercise, it is that you have taken it upon yourself to publish a highly questionable document *as if* it were uncontestable truth. *That* is the issue here. If you were but a journalist I could understand your motive, but you're much more than that, aren't you? You were a priest in the making, and you were, and still are, a scholar of skill with a responsibility to your profession. On that basis I consider what you've done a double disgrace."

"That is exactly the kind of slipperiness I walked away from all those years ago," said Duggan. "Thank you for reminding me." With that said, he looked away from the screen and, as Archbishop Pullman had done, addressed the audience directly. "Over the centuries numerous authorities have been fabricated by the Church to quieten revolt and stifle discussion. They had the ancient seals at their disposal, and by God they used them to good effect! Ludicrous ideas were established as dogma, partial views consecrated as timeless and irreversible, superstition allowed to take root like a noxious weed. History became a minor branch of theology, the corrective influence of councils swapped for a papacy where the pope's subjective notions were applauded as divine revelation. Scholarship all but disappeared in that climate. Whole generations of students were forbidden to read seminal texts. What you have to understand is that the papal system, as it's come down to us, was founded on forgeries, the greatest of which was the Pseudo-Isidorian Decretals composed in the ninth century. These texts were shown to have been forged by a French scholar in the seventeenth century. He was put on the Index for his temerity. It wasn't until Pius VI's reign in the eighteen hundreds that the truth came out. The pope's right to lord it over everything and everyone is based on the contents of those forged documents."

"That sounds like rabid resentment to me," said Monsignor Rossi.

My article on the Mar Saba Codex was a first in over twenty years. I'm a political animal, not a religious one."

"Something made you break that pattern."

"Circumstances, Monsignor. I replaced someone and got caught up in a situation I did not expect, and to start with didn't even want. It was only when I took a close look at the codex photographs that my interest was stirred. I saw their potential importance immediately."

"You mean you saw your chance to get even," said Archbishop Pullman. "Would that not be closer to the truth?"

"I saw issues being dealt with that my tutors in seminary either avoided or thought of no importance. When I persisted with my questions I was told to exercise faith and hold my tongue. Well, I'm sorry, I couldn't, hence my *insubordination*. I've watched the Church avoid those same issues for over two decades and thought it time to challenge its smugness, its incorrigible complacency and its dereliction of duty. I not only felt justified in doing so, I felt *obliged* to do so."

It was Archbishop Hutch's turn. He rolled his eyes to the heavens and said, "Need we hear more!"

"I didn't take on this business because of resentment, or because of a need for vengeance. I took it on because every so often someone has to take a stand against a dangerous form of certainty, and on this occasion it just happened to be me."

A burst of applause drowned out the first sentence of Monsignor Rossi's reply. When it abated, his stern face filled the whole screen. "Moral certainties are the backbone of society," he intoned. "Undermine those certainties and you open the floodgates of excess. Attack the traditional central doctrine of the Church and you remove the reason for people to view society as anything other than a sideshow for their amusement. *That* is what you are in the process of doing, Mr. Duggan. In relation to the Mar Saba Codex, the writer's historical perspective is faulty, and can be shown to be faulty. He has misread the clues of history as surely as you and others have misread them. Why? How? Because he lost sight of who and what Christ was. Blinded by the argument that the man Jesus was no more than a messiah in the Jewish mold, he gave in to the heresy that Jesus was no more than a man adopted by God to play out a role. In that moment he ceased to be a Christian. And I should point out that two thousand years of Christian history have shown him to be wrong. Belief in the Christ has revolutionized the Western world. Fact is, Mr Duggan, like the writer of the codex, you have lost both historical and psychological focus and are relying on a hotchpotch of facts that do not and cannot add up."

The monsignor's impassioned defense of his faith also drew applause. As it subsided, Don Cooper shifted focus and raised the question of what exactly Duggan had said or not said, to Professor Windle in New York. Had he continued with his subterfuge on that occasion, or admitted that he, and not some other, had done the translation?

"I made Professor Windle aware of my credentials the moment I arrived."

"He did not suggest impropriety on your part? There was still the little matter of the Vatican's embargo on publication. You didn't feel a scholarly need to comply?"

"No. I was there as a journalist with what I knew to be a hot story, not as a scholar, or, for that matter, as someone who had spent two years in a Catholic seminary."

"You mentioned having been in a seminary?"

"Yes. Eventually."

"Why eventually?"

"I found Professor Windle to be the kind of man one can trust."

"A kindred soul?"

"Something like that."

"He didn't mind that you were involving him in the process of breaking the Vatican's embargo on publication?"

"His primary concern was for accuracy of translation. He knew I was going to publish no matter what he said."

"Your past was, as you say, behind you, yet you were engaged in - to use your own words - *a stand against a dangerous form of certainty*. What exactly do you mean by that?"

"Too much certainty bedevils us," said Duggan. "When it arises in religion or in politics, trouble is generally just around the corner. Witness the state of the Middle East."

"Moral certainties are not the backbone of society?"

"Strictures or taboos governed by religious beliefs have a habit of hanging on long after a society has outgrown them. Its a matter of signs versus symbols. Symbols are difficult to dislodge; signs, even if they've been in place for a long time, can be changed by consensus. Symbols sometimes take centuries to peter out; signs allow us to adjust rapidly. Sometimes signs are mistaken for symbols. Some symbols have to be torn down. The swastika would be a case in point."

"Would you agree with that, Archbishop Hutch?" asked Don Cooper.

"We denigrate the great symbols of our civilization at our peril," said Hutch. "There are symbols whose potency never wanes, such as the cross of Christ. As the cross is intrinsic to faith, so also is faith in Scripture intrinsic to the ethical systems we build for ourselves. Sustaining those symbols is therefore a Christian duty."

"And so we continue to persecute gays and women are debarred from ministry," said Duggan. "Is that the kind of sustaining you mean?"

Someone in the audience began to clap very loudly; others joined in.

"You have supporters," said a smiling Don Cooper.

"I think we're being led away from the central issue," said Monsignor Rossi, his voice a booming reminder of his presence on screen. "What we're dealing with here is a print media vendetta to denigrate the Christian faith. There's hardly a day passes but some journalist or other takes it upon him or herself to questions the veracity of the Christian message. What is your English term - *screwball?* If it isn't 'screwball' conspiracy theories suggesting that the Son of God was married, it's academic attempts to rewrite Christian history to suit their own atheistic ends."

Addressing the screen, Duggan suggested that Monsignor Rossi was caught in the same dilemma as Jewish archaeologists trying to deal with the fact that new evidence disputing the ancient story of Israel's birth had just surfaced. Backed by a growing number of colleagues, Professor Z'ev Herzog had been quoted as saying that the Israelites had never been in Egypt, had not wandered in the desert for forty years, had not conquered Palestine and, therefore, had not had this particular piece of real estate earmarked for them by God. According to Herzog, the story of the Exodus was pure fable, King David and the mighty Solomon had been no more than leaders of small tribal fiefdoms, and the Jews had not become monotheists until hundreds of years after Moses. The point of Herzog's statements, of course, was that in the light of such discoveries Israel had a moral duty to reassess its territorial claims.

"Professor Ben-Tov of Mt Scopus University has dismissed Herzog's claims as immaterial to the fundamental achievements of Jewish antiquity," replied Monsignor Rossi. "I and my colleagues agree with Professor Ben-Tov when he says it does not matter if Solomon's state was no bigger than Lichenstein, all that matters is that this tribal fiefdom managed to write the Bible. Such a glorious achievement speaks for itself."

The Anglican Archbishop was in hearty agreement; the Scriptures were *all* -important, he said audibly.

Archbishop Pullman's gravelly voice entered the fray at that point. Why, he wanted to know of Duggan, had he not bothered to mention in his article that Professor Windle had acted as official photographer while at Mar Saba. Knowing where Pullman was headed, and surprised by the sudden twist in direction, Duggan said the only thing he could say: he hadn't thought it of any importance.

"So you did know?"

"It was mentioned ."

"Then why not record the fact? "

"There were lots of things I didn't record," said Duggan. "My article was way over-length as it was. Ask my editor."

"It didn't strike you that Professor Windle had both motive and opportunity to take a few extra photographs? A highly respected scholar in America thinks his involvement in fraud a possibility. Others have voiced the same suspicion."

Shaking his head at Pullman, Duggan said it was one thing to accuse Professor Windle of taking extra photographs, but that it was quite another to accuse him of forging the actual codex. As official photographer he would have taken many extra photographs before getting what he wanted. That was a reasonable assumption. But forging the codex was a different matter altogether. That would have necessitated so many complicated procedures and unlikely associations over months, if not years, it was an idiotic suggestion. Key figures in the monastery would have to have been involved for that to be the case. That wasn't just unlikely, it was unthinkable.

"That still leaves us with a number of unaccounted-for photographs, doesn't it?"

"Given the sensitivity of the material all extra photographs would have been accounted for," said Duggan, aware of how delicate his situation had become. "I think it is professor Merle you should be speaking to about that."

"What I don't understand is this," said Pullman. "You fly to New York to consult with Professor Windle over your translation of the codex, and he not only gives your personal translation his blessing, he also allows you to interview him in depth! Why would he do that, I ask myself?"

"Because he saw clearly where things might end up, and he wasn't wrong. He knew what had happened to others in similar circumstances and wanted his side of the story spelt out loud and clear. That, as I'm sure you understand, required more than one cup of coffee."

"He foresaw the accusation of forgery?"

"Of course! It's a risk any scholar faces when something as controversial as the codex turns up. Not everyone is overjoyed by such a find."

"Did he also mention getting into trouble some years ago over statements he made in support of the Palestinians?"

"Not to me. What's your point?"

"My point is that Professor Windle sometimes treads where angels would fear to tread," said Archbishop Pullman. "He's a man of strong opinions, Mr Duggan. He's been referred to on more than one occasion as a bit of a hot-head, and from your earlier statement about Israel I'm beginning to think the two of you have a lot in common."

Ignoring the slight, Duggan said that he had found Windle a no-nonsense individual with an extraordinary grasp of his field. That could sometimes bother the less astute, he added.

"You really are extraordinarily supportive of Professor Windle, aren't you? Why is that?"

"I like the man; it's as simple as that. I think he's being treated abominably. The last few weeks have been a nightmare for him. As a journalist I can walk away from this; he can't. He's on his own and he deserves support."

"And we, I'm afraid, will have to leave it right there," said Don Cooper, wheeling round to face his audience. Please show your appreciation for what was without doubt an intelligent and revealing exchange." He began to clap and his audience followed suit. "But we're left with something to think about, aren't we?" he added "In fact in good old evangelical style we're left with a decision to make. Either we accept *Dr* Duggan's impassioned claim that Christianity should be re-evaluated in terms of historical evidence - a claim strongly supported by Dr Fisk - or, as Christianity's representatives with us this evening have so eloquently put it, we should respect the Christian faith in it's tried-and-tested form and realize that history can't be separated from that form. However, given the state of religious conflict in the world today, a conflict growing exponentially on many fronts because of rabid *certainty,* we should perhaps be re-examining our cherished religious beliefs and attempting to modify their more extravagant claims. I leave you with that thought, do with it what you will. And thank you for again supporting television's most provocative program. As the Irish comedian Dave Allen used to say, May your God go with you."

34

Beneditti's Cabal

Fr Sebastian Grosjean's book was released with much fanfare on Monday, June 15. Uproar again ensued, the names of the churchmen who had dared challenge the powerful neo-conservative movements in Italy being gossiped across the city in the time it took to drink a cup of coffee. Like everyone else, Cardinal Menenger had had to wait to learn the names of Grosjean's backers, but when that moment came his expected roar of disapproval was no more than a squeak of astonishment. Staring at the august signatures the book carried, Menenger's reaction was not one of anger, but of deep shock.

This in itself would have been enough for him to classify June 15 as a day of treachery and betrayal, but when Secretary of State Valerio Maglione informed him of a second debacle he fell back into his chair as if struck.

"He's done what?"

"He announced his intentions to visit the Holy Land while talking with the Brazilian ambassador," said Maglione. "The ambassador mentioned it to his aide soon after."

"Quash it, Valerio! Explain to the ambassador that the Holy Father's pronouncement is more of a wish than an intention. Make light of it. Point out that his English isn't as practiced as his predecessor's."

Cardinal Maglione huffed a sigh and smiled a wan smile. The Brazilian ambassador was already at the airport, he said. And anyway, the damage was done. The corridors were abuzz with it.

"You didn't think to speak to him?"

"It's not long since I learned about the incident myself. An excited member of my staff asked me if it were true."

"We can't issue a retraction. A retraction would alert everyone to the fact that something of the kind had been said by the Holy Father.

Better to claim ignorance of the event and deny it credibility. Talk to your staff, Valerio. Explain that there has been a misunderstanding. If the press get hold of it, tell them the same."

"What about Benedict?"

"Leave Benedict to me," said Menenger, his resolve to finally steer Benedict away from his irritating hobby-horse set hard like his features.

But it was not to be. What Menenger had not properly allowed for was the legacy of unquestioning obedience to a pope bequeathed to Benedict XVI by John Paul II, a legacy Menenger himself had helped shape to countermand the perceived inadequacy of Vatican II's vision. A pale reflection of his predecessor Benedict might be, but on becoming pope he had taken on the mantle of God's principal representative on Earth, and in combination with his sense of himself as chosen for some great purpose, he was fast learning to extract obedience from those who disagreed with him.

They talked first about the signatures in Grosjean's book, and about the repercussions such an attack would generate worldwide. Benedict mostly listened as Cardinal Menenger railed on and on about betra and worse. But when Cardinal Beneditti's name came up that changed. Of all people to join such a cabal, Beneditti was the greatest surprise, a peeved Benedict said. Hadn't the cardinal from Milan been gifted his own special room in the Vatican because of ill-health? Hadn't he been shown every courtesy in spite of his recalcitrant views? What was wrong with the man? Had he altogether lost his senses?

"He's become more dangerous of recent," said Menenger, surprised by Benedict's vehemence. "But I must admit, I didn't expect him to go this far. Nor Cardinal Pia, for that matter. Pia's defection is a great loss."

"You'll talk to them?"

"I have no option. Their banding together is tantamount to mutiny. If others decide to join them we could find ourselves in schism."

"This is the Devil's handiwork."

"Without doubt," said Menenger.

"Keep me informed on all aspects of this matter."

"Yes, of course Your Holiness," said Menenger. Then, with a certain steeliness, he said, "May I suggest a possible visit to the Holy Land . . . premature."

"It is God's will, of that I am certain," said Benedict. "I have never been more certain of anything in my whole life."

Cardinal Menenger waited for Benedict XVI to continue; it was in his face that he had more to say.

"I received instruction in a dream."

"A dream?" said Menenger, now more worried than ever. Hoping to defuse the issue with some astute analysis, Menenger inquired as to the nature of Benedict's dream.

"I was standing in a terribly broken down-place surrounded by dozens of crying children. It was a war zone. I could hear the crackle of gunfire. I tried to comfort the children, but they were beyond consoling. When I looked up, I saw why. "

"What did you see?"

"I saw the Devil as plainly as I can see you, Cardinal Menenger."

"What did he look like?"

"An ordinary man, but much bigger. He had terrible eyes and a terrible smile. I knew who he was without being told."

Menenger ventured that dreams were not always to be trusted.

"My dream was from God, that is not in doubt," said Benedict imperially.

"How can you be sure?" asked Menenger.

"Because when I looked back at the children they were no longer crying, and when I looked up again the Devil was gone and in his place stood the Golden Gate."

"Jerusalem?"

A nod from Benedict, and a smile.

"An omen, perhaps," said a frowning Menenger, "but hardly a directive for you to visit the Holy Land."

"It's what has to be done," said Benedict stubbornly. "I have to enter Jerusalem, and I have to enter it soon."

"But on what grounds, Your Holiness? We can't tell the Israelis we're returning because of a dream!" Menenger hastened to explain that he was not questioning the source of Benedict's dream, but that it was a matter of protocol which countries a pope visited, and when. Then, drawing his trump card, he said, "Everything that had to be done in relation to the Jews was done by your predecessor, Your Holiness. There is no reason to duplicate it."

"The children's crying must stop," said Benedict obliquely. *"That* is the crux of this matter."

"But Your Holiness . . . "

"See to it, Frederick," said Benedict, his tone as light as a feather. "It *is* God's will."

Hearing his Christian name on Benedict's lips for a first time stopped Cardinal Menenger in his tracks. "Your Holiness," he said, bowing slightly.

* * *

As a Polish bishop had argued, and John Paul II had confirmed when addressing bishops from the Third World, Vatican II's conception of the Church as a community of the faithful marching through history, but not above history, was an ambiguous and deeply troubling concept. The Church should not be conceived of as a community open to the world and its vicissitudes, but as the perfect society imagined by the Council of Trent. The phrase 'People of God' should be exchanged for the more appropriate 'Mystical Body of Christ.' The fundamental structures of the Church had been willed by God and should not be tampered with. The priestly, magisterial and pastoral powers of the Church did not derive from the people, they derived from the Church as a mystical phenomenon grounded in the Cross of Christ.

It was with this in mind that Cardinal Menenger tackled the

problem of Beneditti's cabal, as he now called it, during a specially convened convocation of curial prelates presided over by Valerio Maglione, Secretary of State. He was all in favor of human rights, the dignity of the individual and the value of earthly realities, he said with a ranging look. He was also much in favor of greater laity participation in Church affairs, and in the promotion of women to more responsible decision-making roles within the Church. But there had to be a limit set to such things. They should not be allowed to obscure the greater picture. When all was said and done these things were as nothing when compared to what should be being said about Christ, the Cross, and Grace. For all of its insights, and there were many, Vatican II had been deficient in its proclamation of Christianity's fundamental truths. The principles of moral theology had been abandoned in favor of a brash openness to experience that first diluted, then systematically threatened, the very fabric of the Gospel message.

It was a neatly reasoned argument, but everyone was so used to Menenger's carefully constructed gambits that no one bothered to respond. When, however, after ten or so minutes of diatribe he tried to suggest that 'Beneditti's cabal' should be excommunicated en masse for daring to question the magisterium's long-term intentions, he was met with stronger than expected opposition. An elderly German cardinal struggled to his feet to say that such an act would split the Church as surely as an axe splits wood. Menenger's reply was that Beneditti and his supporters had betrayed Christ's Church as surely as Judas had betrayed Christ in the garden, and that excommunication was the responsible route to take. It was they, not he, who had laid down the gauntlet.

"You would excommunicate Cardinal Beneditti?" said the German cardinal in astonishment. "But for ill-health, Flavio could have been pope."

"Then we are fortunate to have Benedict XVI to guide us through these troubled times," said Menenger, his point only too clear. With that said he clasped his hands in front of him and fell silent.

"Tolleranza," said one of the more flexibly Italian cardinals in a quiet voice. "We cannot in conscience condemn these men for telling what is an undeniably truth - excesses of missionary zeal have marred the Church's image. If only a small number of these stories be true, then the love and forgiveness of Christ has for some been replaced by an almost Manichaean hatred of the world. Such behavior should not be tolerated."

This rather odd juxtapositioning of 'tolerance' and 'intolerance' caused someone to snicker.

Cardinal Menenger again got to his feet. Fr Grosjean's book was much, much more than a general criticism of the charismatic movements, he said, addressing his remarks to the cardinal who had spoken. It was also a not-too-subtle rejection of John Paul II's wish to see the whole Church return to the basics of the faith. That was what was at stake here. Every other page contained some gripe against moves to overcome the pernicious separation between professed faith and daily life. This was what rankled most with the cabal; they wanted to institute a freedom of expression antithetical to the Church's teaching. In a word, Grosjean's book - its title was sufficient proof in itself - was little more than an excuse to vent their desire for a democratized Church. But as everyone present knew only too well, that was not a realizable aim. The Church was not a democracy, and could not be a democracy for the simple reason that Divine Truth was not something one could vote on. Truth did not change. It could not be one thing on a Monday and something else on a Wednesday. When that was properly understood, or *remembered*, the whole business of the movements and their boldness in spreading God's wonderful truth would take on a different aura. Yes, there had been excesses, no one was denying that. But it should be kept in mind that even the disciples of Jesus had been thought drunk when they emerged spirit-filled from the Upper Room. With that said, Cardinal Menenger sat down again.

"I should remind you that this is not a formal consistory," said the Secretary of State. "It has no canonical status, so there is no requirement to vote on the issues under discussion. I mention this only in the context of reminding you that a vote will eventually be required. In that context, I ask you to be scrupulously honest and forthright in your deliberations, for what we take from here this afternoon will inform the decision we eventually make."

It was an unusual request in some ways, and it caused Cardinal Menenger's brow to furrow. Nicknamed *la dechiffreuse* - the decoder - behind his back, the Prefect of the Congregation for the Doctrine of the Faith scrutinized Valerio Maglione's face in search of a clue. What was the Secretary of State actually saying, he wondered. Was his request for scrupulous honesty a form of code, a directive of some kind? That he did not considered John Paul II's visit to the Middle East a resounding success had been all but admitted on one occasion, but Menenger now suspected a deeper and more profound level of disenchantment. Bothered by this, he waited for a lull in proceedings, then suggested that all future bulletins to do with Grosjean and his supporters be submitted to a select committee of the Curia.

There was a murmur of approval from those who admired Menenger's ultra-conservative stance, but their hopes were immediately dashed by the Secretary of State. They were dealing with facts, not with opinions on moral theology, Maglione said. Fr Grosjean's book had been carefully constructed to avoid just that kind of accusation. He would therefore not grant his permission for such a move.

The murmuring of Menenger's supporters intensified, but he elevated a hand, and it fell away.

"If thine eye offend thee, pluck it out," said one of the murmurers.

"*Tolleranza,*" repeated the quietly spoken Italian cardinal.

In response to this, a staunch supporter of Menenger's got to his feet. He was a tall, lean cardinal by the name of Vincenzo Borghini, and he was known for his unquestioning allegiance to the Pontiff. Picking up on a previous point of Menenger's, Borghini said that it

was implicit in Fr Grosjean's text that John Paul II be held responsible for encouraging the worst of the charismatic movements in
their missionary activities. Whatever one might think of the
movements, that accusation - he had noted no less than six such
references in the text - was in itself enough to charge those whose
signatures adorned the philosopher's book with rank disloyalty to
the Holy Father. And not just the Holy Father, but the Church as a
whole. As it was they who had separated themselves from the
magisterium through such an act of folly, it should come as no
surprise to anyone if this separation were made formal through the
Holy Office.

"It would immediately limit their ability to enlist supporters,"
said Cardinal Menenger. "Leave them untouched and the possibility
of schism through further infection is all but certain."

"In my opinion their expulsion would result in schism faster
than it takes to blink a mote from one's eye," said the Secretary of
State pointedly. "It would be an unprecedented move, and it would
call in question the integrity and honesty of the magisterium. For
that reason I cannot countenance it."

"It's hardly a precedent," remarked a history buff. "Pope
Innocent III excommunicated most of the English nation over the
Magna Carta."

The someone who had snickered smothered a laugh, a glance
from the Secretary of State having snuffed it like a candle flame.

"We are accused of returning to the excesses of the Middle
Ages," said another. "That is a downright idiotic suggestion!"

"And it is an accusation made with specific reference to the
Pope, to John Paul II," said Cardinal Borghini. "Which is to say that
what we're dealing with is a liberal conspiracy of dangerous proportions that threatens everything John Paul worked for during his
pontificate."

"It is not the Church that is being accused of returning to the
Middle Ages," said the Secretary of State. "It is the Children of the
New Catholic Dawn who are being accused of such, and if only a

small percentage of Fr. Grosjean's claims are shown to be true, then that particular movement should be censured within an inch of its life."

The murmuring broke out again, and the Secretary of State had to ask for silence. When he had it, he rejected the idea of a liberal conspiracy on the grounds that more than half of the signatories were conservative cardinals of longstanding. Yes, there were hardline liberals involved, and fence-sitters, but the very fact that conservative and liberal forces had seen fit to join ranks suggested real concern among senior churchmen. A moment of self-examination had been arrived at, and it behooved everyone present to face the necessary rigors of that moment with every element of their being.

"The foreign press are badgering for a statement in response to the book's more serious claims," said a small, dark-complexioned cardinal recently arrived from Spain. "*Sala Stampa* has been inundated with telephone calls and requests for interviews, and approaches have been made to certain members of staff. The Italian press, as I'm sure you are all aware, is already speculating madly on outcomes."

"Hence this meeting of minds," said the Secretary of State. "If nothing else, we must at least *appear* uniform in our responses. It's imperative that we tread carefully on this."

"Excommunication has already been mooted in one Italian newspaper," said Cardinal Borghini.

"I consider that out of the question," said the Secretary of State. "It's a recipe for disaster."

"The document they signed *also* undermines the authority of the magisterium," said Cardinal Menenger. "That cannot go unpunished. Fidelity to the magisterium is *all*."

"It could be argued, and I think effectively, that their demands for redress are directly related to the excesses of CNCD," said the Secretary of State. "These men are not fools. They are, like yourselves, highly skilled individuals concerned that their faith's integrity is being dragged through the mud. I disagree with their action, but I must admit to having sympathy for the stance they've taken."

Given the circumstances, and the Prefect's condemnation of Grosjean's supporters, it was a surprising thing for the Secretary of State to have admitted. Not a few glanced in Menenger's direction to gauge his reaction.

"I believe them culpable in that they have shown open rebellion to the magisterium," said Menenger, changing his tack slightly. "One cannot sign one's name to something like this and expect to get away with it."

"They have exercised conscience on behalf of the Church," someone ventured.

"Conscience does not belong to the individual *as* an individual," said Menenger, mounting his hobby-horse. "It is gift of discernment allied to the structure of faith."

"But of course," said the speaker, whose statement had in fact allowed for that fact, although in an oblique manner.

There was a silence. Secretary of State Maglione broke it by reminding those gathered that they were there not only to deal with CNCD excesses, or with the problem of what to do with those who had so forthrightly supported Fr Grosjean, but also to acknowledge what everyone present knew to be a fact. There really was a powerful neoconservative power bloc at work in Italy, and its stated - Maglione corrected himself - its *understated* intention by way of books, papers, lectures and general interference was to for ever change the way in which Catholicism was viewed by Catholics and by the world at large. Whatever one thought of Beneditti's cabal, there was no getting away from the fact that there were those in their midst whose theology, if not their mentality, belonged to an another age.

Having shifted the emphasis away from Grosjean's supporters, Maglione waited to see how Cardinal Menenger and certain others would respond. He did not have long to wait. Huffing at what had been suggested, Cardinal Borghini immediately cast doubt on the claim that a neoconservative power bloc was at work. There was no real evidence for such a thing, he said dismissively, just an interpretation of events which most others perceived as perfectly innocent. The understatedness detected in the literature of the movements was not subterfuge, it was just old-fashioned humility, the paranoia of certain American journalists no more than a thinly disguised hatred of religion in general.

"That is the public face of the movements," said the Secretary of State. "Their behind-closed-doors activities are apparently quite another matter."

"*Apparently,*" said Borghini, only just avoiding sarcasm. "I would suggest that most of this is in the eye of the beholder. We're fast becoming afraid of our own shadow."

"There's seldom smoke without fire," piped a Maglioni supporter. Then, with reference to the *Washington Post* expose that Borghini had lumped in with Fr Grosjean's book, he added, "There are too many scorched corpses lying around the world for this little matter to be ignored any longer."

"Conservative? Neoconservative?" said a seemingly bemused Cardinal Menenger. "To whom exactly do such terms apply? As Prefect I would be hard-pressed to differentiate on occasions."

"We are in the middle of a multi-pronged scandal that is not going to go away," said the Secretary of State. "Cases of sexual abuse by priests, even bishops, have been surfacing by the hour. And now we have this debacle and the furore over the codex found at Mar Saba."

"The codex is no longer a problem," said Menenger. "Recent investigations have produced some very damaging intelligence on the journalist involved." He explained what he meant by that and added, "More importantly, we also have proof of a connection between the Australian and one of the American journalists who kick started this nonsense about a neoconservative conspiracy."

"Your source is?" asked the Secretary of State.

"Someone who witnessed them together when the Australian visited the States in April. Someone reliable. We're pursuing the matter."

"Fr Grosjean's book is too well documented to be dismissed as paranoia," said the Secretary of State.

"Something untoward is going on and I intend to get to the bottom of it," said Cardinal Menenger.

"What of the rumor that the Holy Father is soon to visit Palestine?" asked the diminutive cardinal from Spain. "That, too, is being asked about. Is there any truth in it?"

"Quite unfounded," said the Secretary of State "A misunderstanding. The Holy Father and the Brazilian ambassador were conversing in English."

There was no need to explain further, Valerio thought. Everyone was aware of Benedict's faulty English.

"It may just be that the Holy Father's . . . " Cardinal Menenger searched for the appropriate word or phrase, " *apparent slip* was an inspired one."

All eyes were back on Menenger.

"I may have miscalculated as to the viability of such a venture." Menenger flashed an apologetic smile at Maglione. "The Holy Father suggested such a visit to both myself and the Secretary of State only recently. I advised against it. The Secretary of State was . . . less certain. I now think I may have been hasty in my judgment."

A dumbfounded Secretary of State was staring hard at Cardinal Menenger.

"The idea has perhaps hidden merit, Eminences," continued Menenger, who had racked his brains over how to accommodate Benedict's *fait accompli* directive. "It is the most unexpected thing His Holiness could possibly do, and being such it could establish his pontificate like no other."

"And the reason for such a redundant venture?" The speaker was Angelo Cardinal Zanghi, a sometime political adviser to the Secretary of State.

"A pilgrimage," said Menenger.

A puzzled silence followed his suggestion.

"A *personal* pilgrimage to the Holy Land. And soon."

The murmuring started again.

"It would certainly redirect the press's energies," said Cardinal Borghini. "It may well have merit as you say."

Astonished by Menenger's change of mind, and by Borghini's willingness to so quickly support the Prefect, the Secretary of State asked how soon he envisaged 'soon' to be.

"As soon as possible," said Menenger. "His Holiness senses that it should be arranged for before the end of next month."

There were gasps of disbelief from those present.

"The Middle East is even more unstable than it was when John Paul II was there," said the elderly German cardinal. "Would such a trip be advisable?"

"The Holy Father would not be put at risk," said Menenger. "It would all be over in a few hours."

"It's an extraordinary suggestion," said another. "You surely can't be serious, Eminence!"

"It is the Holy Father's dearest wish that we make this happen. After prayer and much thought I have come to realize the wisdom of it." His smile took on a beatific edge. "I have come to see his request as a spirit-directed act of genius. It would capture everyone's imagination and set the new pontificate's agenda for years to come. It would also personalize the Catholic faith in a manner not seen for decades. Pilgrimage would become a beacon to the faithful and a light to those who do not yet know the Christ."

The reason for their being there was suddenly of little importance; it was as if someone had waved a magic wand. Not knowing what to make of what he was hearing, Valerio Maglione sat in silence as Cardinal Menenger further promoted the pope's fixation.

"It is a truly inspired idea," said Borghini at last. "It lifts my heart to think of it."

"And that is what we need in this hour of cunning persecution," said Menenger. "I can think of no better way to offset the unfair and often unfounded accusations presently being made against the Church than by offering the world Benedict XVI's personal act of devotion and contrition. It is, as Cardinal Borghini has so rightly said, a truly inspired idea."

"The Israelis may not go for it," said the Secretary of State.

"Oh, I think they will," said Cardinal Menenger. "A pope on his knees in Jerusalem praying for peace in the midst of such disorder is worth its weight in gold."

35

A Modicum of Dignity

"I think I've worked out how they became aware of my seminary days so quickly," said Duggan, articulating something that had been bothering him since his confrontation with Monsignor Rossi. "Robert Carter saw David and I together a number of times during the Santa Rosa conference, so when he saw David's name alongside Holly's on the *Washington Post* expose, then learned that it was me who had broken the Vatican's embargo on publishing the codex, he must have done a double-take. Could be he tipped someone off. He's a sworn enemy of David's. Question is, what made them dig so far back into my past?"

"They were obviously looking for something to nail you with," said Jane. She was standing at Duggan's curtainless window sipping coffee and staring out into the narrow, tree-intertwined gardens that backed Glebe's old, narrow houses. When she spoke again it was to say that she had breathed a sigh of relief when Rossi's failed to pursue the possibility of her father having been the source of the photographs.

"They've scuppered themselves through buying into the forgery claim," said Duggan, aware that the other accusation might still arise. Then, memory stirring, he said, "On the score of their checking so far back into my past, it might be I was little too clever when interviewing Carter. I may have aroused suspicions."

"That crossed my mind before Monsignor Rossi dropped his bombshell. You sounded much too well informed on matters of religion."

"I'll keep that in mind."

She was silent for a moment, then she said, "David's targeting of Carter's connection with CNCD must have gone down well. He did a real dust-up job on him."

"And discovered doing his tricks in Donaghue's backyard no less!" Duggan laugh was sardonic. "I wonder if they're still talking?"

"Donaghue's since denied in an interview having any knowledge of Carter's link with CNCD. Is that possible?"

"It's probable. Bishop Peters told David and I that the archbishop didn't know what Carter really stood for, or what he was up to. He describe Donaghue as an old-fashioned conservative that Carter was using as a front for the neo-conservative cause. My impression is that he's a man caught between the Devil and the deep blue sea. I don't think Peters knew about CNCD as such, or how influential it had become among Curial prelates. He talked about liberals, conservative and neoconservatives in general, but never of any particular neoconservative group. He just seemed to sense the general drift of Catholic thinking towards a more rigid formula."

"He wasn't wrong."

He had put his arms around her from behind and leaned his chin on her right shoulder. She turned her head and kissed him on the cheek, then drew back slightly to look at him.

"What?" he asked.

"Do you mind being out of the closet?"

His gaze wandered back to what lay beyond the window. It was a relief, he said. It had left him feeling curiously whole.

"You were in hiding?"

"Something like that."

She turned to him and they kissed properly, he with his hands on her hips, she with her right arm stuck out to avoid spilling what remained of her coffee. It reminded her of an equally awkward moment in the Bentleys' kitchen.

"I'm glad it's out in the open," she said at last. "There was something a little furtive about your not telling anyone."

"I told David."

"David has a way of winkling stuff out of people." She smiled an odd smile. "When he told me about your past I didn't believe him at first. I thought it was a joke."

"Synchronicity?"

"Synchronicity is a euphemism for *I don't know either,*" she said back.

"You read Jung?"

"Less than I used to." Apropos of nothing, she added, "I had so many relationships at one point my father despaired of me."

"Is this a confession?" he asked.

"It balances the books," she replied. "It started just after my mother died. I went haywire for about eighteen months."

"That's understandable. You had lost her love."

"No, it wasn't quite that . . . I'd lost her presence." She reconsidered his remark. "Yes, in losing her presence I lost her love, too, I suppose. All I had left was my memory of her."

"Your father said something about your being a bit wild after your mother's death. Headstrong was how he described you."

"He used stronger language at the time." She made a face, disengaged from him and finished her coffee off. "I was out of control, Jack." She placed her mug on the window ledge and pushed her hands into the pockets of her jeans. She was now in profile. "I dread to think what would have happened if George hadn't turned up." She glanced at Duggan and smiled, looked down at the floor and up again.

He found what she was saying difficult to take in. It seemed so unlike her. She seemed so level-headed now, so capable, so centered.

That was when she had painted the little floating, fleeing girl the Bentleys' had in their dining room, she said. It exactly captured how she had felt. Turning from him, she half-sat on the narrow window ledge.

"Elspeth won't ever be able to look at that picture the way she did prior to your comment," he said, remembering the look of shock on her face.

"It just slipped out. Looking at that picture brought it all back."

He reached for a nearby chair and straddled it wrong way round.

"I started writing my novel feeling pretty low," he said "It helped, but it's a dreary old read!"

She laughed at his expression, asked what it was about.

"It's psychological twaddle mostly," he said. "I can't bear to look at the damn thing."

"Is it religious?"

A shake of the head. He had avoided all mention of religion.

"Can I take a peek?

"If you'll let me watch you paint a picture from start to finish. I'd like to see you do that."

"Why?" she asked.

"I want to see how you do what you do."

"Why?" she said again.

"I want to see the magic happen."

"It wouldn't. Not with someone watching."

"Can you describe what happens?"

She did not immediately reply. Frowning, she said after a moment that she sometimes got lucky, that she sort of woke up in the middle of it all and knew exactly what it was she had to do, or, conversely, what she had to undo. That was really all she could tell him. The rest of it was about searching and probing. Looking. You just had to look and keep on looking until what was there, or what ought be there, surfaced. Quite often it didn't. You could work for hours and get absolutely nowhere.

"You've just described the writing process at its most intense," he said, watching her face.

"Then you know what I'm on about. Most people haven't got a clue. They would be shocked to find out how much fumbling goes on in art. Any kind of art."

"There isn't a single painting in the house," he said, wondering what she had made of that. "I've just never seen anything I felt I could live with." A laugh. "One that I could afford, that is."

"You can have anything you like of mine."

"No dolls," he said, raising a finger.

"It'll mean coming to Ohio."

"I've already said I will."

She seemed to be searching his face for something; it made him feel vulnerable. Then out of the blue she said that she'd like to meet his father.

"I'll arrange it."

"Have you seen much of him since we got back? You haven't mentioned him."

"I see him whenever I can. He's very independent. I ring him regularly."

"Does he know about me?"

"Of course. It just hasn't been convenient with so much going on. He lives well out of Sydney. It's a bit of a hike."

"What does he think of your sudden fame?"

"His only comment was *steady as she goes*. He's a wise old bird. I think you'll get on."

"He sounds nice."

"He's content with his lot. Probably because he's a reader; that helps, I think."

"Like father, like son."

"I don't have his quality of patience," said Duggan. "I'm more like my mother on that score. I move a little too fast at times."

"You don't have any photographs on show either," she said quizzically, but with a bit of a smile. "Do you have some?"

"They're somewhere," he said, looking away in an attempt to remember exactly where. "I'll look them out for you."

"A man without images," she said playfully. She paused, then jumped rails again. "I think my father's heading for trouble, Jack." Her expression was one of concern. "They're going to find out what he did, aren't they?"

"He's joked more than once about that possibility."

"It would ruin his career. No one would trust him ever again if the truth of the situation got out."

"He has moral indignation on his side," said Duggan. "That's worth more than you might think. He'd be seen by some as a hero for doing what he did."

"Perhaps," she said, sounding not at all convinced. "But his professional reputation would suffer. He'd lose his research post in Essen. He'd be forced into an early retirement."

"Not if it could be proved the other side were involved in burying the codex for fear of a few home truths getting out. That is in fact the case, Jane, and most scholars are aware of it. The penny's beginning to drop all round."

"He sounded dog-tired when I last spoke to him."

"He was in the thick of it at that point. Things have eased off since then. And he's still got Merle's backing. That more than anything else undercuts the *Department of Antiquity's* claim that the codex is no more than a modern forgery. Also, the Vatican Press Office now has its hands full on two fronts, thanks to David and the ubiquitous Holly Parks. Cardinal Peronio must be pulling his hair out."

She sat backed by the brilliant light of the sky and he was suddenly aware of her again as a person, as an individual carved in the likeness of the mother she missed so much. That seemed to jog his memory. Pushing up from the chair, he said that he remembered now where he had put the few photographs he had.

When he returned with the little cardboard box and opened it, Jane took the photographs from him one by one and studied them with a kind of puzzled frown.

"I was about twelve when that one was taken," he said, remembering the moment. "I could feel my mother's fingers digging into my shoulders."

"She's obviously very proud of you. Look at the expression on her face."

"She was, then," he said. "Little did she know what was round the corner."

"This is your father?"

"Yup."

"He's different from what I imagined. I thought he'd look something like you."

"Afraid not." He stared at the image of a much younger father. "As you can see, I'm my mother's boy in looks."

"So what did you get from your father?"

He thought about that. An analytical eye, he said. He was apt to weigh up all the variables before committing himself on anything. His mother had found that particularly irritating.

"You got the best of both worlds by the sound of it."

"I fluctuate. I'm terribly patient when it suits me, far too speedy when it doesn't."

She did not ask him to expand on that; it sounded too awkward for a Saturday afternoon.

"I only have one photograph of them together. I'm not quite sure why that is. The others probably got lost." He rummaged again, came up with one of himself. "Here's one of me at university. Don't I look smug."

"You had every reason to be pleased with yourself."

"Truth is, I already knew the priest thing wasn't going to work. I just couldn't admit it to myself. I could have saved my mother a lot of grief if I had."

"You knew before you went into the seminary?"

"It would be more accurate to say that I *sensed* I wasn't a suitable candidate."

"So why do it?"

I didn't want to let my mother down. Or our local priest for that matter. Or my own crazy idea that I'd been called of God." He struggled to explain his dilemma. "It was no more than a feeling of unease way down deep that I couldn't properly interpret."

"You regret the whole thing?"

A pause before he replied. In retrospect, no, he said. He was what he was because of what he had had to battle his way through. If nothing else, it had helped knock the smugness out of him. Another pause. He sometimes thought he was solely constructed of flaws that had managed to heal. That's what it felt like at times.

"*Oh what a tangled web we weave,*" she said, lifting a strip of identical images from the box. "Is this you, too?"

"I'd be what, seven?" He took the strip from her and scanned the images taken while at primary school. "Do you know I can actually remember wearing that V-neck jersey. It's scary. I can even remember the exact spot on the playground where our photographs were taken that day. It was summer and we went round to a side of the school where the sun was behind the photographer's back. A group photograph was taken on the same spot. Then individual ones. There was a big white sheet behind us I remember. My favorite teacher was in the group photograph. I thought for a while that I was in love with her."

"You look so innocent."

"I was, and I wasn't. I was just waking up to the fact that I could think, that arguments could also be won with words. That was quite a discovery for a seven-year-old. It revolutionized my relationships. I found out how to make people listen to me. You don't have to be a hypnotist to hypnotize people. They can be hypnotized with the right combination of words. It's how magic was born, I think. Ritualistic incantation is magic whatever its form. I picked up on that through listening and watching our local priest do his stuff. He could have told us just about anything and we'd have believed it. He was a little bit of God talking to us according to my mother."

"Is that what made you want to be a priest?"

"I suppose it must have been. I thought being a priest meant knowing God in a special kind of way. I wanted to experience that. I wanted God's telephone number."

Jane smiled at Duggan's choice of words.

"You can imagine the shock I got when I entered seminary and discovered that it was all an illusion, that priests told dirty jokes just like everyone else."

"What did you expect?"

"Sanctity. I'm not quite sure what I thought sanctity was, but that's what I wanted to experience. I thought they'd show us how to attain it. In my naivety I thought all priests *had* attained it."

"You really thought that?"

"More or less. My mother had drummed it into me that priests were special human beings touched with the ability to see right into one's soul. The atmosphere of the whole house used to change when our local priest paid us a visit. I can remember staring at him in awe. I still had remnants of that in my system when I left university."

"What a let down it must have been."

"Biggest of my life. Fr Michael Flynn put paid to any romantic notions I had in the first week. It was like being doused with cold water. Mind you, he treated everyone badly, it wasn't just me. He seemed to delight in making people's lives a misery."

"Were they all like that?"

"Not at all, but there seemed to be no way of escaping Flynn's vindictiveness. He was always there or thereabouts. It was either him or one of his acolytes scolding you for some perceived misdemeanor. It was all petty stuff. Inconsequential nonsense drummed up into a drama. I took it for a while, then rebelled." Duggan huffed a laugh. "I'll never forget the first time I faced up to him. I thought he was going to have a fit."

"I find what you're describing difficult to take in."

"It was part of a mentality that thought punishment was good for the soul, Jane. It was flagellation swapped for organized cruelty. It was the end of an era."

She lifted more of the images from the box and scrutinized them in silence.

"I was one of three who bailed out," he said, watching her face. "I was the only one to be suspended prior to deciding to throw in the towel."

"What's this one?" She handed him a mottled photograph of two men in dungarees standing side by side.

"That's my father and his father," Duggan said. "Aren't they alike. My father's about seventeen there. It was taken somewhere in

Ireland. I've forgotten where."

"People's lives scare me when I see them captured like this." Jane dropped the photograph back into the box and lifted another, then another. "It all seems so pointless." She lifted the photograph of his father and grandfather again. "The shadows suggest early evening. A summer's evening."

"Pointless?" he said.

"Relentless?" She looked back at the photograph. "Generation after generation battling it out? It's scary stuff, Jack. I caught a glimpse of it when I was ill and freaked out."

"Caught a glimpse of what?"

"The possibility that none of it matters one whit?"

"You were ill?"

"Strung out like you wouldn't believe." She laughed uneasily, glanced at him. "Mad as a hatter was how my father put it."

"What's it all about, Alfie," he said, trying to make light of what he was hearing.

"That's when I did my best work. It was the turning point in my career."

"You had an epiphany."

"Yes, I woke up," she said, translating 'epiphany' into something a little more basic. "I didn't know what was happening to me, but that's what it was."

"Some are luckier than others."

She looked again at the photograph she was holding. "They're hurting, Jack. It's in their faces."

"They should have painted a picture," he said with unintended flippancy.

"It's a doorway, Jack," she said. "Some use it, some don't. It doesn't have to be anything tangible."

"Fr Flynn would not have disagreed with you on that. He was a great believer in suffering.""

"You can't inflict an epiphany."

"No, you can't," he said, remembering his anguish as they tried to bully him towards God.

* * *

Bishop Samuel Peters' third article for the *New York Times* proved to be as controversial as the other two. Having argued that the Church was engaged in a Vincentian-type subterfuge where reality was forced into the straitjacket of revealed truth, he had then accused the hierarchy of shutting down the intellectual renaissance experienced by the Church during the previous century, and capped it all off by contending that 'love' and 'compassion' - the central focus of Jesus' message in the Gospels - had been exchanged for a fear-based grab at personal salvation and the rewards of heaven. There followed a grocery list of objections to this kind of thinking, an attack on the Church's supernatural Jesus, and a challenge to all thinking Catholics to reject the conspiracy of silence over the historical Jesus' raw humanity.

This of course was no easy task, Peters admitted. Christian thinkers had so mythologized their faith's history that it was all but impossible to detect any sensible basis for the Jesus they lauded. Their Jesus was a theoretical construct, an imaginative portrayal of a flesh-and-blood man progressively inflated to a point of absurdity. But alas, Jesus had never claimed any of the things claimed on his behalf, and as the original Gospels had been copied several times - the earliest available dated to 175 years after Jesus' death - their more extravagant claims were obviously due to later elaborations.

The situation today was that most individuals led perfectly satis-factory lives without the Church's magical Jesus. For that, in effect, was what a supernatural Jesus amounted to, a magical figure. In earlier centuries faith and life had overlapped to such an extent that belief in this magical figure had seemed both natural and necessary, but with the advance of knowledge that had become an all but impossible position to hold. We might still believe in God, we might even still attend a church, but the idea that God and the man Jesus were, ultimately, one and the same being no longer carried the certainty it once had. The symbols of traditional Christianity had lost their ancient charge; the faith of many centuries had undergone a subtle metamorphosis, its supernatural claims either smiled at or disparaged.

The bishop's final point was that truth changed in the same way language, people, societies and methods of communication changed. It could not do otherwise. Hence the need to get away from a creed-based Christianity where any change to the formula was seen as a betrayal of eternal verities. Rely on a fixed religious creed and you closed the door on being able to deal with the changing needs of people. It was people who had to be protected, not words on paper. The fear was that any change in language would subtly change the nature of Christianity's truth claims, but that was just magical thinking; it was the notion that truth could be cast like a spell upon the world, that any change to the truth-spell would somehow reduce its spiritual potency. But the dilemma facing Christians wasn't about spiritual potency, it was about falsifying reality. Had everyone forgotten Jesus' claim that he was the way, the truth and the life? asked Peters. This was thought to be a veiled divinity-claim, but it was nothing of the kind. It was just Jesus reminding everyone that truth resided in people, not in syntax. When asked to explain the meaning of truth by Pilate, Jesus had remained silent. To understood that silence was to arrive at a whole new comprehension of self and other.

* * *

The kiss was fleeting, no more than a glancing blow on Duggan's cheek, but the repercussions were startling. Unaware that their affectionate parting had been captured by telephoto lens, Duggan watched Jane drive off in her hire car, then turned to deal with another Monday. By six that evening, however, he was well aware of what had taken place, for the *Sydney Evening Gazette* had somehow managed to match Jane Windle's image with a recent photograph from the *Washington Post,* and the heading was, to say the least, provocative. That the photograph of Jane the artist had been in the *Gazette's* possession prior to taking the other went without saying, and their launching straight into the fact that she was the daughter of Professor James Windle, the American scholar suspected of having forged the now infamous Mar Saba Codex, showed that they were angling for something juicy.

Two questions followed: What was Jane Windle doing in Australia, and what was she doing in the company of the journalist who had so unexpectedly broken the story of the codex - the codex Jane Windle's father claimed to have been tipped off about. Was she in Australia on her father's behalf? Or was she here for some other reason, an intimate attachment perhaps? Leaving those questions open (the photograph of Jane kissing Duggan on the cheek was sufficient testimony in itself), the writer then upped the ante with a series of deft strokes. Linking Duggan to David Mayle, one of two American journalists who had recently caused a furore in the States with their expose of Catholic fundamentalism, it was revealed that Duggan and Mayle had been seen together at a Catholic conference in California during April, and that this had been the occasion illicit photographs of the codex were passed on to Duggan by a person or persons unknown. So how interesting that later in April, Mayle, according to the editor of his old newspaper in San Francisco, had visited New York, and that Duggan, too, had been there to check his translation of the codex with Professor Windle. Officially on leave for two weeks, Mayle had then surprised former colleagues by joining forces with *Washington Post* journalist Holy Parks, and without notice dumped his former employer. All in all a remarkable set of coincidences, and compounded by the fact that Holly Parks had also been in New York at this time, and, surprise surprise, had interviewed both Professor Windle and his daughter about her recent success as an artist. All too neat, surely. All too coincidental to be accepted uncritically, suggested the writer.

So what was going on? Why had all five individuals chosen to visits New York at the end of April? Was there perhaps more to their being there than met the eye? Could it be that there was some kind of connection between publication of the codex and the attempt by Parks and Mayle to blacken the name of Catholicism's most powerful spiritual movement? Could it be that the accusation of forgery made against Professor Windle went deeper than anyone suspected? Could it be that these separate parties were somehow in collusion, that they were engaged in a cynical exercise to harm and humiliate the Catholic Church? And last, but not least: Was the Australian journalist Jack Duggan really as impartially involved in the whole business as he made himself out to be? Or was this ex-seminarian exacting a particularly hurtful vengeance on the Church for perceived mistreatment in the past? Desire for vengeance had been strenuously denied by Duggan while on the Don Cooper Show, but he had perhaps protested too much. Whatever his motives, Duggan appeared to be involved in a very messy business indeed.

On this note the article ended, the writer's cleverly constructed conspiracy theory left to hang in the air.

"It's tip-offs all round," said Duggan. "It's got Carter's prints all over it. Has to be him. What I said earlier about Carter spotting Holly's article on you, then David's name alongside Holly's must have rung alarm bells. But seeing my name on the Mar Saba story must have clinched it for him. David said to me at the time that our being seen together could come back to haunt me."

"Is there anything we can do about this?" Jane's anger was obvious. "Could we sue?"

"I don't think so. This stuff's been carefully phrased to avoid just that. It has the mark of legal all over it." He shook his head at the implications. "Being able to connect up the dots in this way makes us look damned suspicious - I'd be suspicious myself if given the same facts." He paused, and added, "We've perhaps been a little naive in thinking we could beat them at their own game. They've had a lot of practice at this kind of thing. This is a clever maneuver.

It's designed to sink all of us with one torpedo."

"You really think Carter's behind this?"

"Well I'm pretty sure it isn't the Vatican Press Office; they're too damned canny to dirty their hands in this way. It's got to be Carter. Carter revels in this kind of play. He's a big-time barrister with a street-fighter's mentality and he's got Cardinal Menenger's ear. Need I say more."

"They can't hope to prove conspiracy to subvert Catholicism against all five of us. It's a ridiculous assertion."

"They don't have to prove anything. All they have to do is insinuate a connection between groups A and B. The claims made here are vague and circumstantial, but they're enough to sow a reasonable doubt in the public mind."

They fell silent, then Jane said, "Truth is, Jack, we are in collusion, aren't we? But not for the reasons they've drummed up." She sighed out her frustration. "This is one of those damnable situations where lies and truth have coincided."

"Don't I know it."

"Do you regret getting involved?"

"I'd be sitting here by myself if I hadn't. I get goosebumps when I think how easily I could have missed out on meeting you,"

"You exuded a kind of violence the first time I saw you. You looked really annoyed."

"I'd just walked out on Atkins's reassessment of evil. I was appalled by what I had heard. He believed evil to be an intelligent force that could invade a human life."

"He debunked soul-making through life experience in his seminar. It was clever, but similarly bleak."

"I missed that one," said Duggan. "I was busy writing up what Bishop Peters said when David and I visited him in hospital. That was the first I'd heard about the shenanigans of the neoconservative groups. Peters had a really good handle on what was going on there. That's when he told us Donaghue didn't know what Carter was really up to. I think he's been proved right."

"And here we are in Sydney, the two of us," she said, studying his face. "Who'd have guessed it?"

"Not me, that's for sure. When I saw you at Kennedy all dolled up like Lara in *Dr. Zhivago* I didn't think I had a chance. You looked stunning."

"I hadn't made up my mind at that point."

"The way you greeted me made me think I had a chance. The way you acted in the cab totally confused me."

"I got frightened."

"What changed your mind?"

"Elspeth said you were okay."

"God bless Elspeth."

"He has; she has George. He was the other reason I knew you were okay. I asked him what he thought of you when you went off to bed that first night. He said any man who could stand up to Elspeth and retain, as you had obviously done, her high opinion, was worthy of my favor."

"Good old George."

"He has the artistic eye; she has the eye that discerns fools at a hundred paces. They're a highly unusual pair."

They were standing close now. Taking her in his arms, Duggan said, "Having you here with me is so unlikely I'm almost persuaded to believe in fate."

"I prefer chance," she said back. "It leaves one with a modicum of dignity."

36

Fighting Fire with Fire

That he was not going to win the day was obvious to Robert Carter within seconds of entering Archbishop Donaghue's study. The archbishop's response to the accusation of betrayal was one of immediate fury. Silencing Carter with a raised hand, Donaghue said he did not appreciate being preached at by a self-aggrandizing upstart. Who the hell did he think he was waltzing into the presence of an archbishop and making such an assertion? It was an impertinence of the first order, and he would see to it that the appropriate authorities were informed.

"My good name has been dragged through the gutter as a result of the interviews Your Grace and Fr Brentano gave to the *Washington Post*," countered Carter. "Not a single word was uttered in my defense!"

"What you were engaged in *was* indefensible," growled Donaghue, "and what I find alarming, Robert, is that the nonsense you set in motion here continues as we speak! Fr Brentano's once-successful parish has been rent asunder by these idiots of yours, and they're still at it!"

"I'm hardly in a position to dictate protocol to a spiritual movement blessed by the highest ecclesiastical authorities in Rome!"

"*You* let them off the leash, so I hold *you* responsible!"

Carter was silent for a moment, then with the air of one who is aggrieved, he said that the spirit of renewal at work in Brentano's parish would survive all attempts to quench it. What God had set in motion, man would be hard pressed to stop.

"You still dare to equate what these people are doing and saying with the will of God? Are you serious?"

"They are a rectifying force, Your Grace."

"Disallowing love between husband and wife is a rectification? A rectification of *what*, exactly?"

"Individualism," said Carter, as if that were so obvious a fact it hardly deserved mentioning. "Love for family or friends is *cadere nell'umano*; it is to lapse into a human attitude and displaces God from our affections. We must be ready to renounce anything that gets between God and ourselves."

"Oh, that *does* sound grand," said Donaghue, his emphasis bitingly sardonic, "but it is in fact a perfect example of the kind of rampant individualism you yourself are attempting to eschew. You don't think so? Think about it, Robert. It is *you* cornering God for your own benefit. *You* dictating to God the terms of the relationship! Very cozy! What could be more self-centered than thinking you've got God all to yourself?"

"I can hardly believe you're saying what you're saying," said Carter, staring at Donaghue in alarm. "I thought we were as one in our desire to see the faith strengthened across America. You yourself spoke on the necessity of strong discipline at the conference."

"That is not the same thing at all!" said Donaghue. We're talking about something completely different here. I was arguing for self-discipline."

"And that is exactly the New Dawn's directive," said Carter, his face full of concern. "As Catholics we have to overcome our laxity and rediscover our spiritual roots. The spiritual movements are the key to realizing that objective."

"Not if they're hounding and harassing Catholics of good faith at every turn! The scrutinies and confessions being held behind closed doors in Fr Brentano's parish were brutal in the extreme, Robert. They cannot be condoned. It shocks me that you can stand there and attempt to defend such goings-on. And from what I can make out these goings-on were only the tip of the iceberg. Some of the accusation made against the movements in Fr Grosjean's book beggar the imagination!"

"We are engaged in a battle for the faith, Your Grace. Rationalism has invaded modern theology and all but disabled it. We have to fight fire with fire. We are engaged in a great battle for the soul of humanity, a battle between God and his Logos, and the infernal anti-Logos. There's no room for rearguard action in this fight. We have to meet the enemy eye to eye! God's salvific initiative is being hindered by human blindness. We —- "

"Yes, yes yes," said a thoroughly annoyed Donaghue. Then, deciding that it was time to lay his cards on the table, he said, "I am as adamantly engaged in the task of renewing the faith as I have ever been, Robert. I believe in tradition, continuity and discipline, but I cannot in all conscience stand by and watch Catholics of good faith being trodden underfoot by fanatics. For that's what we're dealing with here, fanaticism of the worst ilk, and it has to be dealt with. Fr Brentano's parish is only one of many across the US to suffer at the hands of these so-called missionaries. There are dozens of parishes undergoing the same unnecessary trauma. And don't mistake what I'm saying, Robert. I haven't gone soft on my mission, and neither have I turned into a closet liberal. God forbid! I've simply pondered this matter long and hard, and on the evidence before me have been forced to conclude that the New Dawn movement is undermining the Church's good reputation in America and elsewhere No, no, let me finish! This is not, as you obviously believe, the Church renewing itself through special effort. Such a claim couldn't be further from the truth. It is a case of collective paranoia being mistaken for a movement of the Spirit. In a word, Robert, it is a sickness, a contagion, and I for one will not be party to its machinations."

Carter raised his hands in what appeared to be sad resignation, but nothing could have been further from the truth; he was in fact preparing to deliver his knockout blow. "Is that really your final word on the matter, Your Grace?" he asked.

"It is," said Donaghue.

"Then I can only say that I am truly astonished. I've considered you a champion of the faith for as long as I can remember. This . . . *capitulation* comes as something of a shock."

"I'm still the same man," said Donaghue. "Nothing has changed,

Robert. I wouldn't have tolerated this kind of nonsense as a bishop, or as a priest. Hence my support for Fr Brentano."

"Which brings me to the point of my visit," said Carter.

"I was under the impression the point of your visit was to accuse Fr Brentano and myself of betrayal."

Carter ignored the jibe and continued. "Fr Brentano has a brother studying at Gregorian University. Were you aware of that fact?"

"Of course."

"Are you also aware that he is a friend and confidant of Fr Sebastian Grosjean, the professor of philosophy whose book ridiculing the spiritual movements has caused such consternation in Rome?"

"No, I was not," said Donaghue. "Your point is?"

"My point is this, Your Grace. The Brentano brothers are very much in sympathy with the views expressed in Fr Grosjean's book, and that explains Fr Brentano's knee-jerk reaction to the spiritual insights of the missionaries who came here. He was quite simply predisposed to reject their charismatic zeal. He – "

"That is abject nonsense," said Donaghue, cutting Carter short. "For a start, Fr Brentano welcomed these emissaries into his parish. It was only after they proved themselves to be incorrigibly disruptive that he complained to me. He gave them every chance to prove their worth. He even gave them a second chance at my instruction."

"He could hardly go against your wishes, Your Grace."

"It was all done at your request, Robert. That's why I hold you responsible for what's happened here! I invited them here on your recommendation, and I've regretted it ever since! Given their track record, you must have known what they'd get up to!"

"What I've said about Fr Brentano is true," said Carter, forcing the issue back to Brentano to avoid the point. "He is not the quietly obedient priest he appears to be."

"How can you possibly know such a thing?"

"Because walls have ears, Your Grace. And eyes." Carter's smile carried the pain of revealing a sad truth. "The brother has been unwise enough to confide in the wrong people from time to time. He has talked to others about his and his brother's views, and he has been foolish enough to openly criticize the magisterium while in class."

"Students are sometimes rash in their judgments," said Donaghue, his mind racing. "Particularly the bright ones."

"Undoubtedly, but this is a little more serious than that. The brother has been identified as a subversive element, and is about to be censured."

"In what way censured?"

"That depends on what Cardinal Menenger decides to do with Beneditti's cabal," said Carter, using the phrase he had last heard Menenger use. Then, doubling back. he said, "You've obviously talked to Fr Brentano about his brother."

"He was mentioned in passing."

"Your assessment of him suggests more than a passing comment."

"You're reading more into that than is actually there," said Donaghue, realizing with a jolt what Fr Brentano had meant when he said his brother moved in 'exalted company'.

"Intellectually bright?" Carter's question was rhetorical; he continued with his attack. "Hence his close association with Professor Grosjean, no doubt."

"Where are you heading with this?" asked Donaghue.

"To the possibility of an official inquiry into Fr Brentano's behavior."

"Brentano's behavior?" Archbishop Donaghue's astonishment was patent. "By whom, might I ask?"

"Cardinal Menenger, of course."

"Menenger? You know that to be a fact?"

"The *Washington Post* article highlighted Fr Brentano's forcing of the issue. Cardinal Menenger has taken a personal interest in the matter."

"Brentano only did so because of endless complaints from members of his own congregation. And I should point out that the *Post's* expose also records my firm backing for Fr Brentano. When I learned the nature of the complaints lodged against the New Dawn's missionaries, and checked them out for myself, I had no option but to suspend the activities of these people. The fact that they are again operative in my diocese shows the level of respect they have for episcopal authority."

"Am I to conclude from that that you are also in sympathy with Cardinal Beneditti and those who support him?"

Donaghue's reply took on the finesse of someone in the dock. To the extent that Beneditti's views coincided with his own over CNCD outrages, then yes, he said. How else could it be under the circumstances?

"You're ignoring the fact that a substantial number of Fr Brentano's parishioners are not in agreement with his perception of things."

"The New Dawn's policy is divide and conquer, Robert. It's on record as a tactic they use wherever they turn up. It is, in other words, a blatant and calculated manipulation of innocent minds. I can't stand idly by and watch that happen."

"You intend to act further?"

"They've defied episcopal authority! They've acted outside of the protocols so clearly defined for groups of this nature, and they are in defiance of my most recent order to leave my diocese. Need I say more?"

"I suggest you speak with Cardinal Menenger as soon as possible." said Carter. "This is a complicated affair with dangerous ramifications for the Church."

"I'm well aware of the dangers."

"They are perhaps greater than you think."

"I very much doubt it will come to schism, if that's what you're hinting at."

"It's an act of willful disobedience to go against what the Holy

See has deemed appropriate. Written approval from the late Holy Father as far back as 1990 recognized the movements' practices as valid for today's society and times. "

"The late Holy Father was obviously ill-informed as to those practices. We are not, thank God. Leave things as they are and you'll have schism before you can blink, Robert. The Church is not in danger from Cardinal Beneditti and his supporters, or from Fr Brentano and his outspoken brother, but it will be in very great danger if it fails to deal with CNCD's unconscionable bullying and the looming scandal over sexual allegations. That's where the danger lies."

"That is to misread the situation, in my opinion, Your Grace. Dismantle the spiritual movements and you dismantle the Church's ability to defeat rationalism. The movements are our frontline troops."

"And still you try to sidestep the facts, Robert! Why is that, I wonder? Are you so under the influence of these people you can no longer think straight?"

"I strongly advise you to speak with Cardinal Menenger about these matters."

Donaghue stared at Carter for a moment. Then in a tired voice, he said, "Have you bothered to read a single page of Fr Grosjean's book?"

"I have not, Your Grace. I am more concerned with the larger picture. As is Cardinal Menenger. The peccadilloes of the few should not be used to malign the many. We are at war, Your Grace. War is sometimes a messy business."

"Peccadilloes? Is that really how you perceive this situation, Robert?"

"It is, Your Grace."

"Then you are without doubt blessed with an innocence that defies logic. I almost envy you."

It was Carter's turn to smile. "The envy of an archbishop is something to be cherished, Your Grace."

"I said *almost*," replied Donaghue, having heard all he could bear to hear.

* * *

L'Osservatore, the Vatican's official daily newspaper, published its in-depth review of Fr Grosjean's book *The End of Catholicism?* fast on the heels of a biting editorial in *Corriere della Sera*, Italy's equivalent of the *New York Times*. Describing the book's meticulously documented attack on the New Catholic Dawn as 'deeply flawed in its final argument, but a necessary corrective nonetheless', Cardinal Borghini proceeded to analyze what he perceived as 'mistakes' and 'exaggerations' in Fr Grosjean's lengthy text. There was seldom smoke without fire, he admitted, but the sheer relentlessness of the argument presented by this professor of philosophy ought surely to ring alarm bells. No group or organization was ever perfect, but the litany of objections brought against CNCD and its sister movements was, to say the least, bewildering. The excesses cited would of course be investigated; the Church would not, could not tolerate behavior that brought its integrity into question.

No reference was made by Borghini to the august signatures the book carried; it was as if the opinion of Fr Grosjean's backers mattered not one whit.

This was in direct contrast to the *Corriere della Sera* editorial where the banner heading had spelt out the possibility of schism. Recognizing straight off how serious the situation had become, the writer had carefully sifted the evidence and come to exactly the opposite conclusion to that of Cardinal Borghini: the evidence supplied had been handled by Fr Grosjean in a thoroughly profes-sional manner. Startled by the broad spectrum of high-ranking clergy supporting Grosjean's contentions, and inundated with letters from readers who claimed to have experienced the abuse and harassment cited in the priest's book, this prestigious newspaper had called for an immediate public inquiry into the allegation of systematic brainwashing. Singling out CNCD missionary activity, *Corriere della Sera's* investigator challenged Cardinal Borghini to meet and talk with those who had experienced, at first hand, the New Catholic Dawn's tender loving mercies, and with a boldness equal to that of its sister paper in the US, concluded that the Church's attempt to escape censure by arguing individual malfeasance was to shirk its responsibilities. Yes, there was seldom smoke without fire, the writer agreed, and there was every indication that a fair little blaze was burning in curial ranks.

In reply to this, *L'Eco de Bergamo,* one of Italy's traditional Catholic newspapers, blasted back in support of Cardinal Borghini. This in turn drew fire from *L'Unita,* the historical organ of Italy's communist party. Within a week of publication, *The End of Catholicism?,* in conjunction with Borghini's apologia and Italy's premiere wire service *Ansa,* had incited a journalistic war with newspapers, magazines, broadsheets and broadcasts of all hue wading into the debate. And not just in Italy. As sales of Fr Grosjean's book soared, foreign newspapers, too, began to discuss the issue of Catholicism's drive to reinstate hardcore conservative values on a wide front, the verdict of most commentators being that this kind of thinking had long since reached its use-by date.

But there were also those who stoically upheld the Catholic Church's right to stamp its authority and values on its congregations, and through its congregations on the society at large. Conservative and neoconservative priests and bishops surfaced across Europe, in Britain, Australia and in America to argue against the noticeable media trend to rubbish Christianity at every turn, their shrill message of moral decline adding to the ferment. The secularization of modern society by the media was the culprit, they argued in unison, but it was a trend that had produced an unexpected result - an increased craving for spiritual certainty. New Age faddism and Eastern enlightenment techniques might suffice for a while, but in the end only Christianity's old, old story could satisfy the thirsting soul. In alignment with this, a religious correspondent for a magazine in Ireland wrote that Christendom's sorry state could be righted only by living one's faith in a 'forceful manner'. When pressed to explain what he meant by that, he failed to properly define his meaning

The fundamental argument offered by those who perceived their Church to be besieged by secularism was that tolerance and openness to all opinions and perspectives on the truth led to indifference. Christianity's worldwide crisis of faith was due to indifference, an indifference born of secularist propaganda. There was nothing wrong with tolerance, but if it led to a flawed view of Christ's nature and mission, to a bland acceptance of alternative views, then it had gone too far in the direction of accommodation. Christianity's fundamental truths were sacrosanct. They were revealed of God, not begotten of the intellect. Being such, they should not be tampered with.

So ran the hardliner's argument, and as it gathered momentum, a confused and sometimes quite garbled picture of what it was Fr Grosjean had actually attacked in his book began to emerge. And all done by the trick of leading the eye away from the matter in hand, by the tactic of reading into the text of *The End of Catholicism?* the erroneous notion that that was in fact Grosjean's extraordinary aim, not the saving of Catholicism from a powerful extremist lobby. And that in spite of the question mark in the title. Whatever the book might claim as its subject, went the argument, its long-term objective was a watering-down of Catholicism's great truths. By default, therefore, those who had lent their names to Grosjean's carefully constructed text had to be viewed as similarly tainted.

* * *

"He may be angling to make good his threat of excommunication," said Secretary of State Maglione.

"He wouldn't dare." Cardinal Beneditti's tone was scathing. "Menenger isn't a fool, Valerio. It would bring the roof down about his ears, and he knows it. No, his ploy is to cloud the issue in every way possible. He can't afford to lose CNCD muscle."

"Then he's succeeding," said Maglione.

It was evening, and they were seated across from one another in Beneditti's private accommodation, the small apartment within the Apostolic Palace bequeathed to him for reasons of health.

"He has succeeded in some quarters, but not all," said Beneditti. "As with Peronio's convoluted attempts to discredit the codex that's been discovered, so with Borghini's campaign. But the public aren't stupid. Our politicians have schooled them endlessly in the detection of empty rhetoric. If anything, the pendulum has swung in the opposite direction."

"It is a confused sea nonetheless."

"The intelligence of ordinary men and women should not be underestimated. They are no longer the frightened sheep they used to be. It is they who will bring us to book for our crimes, they who will remind us of our frailty. The fact that Borghini failed to meet *Corriere della Sera's* challenge did not go unnoticed. To have accepted it would have been to wade into a very murky pool indeed. He could not afford to take that risk."

"You could so easily have been pope, Flavio."

"But for the will of God!" Beneditti's laugh was full of self-mockery. "Or an astronaut, if I'd obeyed my own impulses."

"Benedict is dying, Flavio. He has a brain tumor."

Cardinal Beneditti absorbed the news, then with characteristic playfulness he said, "We are everyone of us in the process of dying, Valerio. It is nothing new."

"If only you had kept news of your illness to yourself."

"And what then? The Lord would have changed his mind and loaded the dice for my benefit?"

"You know what I mean. You could have done *so* much."

Beneditti's reply was circumspect. Choosing a new pope was not unlike throwing the *I-Ching*, he said. The act of conclave opened up something deep in those who took part. It was a *seeing* rather than a choosing. Such was the nature of the Holy Spirit. The little Umbrian had had the finger of God on him.

"Has it reached you that the little Umbrian intends to visit the Holy Land at the end of August?"

The laugh that issued from Beneditti was almost coarse. "Would *I* have done such a thing, Valerio?" he asked.

"When he first voiced the idea I thought it interesting. Now I'm not so sure. He claims to have been instructed in a dream."

"Ah," said Beneditti.

"How can one argue with a dream?"

"Mary the Virgin's physical acceptance into heaven after death was the result of a dream. And made by an infallible pope to boot!"

"I've heard it said that like Joan of Arc you have your own voices."

"It's true, I do, Valerio! But the voices I hear are the voices of history clamoring for attention. My dream life is utterly banal."

"Cardinal Menenger has undergone a change of mind on the Holy Land question. He sees it now as an opportunity to establish this pontificate's spiritual credentials through pilgrimage. He wants to promote Benedict's visit to Palestine as an act of personal contrition, a grieving over his own private shortcomings in the sight of God and in the sight of man. It's Menenger's hope such an unexpected act will inspire the faithful to follow suit."

"How do you read it?"

"I'm not averse. But I am fearful Menenger will use it for his own purposes. A contrite heart before God is one thing, a will subjugated to the maniacal demands of the movements is another. If the movements are involved, which I think they would be, it could spark off scenes across Europe reminiscent of the thirteenth century."

"There's a general theory of charisms among the movements that could bolster such happenings," said Beneditti. "The founder of CNCD claims to have been bequeathed a charism, or gift, from the Mother of God: the gift of bestowing sanctity on members of the movement. But not just sanctity. In the context of CNCD the leader's charism guarantees purity of doctrine and authority. It's exactly here that it all becomes dangerous: the leader's pronouncements cannot be changed, and they cannot be questioned. Even Church authorities have to keep their distance. It's something that's even caught on here in Italy with well-established groups like Catholic Action."

"Yes, it's something to be watched," said Maglione. And then, "So much to watch over. So much."

"I could not have signed Fr Grosjean's book as pope," said Beneditti, completing his answer to a previous question. "Dying has its advantages."

"I have the feeling Benedict agrees with you."

"Had you met prior to his elevation?"

"No. He chose me on the basis of my record in the Secretariat, particularly on my time as office chief for general affairs. I was one of three equally experienced candidates to be considered. I got lucky."

"You have many other qualities, Valerio. They did not go unnoticed. You are also a first-rate diplomat."

"Your Eminence is kind to say so."

"His Eminence would like a little more white wine."

Maglione laughed and poured some wine into Beneditti's glass. Then, settling glass in hand, he asked about Fr Grosjean and the others who had signed their way into history.

"They're ready to do battle with Menenger if necessary. He must know that. His spies are everywhere. He's probably waiting for one of us to say or do something quite stupid. He's a man of considerable patience. He thinks us dolts."

"The media have been unkind to all of you at times."

"The media are by necessity Janus-faced. I've learned to live with that fact."

"In different circumstances I would have gladly added my name to that list."

They laughed at the fickleness of their situation, at the way in which moral responsibility constantly changed focus. Yes, there were constants, but circumstances could arise where even they frayed and fluttered. Beneditti offered Maglione a reminder of this fact. While acting as Apostolic Delegate to Turkey and Greece in 1934, Angelo Roncalli - later to be John XXIII - had contravened everything he had been taught by issuing false baptismal certificates to some four thousand Jews, so enabling them to escape the Nazi holocaust. Theologically, canonically, diplomatically, pietistically, he had been wrong to do so. Humanly speaking, what he had done was to the highest degree an act of love that disallowed moral rigidity. It had been an eye-opener for some.

"He was a man of enormous heart," said Maglione.

"And talent," said Beneditti. "His skills in communication were extraordinary."

Maglione nodded slowly. "As Secretary of State I'm bound hand and foot by the protocols of office," he said, his eyes on Beneditti's eyes. "I sometimes wish I weren't. I sometimes wish I could shrug it all off and do the unexpected."

You are engaged in an honorable task, Valerio. Holding the Church steady in such times is something few are fitted for. I admire your ability to juggle so many factors with such skill. Even Cardinal Menenger has been known to sing your praises."

"We are not actually enemies."

"That's as it should be."

"He is a man of strong opinions - albeit ones I consider dangerous in the present climate. But that is perhaps the reason for his attempts to stamp doctrinal certainty on everything. He fears the Church may collapse under the strain of too many opinions."

"Are you chiding me, Valerio?"

"No; I would not be so bold, Eminence. I'm merely voicing aloud the concerns of others. There are those in our midst who would question what Angelo Roncalli did in spite of its outcome. I suspect the Prefect might be one of them."

"It's the anachronisms we carry and continue to flaunt that are crushing the life out of us, Valerio, not opinions. Opinions punctuate truth, they do not constitute it."

"And schism?"

"I prefer to think that we're on the verge of a second Reformation. Schism might prove to be the necessary trigger. It all depends who gets there first. If the neoconservatives win the day, then the planet's in for a long, cold spiritual winter. I dread to think what that would be like. Imagine that kind of Catholicism informing public opinion, the havoc that would be loosed in our institutions. It would be a nightmare, Valerio, a disaster of cosmic proportions. They'd drag us all down into the pit with their mad literalisms."

"Menenger may consider making an example of you in particular. He may see excommunication as the only viable alternative to having you, the most powerful of the signatories, publicly challenge him. Robbing you of your status would cripple your ability to mount a serious challenge and act as a warning to the others."

"We've already considered that possibility. If he takes that route he faces the prospect of prelates of distinction resigning on the spot."

"You can be sure of that?"

"As sure as it's possible to be in a mad, bad world."

"As rector of the Pontifical Institute, Cardinal Borghini will rally the most able of the conservative thinkers against you. I doubt you could match him man for man?"

"We don't have to, Valerio. We won't be arguing theology. That's what Borghini and Menenger are angling for, but they aren't going to get it. At least not right away, and not in the manner they obviously hope. First and foremost we'll be arguing infiltration of the Vatican at the highest levels by movement sympathizers. Next will come a testimonial-backed barrage concerning the unconscionable practices upheld by the movements. When these practices and their repercussions are established beyond doubt, then, and only then, will we tackle the theological issues such practices raise. This is not one man against the Holy Office, Valerio, it is a group of fully experienced Curial members, many of them with law degrees, calling on the

Church to put its house in order. There has never been such a confrontation in the whole history of the Catholic Church."

Secretary of State Maglione was silent for a moment, then in a hoarse whisper, he said, "Do you *really* expect to win this joust, Flavio?"

"If we don't, then all is lost," Beneditti replied.

Part Four

Into the Lion's Den

37

A Higher Authority

The 1946 Isaac Voss edition of Ignatius of Antioch's collected letters, plus Theodore's controversial letter to the heretic Pelagius, was found quite by chance in a section of the Mar Saba library well away from its original location on Saturday afternoon, July 20. On receiving news of the find, a not exactly pleased Monsignor Rossi passed it on tersely to a relieved James Windle by telephone. A few days later, the Vatican Press Office issued a short bulletin saying that two acknowledged authorities on fourth-century documents had been dispatched by the Vatican to Jerusalem where the Codex was being held for safekeeping in the Patriarchate library. In conjunction with Israeli specialists, it was hoped the question mark hanging over the codex's authenticity would soon be removed.

That the whole bag of tricks had been spirited away by some irate monk was pretty certain - outsiders entering the monastery library were fully accounted for - but who that monk was might never be known.

Buoyed by Rossi's call, Windle rang Duggan with the good news, and after three tries managed to catch him in his office. He and Merle were about to be vindicated, he said, relishing the monsignor's discomfort. There was light on the horizon at last. His accusers would soon be silenced. Doubters, too.

Duggan had rung Windle after the Don Cooper Show, but had not spoken to him since. Giving him the gist of the *Sydney Evening Gazette* article, he said he suspected the canon lawyer he had mentioned of having entered the fray. The paper's contention that they were all possibly involved in some kind of grand conspiracy to humiliate the Catholic Church sounded like something Robert Carter would dream up. It was a bizarre claim, and almost impossible to prove, but it was also clever due to the crossover pattern of their separate investigations. As it was a likely Carter gambit, he had passed on his suspicions to David and Holly, and now counseled that Windle, too, be prepared for a similar attack.

They mulled over how to deal with that if it happened, and agreed that the *Der Spiegel* interview scheduled for later that week had come at exactly the right time. Emphasis would move back to the codex of its own volition when news of its recovery got out.

"We're lucky it wasn't just the codex itself that was moved," said Windle. "It would never have been recognized separated from the Ignatius letters."

"Question is," said Duggan, "did whoever move it know what was in it? Had they read it? Or did something alert them to its importance?"

"The latter's more likely," said Windle. "Merle and I may have been overheard discussing what we'd found. We were under-standably excited." He paused and added, "The way the codex was hidden suggests someone in a hurry, the fact it wasn't destroyed indecision over what to do with it."

"A monk struggling with his conscience?"

"Something like that."

"Merle was excited?"

"As much as Fr Merle is ever excited about anything, he was excited. He doesn't show much emotion. We knew at a glance that what we'd found was historically controversial, but not immediately to what extent. Merle's reaction was more one of amusement than anything else."

"Amusement?"

"Priest he may be; pie in the sky merchant he is not."

"You said something about Merle during our farewell dinner at the Bentleys' that interested me. You said he felt the whole point of Christianity had been lost; or words to that effect. In what sense lost?"

"Merle's catch phrase is *vitalis vigilque sopor* - 'a sleep alive and watchful'. It's a quote from Bernard de Clairvaux. Merle's a big fan.

Bernard was the first to systematically analyze and classify contemplative experience. He was very modern in his approach. It's said that he learned more about God from nature than from books."

"You wouldn't think so from some of the authorities I've read."

"He's not as well understood as he should be. Quite misunderstood in fact. There's been no close reading of his writings. What's unique about him is his ability to always find fresh ways in which to rephrase an argument, or statement. That's a telling point. He's never repetitious. He plays with words. In that sense he's highly creative, and being creative he isn't bound to fixed formulas. It's thought he may have broken with orthodoxy on a number of levels."

"He's also one of your favorites, according to Jane."

"How did that come up?"

"She presented me with a book on Bernard not long after we met; something she'd found in a second-hand shop in Height-Ashbury. It was her way of saying thank you for agreeing to help."

"She met Merle once, when she was very young. He came to New York to give a lecture and I had the pleasure of looking after him."

"Does she remember?"

"I've no idea. I've never asked. He was very taken with her. In fact he was quite fascinated by her. He seemed to know she was going to be an artist. He said as much at the time."

"Did he say how he knew?"

"No. And I didn't think to ask. I thought it was just one of those things people say. I got to know him better after that."

"And?"

"I began to realize just how unusual he was."

"In what way?"

Windle's unwillingness to go any further came across the line as a strange little sound in his throat. " . . . Not stuff for the telephone, Jack," he said at last. "Some other time, perhaps."

"No problem." Duggan changed gear. "Did you manage to catch Jane?"

"Yes. We had a long chat. She seems in good spirits."

"That's good to hear."

"I miss having her around. That was the highlight of being back in New York. Seeing her, listening to her rattle on the way she does. She's so vital in herself, so like her mother."

Duggan didn't know how to respond; it was possible Jane might end up living in Australia. Blinking that thought away, he asked how things were going in Essen.

"Better now that the codex has turned up. That was a relief to all concerned."

"They were getting shirty?"

"It was a difficult situation for everyone. Having a colleague accused of forgery is, if nothing else, embarrassing."

"Difficult times," said Duggan.

"And no telling what the future holds," said Windle. "Imagine the mess if it does prove to be a forgery!"

"You wouldn't have done what you did if you'd thought the odds were against you on that."

"Paul's nod of approval cemented it for me. His scholarship is impeccable. But let's face it, in this business forgery's always a possibility. Remote, in this case, but still possible."

It was the first time Windle had referred to Fr Merle as Paul; Duggan registered the fact without comment. "But you aren't actually having second thoughts?"

"No, no. Not at all. I'm just being appropriately paranoid. As you said, difficult times."

"You're in regular contact?"

"Yes, we are now. I spent a few days with him at the end of June. You would have enjoyed the chat. We covered a lot of territory. It turns out he's also an authority on the troubadour poets. He was interested to hear about your background."

"Maybe we'll meet someday."

"It could be arranged. You'd find him interesting."

"I don't doubt it," said Duggan.

There was a moment of hesitancy; Windle responded first.

"Anyway, got to go, Jack. It's been good to talking to you. Keep me up to date with what's going on."

* * *

Fr Timothy White's crisis of faith had resolved itself late one June evening with the exhausted cry "I BELIEVE!" roared out into the darkness of his bedroom. Gone were the words "I believe, help thou my unbelief". Having fallen into the trap of thinking that what he had previously believed about Jesus was too small and limited a concept to accommodate reality, he had given in to the complaints of reason and allowed modernism's poison to do its work. Then, suddenly, as if by way of illumination, he had realized it did not matter one whit that Catholic doctrine flew in the face of just about everything commonly thought sensible, all that mattered was one's acceptance of the sacred story locked up inside the pages of the New Testament. Surrender of the will to God's revelation about the Christ was what faith was all about; it was not a balancing act between doctrine and education. St Paul may have suggested that faith should also be reasonable, but reason, as we had come to understand it, had the bad, bad habit of exceeding its brief. He, Fr. Timothy White had lost his spiritual bearings and attempted to reconcile what could not be reconciled, but he was now at peace.

It was in this state of mind that he had contacted *Sala Stampa* and informed Cardinal Peronio that the journalist at the center of the furore in Australia was known to him, that he was in fact an ex-seminarian fully qualified to translate the Mar Saba Codex on his own. Rossi had been delighted with the news, and had plugged away at Timothy until every skerrick of scandal surrounding Duggan's suspension and dismissal was known. On putting down the phone, Timothy had stood for a moment considering his action, then gone about his business, the fact that he was annoyed with Duggan for failing to have that promised drink only barely conscious. He had done the right thing, he believed. He had helped make a crooked path straight. He had perhaps even set in motion the circumstances through which Duggan could refind the faith he had so obviously lost.

* * *

When informed by Cardinal Menenger that Benedict had had another dream in which the imperative to visit Jerusalem had been reinforced, Cardinal Maglione huffed a sigh and looked ceilingward, which was in fact to look heavenward given that the corridor's vaulted ceiling sported a painted sky, clouds and winged cherubs. He had already inquired of the Israelis as to whether such a visit was tenable, he said, and had been informed that it was not. In fact the proposal had struck the Israeli Foreign Affairs department as downright odd. A personal pilgrimage? It would hardly be that, they had argued. World attention would again be galvanized, and to what end? In the most generous of terms a visit to the Holy Land by Benedict XVI would be no more than a replay of John Paul II's visit minus the apologies. They could not quite see the point of that.

"They're beyond persuasion?" inquired Menenger.

"Hamas has stepped up its attacks; they don't expect the situation to improve."

"Benedict has all but officially announced his visit."

"A misunderstanding. We'll stress his fluency in Spanish to make up for his deficiency in English."

It was Menenger's turn to sigh; he was silent for a moment. "It feels right, Valerio."

"I remember you being of quite the opposite opinion."

"I was thinking like an Israeli; now I'm thinking like a Catholic cardinal."

"It's unlikely they'll change their mind."

"It's unlikely Benedict will change his."

"You expect a miracle?"

"I expect compromise."

The Secretary of State's smile was tinged with concern. "In the event that the Israelis won't budge, and I don't think they will, it might be wise to prepare Benedict for a letdown."

"He's being particularly stubborn over this issue."

"The Israelis invented stubborn."

"Speak with him, Valerio. Explain the difficulties, but stop short of saying that it will not happen."

"Is that fair?"

"Speak with the Israelis." Menenger's look was direct, his smile meager. "Stress the fact that a visit from Benedict would help strengthen the peace process."

"The peace process is in tatters, Eminence. It's going to take more than a token visit by Benedict to resuscitate it."

"He genuinely believes the trip to be God's will. He is as adamant in his opinion as John Paul ever was."

The Secretary of States's reply was terse. It was no doubt God's will that sin should vanish from planet Earth, and that all suffering should cease, he said, offering Menenger some off-the-cuff theology, but there was the small matter of the human will to contend with.

"His will is accomplished through our will," said Menenger, parrying with an oddly inverted reference to the Lord's prayer. "Hence the need for our will to be subject to His in all things."

Maglione decided that caution was the better part of valour and did not reply.

"Speak with His Holiness, Valerio. Assure him that all that can be done is being done."

"Of course," said Maglione, his dislike of Menenger's calculated familiarity almost discernible. "I'll arrange to see him this afternoon."

"He's free, now. I've just come from his apartment. He's having a light lunch. Ask him about his dream."

"If you think it would not be an inconvenience, Eminence."

"He likes a little company over lunch. Put the blame on me."

With that said, Menenger delivered a curt bow of the head and was on his way, his robes swishing, his gait and forward-leaning torso suggesting he already had some other business to attend to.

Maglione watched the receding figure for a moment, then, turning, he headed for the pontiff's private quarters and the task of gently leading Benedict away from his obsession. As things turned out, however, he need not have worried, for Benedict received the news of Israeli intransigence with what the Secretary of State later described as 'calm detachment'. The Lord would have his way, His Holiness said in response. It was out of everyone's hands. His reaction to the news that Hamas had upped the ante was however quite different.

"They're all as mad as one another," he rasped. "It's Jewish extremists versus Palestinians extremist with ordinary folk caught in the crossfire."

"Indeed it is, Your Holiness," said Maglione.

"It's a stalemate, Valerio. The Palestinians want their own state, they want East Jerusalem as their capital, and they want free entry for the return of Palestinian refugees and exiles. The Israelis, on the other hand, are determined to retain military control over the whole of the Holy Land, particularly Jerusalem, and their hardliners find it all but impossible to conceive of an independent Palestinian state, never mind the need to dismantle all Jewish settlements on the West Bank and the Gaza Strip. I ask you, how can such a situation be resolved without God's help?"

"Your Holiness has understood the heart of the problem exactly," said Maglione, surprised by Benedict's fluency. "It's the extremists that have created the present impasse."

"Yet prior to World War I Christian, Jew and Muslim lived in relative harmony. Each had their own quarter within the walls of the Old City. Each followed their religion and respected the religion of the other. Harmony is possible."

"Indeed," said Maglione. "It was decisions made later by the Western conquerors that undermined that harmony."

"The Western conquerors are in the process of learning that domination by force may quell violence for a time, but that it cannot initiate a lasting peace."

"Jerusalem is the fault-line between two great civilizations," said Maglione, quoting something he had read. "In that sense it is a microcosm of the world at large. Its tensions are our tensions. Its descent into chaos is our descent into chaos."

"That is my fear," said Benedict.

The Secretary of State hesitated, then he said, "I had no idea you were so interested in Middle Eastern politics, Your Holiness."

"I sense a calamity in the making. It disturbs me."

"As a result of your dream?"

"A general sense of unease that has accompanied my dreams, Valerio. I am sometimes overpowered by it."

"I am informed by Cardinal Menenger that you have had a second dream, Your Holiness. May I inquire as to its nature?"

"You may," said Benedict. Turning from Maglione, he picked up a sliver of apple from off his plate. Then, glancing at the Secretary of State, he said, "There was nothing at all grand about it to start with, just a feeling of great peace. I was somewhere in Rome, some back street or other, and on my own. It was late evening and very dark. The street was deserted. There was a flash. I looked up and saw a large, brilliant star on the horizon. As I watched, it began to move in my direction, getting bigger and bigger as it approached. Then, suddenly, it was at the end of the street and travelling towards me, all the while growing in size and changing in color. It was magnificent and totally silent, Valerio, a huge flame of a thing moving through the sky with silent intent. That's when I realized it was intelligent, that in some inexplicable sense the flame was a being of great power, and that it was speaking to me personally."

Secretary of State Maglione watched the Pontiff struggle with the memory of what he had experienced. Then the grey eyes swiveled to meet his.

"It was *so* real it astonishes me to think of it, Valerio. I realized fully in that moment that we are not alone in this forbidding place. That we are, as the Scriptures say, surrounded by a cloud of witnesses."

"You felt this dream was in some way related to the other dream?"

"By the very fact that it had happened, yes, Valerio."

"It spoke to your heart?"

"It *ravished* my heart, Valerio!"

There was a silence. Valerio Cardinal Maglione, Secretary of State and guardian of the Church's welfare in a mad, bad world, stared at Benedict XVI in much the same way as Cardinal Menenger had done. Then, after a respectful pause, he said, "If Your Holiness pleases, I'll refer the matter of your Jerusalem visit to a higher authority." To which Benedict replied, "It is already in the hands of a higher authority, Valerio."

38

Complicated Times

James Windle's *Der Spiegel* interview went well, but not quite so well a television interview set up soon after by *Die Welt*, a top-ratings German news program with a reputation for straight talking. Hosted by Wolfgang Pauli, a sallow-faced, dark-haired, dark-suited, white-shirted individual with far too much cuff showing, *Die Welt's* approach to the codex came as something of a surprise. Windle, Pauli advised his Germany-wide audience, had written an article for the *New York Times* in '88 critical of Israel's handing of the Palestinian question, an article considered harsh and unhelpful by many American Jews. So what had prompted him to say what he had said? Why the sudden pro-Palestinian outburst? Why the lapse in scholarly impartiality?

Backed by silent archival footage showing unrest in the West Bank and on the Gaza Strip during the Spring of '88, Windle admitted to venting his ire over the killing of more than one hundred Palestinians by Israel's security forces. He had felt duty-bound to offer an historical overview to help even up the playing field, he said. Israel had every right to defend herself against attack, and there was no excusing the many unconscionable acts perpetrated against her by fanatics, but the history of the region was such that some hard thinking was required on the question of land possession and much else. Anyone familiar with the history of the Middle East between 1917 and 1948 knew, or ought to know, that the Palestinians had as much right to a homeland as their Jewish neighbors. The loathing and hatred generated as a result of innocent Israelis being slaughtered on buses, in cafes and at checkpoints was understandable, but the raging of Jewish fundamentalists, the building of illegal settlements and the rhetoric of the Israel's right-wing politicians had also played their part in the debacle. Given the mounting climate of violence on both sides - a violence now showing signs of spiraling out of control - he had thought it expedient to remind everyone of a few simple historical fact. To his way of thinking, that was not a lapse in impartiality, it was a balancing of the books."

"Would you also classify as impartial your aiding and abetting of the Australian journalist responsible for publishing the now infamous Mar Saba Codex?"

"We live in complicated times. I respond as best I can."

"So your teaming up with the Australian journalist wasn't just another example of a career punctuated by unguarded moments?"

"I don't think that's quite how my career is generally perceived."

"Your judgment has been questioned in relation to the Mar Saba Codex, and your pro-Palestinian article in the *New York Times* suggests, . . . impetuosity?"

"It was my duty as a historian to help set the historical record straight. With regard to the Australian, I was faced with a scholarly *fait accompli*. His translation was going to be published whatever I decided. To avoid a potentially misleading translation reaching the public, I agreed to vet it. He approached me in good faith; I responded in kind. It was to his credit that he even bothered to contact me."

"You're quoted as saying it was a very good translation. How good was it?"

"It was a very good translation indeed. There were differences aplenty in phrasing, but that's to be expected. As in any language, the same thing can be said in more than one way. But there's a limit. A single word can also have more than one meaning depending on context. In translation, context is all. A good translation requires more than skill, it requires a kind of artistry to determine meaning."

"So it wasn't that you saw an opportunity to speed up the process because you were annoyed with the Vatican's embargo on publication?"

Windle's laugh was uneasy. "There's no denying that I thought sooner was better than later. With the codex missing and little chance of it being recovered, it was a foregone conclusion that a translation wouldn't surface for months, perhaps even years."

"Yet you thought it should be made available to the public in spite of the original document being lost. Wasn't that a bit foolhardy?"

"You're overlooking the fact that Professor Merle and I handled the codex. We studied it at first hand. All the others have had to go on are photographs. Good photographs, but photographs nonetheless. We were as sure of the codex's authenticity when we left Mar Saba as it's possible to be outside of ink and paper tests."

"Which are now being run."

"Thankfully, yes."

"But even then you would have been taking a bit of risk on everything working out in your favor. You still are. Why take such a risk? Forgery is still being mooted. You yourself have been accused of colluding with others to humiliate the Catholic Church. The Australian journalist lied about his role in the whole affair. You withheld the fact that Mr Duggan was skilled enough to translate the document himself. I ask you, what are people to think?"

"First, forgery is highly unlikely - it would require the collusion of so many experts it's a ridiculous suggestion. Second, the idea of my colluding with others against the Catholic Church would be laughable if it weren't so pathetic. My fear was that interminable delays in publication would undermine the codex's stature. Out of sight, out of mind, kind of thing. It was a ploy used to withhold and diminish the importance of The Dead Sea Scrolls, and I saw the codex heading in the same direction. Truth is, there are those who would be only too pleased to see Theodore's most interesting letter sink without trace."

"I take it you're referring to the Vatican's Department of Antiquities?"

"No, I'm not. Not specifically. It was they who funded our research program, but it would be ingenuous of me to ignore the fact that some specialists in that department view the codex as dangerous in terms of faith and doctrine. Some would tend to dismiss its contents as spurious on the grounds that it does not support the Church's historical claims. They would hunt out an excuse to reject its findings. Do I have to remind you that most of these specialists are churchmen? It stands to reason that some would find Theodore of Mopsuestia's explorations threatening. I'm not blaming them for that, merely pointing out a fact of life."

"You were brought up Catholic. Is that correct?"

"It is. But only nominally so. I was brought up to respect both faiths. I do respect them."

"Back in '88 Israel's ambassador to Bonn said that Germans had every right to criticize Israel so long as they were tactful about it. Do you think your comments back in '88 were tactful?"

"I'm not German, I'm a New Yorker born and bred."

"Your parents were German, you are presently speaking fluent German, you are a professor doing research in a German university. Your criticism of Israel in '88 was penned while here in Germany and syndicated via *The New York Times* to German newspapers. It was comments made here in Germany by Jitzhak Ben-Ari, Israel's envoy, that sparked your fiery response. Need I say more?"

"Hardly fiery. And you know as well as I do that what I wrote was not directed at the Jewish nation as a whole; it was a carefully considered criticism of the then-Israeli government's over-sensitive tendency to dismiss any criticism of its West Bank and Gaza Strip policies as *tactless*. Only Germans who had no responsibility for the holocaust were given the right to criticize, and then only if they too were *tactful*. Well, I'm sorry, but that didn't apply to me. My Jewish grandparents died in the holocaust and I considered myself then, and consider myself now, to have every right in the world to speak my mind on issues affecting a nation for whom I have the greatest respect. End of story."

Without wavering, Wolfgang Pauli changed course. Was it respectful to suggest, he wanted to know, that some Vatican specialists would feel so threatened by the Mar Saba Codex as to willfully deny it credence?"

Windle shook his head and ploughed on. It was just how things were, he said. If you accepted the Christian message of salvation through Christ, then you tended to question or dismiss what didn't support that message.

"Are you anti-Christian in your beliefs, Professor? Do you actively dislike Christianity?"

"I dislike historical distortion wherever it turns up. If it turns up in a Christian context, then I name it for what it is."

"There must be times when the other side, for want of a better term, is right, and you are wrong."

"You're mixing categories. There's a helluva difference between disagreeing over some fact or other, and disallowing what may be a perfectly respectable set of facts because they somehow contradict the tenets of your faith. *That* is not the same thing at all."

"Preconceived idea aren't always religious."

"No, they aren't, but they're more likely to impede exploration and discovery if they are. My preconceived ideas - call them prejudices if you like - can and must change when strong evidence to the contrary is presented. As a historian I have no option but to change my mind if the evidence is strong enough. That does not generally apply to religious prejudice. The tendency of religious prejudice is to envelope the problem in convoluted explanations. The three Abrahamic faiths would be other than they are if that weren't the case"

"Christianity is historically distorted in your opinion?"

"Elements of Christianity have quite obviously suffered distortion, there's hardly a scholar in the world who would deny that. It's the hazard all three Abrahamic faiths have to deal with as they try to understand their history through the prism of a developed theology, or mythology. All the great religions face the same problem. Theology does not fall from heaven; it develops out of the view that God involves Himself in history. That is not a view professional historians dare take on board. The origins of

Christianity cry out for re-evaluation for that very reason."

"Not a few American Jews found your *New York Times* article in '88 very confronting. Some found it downright offensive. It re-evaluated the Middle East crisis and all but said that Israel should pull its head in. That didn't go down well. You were accused by some of being an Arab-lover. How did you react to that?"

"I was annoyed. Bloody annoyed, to be frank. All I'd done was lay out the factual story of how we had all arrived at this mess, a story that is on record for anyone with the inclination to read it. I expected a sensible debate and got shouted down for my efforts. The din drowned out the voices of Jews who thought like myself."

"You keep talking about facts as if they're solids of some kind. But they aren't, are they. Like beauty, facts are often in the eye of the beholder."

"The Balfour Declaration is on record. It is an indisputable fact. So also is a letter to the Emir of Mecca from the British government promising independence to the Arabs in 1915. These are the kinds of facts I'm referring to. And so with the Mar Saba Codex. Many of the things alluded to in Theodore's letter are only now beginning to surface as facts of history, facts that have either been distorted or ignored because they didn't fit in with the Christian paradigm. It's a time of reassessment all round. Hence my interest in making sure the codex doesn't end up discarded for all the wrong reasons."

"You've been referred to as a revisionist historian by some biblical scholars. Isn't that almost an insult to someone like yourself?"

"It's my job to reconsider the past. It's an inescapable necessity. Sometimes that requires me to question things that seem beyond question. With regard to Israel, it *seems* beyond question that Israel is in the right and that the Palestinian Arabs are in the wrong. But that's only to look at the surface of the situation; it's to see it only in terms of what's happening now. But the past is there. It's in the veins of young Palestinians. It's in the beating of their hearts. As a people flung together by circumstances, they're now at the end of their tether. That does not justify terrorism morally, but it does explain it psychologically. The Palestinians have reached a point of no return. The irrational anger seething in their hearts and minds *is* irrational *because* the facts of history have been ignored. These facts are still being ignored. Hence the brutality, the mindless killing, the unwillingness to listen to reason. It's a form of mental anarchy and its roots are buried deep in the debris of broken promises and smashed dreams."

"Eloquently put, Professor, but you must have known you would be attacked for questioning the legitimacy of a Jewish homeland. "

"I didn't question the legitimacy of a Jewish homeland. What I questioned was the legitimacy of the whole of Palestine being converted into a Jewish homeland. That was not the original intention."

"Didn't the Second World war make an extended Jewish homeland inevitable?"

"It complicated an already complicated situation. You have to go back to 1921 to understand the present debacle. The British view at that time was that a homeland for Jews should be founded *in* Palestine, not that the whole of Palestine become a Jewish homeland. That had been implicit in the Balfour Declaration of 1917. The problem in 1921 was that the British government rejected Arab demands to repudiate the Balfour Declaration in spite of anti-Zionist riots in Jaffa over immigration and land purchases made by the Jewish National Fund. That's when the eviction of Arab peasants started. In 1922 the League of Nations accepted the Balfour Declaration, stressed the historical connection of the Jews with Palestine, and in that moment Palestine became a political entity aligned with Jewish needs. These needs were real enough, but so also were the needs of the indigenous Palestinians. The Arab proposal in 1921 was for a national government and parliament democratically elected by the country's Muslims, Christians and Jews. If that route had been taken things would be very different today, as would they be if Britain had kept its promise of independence for Palestinian Arabs in 1915."

"Is it not a case of what's done is done? You can't hope to turn the clock back."

"No, I can't, but that does not mean we shouldn't acknowledge what happened in the past. A modicum of understanding could modify attitudes sufficiently for a proper dialogue to begin. The present hostilities stem from mistakes made by the British government. They not only reneged on their promise of independence to the Arabs, they progressively ignored Arab needs and allowed the legitimate need of a Jewish homeland *in* Palestine to turn into something quite other than what had earlier been proposed. It took until 1930 for the Brits to wake up to their mistake and call a halt to Jewish immigration. That's why they did it. But things had gone too far by then."

"The British did try to stem Jewish immigration. Didn't they sink two Jewish refugee ships?"

"That tragedy took place much later. The *Patria* was sunk in November 1940, the *Struma* in February 1942. And so was born the Irgun and the Stern Gang, small but effective Jewish terrorist groups. Their activities culminated in the assassination of Lord Moyne, British minister of state in Cairo in 1944. But to return to the point. The royal commission set up in 1930 by the British acknowledged that the Arabs had not been fairly treated, but as a result of pressure from the Zionist lobby in London, those findings were nullified by the then British prime minister, Ramsay MacDonald. Three years later the persecution of Jews across Europe made a Jewish national home imperative. Between 1933 and 1936 Jewish immigration into Palestine was such that the Arabs revolted. Between 1936 and 1939 things got so tense that 20,000 British troops were shipped into the country to hold the peace. It's estimated that during this three-year period more than 5,000 Arabs were killed, fifteen thousand wounded and thousands imprisoned."

"You're placing a lot of faith on people understanding and appreciating the past. Is that likely, given the mess the Middle East is in at this moment?"

"If both sides are allowed to forget the historical origins of the problems they have, then I dread to think where they'll end up." Windle sighed out his frustration. "Problem-solving isn't always a matter of working from the present towards the future. You sometimes have to decrystallize before you can crystallize. That's the problem facing New Testament scholars. That's why the Mar Saba Codex is so damned important. His writings are a window into the past."

"It's one man's view against the many."

"That man just happened to be a Christian bishop and one of the best minds of his generation. What he has to say shouldn't be ignored. There were others who thought like he did. Some of the most important questions being discussed in the fourth century were first mooted by Theodore of Mopsuestia."

"He was nominated a heretic."

"He asked the right questions."

"But came up with the wrong answers."

"In the view of conservative thinkers, yes."

Wolfgang Pauli smiled and returned to his previous topic. Hadn't Windle also been attacked for suggesting that the Palestinians did not have a common ethnic origin?

"I was under the impression the point of this interview was to speak about the codex."

"Not just the codex. If this interview has a point, a central point, it is to find out what makes you tick as a man, Professor. Your character has been impugned, your way of handling things called in question. You've been accused of colluding in forgery and much else. You're passionate and sometimes dangerously outspoken. Need I say more?"

"I try to tell it as it is. That is not always easy."

"And sometimes unwise."

"In the eyes of some."

On the monitor, Windle's face filled the screen. Pauli paused to allow Windle's discomfort to clearly register.

"Statements made by you over the last few years show you to be anti-Church if not actually anti-Christian in your views, Professor. That could hardly be called a strength, given your profession."

"We're at a crossroads in biblical scholarship. I'm one historian among many trying to reassemble a giant jigsaw puzzle that's taken two thousand years to get into the mess that it's in. That sometimes requires a bit of push and shove. The sky is where the ground should be. The trees are upside down. The windows and doors have swapped places. Most of the bits are there with which to build a coherent picture of the past, but their placement has been governed by an overview which bedevils researchers at every turn. That overview is theology, the so-called queen of the sciences, and it has systematically blocked rigorous scholarship from making the necessary adjustments and modifications Christianity so urgently needs at the end of the twentieth century."

"You seem to see Judaism in a similar light."

"I do. My Jewish father alerted me to the problems inherent in Judaism. Islam is in the same boat. All three Abrahamic faiths need to take a hard look at themselves."

"And the Palestinians?"

"Case in point," said Windle. "The Palestinians are a reflection of the region's history. They are at once Roman, Byzantine, Arab, Crusader and Turk. The Jews are in much the same boat. All one has to do is take a close look at the history of ancient Israel. Israel was a fusion of indigenous Canaanites, Aramaean tribes and other ethnic groups. Solomon's boast at having many foreign wives says it all, and the prophet Ezra's consternation over intermarriage practiced by those who escaped the Exile helped Judaism - Ezra's own creation - to displace Israelite monotheism. That's where the Jewish idea of racial purity stems from: from a promise made in writing to obey the law and keep away from the women of other cultures. The problem isn't ethnicity in the sense of the Jews being purebred and everyone else being mongrel, the problem is and always was *land possession.*

It's land possession that gives both the Palestinians and the Jews their sense of coherence, their sense of unity, and it's land possession that has bedeviled both cultures for centuries. The peace process initiated by Shimon Peres was known as 'Land for Peace' for that very reason."

"God didn't bequeath the Holy Land to the Jews?"

"I've always had difficulty with a God who dishes out real estate to His favorites."

"That's an interesting perspective."

"It's what Jews of a radical religious bent have believed for centuries, and it's what Jewish fundamentalists believe today. But not all Jews are religious fundamentalists. Many aren't religious at all. The idea of a God who muddles about inside history and hands out parcels of land is now being seriously questioned. Both Christians and Jewish scholars are taking a close look at that one. Anyway, in terms of land-grab, it isn't just a matter of Jew versus Arab, is it? Christian Palestinians constitute about ten per cent of the population. They trace their ancestry back to the Byzantine period when the whole of Palestine was Christian. Or the Druses, for that matter. There are around 200,000 of them separated from one another on the borders of Lebanon, Syria, Jordan and Israel. So what belongs to whom, and to what extent? They're all descendants of people who have long inhabited Palestine. And that's to overlook the Samaritan remnant. If any group can lay claim to continuity, they can. They've retained their identity through all the periods of history right down to the present. Problem is, there's only about five hundred of them left."

Wolfgang Pauli paused, then in a soft, almost intimate voice he said, "So what exactly are you trying to tell us, Professor?"

"I'm saying that everyone and no one has the right to claim precedence in the Holy land. Holy the land might be, but the acts of barbarity being perpetrated on it are anything but holy. That ought to tell us something."

"You expect people to discard their religious beliefs?"

"Hardly. What I'd like to see them do is explore the historical and theological contradictions embedded in their religious beliefs - that's a task their religious leaders ought to be helping them with. They aren't. If all your religion does is cause endless conflict with your neighbor - and I'm pointing the finger at both Arab and Jewish hardliners - then there's something intrinsically wrong with your religious ideas. I have a wonderful example of that. It's on record that in 1841 nearly all British Anglican bishops were in favor of converting Jews to Christianity to speed up the Second Advent. So was born the Jew's Society under the Earl of Shaftsbury. In alignment with the aims of this society, Lord Palmerson, the then British Foreign Secretary, backed the idea of Jewish settlement in Palestine for his persecuted *fellow Jews* in Poland and Russia. In that moment, Christian and Jewish aspiration amalgamated to produce a hybrid situation that steadily ran out of control. That's a perfect example of how religious ideas can inadvertently produce mayhem further down the track."

"There isn't a grand religious truth superior to all others?"

"I doubt very much there's any such thing."

"God does not interfere in history?"

"God is by definition transcendent. I think that speaks for itself."

"He isn't interested in what we get up to?"

"I very much doubt it."

"We are all alone in an uncaring universe?"

"It's perhaps our job to do the caring."

Delivering his second smile of the evening, Wolfgang Pauli thanked Windle for participating and turned towards one of the two cameras that had covered their interaction. Professor Windle had given them a wealth of things to think about, he said, glancing at Windle appreciatively. To which Windle gruffly replied off camera, "A little thought is all it takes".

39

Freedom

"The Holy Father is no where to be found."

Cardinal Menenger looked up at the Secretary of State uncomprehendingly.

"He isn't in the Apostolic Palace, Eminence."

"He must be!"

A shake of the head from Cardinal Maglione. He and two others had checked every conceivable location and got nowhere. The search continued as they spoke.

"What are you saying to me?"

Maglione remained silent.

"He's gone off somewhere on his own? How? When?"

"His bed hasn't been slept in."

"What!"

"I fear the worst, Eminence."

Cardinal Menenger did not reply; he had already considered the same extraordinary possibility.

"He's not yet well enough known to be recognized. If he uses his old passport he might just get away with it."

"Pray God there's another explanation, Valerio."

"If his passport's gone, then we have a crisis of unimaginable proportions on our hands."

As if afraid to respond, Menenger covered his mouth with the fingers of his right hand and slumped back into the black leather of his chair - it was as if he were signaling secrecy.

The Secretary of State continued with his assessment. They could not, indeed should not, alert the civil authorities. The Italian police were notoriously talkative. Maglione glanced to his right as if expecting some invisible personage to reply, some divine voice to instruct him further. When the grey-green eyes returned to

Menenger's angular face, it was to articulate the thought already in Menenger's head: the Vatican's own domestic police force, the Vigilanza, were insufficiently expert to deal with such a delicate and potentially explosive matter. Criminal investigations were one thing, a missing pope was quite another.

Cardinal Menenger was in agreement. If the Holy Father's old passport was missing, he would speak with the General Secretary and have him inform the Italian Secret Service. There was nothing else for it. He would also speak with Fr Gozzoli, Benedict's private secretary and known confidant. If anyone knew what was going on in Benedict's mind, he probably did. Menenger smiled and added the gratuitous observation that Fr Gozzoli was related to the famous Tuscan artist Benozzo Gozzoli, and that he, too, had exhibited a certain talent for the canvas. The smile evaporated. But first they must make sure the Holy Father was actually missing, and not merely mislaid. A further search of the Apostolic Palaces would be carried out by senior Vigilanza. For what if the Holy Father had merely wandered off and was lying unconscious in some dark corner.

"I think that unlikely," said Maglione.

"As unlikely as him leaving this building unobserved?" Menenger's smile was dismissive.

The Secretary of State acknowledged Cardinal Menenger's point with a tilt of the head.

"If anyone asks, Valerio . . . His Holiness has the flu and is confined to his quarters. Have the nuns who attend him briefed to that effect." Menenger got to his feet and stood in silence for a moment. Then, with a weary shake of the head, he said, "May the Lord have mercy on all of us."

* * *

Fr Merle welcomed Fr Grosjean into his Sorbonne office with just a hint of a smile; the pupil had returned to his teacher. Suspended from his post at Gregorian University, the philosopher/priest had headed for France, and home, but had decided *en route* to consult with Fr Merle in Paris.

"It's rumored Cardinal Beneditti may be excommunicated for incitement to schism," Grosjean said, when they were settled. "It's a cunning charge. It would get Beneditti out of Menenger's hair and partially defuse the growing row over CNCD. With Beneditti gone the others may well capitulate."

"Saints have been thrown out of the Church for less," said Merle. He laughed and added, "As for Their Eminences, this will test their mettle. If they falter . . ."

"Schism is not an attractive alternative."

"That is the substance of the threat posed by the combined signatures in your book. There's no precedent for such a move."

"We expected a more circumspect response."

"From Cardinal Menenger?"

"He's shifted the focus away from why this situation has arisen, to how those involved have responded. He doesn't seem to understand what's at stake."

"He perhaps understands only too well. He smells a return to the bad old days when the Holy Father's whims were tempered by the episcopate in Council. He is an advocate of maniacal certainty. We talked of this before, you may remember. Menenger believes almost ruthlessly in *plenitudo potestatis* - the fullness of power. To his way of thinking all human beings are subject to the Pontiff's will."

The words of Pius V's rendition of Boniface's fourteenth-century conception of papal power rose in Grosjean's memory like sharpened spikes. He intoned them, and felt a shiver pass through the nape of his neck. 'He who reigns in heaven and on Earth, gave the one Holy Catholic and Apostolic Church, out of which there is no salvation, to be governed, in the fullness of authority, to one man only, that is to say, to Peter, the Prince of the Apostles and to his successors, the Roman Pontiff. This one ruler He established as prince over all nations and kingdoms, to root up, destroy, dissipate, scatter, plant and build . . .'"

"And so they continue to face one another across the divide of centuries, Father. I suspect it will always be so."

"Beneditti is attempting to break through that impasse."

"It surprises me he found so many backers."

"He is revered."

"As long as he doesn't turn into an alternative pope." Merle's glance was accentuated by his rimless spectacles, which were perched low on the bridge of his nose, and by the dipping of his head. "The Adversary is forever looking for an opening."

"I think that unlikely," said Grosjean, well aware that Merle's use of 'Adversary' was metaphorical. "What I fear is Menenger's ability to turn this situation to his advantage. He would have us believe that CNCD and its parallels are a sign of pluralism in the Church, a sign of liberty, and not bondage. He admits that excesses have been committed, then immediately clouds the issue with rubbery statements like *the tonality of the movements is more charismatic than functional.* I ask you! Have you ever heard such tripe? And Cardinal Borghini has taken to supporting his every utterance."

"It's their way of controlling the laity and annulling the move towards democratization. Allow the laity a voice and the game of centuries is all but up. The late Holy Father's wishes are still operative. He spoke of loosing whatever *needed* to be loosed in the vast sphere of the laity. That was code for insert the bulk of the laity into the movements and bring them under control."

"The old guard is driven by the divide they perceive between professed faith and daily life," said Grosjean, all but quoting from his book. "It's an obsession. Daily life is interpreted as pernicious, as rotten to the core. They are life-haters, Father. Menenger has christened the laity's move towards democracy as *clericalization.* In Vatican-speak that's don't for one second think you, the ordinary person, has the right to tinker with Church government." Grosjean's gaze dropped to the floor, then returned to Fr. Merle's face. "The third World Congress for the Apostolate of the laity held in '67 sent shock waves through the Church. Delegates representing the laity called for a greater degree of democratization and elected representation. There hasn't been a gathering like it since. Even the authority of priests and bishops is being eroded as the movements grow in strength. That's only now becoming evident. Problem is, most senior clergy take the movements at face value. They accept what the movements say about themselves. The joke doing its rounds a few months back was that new wine bursts old wineskins. I had that said to me when I complained about the behavior of the movements."

"Human beings as the play-things of God," said Merle. "What would be the point if that were the case?"

"Cosmic chess," said Grosjean.

"It's all out in the open now. Thank you for sending me a copy of your excellent book."

"It was the least I could do." Grosjean's gaze returned to the pattern on the rather worn Persian carpet. "I didn't expect suspension for my efforts."

"Limbo is a region on the border of hell where one is expected to consider one's mistakes."

"My book was not a mistake. I stand by everything I wrote."

"The signatures it carries challenge the prevailing power bloc. Your text has been elevated to the level of a Lutheran slap in the face. You have earned Cardinal Menenger's attention, and that is seldom for the best."

"The Holy Father hasn't commented on the book's claims."

"He may not be aware of its existence. He is no more than a breath between factional bouts."

"Cardinal Borghini is supporting Menenger at every turn."

"That surprises you?" Fr Merle's laugh was hearty. "The Pontifical Institute jealously guards doctrinal purity via the Holy Office; it is an extension of Menenger's brain. Borghini and his underlings safeguard the faith by warding off attacks from scientists, archaeologists, linguists, Semitic scholars and Bible theologians. People like ourselves, in other words. In conjunction with the

Department of Antiquities the Institute forms a bulwark against modernism's attempt to rewrite the Christian imagination. It is they who have supplied Cardinal Peronio with much of his reasoning on the codex. They've also helped hound my American colleague with carefully constructed objections and convoluted counter-offensives."

"They've left you alone."

"They have little interest in me. It's Professor Windle they're after. He has become the focus of their ire."

"You've continued to support the American."

"I've continued to support the codex, but will defer to the collective wisdom of my peers if their findings can be shown to be the more accurate. I'm not a one-man band, Father. I cannot dictate the nature of truth."

"That's perhaps what I've tried to do with my book."

"In moments of weakness it's what we all try to do. Even popes. " A smile from Merle. "It's a good book, Father. Don't despair."

"Do you think I have a soul?"

"Do *you* think you have one?"

"I don't know how to answer that. I feel empty. I don't think I've ever felt this empty."

"You can't abandon the intellect until the intellect knows why it must be abandoned. That's an emptiness to be desired. Their emptiness is altogether different - it is driven by fear. They've read the entrails of birds and noted their own probable demise."

"In spite of everything they think the movements are the answer? How can they possibly entertain such an idea?"

"Because the movements are the only corrective they're left with; they're still trying to contain what they conceive of as the chaos of exultation and irresponsibility let loose by John XXIII's pontificate. In their view, John XXIII gambled on his charisma of love accomplishing what Pius XII failed to accomplish with his charisma of power, namely, unity of the faithful. In their opinion John XXIII opened the sluice-gate of nonconformity. In an attempt to sustain the illusion of unity, Paul VI chose the charisma of unity as his archetype, but in the wake of John XXIII's endeavors it quickly fizzled out; it could not halt the breakdown in authority and jurisdiction unleashed by the Second Ecumenical Council. That's what the present situation is all about. It's about wresting back the Church's ancient right to decide what is right and what is wrong on behalf of the individual."

"John XXIII initiated a movement of the Spirit that breathed new life into the Church."

"Not for Cardinal Menenger it didn't. He and his fellow prelates - which was most of the Roman Curia after the debacle of Paul VIs reign - felt a cold breath on their necks and knew immediately what lay ahead. All they could see was looming nonconformity, irresponsibility, disintegration and chaos. In their interpretation of events it wasn't the Spirit of God that had been loosed, it was a disabling spirit. It was, in other words, the Adversary up to his old tricks."

"How can they give their unconditional blessing to the movements knowing what they now have been forced to acknowledge?"

"Because they don't see what you and I see. They see unity in shreds, obedience abandoned, sacred communities secularized. They see the one Holy and Catholic Apostolic Church dying amidst a plethora of freedoms - false freedoms in their estimation."

"That doesn't give them the right to brutally coerce whole congregations to their way of thinking!"

" Shock troops are intended to shock, Father. The neo-conservatives are willing to turn a blind eye to excess because they know only excessive zeal can put the Church back on its old authoritarian path. Fear works wonders. It's all or nothing as far as they're concerned. When the dust settles on your book and its claims, the conservatives, believing that all is well again, will fall back into stride with their neoconservative brethren as if nothing has happened. But of course nothing, or very little, will have changed. And that's not to mention those who haven't even noticed that there is a problem. The neoconservatives believe they can ride out this storm. I'm not so sure. Not this time. Not in this day and age. The bulk of people are no longer susceptible to their nonsense. They'll end up huddled around a corpse, the corpse of a faith hardly anyone can believe in any longer."

Fr Grosjean's gaze returned to the carpet; his own faith was in tatters, and he knew it. His gaze leveled again. "Maybe they're right. I've lost everything I once held dear."

"Being empty isn't so bad," said Fr Merle. "Emptying is ultimately what the faith is all about. If the only choice we have is between an emotionally-driven certainty and an arrogant intellectualism that leaves us as brittle as an autumn leaf, then we are indeed lost. Neither state is worth a button. As I said to you the last time we met, we are mostly unconscious while consciously engaged. Which means we're not all that different from our pre-conscious ancestors. Unlike them, however, we can and do wake up at intervals."

"Surely we have no option but to consciously attend to things. Self-consciousness disrupts our ability to *do*."

"And a submerged sense of self disrupts our ability to *be*," said Fr Merle. "Is that really the best way in which to live a life? Epiphanius observes that the second-century Ophite-Nazoraeans had an excellent grasp of how the human senses worked. They used a code. 'Paradise' was the head, 'Eden' was the brain, 'Heaven' was the brain's hemispheres. The human senses were likened to a river with branches flowing out of Eden. The eye was the river Phison. The ear was the river Geon. The breath was the river Tigris. Egypt equaled the evil of matter."

"I don't accept that matter is evil."

"It can be conceived of as such if you keep getting lost in it! "

Fr Grosjean's frown returned.

"Usurped by the world, Father - that's all I mean by that. These ancient explorers equated 'being' lost in matter with being dead, with being deadened to the experience of our own aliveness. This is quite literally the death of being you philosophers talk of in such convoluted terms. To surface from the death of being is to experience a momentary resurrection of the self to the self. It is to sustain the experience of resurrection, the experience of *coming back to life* for a few seconds at a time. Problem is, Father, we are so enthralled by the world and its demands we find it difficult to detect our plight."

"This is what you've come to believe is important?"

"Yes."

"But it can't really be otherwise, can it?"

"Conscious *of*, but not conscious *as*," said Fr Merle, annunciating the words carefully. Then came a bold evaluation that made Grosjean wince. "You're empty because you've swapped the outside for the inside. You've been turned outside in and haven't noticed. Your interiority has been usurped by the external world to such an extent you think thinking about the external world equals having an inner life. It doesn't. It's a lie. It's a misreading of reality. The 'I am' of your being is not properly in place. 'Recognize what is before your eyes, and what is hidden will be revealed to you.' That's a quote from the Gospel of Thomas. The person who wrote those words was *wide awake.*"

"I hear what you're saying, but I don't understand the words."

"That's how it is. You either get it, or you don't."

"You could say that about any idea."

"It isn't an *idea*, Father; it's a change in perception. Dullards and geniuses experience the same level of difficulty in comprehending it. As experiences go, it is truly democratic."

"Resurrection still seems a rather inflated term for it."

"It's an entirely new faculty of attention coming on line. It's what was once understood as the Christian *gnosis*. It's what the early Fathers understood as the struggle of prayer. It's what St Paul calls *the renewing of the mind.*"

"That flies in the face of everything we've been taught."

"It's the Christianity behind Christianity. It's what's been lost to doctrinalized Christianity for centuries."

Grosjean looked away for a moment. Then he looked back at Fr

Merle, and said, "What you're saying suggests that our most concerted efforts to lead a spiritual life amount to very little in real terms."

"We've sold our birthright for a mess of pottage, Father. We're worlded and worded out to such an extent that the outer has all but replaced the inner. We spend most of our time talking or arguing with imaginary people in our heads. Or dreaming of success in our profession. Or of having lots of money. Or of gratifying sex. And if we get round to thinking about our spiritual welfare at all, it's generally in terms of what to believe or what not to believe. That isn't to have an inner life. That is to be usurped and fooled and led away from ever realizing that's there's a problem to be solved."

"But thoughts and feelings are all we have. They're what makes us human. They're what differentiates us from the animals. We *know* what we think, and we *know* what we feel. That has to mean something!"

"And if our thoughts and feelings are no more than reactions to external stimuli, experiences and sensations had while consciously usurped by the flow of events? What then?"

"They're still part of our inner life."

"Correction. They have taken the place of our inner life. We engage with them and disappear into them as readily as we do while looking at a pen or a sunset. There's no intrinsic difference, Father. Engagement is engagement is engagement. We have to wake up *out of* our submerged state of mind, and that means being resurrected *along side* our thoughts and emotions. The moment we subjectively engage with them, we're at their mercy."

"And if we do manage to wake up?"

"Then we have our first real taste of freedom, the freedom Christ promised us."

Fr Grosjean's reply was slow in coming. Hesitantly he said, "You've managed to integrate this kind of thinking with your faith?"

A shake of the head from Merle. It was not a matter of integrating anything with anything, he said. It was a matter of experiencing that freedom and appreciating its far-reaching implications. When those implications dawned on you, fully dawned on you, the rest took care of itself.

* * *

"His passport and his white vestments are missing." Maglione was out of breath from hurrying. "I would say it's fairly certain he's headed for Israel."

"Do we know what clothes he's wearing?"

"A standard clerical suit, Eminence. Roman collar and purple stock. At least that's our guess. The other possibility is a simple soutane. His valet is almost certain it's the former. He may have one or the other with him."

The Prefect's head went back in despair; he could not believe they were in the position they were in. It was absurd. It was beyond belief. It was in every respect terrifying.

"The Vigilanza have been informed?"

"A search of the Apostolic Palaces is being arranged as we speak. When that is complete, and as I expect, unfruitful, I'll have the General Secretary inform the appropriate government agency. They'll be tracking the movements of one Angelo Cardinal Rinaldi because he's left vital medication behind. Only senior officials will know the truth. It's unlikely any rank-and-file agent will realize the significance of that name."

"And if they do?"

"A fluke. A coincidence. A relative? I can't imagine anyone putting two and two together and coming up with such a preposterous scenario as a lost pope! A pope travelling incognito under his birth name and previous title is all but inconceivable."

"What do you think he's up to?"

"I dread to think," said Menenger. "It could be anything. It scares me to think what might be running through that Umbrian brain of his."

"He has a clear grasp of Middle Eastern politics. He laid the whole problem of the Middle East out for me in a series of deft strokes. I must admit to being surprised."

"All I've had from his lips are those ridiculous dreams of his."

"You think them ridiculous?"

"They're the ravings of a sick mind, Valerio."

"He believes himself touched by God."

The tumor is perhaps growing faster than expected."

"His concern for the suffering can hardly be blamed on his having a tumor in his brain," said the Secretary of State. "He is a man deeply disturbed by what extremists on both sides are doing to their people. He is convinced the situation will only be resolved with God's help."

"Ah," said Menenger.

"You doubt his humanity?"

"No, I do doubt his sanity. Would a sane man do what he's doing? The credibility of the whole Church will be in question if he isn't intercepted and stopped."

Maglione straightened in preparation for retreat, but Cardinal Menenger had a final request. Cardinal Borghini was preparing a carefully worded statement for the press, he said, raising his dark, sunken eyes to engage the Secretary of State's full attention. If he had not already done so, he might perhaps ask Benedict's private secretary to speak confidentially with those who regularly attended His Holiness. Menenger offered a correction to his earlier suggestion. Benedict was *indisposed*, that was all. There should be no mention of his apartment, no reference to where he might be located in time or space. Indisposed would suffice as an explanation to whomever might inquire.

"I understand what you're saying," said Maglione. "We must not be caught out in a lie if the situation runs out of control."

"Exactly." Cardinal Menenger reached for the telephone. "I'm hoping against hope this will take no more than a day at most, Valerio. A few hours if we get lucky."

"He's got a head start, Eminence. He could easily have reached his destination by now - there are no visa requirements for Italians entering Israel. Did he have access to money?"

"I've no idea."

"Could he have borrowed money from someone?"

Menenger's mind whirled. "His personal secretary?"

"It's possible."

"Speak with him again, Valerio." Menenger was suddenly crestfallen. "We could be too late. He may indeed have already reached his destination."

"If he has, picking him up inside Israel will be like looking for a needle in a haystack," said Maglione "Care will have to be taken when speaking to the Israelis; they're suspicious of anything out of the ordinary. It would put us in a very awkward position if they realized who Angelo Cardinal Rinaldi really is."

"We have people in Jerusalem," said Menenger. "They may be able to help. He may seek refuge with some Catholic institution known to him. As a Franciscan, he may well head straight for the Terra Sancta Convent in Jerusalem."

The Secretary of State stared down at the Prefect's drawn face. In all the years he had known him, he had never seen Menenger so tense, so agitated, so nearly out of balance. He almost felt sorry for the man. "I'll speak with Fr Gozzoli right away," he said, watching the Prefect punch in some numbers. "He may know what he has in mind to do."

"Speedily," said Menenger, glancing at the man he knew to be at odds with him on many an issues. "This crisis must not be allowed to develop further than it already has."

40

Crossroads

A clerical-suited Angelo Cardinal Rinaldi, alias Pope Benedict XVI, stepped out of an Arkia Airlines jet and onto the tarmac of Ben-Gurion airport in the early hours of Wednesday morning, July 1st, and headed for Customs. His only luggage was the brown belt-strapped suitcase that had travelled with him since his seminary days in Perugia. Born in the nearby hilltop town of Montefalco, an Umbrian town that had existed since Roman times, he had applied himself to his studies and scraped passes in Greek, Latin and mathematics, and like many another found himself dressed, at the age of eleven, in a black soutane, culottes, black stockings, black boots and a black broad-brimmed hat. Nicknamed 'the little cleric' due to his small stature, he had accepted the domineering and domination of others with unusual humility, never suspecting that he would some day rise to the dizzying heights of cardinal, and then to the unimaginable position of Supreme Pontiff, Vicar of Christ and God-appointed protector of the Catholic faith. As he walked towards customs, however, Angelo Rinaldi felt nothing of the confidence such an august figure was supposed to feel; all he could feel was his heart thumping in his chest.

The quite extraordinary idea of travelling to Israel on his own had occurred to him as he showered. Naked before God, his head bent as if in prayer, his longish black hair streaming rivulets of steaming water, this altogether mad notion had formed without prior warning. When he emerged from his shower, however, what had seemed like the most preposterous of notions was no longer quite so preposterous. If it was God's will, he had reasoned, then it could be accomplished. Only then had he asked himself the more important question: to what end such a journey?

Late that evening, after a tiring day of audiences, ceremonies and diplomatic exchanges, he had returned to this pivotal question and probed at it. A momentary aberration? An intimation? He was at a loss to know which, yet at the same time unable to shake off the suspicion that this craziest of ideas was somehow linked to his dreams. And so he prayed for clarity, and in the night found himself again at the Golden Gate, the gate through which it was said Jesus had entered the Holy City.

In the morning, when he awoke, it was with a sense of having been spoken to. Did the 'Why' really matter? he asked himself. Was it not, as he had been taught, better to obey than to question? With that thought as his compass, Benedict had turned his attention away from the 'Why' and concentrated on the 'How'. He was God's servant, he reasoned, and servants were seldom given explanations for anything.

* * *

Duggan's father died of a massive heart attack around two in the morning. He was found by a neighbor all crumpled up on his living room floor, in his blue and white striped pyjamas, having failed to reach his tiny kitchen. Duggan took the fateful call at the office, informed Elliot and headed out of the building for the carpark feeling as empty as he had ever felt in his life.

"He's donated his body, his *whole* body, to medical science," he said over a stiff whisky later that evening. "I signed the papers about six months ago." Another gulp of single malt, and a glance at Jane, who was sitting across from him in one of the big fifties armchairs. "*Spare parts for the use of,* was the way he put it. I think he knew it wasn't far off. Which means of course there won't be a funeral; at least not immediately. Not until they're finished with him."

"I'm glad I met him. He was so nice to me, Jack. "

"He thought you were a bit of all right. Said so. Kept smiling and nodding at me when you weren't looking."

Jane did not reply; she just made a strange little shape with her mouth.

"My mother had what she termed *a proper burial*. She didn't approve of cremation. She perhaps saw it as a forerunner of the hell she so ardently believed in, and hoped to avoid."

"Did your father have any kind of religious belief?"

"If he did, he kept it to himself."

"What a strange pair they must have been. What made them get together?"

"Now there's a question." Duggan paused to think about that. "They say opposites attract. I think they were the ultimate test of that maxim. Their first night together must have been an unmitigated disaster."

"Was she attractive?"

"I suppose she must have been when she was young. Just about everyone's attractive when they're young."

"The photographs are all of her as a married woman. She looks quite nice in some of them."

"She had nice moments. People aren't all bad or all stupid all of the time."

"How do you remember her?"

"I remember her as dreary. I remember overhearing a relative say that she could dull a summer's afternoon with her presence. That's what sadness does for you, Jane. It eats the heart out of you."

"She was sad. Why?"

"What else was there? God was on his throne high and lifted up, and the Devil was raging down here like a mad bull. I think all she could sense was the hypothetical worst in every situation. The worst in herself. There was no way she could make a fist out of life. She was, as the old song goes, a puppet on a string."

"Did you ever talk with your father about her? About how she was in herself?"

"There was a good old-fashioned Irish wake to send her off. A lot passed between my father and I that night." He pursed his lips as memory stirred. "They didn't consummate the marriage properly for about a year, and then only to produce me. She was of the opinion that sex was only for the purpose of procreation."

"He didn't know how she thought about sex until after they were married?"

"I don't think *she* knew how she felt about sex until after they were married. What it involved seems to have come as a bit of a shock to her. It was of course all too late by then."

"She didn't approve of contraceptives?"

"What do you think?"

Jane let out a groan and reached for the glass of white wine she had put down earlier. After a sip, she said, "So what did they do?"

"They didn't *do* anything after that. They tried for a second child, and when that didn't work she concluded it wasn't God's will and brought the whole sex thing to a halt."

"Why didn't they separate?"

"Wasn't the done thing in their day."

"People did separate even then, Jack."

"Yes, but infrequently. You were looked down on if you couldn't make it work. Particularly the woman. A married woman without a husband was viewed as a threat by every other woman in the neighborhood. It was a matter of grit your teeth and keep your dirty washing out of sight. That's a quote from my father."

"You're admitting to have being brought up in an emotional refrigerator."

"Kids don't know what's going on half the time. I didn't. I was oblivious to their problems. Their *actual* problems. I was too busy dealing with my own rising sap."

Jane thought that an original way of describing adolescent sexuality. Then with a shake of the head, she said, "All these years living like that."

"And all for my sake," he added with a smile. "Two whole lives wasted for my sake."

"They probably didn't see it that way."

"No, but that's how it cancelled out. She died bitter and disappointed. He died oblivious to all the joy he should have known."

"I saw the way he looked at you. He thought the world of you."

"I thought the world of him." The tears bulged in Duggan's eyes. "If I end up with half his dignity I'll do well."

* * *

Israeli airport security was strict, particularly for Palestinian Americans entering the country, but not quite so strict for those coming in from Europe. Visitors from Italy had no visa requirements, but they could nevertheless expect careful scrutiny of their travel documents. Angelo Cardinal Rinaldi was no exception.

"The purpose of your visit, Eminence?"

"To-visit-the-holy-places." Benedict smiled his most winsome smile; he had practiced the lines in English *en route.* "It-is-my-first-time-to-the-Holy Land."

The young official's eyes stayed on Benedict's face. No other business?

"No."

"Rental accommodation in Moshav Bet Zayit?"

"I-am-here-at-my-own . . . *cost?* It-is-a-*personal* -journey."

His passport was returned with a glimmer of a smile; the Italian presence in Palestine boasted a long tradition. "Welcome to Israel, Eminence. Enjoy your stay."

"*Grazie,*" Benedict made to turn, but changed his mind. "Is-my-place-of . . . *stay* very far?"

"Thirty minutes from Ben-Gurion, ten minutes from Jerusalem." As if in reply to a telepathic inquiry, the official added, "Distance to the Dead Sea, thirty kilometers, from Bethlehem, ten kilometers."

"*Grazie, laringrazio.*"

His case was not opened. Had it been, his white vestments would not have aroused suspicion. He was, after all, a Roman Catholic cardinal; they wore all kinds of things. And under the white, the black of a priest's soutane, a necessary subterfuge when the alarm bells began to ring.

He mostly couldn't feel the tumor in his brain; only occasionally did it announce its presence. And there was nothing they could do about it. It was buried deep, and too dangerously situated for even the most skillful pair of hands. It was just a matter of time, they said. A year or two at best, a month or two at worst if it suddenly disrupted the normal functioning of his brain. No one was sure which it would be.

He did not hire a car. He caught an airport bus travelling Route No. 1 and sat very straight watching the dry, sandy landscape roll by. A flickering smile. He was in the Holy Land and headed, at last, for Jerusalem. Jerusalem. No ordinary word, that. A combination of letters capable of producing all kinds of emotion, all kinds of deeds. A crossroads, not only of geography, but also of the mind, and the heart. His landing card named accommodation in Moshav Bet Zayit as his destination, but he had booked that on the internet and had no intention of turning up. His defense would be that he had changed his mind. One was allowed to change one's mind in a democracy.

It had been difficult getting money out of Fr Gozzoli. A friend of his youth from Montefalco, his private secretary had been full of questions. What on Earth did he need money for? He was the Pontiff! Pontiffs did not require money. They travelled the world without a sou in their pocket. It was not something he could talk about, he had said, smiling his smile. It was a little thing he just had to do, a private thing. It would be their secret. He would see to it that he was reimbursed.

Someone close at hand must be in financial trouble, Fr Gozzoli had conjectured. A member of staff? One of the nuns who attended the Holy Father? It was all very mysterious, and not a little endearing. He would make a note of it in his diary.

Walking out of the Apostolic Palace at a late hour, Angelo Cardinal Rinaldi had acknowledged the Guardia Svizzere's salute and sailed out into the sweet Roman night a man free of the trappings and restrictions of the papal office. To the ambitious, the role of pontiff was the final prize in God's lottery. To the discerning, it was a duty, a responsibility of vast proportions few men were either worthy or capable of shouldering. To Benedict XVI, newly installed and looked upon by most as no more than a stop-gap pope, it was an opportunity to prove that the machinations of men's minds could not hope to vie with the Holy Spirit's inscrutable ways. His favorite verse of Scripture said it all: *The wind bloweth where it listeth, and thou hearest the sound thereof, but thou knowest not wither it cometh, or whether it goeth. So also are they who are born of the Spirit.* That, surely, was the crux of the whole thing. It was a matter of being open to the still small voice of the Spirit. No one knew for certain what God ultimately had in mind for the faithful, we could only guess at what that might be.

Benedict's guess was that his dreams were more than mere ramblings of the night. The sense of majesty and purpose they purveyed could not be explained in terms of what he had eaten for supper, or of a tumor pressing on some vital part of his brain. Never had he had such dreams. Never had he sensed the presence of God in such a direct fashion. Overwhelmed by mystery, by love, by subtle illumination, he had surrendered himself to God in a way he had previously not thought possible. A tumor could not be responsible for that, surely. If it could, then nothing could ever again be trusted. The very fact that they had not relieved him of his duties after the diagnosis and prognosis proved he was of sound judgment. They would not have left a deluded pope in charge of Mother Church. No, he was not deluded. He was in receipt of intimations that could be explained only as an inner directive, a subtle nudging of his spirit by the Spirit of Truth. Jerusalem, for whatever reason, was where he had to be. Jerusalem was his destiny, and even if it took his last breath, he would fulfill that destiny.

Looking again at the dry landscape he saw, due to a change in the light, his own lean features reflected in it. As if in response, a tremor of uncertainty ran through his spindly body. Could he be wrong after all? Could it be that he *was* a little bit mad, a little bit deranged?

Could the tumor's presence explain everything he had experienced, everything he was engaged in? Closing his eyes, Benedict felt alarm spread through his frame. What was he up to? What did he think he could accomplish? How could he possibly have believed that he, the little cleric from Montefalco, could be God's instrument in this tortured land? He felt his panic mount. His being here was a travesty of everything sensible, a mockery of everything sacred. He was a nobody pope. A fill-in. A stop-gap. A mere prop with no future. They would track him down within hours and it would all be over. He began to pray, haltingly at first, then more and more fervently, the words forming silently on his lips. Then, almost magically, he was calm again, as calm as he had ever felt in his life. The grey eyes opened, and a smile formed on his thin lips. Satan's promptings had failed to accomplish their objective.

41

Why?

Cardinal Borghini, director of the Pontifical Institute in Rome, weighed into the debate over the codex's authenticity in a syndicated article designed to support Cardinal Peronio's ten-point dismissal of the codex as unimportant and probably fraudulent. There was only *one* divine truth, he opined, and it had not formed in a strife-ridden sectarian milieu as Theodore's letter seemed to suggest. It had, rather, been born in the mind of God, and as such was immutable. That fact more than any other undermined the currently popular notion, or 'pop' notion, that the Early Church was composed of disparate sectarian groups welded together into some kind of artificial alliance. Never had he heard such nonsense. Such a view did not accord with the New Testament, and neither did it accord with the consensus view among scholars. The Standard Model interpretation had proved itself all but invulnerable against vested-interest attack, and he was confident that that would remain the case for a long time to come.

Windle's argument was that Cardinal Borghini was advocating a scholarship based on *appropriateness*, as opposed to the favored investigative form. As a method for sidestepping difficult issues in theology, 'appropriateness' and 'inappropriateness' were without doubt useful mechanisms, but when dealing with the hard facts of the first century, or any other century for that matter, it was a decidedly unhelpful methodology. For what, in essence, was the difference between Borghini's make-everything-fit-the-Catholic-paradigm approach, and that of National Socialism's takeover of archaeology in Germany for propaganda purposes? None, as far as he could see. Both were guilty of bending reality to secure and sustain an ideological stance. In this day and age, that was not only unacceptable, it was a travesty of everything intelligent men and women had fought and died for down the centuries.

As Windle penned his rejection of Cardinal Borghini's convoluted reasoning, Benedict XVI donned his black soutane and prepared himself for a sortie into the winding, jasmine-scented alleyways of Jerusalem's Old City. After an hour or more of aimless wandering the previous evening, he had secured, as a result of stopping to admire some marigold-crammed window boxes, a room with its own bathroom in a small family hotel not far from the Jaffa Gate. Within seconds of lying down, he had fallen into a deep, dreamless sleep, and awakened to the sound of corrugated shutters being raised, and to the drone of engines and voices. Alert to every change in rhythm beyond the shuttered windows, he had lain open-eyed and attempted to digest the magnitude of his actions, but without success. The Catholic Church's most powerful representative had deserted his post, and there was no way to logically explain why that had happened.

Staring up at the revolving fan above his bed, he watched its lazy motion and was reminded of his father's love of aircraft. Then, with a quickness and sense of purpose that surprised him, he was out of bed and standing before the bathroom mirror, his fingers rubbing at his bristly chin, his eyes fixed on the green eyes of the elderly man in front of him. Whatever the truth of the situation, there was no way back. It was now a matter of faith. He was either mad, or stupid, or both. Or, if one believed in the efficacy of dreams, exactly where God wanted him to be.

* * *

"Their preliminary finding is that the codex is most probably authentic. One of the team working on it admitted as much during an interview."

"Most probably authentic?"

"It's subject to further tests. But as he pointed out, carbon-dating can only authenticate the material, not the content. A positive fourth-century dating will only confirm the conclusion they seem already to have reached."

Cardinal Menenger was well aware of the Secretary of State's antipathy towards him; it was sometimes in his eyes and in the way he moved his body. And in that slit of a mouth. And, occasionally, in a decision that ran counter to the Prefect's wishes. But it had never been clear to Menenger what the basis of that veiled aversion might be, just that it was there, intangibly *there* when they interacted. Cardinal Borghini had ventured that it might be jealousy, that in spite of the Secretary of State's Olympian detachment while caring daily for the Supreme Pontiff and a billion human souls, he did not wield the raw power entrusted to the Prefect of the Congregation for the Doctrine of the Faith. It might be that. It might even be that Flavio Cardinal Maglione had his eye on the top job and saw the Prefect as competition.

There was a silence. The Secretary of State's mentioning of the codex had been no more than an aside, a *you'll never guess what?* filler to cover his despair over the predicament they were in. The Italian security services now knew for certain that the Holy Father was in Israel, that he had caught a bus from Ben-Gurion airport into Jerusalem, that he had alighted with some other passengers outside one of the fashionable hotels and bought himself a paper cup of tamarind juice from a street vendor. But after that it was a complete blank. He had vanished into a side street carrying a brown suitcase and hadn't been seen or heard of since.

"He must be sleeping somewhere." Menenger's frown was of the deeply furrowed type. "It stands to reason he's not sleeping rough."

"He knows we're trying to track him down. He may lie low for a couple of days."

"Question is," said Menenger, voicing the problem put to him on the telephone, "did he go far after leaving the bus? Did he get lost? Did he wander for one street or twenty?" A crisp laugh "We'd find him in no time at all if we told the Israelis what's going on, but we can't do that. Too risky. Someone would blab and we'd have an inter-national incident on our hands. And we can't involve the Israeli police in hunting for someone in need of medication. They'd wonder why a cardinal wasn't staying in one of the usual catholic centers, or in one of the big hotels. They'd wonder why someone so important didn't have a cell phone. They'd wonder why no photograph of Angelo Cardinal Rinaldi was available. They'd wonder all kinds of things."

"Wasn't the medication bit used"

"Yes, but we were too late. He was already in Jerusalem when that was passed on to Israeli customs. We didn't let it go any further." A sigh from Cardinal Menenger. "We should have stressed that we were pursuing every conceivable diplomatic angle to make a trip to Israel possible for him."

"I told him we were about to take our request to a higher authority. He told me he already had. I didn't think that was partic-ularly meaningful at the time."

"But to what end, Valerio? Why this fixation with Israel?"

"It's the suffering that's got to him. The suffering on both sides. He thinks he can help in some way. Don't ask me how."

"All he'll do is make a fool of himself."

"He obviously intends to surface at some point. Why else take his white vestments?"

Menenger picked up a sheet of paper and flapped it. "There's nothing particularly important on the Jewish calendar for July. There's a festival of commemoration on the 24th, but in comparison with the other Jewish festivals it doesn't rank as particularly signif-icant."

"Which one is it?"

"Tammuz. It designates the occasion when the Babylonian army, and later the Roman army, breached the walls of Jerusalem. It's basically about the destruction of the First and Second Temple by those armies. Historically important, certainly, but an unlikely trigger for someone in Benedict's state of mind."

"Anything political?"

"Again, nothing of note. My guess is he's there for no other reason than to be there."

"Because of his dreams."

A nod from Menenger. "There are thirty-nine Catholic masses going on in Jerusalem on any given day of the week. He may seek out one of those. They range in location from Jerusalem to the back streets of Ramallah. Updates on the situation as a whole are coming to my desk every hour."

"May I ask in whom you've confided?"

"Too many for comfort's sake, Valerio. I had no option." Menenger counted off those with a need to know. The Vigilanza. The Italian security services. Four members of the Curia with a contacts in Jerusalem. Then, with a terse smile, he added, "The debacle is of course also known to his personal secretary, his valet, the nuns who attended him, and ourselves. Others will have guessed that something is amiss. The rumourmill is already at work. We've had enquiries from the press as to the state of the Holy Father's health."

"He's being looked for in Jerusalem?"

"Watched for by discreet eyes would be a more accurate description. Although it is possible the Italian security services are more actively involved."

"With or without Israeli knowledge?"

"I very much doubt they'll announce their presence, given the circumstances."

"And if he heads for the occupied territories?"

"The Italian government has, as you are well aware, strong relations with the Palestinian National Authority, and with munici-palities in the West Bank and the Gaza Strip. I'm sure our people . . . the Government's people, have that angle covered."

The Secretary of State's feeling was that Frederick Cardinal Menenger, Prefect of the Congregation for the Doctrine of the Faith was, in spite of his frowns and sighs, enjoying the cut and thrust of the situation. But it was changed days. The Grand Inquisitor's powers were now somewhat curtailed. Possess an intelligence service of his own he certainly did - the Vatican's intelligence service was rumored to be busy on five continents - but the home body was a pale reflection of what it had once been. The power of arrest was gone. The right to harass, torture and kill, was gone. The right to excommunicate children because they did not denounce their parents for consuming meat and milk on feasts days was gone. But it was still a potent force. It still had teeth. You still had to tread carefully when dealing with it.

"You have some of your own people in Jerusalem?" The Secretary of State's question sounded innocent enough, but it was a little too direct for Menenger. He tilted his head and grimaced, which of course was admission enough. Then, as if in reply to a quite different question, he said:

"He's going to lead us in a merry old dance, Valerio. I can sense it. He's an Umbrian peasant whose father probably drank too much sangrantino. The word 'Umbria' is near to the Italian for 'shadow', and he is already living up to being *ombra*."

"He didn't seem like much of a threat when he was chosen."

"Neither did Angelo Cardinal Roncalli." Menenger mused on John XXIII's birth name. "Angelo Roncalli? Angelo Rinaldi? Is history playing the same joke on us twice?" A shake of the head. "I had come to have high hopes for Benedict. His lean, classically Italian frame reminded me of Pius XII. With training, quite a bit of training, the little Umbrian could probably have done quite well."

"You're writing him off?"

"He's written himself off. He may as well be dead. It's unlikely he or the Church will emerge from this extraordinary situation unscathed."

"I doubt very much he's another Roncalli," said the Secretary of State, whose opinion of John XXIII was also already formed. "By nature he's ultra conservative."

"Conservative he may be, but he's presently running around the back streets of Jerusalem with the Lord only knows what in mind!"

"He's ill, Frederick. He can't be held responsible for his actions."

It was seldom that the Secretary of State used Cardinal Menenger's first name, or anyone's for that matter. Only in what he considered moments of existential need did he feel it an apt requirement. Menenger, on the other hand, used first names almost as a matter of course - it was his method of manipulating situations and people that might otherwise be difficult to handle. Some unfortunates mistook this for friendship and quickly paid the price.

Cardinal Menenger's reaction was to glance at Maglione, for whom he had a grudging respect, then launch into a diatribe on Angelo Roncalli's failings. According to the Prefect, he had been responsible for just about every bit of nonsense to inflict the Church since the Second Vatican Council closed its doors. That included homosexual marriages, denials of the Virgin Birth, the Resurrection, papal infallibility, masses celebrated by women, Christian yoga, female Holy Spirits, touchy prayer, rock masses, nuns in mini-skirts, the exit of whole groups from religious communities and, last but not least, the revolt of Northern European theologians. All in all, a damning legacy in anyone's terms.

"You see no good in the man at all?"

"By their fruits ye shall know them."

"He inherited the dry rot of Pacelli's Church."

"He let the genii out of the bottle and we've being paying for it ever since."

"The genii being?"

"The clamor of the human, Valerio. We've packed away our message from beyond the stars and replaced it with a socio-political grocery list of human demands. It's no longer a matter of transformation through the blood of Christ, it's now only a matter of constant, imbecilic change. What refuses to change has to be chucked out with the rubbish."

There was a genuine edge of sorrow in Menenger's words, and the Secretary of State was not deaf to it. "I agree, of course," he said, dropping his gaze, "that rampant humanism could severely disable the Church; but we can't turn the clock back to Pacelli's days of petrified glory, can we? The hard crust of power has split open and its inners can't be pushed back into place."

"Perhaps not," said Menenger, who was now almost impatiently standing behind his desk. "But it's a fine line you're advocating, Valerio, and a dangerous one in my opinion."

"I haven't advocated anything."

"You seek fairness; fairness is not always possible. It is sometimes required of us to be as hard as granite."

"But not monsters. We've had our share of monsters."

"And our share of angels," Menenger said quickly. "Angels and devils. Manifestations from another realm. The Church exists primarily to focus attention on those other realms. We are at war, Valerio, and we should not forget it."

"Mostly with ourselves," said the Secretary of State, who understood the battle better than many supposed.

"Which is to be at war with a usurping force, a capricious force," said Menenger, fiddling with things on his desk. "Man the rational machine knows no bounds to his ingenuity, his creativity, his insatiable appetite for the new. He is ever searching, testing and experimenting, hoping to uncover or unveil the cause of his existence, the meaning of his mind, the driving mechanism in his cells." The Prefect's eyes came up to meet those of the Secretary of States. "He is usurped by his own image, mesmerized by his capacity to reshape his world. But it is not this life that matters, is it? In the greater scheme of things it isn't what drives our cells that matters, it's what drives our actions and our motives that should concern us. Hence our need to hold steady in the face of liberalism's attack. The Second Vatican Council unleashed the chaos of liberalism. The result was a hall of mirrors where the bumbling, frightened, helpless human self became the center of attention. Angels were displaced by angles, and the result was the rampage of human thought."

Valerio Maglione could remember a time when he would have given quick and enthusiastic assent to Menenger's fateful grocery list. But not now; he, too, had undergone change. Yes, modernism's dangers were plain to see, but the idea of a grand cosmic war being fought out in some parallel universe was, for him, no longer a tenable description of spiritual reality. Such thinking belonged to another age, another time, another mental clime. There was no avoiding the scholarly advances being made, the discoveries and insights arising from honest research. Push the idea of individual freedom too far and all kinds of trouble would surface, there was no denying that. But that could not and should not be used as an excuse to further burden the gullible and the insecure with religious fairy-tales. The attempt to push everything into the box marked 'human' and disallow it for that reason was inadequate.

The repercussions on the faith would, Maglione knew, be severe if even a few of those discoveries and insights were allowed to register. The faith of centuries would take a battering. But wasn't the uncovering of God's ongoing truth for humanity the Church's age-old claim, aim and responsibility? If its conception of truth could be shown to be inadequate - everything said or written had, after all, been filtered through the human mind - then in all conscience sensible adjustments to doctrine and attitude would have to follow.

Cardinal Menenger's fear of the Mar Saba Codex was a case in point. Not only did Theodore's letter offer further proof that the Early Church of the Apostles was not at all as previously imagined, it quite forthrightly questioned the notion of those apostles being the basis of a divinely appointed priestly succession. That was the crux of the matter. In the place of this grandiose scheme rose the specter of that succession being no more than a monarchical succession, a succession of individuals from one particular Jewish family who believed themselves eligible to reign as the future kings of Israel. Why else had the words KING OF THE JEWS been sarcastically affixed to the cross by the Roman procurator? Of an admittedly priestly nature this succession had certainly been, but the idea of it leaping from its sectarian Jewish milieu into the Gentile world via the Apostle Paul was not just unlikely, it was, as a growing body of evidence now revealed, embarrassingly inaccurate. As was now being admitted by many a Catholic scholar, the Early Church had been at loggerheads on how Jesus the Jewish Messiah should be perceived, and everything pointed to a radical and uncomfortable reassessment of how this enigmatic figure had perceived himself.

" . . . A veritable *rampage* of the mind threatening everything we stand for," Menenger added with a kind of fury. "Fail to understand that and you fail to grasp the nature of the threat we face."

Maglione's smile was genuine, almost kindly. "May the Lord guide us in everything we do, Eminence," he replied, aware of Menenger's impatience to be alone.

* * *

Angelo Cardinal Rinaldi entered the rectangular grid of the Old City of Jerusalem by the Jaffa Gate, and immediately found himself engulfed in a hubbub of shopkeepers, mounted police, green-bereted Border Police, soldiers, traffic and black-clad Orthodox Jews. Pilgrims heading for the Church of the Redeemer or the Holy Sepulcher jostled with a babble of humanity crossing David Street for the Zion Gate, their voices, like their clothes, intimating a range of countries and cultures. To right and left, slung machine guns caught his eye. On the rooftops, more green berets. At strategic points along whichever route one chose, soldiers, police, closed-circuit cameras and electronic sensors. And all the result of new-millennium fears, fears based on the influx of fervent religious pilgrims and madcap apocalyptics that had not, in the end, amounted to anything particularly alarming.

Absorbing the sights, smells and noisy bustle of the Old City, he stood for a moment outside the tourist office, then, instructed by his little map, headed down David Street and into the Arab market, or *souk*, his intention being to turn left at the Dome of the Rock, then right onto the Via Dolorosa. Simple as this seemed, however, he was soon lost, his sense of direction disrupted by the twisting alleyways and the constant hassling of the shopkeepers. A crush of humanity and a dizzying array of clothes, shoes, baskets and trinkets, the narrow, shadowy alleyways and stepped pathways demanding constant reorientation. On his right, somewhere, St James's Cathedral, the Armenian Quarter and the Jewish Quarter. On his left the most holy sites of the Christian Quarter topped by the Muslim Quarter. Ahead, but equally invisible, the Wailing Wall, the Dome of the Rock and the al-Aqsa Mosque.

It was his intention, at some point, to visit the Garden of Gethsemane, which lay off to the right of St Stephen's Gate, or Lion Gate, on the opposite side of the Old City, but not on this occasion. It would be too much to ask of his frail body. His more immediate plan was to walk the length of the Via Dolorosa and try to take in the magnitude of what his Lord had experienced. He would be inter-secting his Lord's path of suffering where the Al-Wad Road cut into the Via Dolorosa. This would require him to turn left, then, later, after visiting the five stations of the cross in the Christian Quarter, retrace his steps along the Via Dolorosa towards the Lion Gate where the remaining seven stations were to be found. On accom-plishing that he would be well situated to reach the Lion Gate, and from there the Golden Gate, or East Gate. Tucked into the rear wall of the Haram Ash-Sharif, or Temple Mount - the spot where Abraham was said to have prepared his son for sacrifice, and Mohammed was believed to have ascended into heaven - this gate was the gate he had seen in his dream.

It was also, he now knew from the tourist brochure he had found in his hotel room, the gate through which the Jews expected their Messiah to pass, and, of course, the selfsame gate as used by Jesus when he first entered Jerusalem riding on a humble donkey. Blocked off by the Ottoman Turks to stop the Jewish Messiah's return, it was fronted by a small cemetery which, the Muslims hoped, would further deter this grand event from happening. Benedict had smiled at such a crude attempt to stay the Almighty's hand. What a surprise the Muslims would get when the man they thought of as their penultimate prophet turned out to be a somewhat more important figure. What a surprise the Jews would get when the man they had turned over to the Romans as a political and religious trouble maker turned out to be their long-awaited Messiah. What a beating of breasts would take place on that day!

Only later, and after much difficulty, did he discover that the Lion Gate could not be approached directly, but only through a courtyard attached to the Church of St Anne. As a result of this mix-up, he found himself first in the Muslim Quarter, then in the area where the Ethiopians lived, then back in the Muslim Quarter. On walking through the Ethiopian section, however, he stumbled on some Crusader crosses carved into the walls of a stairway, then, to his delight, his gaze fell on the Chapel of St Helena. According to legend, it was Helena, mother of the Emperor Constantine, who had discovered the true cross on which Christ had hung.

At every step a discovery, a reminder that this was the city in which Jesus of Nazareth had met his fate on behalf of sinful humanity. But reminders also of the present, for in the Muslim Quarter he had been confronted again and again with crescent moons and statements in Arabic colorfully stenciled on white walls. What had been their meaning, he wondered.

As a boy, Benedict had looked at pictures of the holy places and imagined what it must have been like to be with Jesus in the Upper Room, or as he crossed the brook Kedron after the Last Supper, or in Gethsemane as the temple guard, torches elongating the shadows, came to arrest him. These stories had captured his imagination, and still did. There was something magical about them. They carried a charge like no other stories he knew. They belonged to some other level of reality. They were, in a word, God's 'word'; they were sacred, and they should not be tampered with.

Benedict knew nothing of the Mar Saba Codex; he had been oblivious to all but his own concerns, taken up with his own particular choice of problems. Consulted by the Secretary of State over what to do about the Children of the New Catholic Dawn's excesses, about the alleged abuse of children by priests and other tiresome issues, he had, without hesitation, followed his predecessor's lead and blamed America. It was the American media that had blown the priest thing out of all proportion, the American media that had struck up the band on behalf of female priests and the recognition of gay rights, the American media that had stuck their nose into the Church's affairs and concluded, wrongly, that the wonderfully enthusiastic responses of the spiritual movements were an affront to democratic sensibilities. Priests who had given in to carnal desire should be disciplined and punished as a matter of course, particularly those who had molested children, but they should also be forgiven and rehabilitated. Anyone who besmirched the Church's good name should be so treated, but that was not a task for journalists or wayward Catholic organizations. Only Holy Mother Church had the right to discipline and punish her servants. Only she, it should be realized, carried that inalienable right.

Returning to the Al-Wad intersection, Benedict re-entered the Muslim Quarter and slowly identified the remaining stations of the cross. Exhausted by the long walk, by the fact that he had had little to eat, by the crowds and by the midday heat, he began to sense, for a first time, something of what his Lord must have experience as he headed for Golgotha along those narrow, people-choked streets. But what also must it have been like to undergo a Roman scourging and be forced to carry a heavy wooden cross? He could not properly relate to that; it was too dark and horrible a reality to imagine. What he could imagine was the hushed silence that must have fallen on the crowd as this bloodied figure struggled to stay upright. Simon of Cyrene would have been shocked and fearful when the Roman guards pulled him out of the crowd to assist Jesus, but what a privilege that had turned out to be. He had looked into the face of the Son of God and witnessed, surely, the depths of eternity in His eyes.

Entering the courtyard of St Anne's Church, Benedict found himself in a tiny oasis where trees and flowers grew amidst an unexpected and welcomed silence. Directly ahead of him lay the Crusader-built Church of St Anne with its little dome, its tower and its stone staircases skirted with metal railings. On his left, nothing but outcrops of ruined walls and half-buried arches. On his right, a flat, open area with trees and flowers flanked by a huge building, or wall, filled with windows.

According to a second century Christian tradition, it was where St Anne's now stood that the Virgin Mary had been born, but that idea was to be found only in the apocryphal gospel of James, and for that reason Benedict did not take it seriously. What interested him more was the adjacent Pool of Bethesda, the pool where Jesus had healed a paralytic, an incident clearly recorded in the New Testament, therefore beyond dispute. He would spend a few minutes there, then make his way through the Lion Gate, which was close at hand, and follow the eastern wall until he came to the gate in his dream.

What he would do once he got there had not crossed his mind. His only concern had been how to get there, and with God's help he had accomplished the impossible. That in itself, surely, was proof enough that his dream had been of God, not just some crazy notion generated by the thing in his head.

The Pool of Bethesda had provided water to both the town and the Temple in Jesus' day, and was reputed to have healing powers. The story was that an angel passed over the pool at intervals, and as it did so the waters were miraculously stirred. Enter the pool in that moment and whatever your ailment, it would be healed. No pool existed now, just an excavation, but it was no less sacred for that. Destroyed by the Romans during the capture of Jerusalem in AD70, it had been rebuilt as a healing sanctuary in AD135 by the Roman emperor Hadrian. Even a Roman emperor had sensed the pool's sacred nature.

After a few reverential minutes by the excavated pool, Benedict headed out through the Lion Gate and stood at the Jericho intersection staring towards Gethsemane and the Mount of Olives. It took his breath away to think of what had happened out there in the Kedron Valley, of how his Lord had prayed until he sweated blood, of how he had reprimanded his disciple for falling asleep. Asleep? Imagine their having fallen asleep in such circumstances! Had the wine consumed at their last meal gone to their heads? Or was it that Jesus' words should, or could, be understood in some other way?

Taking the Ofel Road, which ran near to the wall of the Old City, Benedict mustered all of his strength and trudged towards his goal. It was only a matter of a thousand yards or so, but as he quickly discovered, it was almost a thousand yards too much. Tired out by the heat and his circuitous trek across the one-kilometer-square network of Jerusalem's most ancient streets, and by the fact that he had eaten nothing substantial since leaving his hotel, he arrived adjacent to the cemetery fronting the blocked-off Golden Gate in a state near to exhaustion. He was, he believed, exactly where God wanted him to be. The only remaining question was: Why?

42

Blitz

As there could not be a proper funeral, Duggan arranged for a few close friends of the family to meet at his flat on the Sunday afternoon. Five were able to make it; two men and three women. They dribbled in just after two and chatted quietly for ten or fifteen minutes before he formalized the occasion. As he spoke, his face underwent a subtle change of expression. Jane remarked later that it was as if all the anger had suddenly drained out of him.

"I would have preferred a proper wake, as I'm sure you all would have done, but we'll just have to make do." He was referring to the fact that his father's body was already in the hands of the medical establishment, and that the unthinkable was probably already under way. Looking down into his glass of whisky, he tried to explain, "It was what he wanted." His head came up. "We discussed it some months ago and I countersigned the papers. I didn't argue. I knew there was no point."

"He told me he was going to do it," said one of the women. "I didn't argue either."

Duggan smiled down at the woman he had long called Aunt Margaret, but who wasn't actually an aunt. No close relatives had followed his parents out to Australia.

"He was a very practical man," said Duggan. "He summoned it all up for me in a sentence. 'If you're going to give one organ, then you might as well give the lot.'"

"Mary wouldn't have approved."

"No, I don't think she would have. My mother believed in a literal resurrection of a Christian's body come Christ's return. She would not have approved of bits being used by other people." He returned to the loose script in his head. "He told me once, when I was a kid, that a good wake did the heart a lot of good. It was a time of re-evaluation, he said. And not just of the person who had died, but of oneself. I think I understand what he meant by that now." A smile from the man they had all known as a boy, the boy who had been 'too clever for his own good', as someone had remarked way back then. "There are a lot of things about my father that I appreciate now that I didn't appreciate when I was young. For one, his patience. I've never met anyone with his quality of patience. He had an ability to wait. It was a gift." Another smile. "Some would say it evolved into a safety mechanism to avoid fighting with my mother, but I think it was more than that. I think my father was gifted with insight. I'm not saying my mother wasn't a good mother. She was. She did every-thing a mother was expected to do. And more. Much more. But she was a woman driven by a deep need for security, and she abandoned herself to religion in her search for it. I regret to say she was encouraged in this by people who ought to have known better. My father, on the other hand, was, in her terms, maddeningly secure without good reason. She never ever got to grips with that." A pause as Duggan struggled with his emotions. "I've got one more thing to say. My father had an unerring instinct for when I was hurting, and I hurt a lot in my early years." Duggan's eyes glistened with tears. "What I'm trying to say is that when I needed him he was there, unfailingly *there.*"

"He's with us right this minute, son." The speaker was an elderly man, an Irish Catholic neighbor of his parents who had kept up a friendship with his father. A bit of Irish humor followed. "He's not the kind of man to skip off without a peek at what's going on."

Duggan raised his glass and smiled. "I'll drink to that," he said.

"To Francis," said the same man, whose name was Frank. "May the good Lord look after him."

"Francis!" they chorused.

Duggan had not been able to attend Dave Perry's funeral, but within a few days of getting back had stood before Dave's laden bookshelves and communed silently with the man. "Why me?" he had asked, staring at the rich assortment of carefully categorized volumes.

He had introduced Jane as 'his lady' when his guest arrived. They had smiled at the term and shaken her hand and looked her up and down when she wasn't looking.

The women were all in agreement about how handsome his father had been. And how intelligent. "You got your brains from him," one of them said. "Mary didn't appreciate his intelligence," said another. "I don't think she ever really got to grips with the fact that he was wasted in that job of his."

The other man, Jim, said that he had always enjoyed his father's dry sense of humor. A genuinely good man, he added. You couldn't say that about many. Frank looked suddenly distraught, so one of the women, Sara, who had only recently lost her own husband, put a hand on his. She kept it there quite unselfconsciously until he steadied.

Jane stared hard at the floor. When she looked up, Duggan was standing glass in hand much like his father must have stood on just such an occasion.

"There's no doubting your mother could be difficult," said Rosmary, who was a retired teacher. "I really don't know how Francis put up with her mania. I tried to speak to her about it, but she wouldn't listen. All I could get out of her was Jesus this and Jesus that. I think she went a bit loopy in the end, Jack."

"I only ever saw him get really angry once," said Jim, who was English by birth, and a New Australian in spite of his advanced years. "A man they knew was rude to your mother in the street and your father faced him down. It took everyone by surprise."

"What happened?" asked Duggan.

"He sent him packing."

"Even good men get angry," said Frank. A smile spread across his lean features. "I saw him angry a deal more than once, Jim."

"Really?"

"Stupid ideas angered him."

"Like father, like son," said Sara.

The other two women murmured agreement.

"He was an armchair philosopher," said Duggan. "I learned a lot from him early on. He was better read than many you'd think should be well read."

Margaret observed that Duggan's father had also loved horses.

"He tried to get me interested," said Duggan. "I didn't take to it. I didn't like all that bouncing up and down. I saw him gallop once. I don't think I've ever seen anyone so concentrated. He went by like the wind itself."

Jim offered the thought that kids never really knew their parents, that they didn't see them as people who had lived real lives. That hadn't dawned on him until late on, he said, his face carrying its own stock of private memories. It had hit him while looking at some old photographs.

"It's seeing the world through their eyes instead of your own," said Jane.

"Exactly," said Jim. He added a twist. "I got the same feeling last night watching a mob of people rioting in Jerusalem. For a split second I was there. I was one of them."

"'I sat where they sat, and I was astonished'," said Duggan, quoting Isaiah.

"Poor buggers were just about out of their minds with grief and hate."

"An absolute mess," said Rosmary.

Jane went round with a particularly good Irish whisky at that point. "Sandwiches on the table," she said to everyone. "More in the kitchen when that lot's gone."

The women had each brought a plate of sandwiches.

When Duggan next looked, Phoebe was spread out on Sara's knee purring.

"She's beautiful, Jack!"

When he came over, Sara reached up and touched his hand, which was her way of saying sorry.

"I didn't do enough for him," he said, looking down at her.

"He didn't let anyone do much." She smiled a taut smile. "At least it was quick, Jack. None of this hanging around all clenched up. He would have hated that." Her attention returned to Phoebe. "It's what we all dread."

"You're keeping well yourself?"

"I've got cancer," she said, glancing up at him. "It's okay, I've known for a while. If it wasn't that it would be something else, wouldn't it?"

Words deserted him.

"Your father was very proud of you." She was looking at him again. "He told me your accomplishments made him feel as if he'd accomplished something. I think he was referring to the kind of person you've turned into as much as to your achievements."

"I'll never measure up, Sara."

"Nor should you try," she replied. "Goodness isn't something done, Jack; it's what we all are in here somewhere." She patted her chest. "All we have to do is let it out."

The phone rang and he excused himself. It was David Mayle ringing from Washington.

"David!"

Jane glanced in Duggan's direction and he beckoned to her.

"She's right here, David."

"The shit's hit the fan, Jack. There are CNCD operatives being investigated across the States as I speak. Not a few have had criminal charges laid against them. It's in all the newspapers here, and there hasn't been a peep out of the Vatican. Biggest story in years, and it's only just getting going. The stuff that's coming out is *un-be-liev-able.*"

"Where are you right this minute?"

"I'm sitting on the edge of Holly's desk at the *Post.* We're having a congratulatory drink.

"Look, I'll put Jane on and you can tell her the good news. Speak to you again in a minute." He handed the phone over and listened in as best he could.

"*Wonderful* news!" said Jane, when she had the details. "Well done you two!"

"It's just getting going," said David, relishing what lay ahead. "God knows where it'll all end up. Italy will be the big one. If the satellite organizations are this bad, what's the central hive like?"

"Have you been in contact with my father?"

"Talked to him about an hour ago. He sounded a bit down."

"Did he say why?"

"The German press haven't been kind."

"I'll ring him this evening."

"Good idea. He misses having you around."

They talked on about her father for a moment or two, then with a 'bye bye' Jane handed the phone back to Duggan.

"Did you follow that?" asked David.

"I got the gist of it."

"I think he's under pressure from the university."

"Jane'll find out." Duggan glanced at Jane, then he said, "I'm going to have cut this short, David . . . My father died and we're having a bit of a get-together for some of his friends. Could you ring back this evening? Around six, say?"

"Yeh, sure. Sorry Jack. You should have said."

"Life goes on, mate," said Duggan.

* * *

With its so-carefully constructed mystique being revealed for what it really was, the New Catholic Dawn began to split open like a ripe peach, its policy of 'the end justifies the means' laid before the American public in articles, media debates and a series of damning court cases. Reeling from an avalanche of accusation over the organization's Orwellian methods, this vast and sprawling organization began to disintegrate before everyone's eyes. But it did of course fight back, and its fighting methods more than confirmed its disregard for those so guilefully drawn into its ranks.

What emerged was that CNCD had, through gaining hierarchical approval, aggregated to itself maximum autonomy and an aura of authority that extended far beyond the known rules and statutes of the Catholic Church. Evolving its own language, gestures, modes of behavior and even inflections of speech, the Children of the New Catholic Dawn had become all but unaccountable to the hierarchy that had legitimized it. A lay organization it might claim to be, but it was run by self-declared celibates and priests, and as such was hardly representative of average men and women. As one particularly penetrating article in a mid-West newspaper had observed, the new caste of priest being born out of CNCD seminaries would, in the near future, occupy positions of real power within the Church. This was not a lay organization with ordinary lay objectives in mind, it was a breeding ground for an alternative future hierarchy such as had not wielded control of the Church for centuries. The very fact that CNCD seminaries existed spoke for itself - seminaries were the province of Orders, not of lay institutions.

Most worrying of all were reports of blatant psychological manipulation and coercion. Tapping into people's fears and anxieties, movement leaders had encouraged people to reveal intimate private details in group confessions, so gaining the ability to sustain in these individuals a state of shame and self-loathing. As the rules of the confessional did not apply to these sessions, gossip between individuals and parishes was rife. This had resulted in a significant number of people seeking psychiatric help, not a few resorting to the courts when the movement's incorrigible behavior became public knowledge.

With the lid on CNCD practices blown off, leaked letters between priests and their bishops began to surface. In all cases there had been real attempts to still troubled waters, but in the end the sheer weight of evidence showed CNCD to be recalcitrant on just about every level imaginable. The grocery list of objections lengthened steadily, and was punctuated with words like *inflexible, authoritarian, exclusive, secretive and elitist.* Impervious to criticism, indeed contemptuous of those who dared criticize them, movement leaders and officials roundly condemned even high-ranking members of the Catholic hierarchy who disagreed with their evangelizing methods.

One letter in particular caught David and Holly's attention. It was from Archbishop Donaghue of Nevada, and it was a sorry tale. Having tried to accommodate CNCD in his diocese, the archbishop now deeply regretted having proffered an invitation to these 'intolerant buffoons'. The situation in his own diocese was that in spite of having issued a decree demanding that CNCD discontinue its activities, they were not only still operative, but were refusing to budge on the basis of their having been officially approved by Rome. With one parish split in two, and another under threat, the archbishop had no doubts as to CNCD's real nature - it was a direct threat to unity in any parish and should have it credentials withdrawn forthwith.

Cardinal Menenger's reaction to this debacle was swift, and a little too subtle for some. Contemplation and combat belonged together, he said at a specially convened crisis meeting. What had to be realized was that the spiritual impulses of the lay movements acted as a wholesome disturbance to the traditional order of the Church. The Church and the society's institutional authorities found that a difficult fact to absorb, but it was something they would, in the end, learn to live with in spite of the present furore.

Of the five cardinals present, four were Menenger supporters. Secretary of State Maglione was not present, the parallel crisis of a missing pope having usurped his presence. The independent cardinal immediately spoke up. Was His Eminence denying that there was a problem, asked this distinguished but aged member of the Curia.

"Not at all!" said Menenger. "The misplaced enthusiasm of some is to be deplored. But in another sense the gloves are off, Eminence. The Holy Spirit is on the loose and the Devil take the hindmost."

Dumbfounded by the Prefect's reply, the speaker asked if no differentiation was to be made between the Spirit of God and the spirit driving those condemned by the American courts for practicing spiritual bastardry.

"I am informed that grossly exaggerated claims have been made against CNCD missionaries, and that in most cases this will be shown to be the case." Menenger straightened like a soldier on parade. "In all conscience, Eminences, I cannot allow my judgment to be clouded by these hysterical reports. Yes, mistakes have been made, some grievous, but I am assured that these are not policy in the sense that the American media are contending."

"The Holy Father has nothing to say on this matter?" asked a worried compatriot.

"The Holy Father is presently unable to deal with this problem. The burden of response has fallen on me."

"Is it true he is very ill?"

"An exaggeration, Eminence. The prognosis is that he will make a full recovery."

"From what?" asked another.

"Exhaustion. He is as yet unused to the pressures of office, which, as you know, are considerable. He is of a frail constitution, but is recovering well for a man of his age."

"Odd rumors are emanating from the Apostolic Palace, Eminence." The speaker was a newly elevated cardinal. "I've heard it mooted that he isn't there at all, that he is neither in his apartment nor in any of the usual clinics."

"I can assure you that everything is as it ought to be," said Menenger, the movements of his head and his smile indicating that he wanted to move on.

The first speaker obliged. If only a small percentage of what had been claimed about CNCD's behavior was accurate, he said, then shouldn't this movement be censured. The accusations made against it were serious, and as they had mostly come from within the organization itself, just as what had sparked it all off had come from within their own ranks, then shouldn't the assumption that this extraordinary state of affairs amounted to nothing more than hysteria be treated with a greater degree of caution.

"No one is denying that mistakes have been made," said Menenger, "but care should also be taken to separate out media chaff. Those who have dedicated every moment of their lives to Christ should not be abandoned on the basis of malicious gossip. The American media is deeply influenced by leftist propaganda; theirs is a mindset embedded in the mire of democratic excess. And I would remind you, Eminences, we are living in the Last Times. If the church is to mean anything as we approach the moment of our Lord's return, then it should be meaning bathed in the spirit and passion of the early Christian community. That requires a certain rigor, don't you think?" A smile. "It is for this that the New Catholic Dawn is being called in question; they have taken it upon themselves to pursue the enlivening spirit of the early Christian community and have laid down the gauntlet on Christ's behalf." A pause to let his words sink in. Then, "It will be interesting to see who has the courage to pick up this gauntlet as the democracies descend into self-inflicted chaos."

There was a general murmur of approval, but not from the elderly cardinal. CNCD was not then a sect run out of control? he queried.

"*Secta* or *sectus* ?" asked Menenger. Before the other could reply, he added, "*Secta* is the past participle of the verb *sequor*, which means 'to follow'. The sense in which the American media are using the word is quite different. They, in their wisdom, are using the Latin *sectus*, which is the past participle of 'to cut'. In their sense of things a sect is a group which has cut itself off from the major body, hence, CNCD is a sect cut off from the Church. If the word 'sect' is to be used at all, and I personally think it should not, then it should be used in the sense of the faithful following the Gospel injunction to preach and teach Christ to the ends of the Earth. To my way of thinking, that is hardly an indictment."

"What then do you think should be our response?" asked the same cardinal, amazed by Menenger's tightrope-walking.

"That no such sectarian nonsense has been detected across

Europe," said Menenger. "I think that speaks for itself. Don't you? If there is a problem, and I'm not saying that on some level there isn't, then it is a problem peculiar to the United States of America."

* * *

David Mayle phoned back at six; he sounded a little drunk. Duggan chided him playfully, then admitted that he too was slightly under the weather.

"I'm real sorry to hear about your father," said Mayle. "I know what it feels like."

"His heart wasn't good; I knew it was a possibility."

"You can't prepare for it," said Mayle.

"No, you can't," said Duggan.

"Okay if I put Holly on?"

"Yeh, of course."

"Hi, Jack," said Holly.

They went through the business of condolences. Duggan reached for normality. "Sounds like you've pulled off the big one, Holly," he said, aware of how her career would be affected.

"Hasn't done me any harm, Jack," she said back. "But I couldn't have done it without David on side. I knew what was going on in his head. He's a pro, Jack. He saw the possibilities in this one."

"His paper won't be pleased."

"They'll be jumping mad; who could blame them."

"The Post will take him on?"

"What do you think?"

He was hearing a different voice; it was as if Holly had suddenly grown up. "Things aren't quite so well resolved this end," he said.

"I managed to get a copy of your article, Jack," she said back. "It was brilliant. I don't think anyone else could have got it across the way you did."

"I'm lucky it wasn't cut. It took up half of the bloody magazine!"

Duggan's fear had been that Holly's competitive nature would make her run with what she had of his story and botch it, but he had been wrong about that. Her instincts had saved her from making that kind of mistake - her instincts plus David Mayle. She had instead gone after what appeared to be the secondary prize, and in conjunction with David had landed the Post's biggest story since Water Gate.

"We have it on good authority they've been doing their thing in Australia for about the ten years. Heard anything, Jack?"

"Nothing."

"They have a low profile policy. They shun the limelight. If you check things out I think you'll find they've got their fingers in quite a few pies."

"If I took up cudgels against CNCD here in Australia it would be read as confirmation of a pact with you guys. They'd see it as me jumping on the Catholic-bashing bandwagon. I've already been accused of colluding with Windle and yourselves to harm the Catholic Church because of my background. One of our Sydney newspapers had a go at me only recently on that one."

"They linked you with us?"

"They knew Jane was with me here in Sydney, and they knew who she was. They also knew we had all been in New York at the same time, and that David and I had met at the conference in Santa Rosa. It struck me as the kind of thing Robert Carter would get up to."

"It was Carter who messed up Donaghue's diocese. We outed him big time and he's been trying to nail us ever since."

"Watch your back, Holly. He's a nasty individual and he's got it in for David."

"He's flailing, Jack. He's lost face all round. He's out of his depth this time."

"Then he's at his most dangerous, Holly. The Sydney article was an attempt to cast doubt on our collective integrity. It's what I term *subtle mischief*. If Carter was behind it, and I think it very likely that he was, then we haven't heard the last of him."

"I'll keep that in mind," she replied. Then, "We've spoken to a lot of *very* unhappy ex-CNCD people, Jack. Scores of them. We now have documents we're not supposed to have. In-house directives. Letters deploring their activities from priests and high-ranking churchmen. It's damning stuff all of it. It shows a mentality so utterly out of step with democratic values it's frightening. And it's been going on behind the scenes for years. There have been complaints galore and they've all but been ignored."

"And no response from the Vatican? They must be burning the midnight oil on this one."

"What's surfacing now is CNCD's long-term plans for Catholic youth. Most of the mass rallies for young people are CNCD-driven. They bus in their indoctrinated members by the thousand and get them to mingle with kids of their own age from different parts of the Church. It's very well organized, and on the surface quite innocent. But it isn't innocent. It's a full-scale blitz on the innocent, and it appears to have Cardinal Menenger's blessing."

"The whole point of the exercise is converts, Holly. Always has been."

"Yes, but to what? The Gospel message? A bucketload of imaginative theology? CNCD's particularly odd take on the whole shebang?"

"It's all a bit odd, when you think about it."

"Yes, but there used to be rules of engagement. I was never bludgeoned into believing what the Church taught. It was just *there.* It was my decision whether I ran with it or not."

"Thanks to Vatican II."

"Yes, I suppose."

"'A pluralism of movements masquerading as a pluralism of ideas'," said Duggan, paraphrasing Bishop Peters. "More subtle mischief."

"Mind if I use that, Jack? It's good."

"Be my guest," he said back.

43

Majnoon

Benedict XVI lay staring at the ceiling, his gaze fixed on the slowly revolving fan. He had waited for over an hour at the Golden Gate, then, realizing that he was perhaps tempting God, had retraced his steps and had again become lost in the Old City's maze of shops and alleyways. Losing judgment altogether, he had wandered into a small courtyard with arched windows and filigreed screens and found himself confronted by a group of silent, white-turbaned men. Arabs, he immediately realized. They had gaped at him in surprise, one of them indicating, after a moment, in which direction he should depart. He would have dearly liked to talk to them, but knew instinctively that they would not have responded, that his black soutane was not welcome in this particular neighborhood.

Nothing had happened at the Golden Gate. The more he thought about that the more it seemed unlikely that anything could have happened, or should have happened. Yet he had felt compelled to go there and wait, and he had obeyed, just as he had obeyed the impulse to head for Jerusalem.

A small explosion of laughter escaped Benedict's lips as the madness of his actions again hit home. He was truly mad; he had to be. He had lost all reason and would be carted back to the Apostolic Palace in a straitjacket. Imagine, the Holy Father in a straitjacket! How tongues would wag.

The Arab had pointed back the way he had come, his dark-eyed face as severe as any Benedict had ever seen. There had been a look of incomprehension in those eyes. What was this fool of an infidel doing in his courtyard, he seemed to ask. He had hesitated for but a moment, then with a courteous nod turned away, their collective gaze pushing at him like an invisible hand.

The fan's lazy movements were mesmerizing. Benedict closed his eyes and observed the images that arose in his mind. Streets and crowd scenes predominated at first. These gave way to this or that Station of the Cross, to the Crusader crosses he had seen not far from the chapel of St Helena, then, with a twist, to the colorfully stenciled crescent moons with their messages in Arabic. Then, with a further twist, to the face of a small child he had glimpsed in a doorway. Arab? Jewish? He hadn't been able to tell.

Opening his eyes, he thought about his dream of the crying children, and of how their crying had stopped. The Devil had vanished and their crying had stopped. Was it as simple as that? He got up and went to the window, opened the shutters and looked down into the street. It was early evening, still light but touched now with the dusk's dunning down of the day's sharpness. He had eaten late in the afternoon and returned to his little room to sleep, and was now ready for another adventure. Far below - he was on the third floor - the window boxes of marigolds that had first attracted his attention stared up at him. Above his head lay the flat roof area with its whitewashed parapet, wooden bench and tubs of assorted trees and flowers. A nice place to catch the cool of the evening, he had been told.

His cardinal's credentials had not been questioned by the landlady of the Gideon Hotel; it had been as if his passport had said 'computer salesman' or 'carpenter', for all she had cared. He had nevertheless explained his position. He was on a personal pilgrimage to the Holy Land and wanted to keep it strictly personal - hence his being off the beaten track. She had smiled and treated him, he thought, with a little less reserve after that. And when he shed his expensively cut clerical suit and purple stock, and appeared in an ordinary black soutane and broad-brimmed hat, she had positively beamed at him. A simple priest again, he had smiled and doffed his hat for her with a cavalier's sweeping bravado.

There had been a disturbance at the Lion Gate as Benedict bussed in from the airport. Israeli police had fired rubber-coated bullets at stone-throwing Muslims and the situation had escalated out of control. Not long afterwards, some Palestinians had hurled stones from the compound of the Al-Aqsa Mosque into the neighboring Western Wall plaza, a site thronged with Jewish worshippers. More clashes had followed. In spite of incitement, the West Bank Preventative Service chief, conscious of the bloody clashes that had taken place on the Temple Mount during October of the previous year, had urged Israel to refrain from shooting at Palestinian demonstrators.

Unaware of the uncertain truce that reigned that evening between Palestinians and Israeli security forces, Benedict, intent on nothing more than an evening walk, entered the Old City by the Jaffa Gate and headed up Christian Quarter Road towards the Holy Sepulcher. On his left, according to his map, lay the Greek Orthodox Patriarchate, on his right, the Mosque of Omar. As before, an apparently simple destination proved difficult to find because of the endless vaulted alleyways and the crush of humanity which, thankfully, did thin occasionally. Within the 218 acres of the walled-in Old City lay a plethora of churches, mosques, synagogues, monasteries and holy sites, interwoven with a density of residential living equal to anything elsewhere in Israel. As with any densely populated area, crime, poverty and drugs combined to produce a sometimes uncertain atmosphere.

As he wandered, aimlessly and, to an extent, innocently, through these still crowded streets, Benedict would have been horrified to learn that old Jerusalem's Latin Catholic, Greek and Armenian religious communities had, a few days prior to his arrival, collided in bloody confrontation over rights to the Holy Sepulcher. Having divided the Sepulcher up between themselves (circumstances over the decades had given one, then the other dominance), the factions guarded their section of the Sepulcher with a ferocity worthy of East Jerusalem's more colorful inhabitants. Heads had been cracked as they jostled to retain some minor advantage or privilege, and all because their theologies and rituals were tangentially different, their claims on divine truth considered the more ancient. For the sake of peace-keeping, the Jews had put the keys to the Holy Sepulcher's great wooden entrance door in the hands of a Muslim family, the irony of which seemed lost on those demanding that they, and only they, should have custody of the keys.

A parallel irony was that Benedict believed he had custody of the only set of keys that really mattered: the keys to God's kingdom. In whatever fashion he so wished he could extend or curtail the rights of every believing Catholic on Earth. Unbeknownst to Christians who were not Catholic, this right also extended to them by proxy: the Catholic Church was, by definition, the *only* legitimate source of salvation on the planet. Popes could pray alongside Anglicans, Jews and Muslims, visit their separate establishments and make comforting noises, but the price of full reconciliation could only be absorption: co-existence in the sense of spiritual parity was a hoped-for, but unrealizable dream. God had shifted His allegiance from the Jews to the first Christians, and that was the end of the matter.

Muslims were of course of much the same opinion. God had later shifted His allegiance to them, Jesus being the penultimate prophet, not, as Christians claimed, the incarnate Son of the God. Jews, ever the wittiest of the three Abrahamic faiths, shrugged their shoulders and waited for the other two to recognize that history validated their sovereignty in all religious matters. Had they not started the ball rolling? Was it not to Israel that God had promised the final joys, or toys? Who could argue with Scripture?

Suddenly, in the crowd, in twos, young men in green berets with slung machine guns. Then, from the Temple Mount, as if in dismissal of these slouching figures, the distantly amplified call to prayer.

Amidst the color and unfamiliar smells of the alleyways, Benedict heard that call and looked up as if to catch it in the air like a fragrance. Although faint, he knew immediately what it was, and in his heart of hearts respected its constancy. If Catholics were half as concerned with their prayer life as Muslims, then the Church would not be in the state it was in, he had said to Fr Gozzoli, his private secretary and confidant. Imagine, five times a day on your knees before your God!

Benedict looked as if he knew where he was going; his step had changed from a leisurely gait to that of someone moving along with purpose. He was aware of this change in rhythm, but not of the reason for it. It was as if the collective consciousness of the crowd had registered some deep-seated psychic disturbance, a subtle seismic tremor beyond the grasp of the conscious mind. One minute unaware, he was the next acutely aware of a general restlessness, an unease and sense of foreboding. Something indefinable had passed through the crowd, and it was on edge. Incongruously, it made him think of the now empty Pool of Bethesda, the excavated hole near to the church of St Anne that he had stared down into for some minutes. Known in Jesus' day for its healing, angel-stirred waters, it signaled what he had come to think of as a little-understood human capacity for sensing the Holy Spirit's presence.

The burst of gunfire, when it came, made everyone duck, and for good reason - the whine of rubber-coated bullets slamming into walls and ricocheting was unmistakable. Screaming women, some in full djellaba, added to the bedlam, the commands of green-bereted soldiers and the crackle of hand-held radios mixing with the shouting of men and the startled cries of children.

The incident would later be written up in the *Jerusalem Post* as minor, as a false alarm, as an unfortunate mistake made by nervous Israeli security forces. But a threat of retaliation by militants angered by what they considered heavy-handed police action at the Lion Gate had in fact been made, and there had been no way of knowing what these hot-heads had in mind, or where they intended to strike next. Over as quickly as it had begun, the fracas had nevertheless resulted in a number of injuries, some of them quite serious.

Benedict was one of the injured; a bullet had grazed his temple and knocked him unconscious. When he came to he was on a stretcher and being hurled into the emergency ward of a local hospital.

"You were *very* lucky, Father. Or, depending on how you look at it, unlucky." The doctor's humor was lost on Benedict. He blinked his incomprehension at the man's American-accented English. "You could have been killed."

"I-am-live, thanks-be-to-God," said Benedict.

"You suffered a light concussion," said the doctor. "It would be better if you hung around for a few hours. Just in case. Okay, Father?"

"O-kay," said Benedict.

It was all down-hill from there; the nurses questions when they came, proved difficult to answer; they concerned his identity. His head bandaged and throbbing, his grasp of what was being said to him at times wayward, Benedict admitted to being Angelo Rinaldi, to being Italian, and to being on a personal pilgrimage to the Holy Land.

"You have your passport on you, Father?"

"It-ees . . . " Benedict searched for the correct word, failed, and snatched at something roughly equivalent. "It-ees-in-*spec-ial-box*-at-hotel," he said triumphantly.

"I see. What is the name of your hotel?"

"Hotel-*Gid-eon*," said Benedict. "Ees-small."

"Do you have any other form of identification on you?"

"No, Signora."

"No credit cards?"

"No, Signora."

The nurse placed another cross on the form she was filling in and looked up. She was frowning. "You have traveller's medical insurance?"

A blank stare from Benedict.

"Medical insurance?"

"I-leeve-Rome at . . . speed?"

"You were in a hurry?"

"Yes, *hur-ay.*" A smile from Benedict. "At-last-minute . . . I-go." A ball of panic was forming in the pit of his stomach; he could feel the net closing. "Big-rush," he added, trying to sound casual.

The nurse's parting smile was quizzical; Benedict knew she had gone off to report an anomaly in procedure, that she sensed there might be a problem with her little priest. When she returned a few minutes later with a hospital administrator, it was to find the cubicle empty. Her little bird had flown, as bizarre a series of events as could be imagined by anyone already taking shape.

The police were at the Gideon Hotel within minutes of being informed that someone dressed as a Catholic priest had acted suspiciously after being treated in hospital for a light concussion. The circumstances of his injury had caused them to move quickly, but as they soon discovered, Fr Rinaldi had not lied, he had just been unforthcoming about his superior rank.

The hotel owner ventured an explanation. He had admitted to being on a personal pilgrimage, she said. For that reason he desired anonymity. Why else stay with her when he could have been wining and dining at any of Jerusalem's five-star hotels .

"Anonymity is one thing, trying to avoid paying for medical treatment is another."

"He's a lovely little man. Very friendly."

"So where is our lovely little man right this minute?"

The landlady shrugged and pulled a face.

"We'll hold on to this," said the other policeman. He pocketed Benedict's old passport and glanced at his companion. "We'd better take a look at his room."

What they found was at first glance innocuous: two changes of clothes and some underwear.

"The suit's good quality."

"Must be expecting to officiate at something important by the look of this." The talkative policeman had laid Benedict's white vestments out on the bed and was examining them. Picking up the skull cap, he placed it on his head and straightened, "He could pass for a Jew wearing this."

"I thought only popes wore white," said the other, remembering John Paul's visit to Israel.

"Sure travels light."

"The passport could be fake."

"Or stolen. Apart from that there's nothing suspicious here that I can see."

"Unless he has more than one."

They mused on that for a moment, then admitted that it was an unlikely scenario, that they were more than likely dealing with a cleric who just wanted some time to himself. Why else name the Gideon Hotel. Maybe the injury he had received was more serious than first thought; concussion could cause all sorts of problems.

As they reached this tentative verdict, an again exhausted Benedict entered the foyer downstairs and dinged the counter bell. As he waited for the proprietor to appear, he removed his round-brimmed hat and touched gingerly at his bandaged temple.

When she appeared she said straight off that the police had taken his passport and were that very minute in his room. Her wide-eyed stare suggested she thought he might bolt for the door.

"Ah," he said. Then, "I-am-sor-ray-to-have-caused-this-to-happen. Very-sor-ray."

"You had better go up stairs and sort things out," she said back. Then, focusing a little more on the human being before her, she said, "Are you in pain?"

"Some," said Benedict. He turned away, then back. "I am sor-ray," he said again. "You-will-understood-soon."

The two policemen looked up surprised to see him; the older one stumbled over how to address him.

" . . . Angelo Rinaldi?"

"That-ees . . . true," said Benedict.

"There are a few question we would like to ask you."

"I-am-here," replied Benedict.

The younger policeman, who was forever doing courses, took over. "You're attached to the Vatican in some capacity, Eminence?"

Benedict's head tilted in recognition of being addressed properly. He was so attached, he said.

"Why have you come to Israel?"

"Because-thees-ees-where-I-have-to-be," said Benedict.

"You're here officially?"

" . . . Per-haps, yes."

It was a very odd reply; it made the older policeman frown.

"Is there something you're not telling us?" said the younger policeman, sensing a possible caveat.

"Thees-ees-also-true," said Benedict.

"You're here for a particular reason?"

"Yes."

"So why don't you want anyone to know you're a cardinal?"

"Be-cause-I-am-not-a-cardinal."

"Your passport is a fake?"

"It-ees-*old*-passport," said Benedict.

"It still has two years to run."

"I-am-not-same-per-son. I-am-now-diff-erent."

"You were a cardinal, but no longer are. Is that it?" said the older policeman.

"Yes."

"So why are you here?"

"That-ees-not-yet-re-veal-ed-to-me."

"You're waiting for instructions?"

"Yes."

"From whom?"

"God."

The policemen stared at Benedict, then the older one said, "You'll have to come with us for further questioning."

"I-am-redee-for-this," said Benedict, who was now resigned to whatever his God willed.

"Get your stuff together. Everything."

"I-will-not-re-turn?"

"I wouldn't think so."

"I-will-pay-now?"

"For your room? Yes, I suppose so," said the older policeman. He smiled, glanced at his companion and shook his head in disbelief.

"I-change-cloth-es?"

"Back to being the cardinal you aren't?"

"To-be-self," said Benedict.

"And what would that be?"

"Pope," he replied innocently.

"Now you're the pope?"

"That- ees-my . . . hon-er."

The younger policeman thumped in the direction of the Benedict's white vestments and skull cap. *"Majnoon,"* he said, referring to the religious crazies who kept turning up with the tourists.

Every policeman and soldier in Israel was familiar with the term; it signified a psychological disorder prevalent among Christian pilgrims. Otherwise known as the 'Jerusalem Syndrome', those afflicted believed themselves to be biblical characters or divine agents on a mission from God. Abandoning friends, families and tour groups, they gave away their money and possessions and adopted a peripatetic lifestyle of poverty and street corner evangelism. Most were successfully treated and sent back home. Some remained enslaved to their delusion for years.

"Don't they generally think they're Jesus, or Moses?" said the older policeman.

Turning away from Benedict, the younger policeman said in a low voice that it was Protestant Christians who went in for that kind of identification. This one was Catholic, and he was a cardinal. Or had been a cardinal. It followed that his greatest desire, perhaps his secret desire, was to be pope.

"I-am-*not* -mad-man," said Benedict.

The young policeman replied not unkindly that popes did not travel on their own, particularly to the Middle East. He smiled and added that the Israeli government would have been informed of any such unimaginable intention. Knowing that it was useless to argue, Benedict remained silent.

"I'll pack his case," said the older policeman.

He was not allowed to change into his white vestments; they preferred him as he was. Stepping onto the tiled floor of the foyer, leather case in hand, Benedict paid his bill and was ushered out into the night like a common criminal. Whatever lay ahead was now entirely in God's hands, he reasoned.

News of Benedict's incarceration in the special clinic for *majnoons* reached Cardinal Menenger the following morning. The police communiqué was abrupt. They had intercepted what appeared to be a genuine cardinal suffering from the delusion that he was Benedict XVI. It was hoped such a delicate matter could be speedily resolved. Would they please confirm that the man now being held by the medical authorities in Jerusalem was Angelo Cardinal Rinaldi, and if so, arrange for him to be escorted back to Rome. Accompanying this communiqué was a head and shoulders photograph of a weary-looking Benedict taken at the police station.

44

Lies and Deceit

The Catholic Archbishop of Sydney's attack on James Windle on the Don Cooper Show had been specific: he had had both motive and opportunity to take a few extra photographs of the codex and pass them on. Duggan had sidestepped this awkward moment by claiming that all photographs would have been accounted for. He had then focused attention on the follow-up claim that Windle may have been involved in forging the codex - a much easier point to handle - and Archbishop Pullman had taken the bait.

Robert Carter's attack, when it came, chose the former rather than the latter angle. Coming into the argument hard on the heels of the announcement that ink and paper tests had also confirmed the codex to be a genuine, his carefully sculpted accusation in the national press was that Windle had most probably been involved in 'deceitful practices'. Hacking away at Windle's reputation, Carter then borrowed Pullman's 'motive' and 'opportunity' argument and returned to the idea of under-the-counter photographs being handed on. Windle had an axe to grind, he contended, and that axe was a cleverly veiled hatred for the doctrines of the Catholic Church. When aligned with the harebrained contents of Theodore's codex, the result was the disastrous revisionist nonsense already dumped on the general public by the Australian journalist Jack Duggan. As Duggan had been guilty of subterfuge - a fact now on record - the question was: to what extent had Professor Windle also acted unprofessionally while at the monastery of Mar Saba? An authentic document the codex may well be, but its contents were as malicious a form of anti-Christian propaganda as could be imagined, and this fact should not be allowed to slip by unnoticed. In a word, the codex was being used by unscrupulous people to further sideline Christianity's hard-won place in Western civilization.

If this had been Carter's main focus, it would have been bad enough, but the scope of his attack also tellingly reiterated the *Sydney Morning Herald's* conspiracy claim. Concluding that James Windle, Jack Duggan, David Mayle and Holly Parks were all part of a concerted effort to discredit Christianity in general, and the Roman Church in particular, Carter damned this 'coterie of unbelievers' and boldly admitted to being in favor of the New Catholic Dawn's evangelizing spirit. The present media hoopla surrounding this important spiritual movement was, he said, " . . . a cleverly orchestrated paranoia hatched to do maximum damage to Christianity's message of love and salvation".

Hoping to save face through this kind of maneuver, Carter then took to criticizing Archbishop Donaghue. Accusing the archbishop of being an inadvertent supporter of Fr Sebastian Grosjean, the now suspended Gregorian-based philosopher who had penned *The End of Catholicism?*, he questioned the archbishop's perceived role as guardian of the Catholic soul in America, and finished off with the claim that Grosjean's supporters in the Curia were nothing more than closet modernists. Inadequately informed and prejudicial in their many claims and assessments, these self-appointed judges had shown themselves to be irresponsible in the extreme. As a result of their machinations, good people had been pulled down into the gutter, and he, Robert Carter, would see to it that justice was done on their behalf. A missionary spirit was again burning brightly in the Church, and it should be nurtured, not quenched.

Carter's line of reasoning caused an immediate uproar, particularly in Germany's tabloid press. Windle was forcing an atheist's perspective on biblical scholarship, one paper suggested. He was a lone-wolf scholar, a 'maverick' whose interpretation of ancient history was dangerously revisionist, said another. Alarmed by such reports, and by the barrage of abuse he had received over his remarks on the Middle East, Windle arranged another interview with *Die Welt*. Sensing an historic moment in the making, Wolfgang Pauli dropped the scheduled prime-time Saturday night interview and slotted Windle in instead. It was hard to say what this American history professor had in mind, he admitted to his board, but if his last appearance on *Die Welt* was anything to go by, then they were in for an interesting ride.

"So how do you want to handle this?" asked Pauli, as he and Windle shook hands. "You obviously have something in mind."

Windle paused before replying, then he said, "It's time to clarify certain issues."

"A few more home truths?"

"Not quite. But yes, that too."

"I'll take my cue from you," said Pauli, acknowledging a five-minute signal from his producer. As he and Windle walked across the brightly lit studio towards the program's iconic black leather chairs, he added, "Can you give me some hint as to what you have in mind?"

"I'll know when the moment arises," said Windle. He then added mischievously, "I'll take my cue from you."

Ever the professional, Pauli merely smiled.

Settling into his chair, Windle said, apropos of nothing, "It's thought that the first act of intelligence may have been a lie; in the sense of it being something that gave one individual an advantage over another. It makes sense, don't you think? And so we advanced, lie by lie, towards the truth, yet remained doomed to lie for ever."

"Your point?" asked Pauli.

"That lies are part of our power play at the same time as they are part of our search for the truth. We simply can't avoid them. It's possible for someone to live a transformed life through sincerely believing in a particular lie. That makes some lies potentially transformative in spite of the motives that may drive them."

"Myths are thought to be transformative," said Pauli. "A myth is a lie of sorts, isn't it? Myths are exaggerations, inflations of ordinary reality."

"It depends on the myth. Some myths are universal, others are tribal. Universal myths unite, tribal myths separate. Every culture has its share of both. The problems arise in not recognizing which is which, in getting them mixed up. Religion is invariably an undifferentiated mixture of the universal and the tribal."

"Tribal in the sense of local?"

"Exactly. We are bedeviled at every turn by parochial myths."

"Christians flatly reject the idea of their faith being myth-based," said Pauli.

"Christianity's greatest weakness is that it recognize everyone else's myth but its own. It has a blind spot. If it could accept the role of myth in its own makeup, most of its dilemmas would evaporate."

Pauli glanced past Windle and nodded to the floor manager, who was signaling two minutes to go.

"I'm obliged to you for having me on your program a second time," said Windle. "My thanks to you for that."

Indicating that their little chat was over, Pauli withdrew into himself as if into a shell. In the same moment, the studio lights dimmed and a small cone-shaped light on top of one of the two cameras came on. Windle braced himself; he could see the show's introductory credits scrolling across their silhouetted figures on a nearby monitor. When the lights came up again, Pauli turned towards the lit camera.

"Welcome to *Die Welt*. Our guest this evening is Professor James Windle, someone I'm sure most of you are now familiar with." Pauli then turned to Windle and the two men exchanged pleasantries. "As the historian at the center of the Mar Saba Codex controversy, or scandal," said Pauli, "would you care to comment on how this sad state of affairs has arisen?"

"What scandal there is resides in the attempt to disparage the importance of the Mar Saba Codex by disparaging me personally," said Windle. "Particularly now that the codex's authenticity has been verified, and the insinuation that it may have been forged by myself and others abandoned."

"Verified in the sense of stemming from a certain hand, of being on the correct paper and written with the correct squiggles using the correct inks, certainly," said Pauli, getting into stride, "but not, surely, in the sense of it being either true or untrue. Isn't the truth or falsity of what the codex contains an altogether different proposition? Doesn't it ultimately become a matter of interpretation?"

"To a certain extent that is true," said Windle, "but any interpretation made has to be based on evidence, not on wishful thinking. Our whole conception of Christianity as practiced by the Jerusalem Church of the Apostles in the first century is governed by a theological overview. What's come down to us via Church historians and theologians is, on many levels, a distortion of historical reality. Put in kindly terms, it is an inadequate appreciation of first century Jewish sectarianism."

"This is now the consensus view of biblical scholars?"

"It is the view now burgeoning for attention among biblical scholars. It —- "

"But not yet broadly accepted."

"No, but —- "

"Isn't to doubt what the faith teaches about Jesus and the Church to be in error?"

"Doubt is not the same as error. Skepticism is healthy; it's the hallmark of a discriminating mind. Jesus said 'Seek and ye shall find". You can't seek without questioning, and you can't question without doubting."

"Thomas got into trouble for doubting."

"That's the story."

"You don't believe it?"

"It smacks of politics. It's thought to be a contrived story designed to sell the later theologically driven view of Jesus as a miraculous being."

"The New Testament isn't literally true?"

"The notorious anti-Jewish curse in Matthew 27:25 is no longer accepted by Church thinkers as literal truth. Why should it be? It's an obvious exaggeration. It's caused endless suffering down the centuries and had to be seen for what it was, a literary expression.

That alone sets a precedent, don't you think?"

"That's not in quite the same context."

"No, it isn't, but it serves to illustrate a point: the New Testament should not be swallowed whole. The Thomas story is a window into what was going on behind the scenes, as are many other stories in the Gospels and the Epistles of Paul. The identification of textual windows that throw events and happenings into sharper relief is an important part of biblical scholarship. "

"Why bother to include the Thomas story at all? Wouldn't it have been safer to drop it?"

"It's a veiled warning against taking Thomas's highly controversial gospel seriously; it flatly contradicts the synoptics in form and substance. The gospels thought to have been written by Matthew, Mark, Luke and John weren't written until decades after Jesus' death. Hence the reprimand to Thomas about believing without seeing. That tells us that Thomas's gospel was probably already in circulation, and that its contents were so threatening it had to be refuted."

"Thomas's gospel is written off by the Church as apocryphal."

"It's classified as apocryphal to stop anyone taking it seriously. It presents us with a very different kind of Jesus. Some of the statements made by Thomas's Jesus are quite startling."

"Can you give us an example?"

"*'If you bring forth what is within you, what is within you will save you. If you do not bring forth what is within you, what is within you will destroy you.*"

"Thomas said that?"

"Modern, isn't it?"

Wolfgang Pauli stared at Windle for a moment, then in that dangerously soft tone he sometimes used, he said, "You've been accused of hating Christianity and everything Catholic, Professor. Is there any truth in that claim?"

"No, there isn't," said Windle. "I've been fascinated by Christianity since I was a young man. I've spent the better part of my adult life studying its history and its claims. I respect its aims and aspirations, but I cannot in all honesty say the same about its attitude of superiority to all other religious forms. The evidence for a very different view of early Christianity is there for anyone who wants to look, but you have to want to look. It's not something that will jump out at you of its own accord. It's hidden among the stories and statements of the New Testament. It's a treasure that has to be unearthed. It requires work, thought and study."

"Can you give us the *burgeoning* view of scholars like yourself in a few sentences?"

"Yes, I think so. It's a matter of realizing that the Apostles were Jewish sectarians, not Christians in the sense now understood by that term. The title Christian was a term of abuse coined against followers of St Paul by opponents at Antioch in the early sixties of the first century. It had no bearing on the Jerusalem Church of the Apostles, and it cannot be back-dated. It is a major mistake in group identification to do so, and the attempt to sidestep this problem by calling the Apostles 'Jewish-Christians' only makes matters worse. That confuses the issue and allows the identification mistake to continue unchecked. Yes, the original apostles of Jesus were Jews, but they were part of a sectarian milieu called 'the Way', and they did not think their Messiah was Israel's God paying them a personal visit. That formulation grew out of the Roman Church's inability after the war of AD70 to properly decipher what had been going on in those early years. They quite simply lost track of their faith's roots, misinterpreted St Paul's bridging terminology with regard to salvation, Israel, and the role of Messiah, and as a result turned the sectarian Messiah into a pagan-styled god-man risen from the dead. The question being asked now, of course, is whether Paul was actually referring to Jesus at all, or to a figure earlier in Jewish history, a figure to which the transcribers of Paul's letters appended the name of Jesus."

"Many will consider these to be outrageous claims."

"Well, you asked for the burgeoning view of scholars like myself.

That's basically it. The underlying argument between Paul and the Jerusalem Church was over how Gentiles fitted into God's scheme of salvation. Just about everything that makes Christianity so distinct now - its doctrine of personal salvation in particular - grew out of early attempts to solve that particular problem. If we want to understand what was going on between Paul and the Jerusalem Church, we have to read Jewish and Christian literature in tandem, not just assume that Christianity superseded Judaism and dismiss the Jewish context as irrelevant. There were lots of groups within orthodox Judaism, and they each had policies or theologies that involved Gentiles. The Christian position on the Gentiles can only be understood in relation to the different arguments presented by those Jewish groups, and by the Jerusalem Church's approach to that question. The whole thing was about how to get non-Jews under the canopy of the promises made by God to Israel. That was the essence of the salvation under offer, and in relation to the apostles of Jesus, that required an acceptance of their choice of Messiah."

"Jesus."

"Yes, Jesus. The Messiah figure rejected by orthodox Jewry *because* of his sectarian background."

Smiling in a pained kind of way, Pauli again paused; then, with a glance at the camera, he said, "I should tell my listeners, I suppose, that it was your idea to come on *Die Welt* this evening. Is that correct, Professor Windle?"

"It is."

"What was it you said while we were chatting earlier? You wanted to . . . clarify certain issues." A smile, and a tilting of the head. "Are the issues you wanted to clarify the ones we've been talking about? Or did you have something else in mind?"

"I had something else in mind," said Windle, accepting Pauli's lead-in. "Before I tell you what that is, however, let me describe a scene that's been bothering me, something we now know to have taken place at the monastery of Mar Saba after Professor Merle and I left the premises. It involves the person who removed the book containing the codex from its niche in the library and hid it, the person who triggered off the initial suspicion that Professor Merle and I might somehow be implicated in its disappearance. We still don't know who that person is, but it was almost certainly one of the resident monks. The hurried way in which it was dispensed with speaks of someone in a state of panic, a state of indecision over what exactly to do with this hot little item."

"It must have come as some relief to know it hadn't been destroyed."

"Yes, indeed. That would have been a calamity."

"And its authentication by a team of international experts must also be pleasing. It means that the accusation of forgery made against you, and by default others, has been apologetically dropped."

"No worse accusation can be made against someone in my position," said Windle. "It was a nightmare while it lasted."

"And the point you wish to make?" asked Pauli.

"That the actions of the person who moved the codex were grounded in fear and confusion, a deep-rooted fear and confusion of mind which caused him to do what he did. That's worth thinking about. It's a prime example of why honest scholarship is so necessary, why we have to dig down into the entrails of our religious beliefs and test their validity. If we don't, we'll never succeed in eradicating religious fear and the confusions that attend it. We have to learn to face the difficult questions. We have to learn how to ask these questions. Simplistic solutions only multiply the confusions and deepen people's fear of reality. Complicated, contortionist solutions designed to sidestep the sometimes confronting conclusions of honest scholarship are counter productive, they inevitably buckle before properly conducted research. The calculated avoidance of findings which do not tie in with your faith claims is an abuse of the mind every bit as serious as sexual abuse, it's more frequent, and it's doubly insidious in that it leads to a shutting down of the mind on many other levels. If what you're selling is a God who runs the universe to a pre-ordained plan, a kind of blueprint, then everyday reality turns into a gigantic cosmic plot from which there is no escape. God becomes the great jailer, the overseer who whips us back into line through threats or through the devastation of cataclysmic natural events. We are at the mercy of an omniscient, omnipresent tyrant who will use any means to herd us back into this or that religious fold. The sheep metaphor is particularly apt in this context."

"Secular scholars are immune to such prejudice?"

"Not at all. But the same rules apply. Any attempt to force reality into a false shape will inevitably come to grief. The world of scholarship moves on relentlessly; there's no stopping it. Reality always catches up with us."

"There's security in knowing for certain that you are headed for heaven rather than hell."

"I would take you back to the image of that man scurrying through the book stacks to hide Theodore's letter. Can you see his face? Can you see him frantically shove that document into its makeshift hiding place and make his way back to his cell? He's at his wit's end. Should he return and destroy the codex, or just try to forget about it? His whole mentality is encapsulated in that act. He is at the mercy of notions that have disabled his critical faculty. Is that really the kind of mentality we want to promote? I don't think it is."

"The images you're painting are quite fascinating, Professor," said Pauli. "Your little monk has set more in motion than he could ever have imagined."

"Our little monk represents a more than decent proportion of Western society," said Windle. "He is what many of us are in our weakest, most vulnerable moments. He is given over to a vision of things which disables his ability to face reality and accept, as a human being, responsibility for what takes place in the human sphere. We can say that it's a miracle that this or that person escaped death in some terrible incident, and mean by that that God intervened, but we all know damn well it wasn't a miracle at all. It was nothing more than a fluke of circumstances. Facing up to a small fact like that is a step towards the liberation of our mind. Put succinctly, the weight of our awake observations eventually outweigh the weight of our imaginings and we stutter into the light.

Windle fell silent, but Pauli did not come back in. It was as if he had decided to let Windle self-destruct on camera. Aware of the growing tension on the set, and of his now enlarged face on the monitor screen, Windle looked straight at the camera responsible for the close up, and said:

"As someone who was awake to the possibility of the Mar Saba Codex being devalued and kept under wraps for months, perhaps even for years by the Vatican's Department of Antiquities, I took it upon myself to make sure that that did not happen."

"In what way?" asked Pauli, rallying.

"By taking extra photographs of the codex with the intention of breaking the embargo I suspected would follow."

"You're admitting on national television that you took extra photographs of the codex with the intention of passing them on?"

"Call it an insurance policy. I knew roughly what would take place; I'd seen it all before. An exegesis dismissing the codex as unimportant because heretical would be fed to the general public. Church experts would consign it to oblivion on the basis that it contradicted the accepted scholarly position on what constituted the Jerusalem Church of the Apostles in the first half of the first century. That would be the end of the matter. Any voice raised in opposition would be met with ridicule, or by a deafening silence. Ridicule and silence are the Church's standard procedure when faced with questions that prove too difficult to handle."

"Why take on the commission in the first place? It was after all a Vatican-sponsored research trip."

"It was Professor Merle's suggestion. We'd worked together before and got on well. Priest he may be, but he's also a world-renowned scholar who does not shirk his duty in relation to a text.

It's also not easy to find financial backing for such trips."

"So how come it was you, and not he, who was tipped off about the codex's existence?"

"I wasn't tipped off about its existence. I was told that if I looked in a certain place I'd find something of interest. I passed that information on to Professor Merle and we decided it was worth looking into. To be frank, I didn't think we'd find anything. I thought it was a hoax, a bit of a joke to start with."

"And when it dawned on you that it wasn't a joke?"

"We were dumbfounded. Particularly when it turned out to be a letter in the hand of Theodore of Mopsuestia. Professor Merle is a recognized authority on Theodore's writings. That rang alarm bells, of course. Was the letter a forgery? Was Merle being targeted through me? We discussed that at length and made sure that we did a thorough job on the codex before sending photographs off to Rome. Merle's conclusion that it was probably authentic came as a relief to me."

"Probably authentic?"

"We did the best job we could in a short space of time. Confirmation still had to come from others on paper, ink, style, that kind of thing. We knew the manuscript would have to be submitted to rigorous testing on numerous levels before anyone would take our conclusions seriously."

"So why the extra photographs?"

"Because it wasn't certain that we'd ever be allowed to make those tests."

"Why not?"

"If proved to be authentic, the repercussions would have affected Jewish scholarship as well as Christian. Christians aren't the only ones with an invested interest in their particular view of history."

Pauli sat back into his chair and surveyed Windle with interest. "What exactly are you saying?" he asked.

"I'm saying that a lot more hinges on a document like this than many would think."

"You weren't surprised when the codex went missing?"

"I was surprised at the swiftness of the event. It's swiftness worried me."

"And that made you feel justified in having taken the extra photographs."

"Somewhat. It was too important a document to leave things to chance."

"But you already had a set of legitimate photographs in your possession. As did Professor Merle. Why break the rules and run the risk of censure?"

"Because there was a very good chance the Vatican's Department of Antiquities would decide to hold back on publication. Perhaps indefinitely - witness what went on with the Dead Sea Scrolls. The photographs belonged to the Department of Antiquities, they did not belong to Merle or myself."

"You're admitting to having had copies of the codex passed on to the Australian journalist Jack Duggan prior to proper testing. Wasn't that to jump the gun?"

"There was no reason to think the codex would ever be recovered. I had to do something to break the embargo on publication that I knew could go on for years." Windle's exasperation began to show. "The game of prevarication was already under-way. I had to do *something*. I knew I was putting my career on the line, but I considered that a small price to pay considering the probable importance of the codex. When I learned that the recipient of my photographs, a journalist, had the skill to do his own translation there was no one more surprised than myself. When he turned up in New York and asked me to vet that translation, I had no option but to comply."

"What you're saying, Professor, is that you feel no remorse for acting unprofessionally."

"On the contrary, I feel decidedly bad about it all. But in another sense I did act professionally. I did what I had to do to safeguard the contents of what I believed to be a very important fourth-century document. If it hadn't been recovered, the extra photographs I took would have kept the codex before the public eye."

"But not in themselves prove that the codex was authentic."

"Correct, but not altogether correct. If Theodore's letter hadn't been recovered, that would have strengthened the suspicion that it had been removed for no other reason than to render the photographs we already had inadmissible as evidence."

"Or bring about just such an impasse and make a clever forgery appear authentic. Wasn't that also a possibility?"

"Yes, it was. But having handled and studied the original, Professor Merle and I were in a strong position to vouch for the codex's probable authenticity. Anyway, now that it's been recovered such speculation is altogether academic."

"So why own up now? You were in the clear. No one would have been any the wiser. There was no need to confess to anything."

"I knew what I had done, and I knew it was borderline. I admit that. I've thought about it long and hard over the last few weeks and knew that I'd eventually have to own up. It's not in my character to lie or be deceitful."

"But you did lie, in a sense."

"I didn't tell all of the truth - that's the deceitful bit. That's the bit I'm now trying to rectify."

"You wish to be thought of as a man of conscience?"

"I'm not an ideologue; that's the point I'm making. Ideology is the corruption of reason and is morally akin to lying. I read that only recently and thought it so good I memorized it."

"What do you expect will happen to you now?"

"I've no idea. All I can do is claim extenuating circumstances and hope for the best. Others have found themselves in the same position and managed to survive. It's my suspicion that this kind of situation will arise much more often in the future."

"Why should it?"

"Because our society is evolving and the Church is standing still. It's not listening. It's afraid of being relevant, and that fear is making it progressively irrelevant."

"Is relevance the point?"

"It is if you're living in the real world. To stubbornly deny your obvious failings is to add an insurmountable failing to all the others."

Pauli fell silent suddenly. Windle braced himself for the unexpected. After a moment's cogitation, *Die Welt's* presenter said, "Does the person who passed on your illicit photographs to the Australian journalist in Santa Rosa now work for the *Washington Post?*"

"Yes, I believe so."

"His name is David Mayle?"

"Yes."

Another pause before Pauli continued. "Ill-will towards the Catholic Church has already been denied, but is it not true that David Mayle, yourself and the Australian journalist combined forces with Holly Parks - also of the *Washington Post* - to mount a two-pronged attack on Catholicism's truth claims? Isn't the brouhaha over the Catholic Church's spiritual movements - the Children of the New Catholic Dawn in particular - at heart a group effort to ridicule Catholicism and question its historical validity? Has not a straight-forward scholarly situation turned into something altogether nasty?"

"Not at all," said Windle. "I know the source of that rather silly idea, and I can tell you here and now that it is not true."

"All of you being involved with one another is pure coincidence?"

"From start to finish. What were the odds of David Mayle bumping into an Australian journalist in California who was also a specialist in fourth-century manuscripts?"

"Which raises the question as to why David Mayle was there in the first place," said Pauli. "Why that conference in particular? Wasn't it a gathering of highly conservative Catholic churchmen and scholars attempting to reinstate a more conservative theology among the faithful? Did he really expect to find a scholar in that mix of hardline and ultra-hardline thinkers who'd be willing to take on the task of producing a separate, clandestine translation of the codex?"

"Not everyone was hardline. Some were there because they knew a certain American bishop was about to challenge the conference on education policy - there are a lot of gradations between hardline and liberal. Out of those present two possible candidates had been identified as approachable. But given the nature of the request we had in mind, it would have been a risky business."

"So what happened exactly?"

"Only one of the two potential candidates turned up. Before David could get to the other one he bumped into Jack Duggan. On hearing about Jack's past he realized immediately that he had struck possible gold. Not only could the Australian do the translation, he could publish the codex as well. It was perfect. And when I finally met and talked to the guy, and was able to view his work, it was obvious we had been very lucky indeed."

"You're now friends."

"Indeed we are."

"And the much-publicized collapse of CNCD across the US?"

"Couldn't have happened to a nicer bunch of people. I was *delighted* to hear they'd got their comeuppance."

"The Church is in damage control over its charismatic movements. They're trying to blame the American media for the whole disaster."

"They're doing the same with the sex scandal that's presently breaking hard on its heels. It's all the fault of naughty journalists, according to Vatican sources. Which rather suggests they're trying to ignore the book that cracked the case against CNCD wide open. That's the only point of overlap between Holly Parks and the rest of us. Not long after interviewing me in New York she got wind of Sebastian Grosjean's book and headed straight for Rome. The story was there for the picking."

"So what's the upshot of all this for you?" asked Pauli. "Have your actions achieved what you hoped they would achieve?"

"Only time will tell," said Windle. "If the contents of Theodore's letter are treated with the seriousness they deserves, then who knows what the outcome might be."

45

Tea and cake

Benedict hadn't known where he was when he arrived, just that he was being escorted into what looked like a hospital. Fascinated by their charge, the two Israeli policemen had chatted to him nonstop as they negotiated the heavy evening traffic, the little Umbrian further enlightening them as to his identity. Handing him over to the on-duty doctor in the hived-off *majnoon* clinic, they had commented wryly on Benedict's inflated claims, and left him to his fate. Later, in a spacious interview room through whose open windows wafted the heavy scent of jasmine, the doctor had asked Benedict in English if he was, as his passport stated, Angelo Rinaldi, a cardinal in the Catholic Church recently arrived from Rome. Benedict's reply had surprised him. His gaze straying, as he spoke, to a nearby window where a sparrow sat chirping, he had confirmed his passport identity, but again pointed out that it was his old passport that was being examined. It was hardly old, the doctor had replied, turning a page. It didn't expire for another two years. He had meant that he was no longer a cardinal, Benedict explained. He was actually Pope Benedict XVI, and he had travelled to Jerusalem under his old passport to avoid detection. As a result of this bizarre claim, and others, he was assessed as a special category *majnoon*, his awareness of himself as Angelo Cardinal Rinaldi *and* as Pope Benedict XVI an interim state of derangement. It was an unusual case, the doctor admitted in his notes. An obsession with power, perhaps. He had never come across anything quite like it before.

By early Saturday morning, with confirmation from Rome that the person they had under observation was indeed Angelo Rinaldi, the little Umbrian had been placed in a comfortable ground-floor room to await the arrival of those designated his carers. When the two Salesian Fathers sent to collect him arrived, however, it was to find their charge gone. Exiting by way of an unlocked window in the adjacent interview room, he had lowered his slight frame into the garden backing the clinic and quickly found his way out onto the street. Shorn of passport and belongings, and with only a little of his money left, he had trudged back to the Old City of Jerusalem with no clear idea as to what he should do next. Everything was now in God's hands, he had reasoned. Any attempt to contact the authorities in his role as pope would result in his being shipped back to Rome. It was a matter of hide and wait. He still had his credit cards, of course, but knew it was inadvisable to use them. He would find a quiet spot and stay out of sight, lie low until evening and use the time to pray, and fast.

That was when he realized what a mistake it had been to return to the Gideon Hotel. It had been a moment of weakness, a moment of panic. To be without a passport in a foreign country was to be without country as well as identity, and fear of that had driven him into the hands of the Israeli police. And for what? From being Angelo Rinaldi, little known Umbrian cardinal, he had been elevated by men to the dizzying heights of supreme pontiff, and at a stroke by God to being no one at all. No one at all. Smiling to himself, Benedict the nobody had headed back towards the Old City, back to the narrow streets of the *souk* where he knew he could become invisible.

* * *

"They had him and lost him." Cardinal Menenger's tone was one of suppressed astonishment, his expression that of a man in a state of mental upheaval. "They thought he was suffering from the Jerusalem Syndrome."

"Unbelievable," said Cardinal Borghini.

Cardinal Maglione shook his head and smiled.

"It's the peasant in him," said Menenger. "It has to be. He's reverted to type."

"Harmless as a dove; cunning as a fox," said Maglione.

"The Israelis are getting suspicious," said Menenger. "They're asking awkward questions."

"No more so than the Italian press," said Maglione, who, in conjunction with the General Secretary was trying to keep the lid on palace gossip.

"They haven't tumbled yet to who he is?" Borghini was incredulous. "It's bound to dawn on them pretty soon."

"The unthinkable is imminent," said Menenger, more or less admitting defeat. "We should prepare ourselves for the worst."

"A nervous breakdown due to the pressures of office," suggested Borghini. "It would be true enough." He added that he and Cardinal Peronio had drafted a press statement to that effect. It was his hope that His Eminence would find it satisfactory.

"I'm sure I will, Vincenzo," said Menenger. "Thank you." Then to Maglione he said, "We may have to inform the Israelis as to what's actually going on. It may be the only way to speed things up."

Maglione, who sometimes had dealings with Italy's senior intelligence services, was in agreement. If the Holy Father hadn't been picked up within a few hours, he said, that would be the route to take.

"Pray God it doesn't come to that," said Menenger, whose greatest fear was that news of the fiasco would get out and the Church would become a laughing stock.

"I'm sure the Israelis will be sensitive to our needs," said Maglione. "They need everyone's goodwill in their present situation."

"I had hoped our own people would have found him by now," said Menenger, referring both to the Italian Secret Service and to elements of the *Sodalitium Paianum*, the Vatican's own spy network. Said only to monitor and report to the Holy Office deviations from orthodoxy, this organization was also thought to sometimes engage in duties of a more worldly nature. Close to the CIA during the seventies and eighties, *Sodalitium Paianum* had become of interest to spies from Eastern Europe, its present-day network of 'observers' suspected still of being involved in regular spying activities.

"You've spoken with the Council for Public Affairs?" asked Borghini, addressing Maglione.

"And with senior officials of the Secretariat," said Maglione, whose job it had been to summon these men to a council of war. "They were, as you can imagine, shocked by the news. Some were annoyed at not being informed earlier."

"Too many people know about this mess already," rasped Cardinal Menenger. "One loose tongue and the roof will cave in on us."

"I wonder what the Holy Father is doing right this minute, as we speak," said Maglione, forcing his companions to consider something they would have preferred to not think about. "What's running through his mind, I wonder?"

"I dread to think," said Menenger.

"Does he really believe he's doing God's will?"

"He's ill," said Borghini.

"It must have taken every ounce of courage he had to do what he's done. His getting out of the Apostolic Palace without being recognized is almost a miracle in itself."

"He is spectacularly ordinary in appearance," said Menenger.

"You referred to him once as potentially classical in appearance."

"With the right robes and a deal of schooling he could have passed muster. As himself he is a nonentity."

"He lacks bearing," said Borghini.

"Bearing is an attitude," said Menenger.

They fell silent for a moment, each concerned with his own thoughts. Then with a ferocity that surprised even Cardinal Borghini, Menenger's anger burst into the open. It was intolerable what this idiot of a man was doing to them, he said, the lips of his thin mouth curling in to reveal perfectly aligned teeth. If he was returned to them in once piece he would see to it that no such incident ever happened again.

"I think it unlikely that anything approaching this level of absurdity could ever happen again," said Maglione. "It's a situation quite unlike any other in the whole history of the Church."

"I remember you were in sympathy with his idea of visiting the Holy Land," said Menenger, his intention in saying so not at all clear.

"As you were, later," said Maglione, parrying.

"He had become obstinate. I had to think of a reason that would make such a trip acceptable if he forced the issue.

"Pilgrimage was an excellent idea," said Maglione. Then, with a twist that made the two men stare at him, he said, "Isn't that exactly what he's done? Isn't that what we should say if this whole thing blows up in our face?"

Menenger's smile, even when fully formed, remained slight, but there was no doubting that he liked Cardinal Maglione's take on things; it was in his face and his eyes that the Secretary of State had hit upon something important. Turning to Borghini, he asked that the point be noted.

"To what end?" asked Borghini.

"As an explanation for everything that has happened, and will happen, Vincenzo. You may remember I described the Holy Father's desire to visit Jerusalem as *inspired*? Well, in the sense articulated by his Eminence, it was exactly that. It was the pilgrimage of all pilgrimages, and it required him to do exactly what he has just done to make it so." There was almost friendship in Cardinal Menenger's eyes when he turned back to the Secretary of State. "We see through a glass but darkly, Valerio. Then, suddenly, unexpectedly, there is light."

"The Spirit bloweth where it listeth," said Borghini, getting in on the act.

Satisfied with his efforts, Cardinal Maglione prepared to excuse himself. In the event of the Holy Father remaining at large, he said, he would, as agreed, have the Israelis informed of the situation.

"We could use our own diplomatic channels," said Menenger, who liked to keep things in-house.

"I think it would be better if this were handled by our mutual intelligence services," said Maglione, who knew more about these things than he was letting on. "If it happens to suit their purpose, politicians can sometimes be a little wayward."

"Ah," said Menenger.

Cardinal Borghini nodded sagely.

"If there is nothing else, Eminence?" said Maglione.

"It is in your capable hands, Valerio," said Menenger.

* * *

Ruby Weizacker took one look at Angelo Rinaldi and came out from behind her counter in a rush. The man was obviously exhausted, perhaps unwell. "Sit down here," she said, directing him to a chair. "The police let you go in this state?" She fussed over him, fanned him with a newspaper, then told him to stay put while she fetched her husband. When she returned with her husband, Benedict was sitting with his head back against the wall; his eyes were closed and his mouth was slightly open. "Can you make the stairs?" Ruby asked. Benedict shook his head and she told her husband to carry him upstairs. He had seen to it that his bill was paid before he left and that spoke volumes about the man, she said, hurrying her husband on.

Later, when he had eaten a little and recovered his wits somewhat, he thanked them for their kindness and explained how his head had come to be bandaged. He had been very lucky, he said. The bullet had scraped his temple and knocked him unconsciousness. The exact fashion of his words had been quaint, almost comical as he scoured his memory for the appropriate combinations, but they had got the drift of what he was trying to say.

"Why were the police looking for you?" asked the husband.

"They-mis-take-my-leav-ing," said Benedict.

"And your things?" said Ruby, referring to Benedict's brown case. "Where are your things?"

"The-pol-ice. I-will-get-back."

He had spent the whole day in the *souk* avoiding policemen and soldiers and by way of penance had eaten nothing. Then fatigue had set in, and his head had begun to pound, and he had been forced to seek shelter when it got late. Standing just inside the globe-illuminated entrance of the Jaffa Gate, the palm trees backing the all but empty carpark casting their shadows on the gigantic wall of the Citadel, he had hit on the idea of returning to the Gideon Hotel. It had struck him that they wouldn't think to look for him there.

"What you need is sleep," said Ruby.

"I-sleep-now," agreed Benedict. He closed his eyes and his mouth fell open again in search of air.

Next morning, Ruby confided to a friend that Benedict had probably been asleep before they reached the door,

"And up and on his way before the birds had a chance to serenade the dawn," her husband added.

"Anything missing?" asked the friend.

"Soap," said Ruby. She glanced at her husband. "Not exactly what *I'd* call a crisis."

"We should nevertheless inform the police," he said back.

"About what?"

"He's up to something."

"He's probably gone off to fetch his case."

"Perhaps."

"What are you suggesting?"

"I'm not suggesting anything. I'm just being careful."

"He wouldn't hurt a fly!"

"He gets himself shot. The police come looking for him. He turns up here exhausted and then disappears without a word? Who's to say what he's capable of."

"He paid his bill," she replied, hanging on to her little truth. "If he'd been anything other than what he said he was he wouldn't have done that. Anyway, who escapes from the police!"

* * *

When news of the Vatican's dilemma over Benedict XVI reached the head of Israeli Intelligence, the resulting mirth among senior Mossad officials was raucous but short-lived. The idea of their having an incognito pope to catch was certainly ridiculous, but his having already been in police custody once, and his having outmaneuvered their medical authorities twice, threw the whole incident into a less than funny perspective. Cardinal Angelo Rinaldi, alias Benedict XVI, was obviously a resourceful man, and in his present state of mind perhaps even a dangerous one. And so a general alert was sounded, every eye that could be mustered set the task of finding a pope in priestly garb among the many priests who daily wandered the streets of Jerusalem.

Benedict's resourcefulness surfaced the moment he left the Gideon Hotel. Passing through the Jaffa Gate once more, he headed for the Arab Quarter; he knew the presence of Israeli soldiers and police all but petered out in that area. Yes, he was apt to get strange looks from the locals, but that was a small price to pay for anonymity.

Anonymity.

He was back with the dilemma of his having become a nobody, a non-person wishing now to sink even further into anonymity, if that were possible. And all so that he could be where he believed God wanted him to be, in Jerusalem, the spiritual hub of the world. Jerusalem embodied the hope and dream of a dialogue between cultures, civilizations and spiritual traditions, but the children were crying and that had to stop. They had stopped crying in his dream, but only because the Devil had been made to vanish.

Benedict believed wholeheartedly in the Devil, and in exorcism. As a youth, he had witnessed demon possession in his home town of Montefalco, and it had had a profound effect on him. To see the Devil in someone's eyes and hear his blasphemies pouring from twisted lips was to know the Father of Lies at first hand; it was to know for certain that the cornerstone beliefs of one's faith were irrefutable.

A sign of Israel's dominance even in the Arab Quarter of the Old City was that of Stars of David stenciled on top of stars and crescent moons by Jewish settlers. Intent on asserting control over their Muslim neighbors (some were also Christian), the Israeli's made regular sorties in the area armed with templates and spray cans. The star and crescent moon graffiti signified that someone was celebrating the completion of a pilgrimage to Mecca, the Star of David that a deep antagonism existed between communities. The graffiti of Palestinian Christians - Christmas trees, crosses and wishes for a happy new year - were generally left alone.

The Old City of Jerusalem was in fact awash with graffiti. Political graffiti by Muslim Palestinians included cleverly drawn images, some with the highly stylized Arabic lettering extending into a map of Palestine, the outlawed Palestinian flag or the minaret of a mosque. But it wasn't all bad news. A dialogue between Moslems and Jews was in fact easier than one between Moslems and Christians, and in the past had been quite extensive. What was missing was the atmosphere of intellectual rigor that had once dominated the relationship, the rigor of a scholarship that allowed Islamic theologians to read Buber or Levinas, and Jewish scholars to study the works of Sha'rawi and Ashmawi. The common features to be found in the development of Kabbalah and Tasawwuf were being overlooked, the mutual influences in Jewish Halakhah or Islamic Sharia all but forgotten due to political strife.

Not that Benedict was particularly interested in such niceties; his was a made-up mind, a mind enthralled by his faith's certainties. Any dialogue with the other Abrahamic faiths had to be filtered through the uncontradictable belief that Jesus the Jewish Messiah had actually been Israel's God made manifest in flesh. Reject that Great Truth and, as far as he was concerned, there wasn't really much left to talk about. There had been a New Covenant with God, and Christianity had taken over from Judaism.

As he walked further into the Arab Quarter with the drifting crowd, the air heavy with fresh mint, sizzling meat, cloves and perfume, Benedict considered the problem he faced. Exorcism was the Church's usual method of overpowering the Devil, but in this instance the Devil was not an entity, it was an attitude. Yes, the Devil was behind that attitude, as his dream so clearly intimated, but one could hardly exorcise the Devil from so many minds and hearts. So what to do? He was where he knew he ought to be, but he was still in the dark as to exactly why. What did God have in mind, he wondered. For how many days and nights would he have to evade those looking for him before His purpose was revealed?

He had bought some tamarhindi juice, hot bread and fruit from vendors in the *souk* where Arab music blared out of the stores, and ate some of the bread now as he edged his way aimlessly through the congested and claustrophobic alleyways. His little stock of food was in a cheap raffia bag, his penitential attitude of the day before replaced now by the need to stay fresh and alert.

A new piece of graffiti caught his eye; it was in Arabic, and it contested the right of the Israeli municipality of Jerusalem to approve the construction of new buildings near the Bab Al-Saharah Gate, also known as Herod's Gate. The Palestinians saw this as a blatant attempt to displace them and redraw the boundary lines in Israel's favor; the Israelis saw it as their ancient right to reoccupy these areas and put a stop to the many illegal constructions in cellars and courtyards that threatened to upset the delicate population balance. Like Benedict, in that moment, the world at large was unaware of the grassroots problems facing Palestinian and Jew on a daily basis. All it knew were the blood and gore incidents that made the headlines, the attempts made to tear the heart out of the peace process. The extraordinarily brave attempts made by others, Muslims and Jews, to defuse the situation and revive the peace process tended to be washed away in a river of mad, bad rhetoric.

The alley crowds had been progressively thinning, many of the tourists turning back for fear of straying too far into this unfamiliar domain of swirling cloth, taut veils and averted faces. Not so

Benedict, whose reaction, due to his sense of mission, was quite the opposite. Fascinated by the almost fairytale-like atmosphere of the narrow streets and silent courtyards, by the arched windows and filigreed screens, and by the slip-slap of unshod feet on stepped pavements, he stayed with what remained of the crowd until it too thinned and he came to a small, hole-in-the-wall tea house. Having not seen a single Israeli policeman or soldier for some time, he decided to spend what little money he had left on a rejuvenating glass of hot tea among its many water-pipe smoking, card-playing customers. Placing his raffia bag on an adjacent chair, he sat down among the cafe's patrons. Some turned to stare at him, most continued to drink and talk as if he did not exist. Closing his eyes, he sat for a moment or two in the friendly darkness. When he opened them again, it was to find a tall, swarthy man in Arab garb staring down at him.

"Tee?" Benedict said immediately.

"I am not an employee," the man said quietly, and not unkindly, in English. "I would like to sit here, if I may."

"Ah!" Benedict reached for his raffia bag and placed it at his feet. Then, gesturing towards the now empty chair, he said, "It-is-for-you."

When seated, his companion sat silent and unmoving, his gaze fixed on some indeterminate point; it was as if he had been switched off internally, as if his systems of functioning had been given the command to shut down. Unable to resist a glance or two, Benedict was reminded of the tall, turbaned men in the courtyard who, standing like gowned statues, had treated him with such disdain. Yet there was something different here; this was not willful rejection, it was, he began to realize, a form of politeness.

"It is unusual to find a priest comfortable in these streets," the man said suddenly.

"Should-I-be . . . of-fear?" asked Benedict.

The stranger shook his head. "I am Sheikh Abdul Eflaki," he said, proffering a hand. "You live here in Jerusalem?"

"I-am-Angelo-Rinaldi," said Benedict, reinstating the rudiments of his identity. "I-am-Itali-an." They settled back from their greeting. "Jerusalem-is-your . . . place-of-stay?" asked Benedict.

"I am also a visitor," said the sheikh.

The proprietor, who doubled as waiter, appeared to take their order.

"You wish tea?" said the sheikh.

Benedict nodded and Sheikh Eflaki ordered tea and cake in his native tongue. By the time it arrived they were chatting freely in Spanish, English having proved too laborious. Surprised and delighted by the Arab's fluency in that language, Benedict remarked on the fact.

"We Muslims have a long association with Spain, you may remember. I lived and worked there for three years." The sheikh added mischievously, "I believe even the great Aquinas studied with us in Spain."

"Aristotle," said Benedict, something of his past studies returning to him.

"We preserved him for you," said the sheikh. There was a silence. They sipped at their tea. "You have hurt your head?"

Benedict touched the bandage and smiled. It was only a scratch, he said.

They talked on and came, bit by bit, to the problem of Muslim and Jewish antipathy. It was time for them to recognize that they stemmed from the same tree, Sheikh Eflaki said. They were, after all, brothers descended from Abraham their father. The more they discovered their common roots, the more they could hope for a common future of peace and prosperity. Had not Muslims regularly read the Torah alongside the Koran during the first two centuries of Islam? Muhammad had perceived Jews and Christians as spiritual cousins; he had even borrowed from Jewish dietary laws and purity requirements.

"Brave words," said Benedict. "In speaking them you do not fear for your life?"

"I speak what every Muslim knows to be true. Why should I fear to speak what is true?"

"There are Jews as well as Muslims who would find such an enlightened view unacceptable."

"Many Muslims now admit that hostility for Israel has been a great mistake, perhaps the worst mistake we've made in the last fifty years. That is of course an educated opinion, not a local one. We are all engaged in a difficult transition, a waking-up to what and who we are."

"It's the children who suffer most," said Benedict.

"Alas, yes," said the sheikh.

There was another silence.

"Will there ever be a real peace, do you think?" asked Benedict.

"The idea that Muslims, because they are Muslims, are prevented from recognizing the right of Israel to exist as a sovereign state is quite recent. It cannot be found in classical Islamic sources. Our Scriptures are specific in this regard. The Koran states that God, through Moses, freed the offspring of Jacob from slavery in Egypt and made them inheritors of the promised land. The Koran also recognizes that Jerusalem is to the Jew what Mecca is to the Muslim. The current problem is purely political. It is the result of bad political decisions in the past, and it will only be resolved by humane political decisions in the future."

"I was almost killed yesterday," said Benedict. "A bullet shaved my temple. I was knocked unconscious. I've since heard that others were more seriously injured than I."

"The anger goes deep," said the sheikh. "It has a long and complicated history. It boils the blood. "

"The children are crying, and dying," said Benedict.

Sheikh Eflaki paused, then he said, "I am in agreement with the late King Hussein. He proposed that Jerusalem 'within the walls' be removed from all political sovereignty. His recommendation was that the Old City be considered a holy site in its own right, and that it be administered by a joint council of Jews, Christian and Muslims.

Holy Jerusalem, he said, should not belong to any country or religion, it should belong to the whole world." He took a sip of tea and continued. "Moshe Dayan had the right idea. In '67 he gave control of the Temple Mount to Islam in the hope that religious conflict could be avoided. A territorial conflict between Israeli and Arab was one thing; a religious war between Judaism and Islam was quite another. Over recent years idiotic decisions made on both sides have eroded the territorial status quo to such an extent that Arabs now act as if the Temple Mount had been officially handed over to them. It wasn't. Israel is still the landlord. They handed over control of the Temple Mount on the condition that all religions would have access. They even agreed to bar any outward show of Jewish prayers or rituals on the site. That has been policed quite effectively by the Israelis. What you got caught up in was a disorganized protest over bloody clashes on the Temple Mount in October of last year."

"It has become the flashpoint."

"Indeed it has. It has the greatest potential for interreligious friction in Jerusalem, perhaps even in the wider world if territorial conflict is allowed to degenerate into a religious war."

"That seems almost to be the case already?"

"Arab patience is threadbare. But there's hope. It's rumored that unofficial channels have been opened between the Israelis and the Palestinians. That may result in an interim agreement at least."

"You're involved in some way?"

"I am an educationalist. I am here by invitation of the Palestinian Authority to advise on matters of education. As you said, the children are suffering."

Benedict considered what he was about to say carefully, then he said, "Is it right that small children should be trained as killers?"

"Desperation is the killer. It twists our capacity to think."

"Suffer the little children to come unto me."

"Occupation is suffering. Loss of dignity is suffering. Humiliation is suffering."

"The world sees Israel as trying to do the right thing and being thwarted at ever turn."

"Israel has its doves, but it also has its hawks - hawks backed by one of the strongest military machines in the Middle East. The world sees and hears only a fraction of what goes on here."

"I find the history of Palestine difficult to untangle. There are so many views, so many angles. I read what the Israelis say about the past, and I believe them. Then I read what the Arabs have to say, and I believe them."

"Many Jews and Arabs are faced with the same dilemma. They see through the cracks in their own history. Hardly anything is exactly as we have been brought up to believe it was. Most of the arguments on both sides are excuses clouded by hate, prejudice and opportunism. But these brothers of mine have been living in a state of subjection for over thirty-five years. That is an intolerable state to be in. Now you can argue, as the Israelis do, that Palestine was underpopulated and underdeveloped when the Jews began to return to their ancient homeland. I don't disagree with their returning. What I disagree with is the idea that because the Arab population was relatively small that that somehow disallowed Arab anger over being swamped by Jewish immigrants. That's what eventually happened. Arabs had every right to complain about such an invasion, for that was what it was, an invasion. It can of course be argued that the Jews are the inheritors of the promised land, as I have already admitted they are according to Scripture. But even in the middle of the nineteenth century that no longer meant, or should have been allowed to mean, *at the expense of every other human being in the country.* The British woke up to that fact far too late, and the Americans, driven politically by their own massive Jewish population, sealed the fate of the indigenous Arab population by persuading the British to allow the mass immigration of Jews into the country."

"They saw Palestine as their home."

"As did the Palestinians."

Benedict admitted that it was all very difficult. Then, more forthrightly that he intended, he said, "There seems to be an inability in the Palestinian camp to control their religious hotheads."

The sheikh laughed in response. Had he seen any of that day's newspapers? Benedict said No and was enlightened as to their content. The Vatican was trying desperately to distance itself from an organization called The Children of the New Catholic Dawn, the sheikh said. Court cases in America had revealed the most horrendous disregard for human rights. Some members had broken ranks and admitted to all kinds of outrageous behavior, some of them criminal. His Church was in crisis, and their were rumors of worst to come.

"I heard something of these people before I left Rome."

"One newspaper said they had been operating under the nose of the hierarchy for decades, another that it was their declared intention to take over the Catholic Church and run it their way."

Chastened, Benedict withdrew into himself.

"We all have our hotheads, Father. There are always those who think their particular brand of the truth is better than anyone else's. Some become deranged because of it."

"The God of Abraham does not sacrifice children."

"Indeed he does not," said the sheikh. "We Muslims have been pointing that out for centuries."

Understanding only too well what was being said to him, Benedict sidestepped the issue, and said, "We're receiving looks".

"I am drinking coffee with a Catholic priest in the heart of the Muslim Quarter. They are intrigued by that fact, and by the fact that we are not speaking in English."

"Have you said to them what you've said to me?"

"They are very patient with me. Polite. They listen and nod their heads knowing that I will leave this city and that they will remain to face yet another day, then another."

Placing the last of his cake in his mouth, Benedict sucked on it; it was as sweet as anything he could remember.

"You're here to visit the holy sites?" asked the sheikh.

"I'm here because it is where God wants me to be," Benedict said in his mind. Then, with a little smile he said almost casually, "A personal pilgrimage."

"I'm on my way to meet with people who feel as I do, as you do." The sheikh's eyes were suddenly piercingly brilliant. "You would be most welcome to join us."

"That is most kind, but —- "

"It is a mixed group. There will be Israelis present. The views of a Catholic priest would be greatly valued."

"In what way?" asked Benedict.

"In drafting our wish that a lasting peace be brought to this pain-racked country," said the sheikh.

"I thought you weren't involved politically?"

"A dialogue between men of goodwill and good heart transcends politics," said the sheikh. "We talk. We drink tea and eat cake like we are doing now. We are brothers in our father Abraham. We have recognized our responsibility as educators, and as fathers."

Looking into the sheikh's handsome face, Benedict read the moment as clearly God-given. "Then I will come with you, for the cake," he said, revealing that he had a sense of humor.

46

A Work in Progress

News of the shootings broke in Jerusalem around teatime on the Sunday, and around the world soon after. The dead had been identified as a Catholic priest and an Arab scholar about whom very little was known. They had each died instantly, shot through the head from a distance by what was believed to have been a professional sniper. No party or group had as yet claimed responsibility for the killings. Those with whom the dead men had been in conference - a mixed group of intellectuals and artists despised by Israeli and Arab hardliners alike - were now under police protection. With a promise of further information as it became available, the bulletin stopped there. By ten that evening, however, the promised update had become somewhat confusing: the priest had turned into a Rome-based cardinal around whom a bit of a mystery was developing, the dead Arab scholar in whose arms he had been found into a professor of Islamic studies at the American University in Beirut. The Vatican had so far not commented on the death of their Cardinal.

"Some of them don't want it to end," said Jane. "They've got so used to the killings it's become a way of life. They each want it all - right down to the last blade of grass. It's either bludgeon the Palestinians into silence or drive the Jews into the sea."

She and Duggan were eating a late-evening pizza out of the box and drinking red wine. The television news droned on as they talked.

"I've almost finished your novel."

"I know. I looked to see where you were up to."

"It's good, Jack. I'm enjoying it."

He glanced at her and reached for another slice of pepperoni. It was like reading something written by someone else, he said. He'd given up trying to determine whether it was any good.

"Have you read through it recently?"

"Not recently," he admitted.

"You should."

"I'd probably want to burn the damn thing."

"That's carrying editing a little too far." They laughed together and she got to the point. "All it needs is a little editing."

"I thought it was quite good when I finished it," he said, squinting a look at her. "A month later I thought it was crap."

"How long ago was that?"

"Fifteen, sixteen years ago."

She scolded him for leaving it so long.

"I was still trying to nut things out. It was ages before it dawned on me that not everything could, or should, be worked out to the last decimal point."

"It's worth reworking."

"I was still smarting from the treatment I received. It hurts just to read it."

"Anger isn't all bad."

"That kind is," he said, pointing at the television screen where a blonde woman in a neat blue flak jacket was giving a more detailed breakdown on the double killing in Jerusalem. There was now reason to believe the cardinal so brutally killed was a close relative of Pope Benedict XVI, she said, glancing back at the spot where the bodies had lain. The Vatican had so far refused to comment on the tragedy, but reliable sources in Jerusalem had identified the slain cardinal as Angelo Rinaldi, a probable brother, or cousin of the pope's.

"The all-but-invisible pope," said Jane.

"It's unlikely the poor sod was called 'Angelo'," said Duggan. "That's the pope's first name. They've got that wrong for sure."

That the media had not got that fact wrong became clear around midnight. A startled-looking broadcaster interrupted the late-night movie to say that Cardinal Angelo Rinaldi had now been properly identified. He was not, as previously thought, a brother or cousin of

Benedict XVI, he was in fact none other than Pope Benedict the XVI himself. Having travelled incognito to Jerusalem to assist with the peace process, his act of love had inadvertently turned into an act of self-sacrifice. How such an extraordinary thing could have come about was already being furiously debated, the Vatican's preliminary explanation being that he had embarked on a personal pilgrimage that had gone terribly wrong.

"There's no such thing as a pope who travels on his own," said Duggan, staring at the screen. He turned to Jane. "A personal pilgrimage? What's that supposed to mean?"

"There's more, Jack," she said.

"*Conflicting reports are now coming in from Jerusalem on the death of Benedict XVI. The Israeli Government has denied any knowledge of the Pope's visit, but it's thought Israeli Intelligence may have been aware of his presence in the country. This has not yet been confirmed. What has been confirmed is that His Holiness met with a group of intellectuals and artists drawn from both sides of the Israeli/Palestinian conflict. The declared intention of this group is an immediate and lasting peace between the warring parties. A spokesperson for this group has described Benedict XVI's peace making journey to the Middle East as an astonishing act of courage. As a result of this extraordinary happening, thousands have gathered in Rome's St Peter's Square to pray for an immediate cessation of hostilities in the Middle East.*"

They watched the screen hoping for further revelations, but there were none.

"It's too bizarre to be true surely," said Duggan, his reaction one of genuine bemusement. "We hear next to nothing about Benedict, or from him, then he goes and does something like this?" Reaching for the bottle of red, he topped up Jane's glass, then his own. "'A personal pilgrimage that went terribly wrong?' What's that supposed to mean?"

By the following afternoon, articles, television news reports and discussion groups attempting to analyze the pope's 'flight of mercy' had swamped the media. Some lauded his extraordinary behavior, others questioned his sanity. In response, the Vatican issued a carefully worded communiqué: The Holy Father's deep desire to visit Jerusalem had been known to those closest to him for some time, but due to the pressures of ill-health, and the insistence of the Spirit - Benedict had spoken of a directive from God - he had felt compelled to sidestep the usual protocols. Whatever one might think of his actions, it should be noted that his death had had an immediate effect on the Israeli/Palestinian conflict. The many disparate groups involved - whether intafada or settler-driven - had forthrightly condemned whoever was responsible. The bullets that had felled Benedict XVI and his companion Sheikh Professor Abdul Eflaki had been fired, so it seemed, by a phantom.

What fascinated everyone was the nature of the group with whom Benedict and his Arab companion had spent the latter part of that fateful day. Who were they? What did they stand for? How were they perceived by the Israeli government? Had they been previously marked down as problematical by the intelligence services? Had they been infiltrated? Were they, as they themselves claimed, a halfway house where men of goodwill and good heart met to discuss and debate the fine print of a lasting peace? Or were they merely head-in-the-clouds merchants, intellectual dreamers out of touch with a tough, unbending reality?

The questions rolled out, the group visited by Benedict and Eflaki reluctantly described by some as necessary, by others as an impediment to gaining what was rightfully theirs. But something was in the air, something not imagined prior to the shootings: had both sides of the conflict perhaps reached the end of the road as far as the constant killing went? It was not that the pope's life was any more valuable than that of a child's; it was that it somehow symbolised a turning point; or, to be more exact, a point of no return. It was either a case of go forward constructively, or descend into chaos. Whatever God or Allah might be thought to want, it was through the finite minds of men and women alone that the result would be delivered.

It would have been shocking to some to realise that Benedict and Eflaki had met so casually over tea and cake only a few hours prior to their deaths; their entangled bodies seemed to suggest so much more. Benedict had been shot first, and Eflaki, with no care for his own safety, had gathered his priestly companion up in his arms. He, too, had then been shot, and the scene had been transformed into what one shocked commentator described as ". . . a grotesque parody of Michaelangelo's *Pieta*".

Even more shocking, however, would have been the reaction of many to things said at that meeting of minds. Sheikh Eflaki's views in particular would have dumbfounded some, for he had not only condemned the perpetual killing that went on in the name of God, or Allah, he had also suggested that the war being waged between Israel and her Arab neighbors was more intrinsically a war deep within these different religious traditions themselves. Yes, there had been mistakes of consequence made on both sides over the last few decades, and these mistakes had exacerbated an often difficult to disentangle set of historical events, but the war presently being fought was at base an internal war, not an exteral war. The three great Abrahamic faiths were as much at war within themselves as they were with one another. It was in essence Jew versus Jew, Christian versus Christian and Muslim versus Muslim. The carnage being witnessed daily was without doubt territorial, sometimes local and parochial, but it was also significantly psychological - the psyches or souls of all three religious traditions were going through the painful process of being born anew. It was a time of transition holding great promise, but it was also an ugly street brawl with the potential to drag other nations into its ever-widening circle of influence. Abraham, Eflaki had said, his eyes brilliantly hypnotic, was being forced to sacrifice his son all over again, only this time there seemed to be no ram in the thicket.

After some two hours of discussion during which Benedict talked of his dream, they had, as promised, partaken of tea and cake. Addressing the pontiff in a manner meant to be shared with those present, Eflaki had probed him on the meaning of his dream: Did he believe himself spoken to by God? Benedict had offered a slow nod in return. But why him and not some other? the sheikh had asked. Out of all the Catholics on the planet, why had God chosen to speak to him alone? Avoiding the small matter of his true identity, Benedict had suggested that perhaps an open heart had been the reason. Was it not then his heart that had done the speaking? suggested Eflaki. The sheikh's reply had so surprised Benedict he was silent for a moment. Then, frowning, he had asked the sheikh if he thought God had not spoken to him. There were those, said Eflaki, who killed because they believed God had spoken to them. If it were true that He had spoken to him, a Catholic, why not also to these desperate souls? Had he not also spoken to Jewish settlers, telling them to build their little houses on Palestinian land? And to Muslims, giving them the right to drive Abraham's other children into the sea? Benedict's answer had seemed lame even to himself. It was a matter of faith, surely, he had replied, his discomfort obvious to everyone in the room.

They continued to speak privately after that, in Spanish, the sheikh taking Benedict aside for that purpose.

"Your remarks surprised me," Benedict admitted. "I would have thought you a believer in God's ability to speak to his servants."

"We speak mostly to ourselves, I fear," said Eflaki.

"God's role in human affairs is not well understood," said Benedict. "He wills constantly that we become his children."

"We have no will to speak of."

"Hence our need of religion."

"Which may only be an endless detour."

"Augustine's argument stands," said an adamant Benedict. "We human beings are incapable of figuring out the meaning of life for ourselves. All spiritual decisions have to be made on our behalf by a spiritual authority. Spiritual discrimination and insight cannot be drawn out of the mental depths of the human, they can only be found in religion's grand vision of ultimate truth. Revelation faithfully received is the cornerstone of faith. In being received, it is unalterable for all eternity."

Sheikh Eflaki did not immediately respond; he just stared at Benedict. Then, with a smile he said, "God has become our excuse for murder, and worse. We have turned Him into a common criminal. We claim guidance from Him in all kinds of matters, but obey only the whims of our own duplicitous natures."

"God speaks to us through His word," said Benedict. "We are not altogether bereft of His guidance."

"We are intoxicated by the world and tend to read badly," replied the sheikh. "We have to deepen the question."

"In what way?" asked Benedict.

"We must inquire as to the true nature of the soul."

"Which is what?"

"Which is not what we think it is," said the sheikh. "It is not a finished work. If it were, we would be of God and our thoughts and actions would be very different. We would be complete in ourselves and have no need of instruction. Our thoughts would be pure, our actions admirable, our grasp of spiritual truth unchallengable. As that is not the case, our souls are obviously rudimentary in form."

"That is a unique perspective," said Benedict.

"Hence our futile attempts to perfect our thoughts and our emotions; we simply lack a center from which these things can be accomplished."

"We renew our mind through Christ," said Benedict.

"Without soul the mind gallops wherever it wills. There is no end to its disasters."

Benedict hesitated; their conversation had taken an unexpected turn, and he was unsure as to its outcome.

"Soul is presence," said the sheikh.

"My soul was redeemed by Christ," said Benedict.

"Experience without presence lacks a redemptive quality," said the sheikh. "It is what St Paul called 'the body of death'."

"You have read the New Testament?"

"You have not read the Quran?"

Benedict blinked at the Sheikh's question; he had never as much as touched a copy of the Koran. "What you're saying is difficult to follow," said Benedict, avoiding embarrassment. Then, almost tartly, he added, "There is a point to your obscurity?"

"To be without presence is to unwittingly squander the energy of being; it is to waste our *substance* in a far country."

"You are speaking in riddles," said Benedict, "but I think I perceive something of your meaning. You are speaking of the prodigal son, and his return to the father?"

The sheikh dipped his head in acknowledgement.

"I must confess, I am no philosopher," said Benedict. "All I can say to you is that Christ's presence sustains me."

"Then I will speak plainly," said the sheikh. "We abort soul a thousand times every day because we are robbed of presence."

"Christ's presence," said Benedict.

"No, our own," said the Sheikh.

The word 'abort' so shocked Benedict's he did not at first take in the sheikh's meaning.

"We are unaware of our loss," continued the sheikh. "We live and die without real presence and hardly ever notice. It is as if we never really existed at all."

"That is a bleak vision," said Benedict.

"It is a hidden catastrophe," said the sheikh. "To grasp its implications is to be in receipt of a revelation."

"I have no need of further revelation," replied Benedict. "It is, as the Lord said on the cross, finished."

"Notice how quiet it has become," said the sheikh suddenly. "And how transformed the light is."

Benedict looking towards the window where a rosy tint had touched the buildings.

"Eternity's moment," said the sheikh.

Sensing something untoward, Benedict remained silent. Everyone had stopped speaking. It was if the room had been invaded by some strange being, as if the world had again been made to stop revolving under Joshua's command. Twenty minutes later both men were dead, their heads shattered by a sniper's expertise.

* * *

In Rome, Frederick Cardinal Menenger prepared for the funeral of all funerals; and for what he believed would be the conclave of all conclaves. The pope was dead; long live the pope.

It seemed unlikely that he himself would ever sit in St Peter's Chair - even among conservatives his views were considered too unbending - but given Angelo Rinaldi's unexpected elevation, who knew for certain what the Holy Spirit had in mind? Announcing a personal wish to see Benedict XVI canonised as quickly as possible, Menenger began to build Benedict's alternative image: the image of a pope driven to fulfil the will of God like few others in the Church's long and turbulent history. Relying on God alone, the Holy Father had shown the world what an unquestioning faith could do. And that, in essence, was the key to understanding what had taken place in Jerusalem. Like Christ himself, he had obeyed the promptings of the Spirit even unto death.

Due to the brouhaha over Benedict's death, a long and convoluted evaluation of the Mar Saba Codex published by the Vatican's Department of Antiquities went all but unnoticed. Theodore's letter had been declared genuine, the writer admitted, but the drift of this fourth-century Bishop's argument verged on the ridiculous. Only maverick scholars and ill-informed researchers would find such material convincing; scholars of repute would have more sense. There followed a line-by-line refutation of the letter's contention that the early Apostolic Church in Jerusalem had been Nazoraean sectarian and not Christian in any sense that would make sense today. The contents of Theodore's exposition to the heretic Pelagius Britto had without doubt been painstakingly pieced together, but in the end it was no more that a fantasy construction, an odd and unconvincing amalgamation of disparate pieces of information. There was nothing to concern Catholics here, the writer advised; such garbage had been more than thoroughly dealt with in a host of other contexts.

Then came a shrill note of warning: the confusion caused by the premature publication of this material in Australia should not go unnoticed, and neither should the illicitly procured photographs used in that instance. Professor James Windle's attempt to shed responsibility for his actions on the basis that Christian scholars were often biased in their approach was a slight that could not be ignored. The Mar Saba Codex had been treated, as the Department of Antiquity's lengthy report clearly showed, like any other ancient document: and most speedily at that. To suggest, as he had done in a newspaper article, that there was a subtle form of censorship in operation when it came to dealing with the early Christian Church's origin and development, was surely another example of this scholar's tiresome prejudice.

Duggan had not been surprised when Windle phoned to say that he had owned up to taking extra photographs of the codex; the big New Yorker had, on a number of occasions, exhibited unease about the ethics of his behavior. But doing so on a program like *Die Welt* had come as a surprise. Why choose to do it that way? he had asked. Windle's reply was that the public should be made aware of the difficulties scholars faced when dealing with areas of research sensitive to the Church: they ran the risk of a disabling mockery and even vilification if they applied too much pressure. The unwritten dictum was that the moral underpinnings of Western civilization might collapse if Christianity's faith-claims were too savagely contradicted.

Windle was scathing of such a view; it was Christianity's own retrogressive behavior that had been oiling the wheels of such a disaster, he claimed. Secularism by itself could not be blamed for the West's present state of moral and spiritual decline. The culprit was not modernism, or secularism, it was a spiritually bankrupt

Christianity stuck fast at the adolescent stage of its growth - it had abrogated its right to instruct through refusing to grow up. At its best, all it had to offer were worn-out myths, at its worst nothing more than emotionally-charged literalisms. Witness what had happened to Bishop Peters when he tried to argue some sense into the situation. If the hardliners had been able to tear the robes off his back in some kind of public ceremony, they'd probably have done so. Having followed the whole sad story in the German press, Windle had written a long letter of support to Peters. They hadn't been able to shut the man up, he told Duggan, so they'd stripped him of his bishop's authority to speak on Christianity's behalf.

The magazine would support Windle as best it could in the next issue, Elliot told Duggan on the Friday afternoon, but his professional survival would depend on whether the Department of Antiquities decided to take up the gauntlet he had thrown down. By challenging their integrity when dealing with texts at odds with standard Christian belief, he had left himself open to the possibility of a challenge in the courts.

"He's well aware of that possibility."

"He said so?"

A nod from Duggan. Windle had the bit between his teeth and he wasn't the kind of man to avoid chomping on it.

"To the extent of facing the courts?"

"If that's what it takes, I think he'll go for it. He feels he has nothing to lose at this point."

Elliot said nothing for a moment, then, frowning his special frown, he said, "What do you make of this pope thing?"

"It's extraordinary."

"They were on the ropes before this happened."

"They still are. What CNCD was up to behind closed doors isn't going to go away. The American courts are humming with it. Condemnation for the group has spread into Europe."

"The board's delighted, Jack. Circulation's gone through the roof. Question is, where to from here?" Elliot paused, then with a devilish smile answered his own question, "There's the Sydney youth conference, of course, at the end of this month. I think Donaghue's unliklely to turn up for that knowing now what we all now know about CNCD's influence in mass rallies of this kind; it'll be wall-to-wall Archbishop Pullman."

"I . . . don't think so."

"Come on, Jack! There isn't anyone else. It's got to be you. Dave would want you to do it."

"*That* is blackmail."

"No it isn't. Who out of that bunch of ratbags out there could I possibly send?" Another smile. "Anyway, Archbishop Pullman would be real disappointed if you didn't show up."

* * *

Further information on Sheikh Eflaki and his group dribbled out over the weekend. Not only had the sheikh been a respected professor of Islamic studies, he had also, it seemed, been a practising Sufi. Try as they might, the probing of journalists failed to produce anything beyond this simple fact, and no Sufi group claimed him as their own. Earlier in the week, however, Benedict's lying in state had been vividly contrasted on television with sheikh Eflaki's simple funeral - more an accident of images than an intended effect - and the beautifully sculpted Arabic letters that adorned his simple tomb had revealed more about the man in the form of a poem by the Persian poet Rumi.

The one who wants to be awakened
Is the one who sleeps in the middle of the garden.
But for the one who sleeps in prison,
To be awakened is only a nuisance.

Less obscure in meaning was Benedict's involvement in Middle Eastern politics, a British journalist argued. His concern for the suffering of children on both sides of the Palestinian conflict had obviously radicalized him. It was therefore conceivable that he had arranged to meet with sheikh Eflaki in Jerusalem, and that in turn suggested prior contact with key figures in the peace movement. There was an immediate uproar; Vatican sources dismissed the claim as preposterous. Would they then please explain how two such men had managed to find one another in a city the size of Jerusalem, was the reply. Had they perhaps bumped into one another by chance in a cafe?

As conspiracy theories went, it was a beauty, and it had an immediate effect. Tracking down members of Eflaki's group, journalists tried to uncover the truth, but to no avail. The more they probed and pestered, the less they seemed to end up knowing, or grasping. The same applied to Angelo Rinaldi's time as cardinal, and as parish priest; there was nothing there either to uphold the idea of a closet activist. So perhaps, one journalist grudgingly admitted, there was something to the claim that he had been spoken to by the Spirit.

"Rumi's considered a bit of a heretic by some Muslims," Duggan said over breakfast on the Monday, which was dull, rainy and wind swept.

"Fr Merle's a fan of the Sufis," said Jane. "My father thinks he may even be one."

"Catholic priest *and* Sufi?"

"That's what he said."

"He's hinted to me on occasions that Merle's ideas aren't all stock-in-trade."

"They're both renegades at heart, Jack. Merle's full of surprises"

"I began to wonder if he'd ever put his head above the parapet on your father's behalf. He must have realized he was heading into troubled waters with the codex. The whole thing was *Boy's Own* stuff."

"My father's enthusiasm is his greatest strength, and his greatest weakness."

"What's mine?" asked Duggan.

If he could have retracted his question he would have done so, but it was out of his mouth before he could censor it

"You feel things very deeply, but disguise your feelings at every turn."

"That was quick"

"It was an easy question, Jack. Everyone's strong point is their greatest weakness."

Her reply made so much sense he just stared at her.

"Mine's forthrightness," she said. "It far too often ends up with my being unintentially rude to someone. It turns into impatience."

"Know thy self," he said back.

"My mother's was the opposite. She was the long-suffering type."

"I thought you two were supposed to be alike? Peas in a pod is how David described the two of you."

"To look at. I'm my mother all over again physically." She laughed and expanded on a family truth. "It wouldn't have done much for the marriage if she'd responded the way I did. I was always in trouble with my father."

"He dotes on you."

"He despaired of me back then. I was an adolescent tearaway." She corrected herself. "*And* a teenage one up until about the age of forty. The moment I feel hemmed in there's trouble."

"In what way?"

"I bolt, Jack."

He was looking up at her and she smiled her brilliant smile, but there was a warning in what she had just said in it, and he felt cautioned.

"I hear you," he said.

"You're the only man as far back as I can remember who hasn't pulled the possession thing on me. I kept waiting for it, but it never happened."

"Where do you place commitment?"

"In a different box entirely. Commitment isn't possession; it's respect. You can't claim respect for the other if you've got them shackled to you as an object. There's no point in that. It leads to resentment, and worse." She looked away, then back; there was a struggle of some kind going on. "I'm with Buber on that one, Jack."

"Buber?"

"I picked up on what he was getting at when I was about seventeen. He's the major influence on my work."

He shook his head amazed by this new discovery.

"There are two ways to see the world, Jack. As an instrument of our purpose, or through genuine mutuality. I prefer the latter."

"Martin Buber's pretty heavy fair for a seventeen-year-old."

"My parents' books were scattered all over the house. You'd be surprised at some of the stuff I read as a kid." Her smile blossomed again. "I'm not trying to wriggle out of what it takes for two people to stay together. I don't want you to think that for a minute. "

"I know exactly what you're getting at."

Possession was all Duggan's father had ever known; his mother had spent much of her time forcing her way into his head with complaints and demands. How dare he sit there reading that paper? How dare he stand silent at the window looking out. How dare he, how dare he . . .

"Which brings me to my brother's conversion to Judaism."

It was a sudden and an unexpected twist. He frowned a question at her.

"It isn't really surprising," she said, sliding into the chair opposite. "He went out there to hunt for his roots. Seems he's found them."

"When did you hear about this?"

"Last time I spoke to my father. I've been mulling it over for days. I don't know how I'd have reacted if he'd told me himself." She eyed the ceiling as if in search of something, then seemed to change her mind. "My father mentioned it like he would have done a rise in the stock market. "

"I doubt he's that disinterested."

"Paul's a peacenik, Jack. He's up to his neck in politics from what I can make out. He's been politically active since the moment he arrived in Israel. He was disgusted by the stalemate in the Kenneset. Really passionate about it. He said it would take a complete realignment of the political parties to break the impasse caused by the minority religious groups. He said idiots on both sides were holding everyone to ransom. He seemed hopeful that might end soon."

"Did he give a reason for thinking that?"

"Not really. But he sounded as if he knew something. I could sense that he was holding back."

"There's been an unofficial ceasefire since Benedict's death. It's being suggested his death will initiate the peace they've all been after."

"There's more to it than that. Paul hinted at some kind of impending breakthrough weeks ago."

Duggan reached for another piece of toast, but didn't do anything with it. "Rumor has it that something's about to break politically. There's been talk of a new political party emerging. I picked up on that from someone who's just been out there." He returned to the subject of Paul. "I'd like to meet this brother of yours. What's he like?"

"Very much like my father."

"In looks?"

"Nature."

"The conversion thing was spur of the moment?"

She shook her head. She didn't think so. What she knew for sure was that he wasn't a stand-in-front-of-an-Israeli-bulldozer-type. He was too bright for that.

"A pragmatic peacenik?" Duggan mused on his own words for a moment, then he said, "When I've plucked up the courage to tell Elliot that I'm leaving, that I'm going freelance, would you consider a trip to Palestine?"

"Seriously?"

"Yup."

What brought that on?"

"I'm intrigued by this whole Benedict thing."

"And my brother Paul's political associations?"

Duggan's smile was intentionally disarming. "We could visit the monastery of Mar Saba. I'd love to see the place for myself."

"A woman wouldn't be very welcome."

"Probably not," he replied. Then, "An adventure, Jane. Just the two of us."

"Via Rome?"

"Can't see why not."

"And then what?"

" . . . Ohio?"

She smiled her smile.

fini

BOOKS

O is a symbol of the world, of oneness and unity. In different cultures it also means the "eye," symbolizing knowledge and insight. We aim to publish books that are accessible, constructive and that challenge accepted opinion, both that of academia and the "moral majority."

Our books are available in all good English language bookstores worldwide. If you don't see the book on the shelves ask the bookstore to order it for you, quoting the ISBN number and title. Alternatively you can order online (all major online retail sites carry our titles) or contact the distributor in the relevant country, listed on the copyright page.

See our website www.o-books.net for a full list of over 500 titles, growing by 100 a year.

And tune in to myspiritradio.com for our book review radio show, hosted by June-Elleni Laine, where you can listen to the authors discussing their books.

mySpiritRadio